Kip Manley

CITY *of* ROSES

VOL. 3

IN THE REIGN *of* GOOD QUEEN DICK

SUPERSTICERY
PORTLAND • POINTS WEST

Supersticery Press
Manley, Kip
City of Roses Vol. 3: In the Reign of Good Queen Dick / Kip Manley
ISBN 978-1-7349452-3-2

Originally published as individual chapbook nos. 23 – 33 from 2015 – 2019.

Art is a Gift

www.thecityofroses.com

THE WORTH OF A THING

"Uprights, spinnets, pianos droits;" says Bruno, "I began by buying up office furniture, but in every city and many of the sizable towns, rows of old terrace houses were being demolished to make way for modern council estates. And in the front parlors of these terrace houses, gathering dust since the days before television, before the wireless, before electricity," he reaches across the front of the piano, sliding the central panel to one side. The man within snorts himself startled awake, white-haired head laid back against the rows of hammers poised against tautly angled strings. "Spruce!" he blurts, and coughs, patting the pockets of his crisp white shirt, arms tucked close within the cabinet's confines. "Spruce," he says again, "from the forests about Old Tjikko, long may he reign," and fits a monocle to his eye, "chilled in the hold of an old steamer down through the Baltic and the cold North Sea. Mahogany from Brazil, that baked in breathless heat across the Atlantic, between the Pillars of Hercules and up the Balearic to Marseille. Iron," his smile is beatific, "scraped from Erzberg's slopes, spun to wire in Vienna and brought by rail across Venetia and Sardinia. Sugar pine from the very wilds of Northwest America about us now," reaching out of the cabinet to gently stroke the keys below, "stacked for a harrowing, storm-wracked voyage all the way around the Horn, only to end up a century later right back where it began. The ebony veneer from too many different pieces of wood, some of them once keys from other instruments, but not an ounce of ivory to be found: the natural keys are topped with porcelain, which has left them with the occasional chip and crack, though not a piece is missing."

Chilli's stepped back, pressed against the draped piano behind him. Bruno's tugging something from another pocket of his vest, a tiny glassine envelope. "I've kept in tune as best I can," says the man within the piano, with a gesture to the strings arrayed behind him. "Shall I play you something? In a rag-time, perhaps?" Bruno steps close, holds up a fingertip glimmering gold, which the man in the piano seizes and brings it to his lips for a kiss, and a slow and savoring lick.

the TABLE *of* CONTENTS

a FOREWORD

THERE'S THIS CARTOON by, oh, let's say Don Martin: a comedian on stage holds up a sign that says I'M FUNNY. —Noncommittal titters from the audience.

Next panel, the comic's swapped signs for one that says YOU'RE FUNNY. The audience hisses and boos. ("It's interesting to note," says critic Marjorie Garber, "that the entities most usually described as 'hissing,' in the early modern period as also today, are devils, serpents, and audiences.")

Third and final panel: the comic, dripping flop sweat, swaps signs one more time: THEY'RE FUNNY.

Cue the gales of laughter.

Every text is written in the first person.

Yes, all of them: even soi-disant experimental second-person narratives; especially those ostensibly in the third: *every* text is a first-person text. (Yes, and also those in the fourth. Hush, you.) —Every narrative must have a narrator, somewhere—did you check behind the curtain? If you're still unclear, approach it as you would any other criminal enterprise: ask yourself, cui bono? Who chose the matter, wrangled the theme, pondered characters and angles of approach, began as they meant to go on? Such a constellation of considerations can't help but cohere into a point of view, and that's where, much as a sniper in a nest, you'll find your narrator. (And if you shrug and say, with a quizzical cock to your brow, you mean the author? I'll sagely shrug and answer back, perhaps.)

Once you've found the narrator, you've found your I in the sky: first mover, first shaker, first person.

"Did you notice?" said the Classicist. I don't talk about the Classicist much, do I. And I have to be honest, here: while I remember having *had* the conversation, I don't remember what we said, exactly, or where we were, not even a general sense of the circumstances, anymore. So let's say we were having coffee in what I think was the only diner in town. "She pulled the whole thing off," said the Classicist, with an emphatic gesture of her cigarette (menthol, which she would've bought next door, at what might've been called a bodega if we'd been in New York, but was called a bakery when the protests erupted years later), "the *whole thing,* without *once* telling you what was going on in anybody's head." —The SHE in that statement being Patricia McKillip, and the WHOLE THING being PULLED OFF the Riddle-Master books, and the statement itself not entirely correct, or right, or true: after all, when Morgon wakes up after the shipwreck, we're told:

> He tried to answer. His voice would not shape the words. He realized, as he struggled with it, that there were no words in him anywhere to shape the answers.

That's from the first page of chapter three, and while it might be the first time we're told something about someone's state of mind that couldn't be directly observed, or inferred from what's been shown or told, it's not the last. (And if you'd aver that the struggle described and the insight realized might well enough be inferred, perhaps by someone especially empathetic, I'd invite you past the next paragraph to read what follows: "A silence spun like a vortex in his head, drawing him deeper and deeper into darkness.")

No, what the Classicist meant, if you'll trust me to speak after all these years for her (and I'm not getting her voice right, not at all): in the writing of the Riddle-Master books, concerned as they are with identity, and selfhood, McKillip nonetheless eschews the free indirect: she never once presumes to speak for her characters, by making like their interiority's seeping through the narrative. —You know. The bits Stephen King puts in italics. (Talking about King is probably how we got to this emphatic statement in the first place.) —Anyway. True or right or correct or not, it stuck with me.

As perhaps you could tell.

Every narrative has a narrator. This may seem a ravelled tautology, but tug the thread of it and so much comes undone: a narrator, after all, is just another character, and subject to the same considerations. What might we consider, then, of a character who strives with every interaction for a coolly detached objectivity that's betrayed by every too-deft turn of phrase? Who lays claim to an impossible omniscience, no matter how it might be limited, that's belied by every Homeric nod? Who mimicks the vocal tics and stylings, the very *accents* of the people in their purview— whether or not they're put in italics—merely to demonstrate how well it seems they think they know their stuff?

It's only those texts that admit, upfront, the limitations and the unreliability of their narrators, that are honest in their dishonesty. —The third person, much like the third man, snatches power with an ugliness made innocuous, even charming, by centuries of reading protocols: deep grooves worn by habits of mind that make it all too lazily easy for an unscrupulous, an unethical, an unthinking author to wheedle their readers into a slapdash crime of empathy: crowding out all the possible might've beens that could've been in someone else's head with whatever it is they decide to insist *must* have been.

The first few sketches of what would become (distractedly expansive gesture) all *this* were written on a clunky laptop lifted from an unlit room, filled with abandoned computers, just off the elevator lobby where I worked for a couple of weeks as a temporary receptionist. They were scraps of scenes, beginning after a beginning and never finding much of an end, but suggesting strongly where they'd come from, where they might go: our protagonist, Jo Maguire, already surly and underemployed, out for a night on the town with Becker, her gay best friend (making a stab or two at what would become his "epitome of mediocrity" speech); staggering back from the bathroom in time to see Ysabel, our protagonist, winding up the dancefloor with the slow-burn opening of Cassilda's Song—only it was YSABEL, and BECKER, and JO, because these sketches all were written in screenplay form.

I was already writing a screenplay—it was why I'd stolen the laptop; some folks I knew were vaguely acquainted with a pot of techbro proceeds, and thought maybe a micro-budget horror film might prove an attractive tax shelter. It only made sense, when I was procrastinating the one, to sketch this incipient other in the same medium, and anyway, there's room to play, in a screenplay, with voice, with performance, because the performance isn't the point: it isn't the final product, it's instructions for assembling the final product. And who knew? Maybe I'd find some techbro money of my own (it was thicker on the ground, in those days), that might want to shelter itself in a micro-budget pilot for a syndicated television show. —My dreams were so much larger then, if simpler.

But the money went in another direction, and all I had to show for it was a screenplay no one would ever watch, and this, this *thing* that, if it was ever going to be anything, would have to become something else.

As I was considering how best to go about getting done what I wanted to do, I thought once more of the Classicist's emphatic statement—maybe because these things had started as screenplays, concerned with the movement of bodies and objects in space, with words spoken out loud, not left to echo in somebody's head—but I'd already played once or twice with the techniques suggested, in other, shorter pieces, elsewhere (much as writers today come up through fanfic, I'd done some time in the graduate seminars of alt.sex.stories.d). The strictures they impose—the pragmatics of blocking, the seamless exteriority, the relentless focus on precise, specific moments—that make it necessary to deal only by implication with what it is prose is supposed to excel at, by talking outside the glass: they can't help but appeal to a scrupulous fool like me. So I decided to pull the whole thing off without ever once telling you what's going on in anyone's head.

But now I'm worried: having said this out loud, have I tipped my hand? Given the game away?

"I just don't get it," I said, and here we can suppose I gestured at the magazine on the table between us with a cigarette of my own (clove, filterless, bought at the drug store on the corner, where they kept the porn under a shelf behind the counter, so you had to ask for it).

"What's not to get?" said the Classicist, and you have to understand, I would never have actually left such a thing lying out like that, but I have to have something to point to. Still: I did speak to her about this. This is another conversation that happened. Trust me.

"Well," I said, and took a crackling drag. "If you had a sister. A twin. Would *you* do something like that?"

"Depends," she said. Let's say she sipped her coffee. "How much are they paying us?"

"But," I said, "I mean, to, to take something, like that. I mean, whether you really feel it or not—actually, I think it might be worse if you faked it—but to take something like *that* and put it on display?"

"Honestly," she sighed, "worse things happen at sea."

This might be the third volume—look, Ma! I wrote a trilogy!— but it's also the first half of the second season, and second seasons are where television programs typically hit their stride, confident in their logistics, but still gripped by their originating dreams. Second albums are sophomore slumps. Second movements are when things take a turn, get contemplative; usually scored andante or adagio, between fifty and seventy-five beats per minute, depending on your metronome. I'm not sure what we can say yet, about second series of epic urban fantasy web-serial 'zines. There aren't that many around from which to generalize. Whatever it might be, we're halfway through it.

This one is for the usual suspects, I suppose, but it's also for the Classicist, who gave me if not the original idea, then a notion around which an idea might articulate itself. (You mustn't blame her for any more than that.) But also, it's for you. You're the one reading this, after all.

Portland, Oregon
2015 – 2019

1. THEY'RE FUNNY

2. I know you are

∴ But what am I

Obsolete in spoken French, the preterite, which is the cornerstone of Narration, always signifies the presence of Art; it is a part of a ritual of Letters. Its function is no longer that of a tense. The part it plays is to reduce reality to a point of time, and to abstract, from the depth of a multiplicity of experiences, a pure verbal act, freed from the existential roots of knowledge, and directed toward a logical link with other acts, other processes, a general movement of the world: it aims at making a hierarchy in the realm of facts.

—Roland Barthes

That happened in the reign of queen Dick, i.e. never: said of any absurd old story.

—Capt. Francis Grose

NO. 23
" – the thin ice – "

SHE SAID YES – TOMORROW, TONIGHT – WITH HIS OWN HANDS – A HATFUL
OBLIGATIONS OF THE COURT – PUTTING IT BACK – "YES," SHE SAYS
HOW MUCH IS ENOUGH – WELUND, RHYTHIDD, BARLOWE & LACKLAND
A REAL MAD-ON – THE RATTLE OF KEYS – CONFUSING, THE TWO OF THEM
HER REASON – "ENOUGH TO GET YOU INTO TROUBLE"
"THE LEAST LITTLE THING" – AN APPORTIONMENT – HER CASE
EBB-TIDE, CINNAMON TWIST, ALL-AMERICAN GIRL – FÉNIUS
UNLOCKING THE DOOR – WHATEVER SHE WANTS

"Y ES?" SHE SAYS. "I guess." Looking over to him, a shrug. "Who
wouldn't." And he smiles. He's smiling already, thinly, lips
unparted under his long thin nose. The black patch over one eye.
He takes her hand, the other woman's hand, in his. "You see?" he
says to her. Light swoops, shadows rush over them, leaping up
walls to hang a moment swirling as the massive speaker stacks begin to groan a thrumbling beat. She leans back, spangles in her
black hair snagging the light that blares her pink bangs, shadows
under hollowed eyes etch disgust, revulsion, and he laughs, the
sound of it swallowed by the revving song, let's go, chirps a
vocoded voice, let's go, he lifts that hand, the other woman's hand,
to his thin drawn lips, let's go, the gesture isn't at all a kiss, let's go,
let's go, oh, I wanna scream at the top of my lungs –

She steps back from the canvas tautly stretched before her.
Somewhere outside a siren whoops, squeals, cuts out, a shiver of
rain. A window's open, a door cracked, somewhere. Her black hair
unbraided now, spangles gone, pink leached from her bangs. The
brush in her hand. Her feet, her thick legs bare, specked with
gooseflesh. Her T-shirt grey, and black letters across the front say
Outing, Thunder in parentheses. She drops the brush to a
makeshift tabouret. The room behind her cavernous, laddered
with rafters trussed and hung over unlit bulks, boxes, equipment,
whatever it is lost in the glare of the trouble light that dangles over

her head, shining on the canvas stretched, slathered black and red the suggestion of an arm, a sleek line there a throat, a chin, a head tipped back, pillowed in madly scribbled hair. She's picked up a tube of paint, she's squeezing it, a dollop of green out onto her fingertip, bright, electric, poisonously pure. Leaning forward to press it carefully, there, and twist: an eye. She steps back. Sniffs.

"Fucking Flashdance," she says.

Stooping in the harsh light, squatting to pry open the rubber-handled clamps that hold the bottom stretcher of the canvas fixed to a straight-backed paint-splattered chair, the canvas bouncing gently, stiffly dangled, stretching up on her toes to undo the clamps holding the top of it fixed to a cable hung across that corner of the space, knocking the trouble lamp, swooping the shadows about as she struggles with the weight of the canvas, the bottom whacking the concrete floor. Turning it about on one corner, letting it fall, clattering against a stack of canvases all of them tacked to stretchers, each of them spattered, crusted with paint, blacks and reds, arms and hands, torsos, breasts, cheeks and noses, throats, all of them anchoring, framed by explosions of hair, and glimmering in each somewhere a single bright green eye.

"Shit," says Gloria Monday.

Up from a cigarette hissing in the damp grass threads of smoke until she crushes it with her slippered foot. Gloom yellowed by little lights strung from the branches of young trees, newly leafed, placed here and there in wooden tubs. A hammered bronze chiminea on spindly legs, a couple of Adirondack chairs, on the arm of one an empty wineglass, stippled with rain. She steps back inside, shuff and snap of slippers, long white cardigan trailing, her black hair short, swept up in front, a tidy stack of curls.

Candlelight licks bedroom walls, gilds petals, leaves, daffodils and hyacinths in a vase atop the dresser. She opens a small brass box and drops a pack of cigarettes inside, a ragged matchbook. "Still raining?" says the woman on the bed, without looking up.

"Well," says Ysabel, stepping out of her slippers. "It's not *not*." Shedding the long white cardigan, slither of satin pyjamas golden in the light of all those candles blazing along the shelves, the window-sill, the footboard of the bed. She lifts the comforter and climbs in next to the woman sitting up against a heap of pillows, chin-length yellow hair severely straight, her face, her breast paled eerily in the light of a laptop. "You're chilly," says the woman, as Ysabel leans close, pressing a kiss to her shoulder, then impish reaches up to poke a nipple bluely pinked, laughing as the woman jerks away, a giggling shriek, "Ysabel! Stop. I promised, I said to Ettie I'd look these over." The laptop screen is tiled with thumbnails, wedge-soled sandal puddle splash, wet hand filthy, lipsticked mouth, two faces, cheek by cheek, and framed by the same severely yellow hair, the same striking noses, the same blue eyes, one looking down, one up and out. "Grimy," says Ysabel. Pointing. "I like that one."

"Derivative," says the blond woman, dragging some images into a folder. "Why do you go outside?"

"What," says Ysabel, "to smoke? The smell. Jo. She's trying to quit."

"Oh," says the woman. Her lips sour. "Jo."

Ysabel sits up, draws back.

Ysabel's opening the door to the apartment, "You're busy," she's saying, "I'm distracted, really, it's best," as pulling on a long brown coat the woman with yellow hair comes down the hall. "You can make it up to me tomorrow night," says Ysabel, as the woman steps out onto the landing, "at the dinner. Christienne?"

Turning, and under that straight yellow hair as she steps back in, steps close, that scowl twists into a pointed little smile, dipped in to kiss Ysabel's mouth softening, opening, starting to return the kiss when Chrissie pulls away. "It's tonight," she says. "The dinner's tonight."

"What?" says Ysabel.

"The clock?" says Chrissie, headed down the stairs.

Ysabel looks back, into the dark kitchen. Green numbers shine over the stovetop, 12:17, striking gleams from a glass half full of milk there by the sink. She shakes her head. "Pedant," she says, closing the door.

In the dim hall she pauses, there by the doorway flickering, candlelit. She turns away, stepping into the other room, unlit, across the hall. There to one side a sword's slung from a leather strap in a plain black scabbard, and the hilt of it netted in wiry strands. From the same nail driven in sheetrock hangs a painted skull-mask, crudely toothed, black mane falling from it almost to the floor. She doesn't touch the sword or the mask but turns to sit on the bed, a low futon opened flat. Over the head of it a shapeless collage, taped and pasted to the wall, post cards, scribbled notes, pages ripped from magazines. Through the closed windows a sigh of traffic, the wash of rain. A click, there in the room, metal against leather. She looks up. The mask on the wall, wobbling, the rustle of its mane. The scabbard beneath it swaying, empty, the hilt, the sword, now gone.

She looks down. She lays herself down, head on a pillow, pulling a corner of the blanket up and over about her shoulders. Hand on the other pillow there beside her. Closing her eyes.

"Be careful," she says.

He shuts off the engine, looks across to her. She's looking out her window rainwater lurid in the light cast from an Oregon Lottery sign, red and blue and yellowed white. KJ Rice Noodle Shop & Restaurant, say the letters underneath. "What does your grace intend?" he says.

A rip of velcro as she adjusts her fingerless cycling gloves, black and grubby grey. She's all in black, black jeans, black shirt buttoned to her throat, a long black coat. Her short hair dyed a cherry red to match the red Chuck Taylors on her feet. "Well," she says, a gesture at the glass door out there, warmly lit up under the blue and red and white. "We go in there, we get the Harper, we come back out. In that order."

"You make it sound easy," he says.

"Well, hell," says Jo Maguire, shoving her door open. "I'm the goddamn Duke, right?"

WITH HIS OWN HANDS – A HATFUL
OBLIGATIONS OF THE COURT – PUTTING IT BACK

WITH HIS OWN HANDS, the King pours from a cut glass pitcher five generous dollops of orange juice into tulip goblets of eggshell porcelain, leafed with scuffed gold whorls. "Wednesdays," he says, and he chuckles. "Hump day," he says. His caftan white, his dressing gown of black and gold brocade, his pinkish orange hair bobbing upright in matted coils and tangles as he moves about the table. "I'd like to acknowledge," he says, "the extraordinary circumstances," setting a goblet before the Marquess in her black leather jacket, hair close-cropped, gunmetal grey, "that have brought us all together again," and another before the Soames in a green tweed jacket, plaid trilby on the table before him, "so soon." A third goblet before the Viscount in his soft blue suit, matted white locks tied into a thick spray at the back of his head. Out past the credenza laden with pitcher and plates, a dish of scrambled eggs, a red clay tortilla warmer painted with white flowers, the vertiginous drop, black trees and wet rooftops soaked in dull grey clouds, the drip of fallen rain. "Your alacrity's a credit to this court," says the King, taking up the last two goblets, stepping around, down to the head of the table. "As well you know. Something happened last night. This morning. Early," and another chuckle, "earl*ier.*" Setting a goblet before Jo, still in her black coat, black shirt buttoned to her throat. "Southeast will fill us in."

An electronic bong as she opens the door, as they step inside, the front room dim, empty, a handful of plastic chairs haphazardly set about a couple of small tables. Blue Chinese characters written on a dry-erase board tacked over a doorway, English translations crowded off to one side, fresh rice noodle, fresh rice noodle rolls, fresh shrimp rice noodle roll, the prices in green, $0.95, $1.00, $1.60. A woman ducks through the doorway from the brighter kitchen beyond, "We're closed," she says, wiping her hands on her apron.

"Wu Song?" says Jo.

"We're closed."

"The Gallowglas," says Jo. "To see Wu Song. He called us. Me." Looking over to Luys, beside her, his hands in his pockets.

"Yes," says the woman, ducking back through the doorway.

"Huh," says Jo.

"It is late," says Luys.

"He called us," says Jo.

"Yes," says Luys.

"He's got fucking Chilli."

"Yes," says Luys.

"I'm not leaving without him."

"Of course," says Luys. His hair a cap of glossy black, his shortwaisted jacket softly brown. Past him against the wall a pile of woven plastic sacks of rice, piled up about waist-high, Elephant Brand, Product of Thailand, Net Wt. 25 Lbs. Shadows shift, shuff of sneakers, a man's stepping out of the kitchen, blank white T-shirt taut about his chest, his thick belly, his shoulders softly round with unflexed muscle. Tattoos at his temples, blocky hexagrams, blurred by the silver stubble of his hair. His brows as lush and dark as his mustache. "Wu Song?" says Jo, and then, "It's good to meet you."

He folds his arms, there behind the glass-fronted counter, the display shelves lined with empty stainless steel trays. "Again," he says, after a moment.

"Again?" says Jo. "I, we – I'm sorry, have we – "

"How long have you held the Hawk," says the man in the T-shirt.

"We, I, I don't," says Jo, and then, "three months. Four. Months."

"You cannot mean to suggest," he says, "that in all that time you have not yet thought to meet with me. Sit down with me. See me."

"I, well, it's," says Jo, "been busy. I – "

"You hunt, as your King commands?"

She looks down, at her red shoes, looks up again, head canted. "The Harper," she says. "Chillicoathe. A knight, in my service. You called. You said you have him. I want him back."

"Four corners, to your year," says Wu Song, unfolding his arms. "At each, I get a dŏu. Enough to fill a hat."

"Yeah, I know," says Jo, a hand up to wave, dismissively, "Chilli was – " The hand stops. "Oh," says Jo.

"Stolen?" says the Soames.

"The owr?" says the Viscount.

"Yes," says Jo.

"By whom?" says the Marquess.

"When?" says the Soames. "And why did he go see him anyway?"

"The bandit wore a mask," says Jo.

"So what are we to do," says the Viscount.

"If I could just," says Jo, but "Do?" says the Soames. "It's only a hatful."

"It's a big hat," says the Marquess.

"It's kind of a," says Jo, as the Viscount says, "There must be a response."

"Please," says the King, and quieting they all look to him.

"Gallowglas," he says. "If you'd continue."

"He is not unharmed, but safe," says Wu Song, then, raising his voice, "not a finger laid on him was ours," over what Jo might've said. "Only helping hands."

"So help him on out," says Jo. "We'll be on our way."

"No," says Wu Song.

Luys jerks a hand from his jacket pocket, but holds it there, arm an awkward crook. Neither Jo nor Wu Song look his way. He straightens his arm, lowering his fingers twitching into an anxious fist. "Yeah, well," says Jo. "Didn't think this was gonna go easy, you calling in the middle of the night and all."

"It goes very easy," says Wu Song. "I get my dǒu. You get your man."

"That," says Jo, "that's not how it's gonna go." And then, "We need to talk, him and me. Figure out what happened. I'm a little behind the curve, here – "

"*A* dǒu was stolen. Not *my* dǒu. Fill another. Bring it to me."

"I," says Jo, "now, you have our assurances, Wu Song, that – "

"You cannot mean to suggest you could not fill one with what you have, now, in the trunk of your car."

"So," says Jo. "That's what this is about."

Something settles in Wu Song's stance, his shoulders, just, his jaw, his mustache. "You are a child," he says, and Luys sucks in a breath. "Yeah?" says Jo, lifting her hand. "Maybe. Still." Her fingers close about nothing at all there before her. "I hunt, for the King." She yanks and light blares washing over the blade appearing sharply bright as Wu Song steps back, a percussive "Ha!" as he claps, turning between his hands a slender staff of dark wood polished spinning green ribbons tied to one end fluttering snapping over up and around to come down stopping suddenly, firmly, fast, ribbons swayed a-dangle. Jo isn't facing him, isn't holding her blade up en garde, she's laying it down carefully on the table to one side, the blade of it whorled with waves of dark steel and light, the hilt of it simple, straight, wrapped in dulled wire, guarded about with a glittering net of wiry strands. "This," she's saying, "isn't how it's going down, either." Straightening, ducking under to one side the ribboned end of that staff, lifting a hand to shift it, gently, aside. Wu Song's lips snarl under his mustache, a snagged smile as he lifts the staff up, away. "The agreement, Wu Song," says Jo. "Between you, and the Duke. And the King. The trust they've placed in you. What you've done, to earn that trust. That's why you get the hat. Not the man. Not the threat. The agreement. That trust." A step closer. "Now. Maybe." Another. The ribbons tremble. "Maybe what you mean to say with this, this threat. Is maybe you don't. Trust. The agreement. The King. Me." Tilting her head. Looking up at him. "It could go down like that," she says. "Or?"

Wu Song steps back, claps his empty hands together. Nods once, to Jo, and looks back over his shoulder into the kitchen. "Mang nó cho tôi," he says, and a clink, a clank, some shuffling footsteps, a woman in greasy whites bowed under the weight of the man leaned against her, limping heavily, one arm slung in a white napkin folded, tied about his neck, one eye swollen yellow and green between a tangle of blond hair and the verge of a big blond beard.

"Chilli," says Jo.

"Come back tomorrow," says Wu Song. "With my dǒu."

"What's still unclear to me," says the Soames around a mouthful of egg, "is why we've been called in."

"We were robbed," says the Viscount, folding a tortilla just so.

"*Southeast* was robbed," says the Soames. "With no disrespect," pointing his fork at Jo, who only blinks. "But I do not understand why we've been called to make her whole."

"It's the court's obligation," says the Marquess, reaching for the marmalade.

"It's our agreement," says the King.

"Satisfaction of which was entrusted to her hands," says the Soames. "It's a hatful!" Sitting back, throwing up his hands. "After you made your well-put point," he says to Jo, "why not just scoop another up and hand it over?"

"A doe," says the Viscount, and the Marquess says, "Döe," as the Viscount's holding up his hands. "About a salmanazar, Thomas," he says.

"Just over a peck," says the King.

"A," says the Soames, looking from one to the other, "peck." Holding up his fingers, looking to Jo, "Four a year."

She shrugs.

"He gets a brace of pins?"

"While I was gone," says the King, "Wu Song did signal work that helped to keep this city safe, work that continues to this day."

"The court has a great many obligations," says the Marquess.

"And we do honor them, all," says the King. "So!" He sets a folded parchment sealed with yellow wax beside his plate. "I've drafted an edict for her majesty my sister. If you all," but the Marquess has already pushed a little plastic tub out into the middle of the table, sloshed with something inside thickly viscous, and the Viscount sets a silver flask beside it. Jo's pulling out a small glass bottle, and maybe a finger within of milky stuff tinged with gold, laced with froth. "Sure," the Soames is saying, "of course," as he sets a paper cup capped with plastic on the table. "But so much, again, so soon – "

"How did you know," says Luys, quietly, "to call his bluff?"

"He wasn't bluffing," says Jo, laying her bare sword in the trunk, over behind the cardboard box, the brown glass growler wrapped in a garbage bag.

"But he didn't hit you," says Luys.

"I'd already put mine down," says Jo. "I mean damn, Luys. You know I can't fight for shit with that thing." She's opening the cardboard box, feeling about inside.

"What if he had," says Luys.

"Hit me?" says Jo, plucking an empty plastic baggie up from the floor of the trunk. "You'd've hauled me out. Patched me up." She's tapping the box, tilting it, daubing up a pinch of golden dust from a corner. "We'd've figured something out," she says, letting it trickle from her fingertips into the baggie.

She tosses the baggie into the back seat, where sprawled in his bulky sweater, one arm held close in a napkin sling, Chillicoathe the Harper catches it with his free hand. "So," she says, as Luys climbs into the driver's seat, "Chilli," as she settles into the passenger seat, buckling her lap belt. "Who was it."

"Wore a mask," says Chilli, with a grunt, smearing a bit of gold over his yellowed, puffy eyelid.

"Just one? Was it a crew?" says Jo, as Luys starts the engine.

"Just the one," says Chilli. "Had a baseball bat. Kneecapped me. Sweetloaf ran, and the other one. Whatsisname. New kid. And then bam! Boot to the head."

"Where," says Jo.

"Right back there," says Chilli, sitting up with a wince, looking back. Blinking golden dust from his unswollen eyes. "I was just about to knock."

"Think it was him? Wu Song?"

Chilli slumps, rubbing his shoulder.

"Doesn't smell right," says Luys.

"But you don't know," says Jo, to Chilli.

"It was a horse mask," says Chilli. "Covered the whole head."

"And a bat," says Jo, blowing out a sigh, "and a boot. Okay," she says to Luys. "Take him home. And then we go see his majesty. You got anything else for us?" she calls back, pulling a glassy black phone from her pocket.

"Whoever it was," mutters Chilli, scowling, "had a real nice coat."

"Ysabel?" says Jo, in the kitchen steeped in grey morning light. A cardboard box in her hands, packed with a plastic tub, a silver flask, a glass bottle, a paper cup, her unsheathed sword tucked under an arm. "You up?" Setting the box down on the counter by a mound of tulips, heavy heads of purple and red and golden orange a-bob, fleshy green stems stuffed in a boxy green glass vase. "You even here?" Leaning her sword against the counter she picks up the glass left by the sink, eyeing the ring of milk left at the bottom. Rinses it out, leaves it in the sink.

Knocking softly on a closed door, she opens it a crack. The room beyond is whitely bright, daffodils and hyacinths a-bloom on the dresser, pillows an orderly stack at the head of the well-made bed, a long white sweater neatly draped over the dressing screen in the corner. "Okay," says Jo. Closing the door. Opening the other, across the hall. Beneath the skull mask, hanging there from the nail, that plain black scabbard, slung from its leather strap. With her free hand she takes the throat of it, the color of a thundercloud, and fits the tip of her sword to it, slipping it home with the faintest of clinks.

"Jo?" says Ysabel, sitting up on the futon.

"I still," says Jo, hanging her head, "don't have the faintest idea how to put it back."

"Are you all right?" says Ysabel. "Are you hurt?"

Jo turns away from the wall, the mask, the sword, "I didn't," she says, "I just – I needed it, to make a point." Looking up.

"We have, I brought, there's. Another batch, to turn. Today. Ysabel, I'm sorry, I – "

Ysabel, wordless, holds out a hand.

Shoulders shaking breath quickening Jo steps to the futon, kneels bending over curling formless in her long black coat to lay herself in Ysabel's lap. Ysabel's arm in white satin settles over her shoulders. Jo lets out a single, strangled sob, and Ysabel bends over her, gently, lowering her head to kiss away a tear.

"Yes," says Gloria Monday, tapping a credit card once against the countertop, "my name is Suzette Wilson? I called this morning about an order for some canvases and paints and there was a problem with my card?" Her jet-black hair tied up in a sloppy ponytail, long black coat pulled over an untucked striped dress shirt. "Yes, right," says the man behind the counter, "eight stretched canvases, plus delivery. The card wouldn't go through."

"I *know,*" she says, "can we," tapping the card again, "try it here?" Holding the card out to him. He takes it, shimmering grey, looks up from it to her, frowning. "It's my *father's* card," she says.

"It's a nine-hundred dollar order," he says, poking the screen of a tablet computer.

"Can we just, try it. Please. It's a platinum card."

He shrugs, swipes. One of the buttons pinned to his red apron says Happen Things Makes Art. The tablet bleeps, he looks up, holds out the card with an apologetic shrug.

"Maybe, try it again?" says Gloria Monday. He's still holding out the card. She takes it back, a snap of her wrist, and opens her purse, a gutted teddy bear slung from a rhinestone-studded strap. "I guess," she says, tucking the card away, "they finally figured out he's dead."

"Dead?" says the clerk.

"I gotta go talk to my lawyer," says Gloria Monday. "I'll be back. For the stuff."

A golden haze of summery light swirls disturbed as a hand sweeps up, claps the rim of the big white tub with an echoing bong. Jo hauls herself up on her knees, clinging to the tub, head hung low, and gold dust settles on her maraschino hair. Dust shimmering in the tub, shifting as Ysabel hoists a knee, sits up, sloughs brilliant tumbles over the stuff beneath, darker and yet damp. Groaning. "You okay?" says Jo.

Ysabel's nodding, face in her gold-caked hands. "Is it enough?" she says. "Did I make enough?"

"It's plenty," says Jo, sitting back on her heels. "More than enough." Clink as she picks up a silver flask from the tiled floor, then a crumpled paper cup, tossing them both into the cardboard box against the wall. Squeak and an echoing thump, a grunt from the tub, Jo whirling, grabbing at Ysabel awkward arms a-tangle rubbing her chin, "ow" she says, and "Ysabel, are you okay?" says Jo, and "I'm *fine,*" says Ysabel, "just *slipped,*" pushing herself back up, a squelch and squeak of dust. Eyes weighted, cheeks drawn, face pale. Teetering there. Jo offers a hand, and after a moment she takes it, climbs out, shivering. Sits, heavily, on the floor. "I just," she says, as Jo drops a white robe in her lap, "need to sleep for a hundred years."

"Right there with you," says Jo, pulling on a white robe of her own.

"But we can't," says Ysabel, elbows on her knees. "We can't." The hair at her temple brushed a stroke of white. "What are you," says Jo, and then, hanging her head, "fuck. The dinner. The fucking goddamn dinner."

"Indeed," says Ysabel.

"Can't we cancel?" Jo leans against the wall, there by the window of frosted glass.

"That would be rude."

"I just, I don't know if I can deal with those two, tonight."

"Did you speak with Bruno yet?"

Jo tips her head back against white tiles, eyes closed. "Not yet," she says.

"You know how important this is."

"Ysabel, please." Jo pushes off the wall. "Luys is running down the guys who were with the Harper, last night, and I gotta talk to them, figure out why it is he doesn't want to tell us who it was that ripped us off, and – "

"Jo," says Ysabel, "you promised," and Jo looks down. "Yeah," she says.

"Well," says Ysabel, sitting up, stretching, "I confess I haven't spoken with the Glaive yet, either." Twisting about to reach into the tub.

"So, what, we're both procrastiwhat are you, what's," as Ysabel turns back, wiping golden crumbs from her lips, "So it's a good thing," she says. Smiling. "That I made extra." Holding up a hand, a dollop of wet dust glimmering on her fingertips.

"Really," says Jo, kneeling.

"I won't tell if you won't," says Ysabel.

Jo bows down to take the laden fingers in her mouth.

"Wait," says Jo. "What?" In her hand a cigarette, doldrummed in smoke. Under her head a tasseled pillow, propped against the slatted wooden arm of a sofa. A man's standing by the desk, just outside the light of its lamp. "This isn't an investment," he's saying. Dark blue bowl of a tea mug in his hand. "That might be leveraged, against anticipated returns?" Rumpled corduroy trousers, moleskin vest. "It'd be a gift, a donation to the Sœurs Limoges." He sits on a pinkish-grey armchair, there by the sofa. Jo sits up, smoke swirling about her, frowning at that cigarette, "Isn't there," she says, "aren't there, ah," and she takes a quick drag. "Won't there be, tax benefits?"

"A mitigating factor," he says, lifting his mug to his lips, "nothing more." He sips. "Which assumes their paperwork's in order. But even so – you have to have it, before you can give it away."

"I don't," says Jo, "understand, we're, we're rich. Right?"

"Wealthy," he says, "but not liquid. You've been most generous, to the King."

"And this is for the Queen," says Jo. "How much could, could I, could we, offer?"

"It's not," he says, and sighs, looking up, lips pursed. Blinking. There's a knock. He looks to the door, exasperated, "I'll tell you," he says, and again a knock. "I'll tell you three," he says, standing. "Because you want to tell her majesty five." He heads for the door lit with a stippled pane of glass that says, reversed, Bruno's, in an arc over Investments.

"And if I do tell her five?" says Jo.

"I'll do what I can," he says, his hand on the knob, "to make it work, your grace." He opens the door.

It's Luys, in his softly brown jacket, and Jo leans over to stub out her cigarette on a saucer on the arm of the sofa. Bruno's nodding, saying something about the weather. Luys steps inside, followed by a kid, a boy in a brown bomber jacket, brown hair popped in a matted pompadour, and another boy, a young man not much older, grey hoodie stained, ragged cuffs, Jo's sitting up, his dark hair's tightly curled, dark cheekbones hunched like shoulders under squinting eyes, "Christian," says Jo, but Luys is saying something about Sweetloaf, and slick pavement, and the boy in the bomber jacket laughs. "Christian," says Jo again. The man in the hoodie's looking down, at his hands, his filthy blue running shoes, the intricate rug laid over the plain grey office carpet. "Chickie *chickie,*" says Jo, and he looks up, and Bruno looks up, Luys is frowning, and "The fuck? Your grace?" says the boy in the bomber jacket.

"Hey," says Christian Beaumont. "Jo." A shrug. "How long's it been? Six months?"

"Well?" says Ysabel, dressed in white, sitting back in a low chair, beige leather slung from a sleek steel frame, there before a wide slab of desk, powerfully empty. Standing behind the desk a tall man, and rotund, a rough linen suit over a shirt of pearly pink, his knit tie plain pale blue. He's looking out the sweep of window, brimmed with dull grey cloud. "Your brother, majesty," he says, scratching the back of his head, rough salt-and-pepper stubble atop his thick neck, the sheen of his collar. "He has been most rash." Turning to face her, an apologetic cast to his mouth, his eyes. "Demanding what's been properly apportioned, that he might throw it at a debt already well in hand."

"You mean the owr," says Ysabel. "I'm asking after cash."

"The court's reserves are stripped, majesty," he says. "And without collateral?" He spreads his hands. "There can be no loan."

After a moment, Ysabel says, coldly, "Owr is not collateral."

"Of course, ma'am," he says.

"Even if it were," she says, "you cannot doubt what I produce."

"Of course not, ma'am," he says, looking down, his hand loosely curled on his desk.

"So I can't but think you mean to speak to me of something else," says Ysabel.

He pushes his own chair back from the desk, a high-backed throne of pale brown leather, and gently sits him down. "All right, majesty," he says. "One might speak of good will. Our agreement with the Court of Engines was soberly negotiated, prudently arranged. To cast it all aside, in one debilitating swoop – "

"We never agreed," says Ysabel, flatly. "Not my brother. Not I."

"Nevertheless," he says, "it was made."

"For a Bride we did not want, and do not need!"

Soft hands spread flat atop his desk, about one wrist a watch, a slender, silvery thing. "The transition, ma'am, was fraught, as I'm sure you will recall. We did what we felt necessary, at the time, to see to the city, and its people."

"Not," says Ysabel, "me. Not the King."

"The court, ma'am," he says.

She looks away, about the office, the two walls of glass, the two of dark wood paneling. "What of the house," she says, after a moment.

"House?"

"Blast it, Rhythidd! Our house! *Our* house!"

"Your father's house, ma'am," he says. "And then the bank's. The foreclosure is complete; I understand an historical society has expressed some interest?" She looks away again, something bitter on her lips. "Now," he says, pushing back from the desk, and standing, and a gesture to the door. "If there's nothing else that I might do to help?"

Gloria Monday black hair swaying turns away from the windowed wall, filled with flat grey sky, back toward the broad conference table neatly set with empty yellow pads, a pen laid at an angle across each, and before each an empty leather chair. She picks up one of the pens, heavy and thick, a burgundy casing printed with precisely serifed letters of cream that spell out Welund Rhythidd Barlowe Lackland. She tucks it away as a glass door opens there in the wall of glass and a woman steps through, a pencil skirt in a windowpane check, crisp black blouse, russet hair framing a narrow pair of glasses with black rims. "Ms. Wilson," she says, as she sets a redweld of files on the table, "I'm Anna Nirdlinger. I work closely with – "

"Where the hell is John," says Gloria.

"Mr. Barlowe," says Anna. "He's in depositions this afternoon. I – "

"Well get him out. This is about my, my father, his money, *my* money, that I need to – "

"I assure you, Ms. Wilson – "

" – I am not *about* to get palmed off on some fucking *secretary* – "

"Ms. Wilson. Gloria Monday." And Gloria blinks, falters, slumps a little. "I am a paralegal," says Anna, "and intimately familiar with every aspect of your father's estate. That I am meeting with you – that anyone is meeting with you, when you show up unannounced, without an appointment – this is a sign of how very important you are, to this firm. Now." She pulls out a leather chair, sits down, pulls files from the redweld, one two three. "What might we do, for you."

Gloria still standing plops her teddy bear onto the table, unzips the belly to spill out a handful of credit cards. Tosses one shimmering grey across to Anna. "It's getting declined," she says.

"A number of issues can occur with the winding down of some of the ancillary accounts," says Anna, taking it up, looking it over. "This isn't your allowance account." Setting it down with a snap. "It's been closed, Ms. Wilson."

"I," says Gloria, "could you, could you stick with Gloria? I'd appreciate it." Folding her arms.

"You have an allowance, Gloria. Two thousand dollars a month, for miscellaneous expenses."

"It isn't *enough,*" says Gloria. "Not for what I need to do – "

"The terms are quite clear."

"Look," says Gloria. "I know what the game is."

"The game," says Anna, looking up through her narrow glasses.

"You want to hold on to as much of the money as you can for as long as you can and I get that, I do. I don't want to get in the way of that. I just, I need – "

"Gloria, I can assure, you," says Anna, but Gloria's blinking, looking past her, out the glass wall of the conference room into the lobby and Anna, turning, sees there all in white Ysabel storming past, headed for the elevators. "What," says Gloria, stepping back from the table, "what is she," back again, a booming thump against the window, and the grey sky.

"She's a client," says Anna.

"No," says Gloria. "You *know* her."

"I used to work," says Anna. "For her mother."

"And one day," says Gloria, "she asked you."

Anna swallows. "Yes," she says.

"And you said," says Gloria.

Anna says, "Yes."

"So," says Christian, looking down, looking over, at the row of filing cabinets behind the desk. "You're, like, the boss, now."

Jo waves out the match, drops it to the saucer on the arm of the sofa, "It's not," she says, taking in a drag, letting out a smokey sigh, "not really."

"That guy, Mason, he's like Sweetloaf's boss? And then Mason, he was all like – "

"The Mason," says Jo. "It's, a title. His name's Luys."

"It's, okay," says Christian, "whichever. He sure jumped when you said boo." Looking over to the door, the pane of frosted glass, the letters, reversed. "And Bruno? He, what, besides letting you kick him out of his own office. Handles your money? You have money?"

"It's not," she says, and "Yeah it is," he says. "You either got money, or you don't. And you," he's shaking his head, looking at his shoes, "you in it. All the way with them that's in it."

She's shaking her head, a puff of a laugh, "Most I'd say is maybe I'm next to it."

"You're like a Queen or something. Admit it."

"They, ah," she says, "they did make me a Duke. Duchess. Whatever."

"Fuck you," he says, with a chuckle.

"The Queen's my housemate," she says, and they're both laughing. "Yeah," she says, "we got a great little place, Hawthorne and Twentieth. Little garden, up on the roof there?"

"Must be nice," says Christian.

"So what kind of mask was it," says Jo.

"What kind a, whoa. Well. Turned a corner, there."

"Just, what'd it look like," she says.

"One a those fucked-up floppy horse-head masks, they make, stupid videos with 'em, you know?"

"Why'd you run?" says Jo.

"What?"

"You were there, with Sweetloaf. Back-up. Muscle. You were," and she looks down, at her cigarette, the lengthening ash on it.

"Run?" says Christian. "He told us to go."

"He." She looks up. "Chilli?"

"Told us to get the hell out. It was personal, none of our business." His brows pinched, a considering frown. "Whoever it was, they got a real mad-on for each other."

"Shit," says Jo. Reaching up to rub, absently, at her chest. Leaning over to tip her cigarette against the saucer, there on the arm of the sofa, but then she grinds it out. "Trying to quit, anyway," she says.

"Jo," says Christian.

"Dammit," she says. "I went looking for you, goddammit. After what went down. Nobody knew where the hell you went."

"Home," he says, looking down, sucking his teeth. "I went home."

"Home."

"Oakland?" he says, put out. "Holidays at my Gram's, what can I say."

"And now you're back."

"Holidays are over," says Christian. "Besides. I don't know anybody down there anymore."

"But here, you know Sweetloaf."

"And you," he says. "I know you."

"Yeah," says Jo. Her hand still at her chest, thumb against her sternum. "Hey," she says. "Christian. What are you doing for dinner."

Sprigs of something green, mint, float among cubes of ice, a glass of water, tall and narrow. Black cords looped about it, wound together in a single hank that dangles over to a bulky headset clamped about his ears, over unruly dreadlocks, fuzzed white dully brushed with gold. "After this morning," he says, "I think it's clear; they are not worried – or, at least, aren't mindful, of their precarity." He picks up the glass of water. "If it'd come to that, I'd've made you whole myself." He sips. "All right," he says. "All right." Setting the glass down. "I detest email," he says, and presses the switch hook on an upright telephone console, silver and black. Drops the headset clattering beside it.

On the sideboard there a rack holds but a single slender glass tube, capped with cork and sealed with pale blue wax, a thread of golden dust within. He opens a drawer, clink of glass as he pulls out an empty tube, and reaches past the rack to lift a weighty plastic freezer bag, careful of a fiendish little basket-box, carved from a single chunk of dark wood. Dipping the tube into the bag, tapping in just enough.

A hallway, and the light diffuse, clouded, morning or midday, getting on toward evening, his footsteps soundless on a long pale rug.

Curtains drawn, and no lights lit, a bed surmounted by a rounded mass of blankets. "Grandfather?" he says. A great pillow, dimpled by a wispy crown of limp white hair. "I've brought your medicine," he says, sitting on the edge of the bed, but in his hand, he looks, the basket-box, black in this dim light.

Back up the hall, down it again, his footsteps muffled thumps. The tube a spark in his fingers.

"Here you go," he says, peeling back blanket enough to reveal a nose, the eyes squeezed shut in all those wrinkles, the mouth, thin lips he presses a thumb against, prying open as he carefully taps the golden owr from the tube, falling a glimmer to dust the bubble of spit that swells and pops. Blankets shift , lift, a breath drawn fluting through that nose, a rumble somewhere under the blankets, and Agravante draws back as the jaw swings open beneath his hand, and a mighty lumbering eructation, a snarl of a cough. Lips smack, relax, settle half-opened. The eyes still closed.

THE RATTLE OF KEYS – CONFUSING, THE TWO OF THEM
HER REASON – "ENOUGH TO GET YOU INTO TROUBLE"

BUT THERE'S A RATTLE OF KEYS at the door to the apartment, it's opening, there's Jo, black coat swinging and bright red hair, saying something to someone behind her, Luys, his brown short-waisted jacket, loose brown check trousers, "Jo," says Ysabel, "you're late," but there's someone else, after Luys, a young man in a soft yellow suit that swallows his narrow frame. "Sorry," Jo's saying, tucking her jingling keys away. "Had to find some clothes for Christian. *Nice* clothes."

"Hey," says Christian, shooting his cuffs, "it's *me* makes this look good," even as his narrowed eyes dart about the kitchen, the steps down to the open room, where a long table's laid with rich yellow cloth, set with gold-rimmed white dinner plates under gold-rimmed soup plates, bread plates, gold-plated forks and salad forks, soup spoons and teaspoons, broad-bladed knives, water glasses and wine glasses and crisp white napkins, and in the center of it all a glass bowl filled with white and yellow roses. Ysabel stands at the head of the table, there where the windowed walls of the open room narrow to a windowed point, a hand on the back of a chair swathed in beige. White flared pants, a shimmering golden drape of camisole. "Christian, Ysabel," says Jo, and "Ysabel Christian, but I bet you both remember each other."

"Yeah," says Christian, "yeah, the Bride, the Queen, I mean, hey. Highness." He nods. "Majesty," says Luys. "Yes," says Ysabel, and then, to Jo, "We need to talk?"

"Sure," says Jo, "let me just catch a shower, get changed," and "Jo," says Ysabel, coming down the length of that table, as Jo's saying, "won't be ten minutes."

"*Jo,*" says Ysabel, coming up the three low steps into the kitchen.

"You've been smoking," says Ysabel, as she closes the door to her room.

"Ysabel," says Jo, sloughing her coat.

"I can smell it."

Jo tosses her coat on the bed. "I went, I was at Bruno's," she says.

"You asked for my help with this," says Ysabel. Then, "What is he doing here."

"What," says Jo, hand at her throat. "Christian?" Undoing the top button of her shirt. "Apparently, he's working for me now."

"So you invited him to dinner," says Ysabel.

"He's," says Jo, "yeah, just, we can set an extra place at the table or something. Seriously, Ysabel, give me ten minutes – "

"They'll *be* here in ten minutes. Jo, you *know* how important this – "

"Ysabel," says Jo. "Ysabel. We can only do, five thousand."

"This is," says Ysabel. "But that's, not enough. Not nearly."

Jo says, "So I'm guessing that you didn't have any luck, either."

"There *must* be more."

"Bruno," says Jo. "It's complicated. Bruno says – "

"It's *your* money. He doesn't tell you. *You* tell *him*."

"It's not," says Jo, and then, "it's all we can do. Even that's a stretch."

Ysabel looks away, turns away, all in white and shimmering gold.

"It's not nothing," says Jo, undoing another button of her shirt. "They can raise more money off of this. It's – Ysabel – " Reaching for an arm, a hand. "Let me shower and change and we'll go out there and we'll – they're not gonna say no, Ysabel. It's a lot of money." Squeezing her hand. "How could she be disappointed?"

Ysabel brushes back a hank of matted bright red hair. "You need more than a shower," she says.

"No," says Jo.

"Yes," says Ysabel. "You'll look fabulous. Go on, get out of this," undoing the next button of Jo's shirt, Jo's shaking her head, stepping back, pushing Ysabel's hands away, "get back there," says Ysabel, pointing to the dressing screen in the corner, a simple frame of whitewashed wood, and panels of plain linen. "Don't make me issue a royal decree. And, Gallowglas?" as Jo strips off her black shirt, wads it, drops it to the floor. "Try not to peek, this time?"

Christian in his yellow suit, sitting at the table, laughing at something, Luys beside him smiling ruefully, sitting up when he sees Ysabel coming into the kitchen, pushing up to his feet with a clatter of plate and clinking glass, "Ma'am," he says, and Christian half-standing beside him, "Majesty," he says, "I don't mean to put anybody out. I can be on my," but Ysabel's saying "Please. Of course you're welcome." At the foot of the table a powerfully built woman in a wing-collared shirt, a black string tie, pours something from a cocktail shaker into a low square tumbler. Her short hair dyed a virulent chartreuse. "As for what happened, last year," Christian says.

"Don't mention it," says Ysabel. "This is to be a pleasant dinner, with friends."

"Okay," says Christian, and Luys leans toward him, "Ma'am," he says, quietly, and Christian says, "ah, highness." The woman in the string tie's pouring the last of the liquor from the shaker and setting it down. *"Ma'am,"* says Luys to Christian again, and Christian nods as he reaches over the table to take the drink from her hand.

"Jo will be ready shortly," says Ysabel, "and our other guests should be here any moment. Iona," and the woman in the string tie looks up, a cube of ice in the tongs in her hand, "if you'd like to join us, as Christian's companion?"

"What of the service, ma'am?" says the woman in the string tie.

"Finish what you're making, there," says Ysabel, "but otherwise, let's let it take care of itself? Mason, if you'd be so kind as to switch places," and Luys nods, standing, and Christian's standing beside him, a clink again of glasses, "Hey," he's saying, "if you need help with the," looking about, "table," and he frowns. "I thought there was just the six places."

"There's eight of us, tonight," says Ysabel, "with yourself and the Chariot." There's a loudly definite knock. Christian, sitting, starts to stand again, but Iona pushes past him, up the three low steps toward the door to the apartment, another knock, and she opens it, a man there on the landing, not too tall, somewhat stout, a grey cashmere topcoat and a great big smile, "This the place? Is this the place?"

"This is the place," says the woman sweeping past him, slipping off her wrap of fake white fur to reveal a brief dress, black, and asymmetrically cut. Her yellow hair chin-length, severely straight. A second woman, also wrapped in white fur, clings to the man's arm, her yellow hair as long, as straight. The first woman with a clack of her heels steps up to Ysabel, a hand for her cheek, a kiss for her mouth, and "Well," says Ysabel, stepping back. "That was nice. But Ettie, I rather imagine you're his date, tonight?"

Ettie laughs, her hand on Ysabel's hip. "You know," she says, "I *do* get the two of us confused."

"Told you," says Chrissie, squeezing the man's arm, letting go. Slipping out of her wrap to reveal a dress as brief and black as Ettie's. "How the hell can you tell them apart," says the man in the topcoat.

"I pay attention," says Ysabel, taking Chrissie's hand. "Ysabel Perry. Pleased to meet you."

"Davies," he says. "Reginald Davies. Reg, to my friends."

"Well," says Ysabel, "Mr. Davies, ladies, if you'd let Luys take your coats, and Iona there can make you anything you'd like to drink, and this is Mr. Christian, Christian..."

"Ah, Beaumont," says Christian. "Ma'am."

"Mr. Beaumont, an associate of our Jo Gallowglas, who'll join us in a moment. Why don't we all sit down." And they move and shift about the table with a scrape of chairs, rattle of plates, clink of ice in glasses, "Vodka martini," says Reg, "dirty as you like," and "Vodka tonic," says Ettie, and Iona nods. Chrissie shakes her head. Christian pulls out a chair for her, and "Christian," says Ettie, letting Reg squeeze past, "how charming. My sister's name is Christienne."

"French?" says Christian.

"Of a sort," says Chrissie, as she sits.

"Tell us, Mr. Davies," says Ysabel, as she takes her seat at the head of the table, "as the person here of whom we know the least. What is it that you do?"

Down the hall Luys, white fur and grey wool draped over his arm, and a door to either side of him, the one to the left ajar, and the room beyond dark, the one to the right closed, and light shining beneath it. He knocks. "Jo?" he says. He opens it, gently.

She's sitting back against the high wide bed, the soft comforter smoothed across it, and the pillows piled at the head of it, white, all of them white. Her dress a sombre chalkstripe, tailored like a suit coat tightly buttoned down the front, and her bright red hair cut short, slicked back. On the floor by her bare feet an insubstantial pair of shoes, all narrow black straps and slender, pointed heels. Her hands tugging closed the lapels of the dress, the top button of it quite low. "I didn't get anything," she's saying, "to wear under it, I was about to raid her drawers for something," and "My lady," he says, laying the coats across the bed, "please, let me," taking her hand in his, and the bit of leather about his wrist. He tugs her to her feet. "Let go," he says, "let me see it," smoothing the lapels as she takes a deep breath, lowering her hands. "It is a fine dress," he says.

"Of course you'd like it," she says.

"It was made for you," he says.

"Well, yeah, I mean – literally – "

"Tú eres hermosa," he says, and she looks away, biting her lips. Smiling, a little. "Still," she says, toeing one of the shoes. It topples over click against the floor. "I'm gonna fall on my ass in those fucking things."

"I think," says Luys, kneeling before her, "a compromise is possible." Fishing one of her red Chuck Taylors from beneath discarded jeans, the other out from under the bed. Loosening the laces, tugging it open, he fits it to her lifted foot. "There," he says, tying it off, and "Luys," says Jo, "you're a prince."

"It's hardly that simple," Reg is saying, as Iona hands him his drink.

"It's marketing," says Chrissie, stating a fact.

"Darling," says Reg, not unpleasantly. "You *know* how I feel about that word." She smiles, sipping her water. "At Maieutics," says Reg, "we're helping clients see how it is they're seen, in the world, and determine how they wish to be seen."

"What, so, like, branding?" says Christian, there beside Chrissie, and she lets out a honk of a laugh. Ettie across from her says, "Oh, now there's a word he *definitely* does not like."

"It's been sucked dry of any meaning," says Reg, but at the head of the table Ysabel's pushing her chair back, standing, and then Iona, after a moment Christian, Chrissie, Ettie tossing her napkin to the table and nudging Reg, there in the kitchen Luys is handing Jo in her dark dress down the three low steps into the open room. "At last," says Ysabel, smiling, "our Jo Gallowglas. The party may begin."

"Something to drink?" murmurs Iona, and "Uh, whiskey sour?" says Jo, letting Luys pass behind her before pulling out her chair at the foot of the table. "Nice shoes," says Christian, wryly.

"Yeah?" says Jo. "You know me. All about the personal branding."

Another honk from Chrissie, and chuckles ruffle the others. "See?" says Reg, holding up a forestalling hand, as Jo takes a tumbler from Iona. "See?" he insists, but he's smiling. "It's a joke, you laugh, but: it's important to you, isn't it. Red. The color. Do you always wear something red, somewhere about you? You've dyed your hair – there's a reason, to go that trouble. A way you wish to be seen. At Maieutics, what we do is help to articulate those reasons. Refine them. Make them legible, at the right time, in the right way, to the right audience. So." Sitting back. *"That's* what I do."

"And people pay you for this, service?" says Ysabel.

"Handsomely," says Reg.

Ladled into soup plates a creamy white, sprinkled with green and black pepper and floated swirls of golden oil. "Delicious," says Ettie.

"Is it, it's a bisque?" says Reg.

"The wine," Ysabel's saying, as Iona pours from a rough clay container into waiting glasses, "is an Albariño, from the rainy northwest of Spain."

"You need seafood, for a bisque," says Ettie.

"You can have a vegetable bisque," says Chrissie.

"I know why," says Jo, looking at Reg.

"I'm sorry?" says Reg.

"Jo," says Ysabel.

"The reason," says Jo. "I can articulate it just fine." Ice clinking as she lifts her half-empty tumbler. "He wore red," she says, and she tosses back the rest.

"He?" says Reg, looking from the foot to the head of the table and back.

"Red, and brown," says Jo, "though sometimes he'd put on black and gold, or purple. He had the most knights enfeoffed and ruled the biggest fifth of this damn town and he's gone now, and he isn't coming back, so it's left to me to carry it all, for her," and Jo lifts her wineglass to Ysabel. "The Queen of the City of Roses," she says. Luys lifts his glass, and Iona, and Christian, looking back and forth, lifts his, and Ysabel inclines her head. "So," says Jo. "There you go."

"Well," says Reg, "that's, yes." Chrissie's taken Ysabel's hand in hers.

The pasta's cloudy knots of translucent, hair-thin strands, stained green with pesto, tumbled with slivers of cheese. "It's rocket, isn't it?" says Ysabel.

"Ramps, I believe, ma'am," says Iona.

"So," says Reg. "Portland has a queen."

"It's like a game," says Ettie.

"A game?" says Ysabel.

"With the titles," says Ettie, "and the etiquette. I think it's charming."

"Leo played it," says Chrissie.

"Leo," says Reg. "Leo Barganax?"

"The Duke," says Jo.

"You knew him?" says Luys.

"We worked together, or rather," Reg smiles, "our money did, in a number of joint ventures. He introduced me to Ettie, and of course, her lovely sister." Looking about the table. "I was saddened, to hear of his passing."

Yellow-glazed ramekins, and within them custards stuffed with dark mushrooms, wilted spinach, and beside each a couple-three halves of baby artichokes, the edges of them charred. "Tofu?" says Chrissie, spooning up a bite.

"Chawanmushi," says Iona. "Egg, and bean curd."

"It's not a game," says Ettie, knife and fork busy with an artichoke.

"Isn't it?" says Ysabel. "What you do is art, isn't it? And isn't art a game?"

"She has you there," says Reg.

"No," says Chrissie.

"It's prurient," says Luys.

"Now *there's* a word," says Reg.

"I cannot see the artistry in what they do. What you do," he says, to Chrissie, across the table. "Forgive me for speaking bluntly."

"So," says Ettie, "you think you could," as Reg is saying, "You've seen them perform?"

"I don't mean to deny the skill," says Luys, "the, the work, that goes into it. It's all very," he sighs, he takes up his fork. "It's an appeal to a gross, simple appetite. A reflex. I don't see, art."

"Maybe you don't see it," says Ettie, leaning around Reg, who's lifting a hand, "You say simple," he says. "You say gross. I say direct. Primal. Universal."

"But it isn't universal," says Luys.

"Everyone loves a beautiful woman," says Reg, and "No," says Jo, "we don't," and Ysabel snorts.

"But think," says Reg, "of, all of the, art, over the years, the poetry, the painting, the songs, the emblems they've employed, all dedicated to, dependent on, the beauty of a woman – "

"So?" says Jo.

"It's there," says Chrissie. "Already. Why not use it."

"Why not add to it," says Jo.

Small salad plates loaded with thick wheels of blood-red tomato, glistening with juice and oil, sprinkled with yellow chunks of roasted garlic, with grey salt and black pepper. "This is fantastic," says Jo, to Iona.

"Actually," says Reg, "you should be looking at video."

"We have," says Ettie, and Reg says, "I'm not talking about the amateur stuff, the stuff filmed by the audience, or whatever."

"This, to me, is magic," says Iona, a wedge of tomato speared on her fork.

"I'm talking professional video," says Reg. "Trailers, teasers, for your overall concept. Your semblance."

"The taste of August," says Iona. "In March." She takes her bite.

"Shit!" says Christian, and then, "sorry, no, I didn't recognize, but – I saw one of those, once. You were both up on a bar, with the hula hoop?" and Ettie nods, a half-shrug. "Damn," says Christian.

"See?" says Reg. "Your ideas, your art, but professionally shot, edited – "

"But we don't do film," says Ettie. "We do theatre, we do dance – "

"Burlesque," says Chrissie.

"Then hire people, for the things you can't do," says Reg.

"Which takes money," says Jo.

Ettie's fork clinks against her plate, and Ysabel sits back, her wineglass raised. Christian coughs. "Yes," says Reg. "Most things do."

"We've been trying," says Chrissie, and Ettie says, "We've been raising funds to get our show off the ground, the Ecdysis – "

"Yes," says Reg, "strippers and a symphony, right. It's a great hook, but that's all it is. Maybe you make a splash, maybe you don't, but – if the show's the culmination, of a campaign, something you make everyone anticipate," and he spreads his hands.

"We'd have to start all over, from square one," says Ettie, as Chrissie says, "We don't want to make commercials."

"Twenty-five thousand sets you up pretty nicely on square one," says Reg.

Luys takes a bite of tomato as Iona stands, and begins to clear emptied plates. "Oh," says Ettie. Ysabel polishes off her wine. "Is that an offer?" says Chrissie, to Reg.

"It's a round number," says Reg. "Enough to get you into trouble. Figure out if any more will help."

Christian lets out a low, breathy whistle. Ettie laughs, a shake of her head. Ysabel sits up, leans forward, reaching for the clay decanter. "Ten thousand," she says, pouring herself more wine. "Right here, right now."

"Ysabel," says Jo.

"But for the show you want to do," says Ysabel, taking up her brimming glass. "The orchestra, the concert hall. Not these pornographic films."

"I'm not talking about porn," says Reg.

"Aren't you?" says Ysabel.

"*Ysabel*," says Jo. "Your grace," murmurs Luys, reaching for her hand. She shakes him off. "That's very generous," Chrissie's saying. Christian's looking from Jo to Ysabel, to Reg, to Jo. Reg says, "Look, you have options, is the point." Ysabel's drinking her wine, big, gulping swallows. "It's a testament," says Reg, "to what you've already accomplished. We wouldn't be here if there wasn't something there."

"Tell me, Mr. Davies," says Ysabel, setting down her empty glass. "Reg. Answer a question for me."

"Okay," says Reg, the world half a laugh, "your, you, you're a queen, so, I should, what, say your majesty? Is that appropriate?

"Do you think I'm beautiful, Reg?" says Ysabel, and he frowns, and opens his mouth to speak, but glass clatters and forks tumble as Chrissie leans over the corner seizing Ysabel's hand *"Don't"* she cries, pulling, and Ysabel blinks, looks down, away from Reg to her hand in Chrissie's, to Chrissie, her blue eyes, her painted lips, "please," she's saying. "Don't."

"The least little thing" – an Apportionment – her Case Ebb-Tide, Cinnamon Twist, All-American Girl – Fénius

"The least little thing," says Anna, fingertips against her forehead, pushing aside a wing of russet hair, "sets it off." On the table between her elbows a round white cup full of steamed milk marbled with coffee and cocoa. "And I'm right back there, that moment, the moment she asked. Time stopped, you know? And everything about her that I'd noticed, without noticing, her smile, the way she holds herself, those – eyes," her own hand dropping, gripping her upper arm, glasses flashing as she looks up, a wan smile for Gloria sitting across from her. "The smell of sunlight, in her hair. It all came crashing down, and I know, I knew," she looks back down, shaking her head. "There was no other answer, there was nothing else to say. There will never be another."

Wrapped in Gloria's hands a pale green mug of red tea, steaming. "It was," she says. Behind her rows of shelves neatly lined with books. Romance, says a sign at the end of a shelf. Paranormal Romance. Humor. "It wasn't anything like that," says Gloria. She sips. "I never met her before. But the lights, and the music, everybody, I just, it was an impulse. I said yes. And, and it was like, everything," she looks away, she licks her lips. Another mouthful of tea. "I can't get her out of my head."

"The," says Anna, "the taste of her."

"We, I, ah, we never," says Gloria quickly.

"Your pardon," says Anna, sitting back. Adjusting the drape of her houndstooth skirt over her crossed legs. "It's not easy, talking about it. I, um, it's – "

"I paint," says Gloria. "It's what I do, with the money. Most of it. Paints. Canvases. I keep, doing the same one? Over and over. I, I can't," setting her mug down, looking away.

"Does it help?"

Gloria shakes her head. "But I can't stop," she says.

"I'd like to see them," says Anna.

Rhinestones flash under fluorescent lights as the man in the peach Nudie suit twists and shoves, and the man with the big blond beard goes stumbling thump against a white suv, squeak of brown boots on polished concrete. "Draw," snarls the man in the Nudie suit, "or shut your bleeding mouth."

"Hey," says the man in the grey sweatsuit, a can of soda in either hand.

The fourth man, his coat of red velvet worn and stained, puckered with intricate embroidery, reaches for the man in the Nudie suit, and more flashes and sparks. "Do *not,*" snarls the man in the suit. "He is a churl, and will answer as a churl, or I will have satisfaction." The blond man, Chillicoathe the Harper, pushes up off the suv to spit at the feet of the man in the suit, who says, "Oh," and lifts his glittering arm, light gathering itself in his curling hand.

"Hey," from behind them. "Hey!"

Chilli looks down, scowling, and the man in the Nudie suit shakes the flare from his hand. "Your grace," says the man in the grey sweats, ducking his head. Jo's marching across the parking garage in her black coat, her sombre chalkstripe dress, a sleek aluminum briefcase in her hand. Behind her Luys in his nondescript brown jacket, and Christian in his softly yellow suit. "Your pardon, ma'am," says the man in the Nudie suit, "but we have business, the Harper and I – "

"Do I look like I care," says Jo, headed past the suv, to the reddish brown car parked beside it. Hefting the briefcase up onto the trunk, thumbing the combination locks, clicking open the latches. "Okay, boys," she says, opening the case, and golden light washes over her as they gather around. The man in the red velvet coat whistles. "Most of this is to replace what got stolen last night," says Jo. "But we got some extra."

"I'll say," says the man in the grey sweats.

"Her majesty provides," says Jo. "Okay. It's portioned out, but since this one kinda took us all by surprise, we're gonna deliver, instead of waiting for pickup. So. Medoro?" Holding up a plastic freezer bag bulging with dust. "This one goes to the – "

"It's Astolfo, ma'am," says the man in the grey sweats.

"You're kidding," says Jo. "You guys're just fucking with me at this point."

"I assure your grace," he says.

"This to the rabbits," she says, holding out the bag. He looks around. "Anybody want some?" he says, holding up the cans. "It's Mexican Coke."

"Um, sure, hey, thanks," says Christian, stepping up to take one, but Chilli puts out a hand to block him, "Sworn knights only, at an Apportionment!"

"Horseshit," says Jo, and they're all looking at her. "Unless Sweets has been hiding a badge in that head of hair he has?"

"Your grace," says Chilli, "this boy should not – "

"He's a friend of mine, Harper, so tread careful. Conary?" She tosses a bag to the man in the Nudie suit, who catches it, alarmed. "How do you feel about the Marquess."

"As, as well as I might, your grace," he says.

Jo looks back, over one shoulder, the other, there's the man in the red velvet coat, rubbing his hands. "Pwyll," she says, handing him a bag, "go annoy the Viscount. As for the King's, I'll see to that, and our own cut has been divvied up, we'll hand it around the next couple of days. Chilli." He's reaching for the briefcase, but she snaps it shut. She's holding up a bag, noticeably smaller than the others. "I'll need you to walk this over to Ladd's. Tonight."

"But, your grace," says Chilli, and a gesture at the briefcase.

"But?" says Jo, still holding up the bag.

"The theft's on me, your grace. I'd set it right."

"Then do as your Duke commands," says Jo.

"All due respect, your grace," says Chilli, "but – you've been upstairs? With the Queen?" and Jo lets the bag drop to the trunk. "What the who?" she says.

Mouth fixed within that big blond beard he says, "You've been drinking."

Jo blinks.

"Ma'am," says Chilli.

"What of it, Harper," says Luys, hands on his hips.

"Mason," says Chilli, "I mean no disrespect to her majesty, but – "

"Or anyone else?" says Jo, as off that way, toward the ramp leading out of the garage, someone whoops. "Do yourself a favor, Chilli," she says. "Take the bag, shut up, and go."

"So where's the party?" someone's calling, and they're all falling still, Conary in his glittering suit and Pwyll, hanging his head, Astolfo, soda in one hand, bag in the other, looking about, and Luys folding his arms as Christian ducks back. Off that way, pinkish-orange pompadour a-bob, comes Lymond in a trench coat over a dull green suit, a black tie loosely knotted about his undone collar. "Did I miss it?" he says.

"Kinda fizzled, a little early," says Jo.

"Gentlemen!" says Lymond. "Always an honor. Don't let me keep you." They're already turning away, Astolfo and Pwyll and Conary, bags in hand, and Chilli picks up the little bag from the trunk of the car, heads after them for the ramp, up and out. "I didn't need that," mutters Jo.

"What," says Lymond brightly. "That? That was nothing. I find myself with a sudden hankering for noodles. Heard you might be making a run."

"Luys?" says Jo, turning away, beckoning him over. Christian throws back the last of his soda. "Get the others. Follow Chilli," says Jo.

"You're certain," says Luys, hands in his pockets, eyes on his boots.

"It's personal," says Jo, quiet, close. "The bandit doesn't want the owr, she wants him. Look," a hand on his shoulder, and he looks up to meet her eyes. "Follow him. He delivers without a hitch, I'm wrong, and you can hightail it across town because we'll maybe need your help. Okay?"

He nods.

"And take Christian with you. Just in case."

"You're off?" says Christian.

"Don't get hurt," says Jo, "but this time, don't run." And then, to Lymond, "We're taking my car."

"Sure," he says. "But I'm driving."

The room now dark, the table gone, the candles and the chairs, the sofas returned beneath the windows left and right in walls that narrow to a point, and there the great maroon chair where she sits curled up in white and gold, a wine glass in her hand. "It isn't locked," she says, and the door to the apartment opens. "I wasn't expecting you back," says Ysabel.

"She was his date," says Chrissie, uncertain on spindly heels, shoulders draped in fake white fur. "I'm yours."

"But still," says Ysabel, sitting back, lowering her bare feet to the floor. "You had to see him off."

"Investment has its perks. Should I go?" Click of a heel, as she comes down a step, and "No," says Ysabel.

"Are you angry?" says Chrissie, letting the fur slip from a shoulder. "We're very grateful." And the other. "He'd never've gone that high without you."

"Yay, me," says Ysabel.

"You *are* angry," says Chrissie, lowering a hand, letting the weight of the wrap draw itself slinking through the crook of her elbow and down to pool whitely on the steps. "Don't be angry." Heel-clack as she comes down another step. "You can still give us whatever you want." Undoing a knot at her shoulder, and an asymmetrical panel falls away, baring a ghostly breast to the dim light of those windows all about.

"How very generous of you," says Ysabel.

"Whenever you want," says Chrissie, unhooking a flap at her hip, opening a zipper, another click of her descending heels. Her little black dress falls away to the floor.

"Give me a reason," says Ysabel, and on those heels quite steady and sure comes Chrissie toward her, streetlight from those windows oblongs and rhombuses slipping up and over naked swooping sway of legs and belly, arms and breasts, "make your case," says Ysabel, and Chrissie stands herself before the chair, between Ysabel's white-draped knees, yellow hair severe about her almost-smiling eyes, lips parting, a breath taken in as Ysabel leans forward, hand on a bare knee, nose brushing belly and lips a briefest kiss the lightly gooseflesh hand against a thigh, fingertips nestle the crease sloping up to hip, thumb beside the sleekly pout of vulva. "I could," says Chrissie, "answer your – "

"No," says Ysabel.

A hiss of a breath. "Thank you, then, for – "

"Don't," says Ysabel.

Chrissie's almost frowning, mouth still open about the words unsaid, until another sharp breath, through her teeth. "I was," she says, "pleased, you didn't," her hands lifting, floating at her sides, "push, things, with Reg," and a shiver, a jerk, trying to keep her balance, one and and the other hand coming about to Ysabel's head, fingers among the black curls. "You," says Chrissie, "you, you're not," and another breath, "you're not going to make this easy," she says. "Are you."

"Stop," says Ysabel against that skin, "asking, for what I've already given away, and yes." Looking up. "I will."

He shuts off the engine, looks across to her, "Chilly?" he says.

She's leaning back in her seat, eyes closed, collar of her black coat up about her throat. "Exposed," she says. The aluminum briefcase on the floorboard between her red shoes.

"You ready for this?" he says, brow furrowed over bulging eyes, one blue, one brown.

"We ain't getting jumped," says Jo. Sitting up, and a sigh, shaking her head. "It's been a day," she says. "I found out, this, old friend? I'd been looking for, for months? He's, well, he's working for me. Has been, for a couple weeks."

"Yeah?" says Lymond.

"I didn't know," she says.

"But now you do. And he's okay? You're taking care of him?"

"Ray," she says. "I didn't know."

He smiles. "Welcome to upper management. The shit I don't know," and he shakes his head. "You could write a book." Looking down, at his hands. "How's my sister," he says.

"How's the new Bride," says Jo.

"She's not," says Lymond, and then, a deep breath, "she's no one's Bride," he says.

"You're just keeping your options open," says Jo.

"And you didn't answer my question," says Lymond.

Jo looks away, out the window, spangled with neon rain. "She tried to give ten thousand dollars we don't have to her goddamn girlfriend."

"She," says Lymond, "tried, ah," his hand up, reaching for a word. "So, she didn't. Which is good. And if she had, actually, I'm sure – you would've figured something out."

"I have to figure out too many goddamn things," says Jo. "You better know what the hell you're doing."

"Funnily enough, I don't?" says Lymond, leaning over the steering wheel, looking up through the windshield at the sign, KJ Rice Noodle Shop & Restaurant, it says, under the lit-up Oregon Lottery logo. "I mean, do we just walk in the front door, or what?"

"Works for me," says Jo, shoving her door open, hauling up the briefcase, kicking her red shoes out to the pavement.

An electronic bong as he opens the door, as they step inside, the front room brightly lit, and there by the empty glass-fronted counter a thickset man in a tight black T-shirt, shoulders softly round, and faded tattoos at his temples. "You have a new man," he says.

"What, Ray?" says Jo, looking over at Lymond. "Don't mind Ray."

"A new man, and you brought it yourself," Wu Song folds his arms over his chest. "Troubles?"

"I ever want advice," says Jo, setting the briefcase on the counter, "I'll be sure to ask."

"Of course," says Wu Song.

And Lymond says, "Wait. That's it?"

"Until next quarter," says Jo.

"But I was," says Lymond, a theatrical pout, "I wanted some noodles."

Wu Song shrugs, then smiles. "Best in town," he says.

Here and there, close to the grass, small signs planted that say, white letters on black, Ebb Tide, Barbra Streisand, Cinnamon Twist, All-American Girl, The Kincaid. Behind each, serried ranks of new green upright rose canes, sprouted from the stubbled nubbins of deadheaded bushes. She stands before them, waiting, wrapped in a big coat, sheepskin collar upturned, and on her head a floppy, goggle-eyed horse-head mask, and a baseball bat in her hand. "Harper!" she cries, muffled by that mask.

He's coming down the middle of the tree-lined street, arms wide, "I want my *coat!*" he bellows, breaking into a run. That horse head wobbles and flops, a muffled gibber of laughter, and she plants her feet, lifts the bat, but a grate and skid of his boots he stops just short of the square and she's turning away, swinging the bat up whock to catch Luys's sword and shove to send him staggering back, "Mason!" cries Chilli, aggrieved, as the woman in the mask ducks under the whick of a dart flung by a figure all in black. "Ambuscade!" she roars through the mask, dancing back between the rows of roses. "Banditry!" yells Luys, sword up, following her. "Gerlin?" says Chilli, as a portly man in a brown and black ski jacket rushes past him, waving a long square-pointed blade above his head, followed by that figure all in black. "Cheat!" the muffled voice, and "Coward!" Crunch and whip and chunk, another pass of sword and bat, more whicking darts, "Spadone!" yells Luys "Cut her off!"

Chilli kneels, his hand a fist he knocks against the pavement, and the twang of a snapped string pulls up out of a flare of light a short-bladed sword, stubby hilt and pommel of it golden, heavy. Standing. He steps up into the garden, picking up his pace, lifting the sword up over his head, shoving past the man in the ski jacket to Luys his sword back for a two-handed swipe and clang, scrape of blade on blade, Luys wrenched around by the unexpected blow, tripping over a line of roses. "She's *mine,*" bellows Chilli, turning but not in time to avoid that square-pointed blade, a cut that rends his sweater, slashing from rib to hip, *"my* fight," he gargles, falling to the grass, as roses thrash about.

"Gradasso," calls Luys, his sword up and ready. "Kern!"

"Lost her," the answering cry. The man all in black, coming up from the other end of the garden. "She went south," he says, pointing with a dart. "That way," shifting, "or that."

"You lost her," says Luys.

"You had no *right,*" snarls Chilli. "Her quarrel is with *me.*" An arm clutched about his shredded sweater, breathing shallow, loud, quick. "She'll name me coward, she'll tell – "

"She's exiled!" cries Luys. Hand to his forehead. "Outlawed. She'll tell no one a thing. But *you.*" Turning about, there among the trampled roses. "Kern, Spadone," he throws a gesture off toward the other end of the garden, "go. Do what you can," and as they head off, he kneels. "You," he says, to Chilli. "Still have a delivery to make."

"I'll need a moment," says Chilli, hands wet in his lap.

"By all means," says Luys. "But take not a pinch, nor the slightest grain, to help it along."

"I would *never,*" says Chilli, scowling over is big blond beard.

"But you would," says Luys, pushing himself to his feet, "put a peck of it at risk, and our friendship with the East, the word of your Duke, all for your petty vendetta."

"Duke," says Chilli, with a barely hidden sneer.

"Be about your business," snaps Luys, and he's off through the roses.

"Who is it," says Agravante, turning a page of the leather-bound book in his lap.

"A delivery, sir," says the glumly narrow man in a black suit, chin tucked in behind a high white collar.

"Awfully late," says Agravante, taking off his spectacles, looking up, the book now closed about a finger. White dread-locks unbound, loose about his shoulders.

"He did not wish a word, but presented this," and the narrow man holds out a shapeless parcel wrapped in brown paper, tied up with string. "With the compliments of Southeast."

Agravante takes the parcel and turns it over, finding a corner of the paper wrapping to pry open, the pleasantly puzzled look on his face fading as faint gold light shines out on his fingers.

"Something amiss, sir?" says the narrow man. His nose and cheeks are appled with extravagant gin blossoms.

Agravante, closing the folded corner up, shakes his head, "Not as such," he says. Setting the book aside. "I'll be retiring now," he says, getting to his feet, tightening the belt of his pale blue robe. The parcel in his hand. "Be so good as to alert the gentlemen: I'll want them here a little before lunch tomorrow." He smiles. "Briefly. Nothing untoward." And then, as the narrow man's turning to leave, "Do you know," says Agravante, "what is worst, about answered prayers?"

"Prayer, sir?" says the narrow man.

"Indeed," says Agravante.

Between the gateposts of that collar, his chin shifts from one side, to the other, and back, "I don't, understand, sir," says the narrow man.

"It's all right," says Agravante, clapping him on the shoulder. "Have a good evening."

Up a long straight staircase in the front hall of the house, pale robe ghostly in the unlit halls of the second floor, Agravante parcel under his arm opens a slender door on a tightly winding spiral staircase.

A round room at the top of it, casement windows all about, cranked open to the night, an uncommitted drizzle stirring the dark trees without. Cardboard boxes full of clothes stacked here and there, and more clothing strewn about the bare wood floor, a wrought-iron bed there, a marble-topped table beside it, an alarm clock blinking 12:00, 12:00, and a reading lamp, unlit. A paperback book, swollen, rumpled with old rain, the edges of it flocked with mold, the cover faded, the title just legible that says Chanur's Legacy. He lifts his arm to let his parcel fall, reaching for the book, but what's landed on the pillow is a fiendish little basket-box, carved from a single chunk of dark red wood. He looks at it a moment. Pulls the chain on the lamp, lighting up its blue glass shade, and sits, gingerly, on the edge of the bed. Turning the basket-box over in the light, the knurled and seamless faces of it, the pips carved into each, a flame, a cloud, a drop of water.

"Fénius," he says to himself. His big white head hung low.

UNLOCKING THE DOOR — WHATEVER SHE WANTS

UNLOCKING THE DOOR to the apartment she leans back against him, head against his shoulder, "It's just," she says, "a more, calculating knight, would've seen the King home. Not a lowly Duchess."

"His majesty has no need of my help," murmurs Luys, looking down on her red, red hair.

"You're saying I do?" says Jo, looking up for a kiss. Arms about each other stumbled steps into the kitchen, kissing, he's undone a button of her dress, she's grabbing his hand, turning away from his mouth, "What," he says, "my lady," but she shakes her head. Looking down the dark hall, the closed doors. The light under the door to the left. Stepping away from him. "I didn't leave a light on," she says.

It's the bedside lamp, an anglepoise affair pulled out to light the small thick book laid open on Ysabel's lap. She's sitting in the corner, pillows piled behind her, knees tenting the blankets, "I'm sorry," she says, looking up to Jo in the doorway. "But her snoring's terrible."

"She came back," says Jo, her red hair skewed, her hand holding closed her dress.

"She came back," says Ysabel, and then, sitting up, "oh," she says, "oh, Luys, he's, you, Jo, I'm sorry," setting the book aside as Jo says "No, it's, just, it's okay, stay. Stay."

"No," says Ysabel, lifting the blankets, "I can stand the noise, let me just – "

"Ysabel," says Jo. "It's okay. It's late, anyway. Just, give me a minute."

Luys stands in the open doorway of the apartment, his hand on the knob of the door. "So," he says, "my place, not yours? What's that?"

She's holding a small plastic baggie, a generous spoonful of golden dust. "I have to give Tommy Tom a call in a minute here," she says. "When he tells me how much it's gonna take, to fix the roses you tore up, I want to be able to tell him you're on the way."

"A vassal's work is never done," he says, taking the baggie from her hand.

"I'll make it up to you," she says. "Breakfast. We'll have breakfast. Just the two of us. A proper meal."

"There is nothing to make up, my lady."

"Get out of here, with your my lady," she says, and kisses him.

"Eres hermosa," he says.

Jo closes the door to her room and stands there a moment, eyes closed, head leaned back against the jamb. "One down," she says. Opening her eyes. "Ninety-eight to go."

"Long day," says Ysabel.

"More'n a day," says Jo, setting her phone on the bedside table, a ring of keys, a money clip pinched about a sheaf of bills. "Since, yesterday? Morning?" Kicking off her shoes, letting her coat fall away. "I feel," she says, turning away. Under the windows the three or four wood crates filled with clothing neatly folded. She's standing there, swaying, a hand on her chest, there between the lapels of her dress half unbuttoned. "Just leave it," says Ysabel, reading her book. "On the floor. It'll be fine."

"Yeah?"

"It looks good on you," says Ysabel, as Jo undoes more buttons. "You should wear nice things more often."

"Yeah," says Jo, stooping over a crate, worming her way into a black T-shirt. "Sure." A red devil leers across the front of it, marred by silkscreen craquelure. Shivering, she crawls under the blankets. Ysabel sits forward, tugs a pillow free, tosses it to the foot of the bed. Leans over Jo to set her book on the bedside table. Lays her head on Jo's shoulder, as Jo switches off the light. "Your friend," says Ysabel. "Christian. You need to do something about him."

"He's," says Jo, "ah, he's on Iona's couch tonight? I think, I don't – "

"No," says Ysabel. "I mean, he can't keep running around with just, whomever. You made too big of a deal of him tonight."

"Did I," says Jo, shifting on her pillow to look down at those black curls. "So," she says, closing her eyes, a yawn. "What do you suggest?"

"We need a new Shootist," says Ysabel.

"I'm pretty sure," says Jo, "he's never held a gun in his life."

"We're also in need of a Dagger, if you'd rather."

"So I can just, do that," says Jo. "Just pick somebody, a freaking gallowglas, I can make him a knight."

"You're the Duke," says Ysabel. "You can do whatever you want."

"Good to know, your majesty." Her eyes pop open, "Shit," she says, switching on the light, reaching for the phone, "almost forgot, I have to call the fucking Soames – "

Black hair loose, bleached bangs, red paint smudging one round cheek, grimy white T-shirt stretched out, handwritten letters distorted that say Miracle Rod and Those Amazing Trumpets. She drops her brush to the makeshift tabouret. Takes up a tube of paint, squeezing out a dollop on her fingertip, a brilliant green, apple and glass, a green like some weird flame. Stepping back, her T-shirt rides up, a roll of belly lopping pilled black satin about her hips. The canvas before her a scramble of hair in thick black strokes, a line of cheek, a mouth, all crowded at the bottom and an arm, a suggestion of an arm, the motion of a gesture of an arm reaching up, and up, a whoop from somewhere behind her, laughter echoing among the shadowed bulks, equipment, boxes, someone unseen in the flare of the trouble light dangled over her head as she turns, peers into the darkness, a hand up against the light, fingers shining with that eye-borne green. "Mar?" she says. "You get it?"

"Who cares!" The voice, contralto, brimmed with mirth, something bangs, clang a bat against a truss, "Who gives a good," bang, "God!" clang, "damn!" and a peal of laughter, dancing up to her down the shadowed aisle, a figure in a coat, a sheepskin collar up about a mass of tangled curls that lighten paling as she prances into the light, a matted cloud of cream about her head. Dropping the bat to the floor, and the flop of an empty horse-head mask. "The oathless reprobate proposed to ambush me! A third of a dozen, against my wooden bat – but I led them such a chase!"

"Cool." She turns back to the canvas, but her green-daubed fingers hesitate over the wild blurred face, there at the bottom of it. She straightens, picks up a rag to wipe them greenly smearing clean. "I went to see the lawyers today," she says.

"Aren't you cold?" says Marfisa, sitting on a nubbled pea-green couch, there at the edge of the circle of light. She starts to work a boot off of her foot.

"There was a problem with a credit card. I met somebody there. Anna Nirdlinger? She, she used to – "

"I know who she is," says Marfisa, setting the one boot on the floor. "The Queen's amanuensis."

"Well, now she's a, a paralegal, there at the firm. She, she wants to come see the paintings."

"Why did you tell her about the paintings," says Marfisa.

"She's, well," that greened rag dropped to the tabouret. "She's like you, Mar. She's like me."

"What does that mean, she's like us."

Biting her grinning lip, looking off in the shadows, "Fucked if I know," says Gloria Monday.

Well, do you ever get the feeling
That the story's too damn real, and
In the present tense?
Or that everybody's on the stage,
And it seems like you're the only person
Sitting in the audience?

—Ian Anderson

NO. 24

" – vilissima et infima – "

BLACK SUNGLASSES ON THE DRESSER, neatly folded, left lens spiraled with spidery letter-shapes written in white. Spidery letter-shapes inked across the mirror above it, an elegant shambles of a paragraph, each line cramping, curling downward to the right, and the last of it trailing in curlicues down toward the bottom of the glass. Behind those lines his reflection, the massy bulk of him fitted in a black T-shirt, his beard a matted mahogany bush in the flat white light of the room, his hair, loosed, eaves of faintly waved curls still crimped from long confinement, all of it a leafless thicket about the upturned plug of his nose, round hillocks of his cheeks, the narrowed eyes, red and brown. "You didn't tell me," he says, a rusted croak.

"You didn't want to know," he says.

"How can you say that," he says.

"You turned away," he says.

"That's a lie," he says.

"You know that's a lie. How can you say that."

"You said that." The tempo of his breathing's picked up, tendrils of beard and mustache lofting, fluttering with each blowsy exhalation, until it catches, with a hitch. "You did it," he says, a thready whisper, and his breath seeps from him in a slow settling sigh. "You *did it,*" he says. "You kept doing it. You knew. You always knew. You just didn't want to know."

He stands. He's been sitting on a narrow bed, discreetly made, a threadbare blanket, beige, folded neatly at the head of it about a single pillow. The walls a dark green rumpled by old over-painted cracks and sagging plaster, the single window bare, warmed by pulsing neon light outside, then off, then on again, and when it's off the weaker, palely yellow streetlight. Through that shifting scrim can just be seen the unlit windows set in other buildings. "You should've said," he says, looking back and forth, his reflection, his shadow, on the glass.

"You stayed," he says, stepping to one side. Away from the window, hand against the wall. There the bed, there the dresser, there the door, before him. "You didn't leave," he says. Another step. "You did not leave," he says.

Those sunglasses tremble on the dresser, bounce, flip over as an arm springs up. His hands up pressing back his stiffly outright hair, as he watches the sunglasses rocking, slowing, stop.

"You need to get out of here," says Philip Keightlinger.

Wings flutter and settle, a chirrup, a chime, the crackle of straw, a shift of weight, seed scatters to the floor. "Boy?" says a gruff voice. Hootings erupt, whitterings and clucks, a crowing whoop, chains rattle, wood creaks, shadows coil and lurch and spread, like wings. "Boy, it's after six. I already got the coffee." Hunkered over a figure shuffles under the low-hanging cages swaying, settling. Seed crunching under a heavy step. At the end of the sleeping porch a low table, a sleeping bag neatly rolled beside it, and on it a radio alarm clock, silent, unplugged. He rubs his bare head darkly bald over a crisp circle of white curls. "Right," he says, turning, "he isn't," and stooped, shuffling, makes his way back through the sleeping cages.

Outside the susurrus of fallen rain, the dripping trickles, crinkling seep, the plops and chimes and a shivering gust-blown spatter from the trees, over the fence. By the door a cardboard box, under that flight of stairs bolted to the back of the old brick building. He leans out from under them, hand out, palm up, looking up, into the soft dark starless sky. A sullen haze, off that way, the lights of downtown. He squats, mindful of the mud, wrestling up the rain-soft box, squelch and plep, duck-walking back, pulling him upright, groan and glower.

Inside, through a cramped kitchen all scarred linoleum and dark cabinets, down a narrow hall lined with shelves, partitioned into cubbyholes, stuffed here and there with mis-matched pairs of shoes. Clatter of a beaded curtain and up to a worktable mounded high with more shoes, where the old man sets the box. Brushing down the front of his coat. He gingerly pries up a soggy flap, reaches in to pull out a shoe, a black and brown leather football shoe, filthy, the collar of it worn to shreds above the heel. He tosses it on the pile, pulls out another, a cognac-colored wedge-heeled pump. Someone's tapping at the door.

"Here," he says, unlocking the door, swinging it open with a jingle of the bell, "here," switching on the lights in the front window, George's, say the letters painted in red and yellow in an arc across the glass. Shoes Repaired. A man in a brown and orange ski jacket pushes through the doorway, dingy red cooler in his hands, followed by a woman in a green rain slicker, carry-ing a plastic storage tub lined with custard-laden ramekins. "Over there," says the old man, "on the counter," as he steps out onto the sidewalk, "Hita!" he calls, to a woman coming down the sidewalk, brown coat wrapped about blue coveralls, long black hair under a kerchief. "Lend a hand?" He's shaking out a ring of keys to find the one that opens the door of a powder-blue town car. The light of downtown off that way fading into the lighten-ing overcast. He lifts a cardboard box from the front seat, printed over with little running coffee cups, and a spigot on one side. Hands it to the woman in the kerchief, and leans in to fetch out another. "I'll get the donuts," he's saying.

The front room of the shop's now filled, raincoats and overalls, uniforms brown and taupe and beige, styrofoam cups a-steam. "Better than ever I can remember," says a man, his navy work-shirt blazoned with a white patch, Atlas Facilities Maintenance, it says, under a stylized globe.

"First flush," says a woman with grey-tinged curls, lifting a bar-shaped pastry from a big pink box. "It'll all settle down, soon enough."

"She's been flushed all winter," says a man in a denim jacket, munching something darkly chocolate under a white piped-icing pentagram, and "Have you seen the Bride?" says a man in brown and orange polyester, and "She's no Bride," says someone, and "No one sees the *Princess,*" says someone else, and "I hear she likes butterflies," says a woman in a white formal shirt, bow tie unclipped about her neck. "I hear she's beautiful," says the man in brown and orange.

"Course she is," says the old man to himself, filling a cup with coffee from one of the boxes on the counter.

"How are you, Gordon," says the woman in the kerchief, her hand on his. He grunts, a gesture of his cup at the work table back there, the shoes, the half-open box. "Too much to do, and more on the way," he says.

"You need some help," she says, and he snorts. "Don't we all," he says, but the door's opening again, the bell's jingling again, and the laughter's dying, sentences falter, stop, they're looking down, away from the four men pushing into the front room. "Gordon," says the one at the head of them, short and wide in a bulky cardigan, bald head ruddy.

"Dogstongue," says Gordon. "You're with the Gaffer now?" A man in a pea coat nods once, crisply. "Moving up in the world," says Gordon.

"We just got done, putting a rose garden back together?" says Dogstongue. "For the Duchess?" He isn't looking at Gordon, but about the room, the men and women in coveralls and uniforms, cups in hands, napkins, donuts. "And while I know you prefer the company of domestics," he says, and none of them meet his gaze, "well." Dogstongue smiles, then, at Gordon. "You always did have the cheapest coffee."

Gordon looks about the room, at all of them silent, looking to him from the corners of downturned eyes. He sighs, turns his back, stumping around behind the counter. "Free country," he says.

He isn't the first person off the bus. He isn't the last. Right there in the middle of them, coming down the steps, brown dungarees and a jacket of army-surplus green, an emaciated duffel slung from his shoulder. Rain loud on the great awning over them, and another bus snoring in the stall beside, all dark blue and grey, a leaping hound painted on the side. Seattle, says the sign on the front of it. Portland, says the sign on the front of the one they're disembarking.

Around the corner of the low brick terminal, the flat roof extending out over the red brick sidewalk, glassy wet in streaks. He runs a hand through his black hair, looking about, greyly morning light, a woman dragging away a wheelie suitcase draped with a plastic garbage bag, somebody sitting over there, on a dry patch of brick, faded black denim and mud-caked boots, a big black broad-brimmed leather hat. A pale grey scrap of kitten tumbles about a bit of string before a cardboard sign. So he turns up the ragged collar of his jacket, heads down the sidewalk to squat, hold out a hand, wriggle his fingers. The kitten rears up paws spread to fall back against the sign. Letters carelessly scrawled across it say, Will Drink for Money.

"Cute cat," he says.

"Oh, hey," says the kid in black denim, looking up. Under that floppy brim a round face fuzzed by a sweep of ginger beard. "Thanks."

He leans back, reaching into a pocket of his jacket, army-surplus green. Under the beak of his nose a pointed smile. He's pulled out a pale green nylon wallet, ripped it open, the inside of it black, card slots empty, nothing tucked in the photo ID window. Slips from it a crisply single twenty-dollar bill and holds it up between them, his smile sharpening as the kid's eyes widen.

"Nice hat," he says.

A SHINING SILVER EGG – SETTLING ACCOUNTS
A SIMPLE ADJURATION

SHINING IN THE RAIN A SILVER EGG of a trailer, there at the back of the mostly empty parking lot. In her long black coat she's knocking at the door of it, rattling the aluminum shell, "Luys?" she says. Red hair a vivid shock in all that grey-white light. "You home?"

The handle turns, the door jerks, opening enough to reveal him big and brown, black hair, blinking, "Your grace?" he says.

"Breakfast," says Jo. "Remember?"

Inside it's dark, the only light from without, and hazed by gauzy curtains over slender windows there and there. "I called," she says. "Your phone must not be on."

He's stepping toward the back, out of the way, sitting on the low bed there in a sort of alcove, umber comforter rucked over yellow sheets. His black hair wet, chest bare, a white towel about his hips. "I suppose," he says.

"We've talked about that," she says, latching the door shut. Head bowed, against the curl of ceiling.

"Yes, your grace."

"I need to be able to get a hold of you guys whenever I, might, need," she says.

"Of course, your grace."

"That's not what I," and she steps into the middle of the trailer. Behind her a booth in the nose of it, two benches, a table bolted between them. "Well. Breakfast."

"Of course," he says, leaning forward, opening a cabinet at the foot of the bed. Pulling out a neatly folded pair of pants. "Wait," she says.

He looks up.

"Before," she says, "you know. I don't know." Hands at the buttons of her coat. "I thought, maybe. Unless you're hungry, I mean."

"I just, woke up," he says, brow furrowed.

"I shoulda got some coffee," says Jo, undoing her buttons, one by fumbled one. "Or tea. Tea. I should've brought some tea."

"My lady," he says.

"I just figured," she says. "You have the food carts next door."
Looking over her bared shoulder at him as she lets the coat slip
down her arms. "Whatever we decide to do."

"Jo, I don't," he says, as she lays the coat over the table, "what *are*
we," he says, as she turns to face him, hands on hips wrapped in a
short kilt, black plaid shot through with red and white, between a
sleeveless black turtleneck and black knit stockings. "Are we," he
says, "to go dancing?"

She hikes up the hem of the kilt an inch and there, the tops of the
stockings, bare skin above. Her lip-bitten smile, eyes wide, brows
up, uncertain, "You like?" she says. Luys blinks. "Borrowed 'em
from Ysabel," she says, letting the hem drop. "Not that I have her
legs."

"I like the legs you have, your grace," says Luys.

She blows out a little laugh. "I cleared the morning," she says.
"Nobody on deck. Nothing on tap. Just," a little shrug. "You
and me."

"Yes," he says. "Breakfast." He shakes out that pair of pants.
"Luys!" she says, and he halts, pants a-dangle, frowning. "I,"
she says, and then, a deep breath, eyes squeezing shut, she grabs
the kilt again, lifts the hem again, up and higher up. He drops
the pants, his jaw, eyes widening, "My lady," he says, "you
came, all this way, here, like, like – "

"No," she says, rolling her eyes, "I yanked 'em off in the parking
lot, where anyone could see. Luys, I just," letting go of the kilt, a
shake of her head, looking away, "I wanted to be sexy," she says.

He leans forward, elbows on bare knees. Looking softly up.
"Your grace," he says, "does not need to be sexy."

"My grace is horny," says Jo. "We got," she says, "I just
thought, we were interrupted, last night, so I thought, we
could take the morning, we could, jump each other, we, and I
tried, to call, and you opened the door in just a, a towel, and
that was, that was," her hand up, weighing the next word.

"I had just," he says, hoarsely, "woken up." Looking to the
narrow stall that alcoves off the bed. "I took a shower."

"Which, is fine!" says Jo. "Just what I would've – thought.
But then, you," that hand, lowering. "Walked away."

"I," he says, and he swallows, "I didn't mean," but "Ah, fuck it," says Jo, reaching for the kilt, yanking something, and it swings loose, falls open, down, she lets it go. "My lady," he says, but one step, two steps, three down the cramped length of the trailer lifting a knee to plant it on the bed leaning to lift the other kneeling a-straddle him kissing, kissing his mouth, his head in her hands, her fingers in his thick black hair, his hands a bit of leather tied about his wrist on her bare hips, brown thumb along the blued shadow of her belly just above an edge of dark curled hair, lifting away as she yanks away his towel, "Oh," he says, and she kisses him again, pushing him back, down, leaning over him, "oh," he says, she's kissing his hairless chest, tilting to run her teeth along the firm undergirding of a pec, he hisses, her hand about lifting the flop of his cock which stirs and swells in her fingers and his head lolls back against the pillow blue and both hands high and "Hanh," he says, and "hup," slapping his forehead sweeping back what little hair he has left and grinning, he's grinning, opening his mouth to let out a whoop, drinking the air in, "ha, heh," the rise and fall of his soft chest sparsely haired, "whoa," he says, looking down, to those grey mustaches between his knees. "Now this," he says, says Arnold Becker, "*this* alarm clock I could get used to."

"What, every morning?" Wiping his mouth with the back of his hand, dull beads of pewter at the ends of his mustache swaying as he pushes to his feet, his belly a thin softening of fat laid over muscle, chest fuzzed with iron-colored hair.

"We could take turns," says Becker, sitting up on his elbows. "I have no qualms about waking you up. I mean, I owe you one," and Pyrocles smiles as he stoops to pick up a salmon-orange towel. "Actually," says Becker, frowning, "if we take last night into account, I'm pretty sure it's two. At least two."

"We'll settle accounts tonight, or tomorrow," says Pyrocles, wrapping the towel about his waist. "Or the day after. But today, this morning, I have a valve adjustment, I have two tune-ups, I have a fifty-year-old Galaxie that needs a new suite of belts."

"What," says Becker, flopping back on the bed, "no swords to forge? No, no breastplates to pour?"

"Cast armor would be too heavy," says Pyrocles. "And much too brittle."

"It was a," says Becker, rolling over, "it's a joke," pulling the heavy blue blanket over himself. "My jokes have to be technically accurate?"

"You have to be getting up," says Pyrocles, "you're going to be late." Padding away from the bed there in the corner of the white-painted loft, and all that light cascading down from the clerestory lining one long wall. "Not today!" calls Becker, snuggling under the blankets. "Finals are over. New term begins next week!" At the other end of the loft Pyrocles draws back a white curtain, behind it a toilet, a sink, a glass-walled shower stall. "But," says Becker, sitting up, as water starts to fall in the shower. "Oh, shit." Lunging over the side of the bed, reaching around for a pair of pants in the tangle of discarded clothing, coming up with a phone. He thumbs it on. "Shit," he says, hauling himself out of bed.

Pyrocles soaping himself turns with a jerk as Becker opens the dappled glass door to the stall, crowding inside, "Sorry," he's saying, "sorry," ducking to wet his head as Pyrocles leans back, blinking water out of his eyes, and the pewter weights swaying and tocking together. "I just," Becker's saying, "I have a shift, at eleven, but I was gonna do some shopping first – "

"Becker," says Pyrocles, hands on his shoulders, water streaming over them both. "Forget the shopping. Take it easy."

"We have," says Becker, "maybe two lemons left? I could make omelets for dinner. Very plain omelets. A little salt," and Pyrocles leans close to kiss Becker's forehead, and then his lips. "Forget dinner," he says. "I'll take care of dinner."

"You're not cooking again, are you?" says Becker, and Pyrocles laughs, sluicing suds from his arms, his back, "Go to work," he says. "Meet me at the garage when you're done." Leaning close again. "Trust in me."

"I do," says Becker, smiling. Kissing him. "Of course I do."

Four of them about a round table, and in the middle a dull grey lily pad of a speakerphone. It's saying, "What? Who was that?"

The man in the striped shirt sits forward. "It's David, George," he says. "That's a list, of key terms, we're gonna want to – "

"What?" says the phone.

"Key. Terms," says David Kerr. "We want to salt 'em in any upcoming statements, go over the stump, then a couple of weeks, we get new numbers, we can assess performance and tweak and tune going into the City Club debate – "

"You don't handle communications," says the phone. The woman by the door, in her pearly grey pantsuit, folds her arms at that. "This is based on Bob's work," says Kerr, and the man leaning against the table might've shrugged at that.

"Avery handles communications," says the phone.

"I'm gonna talk to Avery about this," says Kerr.

"Avery's right here," says the phone. "She's not happy with the list."

"And I'll talk to her about it." Kerr looks at the watch on his wrist, heavy and gold, a big flat dial. Twenty of ten. "This is the Barshefsky polling, George, and the social media analysis. It's, it's impeccable."

"The corpus is solid," says the man leaning against the table. "Nothing more than two months out across the Twitter, the Facebook, the comments sections, message boards, it's," he opens his eyes, looking for a word, "actionable." His suit a dour brown, his shirt ecru, his tie burgundy.

"Avery thinks it's stilted," says the phone. "Awkward."

"Avery," says Kerr, leaning over the phone, "wants to swing for the fences every time you step up to the plate, George." The stripes of his shirt are slate and gold on white, the collar and cuffs starkly white, his carefully loosened tie of white and blue. "She wants the three pointers, no net, every damn time. But you don't get those hero moments without the grunt work. Without paying your dues. That's what this is. These are the dues." Dark circles under his dark brown eyes. "Every time you use one, you remind them out there, whoever's listening, of that term, that phrase, that thought, they've already had. You're saying, we're on the same page. Making a connection, but wholesale, not retail." Cheeks hatched with stubble, untrimmed, black. "Long run? Makes her job easier. Makes you a winner."

"I suppose," says the phone, "it's hard to lead, if no one's following."

"That's right, George," says Kerr.

"And you'll talk to Avery. Convince her, David. Don't steamroll her."

"I'll talk to her."

"I need her buy-in."

"Understood, George," says Kerr.

"All right," says the phone, and a click, and a burr. The fourth of them, a woman in a frilled white blouse, shuts the speakerphone off.

"Okay then," says the man in the dour brown suit. "Ms. Upchurch, I hope that was – enlightening?"

"Of course," says the woman in pearly grey, her voice at once rich and hoarse, but she's looking down at her folded arms.

Out in the main room of the office Kerr sits at an empty glass-topped desk, white-framed platter of a phone in his hand, scrolling through messages, swiping, tapping, sweeping them here and there. "Give me just a minute," he says, without looking up, as the woman in pearly grey looms behind him. She plants a hand deep brown against the white vinyl back of his chair, and he sighs, "Okay, okay," he says, swiveling the chair around against her grip, and she lets go, lets her hand fall away as he looks up at her, phone still at the ready. "It's gonna be like that," he says. Looking past her to see the woman in the white blouse busy with the printer on the other side of the office. "There is no way in hell," he says, quietly, "your name's really Frances Upchurch, and if you actually have anything at all to do with the Democratic Party of Oregon, I'll buy a hat just so I can eat it."

She steps back, looks about. Pulls a chair from the desk across the way and lowers herself into it, nodding to herself, leaning forward, leaning close. Her hair all tiny corkscrew curls, brown and gold, swept back, pinned up. Squeak of the wheels of the chair as she pulls a little closer, even. "What you should ask yourself," she says, "is this: how does a woman, that is so large, enter in through the eyes that are so small?"

Whatever he was preparing to say melts in his mouth as his shoulders sag. He turns away, to set his phone down on the desk. "If this is about that call," he says, very quietly, "it's just a simple objuration. I have some clients, some other clients, who want to change the city's temperature on a couple of issues? If you want, if you want a cut, if you want in, on the wording, we can talk, we can negotiate that."

"Tell me about Charles Leir," she says. Her lips carefully painted the color of brick.

"Leir?" says Kerr. "Dabbled a bit. Fixed things, for powerful people."

"Did he ever fix anything for you?" A thread of startling blue limns each of her eyes.

"We did, favors, for each other, yeah."

"You speak in the past tense."

"Well," says Kerr, and a hint of a shrug. "Haven't heard from him since December. End of November. Now you guys are asking questions? Doesn't seem unwarranted to assume, well."

"The worst?" she says, and she pushes herself to her feet. "Stay out of our way, Mr. Kerr."

"You, your," he says, as she turns, as she's walking away, "*what* way?"

"You'll see," she says, over her shoulder. He watches as she nods to the woman pulling pages from the printer, as she says something genial to the man in the brown suit, as she opens the door to the office, as it shuts behind her, and then he lets out the breath he'd been holding with a "Shit." His hand trembles as he picks up his phone.

"Excuse me?" says the woman behind the counter. "Sir?" A couple of people look up from their plates of waffles, scrambled eggs, the woman at the corner has a half-eaten burger in her hands, the man there at the end in a ragged jacket, army-surplus green, only a cup of coffee. "You're gonna have to step outside," says the woman behind the counter.

"It's," says Mr. Keightlinger, "cold." He shakes his head. "Wet," he says.

"Go on," says the woman behind the counter. "You find some shoes, maybe some pants, you can come on back." Eggs sizzle on the griddle before her, and the ring and scrape of her spatulas as she stirs them about.

"I," says Mr. Keightlinger, "I left, in a hurry. *Not now,*" he snaps, to his right. He's wearing a black T-shirt, and pale blue boxer shorts, and his legs and his red raw feet are bare.

"Go on now," says the woman behind the counter, and then she points to a man in a blue meshback cap, a phone in his hand, "I'd rather you didn't," she says.

"What if he needs help?" says the man, a finger poised over the phone's keys.

"I don't want to involve the cops if we can at all help it," says the woman behind the counter.

"Look, I really think we," says the man, and "I asked you nice," says the woman, and "No," says Mr. Keightlinger, shaking his brown shaggy head, and the man in the ragged green jacket's getting up off his stool, and Mr. Keightlinger turns back crashing through the red-framed door to the diner with a wordless bellow, out onto the sidewalk, under the rain, wheeling about and about again, "What?" he's saying, "I can't, what?" Out in the street a primly nondescript white sedan is slowing to a stop, turn signal blinking, and bouncing off a Willamette Week newspaper box he lurches from the curb, grabbing the handle of the door of the sedan, wrenching it open as someone inside screams. "Sorry," he says, as he falls into the passenger seat, "this isn't, I don't, you have to," as the driver's screaming "What the get the *fuck* out of my car," a woman, black hair, intricate tattoos crawling up her neck, one hand held up curled in a fist a blow that doesn't land as he's looking at her, as she's looking at him, his draggled hair, his rain-wet beard, "Ell," he's saying, and a look of such wonder passes over him, "Ell," he says again.

"Jesus," she says. A car behind them honks once, curtly. "Jesus fucking Christ. Phil. Is that you?"

BERLIN – "HIPPY-DIPPY FOODIE CRAP"
AT LEAST, THE MONEY – THE BAD OLD DAYS

"BERLIN," he says, huddled unbelted in the passenger seat, head against the window, loose hair stirred by the howl of a heater on high, his bare legs, bare arms pricked with gooseflesh, wet bare feet clutched one over the other on the floorboard.

"I thought it was Dubai," she says.

His head rolls side-to-side against the glass, "I was never," he says, and then *"stop* it," and "What?" she says, the car, slowing. "Not you," he says. "Not you. I was never in Dubai."

"I could've sworn," she says.

"The abandoned," he says, "limousines. Himmelblau. Ellenellenellen Ell," he says.

"The show, right, that was the summer Katarci had that amazing," and "Please," he says, quietly, "that sublet," she says, "down by Yaam Beach." Clack and swipe of windshield wipers. She's made a turn, they're sweeping up a ramp. "You'd just met that guy, what was it – that obnoxious little fucker?"

"Charles," says Mr. Keightlinger.

"Really?" Her black hair's spiky short. Her hoodie's black, of some rubbery felted stuff. What can be seen of her tattoo, stretched up along her throat toward the point of her jaw, leaves, branches, a songbird's beak, all sharp black lines. "I thought it was weirder than that."

"No," he says, folding his arms about himself. "It was only ever really Charles." They're going across a bridge. Through the rain-smeared glass behind his head the city, stood up about a curl of river, and more bridges, there and there and there.

When he opens his eyes, he says, "Why."

She's shutting off the engine. "We're here."

"No, there," he says. "Why were you there."

"I want to get you inside," she says.

"At that moment, at that corner," he says, and then, "shut! The fuck! Up!"

"Phil," she says, pulled back, pressed against her door, and "Sorry," he says, "I'm sorry, that wasn't, I didn't, but why. Why then. Why there."

"Three years," she says.

"Why now," he says.

"Three fucking years," she says, "and you, you're a, you, you don't even have any goddamn pants."

"Someone's after me," he says.

"Jesus," she says, sitting up, peering at him. "Who?"

"All winter I spoke to no one," he says, "and then this morning and now that, then, and I, I need to know. How. Why, you were there."

"I don't know," she says. "I wasn't paying attention, I got turned around. I just, happened to be there."

He's tipped back his head, looking up at the finely nubbed beige ceiling, under the faint patter of rain.

"It's not my car," she says, handing him a steaming mug. He's sitting on the bottom steps of a grand staircase, dull dark wood the color of his beard, a green towel about his shoulders, legs wrapped in a rainbow-colored God's eye afghan. He takes the mug in both his hands but doesn't lift it to his lips. The staircase climbs the side of a low broad room columned and beamed with more dark wood. Over there a sofa, a beanbag, a couple of chairs, all crouched before a big black flatscreen television, snarled in a nest of cables and consoles and decks. "Okay," he says.

"It's my cousin's," she says. "He lives out in Gresham."

"Cousin," he says.

"Ben?" she says. "You never met him."

"In Khartoum, it was your aunt."

"Yeah," she says.

"Great-uncle, in Quito."

"Jusshi's more my grandmother's, ex's," she's waving a hand, "what's the point? Here?"

"You got family everywhere."

"Doesn't everybody?"

His mustache lifts a little, under it his lips spreading, in a, almost, but he ducks his head, a chuckled cough. Lifts the mug, and sips. "Might," he says. "Be okay."

"You don't mean the tea," she says, and he shakes his shaggy head. "No," he says. "Tea's good."

"Good things do happen," she says. He takes another sip. "Anyway. I borrowed Ben's car because I had to haul some stuff out to Metro to recycle. Today's, like, my Saturday? And I got turned around, on the way back, trying to remember how to get on the Steel Bridge. Which is why I was there, when you were."

"What," he says, and then, "I am," and then, "what was it? You were taking back?"

"Paint," she says.

"Paint?"

She holds out her hand. "Come," she says. "See."

Up those stairs, and up another flight, up under the very peak of the house. She opens a door for him, the top of it cut at an angle to fit under the slope of the roof. "Go on," she says.

"What is this," he says, wrapped in that green towel, the tea mug in his hands. "Gonna," he says, and then, "yes," he says. "Okay. Good."

"Go on," she says.

The room within, stretching half the length of the house or more, the plaster of the attenuated walls and the long angled ceilings above, the evened planks of the floor planed smooth, all of it painted a flawless eggshell blue, a clear plain cloudless blue, seamless, depthless, clean and gleaming, fresh, the only shadows from the pallet in the middle of it, and the mattress atop that, pillowed in white. Hung to one side a photograph, out in the air of the room, a picture of a hand, the back of it roped with veins in rich greys, crisp blacks, reaching for something, or warding it off. "Oh," says Mr. Keightlinger, stepping into the room, "oh, Ellen," turning about, and again, "Yes," says Phil. "Yes."

A large squared-up white tent over rows of ruddy picnic tables, lit against the midday gloom by strands of yellow lights, each in its own bead-strung little copper-wire cage. Murmurs and low converse here and there, swaddled and slicked in rain gear, the clink of forks and spoons, the clack of chopsticks, white paper cartons of noodles, wraps bound in foil, and sprigs of cilantro and sprouts popping from their seams, red and yellow plates of waffles, fish tacos, slices of pizza yellow and white, studded with mushrooms, bacon, shriveled kale, neatly rounded heaps of mac and cheese. There in the back, by a table fixed up with taps, sits Jo in her black coat, short red hair pressed back, tearing a bite from a sloppy big-bunned sandwich. Looking up as she chews, swallows, waves him over, Christian in his grimy hoodie, carrying a paper bag, eyes narrowed over those hunched-up cheekbones. "You're late," she says, as he climbs onto the bench beside her.

"Busses," he says, stashing the bag down between his feet as she takes another bite. "I see you went ahead and tucked in."

"Yeah, well," she says, chewing, swallowing, "the day I'm having. You want something?"

"Nah," he says.

"Because the food carts here, anything you could want." Putting her sandwich down, shreds of pulled pork glistening on the wrapper, "I swear," she says, "I'm fine with the whole vegetarian thing, but every now and then?"

"I ain't hungry," says Christian.

"Big breakfast? You sleep all right?"

"Well enough," he says. Looking about the tent. She's taking a drink from a plastic cup, "He's got this," she says, gesturing at the table fixed up with taps, "beer? Brewed with chamomile, which, I mean, you'd think, but it's great."

"Hippy-dippy foodie crap," says Christian. "Why'm I here, Jo-Jo."

"Thought you might like some lunch," she says, scooping up some loose pork.

"I work for you now, is that it?"

"You been working for me," she says, licking her fingers clean. "I want to make good on that." She reaches into her black coat, pulls out an envelope, manilla, thick, a little longer than her hand. Holds it out to him. After a moment, looking down at it, he takes it. Reaches in, pulls up a roll of worn bills, then tips out a phone and a slither, a chime, a key on a red plastic tag bouncing out that he manages just to lean over and catch.

"How's that for good," says Jo.

He's shoving the roll of bills back into the envelope, quickly, "What is that," he's saying, "two hundred?" Dropping the envelope to the table, over the phone, the key.

"*And* a place to stay," she says, shifting the envelope over, nudging the key. "It's kinda easier, covering room, and board, than cash? This is just, walking around money. Buy yourself a coat or something."

"You know me," he says. "I like the rain." He's looking about the tent, at each cluster and knot of diners in turn. "Hey," says Jo. "Christian. Christian." He looks at her, those darkly narrowed eyes. "What's in the bag," she says.

A sheepish look, almost a grin, he looks away. Sucks his teeth. "That suit," he says.

"It's yours."

"Nah," he says. "It ain't."

"Christian," she says, but he's saying, "How was this going down, in your head? You buy me a suit, you buy me a beer and I just, hang around, do whatever?"

"And a place to stay, with a bed, and a shower – "

"I can get that shit whenever I need it," he says.

"You can't just, keep doing favors for Sweetloaf, or whatever," she says.

"Why, because you say so?"

"Pretty much," she says. "Yeah. What I'm talking about, listen, you know how, like, Luys has a title? The Mason?"

"Jo," he says.

"We're talking about maybe getting, giving, giving you one."

A snorted laugh, shaking his head, "You're trying to, this, this is how you give somebody a promotion?"

"I'm trying to do you a favor," she says.

"By dragging me into this, whatever this," he says.

"It's a better deal than I ever got."

"And look at you now."

"The hell is that supposed to," she says, but he's leaning back, spreading his hands, "What are you doing here," he says. "Jo-Jo. That shit, last night, your roommate, the Queen, whatever, and this, the fuck is this. It's all like, I went on a run up the Stadium Fred's, come back to find Bambi's the jefe now or something."

"I am *not* some goddamn Bambi," says Jo, her hand to her chest, her black turtleneck under the long black coat.

"Everybody's Bambi, in the right woods," says Christian. "And you sure as shit ain't no fucking Duke." He's pushing up, off the bench, but she reaches for his arm, "Frankie's dead," she says.

"I heard," he says, braced there, half off the bench, her hand on the sleeve of his sweatshirt, "Dammit, Christian," she's saying, "this isn't a game. This is for your own – "

"And how deep in it did he get?" says Christian, tugging his arm free, stepping away from the picnic table.

"Christian," she says. "Christian!" People around them looking up at that, watching as she tosses the envelope flopping at him, and he just manages to catch it. "At least take that," she says. He's glaring, but he's folding the envelope, twisting it about, stuffing it in a pocket of his dungarees. "Come back in a couple weeks," she says, "I'll have more."

"If you're still here," he says.

"Fuck you," says Jo, as he turns and walks away, through the tables, toward the open door of the tent. She looks down, at the paper bag on the pavement beside her. Sweeps the phone and the key off the table and drops them both inside.

Christian heads toward the back of the bus, standing room only, hooks a hand about a pole there by the rear door, lowers his head as they get under way. When the bus says Southeast Belmont and César Chávez Boulevard, transfer to the 66, the 75, the crowd shifts, moving toward the front door, the rear door, and Christian worms his way through them, up into the elevated back end, swinging into a seat by a window. Two Brothers Cafe & Grill, says the sign painted on the red wall outside. Homemade Balkan Food. The envelope's in his lap. That roll of bills in his hands. He's skinning the rubber band off it, undoing and unfolding them, turning them about and folding them up again, all the while looking over the depleted crowd of passengers as the bus trundles on. The man, up front in the feathered trilby, loudly asking the driver about the MAX. Two women just below, draped in red abayat, black cloth shopping bags nestled at their feet. Christian's shifting about, dipping a hand into this pocket, that. The bulky guy across from him, one hand holding a ribbon-bedecked hoop upright in the aisle, long grey socks and a corduroy kilt. Christian leans over to adjust the fit of a filthy blue running shoe, sits up, clapping dust from empty hands. The man in the oilskin duster, laid out across the last row of seats, eyes closed, lips pursed. Christian reaches into one more pocket, pulls out something clamped between thumb and palm, quickly covered by his other hand. One more look about, and then he parts them just enough to reveal a glimmer of gold, lighting the shadows cupped in his hands, a fingertip of dust, caught in a small plastic baggie.

His hand, back in his pocket. His eyes, closed.

It isn't raining when he steps off the bus, onto slick wet brick, under the corner of an office tower. Slender grey columns and the glass sweep of a lobby, Key Bank, say the signs here and there. Over across that street a Chase Bank, and he makes his way behind the bus, jogging through stalled traffic toward awnings that say E-Trade Financial. On down the sidewalk, past the Sterling Bank, the Red Star crowded with diners and drinkers, a piano showroom, nearly empty, mannequins in the windows of a department store, neon-slashed running togs, dresses and skirts in pastels that froth about clean-limbed plastic, business suits in a bewildering variety of greys, stone and cloud, ash, herringboned water. Around a corner, across a street, a nod for a man sitting on a white plastic bucket, blurred sticks whipping a rattled tattoo from the white plastic buckets overturned about him. A bit of greensward slopes up sharply behind a wrought iron fence, and a grey stone pile of a courthouse, and then, there, opening out under the high grey sky a brick-paved plaza, hemmed by low walls and more wrought iron, the wide steps climbing the far side, the cyclopean blocks of a low concrete bunker at the head of it. People dot it, here and there, most of them clustered about food carts at the top of those steps, Shelly's Garden, Cheese Steaks & Burgers, The Completo, say the signs above and about them. Christian turns about there on the corner in his grimy hoodie, jostled against a sudden rush, a dozen or so setting off as the light changes, but he's looking off down the sidewalk after someone turning away, setting a broad-brimmed black leather hat in place, a narrow back in a ragged jacket, army-surplus green, an emaciated duffel, swinging from a shoulder. Christian frowns, shaking off a notion. Sets out across the bricks.

Up the steps to the far corner of the square, a low brick wall under glass awnings. Slouched back against a pale stone column a man in a fur-hooded anorak, dappled in a chocolate-chip desert camouflage, and his face brightens as Christian comes toward him, and he leans up holding out a hand for Christian's hand held out, a slap and a clasp, "My drow!" he bellows, settling back against the column as Christian's cheekbones hunch. "The hell are you?"

"Okay," says Christian, sitting back against the brick wall.

"Yeah?" says the man in the anorak. "How long's it been? Six months? How long you been back?"

"A week?" says Christian, with a shrug. "I figured, if you was still here, you'd be here."

"You know it," says the man in the anorak. "You got a place to stay? You doing all right?"

Christian shrugs. "Could be better."

"I hear that," says the man in the anorak. His jaw salted with stubble, along the one side a white stretch of skin, a scar that skews his smile. Under his anorak brown denim overalls and a faded pink Henley shirt. "Don't know what to tell you, though. Might want to stay put."

"Sorry," says Christian, looking at him squarely now. "Thought I was talking to the xo."

"Hey," says the man in the anorak. "Hey. You go away, you come back – you're in early, and that's good, but you're still at the back of all the lines. And everything's all shook up, fuck knows where it's gonna end up. You like boosting bikes?" Christian shrugs. "Kids over, down by the Esplanade? It's what they're working, these days. Open-air chop shops under I-5. How about the Copper Boys? Foreclosures, man, it's a goddamn growth sector. Though I can't keep straight who they're turfing with anymore. Guy gets stabbed over some fucker's drainpipe." That scar dragging at his mouth as he squints. "Pity you was never any good at the double-tap game, no offense."

"Yeah, fuck you," says Christian, looking away.

"I'm not," says the xo, lifting placatory hands, "I'm just saying. I'm not a racist here. You draw attention, is all."

"I don't need to be told," says Christian.

"It's all *unsettled,* is what I'm saying. They're trying to pass another law to make it illegal to sit on the sidewalk, you know? And meanwhile damn near every empty lot in town it feels like, somebody's started to build something. Where you gonna go?"

Christian's pulled some money from a pocket of his dungarees, a few bills folded together and folded about again, and the xo his lips pursed, tautening that scar, sits up to take them, unfolding them and turning them about, counting them ostentatiously, one, two, three, four twenties. "Okay," he says, slipping the bills into the bib pocket of his overalls.

"I know it'll be safe," says Christian.

"And I know you'll be back for it," says the xo, nodding. "Oh, hey," he says, as Christian gets to his feet. "You hear Moody's back?"

And Christian steps back, steps away, half a turn, looking back down along the plaza, "No," he says, and then, "no. He," looking back to the xo, "he got, like, ten years."

The xo shrugs. "Angie Lil saw him getting off a bus from Salem this morning. The Dread Paladin, his own damn self." That lopsided smile. "Man. Talk about the bad old days."

A FOUR-DIGIT CODE, entered on a keypad, "Hey, Becker?" says the woman leaning in the doorway. "You clocked in?"

"Just about," he says, pressing enter. Arnold Becker, says the screen, the computer a rounded blob all smoked plastic and bondi blue. 11:03 AM 03/21.

"Help Dorena get the lunch out," says the woman in the doorway, "but then you and Tish are on Trans this afternoon." Orange cats-eye glasses hang from a strand of beads about her neck.

"I thought," he says. It's a small room, not much more than a closet, and the wall behind him looming metal shelves, stuffed with jugs of soap and bundles of paper napkins and tubs of powdered milk. "I was on Wobblies this week. With Rose."

"Sam's out early today," says the woman with the glasses, "and no way can Tish handle them by herself."

"Okay," says Becker, pulling on a dark blue apron, the front of it printed with a stylized Y in purple and white. Child Development Center, it says.

"Okay," Becker's saying, "okay," as children swarm about, red and white stripes and blue and green stripes, blue and purple, wild bright blue shirts and solid reds and purples from royal to lavender, flower prints and appliqués and comic book prints and calicos and robots in orange and red, all of them hastening to sit in low little plastic chairs at low wide round tables that come up to about Becker's knee. He's holding up a plastic tray loaded with plates, each with an identical scoop of spaghetti in tomato sauce and a precise wedge of apple, white-fleshed, red-peeled. "Who's ready for worms?" he says, and a lusty chorus of "No!" and "Eww!" erupts. "Who ordered the toad? Anybody?" Beaming as he leans over, setting a plate before each child.

Leaning back against a credenza, paper towels ready in either hand, "Spaghetti," he mutters. "Why'd it have to be spaghetti."

"You know the menu," says the older woman beside him, in a similar dark blue apron, her short black hair caught up in hundreds of tiny braids. "Wednesday is spaghetti day."

"Cobb," says Becker, starting forward, towel up, "not in Brooklyn's hair, not in Brooklyn's hair – "

He's wiping a boy's hands, "If you need help with your juice," he's saying, "use your words," when somewhere up behind him someone's saying, "our Transitional group, between Toddler and Pre-K," and someone else says, "Oh, it's very impressive, a very impressive facility," and Becker stiffens. "And the staff, too," says that voice, deep, about to laugh at itself. "Impressive. Little Kayden's going to love it here."

Becker's standing, turning, as there on the other side of the credenza the woman with the orange cats-eye glasses is saying, "I'm sorry, I thought it was, Hayden?" to the tall man, his back to Becker, a beige fleece pullover, a dress shirt under it, slate and gold stripes on white, and white cuffs. "Hayden, yes, of course," he's saying. An irritated shake of his head, dark hair carefully swept back. Looking down at the watch about his wrist, heavy and gold.

"Well," says the woman with the glasses. "Why don't we head back to the office and take a look at the schedule."

Becker watches them go, down the corridor between credenzas and cabinets, bedecked with crayoned and finger-painted drawings and construction paper gee-gaws. Someone's tugging on his apron, a girl in a blue tunic dress, a yellow lightning bolt zigging the front of it. "Becker," she's saying. "Becker. Teacher Tisha says. It's time a do the cots."

"Okay," says Becker.

It's dim now, mostly quiet, the muttered fluting of lullabies here and there from discreet speakers. Low plastic cots laid out on the floor and on each tiny forms under blankets, quietly restless, deathly still, there's Becker, sitting between two of the cots there by the window, and outside pedestrians hastening past on the sidewalks, and traffic taking its turns through the intersection. He looks to his right, his hand cupping the the pale-haired head of a girl, eyes closed, jaw slack, a tiger clamped under one arm, and he pulls away, gently. She doesn't stir. To his left, his hand clutched by a small boy, large dark eyes looking up through floppy bangs. Becker turns his hand in the boy's hands, tugging it lightly, cocking an eyebrow, and after a moment the boy nods, gravely, lets go, burying his face in his light blue blanket. Becker slowly pushes himself to his feet.

"Hey," he says, quietly, to Tish, sitting at one of those low round tables, papers spread out before her. "I need to take a minute." Distracted, she nods.

Past sleeping toddlers, the corner chock-a-block with cribs, the cramped office, where the woman with the orange cats-eye glasses about her neck peers through a black-rimmed, thick-lensed pair at a computer screen, out through the cramped foyer lined with photos of children, children with their parents, with each other, portraits, holding basketballs or baseball bats, toys, with dogs, with a horse, with a clown. Out the high wood-paneled door into a high wood-paneled lobby, lunch counter to the left, and a great glass wall looking out on the sidewalk, and there, at a table on the other side of the revolving door, that beige fleece pullover, the heavy gold watch, reading a plastic-wrapped hardbound book. Adventures in Unhistory, says the cover. He closes it, sets it on the table as Becker pulls out a chair across from him. "Took you long enough," says David Kerr.

"Why are you here," says Becker.

"Wanna offer you a job," says Kerr, and "I *have* a job," says Becker, as Kerr's saying "It's a perfect match. In fact, you've done it before. In fact, you walked out on this very job last year with five minutes' notice, but don't worry. I know the boss. I'll put in a good word."

"I have a job," says Becker.

"You change diapers," says Kerr.

"Most meaningful work I've ever done."

"Oh, I get it, I do." Kerr leans back, arms folded. "Hubby earns the daily bread, so you can afford to go back to school, find yourself, make a difference. How wonderful." Leaning forward, as Becker blinks, "Doesn't it even begin to bother you? That you don't know why? You don't know how?"

"How, how what," says Becker.

"Tell me, does he stir a pinch in your juice every morning? Your coffee? No, wait – he's a mechanical type, our Pyrocles.

A tinker. I bet he's measured out precise doses in proper little pills for you, hasn't he. All lined up in the medicine cabinet, one a day. Am I right? Tell me I'm right." Sitting back, a finger to his lips, all hatched about with stubble. "And you have no goddamn idea what it's doing to you. Or what it is inside you, that it's doing it to. Or what else it might be fucking up, along the way. Your liver? Kidneys? Your blood, your brain," and "Shut up," says Becker, as Kerr says, "your heart? Tell me. True love. What's that worth – cirrhosis? Stroke?"

"Shut *up.*"

"Cancer?"

"What the fuck do you want," says Becker, leaning over the table.

"What's in you," says Kerr. "What forgets. What doesn't want to know. It's still in there, just, held at bay, by those little," he taps the table, "yellow," tap, "pills." Tap. "And I'm gonna need it, sooner than I'd thought. Which means, I need you." A sigh. "I don't like needing people. I have this weakness, where I want to make sure the people I need are safe? Comfortable, even. So I do stupid things," and he picks up his book, tucking it away in a sleek leather bag, "like call in favors to set up cushy jobs with grotesquely swollen paychecks."

"I'm not interested, David," says Becker, as Kerr gets to his feet. "I know," says Kerr. "I'm not an idiot. But. When you need me, and you will," he smiles, "don't worry about a phone call, or an email. Just," and he's turning, he's walking away, "say my name," he says, over his shoulder. "I'll be there," and Becker watches him push through the revolving door, out onto the sidewalk.

He sits up on that white-pillowed bed in the soft blue room, his beard, his hair now dry, spread out ruddy brown about his head, his shoulders, his chest, his back hatched with darker hair the curves of sagging muscle, thick round waist. Rubbing an eye with the heel of his hand. "Time's it," he says, a gravelly rumble.

"After two," she says. Sitting tailor-fashion on the soft blue floor. "Go back to sleep." Wearing loose black yoga pants, reading a tablet computer resting on the floor. "You need it." Tattoos in black ink swarm over shoulders, her upper arms, down her back and over around her breasts, calligraphic vines and branches, leaves and flowers, birds and animals, magpie and owl, a fox, a crane, rabbit, maple and oak, pear blossoms, pine cones, katsura, elm.

"I'm not asleep," he says.

She looks up, sets the tablet aside. Standing stepping up to kneeling on the bed, straddling him to kiss and kiss him again, taking his head in her hands as she sits on his white-pillowed lap and kisses him once more. "I didn't," he says, between them, "I'm not, I don't," and he kisses her, his hands on her waist, her sinewy ink-shadowed shoulder, and "I don't," she says, "either, I just," and one more kiss. "I missed this."

"You," he says, arms about her.

"You," she says, forehead against his.

On his belly arms spread wide and she's laid herself over him, wrapped around him, fingering the hair on the back of his shoulder. "I left him on the bridge," he says, and she doesn't say anything in return, she waits, as he licks his lips, ducks his head, shoulders rising tense beneath her arm a breath, taken in, and then, "It turned out not to matter but I didn't – know that, when I did. And he wasn't supposed to be a friend, but he was, but at that moment. I turned around. I walked away. I left him. On the bridge."

"Who, him," she says.

"Charles," he says, "Charley, Doctor Charley. Charlock." Lifting his great shaggy head from the pillow. "All one. He played me. He played everybody, but still. I didn't know that, when I walked away. He wasn't even real, but," and "Phil," she's saying, "Phil," stroking his shoulder, he's looking up, all the blue above, "I *left* him," he says. "I *walked away.*"

"From what," she says, and *"Listen,"* he snarls, turning to her, and "I *am,*" she says, arm still about his shoulder, "I just don't *get* it."

"That's not *listening,*" he says, fist clenching white sheets. "That's *hearing.*" His head hung low.

"Magic," she says, after a moment. "I hate magic." Lying down on the pillow, looking up at him. He turns away, eyes clamped shut, "It is," he says, "what it is. I can't change it around just so you can follow."

"All right," she says. "Okay." Stroking his beard, the curl of his cheek. "Just," she says. "Answer one question? Try?"

He falls over, on his side, head on his folded arm, catches her hand, presses it to his lips. "This room," he says. "Ellen, this room. I wish I could never leave this room."

"Phil," she says, taking back her hand. "You said he died. Did you, did, what you did, was that what, got him killed?"

He falls away onto his back, looking up at the blue. She watches him, closely, until under his mustache his lips purse and part and he says, "No."

"So," she says, stretching her arm across his chest, "there's that," but he's sitting up, sweeping back his hair, "I should," he says. "I should go."

"Phil," she says, falling back to the pillow, as he climbs off the bed. "Phil," she says again, but he rounds on her, the hairy bulk of him naked in all that blue, "I can't!" he roars. "Stay!"

She sits up, not looking at him. "You can't," she says, "you can't go, Phil," and she swings her feet to the floor. "Not like that. You need some clothes."

"I'll think of something," he says. "Ellen. Nothing you have will fit."

"I have housemates," she says, padding away across the soft blue floor. When she opens that angled door, he winces.

Grey clouds now a chilly ceiling, high above. He looks away from it, tugging the broad brim of that black leather hat down over his eyes. Striding across the mostly empty parking lot toward a simple arch at the far corner, a green sign that says Springwater Corridor hung over a narrow paved path. Railroad tracks to the left, and the fenced-in yard of a gravel plant to the right, towering tanks and pipes, virgules of conveyor belts, all of it silent and still.

Him, in his ragged jacket, army surplus green, duffel swaying, passing under the arch. Another sign, low, white, says Stop! Please Use Caution – Heavy Truck Traffic.

Past the plant the fence to the right is swallowed in brown vines dotted over with swollen buds, purpled, tipped with impossibly potential green. Over beyond it the river, dull steel scraped by wavelets rippled, dark. To the left now a slope rising steeply above the railroad tracks, grey and brown with mud, brushed with green. Shadows ahead, beneath a high bridge, and traffic hissing and booming over it, the concrete pillars of it tattooed with grubby rainbows of graffiti, signatures, sigils, cartoons. He lifts his hat, a salute, and pushes on.

Calved from the bridge an offramp on spindly pillars curls through the air above to merge with a freeway along the top of that steep slope. He's eyeing it, as he comes out from under the bridge, every now and then looking down to the railroad track, and the fence along it. The river, ignored, runs sluggish, high. Down a ways something's fastened to the fence, about the brightening grass, and he fixes on it: a green plastic cat bowl, set in a gap cut in the cyclone fencing, so it might be reached from either side, a clear plastic reservoir filled with kibble wired to the post above it. He stops there, nudging it with a worn black boot, looking up and down the paved trail. Back that way under the bridge a cluster of cyclists, headed his way. He tosses the duffel up and over the fence, then grabbing the fencepost wire ringing under his boots up it and over it after the bag. Looking up and down the railroad track he darts across it, into the brush, and up and up the muddy slope.

Halfway along there's a path, running along a brow of earth, treacherous under his boots, high above the railroad and the bicycles passing below. Scrubby trees, bare branches touched with green, lean out over the drop. He braces himself against one, a balustrade to clamber the last steep hillock of path, onto the narrow top of the slope, there between the trees and the dark galleries under the freeway – regular bays between concrete walls that uphold the deck, floored with clayey dirt that's studded with gravel, rising abruptly at the back to meet the thrumming, rumbling road above. The first gallery's empty, and a great eye painted on one concrete wall, the iris of it elaborately paned, red paint squiggled over the pupil. A low flat rock's been set at the edge of the overgrown path, and on it pebbles mark out a shape, a crude face, two eyes, the curve of a smile. He laughs, a quiet snort, and picks up one of the pebble-eyes, rough and black in his fingers. He whips it away, zip and slither, lost in the grass. Looks about. The river, so far below.

The next gallery, an old green tent, splashed with mud since dried. Stuffed black garbage bags arrayed before it. He passes by without a second look. Three figures in the next, a-sprawl on blue plastic tarps laid over the hard-packed earth, and here he pauses, tips back his hat. One of them sits up, a man in a long blue-black down coat, scratching his nose above a ragged beard.

"Winks," says the man in the black hat. "Looking for Winks."

The man in the down coat looks over at the figure beside him, a featureless bundle of old blankets, then waves a hand, go on, down that way, away, as he lays himself back down.

Murmurs still themselves in the next gallery, three, four kids in black denim and leathers tinged brown and red, hair shaved and shaped in drooping spikes, tufted braids, grimy hanks, bottles in hands. Past them the raw earth under the highway's been tumbled, piled, a yawning mouth scratched at the base of the concrete piling. The man in the black hat steps off the path, heads up toward it. The kids watch. He looks back, a hand braced on the lip of the tunnel, "Winks?" he says.

No one speaks. Smoke unspools from the joint one of them's holding. He settles the black hat more firmly on his head and ducks into the darkness.

Low, cramped, the floor uneven. He bumps the wall and loose dirt patters his shoulders, plops the brim of his hat. Down a ways a lick of light. "Winks?" he calls.

"Who's that," a gruff voice, muffled.

"It's me," he says, pushing on down the tunnel. "I'm back."

"Who's you," that voice, light leaps, shadows jerk and lurch, "that's back." Light flares, a battery lantern held up, a beardless face, filthy, a squint over rounded cheeks. The lantern dips, the face draws back, up, "Paladin," says Winks.

"They said you was up here," says Moody, doffing his hat. His smile quite sharp.

"I kept her safe," says Winks, backing away.

"Lucinda?" says Moody. "Well. Time I took her back."

The lantern ducks, is lost in sudden darkness. A glimmer, there, off to the right. Moody stoops off toward it, a turning that opens into a low room, one wall of it pitted concrete, the lantern set on a tummock. Winks sprawls in the light of it over the uneven floor, a bundle of sweatshirt over sweater over coveralls, sodden with mud, rummaging through bags and sacks, plastic crates, one sagging cardboard box, all full of clothing, coats and blankets, empty cans, bottles, bundles of newspaper, "I thought," says Winks, tossing a fluttering magazine, "you got the chair?"

"They don't do that anymore," says Moody. "It was only ten years."

"Ten years?" says Winks, astonished, rolling over, sitting up. "Has it been so long?"

After a moment, Moody says, "Yeah." And then, "You haven't changed a bit."

"Told you I kept her safe," says Winks, handing over a slender package wrapped in grubby cloth. Moody takes it, unwinds it, tugs from it glinting a silver handle, wrapped in wire, snug in a black leather sheath. "Lucinda," he says, slipping free an inch or so of the blade. Leaning down to sniff it.

"I am so glad you're back, Paladin," says Winks.

"The Sikes-Fairbourne," says Moody, drawing the rest of the knife free, a tapered poignard. "Only fourteen ever made. MI6 gave 'em out to top operatives. I got one when I was over there, with Echo Force? That's like, Delta, only even more top secret. Need to know."

"Yeah," says Winks. "Kids, these days."

Squatting, leaning back against the muddy wall, blade in one hand, sheath in the other, "Thank you, Winks. For looking after my Lucinda." His eyes quite serious now, and his mouth, under the beak of his nose. "But I'm afraid I've got another favor to ask."

"What's that," says Winks.

The first cry's thready, muffled, and the kids look up, out there under the highway. One of them hands the joint to the next in the circle but then a loud, a frantic scream claws up out of the hole in the mud, cut off in a gurgle, and almost as one they stand, they back away, they turn, flitting off along the top of the slope, some this way, some that. A minute passes, or three, and a scrabble, a hand, Moody pulling his muddy, dusty self out of that hole, straightening in the shadows, looking up at the concrete above. His mouth, his chin, his throat slicked dark with blood. The knife in his hand stained red with it. He wipes the blade on his thigh and slips it back into its sheath, drops it into his duffle. Sets off, picking his careful way downhill.

A Powder-blue Town car – "One does not eat monsters"
something Romantic – how He did get in

A POWDER-BLUE TOWN CAR swings a left turn under the yellow light, jerking to a halt there to the side of a green two-storey clapboard building, backing and filling into a space just past the corner as a couple of cars struggle around. Settling a good two feet from the curb. The old man with some effort climbs out from behind the wheel, closing the door firmly, wiping the chrome handle with a cloth that he folds and tucks into the pocket of his suit coat, a dark brown sharkskin gleaming in the dark grey evening light. The corner of that green building the angled foyer of a modest storefront, and hung above it a blue and orange sign, jutting out over the sidewalk, neon bright against the darkening, Alberta Rexall Drugs, it says. Scowling, he brushes down the front of his suit, his vest, runs fingers through his hair, that circle of crisp curls almost yellow against the reddish darkness of his bare bald head. Takes a deep breath.

Inside, round formica tables each with a candle guttering, some with diners, couples, glasses of wine, water, plates of bread, little bowls of salt, cruets of oil, vinegar, "layered with a pesto," a woman's saying, "of tarragon and parsley," as she's handing a wine list to a man sitting at one of the front tables, but "Excuse me, miss," says the old man, door swinging shut behind him. "Where is she?"

"I, ah," she says, looking up at him, startled. "Do you mind?" says the man with the wine list, affronted.

"'Fraid not," the old man says to him, and then, "Miss?" Wordless she points, back that way, to a door, painted red.

Through that door, a dim hall, clatter and rush of the kitchen to one side, a canvas curtain lifted to reveal an echoing room, opening out, the floor and walls painted an old thin dusty black, brightly lit. Folding chairs in rows on stepped platforms raised up, three sides about the room, and up there behind him, he's turning about, a woman sits in the last row, draped in a thin white gown, her left arm sleeved in polished plate, cop and pauldron, vambraces and cowter. Her hair a close-shorn cap, gunmetal grey. "Gordon," she says.

"Linesse," he says.

"So. Now that you're here," faint squeak and scrape of metal as she gestures, clack, "what do you think?"

He shrugs. "Slap up some paint, pull in some tables, maybe a couple of four-tops, it's a nice private dining room."

"I like the theatre."

"You'll never make any money," he says.

"That's not why I like the theatre."

He shifts, scuff of shoe. "I need a favor."

Smiling, she stands, comes down the steps, whisper of gown, slip and snap of sandals, clank of plate about her arm. "So that's why you've dressed," she says, looking him up and down in his suit.

"This morning," he says, as she passes behind him, "some of Tommy Tom's bravos came to coffee. Boggs Gaffer, and also Swift, and Dogstongue."

"It seems we've got off on the wrong foot," she says, at his side, "if we're to speak of boons. I should've named you Porter, and not encouraged such familiarity."

He stiffens, draws an aggrieved breath, "That's not what I am," he says. "No drop, nor pinch."

"But you did not renounce your office," she says. "You still serve the court." He flinches at the touch of her hand, a ghostly thing beneath the bright cuff of the vambrace. "I wonder," she says, stepping back, and again, "were I to draw on you," two more steps back, in a rush, plated arm lifted before her, shining in the light, and held low in her other hand a sword, the blade of it short, and broad, "were I to cut at your chest, your head," a sliding sidelong step toward him, that sword swung out, and back, and up, "would you block it, with your mace?"

His eyes are closed, his head inclined. His hands at his side. "Marquess," he says. "I would ask of thee a boon."

Clank and squeak as she lowers her arm. "Speak to the Soames," she says. "Your problem's with his men, not mine."

"You know I cannot do that," he says. "But – from one peer, to another – "

"When I've no stake in the matter?" she says, stepping toward him.

"More domestics come to my house from your fifth, than any other," he says. "Do it for them, if not – " but she's taken another step, another dismissive flick of her fingers, "You keep an open house," she says. "Free to all. Even bravos."

"There are limits!" he cries, words ringing in that space.

"Then make them known," she says, moving past him, "and see that they are kept," headed back to the stepped rows of folding chairs.

"If not," he says, and he stops. His hands clasped together, lifted up before his chest, beneath his chin. "For what we've meant, to each other."

One foot on a riser she stops, looks back, over her shoulder, "What's that, exactly?" she says. Turning, when he doesn't respond, to look at him there, in his brown suit, head bowed under all that light.

"I will speak with him," she says, then. "Though it will do no good."

"It is as you say," says Gordon.

Wide noodles slippery under a dollop of red ragù, white feathery curls of cheese, a sprinkle of herbs, his fork, gleaming in his hand. "It's, um, it's fantastic."

"The smell of it?" Pyrocles points with his own fork, a fat round ravioli hanging from its tines, dripping a plum-dark sauce. "You haven't had a bite."

"Sorry," says Becker, scooping and twining up a noodle. "Sorry, I just, a – "

"Did you want something else?"

"What? No! No." Becker takes his bite, slurping, chewing. "Hey," he says, "so," and swallowing, "now I know what wild boar tastes like." A gesture of his fork. "How's, ah, how's your celery root?"

"Delicious," says Pyrocles, forking up another ravioli. "You do not recall, but we met – the first time – at a boar hunt."

"We, we did?" says Becker.

"One the old Duke called," says Pyrocles, "for Erymathos Kernel-Hearted. I was to stand for the Hound, but," a small smile, "the Mooncalfe drew on me, for no reason, and took me with his tricksy stop-thrust." The pewter beads at the ends of his mustaches gleam in the candlelight. "And you, you came and held the cup that caught my offering," and Becker looks away, blinking, and a clatter of dropped fork Pyrocles reaches for Becker's hand, "oh, blast me for a fool – the last thing that I wanted," and "No," Becker's saying, "no," squeezing Pyrocles's hand, "it's, it's," and a sniff, "you don't," he says, "why would you, why hunt a boar? You don't eat boar."

"Of course not," says Pyrocles, brows pinched. "He was a monster. One does not eat monsters," and Becker laughs, a sputtering cough too loud, quickly swallowed. Works another noodle onto his fork but doesn't lift it, yet. "David Kerr found me today," he says.

"The melanchlœnidon," says Pyrocles, and "Ah, yes," says Becker. Pyrocles tosses his wadded napkin to the table. "I would do no murder, love," he says, "but that man I'd leave bleeding in a ditch."

"He didn't *do* anything," says Becker.

"He's done enough," says Pyrocles.

"He just, he wanted to talk. He let something slip, I don't know. Maybe it was on purpose. He told me why it was he wanted me to have that awful job."

"He wants you," says Pyrocles.

"No, no, I mean yes, but, he also," leaning forward, "he wants what I do. When I'm not – the thing that forgets, he said. That doesn't want to know. That's what he – wants."

"He will not touch you," says Pyrocles. "He will not approach you again – he came to your work? The day-care center? I will speak with the Viscount. We will have someone to watch over you, when we must be apart," and Becker's saying, "That's, that's, he just, he didn't try to hurt me, or anything, he just – he rattled me – "

"He means to take you," says Pyrocles. "I will not let that happen."

Becker smiles, a little.

"What is it, love," says Pyrocles a moment later, two.

"That's," says Becker, "that's the question, isn't it." A hand to his temple, his thinning hair. "What *is* it, in me, that does that. Fucks things up. That he wants."

"It is you," says Pyrocles.

"But what *about* me," says Becker. "If we could, figure that out, get rid of it – not just hold it off," and he laughs, takes up his fork again. "I mean, it's not like there's a doctor I can see about this."

"You are what doesn't want to know," says Pyrocles, gently. "You are what forgets. There's nothing to get rid of. It's, you."

"But that's why we, that's why I take the stuff," says Becker. "So I don't lose me. So I don't go away."

"Yes," says Pyrocles, frowning, looking down. "I, yes."

He picks up a pair of sunglasses from the floor, the left lens of them spiraled with spidery letter-shapes written in white ink. "Let me guess," says Ellen. "Those aren't yours."

"They're mine," he says. "But I left them over there. On the dresser." He moves to tuck them into a pocket, but he's wearing a bright aloha shirt, splashes of blue and yellow and white, and no pocket to put them in.

"So," she says, looking about the grubby little room. "You get this by the week or something?" The rumpled green walls, the neatly narrow bed, thin beige blanket tucked and folded, neon blinking shining on and off and on again through the one lone window.

"I gave them a bunch of money a while ago," he says. "They leave me alone."

She's looking at the mirror hung above the dresser, written over in curling, branching, slashed and dotted letter-shapes. "So it pays well, huh? This stuff?"

"You're angry," says Phil, sunglasses in his hand.

"You're back," she says, turning away from the mirror, "you're safe," heading for the door, "there's no bogeyman or pea-soup vomit to clean up, so I'll, just – "

"Dinner," he says.

"I – should go, Phil. I'm sorry. I have to work in the – "

"Wait," he says, "wait," unbuttoning the wildly flowered shirt, "let me – "

"*Keep,*" she says, "the shirt. I never, I hate the way Dan looks in that damn thing."

"You," he says, and then, "you're close."

"You don't get to ask that," she snaps, and he starts to say "I'm" but "God*dam*mit," she says, turning away. "I was really starting to like it here."

"You don't have to," he says, but "North," she says. "I'll just go north. Keep going. All the way."

"Ellen," he says.

"What the hell, right? Yellowknife! I mean, what are the chances you'll."

"Ellen," he says, again. "Don't go. I'll go." Stepping toward her. "Ellen?" She doesn't shift to follow him as he steps to one side, doesn't finish her sentence, lower her hand, blink, doesn't breathe. "It," he says, looking from her to the window, red neon shining balefully, steadily, on. Just on. "Oh," he says. He turns to look at the door. There's a knock.

He opens the door on a woman pugnaciously short, all in pearly grey, who pushes past him into the room, right up to Ellen, hiking up on the toes of her sensible shoes. Peering at the fronds and feathers of black ink that curl about the collar of Ellen's denim jacket. Stepping back the woman favors Phil with a look, brow cocked over blue-limned eyes, something skeptical about the set of her brick-painted lips. "You," says Phil, but she's moving on, peering a moment at the written-over mirror, sliding open the closet door. Rattle of hangers, crinkle of plastic. "Three," Phil's saying, "months."

"Vacation is over," she says, pulling out a suit wrapped in a clear dry cleaner's bag. "Or did you think you'd been let go? Feet first. You know that." She rips open and off the plastic.

"I thought you'd forgotten," says Phil.

"Backlog," she says, laying the suit out across the bed, flat, black, jacket and pants. "Which means work to be done. An entire verse of Antethesis, loose in the world."

"That," he says, and then "I," and then, looking to Ellen, "well. I know where it must be."

"Dormant in a heart, but which?" says the woman all in grey. "The Queen's? Her pet's? Or perfidious Leir's?"

"You," he says, a turn of his head, a shake of it forestalled. "You think Leir?"

"His name's still known," she says. "Antethesis didn't take him. What else could?"

Leaning over the bed, he lays a hand on the black suit jacket, and a breath. Then Mr. Keightlinger takes it up.

He fills the little doorway, and behind him a wild bright blaze. Making way for her he backs into it, candlelight that soaks him golden, white, his plain white T-shirt, yellow cardigan, black hair gleaming, gentle smile. "Jesus, Luys," says Jo all in black, red hair aflame, looking about the cramped trailer, and candles everywhere, along the little countertop, tapers lining the sills of the windows, and back there over the low bed in its alcove, votives scattered over the floor of the narrow shower stall, immensely glossy blocks with three wicks each or four clustered on the table there in the nose of it, and a small feast of take-out boxes arrayed with napkins, chopsticks, a couple of bottles of beer. "After this morning," he says, as he lowers himself into the booth.

"That's," she says, "you didn't, there was nothing to make up for – "

"I wanted to," he says. "To do something romantic."

"It's certainly that," she says, picking up one of the bottles. Taking a swig.

"Well sit down," he says, "dig in. I got you a whole order of, of the garlic broccoli," and he frowns. She's still pulling at the bottle, great thirsty swallows, and most of it gone when she lowers the bottle, wiping her mouth with the back of her hand. "Is everything all right, your grace?" he says.

"I lost Christian," she says, and she polishes off the beer.

"Lost," he says.

"He said no. He walked away. He took the money." She's shucking her long black coat, turning about, careful of all the candles, "Tell me something," she says, her back to him, laying the coat over the low bed. "It's a little weird, but, did you see him, eat? Anything? Last night?"

"At the party?" says Luys, sitting back. "I think so. Yes."

"You think so."

"Yes."

"Yes you think so, or yes you did?"

"Jo," he says.

"Sorry," she says, turning about, sitting there on the bed. "Sorry. It's, it's stupid, but." Looking down, at her red shoes. "I had a dream, last night." He leans forward, elbows on knees, intent on her. "More of a fragment," she says. "An impression. I was, I was back at the bridge, at the World Trade Center, waiting for the sorcerer, and Ysabel, to come up the escalator, only, it wasn't them, coming up? It was Christian, I could see his face, coming up, only he was dressed all in green, and I knew, the minute I saw him, it was too late. I wasn't gonna be able to save him. That I hadn't saved him, because it'd been too late long ago." She looks up at him. "I think something happened, after what went down, last year. I think, I was thinking. Maybe he's a ghost."

"Christian?" says Luys.

"That's a thing ghosts don't do, right? Eat?"

He leans forward, reaches out for her hand. The bit of leather about his wrist, dull against his yellow cuff. "I've never met a ghost, my lady," he says.

"Oh," she says, "I thought," sitting back, her hand slipping free, "I thought maybe," and she sighs. "I don't know," she says. "I just don't goddamn *know.*"

"Lady?" he says.

"Can I," she says, "can I show you something? I just, I gotta," all at once she lifts the hem of her turtleneck skinning it up and off to drop on the floor before her. "Right," she says, eyes closed, "here," fingertips pressed to her sternum, trembling, "just look," she says. "It's not," twisting, wrist, hand, pressing again, "sometimes," and she yelps, slumping, he's swarming out of the both on his knees to catch her, hands on her shoulders, "Lady," he says, and "Look!" she snarls through her teeth. Knuckled fist pounding her chest. "Look!"

He does, and he looks away, and again, and he sighs. "I see nothing that should not," he says, and then, "oh."

"You see it," she says.

"I thought, perhaps," he says, "a shimmer?" His hand, roughly brown, tenderly shades her skin.

"The shine, the rainbows, like, like soap," she says.

"Like oil," he says. She sags against him in his arms about her. "What is it?" he says.

"The, the, it's the quicksmoke," she says, against his chest.

"What is that," he says.

"You don't." Leaning back she looks at him. "You don't know what quicksmoke is."

He shakes his head. "I've never heard the word before this moment."

She leans back against the bed, out of his grasp, closing her eyes. "Well, shit," she says.

What little light there is leaks in from other rooms to catch on dishes piled in the sink, dents in the counter's aluminum trim, the chrome frame of a plastic-backed chair, and abrupt slashes shine across the black and white checkerboard floor, a warm glow struck from the doorknob there in the back, jiggling, rattling, a clank. It turns then, in that oblong of dim light, and the door, shivering, opens.

He steps through, ragged jacket, broad-brimmed hat, moving with quiet care. Slipping a contraption of snarled wire into a pocket. Looking about. A television's burbling, somewhere else in the house. A table, there, piled with loose paper, stacks of mail. He sits, carefully, in one of the chairs beside it, slips the duffel from his shoulder, sets it quietly, on the floor. Doffs the hat, holds it a moment over the crammed table, then sets it in his lap. Leans back in the chair. It creaks. He cocks his head, listening. The television's laughing at its own jokes.

Again, he leans back. Again, a creak. Then he pushes the chair back, a scrape, and listens. A murmur, a cough, something's said, a sharp retort. A thump, a slam, heavy footsteps, coming closer. At the table he smiles, then swallows it, a hand up over his eyes.

Snap of a switch, light flares, "Son of a *bitch,*" says the man in the doorway up there, that awkward corner landing, behind a heavy bannister. "Moody?" His T-shirt says Still Haven't Used Any Algebra Yet. His jockey shorts are purple. "The hell did you get *in* here," he says. His jaw salted with stubble, and along the one side tight white skin, a scar that skews his scowl. "How the hell you even know where here *was,* to get into?"

"xo," says Moody, hand still shading his eyes. "Mind turning off the light?"

"*Fuck* you," says the xo. A short staircase at his feet, mostly covered over with a sheet of plywood, a makeshift ramp. "I told you where to find Winks," he says, coming crabwise down it. A can of beer in his hand. "You're overdrawn at the favor bank."

"I spent seven months in solitary," says Moody, putting his hat back on, "for killing a man on the chow line. He was a rapist and a pedophile and he deserved to die most cruelly, but it brought me to their attention. On my seventeenth day in the hole, a man came to see me."

"I do not care," says the xo, as Moody says, "This man had come up through the ranks in the black site prisons of Antaviliai and Djibouti, and was once in charge of Extreme Interrogation at Guantánamo. He invented half the tricks they use to cause excruciating pain without a single incriminating mark."

"Moody, man, you cannot sit here and keep," says the xo, but Moody's rolling on, "Every day for five of those six months he used those tricks to ask me questions, over and over again, and I. *Never*. Answered. One."

"The hell is that on your *face,*" says the xo. Somewhere else away off in the house another thump, a churning squeal, getting closer.

"But every single one of those questions," says Moody, tugging down the brim of his hat, "was about you. And the co. And the jefes. All the *things,* we used to get up to." Up on that awkward landing a rattling clank, a squeak, a wheelchair backing out of the shadows, grey plastic push handles poking up out of a grey thermal blanket draped over the back of it, over the shoulders of the man glaring over his shoulder at them, "What on earth," he growls, one eye squinted shut by the snarl of wrinkles that radiates from his sunken nose. "Who is this, Chad."

"Just Danny Moody, Dad," says the xo, and then, "sit the hell down!"

"I'm paying my respects," says Moody, half out of his chair. He sits himself back down. "An honor, to finally meet the co," he says.

The old man's chin juts up at that. "You a jefe?"

"He was, Dad," says the xo, as Moody says, "The Dread Paladin, sir. I've been down in Salem the last little while. But I'm back."

"And who was it, asking questions," says the co.

"The feds, sir," says Moody. "My guess, a task force aimed at rolling up your whole network. But they didn't get anything out of me."

"Dad, he's just," says the xo, as the co says, "What do you need." The xo blurts out, "Dad!" Moody's smile is pointed, there under the pointed beak of his nose, over his dark-scabbed chin. "A place to sleep," he says. "I wouldn't say no to a hot shower."

"Make it so," says the co, setting himself to the wheels of his chair. The xo looks down, muttering something, bare legs knobby and pale in the light. "Thank you, sir," says Moody, as the co squeakily wheels away. "You won't regret it."

A Running shoe, blue & brown

A RUNNING SHOE IN ONE HAND, BLUE AND BROWN, a square-toed Oxford black in the other, he stands there, looking from one to the other, "Where was I," he says. Setting them both on the counter, he pushes the running shoe over to the woman on the other side, holding the mate, brown and blue. Her jacket and her long brown hair dark with rain. She puts hers by the one he's given her, "So, now what?" she says. "Do I put them on?" and he shrugs. "You can, if you like," he says. "They're shoes." He drops the lone black Oxford onto the jumbled pile of shoes at his feet. "Welcome to Portland," he says.

Patter of rain against plastic tarps, blue and green, garbage bags stretched over flattened cardboard boxes, a lean-to strapped to the high wire fence along the sidewalk. A curl of freeway overhead, a shadowed mass above the streetlight, and the blank black sky beyond. His grimy hoodie blotched with rain, he kneels at one end of it, lifting a flap, "Hey," he says. "I'm with the xo. Jefe's here?" Three or four figures lying under the shelter, on old blankets, a sleeping bag, more flattened cardboard. One of them maybe nods. "So who are you," says another one, but the fence rings as he curls up against it, sitting himself as much under the shelter as he can get. His eyes narrowed over cheekbones hunched. "I'll tell you tomorrow," he says.

Spitting toothpaste into the sink, rinsing his brush, running it about his mouth, leaning over to spit once more. Stays there, hanging there, bent over the sink. A hand on his shoulder, firm, knuckles yellowed, nails cut short, "Don't forget your medicine," hale, good-humored, and he nods. He lifts himself as the hand's lifted away, opens the medicine cabinet, plucks a blue plastic pillbox from among the bottles of cologne, the shaving bowl and brushes, the pomade-tin. Unsnapping the lid, the light changes about him, warming his face as he lifts it away. Within, clear gel caps each a pinch of glimmering gold. He plucks one up, lifts it to his lips, gingerly between his teeth. A moment, over the sink, hands braced to either side. He closes his mouth. He swallows.

Muttering, open shirt billowing as he moves about the cavernous room, feet bare on the unfinished wood floor. Undoing his white cuffs. The shadowy suggestion of columns about him, glints from the glass of the windows beyond. Throwing back his arms he lets the shirt slip down and off, "architectonically," a word that can be made out of his glossolaly, and then, undoing the buttons of his fly, hopping awkwardly as he kicks one leg free, then the other, "environmentally," and he leaves his pants behind him. Naked but for his heavy gold watch he moves to the middle of the irregular polygon he's paced off in the dust, and kneels, undoing the latch on his watchband, slipping his hand free. "Syzygonomical," he says, letting go of the watch, left hung in the air before him. He lets out a breath of relief. "All right," he says. "Let's see where you've gone."

"Good God damn about anything happening," she says, "in," looking about the grubby, empty little room. "Yellowknife," she says, perplexed. Neon shining on and off through the one lone window. Crimpled plastic, some discarded dry cleaning bags, splayed over the foot of the neatly made bed. "Phil?" she says. Turning about. There, by the door left ajar, splinters of black plastic on the stained carpet. She picks up a pair of sunglasses, one arm dangled awry, and the left lens cracked, gone smokey blank and grey.

Those blazing candles along the sills and counters juddering, flickering, something's shaking the trailer. Under the tiny sink a cabinet door pops open, a worn black orthopædic shoe wiggling out of the narrow space, followed by another, legs in blue coveralls kicking, twisting to one side to allow the hips to fit, fingers wriggling around the edges of the cabinet gripping, pulling, a grunt and a gasp and she's sitting on the floor, coughing once, lightly, tucking a long loose strand of black hair under the kerchief about her head. Grimacing she gets her feet under herself, pushes upright, working her head side to side, careful of the curl of the ceiling above. Looking about, sucking her teeth, clucking her tongue. Leaning over the bed in its alcove, there in the back, tugging the heavy umber comforter up over bare arms, smoothing over twined legs. Looking over them both a moment, the black-haired head on the pillows, the bright red hair spread over the shoulder, the broad chest. Then she licks her thumb and forefinger and sets to snuffing candles, one by one.

Et quia maximum in perfectionibus motibus, et figuris in mundo non est, ut ex iam dictis patent: tunc non est verum quod terra ista sit vilissima et infima, nam quamvis videatur centralior, quo'ad mundum, est tamen etiam, eadem ratione polo propinquior, ut est dictum.

—*Nicholas of Kues*

NO. 25
" – two sweetest passions – "

Slouching through the Door – a Scum of whited sugar
Monte Carlo – the Ell-word, the Jay-word – Crisp little tents
"My sister" – Third Annual – Light; Hope; Truth
the Chords of Tom and Gary – Level A, Furniture
the warmth of March – what's In the Envelope
the Nearest book – "You're it; That's all" – what's On the Radio
an Audience – some God-damned fools – there was a Gate
White towers

Slouching through the door, grey yoga pants and a hoodie under a ruddy down vest zipped up, hood up, head down. Black gym bag in the one hand and the other a quick wave for the man behind the bar, spiky black hair and a faceful of stubble, skinny arm up to wave back. Drums clatter a sashay under a popping fanfare, that's when you know you're close, a woman's voice, sometimes you gotta work hard for it. Past the bar, the mostly empty tables, the tiny empty stage, brushing the column of chain at the corner of it, a gentle ring that's swallowed by the blaring horns. A nondescript door in the shadows there, a narrow hall, dark, beyond, at the one end a door half-open on white light, papers piled atop an old grey cabinet, but down the other end a small room painted black so many times the regular lines, the dimples and pocks of the cinderblock walls are softened, blurred, shining in the light of lamps ablaze about a row of mirrors. Squeezing in, behind a woman blending red and blue in a sloppy arc over an eyelid, behind a woman adjusting a bit of white lace, down to a short red velvet chaise against the far wall. Gym bag up on the chaise, unzipped, thrown open, digging through lace and satin, feathery gauze and fringe and stiff black rubber to pull out a plastic sandwich bag, heavy with golden dust, dropped on the counter with the tubes and the bottles and jars.

"Dead out there," says the woman mascaraing her lashes.

"Thursday morning," says the woman gathering up her thick blond hair.

Lotion white on a rough palm sprinkled with gold. "I can take the first dance."

"You're early," says the woman checking her ponytail in the mirror, arms and thigh, flank and chest all looped and filigreed with tattoos, the largest a black-letter motto arcing her belly that says Der Bauch lügt nicht!

"Weren't you on to close tonight?" says the woman brushing her lips a thickly red.

Lotion on fingertips slender, sleek, lifted up under that hood, a sigh. "It's Thursday." The hood, pushed back. Black hair cut short, swept up in front, those fingers teasing a tidy stack of curls.

"You cut your hair!" says the woman tugging on a long white boot. "When did you cut your hair?"

"Weeks ago," says the woman looking over her painted face from this angle, that. "Where have you been."

"Right there," she says, "right there right there, right yes there," on hands and knees her yellow hair severely straight "fuck yes" whipped up and back, "fucking fuck yes there don't stop don't stop oh *God* don't," flopping to slap the bunched white comforter, hips humped back against Ysabel kneeling behind her, Ysabel leaning over her, one of Ysabel's hands on the small of her back, *"don't* stop *don't* stop," the other reached under to circle, twist, jiggle and slap, *"fuck"* a groan and belly heaving toes clenching head reared up and howling out she trembles shivering slumping into Ysabel's arms about her.

Morning softly grey in the window, clouds closed high above the greening trees, the rooftops black and grey and dark wet red. *"God,"* a breath of a word, and a laugh, "I *love,"* she says, and as Ysabel breaks off a kiss to her throat, "Chrissie!" sitting up, alarmed, but yellow hair spread out on the pillows she's giggling, *"this,"* she's saying, "this, I love *this,* for fuck's sake." Reaching up a hand. Ysabel looking away. "You're so easy to tease."

"You shouldn't play games with this," mutters Ysabel.

"All right," says Chrissie, sitting up beside her for a kiss, "then," and another, rolling, licking, "how about," as Ysabel slowly lays herself down, "this?" her hand at Ysabel's opening thighs. Breaking off suddenly sitting back, hands on her own knees, "I thought you had to ask," she says. "I thought you had to ask, before I could answer." Head at an impish cant. "Do you want to ask? Is that it?"

"What I want," says Ysabel, and a sigh. "Chrissie," she says, but then a yelp as Chrissie falls on her, kissing, kissing, "I'm here," says Chrissie, "right here," lips at Ysabel's throat, her chest, the slope of a breast and as Ysabel hisses a nipple, "Chrissie," she says, "wait, please, it's not," her hands on shoulders, a cheek, and "Please nothing," says Chrissie.

"I have to," says Ysabel, "oh."

"You have to oh," says Chrissie.

"It's late," says Ysabel, a grimace, "I must get up, go shower, oh," and a swallow.

"So like this," says Chrissie, leaning over. Ysabel slaps at her arm, pushing, "I really must," she says.

"Go ahead," says Chrissie, lying back. "I won't stop you. I'll just," stretching up, fingers linked, languorous above her head, "wait here. I'll keep the oven warm. Till you come back."

"*Chrissie,*" says Ysabel.

"All day, if I must."

"All Thursday," says Ysabel.

"Oh," says Chrissie. "Then. I'd better make it quick?" Pouncing on Ysabel's belly again, Ysabel gasping, laughing, and then "oh" the breath gone fluttery in her mouth, and her hand wrapped about in that yellow hair.

The little jar in her hand, the label of it worn, Villainess Soaps it says, in smudged black type, Jai Mahal White Sugar Body Scrub. Tipping it, peering into it, a faint white curl about the bottom, and otherwise empty. Setting it on the long counter marbled red and black and pocked with sinks at regular intervals under the long mirror empty but for herself, there, and down at the other end a woman wrapped in a blue towel, brushing her dishwater hair.

By the jar, the lid, the inside of it scummed over with a white paste. She pokes it, softly pliable, with a finger, then scoops up carefully precisely half of what is there to stroke one cheek, the other, feathery faded white under her eyes. Rubbing those streaks into her skin with both hands, hesitant at first, swiping up across her forehead, down her chin, her throat. Pale hair swept back, limply damp on her shoulders. Beige bra fuzzed with soft sprung thread. "Nice ink," says the woman in the blue towel, passing behind her, eyeing the small of her back. She answers with a nod, a brisk tight smile.

Sitting on a bench before a row of lockers, the bottom one before her open, stuffed full, a swollen brown gym bag stood up on one end, a puffy pink and orange parka crammed in beside it. She's doing up the buttons of a plain white blouse. "He's crazy," someone's saying, "fucked in the head." Next bench down, an older woman, grey sweats, phone in one hand, towel in the other, wiping her face. "The deposition's today. He knows it's today. It can't be done today," turning her broad-shouldered back, "there are *laws* of *physics.*" Four buttons left on the blouse, then three, she pauses, ducks her head, quick sniff at her armpit. A sigh. Two buttons, left undone.

Hustling across the street in that pink and orange parka, leaning the weight of the gym bag slung from her shoulder. The building behind all sharp brick corners and windows relentless, filled with idle exercise machines. Tucked away over a side door a sign that says 24-Hour Fitness, lit up in reds and blues turned richly weird by the morning gloom. A wheezing bus gathers itself, nose swung wide in a left turn beside her, she skip-hops onto the sidewalk, past the bright island of a gas station. Behind the little convenience store store a narrow parking lot, angled stalls to either side between blank white wall and a length of cyclone fence woven through with pale plastic strips. Halfway down she tries the handle of a boxy blue car only to find it locked. Tipping her head back, a sigh, letting the bag drop to the pavement, she knocks, a gentle tap. Then a pound, banging the side of her fist against the glass, "Luke, goddammit, Luke," she says, and inside something moves, a chunk, the lock releasing.

She stuffs the gym bag into a back seat jammed with boxes, bags, a hardshell suitcase, loose books and papers shifting, "Shit," she says. On the driver's seat a grease-stained paper sack, yellow and red, Go-Go Taquitos, it says. She crumples it, tosses it into the back seat. "What," says the man slumped in the passenger seat. "I was hungry."

"Breakfast now means no dinner later," she says, climbing in behind the wheel.

"You're getting paid," he says. A beard, a mustache thick about his mouth, and dark hair dribbled lankly about the shoulders of his warm-up jacket, blue and grey, unzipped over a T-shirt printed with some faded engineering drawing, a feathered wing, its armature. "Friday," she says to him, holding out a hand. "I get paid Friday. Tomorrow."

He looks away, frowning, digging around in his pockets. "Tell me," he says, pressing a key into her palm. "Tell me again."

"No," she says, slotting the key in the ignition.

"Jessie," he says, "dammit, just, tell me something. Tell me something about her. Tell me her name. Say her name. Just, say her name."

She closes her eyes. He's gripping the armrest between them, his breath a hasty bellows. "Annabelle," says Jessie.

"There," he says, relaxing, "that's pretty," as she twists the key, as the engine roars to life.

MONTE CARLO – THE ELL-WORD, THE JAY-WORD
CRISP LITTLE TENTS

MONTE CARLO, says the sign, Pizza, Steaks, the lettering scratched and fading from the filthy windows of the corner storefront. Down the block the other storefront's boarded over with graffiti'd plywood, a rust-raddled chain knotted about the handles of its big double door, under the skeletal frame of a grand awning that once sheltered the sidewalk. Between the two storefronts a demure door painted a brown that melts into the brickwork, and small black squares of tin nailed above it, each printed with a brassy numeral, 1018. It's opening, a man's stepping out, blue and white track suit, running shoes, locking the door, looking up in time to see the woman headed past the Monte Carlo window, around the corner, brown coat, pale bloom of hair.

Quickly after her, around that corner. Letters flaking from a side window above say Live Music Every Nite. The street slopes down, and past the brick the looming blue-grey bulk of a warehouse, long windows high above that stretch between concrete pillars, square panes painted over white or caked with old dust or smashed out, jagged shadowed holes, and the wall beneath illegible with graffiti. A fence has been slapped up against the wall, tipped poles canted drunkenly, an old worn sign hung from the mesh that says Wilson Properties in blocky type. She's maybe a quarter of the way down the length of it, leaning a shoulder against the ringing, squealing fence as she pushes the mesh away from the pole, sharp cut ends of it bright clean sparks. "Hey!" he yells. "Hey! You can't go in there!"

"I assure you," she calls back, "it's easy enough. I've but to lift my foot," and she does, straddling the mesh, careful of the white paper bag in the one hand, the cup-carrier in the other, and three tall white paper cups. A door's cut into the wall above her, three feet up or so, a brief shelf of threshold jutting beneath.

"You're trespassing," he says, coming down the sidewalk. "We don't want any squatters – "

"I may be outlaw," she says, leaning over to set the bag and the cups on the threshold, "but I do no trespass." The sheepskin collar of her coat turned about about her frothy cloud of white-gold hair.

"Yeah, well, we, can," sputtering, standing there, looking about, the warehouse, her, the empty street. He's taller than he seems with that stoop, his dwindling brown hair buzzed close, tipped here and there with silver. "Look," he says. "You can't – it's dangerous. This building – "

"There's no danger," she says, a gesture toward the paper bag, the cups. "It's but breakfast, for those who wait within.

You may join us, if you like, but we'd need to fetch more coffee – or tea, perhaps?"

"I'm not," he says, "I don't. I'd rather, not, call the cops."

"Of course not," she says. "Would you speak with the owner?" Reaching up and over she knocks on the door, the metal of it booming. "She likes chai lattes."

"I, I don't," he says, stepping back. "Just, keep it quiet. I don't want any trouble."

"Who does," she says, as he turns, walking away, jogging away. The door above her opens, groaning. Long black hair dangling loose, pale bare knees smudged, baggy white T-shirt scrawled with handwritten letters that say The Giggling Mountebanks. "Hey," says Gloria Monday. "Who the hell was that?"

Marfisa shrugs. "Neighbors," she says, hauling herself through the gap in the fence.

Wrapped in a white towel Chrissie laughing barges into the room and hurls herself on the bed as Ysabel stately swans in after, short white robe loosely draped. Rolling over and over again, Chrissie in the muted sunlight, the towel falling away from her pale bare back, laughter stilling with a sigh. *"Why* do you have to go see your brother," she says.

"He's the King," says Ysabel, opening a drawer, rummaging through filmy, frothy stuff.

"I don't play that game," says Chrissie.

"When you're with me," says Ysabel, laying out bits of cream satin edged with brown lace, "you do."

"But why *today,*" says Chrissie. "Why Thursday." Yellow hair wetly burnished about her face.

"Merely a coincidence," says Ysabel, undoing the belt of her robe. "The one has nothing to do with the other."

"God, you're lovely," says Chrissie.

"Don't," says Ysabel, laying the robe over the foot of the bed.

"It's a woman, isn't it," says Chrissie, chin in her hand.

"What?"

"Thursday. It's a woman," says Chrissie, as Ysabel bends over to step into her underpants. "And you go to see her, once a week, every week. I bet you let *her* say the ell-word."

"This isn't funny, you know," says Ysabel, opening the doors of an armoire.

"I'm not the funny one."

"But you *are* in a mood." Ysabel lays out a sweater the color of wheat, or oats.

"Triste est omne animal post coitum," says Chrissie, tipping over, on her back, "but not with you. Never with you. With you I feel," knees up, arms up, stretching for the ceiling. "Carbonated? Effervescent."

"Every animal," says Ysabel, laying out a lacy white skirt, "but the cock, and woman."

"Well." Chrissie tips her head back, chin up, looking at Ysabel upside-down. "If you're going to spoil the mood with context."

Ysabel sits on the bed beside her. "You're chattering," she says. Slipping the lace-edged straps of the bra up her arms. "What is it you're not talking about. Is it Davies? Is he pushing you?"

"That," says Chrissie, kneeling up behind her, taking hold of the bra-straps, "would be the jay-word."

"Don't be ridiculous," says Ysabel, as Chrissie hooks the bra closed.

"Let's talk about your secret lover, then. Or is it lovers." Chrissie lies back against the pillows, watching as Ysabel takes up the skirt, bends down to pull it on. "A whole harem of beautiful women, bewitched by your terrible curse."

"You've decided, haven't you." Ysabel bunches up a long white sock, slips it over her foot. "You're going to do his movies, his videos." Pulls it up and up, smoothing it over her knee. "You're going to do what *he* wants," she says, bunching up the other. "Not what you want."

"It's a one-time deal," says Chrissie, with a sigh, "that gets us money, and an opportunity, to – "

"Oh, those are Ettie's talking points," says Ysabel, looking back over her shoulder. "She's the funny one."

"It's a man, isn't it. Your shameful Thursday secret is a man!" Chrissie sits up, leans close, "Does it even work on men?" she says.

"I mean, if you have to *want* to ask," but then Ysabel's kissing her, hard, arms about her crushing tight and eyes squeezed shut.

"Shut up," says Ysabel, after.

"You want to ask right now, don't you," murmurs Chrissie, lips on skin. "What would happen, if you did? What would I say, do you think."

"Why should I?" says Ysabel, and a hissing suck of breath. "Now that I know you're not after my money," and Chrissie laughs into Ysabel's kiss.

Canvases upright, leaned against walls, against crates, against the worktable and the pillar, a staggered circle of them in the glare of the trouble light dangled overhead. She's sitting in the middle of them all, yellow blouse and a houndstooth skirt, black tights, brown hair unskeined about her shoulders. Leaning forward for a bite of burrito, then pushing her glasses, narrow, black-rimmed, back up her nose. Figures splashed across those canvases, form and motion scribbled blackly, redly slashed, swoops of arms and hands, shoulders, clavicles, breasts, the lines gone sleekly slender up along throats, jaws, noses, and in each is caught a single look, quite still, those sole green eyes that gaze out, sidelong or direct, uptipped or a downward regard from each sliver of a moment frozen, and above around about them all the mad wild tangles of hair, curls and spills and splatters of black paint crusted, strobe-lit, jump-cut, scattered dance. Another bite. A white paper cup, lifted, and she blows at the steam lofting up from a notch in the lid. A sip.

"See, well, I mean, it's, it's," says Gloria Monday, off to one side, behind a canvas, out of the light. "It's not, it's, it's just," shaking her head, "it's just not."

"She cut her hair," says Marfisa, sitting up on the walkway in the meagre daylight, a paperback in her hand.

"Yeah, I know, we know, she cut her hair," says Gloria.

"There's something here," says the woman sitting in the middle of all those canvases. "It's just," looking about, "there's, ten of them? Twelve?"

"Fourteen," says Gloria.

"Wow."

"There's gonna be more," says Gloria. "There was gonna be more."

"More," says the woman, sitting in the middle of them all. One last bite of burrito. "Well. It's – relentless."

"Relentless," says Gloria, flatly. "That's, that's not a good word."

"Perhaps if you," daubing her lips with a napkin, "winnowed it down? To three, or four," and she pushes herself to her feet, brushing dust from her tights. Gloria's stepping out from behind the canvases, into the ring of them, bare feet shuffling, "No," she's saying, "you don't, it's got to be," turning about, including them all with a sweep of her arm, *"all* of them, every, it's, it's," hands to her head, black hair shining in the harsh light. "Anna, I *told* you. The music, the lights, the way she, looked, right at me, and, well, you know?" Lowering her hands, an irritated, empty gesture. "Right?"

"She stepped close," says Anna, quietly. "In her mother's garden. She asked me, and I, answered, and brought her five hundred dollars, and a bus schedule."

"And ever since," says Gloria. "You close your eyes."

"I see her," says Anna.

"Over and over," says Gloria.

"You should've slept with her," says Marfisa, turning a page in her book.

"It's not *like* that," snarls Gloria, wheeling about.

"Worked for me," says Marfisa, without looking up.

"The *hell* it did," mutters Gloria.

"Unrelenting," says Anna, her hand on Gloria's arm.

"Yes!" says Gloria, turning back. "Relentless! So." A kick at the dust. "Yeah."

"*I* can see it," says Anna, "but I know what I'm looking at. Some things – "

"This is how it is!" cries Gloria. "This! *This* is how it has to be!"

"Some things," says Anna. "They have to be said, but it doesn't mean they're meant to be heard. That they *can* be heard."

"So," says Gloria, and a deep breath. "Okay." Throwing out a hand, clamping it about the top of the nearest canvas. "So fuck it," she says, and tips it over falling face-down to the floor, smack.

"Gloria!" cries Anna. "You said you wanted to do more. So. Do more. Try again, try something – Gloria!"

"I *can't!*" wails Gloria, tipping another, whack and a billow of dust, grabbing another, "the whole *point,*" yank, topple, crack, "is I don't have the money to *do* any more," and Anna seizes her arm, "Please, don't," but Gloria shakes herself loose, grabs another, "was to see if I could *raise* money," yank and slam, "by maybe *selling* these damn things," and again, toppling, but Anna with a lunge catches it, grunting, pushing it back upright. *"Gloria,"* she says. "The point isn't to sell the paintings. The point is to raise money. Right?"

"You have a better fucking idea?" says Gloria, with a half-hearted kick at a fallen canvas.

"I might," says Anna.

Marfisa turns another page.

"Let's hear some love," the booming voice, as she mounts the shadowed stage, "for the one, the only, Starling!" and a piano riff rumbles from the speakers, left-handed, low, a whoop or two, someone's clapping. Red and black wrestling boots laced up her calves and jagged oblongs black and red that cover her breasts, her belly, her buttocks and thighs, and as that riff circles itself she plants her feet, lifts up a wooden guitar body, a red flying vee, and with a windmilling swing of her arm as the lights flare mimes a strike at the strings. A power chord roars through the speakers, guitar and drums overwhelming the piano. More whoops. The music settles into a thumping march and she struts three steps to the edge of the stage, spins about swinging the guitar over her head, drops to a squat, throttling the neck of it between her knees, I don't wanna let another minute get by, a woman's singing, but she's looking out over the thin audience, they're slipping through our fingers but we're ready to fly, men here and there, a man and a woman at that table, she has pink hair, two more men crowding close to the stage, heartily young, bills creased about their beefy fingers, bills already littering the stage like so many crisp little tents. Standing to spin again, swinging about, and when the morning arrives, it'll all be gone, two more, three more men there, a woman pulling out a chair, shapeless in a green coat, at the bar a woman leaning forward, blond hair cut short, ordering a drink. It's time to put up or shut up, singing out over the speakers, or to pick up the pace, and the Starling dances.

"Urban Restoration Squad," she says, handset of an old desk phone to her ear. Sitting up. "I can do that for you, actually," she says, but brightly chipper, highly pitched. "What's the name? Jessie, yes, Jessie Vitaly. Yes." Her long blond hair, her plain white blouse, the top two buttons of it left undone. "Jessie's been with us for, for three months, yes. Since January fifth. Fourth. January fourth. Yes." Looking about the little office, a couple of desks in opposite corners, shelf of binders and file folders, printer on its podium, nothing stirring in the doorway to the back room. "I'm afraid," she says, clamping the handset between shoulder and ear, "it's policy merely to confirm, ah," reaching down, under her desk, "the period of employment." At her feet a stuffed brown gym bag, and resting atop it a clamshell phone, charging. "Is there anything else?" She unplugs it. "Anything I can, no, thank you. Thank you. Goodbye!" Straightening, hanging up the desk phone. Unfolding the cell phone, laying it on her desk by her keyboard. A stylized hawk's head, red and black, fills its little screen, and numbers along the top of it, 3/22, 11:17. "Hey," says someone, from back there in the back room. "Jessie, how the hell do I," but "Just a second," she calls back, staring intently at the phone.

It lights up, buzzing, a burst of tinny music, whistling synthesized strings that gyrate about a splashing high-hat. She snaps it up, tapping the big green button on its keypad, "Hello?" she says. "This is Jessie." Her voice pitched low now, softer, rounder. "Yeah," she says, "no, yeah, we still are. Of course." Turning about in her chair, looking out the big bay window behind her, the glass taped over with posters and flyers. "Well, yes, the, ah, the landlord, of our, our previous occupancy? Apartment." Outside the corner, the sidewalk. "He, ah," she's saying, "well. He's dead. He died. So. That's, I mean, why we're moving. So. It would be, hard." The empty street, wet with rain. Over across the way a pile of a brick building, three or four storeys, huge high windows dark. "Yes. You did? Good. And everything's?" She's nodding. "Good." Sitting back in her chair. "We can, the, yes. First, last, security, yes, we can, yes. Saturday, we can have that for you. But I was wondering, if," leaning forward, "the keys, if we could," listening, nodding. Looking down. "Saturday. No, that's fine. Thank you. No, thank you. Thank you."

She closes the phone. Closes her eyes. A little smile, and a sigh.

"Jessie," that voice from the back room. "Can you tell me why the hell this piece of shit machine can't open a simple PDF?"

"Because it's a piece of shit," says Jessie, leaning down, plugging the cell phone back in, setting it back on the gym bag. "Send it over to me, I'll print it for you, or whatever."

"I just want the damn thing to open the damn files without making a big production, you know?"

"We probably just need to download something, or update something else," she says. "Hey, Nelson. You mind if I take an early lunch?"

"Just, fix this damn thing first."

"Right," says Jessie, getting to her feet.

"MY SISTER" – THIRD ANNUAL – LIGHT; HOPE; TRUTH
THE CHORDS OF TOM AND GARY

"MY SISTER," says someone, says Lymond, "gentlemen: Ysabel," and the rustle and turn in that high wide room of all those regards to her, conversations checked, chins lifted, and glasses, those dark-suited men brushed with bonhomie in little knots and clusters under the great curving wall of glass. The uncertain grey of the clouds beyond, framed by wet black trees. She's there in the mouth of that room, all in white, hands clasped behind her back, and then, she's smiling, they're looking away, back to each other. Murmurs resume.

"So pleased you could come," says Lymond beside her, smooth white shirt and charcoal slacks, delight in his bulging eyes, one brown, one blue, and his brightly orange hair slicked back.

"I'd thought this was just a simple lunch," says Ysabel.

"It is," he says. "There's food." A gesture toward a table laden with triangled sandwiches, pinwheeled wraps, chips and crudités. Just past it under the great window a man in a pale blue suit, shoulders brushed by white-gold dreads, one hand jabbing the palm of the other as he makes a forceful point to the woman listening intently, draped in a purple gown iridescent with blues and greens, head wrapped in a fine black scarf. "Something to drink?" says Lymond. He's taken her arm, he's squiring her into the room, she's shaking her nodding head, a shrug, "But," she says, "a function such as this. Shouldn't all the court be here?"

"You mean the Gallowglas." He waves to someone, nods to someone else. "This, this is more of a Westside thing. Don't you think?"

"All right," says Ysabel.

He stops, head tipped, brow cocked. "You do know what this is about."

"I'd thought it was to celebrate phase one," she says, quietly.

"There've been some complications," he says, softly, and then, raising his voice, "You know Mr. Sogge?"

"This guy!" growls a man in sharp navy. "This guy." Under his suit coat a heather grey T-shirt, blazoned with a brightly yellow O, and about his chin a scruff of beard too neat to be an afterthought. Clapping Lymond's shoulder, firmly shaking his hand, "Not only have we finally got the crane up over Park West," he says, "the Pearl's back underway. I'm telling you," turning to Ysabel, "three months in and this year's already better than all of the last."

"Your pardon," says Ysabel, "but I've no idea who you are."

"That's all right," says Mr. Sogge. "I had no idea he had a sister." Abruptly he heads off, into the scrum.

"Was he important?" says Ysabel.

"He's not," says Lymond, "irreplaceable. But." He gestures toward a tiny woman in a nubbled grey suit, laughing with a heavyset man in tweedy browns and greens and a yellow mesh-back cap. "The mayor's here," says Lymond, and then, looking around, "and also Councilman Killian, somewhere, so there's at least a couple of reporters in the room? Speak carefully."

Ysabel says, "What's that?"

Past the table laden with food, another, and laid atop it a city, blank white towers jumbled in a curl of broad blue painted river, and delicate white bridges stitched across it. "Rudy brought it over," says Lymond, following Ysabel as she makes her way toward it, through the milling crowd. "Sogge. To give our celebration a little focus."

At the foot of one of those little bridges a bloom of color, towers in red and yellow instead of white, lining a single avenue there at that end of the city. "Focus," says Ysabel. And then, "The Pearl's back underway, he said." Looking up at Lymond beside her, who shrugs and says, "Complications."

"Beautiful, isn't she," says a man over across the corner of it, not too tall, somewhat stout, his dark grey suit shot through with glistening silver.

"Mr. Davies," says Ysabel. "I hadn't expected to see you again so soon."

"I've told you, please," he says. "Feel free to call me Reg."

"You know each other," says Lymond.

"Mr. Davies and I have certain interests in common," says Ysabel, and Reg lets out a snort of laughter.

"I see," says Lymond.

"I gotta tell you, Lymond," says Reg, "the Lovejoy Development? A lot of people in this room aren't happy, if you asked them, honestly, with how long it took you folks to come around. But me?" A gesture over that patch of color. "Gave me a chance to grab a seat at the table. I'm thrilled, I gotta tell you, to be a part of this project."

"Careful, Ys," murmurs Lymond, and she spares him a side-long look as she leans out over the city. "Tell me, Mr. Davies," she says. "Your seat, at this table. Will you merely consult, on the marketing and such, or do you actually have – what's the phrase? Skin, in the game."

"Oh, I'm in," says Reg.

"Well," says Lymond, stepping back, "the Guisarme's arrived, and the Glaive. I should go and welcome them."

"By all means," says Ysabel.

"So," says Reg. "He's your brother."

"Yes," says Ysabel.

"And you're, what was that? The Queen? That makes him, what, a prince? Duke?"

"The King," says Ysabel.

"But he's your brother," says Reg.

"Yes," says Ysabel.

"You know, the two of you look nothing alike?"

"He takes after his father," says Ysabel.

"So this," he says, turning about in that little office, the two desks, the big bay window taped over with posters and flyers, "is what's gonna save the city." His warm-up jacket grey and blue, his navy workpants almost black. "One storefront," he says, hands up, shoving back his lankly coiled hair. "Two desks." Blinking broadly, as if trying to clear his eyes of something.

"Nelson's got his own office," says Jessie, there by the door, shrugging out of her pink and orange parka.

"Nelson," he says, scrubbing his eyes with the heels of his hands. "Stiles? Your glorious leader?"

"There's the board," says Jessie. "And the volunteers and stuff, but, yeah. Day to day, this is it."

"You're fucked," he says.

"Luke," she says. "This is the job." Forcefully, but quietly. "This is what I could get. This is what you wanted me to get."

"The only thing being saved in here is petty cash," he says.

"Come on," she says, stepping toward him. Taking his arm by the elbow. "You go on back to the car. Do, whatever. We just have to make it through tomorrow and Saturday, Saturday we get the keys. Okay?"

"A roof," he says, pulling himself free. "We *have* a roof."

"Someplace to put our stuff, then," she says, reaching for his arm again, but he shakes her off, throws back his head, "What the *fuck* are you even *doing* here?" he blurts. Lurching across the little office toward the shelf full of binders, "Tell me," he says, bang against that other desk there, "tell me *one thing* you're getting done here. Please."

"Keep your voice down," says Jessie.

He's snatched something from the desk, a poster, a mandala in greens and blues and silhouettes ringed below it about a stylized map. Hands Around Portland, it says. Third Annual. "This. You're doing this."

"Luke. Put it down. Come on."

"You're holding hands."

"It's a, it's to raise awareness, you know? Just, put it down, go on, tonight we can – "

"Third. Annual," he says, shaking the poster for emphasis. "Three years, this has been done. Awareness must be pretty fucking high."

"Actually," says someone else, a man in the doorway there to the back room, "that's last year's poster. So this'll be the fourth." Grizzled and jowly, a lump of a nose, tie-dyed T-shirt all reds and purples and a dull grey cardigan. "It's a symbolic gesture, intended – "

"Precisely!" roars Luke, slapping the poster back on the desk, and Jessie, wild-eyed, "Luke," she's saying, reaching for his arm again, "Luke," as he rounds on that man in the doorway, "You!" he says. "In here dreaming up *gestures* to raise awareness so you can then write a grant to beg for the money you need to buy a ticket to the meeting where, *if* you're meek and lucky, you might *politely* get a chance to ask them maybe to think about *stopping,* just for a *minute* – they're *always* gonna have more than you!"

And after a moment the man in the doorway says, "I'm sorry?"

"Money! They'll *give* it to you just to prove that point! You're never gonna get it done like this," and the man in the doorway's

shaking his head, "I really think you ought to," he says, but Luke's plowed on, "you've got to get out there with what you have, with what *they,* don't have, you seize something, take what you need, you force the situation, you *make* them come to *you.*"

"You really need to go," says the man in the doorway.

"This was *my* fucking idea, Nelson," says Luke. "And you're *fucking it up.*"

"Luke!" says Jessie, sharply, and he wheels on her, *"Lake!"* he snarls, but then he shudders, swallowing, nodding. The man in the doorway's frowning. He says, again, "You need to go."

"Yeah," says Luke. Stepping back. "Okay." Turning around. Jessie's backed up against her desk, hands to her face. Luke stalks past her, throws open the door. The jingle of a bell.

It's darker under the bridge, but not by much. The white suv slows to a stop, sits a moment, purring idly, before headlamps light up, front tires turn, crackle of gravel as one corner of it tipping up it mounts the curb, the slightest growl of engine, a threat of power, lifting the other corner of it, pause to hike up the rear wheels, rolling out onto the roughly paved lot, wallowing over old rail lines buried in the macadam. Long aisles of pillars to either side hold the length of the bridge above, a gentle slope and then more sharply down to where the buildings shoulder close to either side, where the suv swerves, lights slicing through the gloom, splashing over pillars, slowing, stops. A sigh as the engine cuts out. After a moment a rear door opens and all in white, Ysabel steps down.

There are things painted on the pillars about her, a wide-eyed owl in a swirl of feathers, clutching ungainly a pen, a black-faced lion awkwardly savaging an antelope, a stoic bust, defaced with yellow paint, under a spray of cartoon bunting, a bird with an elaborate tail perched atop a drawn plinth that says God is Love, and a scroll beneath that says Light Hope Truth April 7 1948.

Behind her the driver's door opens, a gentle warning chime. A woman climbs out there, hair cropped close and dyed a virulent chartreuse, looking about.

"Behold," says Ysabel, "the complications."

"Ma'am?"

"This," says Ysabel, with a sweep of her white-clad arm, "is what my brother means to give them. To Mister Reginald Davies." Walking, slowly, down the aisle. "What they will tear away, to make their little towers." A hand on the corner of a pillar, there by the shoulder of a bearded hermit, wrapped in robes, holding up a sketchy lantern.

The woman steps down from the running board, disappearing behind the spotless bulk of the suv. When she comes around the back of it, in her yellow track suit piped with white along the sleeves and legs, she's holding in her hands the long staff of a fauchard. Looking away, down the length of that shadowed nave under the long dark deck of the bridge, the columned aisles to either side, the glisten here and there of old rails, the street's brief interruption, and there, blocks away, a lone boxcar rusting comfortably. Peering at it, the sickled blade of her fauchard up and ready. Its side a gallery of graffiti, the lowest edge of it rainbow-stained below a spidery great sigil-shape of white.

"Iona?" says Ysabel.

"It's gone quiet, ma'am," she says, stepping back, and back again.

Ysabel looks up. Closes her eyes. The air, still, and not even the thrum of tires, the rumble and mewl of engines, the sing-song whistle of crosswalk alerts or the clatter of a bicycle, not the drip and plash and seep of rainfall settling, not the wind, high above, ushering clouds across the unseen sky. "It has," she says, then the startling clack of her heels striding back toward the suv. "Let's go," she says. "East, over the river to Alberta." Stepping up onto the running board, pulling herself up, one last look this way, that, the columns, the bridge. "My mothers will want to hear of this."

"Yes ma'am," says Iona.

It all goes suddenly blue, and blued she slinks to the front of the stage, sealed in a neoprene wetsuit, blackly sleeved, French cut, and strapped to her thigh a long black knife. Piano vamping from the speakers under a slice of feedback soaring, kettle-thump of drums, the day, that it became, a voice is singing, clear, and she's swaying gently, floating on the music, the first time that I saw you for the, one hundred fiftieth time, a whoop from the audience, three men, four, crowding the stage, a fifth, and the woman with pink hair, but can you blame me? I was reaching, sings that voice, reaching, halfway across the Atlantic Ocean, and pale arms appear about her, pale hands on her breast, her hip in that blue light, pulling away with a whip that spins her around and about, twirling away from a woman draped in tinsel glimmering, the place, it socked my square-jawed face, the tinseled woman swinging her arms, miming a pull at a rope or a net as the wet-suited Starling whirling on bare feet head back arms wide swings inexorably toward her, yanked with each tug of those glimmering arms till she's standing before the kneeling woman who grinning licks at her black rubbered crotch, halfway across the Atlantic Ocean, howls and cheers and applause as the music pounds, pounds, pounds, a half dozen men at the bar or more, that older woman at a table, ripped black T-shirt, white hair tousled, woman in a pink cocktail dress brown leather on her shoulders, woman in a red lace camisole looking away, bored, the man beside her staring, gone, gone, I have enough rope when you're gone, the door's opening, and someone all in white and short black hair but turning, stepping aside, making way for someone else, another woman taller, longer-legged, straight blond hair, and crumpling the Starling closes her eyes, gone, gone, gone.

Lights above the escalator, set in metal cups, and the ceiling about them sooty from years of incandescent heat. At the top the walls close in about a landing where Gloria Monday, all in black, stops, there between getting off the one escalator, onto the next, under a sign on the wall that says Housewares, and an arrow pointing up. On shelves haphazardly set within a glass case there's a grey plaster statue of a young girl with chunky grey butterfly wings and a flock of grey plastic ducks, and on the bottom of it a single bucket filled with dusty silk flowers and a fountain to be hung from a wall, lion's mouth yawning from a molded plaque, by the threadbare greenery of an ersatz topiary pawn, some sort of felted flocking wrapped about a wicker frame. Bracelets clack and jangle as Gloria lifts a hand to press against the glass, "This," she says, and a chuckle, "is *fantastic.*"

"Over here," says Marfisa, eyeing a door the same blank white as the walls.

"Okay," says Gloria, turning away from the glass case, black skirts swaying.

"Now Anna said," says Marfisa, "what did Anna say." Wild pale hair knotted loosely at the nape of her neck, above the collar of her sheepskin coat. "There'll be a hall. Down it to the end, last on the left, four knocks. Wait to be admitted. Speak to no one else," and Gloria's nodding, impatient, "Yeah, yeah," she says. "But then what."

"The truth," says Marfisa. "Close your eyes."

She's pulled from the pocket of her coat a plastic baggie, and frowning leans close to Gloria, tipping a bit of golden dust on each purpled eyelid. Turning to sprinkle a pinch on the knob of the door. "Okay," Gloria says, "so, Mar, do I open 'em now, or," and then, opening her eyes, "oh."

The offices are dim. Cubicle walls chin-high, a dingy, nappy brown, black nameplates by each opening, Offa, says one, in straight white sans-serif letters, Financialisation, and Sceatta, Courts Liaison, says another. Denarey. Manypeny. Light warms a cubicle to the right, "Look," someone's saying, "the show is incomplete without the three of them. Think of the chords, that Tom and Gary knew! The Stromberbrauch's been optimized, not only on the Chip-Ebene, but up and down the line, as well," and Gloria hurries past, hands holding her bracelets still in the creeping hush. Lloyd, says the nameplate by the last cubicle on the left. Accounts. Her knocks against the fabric of it muffled. Someone says, "Come in."

A woman's sitting in a black leatherette chair, flipping through an enormous stack of green-and-white fanfold printout next to an old computer terminal, black screen glowing with amber characters. A grey blouse, a soft pink bow knotted under the collar. She pauses, holding a chunk of printout in the air, takes up a clear plastic ruler, lays it along the lines of data. "Suzette Wilson," she says.

"Ah, actually," says Gloria, "I'm Gloria Monday? I'd rather, I'd prefer – "

"As you wish," says the woman, picking up a mechanical pencil, making a neat notation. "You have no purchases," she says, setting the pencil aside.

"No," says Gloria. "Well. I hope to – I want to – "

"A line of credit, then."

"Yes," says Gloria.

"That wasn't a question," says the woman. "The first question is this: do you love him?"

"Love," says Gloria, looking down, lips pursed, on the verge of shaking her head when her eyes widen, her face settles, smoothed over something fierce, and she looks up again to meet the woman's gaze. "No," she says. "No. He was a terrible – person."

"There's no need to elaborate," says the woman, jerking the ruler down a line. "The second question," she says.

Level A, Furniture – the warmth of March
what's In the Envelope – the Nearest book
"You're it; That's all"

Level A, Furniture, says the sign laid into the floor under her feet, but as she steps off the escalator she isn't looking over ersatz rooms, each on its island of carpeting, the queen-sized beds heaped with clashing pillows, the rectilinear sofas, all chrome and black leather. Tock and plock of bootheels, her houndstooth skirt, her tan trench coat, she heads off to one side, an alcove there where a couple of full-length mirrors in bulky wood frames are leaned against a wall. Cater-cornered from them a swinging door, lit by a small glass square criss-crossed with chicken-wire. She pushes through it into a service corridor crowded with pallets loaded with stuff, anonymous cardboard boxes swaddled in plastic wrap, patio furniture strapped in teetering stacks. She ducks under an enormous plastic candy cane, barber-striped, sidles past a throne all threadbare velveteen and worn gold-painted wood. Pushes away a stuffed reindeer, its nose an unlit bulb. There, beneath a stretch of dented duct, a portholed door, and beside it a boxy intercom grille, and no button or level or latch. Over the porthole blocky letters, carefully painted, say Boiler Room. She stoops over the grimy yellowed intercom, "Ah," she says, "Anna Nirdlinger, from Welund Rhythidd, to see Mousely."

After a moment a squawk from the box, a gabbled squelch in a rising pitch. She leans closer. "Anna," she says. "Rhythidd? Mousely." And then, *"Mousely."*

Far below, something dings, there's a groan and a climbing whine of cable, grind and squeak, a clang as light rises to fill the porthole settling as the noises drop with a thump back to a hum. The door sides open, she steps inside. The elevator begins its descent with a cacophonous jerk, and she resettles her narrow, black-rimmed glasses, clutching her shoulder bag close to herself. A deep breath in through her nose.

The elevator opens on a hall lined to either side with roll-top desks, each with a set of tubes hung above, like the pipes of an organ, sleeved in rubberized canvas, cornered and finished in bent metal joints, and all about a loudly rushing wheeze of air. Clerks in striped shirts bend over each of the desks, taking long capsules from tubes, unscrewing them open, looking over pages pulled from within, deftly selecting additional documents from cubbyholes, stiff cardstock, gauzy wodges of onionskin and carbons, crisply laser-printed forms, cream and salmon, goldenrod and lilac, shuffling all together, stapling here, clipping there, stamping with wide forceful but precise swings of their arms. Some bundles rolled up, stuffed back into capsules, sent with a shunt on their way, others neatly dropped in one of the swaying baskets overhead, hung from the chains that trundle down either side, the creak of them lost in the din from the end of the hall. Flat tables there, and big upright computer monitors hooked with snarls of grey-beige cabling to hulking flatbed scanners. White-shirted clerks hands gloved in blue take stacks from baskets, swiftly disassemble them, slap each page and card and form in turn on the glass bed of a scanner, and scrolling bars of light shine along the walls, then up the papers snatched and tossed into the maw of an enormous grinding shredder. A steep flight of stairs lifts up above their racket to a little balcony, where a stolid figure in a long pink dress, a pillbox hat pinned at a distracted angle, looks back down the length of the hall, beckoning to Anna with a white-gloved hand.

Up the stairs and through double doors into a cozy office, richly paneled, warmly lit, armchairs upholstered in floral prints before a polished desk, and one wall almost entirely taken up by a brick fireplace, the mantel of it crowded with sepia-tinged photographs, a graduated gaggle of matryoshka dolls, a vase top-heavy with stargazer lilies, the pink of them shading to blood red. When the white-gloved woman closes the double doors it's all plunged into silence, and only the merry crackle of the log on the grate. "Some tea, perhaps?" she says, as she steps around behind the desk.

"That would be lovely," says Anna, taking an armchair, and on the little table beside it more lilies, and a gently steaming china cup.

"Is it beastly without? I imagine it must be beastly."

"It's March," says Anna, sipping her tea.

"They're getting warmer, though," says the woman, "aren't they? Marches?" Smoothing papers in a manila folder laid open before her.

"I suppose?" says Anna. "It's good to finally meet you, Mousely."

"There's no need for flattery," says the woman, taking up a little grey plastic card which she fits into a squat black machine on her desk, carefully lowering the weighty lid. "Why are you here, Anna." Pressing a lever on the side of the machine. That lid slams down, a solid chunk.

"Well," says Anna. "I have recently begun work as a paralegal, with Welund Rhythidd," and Mousely yanks the lever up again. "Before that, I was amanuensis to the Queen."

"I know who you are," says Mousely, lifting the card now embossed with a line of numerals.

"Yes," says Anna, adjusting her glasses, "well, I do need to learn more of the firm's operations, and had some time at lunch today."

"A tour cannot possibly be arranged without some sort of notice," says Mousely. Careful of her white gloves, she's squeezing a dollop of something thick and clear from a tube onto the back of the card. "We are terribly busy, as you can see." Lips pursed, she presses the card precisely, firmly, to a square printed on a piece of paper before her in the folder. "If you'd called ahead, we'd've had time to prepare for you." Folding the paper, a bit clumsy with the stiff weight of the card now glued to it, neatly into thirds. "But perhaps that was the point?"

"This isn't anything like a surprise inspection," says Anna.

"Of course not," says Mousely, slipping the folded paper into a plain white envelope.

"Just a whim."

"Whimsy, Anna?" She's moistening the seal of the envelope with a neat little blue sponge. "Not the best of motives, where a bank's concerned," but a sudden grinding rush of noise, the double doors opening, a clerk stepping within, a red folder in her blue-gloved hands, nodding once, crisply, as she lays it on the corner of the desk.

"Blast and rot," says Mousely in the silence that falls as the doors close up again.

"Is there a problem?" says Anna, her eyes on that folder.

"A red jacket," says Mousely, opening it before her, "takes precedence over all other work, and must be approved at the highest levels." Lifting pages, looking over forms. "An impressive acquisition, to be sure, but a terrible bother."

Anna takes in a deep and fortifying breath. "I'd be happy to take it back with me," she says. "Deliver it to Rhythidd myself. Save you that much, at least."

Mousely looks up, a little card of glossy black in her white-gloved hands. "Would you," she says.

A half-dozen dream-catchers dangle before the broad window, and on the sill of it a bright round mirror in an octagonal frame, richly painted red and green. Jessie's sitting on one end of the couch beneath them, arm up along the back of it, looking out at the street, the dimly sourceless light of a cloudy afternoon. From the front room through that doorway a muttering rumble, a sharp retort, a sighing exhalation. She lays her yellow head on her outstretched arm. She closes her eyes.

"Jessie," says the man in the doorway, a hand up, rubbing his lump of a nose.

"Yeah." She sits up, drawing her arm to herself as he sits on the couch beside her. "How are you," he says.

"I can," she says, "I can get back to work."

"I just want to make sure you're okay," he says.

"I'm fine, Nelson," she says. "Thanks. For asking."

"That, was. Disturbing." A vague gesture of his hand toward the doorway, the front room beyond. In his other hand a plain white envelope.

"I'm really sorry about that," she says. "He isn't usually so agitated, but I guess, we've both been under a lot of pressure? It won't happen again. I swear."

A slow nod of his grizzled head. "So he's your boyfriend."

"We're, together," she says.

Another nod, a little higher, a little lower. He still isn't looking at her, not directly. "Do you," he says, "need to talk to someone. Some help. There are phone numbers. I can get you a phone number."

She says, "For what?"

"To, talk?" he says. "If you need it. If it's gotten to that point. There's – I know a good shelter."

"Shelter?" says Jessie, sharply, "we don't need a," and then, "oh. Oh, Nelson. No. It's not like that. He lost his temper, yeah, but like I said, we've both been under a lot of stress. I don't know what set it off. Frustration. But – he's not *violent*. It's not like that."

"Well," says Nelson. "Like I say. I can get you a phone number."

"Is that what's in the envelope?"

He holds it up, sighing, then hands it over to her. The flap's unsealed. She peers inside, looks up at him. "You said no checks till Friday."

"Yes."

"This is a check."

"It's the law, Jessie." He sighs. "When someone's being separated from employment, by end of business – "

"You're firing me," says Jessie.

Another sigh. "You're being laid off. I'm sorry, but – "

"You're firing me because you think my boyfriend's beating me."

"What?" he says, alarmed, looking at her now, beside him. "No," he says. "No, that's, no. No no no, no, no."

"Because that would be wrong," she says, her voice gone thickly soundless by the end.

Hand up, rubbing his face. Up on his feet, over to the desk. "It's," he says, "a question of money. We made a go of it, and, you did a fine job. That's not an issue. I'll be happy to write you a glowing recommendation, but the funding, we just, we can't justify," but Jessie says, "Shut up," and he stops, his gesture hung, unfinished. "I swear to God," she says. "The bullshit."

"Jessie," he says.

"I've been here three weeks," she says. "Three weeks. If it was money you wouldn't've hired me in the first place."

"Jessie, I have to ask you to – "

"No, you fired me, so, fuck that. Fuck that. He told me you were useless, but my God."

"He," says Nelson, and, "you," and, "what?"

"This check," she says, "this fucking check, we had such plans." Crumpling the envelope in her hand. "But we needed the next check, and the one after that, and, well, just, fuck it."

"What do you mean, he told you. What. He knew my name. I thought you told him."

"He said you wouldn't remember," says Jessie.

"He said. Who said. What is going on, here."

"I just," says Jessie, getting up. "I wanted a fucking job."

The receptionist at the desk looks up, an ornate brass telephone headset clipped to one ear. "Anna," he says. "I thought you were out today."

"Had a thing," she says. "It's done. Is Rhythidd back?"

"Still in the hills," says the receiptionist.

"All right," says Anna, holding her shoulder bag close. "I'll be here at least till four," she says. The receptionist nods.

A long and narrow corridor, cream-carpeted, blond paneling to the right, and office doors, slightly ajar, or closed, open carrels to the left, blond desks and cabinets, women typing at computers, and some men. The end of it an acute angle, and a single blond wood door. Her hand on the weighty brass knob of it she's looking back, along the hall, then down the next continuing sharply back to the left, more offices, more carrels, more typing, muttered phone calls. She opens the door.

An angled office, two shorter walls of dark wood, two longer walls of glass, a wide slab of utterly empty desk and behind it a high-backed chair of pale leather. Closing the door, softly, she pulls from her shoulder bag a folder, red, and a pen. Laying the folder open on the desk she flips through the pages within, pausing to initial here and there, quick bold Rs that finish with a curl. At the end, the penultimate page, a long blank line, and she looks up, adjusts her glasses, the pen hovering. Lowering to touch the line, and a single dot of ink, not quite black, tinted red. She signs, with slow definite strokes. Rhythidd.

Glued to the last page a black card, glossy, embossed with a string of numerals. MasterCard, it says, within interlocking circles of red and orange. Bank of Trebizond. Gloria Monday. Good thru 86/75. She unsticks it from the paper, turns it over, peeling off the last waxy dollop of glue as she steps away from the desk, toward the windows, and the expanse of sky beyond, empty, grey, the dark hills of the city below. She allows herself a briefly satisfied smile.

Clomp of wedge heels into the black room, sweat-sheened tattoos, handful of underwear tossed to the floor, "Starling," she says, laughing, and the rest of them turn back to their reflections, adjusting the shape of a wet red lip, the fall of dozens of braided extensions, purple as popsicles, fluttering a wad of grey-green bills. "You're wanted next door," says the sweating dancer, grabbing a robe from a hook on the wall, "your Thursday regular," and "Yes," says the Starling, there at the far end, standing up from the red velvet chaise, sheer négligée held shut by a single bow, and long black fishnet stockings.

"She brought a date," says the dancer, blotting her brow with a sleeve, and there's an exaggerated "Ooooh!" from the woman with the lipstick. "I saw," says the Starling, draping a black cloak over her shoulders as she squeezes her way down the line of them all.

"One of the Limoges sisters," says the dancer, and a dismissive "Pssht," from the woman tying up the last of her braids. "I know," says the Starling.

"How is it you get changed so goddamn fast," says the woman wrapping up the roll of bills with quick twists of a rubber band. "Like fucking magic, I swear." The Starling turns up the hood of her cloak, careful of her tiara, and steps out into the unlit hall, toward the muffled beat.

Her long white coat he takes with hands scrubbed pinkly clean, the nails of them buffed, meticulously trimmed. "It's good to see you again, Chazz," says Ysabel.

"Oh, but here's a paradox," he says, hanging her coat on a hall butler heaped with raincoats and rainshells, all about a speckly mirror. "A poor devil, unable to meet the mark of such a praise, and yet," with a wry smile, bald head pink and shining, his turtleneck spotlessly black, "your majesty, being her majesty, cannot possibly be wrong."

"Are they within?" she asks.

"Even so," he says, with a gesture toward the wide doorway to the side, there, the dim, high-ceilinged room, and the sonorous murmur of someone's voice. Lamps lit, here and there, against the darkening day, one of them harshly bright at the end of a long table, where a little round man sits tailor-fashion, naked but for a pair of Y-front underpants, reading aloud from a slender paperback, "grabs the nearest book," he's saying, "which was, and there are no coincidences, Hegel's Phenomenology of Spirit." Past the table, past the spindle-backed chairs, the man there in the baggy blue coveralls, the woman in a gauzy robe, scrolling through something on her phone, at the end of the room a fire's dying on the grate, and pulled up close by its sullen ember-light a sofa, brownish pink, and two women sat upon it, leaning back against either arm, outstretched legs entwined under blankets and thick rugs. The one, her long white hair wound up in ruthless braids, snaps green beans, dropping halves and thirds into a colander on her lap, and the ends in a paper bag on the floor. The other, long white hair unbound, drifting, whicks chunks of peel from potatoes with swift flashes of a paring knife. "Mothers," says Ysabel.

Whick and snap, snap and whick. "Pretending to arrange his apartment," reads the little round man on the table, "for some purpose other than fucking me," as Chazz takes one of the spindle-backed chairs and draws it over toward Ysabel. "Might I have a word?" she says, as she sits.

"Our daughter requires something of us," says the woman, her hair in braids.

"Our Queen demands an audience," says the woman, her hair undone. Chazz heads around behind them both to stoop by the hearth, taking up a poker, stirring the charred logs. "I read aloud as he rushed back from the bedroom with a plastic laundry hamper," says the little round man on the table, and Ysabel raises her voice, "I was up in the hills this afternoon. A luncheon, hosted by the King."

"Dressed like that?" says the woman snapping beans.

"At least her knees are covered," says the woman peeling potatoes.

"And to find," the little man's saying, "a bottle of *wine* that hadn't gone bad in the fridge. The concrete content, which *sensuous* certainty furnishes," and Ysabel looks over the back of her chair at him and says, "Might we have the room?"

He blinks, lips pursed around an interrupted word. "We're enjoying this?" says the man in the coveralls.

"It is a free house," says the woman plucking an errant peel or two from the rug on their lap.

"Go on," says the woman dropping a handful of bean-ends into the paper bag. "It helps us to work."

The little man shrugs and nods sort of sideways and takes up his book again. "The, ah, the sensuous *certainty,* furnishes, which makes this prima facie *appear* to be the richest kind of knowledge," and "So," says Ysabel. "When did you take up scullery work, Mother?"

Neither of those heads look up. Behind her, the voice, droning, "a wealth to which we can as little find any limit when we, ah, traverse its extent," and then someone else says, "Well, actually, that's, that's washing dishes."

Her chair creaks as Ysabel turns, looking back again, to the man in the baggy coveralls. "Scullery work," he says. "That's washing dishes. Chef de plonge. What they're doing," and beside him, the woman in the gauzy robe's looking up from her phone, "they're legumiers, they prep," and he's faltering under her glower, "the vegetables and such, what. I studied."

"It's a cooperative house," says the woman, her hair in braids. "There's a rota of chores."

"All must do their part," says the woman, her hair undone. "Go on. Read on."

"Ah, yeah, so," says the little man on the table, "okay, its, ah, ex*tent,* in time and *space,*" and Ysabel closes her eyes, takes in a breath through her nose, and abruptly says, "He means to give them the Ramp. The Lovejoy Ramp."

"He?" says the woman with the knife. "He who?"

"Our son," says the woman snapping beans.

"*Your* son."

"You're as much me as I."

"They mean to *demolish it!*" cries Ysabel. "Wipe it away! Put up towers!"

"So they will."

"These things happen."

"They don't!" snaps Ysabel. "They *don't* just happen! They're done, by men, who might be stopped," and both those heads of white hair toss back with sudden peals of laughter, delicate titters, hacking cackles, "By whom?" says the one, and "If his majesty has spoken," the other, catching her breath.

"But you might speak against him," says Ysabel, leaning forward.

"Me?"

"Well certainly not *me.*"

"He is the King, your majesty."

"He has spoken."

"As if," says Ysabel, "you never spoke against my father."

"You have no father."

"She means the King."

"Her brother?"

"No, no, the King Before."

"She means the Queen!"

"Please," says Ysabel.

"It *is* confusing."

"That there's the two of us."

"And not just one."

"No, no," says the woman in braids, lifting a hand, three knurled fingers extended. "Instead of *three,*" and *"Mother!"* cries Ysabel, but someone's knocking at the door, outside, someone's been knocking, Chazz has already gotten to his feet, he's headed down the length of the table, and the woman with the knife still in her hand says, "You *have* no mother."

"We are the Gammer."

"You are the Queen."

"There's no more Bride."

"You're it."

"That's all."

"Enough," says Ysabel, but the word is lost in the sudden scuffle out there in the foyer, the yelp, the scrape of chairs, the chiming crash of bottles as the little man leaps from the table, the "Hey!" and "What the hell!" as Chazz stumbles through the doorway, crashing to his knees, turtleneck yoked in the hand he's reaching up and back, grappling with, the hand of the much larger man in a big black suit, a bright aloha shirt, splashes of blue and yellow and white, and a matted bush of a beard, and brown hair in crimpled eaves that brush his shoulders lifting as he takes in a deep breath, looking about. "I don't," his arm jerked as Chazz struggles, "want to hurt anybody," says Mr. Keightlinger.

WHATEVER'S PLAYING ON THE RADIO dissolves in distorted feedback, a little Ennio Morricone, a little 3 Mustaphas 3, it mutters to itself. She shifts in the driver's seat, leaning forward, watching the man in the black suit through the side windows of the suv. Continuing this exotic kick, murmurs the radio, let's feast our ears on these East African rhythms from the Lagos Music Salon. He's stepping off the sidewalk, there by the welter of bicycles, heading across the greening yard toward the pink-painted house, climbing the steps to the cramped front porch, a big man, unkempt brown hair and beard. Empty hands, one of them lifted to knock. She frowns. Cocks her head. Sits up behind the wheel. Yesterday she said her prayers and thank yous, coos the radio, morning heat crowding her room and thighs, and she leans down again, looks out the side window. The man in the black suit's talking to someone in the doorway. Yesterday the rains were rather heavy, sings the radio, and the man in the black suit yanks his elbow back, leans in to throw a punch.

Her brow quirks.

Her hand yanks open the passenger door feet kick off the seat the floorboard into a shallow dive over the sidewalk tuck and roll to come up running yellow blur foot leaping middle step then hitting porch and barreled through the front door left ajar a pushing leap her running shoe slaps the wall a spring momentum lofting over the bannister tumble a flip over heels over head as one hand pulling flash that lights the hallway steps and clutter through the doorway scuffle black suit pink head feet a-thump the floor her blade a whip swung down and back a half-step lunge "Iona!" and the blade-tip stops dead there, an inch, perhaps, from blinking eye. The man in the black suit's hauled Chazz around, held tight to meet her thrust. "Do you?" he says, voice rough.

"Your pardon, ma'am, Devil," says Iona, taking one step back. Her sword still up. "I did not recognize the wizard."

"Everyone, please," says Ysabel, down at the other end of the dining table. "There's no need for swords, or shields." The others beside and behind her, the little man holding his book to his naked chest, the man in the baggy coveralls, the woman in the robe. "Put up yours as well, mother."

"What, this?" says the woman at the one end of the sofa, white hair wild about her head, and a little silver paring knife in her hand. "What could I *possibly* do with such a wee point."

"Let the Devil go," says Ysabel, to Mr. Keightlinger. "We'll hear you out." But as Chazz leans forward into a step away Mr. Keightlinger tugs him back, tightening his grip full of turtleneck, "Good sir!" cries Chazz, with a choke. "You've secured our attention. There is no need!"

"You," says Mr. Keightlinger, over Chazz's pink bald head, to Ysabel. "You might have something. You might not. I need to know."

"What might this something be," says Ysabel.

"You have it, you'll know."

"But what if I don't?"

He shakes his big brown head. "You won't want to know."

"Ridiculous!" cries the woman at the other end of the sofa, her white hair done up in braids. "Mother, *please*," says Ysabel. Taking a step toward Mr. Keightlinger, toward Chazz, toward Iona wary in the doorway. "Well," she says. "It's you who've pressed most firmly for this dilemma. How would you see it resolved."

"I am *aware*," growls Mr. Keightlinger, a flick of his free hand, annoyed, and then, "Your shirt. Take it off."

She stops, halfway along the length of the dining table. The woman in the gauzy robe lifts a hand, opens her mouth as if to say something. "You address," says Chazz, "a *Queen*, sir," and Mr. Keightlinger shakes him, once, "Your *sweater*," he growls, "take off your *sweater*. I need to see. If you have it."

"Draw, Chazz," says the woman on the sofa, "Iona, go on. Cut him down. Someone!"

"Gammer Duenna, you will be still," says Ysabel, and then, to Mr. Keightlinger, "First, you must let him go."

"He stays in the room," says Mr. Keightlinger. "Everyone stays in the room."

"You'd have an audience."

"Collateral," says Mr. Keightlinger, pushing Chazz stumbling into the end of the table, crash, and steps past him, down the table, up to her standing quite still, and "Ma'am!" cries Iona, and a stern *"Hold!"* from Ysabel. "This will be done in a moment." Mr. Keightlinger doesn't so much nod as shrug, and she lifts her sweater up and over her head and off.

"Bra," says Mr. Keightlinger, but she's already turned her back to him. "You'll need to undo it," she says.

Delicate clasp of it pinched by thick fingers pressing her skin, prodding as satin straps fall away. She holds the cups of it in place. "I have never," says the woman on the sofa, "in all my days," but turns away from a look from Ysabel. Those fingers, pressing the base of her neck. "Please," he says, pushing, turning her about before him as she lets the bra fall to the floor. Looks up, away. In the shadows above, just under the ceiling, styrofoam wigstands and mannequin heads crowd along the picture molding, each of them painted, thick lines and curls in red and black, fixed rictuses of joy, wonder, and delight, and here and there a wicked sneer. Those spatulate fingers twisting, paling her skin, she winces, "Surely," she says, "by now, you know?"

He stops, fingers along her sternum, index snug in clavicle-notch. His small eyes, reddened, squinted, brown, between snag of hair and snarl of beard. "You killed him," he says, and takes a step back. "Didn't you."

She looks at him, then. "I seem to recall swatting something," she says.

"His name's yet known," says Mr. Keightlinger, backing away. "Should've finished the job." Turning to go, past glaring Chazz, Iona stepping aside. The door slammed shut behind him.

The man in the baggy coveralls is the first to make a move, a sound, coughing, and Ysabel snatches up her sweater, shoves herself into it, "Ma'am?" Iona's saying. "Did he harm you?"

"Frost and blight," says one of the women on the sofa, and "Blast and rot," the other. Chazz mutters, "Why is his heart not here in my hand."

"Shall we go?" says Iona, holding out a hand. "Home?"

"Yes," says Ysabel, but then, frowning, "no," she says. "No."

It's dark, up under the rafters. She lifts a paper bag over her head, climbs after it, up a brief ladder bolted to the wall, and crouching out onto planks laid across the joists there, a makeshift floor. Far below a pop and splatter, whoops, shrieks of laughter. On her knees she's striking a match, lighting the fat wick of a small brass lamp, setting the glass chimney in place, the light warming about her, her brown coat, her white-gold shock of hair. She drags the bag over, Powell's, it says, and reaches in to pull out books, thick paperbacks with worn covers and creased, curled spines, star-spattered nightscapes and otherworldly pastels, fiery star-ships, lumpen aliens, The Romulan Way, Norstrilia, the titles say, Floating Worlds, in sober type, in colorful, wildly shaped logos, Caravan Stars, Titan, Brightness Falls from the Air. She sets to methodically peeling off price tags, little perforated squares of yellow and red, big white UPC labels. Someone says, "Hey," and she looks up to see Anna, clinging to the ladder. "C'mon down. The champagne's – not that bad, actually."

"Come on *down,"* roars Gloria, somewhere below, laughter in her words.

"I'm putting these away," says Marfisa, stacking a couple of books by a low wooden box, The Thurb Revolution, The Sardonyx Net, and "So," says Anna, leaning an elbow on the floorboards. "This is what an outlaw's lair looks like." Tucked up close to the rafters, at the flickering edge of the lamplight, a rumpled sleeping bag, some discarded clothing. Leaned against a truss a wooden baseball bat. "I don't need much," says Marfisa, stacking up more books.

"Still," says Anna, "now you can run out to IKEA, get yourself a shelf. Maybe even a bed."

"She can," says Marfisa, her back to Anna, a book in either hand.

"And?" says Anna. "Look, Marfisa. At all we got done, together, in a day."

The sheepskin collar of that coat rises gently, in a sigh, as she sets the last two books with the others. "You gave a pot of money to, her," she says. "We went shopping. For clothes."

"And art supplies," says Anna. "The computer, the champagne – that spark, in her eyes?" A yelp from below, "Ladies, come on! I'm about to fire this thing up!" Anna smiles. "And, also – the books," she says.

"And you?" says Marfisa, turning about, sitting herself on the floor. "What did you get, from all of this?"

"It's not the money, Marfisa. It's not the stuff. Didn't you feel it? We can *help* each other."

Marfisa snorts. "With what," she says. "We're just some God-damned fools who said a wrong thing, once, to, to the wrong damned woman."

"Here we go!" yells Gloria somewhere below, but Anna, stricken, leans her elbows on those planks, "Don't *say* that," she whispers. "It's *more* than that. You know it." Marfisa looks away. "And more than just us," says Anna, a little more than a whisper now. "There's others, out there. Left, lost, in the shadows, when she turned her face away." Reaching out a hand. "We can help them, too."

Marfisa shifts, leaning away, over toward the low wooden box, there by her books. "Are you ready, Anna, for an outlaw's life?" Anna draws back her hand, a pinch of a frown. Marfisa moves something from the top of that box, an empty horse's head, bulging black eyes, flop of a snout. "When the Glaive and the Guisarme find out what you've done," she says, "and for whom," as she lifts the lid of the box, and a wash of golden light spills up and out to overwhelm that little brass lamp. Anna, blinking, catches her breath. "You'll want to take some," says Marfisa. "Against that day."

"The money, is nothing," says Anna, her voice gone husky. "The bank gets its due. And I've signed his name before, at his request."

"Your tracks are covered?"

"I shouldn't," says Anna, looking up at Marfisa in all that light. "Not yet."

"Not yet," says Marfisa. Darkness falls as she lowers the lid.

"It's just the Montage leftovers," she says, leaning back against the counter, sweatpants and a white tank top. Over the stove the microwave's lit up and roaring. "I thought you were going out with Reg."

"You could've asked, is all," she says, there by the shelf in an oversized sweatshirt, legs bare. "It's the principle of the thing."

The gentle chime of a doorbell, and she tips her head, a gesture of that striking nose, "Is that him?"

She shakes her head, blond hair austerely swaying side to side. "Not yet."

"Well, I'm not expecting anyone," she says, as the microwave bleeps, goes dark. She turns to open its door.

Rolling her eyes she heads off out of the kitchen across the open living room, dark wood paneling and grey-green shag that softens her peevish stomps. Again the gentle chime, followed almost immediately by a pounding knock on the door she opens to see Ysabel, in her long white coat, and her scowl brightens into a smile. "Hello, darling," she says.

Ysabel's looking past her. "Is she at home?" she says.

Smile sours to pout. "You could've just called," she says, and then, calling out, "Chrissie! It's for you!"

"Hey," says Chrissie, stepping out of the kitchen, bowl in one hand, fork in the other. "Are you okay?"

"I've had a day," says Ysabel, looking down, away from Chrissie to Ettie there beside her, and then up and back to Chrissie again. "Come out with me," she says, all at once. "Tonight," she says. "Right now."

"All right," says Chrissie, after a moment.

Dim pink light shimmers pulsing from the drumbeat somewhere else, close pink-painted walls, dingy white carpeting, a low white rumpled couch. A silver pole in the middle of the room, bolted to floor and ceiling, and she steps around it, black cloak purpled in that light, and Ysabel's long white coat gone pink and shadowed purple, and the spangles of Chrissie's black dress softened, dulled, her hand in Ysabel's, looking about the little room. "So," she says. "This is Thursday?"

That cloak spreads lifting arms to reach for the hood and "Wait," says Ysabel. "Don't."

"I am her majesty's to command," says the Starling, horsely hushed.

"Your," says Chrissie, almost, a breath of a word, looking from the shadowed wings of the cloak to Ysabel eyeing her sidelong from a step away, letting go her hand. "Go on," she says, to Chrissie. "Look at her."

"I," says Chrissie, "I am."

"No," says Ysabel. "Go and look at her."

A smile creeps over Chrissie's lips. "All right," she says, stepping back. "I guess I'm her majesty's – "

"Don't," says Ysabel, sharply.

And Chrissie says, "All right," and another step back, and then around and past the pole. Leaning down in her brief black dress to look up, into the shadows under the hood, and a glimmer there, pink light shimmering, caught in crystal, on silver filigree. "Ysabel?" she says, a whisper, bare arm reaching up to jolt back as rustling a cloaked arm lifts a hand to meet hers, there, at the edge of the hood, fingers brushing, grasping, drawing back.

"You're," says Chrissie, "you're her – "

"No," says the Starling.

"I've but a brother," says Ysabel.

"Is this some kind of a," says Chrissie, and then, "how," she says, stepping back, bump against the pole.

"Smoke, and mirrors," says the Starling. "Powders and creams."

"I guess," says Chrissie, "we know you're not the funny one," and the Starling frowns.

"Chrissie, please," says Ysabel. "Look at her, and tell me. Do you – think, she's," and the thrumming drums, the half-heard synthesizer stabs. That pink light, pulsing. "Do you," says Ysabel, as Chrissie's fingers interlock with the Starling's, the two of them breathless watching her, the Queen. "Do you want her," says Ysabel.

The Starling closes her eyes. Chrissie, swallowing, lifts her head, a nod, or possibly a sigh.

Two residential streets, a simple intersection, the pavement of it painted in a great circle, yellows and whites, a sunflower faded by weather and traffic, opening under harshly blue-white street-lights. Houses sit comfortably at three of the corners, windows lit here and there against the fallen night, and at three of the corners there by the sidewalks little kiosks built of scrap lumber and windfall, painted in primary colors dimmed with age. He's there by the sign that says Central Square, a bulletin board beneath it papered with notecards and flyers and photos, lost dog, Yamaha keytar cheap, web design made easy, paleo prepped 4 you. A beard, a mustache thick about his lips, dark hair lankly brushing the shoulders of his warmup jacket, blue and grey. Out in the intersection, Jessie in her puffy pink and orange parka, yellow hair struck colorless in the close bright light. They're both looking over the fourth of those four corners, where a new house rises up, sheets of plywood cut around what will one day be doors and windows, paper sheathing wrapped about, yellow and white, and spars and beams of a second storey and a third reaching up, raw lumber pale against the dark night sky.

"There was a gate," she says. "A red gate, and little lights, strung from the trees. There were more trees."

"The Bedroom Spared," he says. "The Second Breakfast Nook. The Singing Room and the Smoking Porch. The Heartstone."

"All the," she says, "rugs, everywhere you went there were rugs on top of rugs."

"We had a Rug Day," he says. "You had to bring something for the floor to get in. Leo brought a strip of carpet from the airport."

"Leo," she says, look over at him on the sidewalk, his hands in his pockets. "John," she says, but then, "no. Michael. Michael John Lake."

"Luke," he says, turning away. Heading back down the side-walk, the cars parked alongside, to a boxy dark sedan. He opens a door and leans in, wrestling with the stuff crammed into the back of it.

She's frowning as he comes back toward her, a roll of sleeping bag in one hand, a wad of blankets tucked under an arm. "Let's go," he says, stepping up onto the curb before the unbuilt house. "I, uh, Luke," she says, hurrying after him, "we shouldn't," up shaky steps onto a narrow plywood porch. "It's all right," he's saying, as he steps through the empty hole of the front doorway, "I doubt they've installed an alarm system yet."

Inside the darkness thick, abruptly shaped by skeletons of walls, enfilades of two-by-fours limned faintly by the street-light. "What if someone sees us," says Jessie, hushed.

"No one saw us," he says. Over there serrated angles, a couple of stringers hung from ceiling to floor out in the middle of what will be a room, and planks laid atop each deckled edge, a makeshift staircase. Creaking up he does. "Shit," says Jessie, following after, careful steps in the middle of each board. "We don't have to stay here," she says, arms out for balance, the drop to either side.

"I won't spend another night in that car," he says, up there somewhere, rustle and thump. He's tossed the sleeping bag up another floor and he's stuffing the blankets up after. "The cash," she's saying, stepping away from the edge. "We don't have to save it anymore." He's jumped up grabbing the floor above, feet kicking for purchase against a lumber strut. "Little help," he grunts. She steps up, hands on the seat of his jeans, pushing, "There's a motel up on Powell," she says. "Let's go get a damn room. Sleep in a bed."

He's reaching down, and grabs the hand that she holds up. "No," he says. "We have a plan. We're sticking to our plan. We're getting the apartment." He braces himself to pull, but she's standing still, "The rent," she says. "Without a job, there's no way – "

"We go on as we mean to go on," he says.

"But," she says, and "Do you trust me," he says.

"Yes?"

"Do you believe me," he says, resettling his grip, and she nods. "Then we go on," he says, and pulls her up.

Out past the unroofed back of the house restless, lightless trees, stirred by the hissing rush of wind. The starless sky above brushed with light from the city below, and off that way, far off, towering buildings lifted, lit up, and rising among them warning lights winking about the towers of idle cranes. "Look at that," he murmurs, low and close, there by her ear. "How do you hold hands around something like that."

"We're gonna freeze up here," she says.

"No," he says. "I'm almost back to myself. Soon," he says. "Soon." And then, "Just," he says, "tell me."

She turns a little, in his arms, to look at him. "I need to sleep," she says. "We have to get up stupid early, so nobody sees us sneaking out of – "

"No one will see us," he says. "Tell me. Tell me her name."

And Jessie says, "Isadora."

White Towers

WHITE TOWERS blank in the lamplight, clustered on the table, a clump of them quite tall at the one end, lowering in the middle, and the one lone tower taller than the rest there at the other end, all spread along the bank of a broad blue curl of river painted along one edge. Delicate bridges of foamcore and thread span the blue, and a little white boat between a couple of them, and at the foot of one, just past the lone tower, a bloom of color, towers and blocks in red and yellow and blue instead of white. In her purple gown she leans over it, her hair wrapped in a fine black scarf. "I'd no idea," says Lymond behind her, "you could get wine in cans."

He's sitting sideways in an overstuffed armchair, the only chair in that wide room, both legs hooked over the one arm, leaning back against the other, and in his hand a plain silver can that says Pinot Gris in clean black simple letters.

"Is his majesty pleased?" she says.

"What, with today?" he says. "Didn't go too badly, I guess."

"Better than the wine?"

"Oh," he chuckles, leaning down to set the can on the floor with exaggerated care. "I'm not about to touch the wine."

"Your sister," she says, stepping away from the table, purple gown glimmering blue and green as it sweeps the polished floor, "did not seem too enthused." The great wall of glass behind her filled up blankly black, struck here and there by reflections of yellow-gold lamplight, pools and whorls of warmth curled up above her and that little white city. His hands in his lap he's poking at the ragged corner of a thumbnail. "How about you?" he says. "How's your enthusiasm?"

"Do you really think you can do this?" she says.

"Well of course I do," he says. "But it doesn't matter what I think. Does it."

"But I defer to his majesty's judgment," she says.

"Y'know," he says, swinging his feet down, sitting up, "I gotta tell ya. You evince a remarkable equanimity, for someone who came to this city thinking she'd be Princess, Bride, and Queen."

"And I may yet," she says, and he laughs, and claps his hands together. "True!" he says. "Yeah. Failure mode's pretty good for you, isn't it."

"It was a marvelous party," she says, heading past him in his overstuffed chair. "A good evening, to your majesty."

"Your highness," he says.

Up an enclosed, spiraling staircase, the loud rustle of her gown, down a carpeted hall lit dimly yellow, photographs hung to either side, a mountainous cloudscape, a stretch of water dimpled by rain, a fog-shrouded copse. She opens a door at the end of the hall on a room almost entirely filled by a canopy of white netting, hung across a corner, a lamp shining within, and shadows fluttering against it. She closes the door, then undoes a couple of velcro fasteners, lifting a flap of netting, ducking within.

Butterflies, a dozen or more, lilt and lop about, white wings and yellow, black and yellow, black and red and brown and beige, unblinking eye-shapes of orange and black, lighting on the netting, the pillows piled at one end of a narrow bed, her hand, held up before her, and all but wonder smoothed from her expression, and her shining eyes.

On a little table by the bed a plate of cookies, a white cup of ruby tea, a little black notebook, a glossy black phone. She takes up the phone, thumbing through the menus to find a list of missed calls from a number beginning with 313. She sighs, taps the number, holds the phone up to her ear.

"Dina," she says. "Dina, tell Mother it was just a – " and she closes her eyes. "Party," she says. "Yes, Mother. Of course. It was the King's luncheon, for the mayor, and –

"Well, yes, it did run late.

"Yes, Mother. Did everything – yes. Did everything, arrive? As they said it would?" She absently waves a butterfly brown and gold from the tendrils of steam faint above the cup. "Good," she says. "Oh, good." Close by the end of the bed, netting rucked up about it, a glass tank rests atop a wrought-iron stand, and inside two white plastic pots, packed with dirt, and clouds of feathery green fronds on slender stalks. "So much," she says. "That's why – yes, Mother. Yes. I will try. I *will,* yes, I will. Good – goodbye, Mother. Dina? Dina. Is Nadia there? Is she, can she, oh.

"I see. Could you tell her. Would you tell her how much I miss her?

"Tell her how much I miss you all."

Setting the phone down. Unwinding the black scarf from about her long black hair. Leaning over that glass tank. Caterpillars brown and black inch and hunch, ravenously nibbling the greenery shivering, trembling, but there, and there, hang still, rearmost leg-pairs sealed to branchlets by daubs of white foam, heads dandled in sleepily protective curls. "Oh," she says, reaching for the notebook. 3/22 she writes, deftly, in blueblack ink. L. lorquini, L. lorquini, R. polynice. Capping the pen, setting the notebook down, she sits, and takes up the cup. A sigh, and a sip of tea.

I think that in a work of art there is a kind of merging between the two things, between the precision of poetry and the excitement of pure science.

—*Vladimir Nabokov*

NO. 26
" – only borders lie – "

"THERE'S TWO WAYS THIS GOES DOWN," she says. Bared finger-tips grip a hilt wrapped in dulled wire, simple, straight, and above it quillions clean straight bars, and over about it all and her gloved fist a glittering net of wiry strands that meet in thick round worked steel knots all gathered together in a cord that swoops to end at the great silvery clout of a pommel. "That's it."

"No," he says, "no, it's not." All in black, black slacks rolled up at his shins, black turtleneck, his pink hands held out empty to either side, and his bald head pinkly shaking, no. "There's but one way we might go out from this moment we have freely, each of us, entered into. Our terrible, freighted moment will come to its ending only when you stick me with your steel, and down I crumble, into dust. For if you will not do this," and one of those hands is lifted, up, and even in this harsh light, bright light flares between his curling fingers. "I will let out your life," he says, drawing down a sneering curl of cutlass from the air.

Her right foot slips back, blade of her sword dipping as she holds her free hand up between them. "That's not," she says, "nobody's, done anything yet, that can't be undone."

"Oh, but Huntsman," he says, a sliding shuffle-step toward her, cutlass angled up and back, above his head. "One of us will."

Another step back, and she settles into her stance, sword up, en garde. His chest swells with a growling breath. A concussive whump shakes the entire room, everything, staggers them both, sends him to his knees, billowing dust, the lamps swaying high above, and one blows in a burst of raining sparks, filing cabinets tipping banging crashing down, the clatter of dropped blades, rising smoke, a scream

"Does it hurt?" – before the Sun – her Grace; his Lady
Back-slaps & Glad-hands – the Candidates

"Does it hurt?"

"What?" says Jo, a dark shape turning away from dark windows. Over on the futon a rustle, Ysabel ghostly sitting up, "Does it," she's saying, and then, "you're up." And then, "You've been smoking."

Jo shrugs. On the sill by her hand a glass ashtray, a scrumble of ash, a single filterless butt. Ysabel's feeling about, lifting blankets, tipping over to peer at the floor, and "Down at the foot," says Jo. Ysabel leans up, hands and knees, reaches out, sits back against the pillows with something glossily white in her hands. "Time is it," she says.

"Almost five," says Jo. "Luys'll be here, any minute." Red shirt in the shadows nearly as black as her kilt.

"Of course," says Ysabel, bunching up the stuff in her hands, pulling it over her head, a shimmering fall of chemise. "The Samani."

"Knights gonna knight," says Jo, and Ysabel chuckles, leans back, her head against the wall. "While Queens cannot be bothered to sleep in their own beds," she says.

"You know I don't mind."

"Still," says Ysabel. "It's not as if we must, anymore?" Something glitters under her eye, a smudge of gold.

"Anyway," says Jo, getting to her feet, "I was gonna go see if the coffee was ready yet – "

"Of course it is," says Ysabel, absently picking at the smudge, peeling away a lacey scab.

Jo's hand on the knob of the door to the room. "Right," she says. On the wall by the door a sword, slung from a leather strap, the scabbard of it plain and black, the simple hilt wrapped in wire, swaddled in a basket of wiry strands. Above it from the same nail a painted skull-mask, teeth crudely chiseled, black mane falling almost to brush the floor. "Want a cup?"

"Bible-black," says Ysabel, "and sweeter than sin," but she opens her eyes. "Jo?" she says, sitting up, "you *do,*" and leaning on that word, she's weighing what she might say next, but Jo with a dismissive shake of her head's already interrupting, "You know," she says, and she opens the door.

The unlit hall, then the kitchen, shadowy grey and blue. There's a slender vase tucked full of cornflowers, and beside it a stainless steel carafe, a couple of travel mugs. Jo thumbs back the lid of the carafe for a sniff, a smile, "I'm sorry I ever doubted you," she murmurs. Frowns. Cocks an ear, looks sidelong at the door to the apartment.

Opening the door Jo leaps back with a yelp as the woman lying across the threshold flops over, tan raincoat, clumsy wedge-soled sandals scraping for purchase, blond hair hung severely straight, a thready whisper, "Ysabel?" A cough.

"Chrissie?" says Jo. Hands on her shoulders, helping her sit up, lean back against the jamb. "What the hell. Are you, okay? Chrissie?"

"Chrissie," says Ysabel, there in the mouth of the unlit hall.

"Ysabel," says Chrissie, pushing shuff and clomp to her feet, "I didn't mean to wake you," and "You can't," says Ysabel, looking up to Chrissie towering in those heels, and "I thought you sent her home," says Jo, as tottering Chrissie drops to one knee, raincoat lopping about a silvery cocktail dress, "I just wanted," she's saying, as Ysabel, arms folded, steps back, and Jo says, "You said you sent her home."

"Chrissie," says Ysabel. "You mustn't."

"She was out there all night?" says Jo.

"I'm sorry," says Chrissie. "But I just couldn't leave."

"Jesus, Ysabel," says Jo. "Did you ask her?"

"You need to go home, Chrissie," says Ysabel, carefully, but "I don't *want* to!" cries Chrissie, crumbling, and Ysabel, arms still folded, looks up to Jo. "Could you?" she says.

"Could I, what, no. Ysabel, I'm leaving. In, like, as soon as Luys gets here."

"Of course," says Ysabel, "he can drive you. It's on your way."

"The hell it is," says Jo. "We have to be in Forest Park before the sun comes up. Ysabel, goddammit, answer me. Did you *ask* her." Something's chiming.

"I'll play the game, I swear," says Chrissie, thickly, looking up. Something's chiming, getting louder. "Whatever I have to do."

"Jo," says Ysabel.

Jo pulls her phone from her shirt pocket, swipes at it, yanks it to her ear. "The *hell* can't you learn to text like a normal person," she snaps, then stuffs the phone away. "Luys," she says. "He's here."

"Then it's settled," says Ysabel.

"The hell it is," says Jo, stepping around Chrissie. "Call a cab, call her sister," past Ysabel, down the unlit hall, "hell, wake Iona up, I don't care."

Chrissie's hands on Ysabel's hips, fingers gripping the glossy chemise pulling Ysabel close. "Please," she says, face pressed to Ysabel's belly. "Let me stay. For the day." Looking up, at Ysabel, looking down. "I *love* you."

And Ysabel, shaking her head, her hands on Chrissie's hands, pulls them loose, pulls out and up, a step back as Chrissie slowly stands, hands in hands to either side. "No," says Ysabel, leaning close, "you don't," against Chrissie's lips.

"Shit," says Jo, in the hallway behind them, and Ysabel breaks off the kiss, lets go. "Okay," says Jo, "fine. Chrissie." The sword slung from her shoulder, and in her other hand the mask, the mane of it twitching restlessly, looping, coiling across the floor. "Let's get you home."

No one looks up as he leaves. On the television screen, a man with greasy hair sews up a bloody gash in his arm.

Outside, the darkness, and low houses. He hunches under the hood of his grimy sweatshirt, heads quickly down one side of the street, avoiding cars and pickups parked along the margins of the regular, unkempt yards. Lights switch on with an audible clunk as he passes one house, chain-link fence about it hung with signs that say Posted and Beware of Dog, and sinuous bars of white wrought iron on the windows of it, and the front door. He ducks away, heads on. The lights switch off.

An overpass ahead, a close horizon brightly lit, and busses snore beneath. A driver leans against one, smoking the end of a cigarette. Past that another overpass, more slender, more dim. He crosses under, looking up, a sculpture on the other side, smooth blue stalks twining up and topped by thistled fronds of plastic about slumbering solar panels. Head down he climbs a stairway along the embankment to train tracks above.

Daylight threatens half the sky up here, off past the houses and low trees. Two hills rise, one there, spangled even now with houselights and with streetlights, the other a hole cut in the burgeoning light. He stands with his back to it all, looking over a ticket machine that's blinking to itself, Select Passenger, it says, Select Passenger. He shrugs and sets off over the walkway across the tracks to the empty platform. No Smoking, says a sign. Fare Paid Zone, Proof of Payment Required.

The train when it arrives is only a couple of blocky cars long, squealing, groaning to a stop. Doors open on a recorded voice that says, This is a Green Line train to Portland City Center. Another look up and down the platform. In the priority seating area, you are required to move for seniors and people with dis-abilities, and then another voice, En el área de prioridad, and he steps onto the empty train, ceda el asiento a personas de edad avanzada, past the couple of seats right there by the doors, y personas con discapacidad, and up a couple of steps into the end of the car, grabbing a pole to swing himself into a seat, but he stops short, blinks, looks back, looks outside. Then Christian Beaumont, pushing back the hood of his grimy sweatshirt, reaches down and picks up the shoe from that orange plastic seat, a shining oxblood monk-strap shoe, a bit of dried mud clinging to the sole.

Doors are closing, says the first voice. Train departing. Please hold on.

Greenery climbing steeply either side, abrupt high wall of it coolly shadowed close on the left, lit up over across a deeply shadowed gorge to the right by the rising sun, a tunnel ahead, white numerals set in mossy stone above, 1940, briefly glimpsed before it closes over them, lamps strung down the spine of it and green daylight at the end of it yawns them out. "You maybe want to slow down?" says Jo.

"We're late," says Luys, leaning the car into a curve.

"We get pulled over, we'll be even later," says Jo. "Look, I'm sorry about the, joggers, joggers!" On the gravel shoulder by a low stone wall bouncing ponytail, light blue jacket, balding shirtless long white socks and gone, another, tighter curve, a demure bit of bridge, another tunnel. "If I might advise your grace," says Luys, sunlight flashing, dappling, "do not apologize." One hand on the wheel, one on the polished wood knob of the gearshift. A bit of leather tied about his wrist. Jo says, "It's my fault we're late. Taking her home."

"You did as her majesty desired," says Luys. The car bottoms out, then soars, a ripple in the road, leans into another curve. "There is no fault in that."

"Jesus, Luys, slow *down,*" says Jo. The engine whines, swallows, growls as he works pedals and gearshift. She leans forward, gripping the armrest, the car's slowing, slows further. The tock-ticktock of the turn signal. "Your grace," says Luys, turning the wheel, "should not apologize."

Gravel crunches as the car noses down into a crowded little lot, a couple of dark blue SUVs, a white one, a boxy jeep atop enormous tires, the long taupe tail of a coupe de ville. Luys wheels abruptly into a space at the end, by a lone black motorcycle.

Opens his door, looks over to Jo, who hasn't unbelted herself. "Shall we?" he says. "Your grace?"

"See, but there's the thing," she says. "It's gonna be a your grace kind of morning. Not so much my lady."

Couple of signs on a wooden post, Wildwood Trail, this way and that, Audubon yonder. Jo leads the way down rough log steps, red shirt billowing unbuttoned over her blacks, black T-shirt, kilt, leggings, her red Chuck Taylors squelching muddy down the slender trail, cigarette in her hand. Luys behind her all in browns, ducking his dark head under low branches. Down they go, and down, switching back along the wall of that deep gorge, into all that green. Far below a chuckle of water, a glimpse of wooden bridge.

Someone's standing on the bridge, thick bare legs and a cloak of fur about hips and shoulders, leaning on a massive cudgel half his height. Jo scowls, dropping her cigarette to the ground. "I'm thinking I'm maybe underdressed," she mutters, grinding it out.

"Your grace is fine," says Luys, and when she steps up onto the bridge he stoops to pick up the half-smoked butt. The man on the bridge lifts his ruddy bald head, wide fur-wrapped chest a-swell with a great inhalation. "Southeast!" he booms. "The Huntsman, and the Mason!" Cudgel-tip banging the planks of the bridge, once.

"Yeah," says Jo. "Sorry we're, uh, late."

Luys closes his eyes, and opens them again. The man on the bridge steps aside, "Your grace," he says, and a sweep of his arm, "is merely the last to arrive."

Across the bridge the trail follows the bottom of the gorge, running along the bank of the creek. Up ahead Jo red and black stumps over rumples of rock and root, and Luys and the fur-cloaked man following after. "You're to take office, then?" says Luys. "But not as Porter, surely."

"Gordon's with us yet," and a shake of that ruddy head, "and as stubborn, and as selfish." A glance spared, back at the bridge. "The Soames thought it best, though, to have someone stand where he won't."

"You swear to the Soames?"

"Four of us," says the fur-wrapped man, "and three to the Marquess. And the Hound's brought a weaselly fellow, all in blue."

"A crowded field."

"But none for the Hawk?"

One boot up on a hunch in the trail, Luys leans an elbow on his knee, "Her grace," he says, "thought it best to wait." Jo's forging on ahead, red hair licked bright by the sun.

"How is she," says the fur-wrapped man, "as, well," but from away up the trail a rumor of astonishment, applause, a distant clang of steel. "They've started without us," says Luys.

"They must not a heard me," says the fur-wrapped man, "I got to warn them," sandal slipping in the mud as he pushes to climb the hunch, but there's the Mason's hand, reached down, and a tight smile sits the Mason's mouth as he hauls him up, "I look forward," he says, "to calling you brother."

The fur-wrapped man nods, and sets off at a run, cudgel in both hands, "Gallowglas to the field!" he bellows. "Gallowglas!" Jo stepping to one side as he barrels past. "Gallowglas approaching!"

The trail bends around a buttress of gorge-wall, turning into the rising sun, climbing up away from the creek. Ahead, the ruins of an old stone house, thick walls softened by vivid green moss and topped by stark gables at either end, shingles beams and rafters long since gone, and with them doors and frames, shutters and window-glass. A new metal railing's been bolted along the edge of what once was a second floor, and braced against it flagpoles bearing banners brightly limp: blue, green, red, white, their emblems glimpsed in listless folds, a hound, a hare, a stark black hawk, an empty helm. Highest and largest of all a yellow banner, a glowering bee, plump stripes and slender wings. A crowd of mostly men's pressed up against the railing, suit coats and sweaters, rain gear, dull greens, dark blues, greys and blacks and browns. Below them, where the trail pools before the ruin, the fur-wrapped man's bent over, hand on knee to catch his breath, and a handful of figures wait, weapons in hands, watching as up climbs Jo, and the Mason at her heels. "Huntsman!" rings a cry from the railing, pink hair bobbing, slicker brightly yellow: Lymond, the King. "You've brought the sun!"

"Yeah, you know," she calls up to him. "So. This is the, thing. The Samani."

"It will be, once you're up here, and safely off the field."

"Oh," says Jo, "right. That." She heads for the steps that stagger up the side of the ruin, but one of those armed figures, a fencer in black trousers spinning bare feet slapping whip-snap of rapiers in either hand beads clacking in her hair, leaps at a man in long white robes his scimitar swung wide to knock aside her first blade but the second, "Hold!" cries someone, the King, and "Zeina!" someone else, and that second thrust's stopped, whicked aside. Jo's hand on the mossy stone corner, a foot on the first worn step. The man in the white robes steps back, lowering his sword. The fencer laughs. "Aw," she cries. "I only wanted to see what would happen!"

They climb the steps, Gallowglas and Mason, up and through a stolid arch onto the second floor, open between those gables, grey stone rusty with moss and lichen, scrawled over with neon-bright graffiti. The crowd mills about, back-slaps and glad-hands, cheers and laugher as with grunts and shouts the clangor resumes below. Jo looks about, arms folded, Luys behind her, nodding, waving someone over, a boy in a brown bomber jacket, brown hair popped in a matted pompadour. "Boss!" he cries, arms flung wide. "They was starting to worry."

"Let 'em," says Jo, still looking about.

"How's the banner look?" says the boy. "I think the old buzzard needs a fucking stitch-up, you ask me."

"Did you find him," says Jo.

"Did I fucking find him. Fuck *yes* I found him."

"Not so loud, Sweetloaf," says Luys.

"You wouldn't a fucking sent me if you didn't fucking think I could get it the fuck done," he's muttering.

"He isn't here," says Jo. "What did he say."

"What he said was, he already told you. No. He said *fuck* no. That was him, the fuck no. Not me."

"Your grace," says Luys. Coming through the crowd there, yellow and pink, the King, big wide smile and a red plastic cup in either hand. "We were starting to worry!" he says, offering one to her.

"Yeah, well," she says, and takes a sip. "It's loaded," she says, blinking.

"We're not going to not have fun," says the King. "You'd rather a mimosa?"

"Let's just get it over with," says Jo. And then, "Majesty."

"You make it sound such the chore, Duchess." Clapping a hand to her shoulder. "But come!" Steering her into the thick of it, "People to meet, flesh to press. We'll start with the Lake Barons."

"The who the what now?"

"Alphons," says the King, pointing, "Alans, and, ah, Medardus, and, well. Good morning, Euric." A grunt from the throat of a stone-faced man, slope-shouldered in a pale green coat, handing a small square envelope, blankly white, to the King. Jo nods once to that impassive face as she's led on through the crowd. "What you have to remember," the King's muttering, "if you ever speak with Alans," as he's prying the envelope open, "he styles himself an Earl." Peering within. "Annoys us all no end, but what will one do. Lighter?"

"What?" says Jo, lifting her cup for a sip.

"Your lighter. Or a match? You still smoke?"

She opens a silvery lighter, flicks it to life, and he touches the small square envelope to the flame, dropping it as it flares. Grinding the curling ash underfoot. "But really," says the King, "unless you're speaking with Alans? Baron is fine."

"Lake Barons," says Jo.

"Well," says the King. "Anything west of the hills. Beaverton and such."

"They have their own court?"

"What? No. No, no no. Medardus! You know our Huntsman?"

"Have not had the pleasure," says an older man, quite tall, head canted as if stooped under some low ceiling.

"Good morning, your, ah, grace," says Jo.

"Oh, dear me no," says that tall man with a cheerful magnanimity, swiveling to one side, looming over the woman beside him, wearing a blue satin baseball jacket much like his. "We're much too low for grace," he says, as she rips a sheet from a notepad and hands it to him, and swiveling back he hands it in turn to the King. "Lovely morning for it," he says.

"We do try," says the King, already stepping away. Jo, hastening after, bumps into someone, thickset, softly rounding a navy jacket, and at his temples blocky hexagrams tattooed, blurred by the silver stubble of his hair. "Duke," he says, with a nod.

"Wu Song!" she says, and then, as he lifts an empty hand, "You don't," she says, but his brow furrows, lips pursing under his mustaches in a frown, and her free hand leaps to take his, give it a shake. "Good to see you," she says, and then, looking off, after the King, "I should," she says.

"Of course," he says.

Off through the crowd, that yellow slicker, bent over the sheet ripped from the notepad. "So," says Jo. "Lighter?"

"No," says the King, folding it in half, and half again, "this one's good. For now."

"He's not playing, is he. Wu Song," says Jo. "Whatever this is."

"I told you," says the King, leaning close. "Lake Barons. West of the hills." Polite applause ripples about them, at some shift in the ringing clash below. "You're certain," says the King, "you've no one to propose today, for Southeast?" The crowd, milling about them both, pressing closer to the railing. "Jo," he says.

She looks up at him, those bulging eyes, one brown, one blue. "I got nobody," she says. "Your majesty."

"Okay," he says. "All right. Let's go."

The crowd parts, stepping back, aside, as they head up to the railing. Jo stands at the King's left hand, there by the Marquess in a long grey gown, her one hand shelled in a polished steel gauntlet. To the King's right, there's the Viscount in a blue and white striped suit, and the Soames in tweedy greens, a yellow meshback cap on his head. The King lifts a hand, and stillness settles, a last few thwacks and clonks as the donnybrook below clatters to a stop. Combatants lower arms and weapons, lift shoulders, feet drawn together, favoring perhaps a leg, here or there, a wince, but "Hup!" and a punch of steel driven through skin, the fencer in black trousers crouched low, one rapier back, a counterweight, the other buried half its length in the belly of the bald man wrapped in fur. Gathering herself her ropey muscles tensing the fencer yanks her blade free, "La!" she cries, and Jo

"Enough," says the King, looking down at Jo beside him. Her eyes closed. Her hands in fists. Her breathing shallow, quick. "Enough," says the King again, his hand laid gently over hers, withdrawn at her flinch. "You have done as we expected, which is to say, you have done well. Let's introduce you all, before tests and games and oaths! Soames! Tell us, who would the North put forth today?"

"Majesty!" says the Soames, leaning out over the railing, adjusting his cap, and his smile. "And such the crowd of gentles here assembled. Hoy! To join the Stevedore and the Gaffer in our service, and see to such Apportionment as we are due, we've drawn lots to propose, to you, these four: the Kamali!" The man in white robes, scimitar still in his jeweled gloves, bows. "The Luthier!" A bow from a man in a black leather jacket, thick chain looped about his fists. "Jackstaff!" A man in a long leather coat, a long staff in his hands. "And Bullbeggar!" The bald man, all in fur, leaning on his cudgel, one hand pressed to the hole in his belly, chuckling as claps politely smatter.

"Viscount!" says the King. "Who from Southwest?"

"But one, majesty," says Agravante, with a sweep of his striped arm. "The Serpent!" A young man all in blue denim holds up a shining squiggle of a blade, another flutter of applause.

"For Northwest!" says the King, and again, that stillness. "We've no one to put forth today. Duchess?" Looking to Jo beside him. "Who from Southeast?"

"No one, your majesty," she says. And then, in a hitch of that stillness all about, "My men," she adds, "my, knights, are as fine a company as anyone could ask." She drinks down what's left in her cup.

The King nods, looking past her. "Marquess!" he says. "Who would the Northeast Marches have put forth?"

"Three candidates, your majesty," she says. "A Dagger!" A man in a pearly grey suit, a long-bladed knife in his blue-black hand. "A Javelin!" A woman in a skirt of bronze sheaves, and a quiver rattling with short-bladed spears. "And a Mooncalfe!" The fencer throws wide her arms, swords high, crossed above her upturned face, and Jo steps back from the railing, opens her mouth, as if to say something, or shout, or

"All right!" cries the King, catching her arm. "A banner day," he's saying, "eight new knights!" Lifting the Viscount's hand, and Jo's, in his own, and the Viscount lifting the Soames', and the Marquess raising up both her own hands gauntlet shining as cheers break out, and applause. The candidates below take their knees, duck their heads. "Now!" says the King. "I believe," loud and clear, "before the oaths, we were promised tests and games?" Whoops at that, whistles and cheers, bottles and cups held high, but faltering there toward the back, stuttering the applause, falling away as with rustles shuffles scrapes the crowd of mostly men parts to one side or the other. Someone calls out, again, "Your majesty!" There under the stolid arch in the one gabled wall a tall man, pinkly, hatlessly bald, and no coat over his black turtleneck. "A word, if I might, slipped edgewise, before you begin to commence?"

"Devil," says the King, still smiling. "How fares our mother."

"Wordless, sir," says the Devil. "Our house is free; the word I bring's my own."

"But weighty enough it could not wait?" The King spreads his hands. "By all means, then. Go to. Unburden yourself."

"There is an absence, sir," says the Devil, "its presence keenly felt." Hands clasped behind his back be comes a little way down the ad hoc aisle dividing the whispers and murmurs that roil to either side. "And once again the perquisites of my office lash me forth, to speak those words that fret on all our lips: where is our Queen?" His pink head cocked to one side, smile widening. "Your sister, sir. Is she upset?"

The King steps away from the railing, into that ad hoc aisle. "Okay," he says. "I can guess what my next line should be, Chazz, but you're working off a script I haven't read. After this? I might need prompts." He folds his arms. "Why, no," he says, perfunctorily. "She's not. Whatever could you mean."

The Devil's smile has curdled. "To stop you, sir," he says. "To leave the Ramp intact. To have Old Tom's weird drawings stay, where anyone might see them, and thwart the dig of any new foundation, along Lovejoy." Unclasping his hands, both gloved in black leather. He sets to tugging one free. "Your sister, sir, our Queen, came just last week to see your mother, and hers, and was most upset about your plans to cede the Ramp. She'd see you stopped, sir, and I?" He holds up the glove he's taken off. "I stand with her," he says, and lets it fall, and the slap of leather against stone when it lands in the aisle between them. "I will await your response, majesty," says the Devil, and no one stops him as he turns to go.

A black Duffel, dragged — Three out of Five with Her in the room — not King nor Court

A limp black duffel dragged across carpet. Dust swirls in diffident light. A pair of pants, withdrawn, a couple shirts, a black leather sheath the length of a forearm, silvery glinting, wire-wrapped handle of a long straight knife. Reverently laid aside. The pants, taken up again, and sniffed. A judicious squint. Pulled on. The louvered doors of a closet half-opened, and a mirror hung inside, the glass of it pasted over with stickers black and grey, and red, but mostly black, and letters white and silver and black in shapes like lightning bolts, like blades, like the printing in old Bibles, White Doom, they say, Hyborian Philharmonic, King-in-Ice, Four Twenty, Iron Thule. Ducking, scooting over, he finds enough of a reflection cleared to smooth his hair, brush down the front of his black T-shirt.

All in black and brown he stands on that awkward corner landing, behind a heavy bannister. Low morning light pours through the windows over the sink, the rush of water, a silhouette there, the xo, nodding, shutting off the faucet. Off back that way there's this drawn-out, reedy groan, cut short by a meaty smack. The xo's drying his hands on his old white T-shirt. The front of it sprinkled here and there with drips of red. "Not mine," he says, his grin skewed by that white scar along his cheek. A querulous voice lifts up off back that way, through the half-open door, loud enough to drive home a couple of words, God's green earth!

"Need any help?" says Moody, coming down the short staircase, careful of the ramp.

The xo shrugs. "Dad's got it in hand," he says. Paid us? from back there. Paid us! "I was gonna maybe get some breakfast, change my shirt. Get some sleep."

Moody's shaking his head. "I'm good," he says. Peel a number off a clock, that voice, what good, any of us, another smack, another groan. "There *is* a thing today, about lunchtime," says the xo. "Dad said maybe you should tag along."

"Tag along," says Moody.

Rip City! howls that voice from off out back.

"Anyone?" says the King, sitting in the passenger seat, looking up in the rearview mirror at the rest of them behind, Viscount and Soames in captain's chairs, the Marquess on the bench at the back, and beside her, in the furthest corner, Jo. The Viscount's leaning forward, elbows on knees, his white-gold locks a-dangle. "I think," he says, "we'd best be served, perhaps," looking up, "by viewing this within the broader context."

"Context," says the King. Outside an engine's turning over, whir and rumble muffled by thick doors and tinted glass. A sleek sedan slowly backs out of the space beside them.

"Consider, majesty," says the Viscount. "This, the first Accolade of your reign, a Samani that sees the court extended to an admirable degree, and yet: we sadly lack for candidates from every fifth. Also." He's holding up two fingers, a second point. "Just this past week your sister had to turn a second portion, to replace what had been stolen by a thief as yet uncaught. And now?" A third finger. "Under the strain of such an effort, our Queen's been led astray by elements without the court to provoke such a display of defiance, as we've seen." Those three fingers held up a moment more, then folded away. In the mirror up there those eyes, one brown, one blue, look from the Viscount to Jo, in the back, her head against the window. "You'd speak of weakness within our ranks," says the King.

The Soames shifts in his seat, sucking his teeth. The Marquess with a scrape of metal lays one hand over the other. "In this context, sir," says the Viscount, with a nod, "it's unavoidable."

The King looks over his shoulder, at the Viscount direct. "You'd've done things differently," he says.

"Sire?" says the Viscount.

"You negotiated the dowry with the Court of Engines, did you not? That we then paid down at once, a swoop most fell?"

"That's not," says the Viscount, "majesty, what I mean – "

"It's the root of our insecurity, is it not? The specter of our empty coffers, that's led the Barons to press you to press their point to me, so forcefully?"

"Sir, I never meant – "

"It's also, I've no doubt, a source of effortful strain? That's led the extensions of this court, that you so richly laud – Marquess, Soames," a nod to each, "to beef over who might best oversee, what is it? A cobbler's shop?"

A cough, from the Soames. "If it's a free house the Porter would keep," he says, but the Marquess, leaning forward, says, "That's not an invitation, excellency."

"The both of you. The three of you. All of you," says the King.

"Majesty, if I might," says the Viscount.

"You might've enough, by now," says the King. "Next time? Try," and a fillip of his fingers, "not to twirl your mustaches so theatrically. Anybody else? Anyone? No?" He's looking over his shoulder again, at them all, and none of them looking back. "We go on. This is not a setback; we will have everything we want. My sister – our Queen – we do know her, I should trust, more better than some banneret, so soon come back from death?"

"What," says the Soames, "of the insult? The Devil's, insult?"

He smiles, the King, to light up his face. "Oh," he says. "It will be answered."

And there, at the very back, her head against the glass, Jo closes her eyes.

The doors of that white suv open, front and back, down at the end of the lot, and Luys stands up from leaning on the fender of a ruddy brown car. They're climbing out, the peers, the Soames, in his tweeds, headed for the long taupe coupe de ville, the Viscount in his blue and white stripes climbing into the back of another suv, smaller, midnight blue, and sweeping toward Luys, past him, the Marquess in her grey gown, gathering up her skirts to straddle the motorcycle there, and settling a plain steel helmet on her head. Luys still watching the white suv, the doors of it standing open. A flash of red, there's Jo, climbing down, backing away, turning away. Luys lifts his head, lifts a hand, not quite a wave, she's looking down, at her feet, arms folded. That big white suv lurches, there's the King's head, pinkly orange, popping up over the roof of it. He calls something to her, and she's nodding. She isn't looking back.

"You won't be going home?" says Luys, as she takes hold of the handle of the passenger door. She shakes her head. In her other hand she holds a lone black leather glove. "Over the river," she says, yanking the door open. "Clown House."

"Of course, my lady," he says, sitting down behind the wheel.

He scoops up the silicone chopping mat and taps chopped onions into the pan a-foam with butter, stirs them about with a wooden spoon. A couple of cracked eggs wait in a silver bowl. He pours in a plop of half-and-half, and a whisking clatter joins the sizzle and spit till he tilts the bowl over the pan, egg-and-cream smoothly poured to smother it all with a satisfied sigh. Shake and jiggle the pan to round it out.

"Yogurt would've been fine," says Pyrocles, behind him.

"What, you thought this was for you?" Becker grinds pepper into the pan, sprinkles on a pinch of salt. "I mean," he says, "I *could* make another, if you *want* this one," as Pyrocles' arm slips about his waist. "Yogurt," he says, "will be – "

"Wait," says Becker, and a shake and jerk of the pan, "hup!" The omelet lofts, flopping a twitch of the pan beneath it folding shook out slop, a browned gold circle rippling pocked with crisped onion, shushing on the flame. "Ha!" belts Becker.

"Finally," says Pyrocles, and a kiss for Becker's cheek. The pewter weights dangling from his mustache-tips brushing Becker's shoulder. "Finally?" says Becker. "I'll have you know I am six for ten, good sir, and," another shake of the pan, settling it all, "the last *four* in a row."

"It looks delicious."

"Say the word, I'll go seven for eleven." Another kiss, for his mouth. Becker hoists the pan over a plate, and a shimmy lops the omelet in a perfect semicircle. "All right," says Pyrocles, but there's a booming knock.

Pyrocles with a sigh pads away, shirtless and barefoot in loose white trousers, to the door to the loft, a mighty thing of beams and planks and a lever that he yanks back clank a grinding screech that cuts off with a thunk. Revealed there on the landing in his blue and white striped suit the Viscount Agravante, smiling. Pyrocles dips his head, a bow. "Well, hell," mutters Becker, shutting off the flame.

"Anvil," says Agravante, stepping inside. "Lovely space," he says. He stomps the white-painted floor once, a muffled thud. "And solid," he says. Looking over to Becker in the kitchen-nook, wiping his hands on a towel, grey boxer briefs and a white T-shirt strained by his bit of a belly. "Bet you can't hear a thing up here when he starts banging away down in the garage."

"How went the colée, m'lord," says Pyrocles, still by the door.

"You'd know if you'd went," says Agravante. "It didn't, in point of fact. Interrupted, by a challenge to our King. The candidates will swear their oaths another day, I suppose. And whatever was intended to placate our friends from over the hills?" A hand, lifted from a pocket, a one-sided shrug. "They are more skittish than before. An entire morning, worse than wasted, all before a second cup of coffee."

"A challenge, sir?" says Pyrocles, unmoved.

"The Devil, of all has-beens," says Agravante. "Something about the Queen, and property. Fret not: the Huntsman's on his scent."

"His," says Becker, still by the stove, and then, "the Huntsman? Jo?" But Pyrocles still looks to Agravante, who still smiles, and says, "As to my purpose, here and now."

"M'lord?" says Pyrocles.

"Your liege has need of your – presence," says Agravante. "This very day, an hour past the noontide. A car will be sent." A hand, slap against Pyrocles' shoulder. "Dress to impress," says Agravante, and then he leaves.

"Well," says Becker, as Pyrocles leans into the lever, shoving the big door noisily shut. "That was, well. He could've just called." Pyrocles is heading away down the loft, through all that light cascading down from the clerestory. "Is," says Becker, "is Jo really going to, fight?" Pyrocles draws back a white curtain to reveal a rack hung with coveralls, white dress shirts, a couple of suits in different blues. "I mean," says Becker, "a challenge, is that, to the King, that, that sounds serious?"

"What did I do with my white bucks?" says Pyrocles.

Becker looks down, at the omelet cooling on the plate. "How about dinner," he says. "When do you think you'll be back?"

"Go on," says Jo, opening the door of the car.

"My lady," says Luys, his hands on the wheel.

"Don't," she says. "Just, don't." One foot out on the sidewalk, looking up to the house they're parked in front of, peeling pink siding, mud-red trim. The welter of bicycles chained together, along the edge of the yard. "Start the car. I get out, you drive away."

"Lady, I cannot leave you."

"What are you gonna do? If he's here." A rip of velcro as she loosens one of her cycling gloves, flexes her fingers. "Talk to him? About what?" Closing it up again.

"The Devil's tongue is hammered silver, and his very breath weaves lawyer's nets," says Luys. "Speaking's not what I had in mind."

"Like hell I let you go at him, with me in the room."

"Jo," he says, closing his eyes. "Lady," he says, beginning again. "I could go in first, alone, to see if he's within." She leans in, across her seat, against his, her hand on his shoulder. "To save you time and," he says, but she kisses him, softly, "trouble," says Luys. "But what if he is not here." His voice a husk.

"Then I'll find out where he is," murmurs Jo, "and go to there."

"But I must take you," he says. "I am your right hand. I do what you need done."

She kisses him, again. "You're the Duke's right hand," she says, pushing back, "but this," climbing out of the car, "this is on the Huntsman. And that's all on me. So go, get out of here," she says, a hand on the door of the car. "I'll call you if I need you." But then she leans down, looks in through the open door. "Actually, pop the trunk first," she says. "I wanna grab something."

The front door's opened by a hugely shaggy monster in a ragged burlap cassock, great glassy yellow eyes under a single black hedge of brow, a waggling felted nose, red thick-lipped mouth with two white dagger-teeth jutting from the lower lip. "Jesus!" yelps Jo.

"You got me mistaken," booms the monster, that lower lip yanked up and down and up again.

"Yeah, okay," says Jo, "nice costume," as the monster steps back, right hand jerked into an awkward welcoming sweep. "Actually, more of a puppet," he says, not so deep, and muffled by the lip no longer moving. "Transfer's still tricky," he says, "between mouth and arm," as those big furry paws pry open the lips. Within, blurred by a screen of black mesh, a wry grin. "But how else'm I gonna get to Carnegie Hall? Whoa." Hiking up as Jo steps inside, pressing his face to the mesh for a closer look. "Killer mask."

"Yeah," says Jo, the skull mask in her hand, the coarse black mane of it brushing the floor. "They inside?"

Past the hall butler, its old mirror pocked and grimy, hung about with light coats and a slicker, through the wide doorway, the dim, high-ceilinged room beyond. In the shadows along the picture molding ragged lines of faces, plastic mannequin heads, styrofoam wigstands, each of them painted, expressions of wonder and delight, joy, and here and there a glare, or glum regret, calligraphed in black and red and blue and yellow, round eye-shapes and mouth-shapes and noses, cheeks harlequinned with diamonds and teardrops, and nowhere any two of them alike. A dining table's pushed against one wall, and in the open space afforded a contraption's being built on laid-out newspaper, gears and chains and bicycle wheels and a couple of frames, welded together, leaned up against a sawhorse. A little round man kneels before it, cargo shorts and a tatty sweater, cranking a ratchet back and forth, whir-click, whir-click. At the other end of the room a sofa, brownish pink, pulled close beside the cold dead hearth, and white heads at either end. "Hello?" says Jo. "Ma'am? Could I, speak with you? Ma'ams?"

Neither head moves. The little man's still cranking away, whir-click.

"It's, it's Jo? Ma'am?"

A clatter as the little man sets the ratchet aside, spins the whirligig he's bolted to the frame. Contemplates it. A whickering slither of mane-tips on newspaper as Jo drags the mask up to her chest, a deep breath, and then up over her head. "Jo Gallowglas," she says, lowering it. "Huntsman," as she fits it over her face, and the mane shivers, lifts. "Duchess of Southeast," she says. The little man at her feet looks up, scrambles back. Shadows flit over the floor, the walls, the ceiling, bare branches tossed by a silent storm. "On the King's business," she says.

Down the other end of the room those two white heads turn to look at her over the back of the sofa, the one of them her long white hair left loose, unbound, and the other her long white hair bound up in glossily ruthless braids. "You have our attention."

"The mask's a bit much."

"Command; do not demand."

"I'm, sorry," says Jo, lifting the mask from her head, and shadows flee as the mane collapses. The little man at her feet hold up an arm against the falling pattering strands. "I don't," says Jo, stepping toward the sofa, "I don't know the protocol, I mean, do I kneel, or – "

"As you wish, child."

"It's dangerous, giving old women airs."

The mask in her hands before her. "I'm sorry," she says, "it's just – "

"Don't apologize, child."

"I wasn't," says Jo, "I only – "

"Never complain," says the one, and "Never explain," the other.

"Right," says Jo. "Except. I mean." Looking from the one, to the other, wild tangles, taut braids. "You named me. You gave me this, ah," the mask, turned about in her hands. "Office."

"I did not give you that."

"That, you took yourself."

"You gave me the, you named me. Huntsman. And, I went about your business. And now, for the King. I'm about his – I'm sorry, that didn't, that sounded – "

"Speak plainly, child. As you would to anyone."

"Whom do you hunt."

Jo swallows. "Chazz," she says. The mane ripples. "The Devil. Is he here?"

They look at each other then, and it's possibly a smile that passes between them. "What would you have of him."

"What has he done."

"He," says Jo, "he claims the Queen's against the King, and that he's gonna stand with her. Is he here?"

This time, perhaps, a frown.

"Can you tell me where he is?" says Jo.

"It's not without the realm of possibility."

"Will you tell me," says Jo.

"Do you ask."

Looking down at the mask, those teeth, the empty eye-holes. The limp mane. "Gammers," says Jo, looking up. "Tell me, the Huntsman of this court. Where will I find the Devil."

"Why do you do this, child."

"What is your reason."

"Not the court's."

"Not the King's."

"Is it for honor?"

"For Ysabel," says Jo, and then, as they share another look, "what," says Jo, "what is it, what's – "

"We were wrong about you, child."

"*You* were wrong about her. I've said she's trouble from the start."

"I don't," says Jo, "what does that, what do you – "

"Out by the airport."

"One of those abandoned markets, left to rot."

"A Circuit World, or – "

"The Best Buy."

"Its livery was blue and gold, as I recall."

"More of a yellow."

"He'd spend time there, days on end, when we wandered in the wilderness."

"When *I* wandered."

"I spoke in a general sense."

"The Best Buy," says Jo. "Out by the airport, okay. Okay. Thank you – "

"*Never* offer thanks, child."

"Gratitude has no place in this."

"What is done as you command is merely what should be."

"What we do has no reason but our own."

"Right," says Jo. "Okay." And then, "I'm not a kid."

"Of course not, child." They both begin to laugh.

His watch chimes softly, and he pushes back the white cuff of his shirt to look over the face of it littered with three or four ticking dials, each hashed with tiny numerals and over them all a single majestic sweep hand quivering as it holds itself still, pointing out, away toward the front of the bus, where someone's stepping through the opened doors, holding up her phone, a woman in black leggings and a short black skirt and a baggy red shirt. In her other hand she's holding a bundle of coarse black hair. He frowns as she swings into an empty seat down toward the front of the bus, shakes his head, looks outside.

There's no one else waiting at the bus stop there on the corner, a repurposed gas station behind it, a tall red sign on the corner, Al's Auto Repair, it says, & Towing, Se Habla Español. "That's, odd," he says to himself, twisting the golden bezel of his watch. The sweep hand spins wildly about to catch up to where it should be. The bus doors close.

His watch chimes softly.

He pushes back his cuff again. Every hand, not just the sweep, trembles, pointing out as he lifts it, beside the bus, tracking the burly figure there, a big man in a black suit pounding on the doors that open with a sigh. He steps heavily onto the bus, brown hair in crimped eaves about his shoulders and an enormous brown beard, and an aloha shirt under his black suit coat. He waves a piece of paper at the driver, blundering past, past Jo Maguire looking out the window at the traffic, up to the well there by the back door to the bus, where he plants himself, one big wide-fingered black-haired hand gripping the pole right there before him where he's sitting, twisting the bezel of his watch again, covering it with his hand.

"Well, shit," breathes David Kerr, very much to himself.

ACROSS THE EMPTY PARKING LOT a looming box of a store, the façade of it a great oblong thrust above the high flat roof, and stained across the front of it where a sign once hung, and now just holes punched in sheet metal where once were struts and electrical conduits. By the blankly dark front doors a sheet of plywood's nailed to a frame of two-by-fours, and a plastic sheet tacked to the plywood, Future Home, say faded black letters, Columbia River Campus Advanced Disaster Management Simulator. A heavy chain is looped about the handles of the doors, and a padlock, bulky with a keysafe. She brushes a finger down the keypad set in the front of it, and it falls open with a clunk. She starts back, looks around, Leans in, twisting the lock free of the chain, and it clanking falls away.

Dust within, and darkness. Light scraped by scratched door-glass falls to thinly flop against a stack of drywall, a couple of buckets that say Sheet Rock All Purpose Joint Compound. Past that, across stained concrete, a shadowed mound of gutted cardboard boxes, glinting with shucked plastic clamshells. What might be a desk lamp's shining beyond, somewhere behind a curling row of slender columns in all that enormous darkness, and the faintly tinny chirps of music playing to itself. "Hey, hello?" calls Jo. "Chazz?"

They're filing cabinets, those columns, a dozen or so in a wide circle about the warm glow of that lamp, tall, five drawers each and each of them painted a dull institutional green, dented, scratched, rusted along the corners and edges. Some of those drawers hang open, crammed with manila folders stuffed with sheets of onionskin and glassine all protecting photographs, glossy photos stuck up, haphazardly tucked away, and more spilled on the dusty floor about, dozens of them, hundreds, and on the desk in the middle of the cabinets, stacks of photos piled atop folders and more folders stacked atop the piles, and a high thin voice singing over stinging strings and piano, William William William Rogers put it in its place, blood and tears from old Japan, and he leans forward to shut off the little radio, dressed all in black, his pink head gleaming.

"Devil," says Jo.

"Why," he says, "that makes of this the storied Inferno, where it's said I rule, and do not serve." Pushing back his chair, an echoing scrape, and shadows swoop as he stands, hands braced on the littered desk. "Huntsman. Welcome! But we cannot have you skulking in such a dismal Abaddon." Looking up, he cries, *"Yehi-or!"*

And chunk, chunk, chunk, that big dark room lights up, great bulbs hung from the ceiling in bells switched on row by row, the glow from them strengthening, brightening, blooming a blue-white glare that swallows the warmth of the lamp. Jo steps out from between a couple of cabinets, red shirt bright, blacks dusty, the mane of the mask in her hand listless. "Vayehi-or," says the Devil, smiling, but his smile folds away as she tosses a black leather glove to slap on the desk. "Dropped that," she says.

"Most deliberately, as well you are aware," he says. "Right!" He claps his hands together. "Where shall we have it. Here, on the desk?" He bends down to press hands and chest against the spill of photos, twisting his head to peer up at her, still there by the cabinets. "There'll be no stain, nor sticky mess, I assure you. Just a bit of dust, easily swept away. But no?" Pushing himself back up. "You'd rather we were out in the open," he says, stepping around the desk, a gesture toward the cabinets, and beyond, "where there's room to swing! Of course. I might kneel, to afford the best blow?"

"What are you doing," says Jo.

"I yet provide whatever assistance I might," he says, and frowns. "You *do* know why you're here?"

"You went and tried to pick a fight with somebody who doesn't have the time," says Jo.

"Even so!" says the Devil. "Where, then, do you mean we should have it? The neck's traditional," his hand at his turtle-necked throat, "though a blow from you to breast or belly should suffice, or even thigh."

"We're not," says Jo, "that's, not what's gonna happen."

"Isn't it?" he says, theatrically quizzical. "Then all this way you've come, merely to return to me my glove?" He leans over to pluck it up from the desk, limply black. "I must say I am touched, that you would take such time from what is a doubt-less busy schedule to see personally to the restitution of my wardrobe. But," he shakes it, the fingers of it jiggling, "thus am I made whole; the matter need trouble you no longer, and nor must I." Then, when she doesn't turn or step away, "Unless?" A broadening of his smile. "Is there, perhaps, some other task to be discharged?"

"You," says Jo, and a sigh. "You need to apologize."

"Apologize!" cries the Devil. "For leaving this behind?" He lets it fall, plap to the photo-strewn floor. "Or rather more, perhaps, the insult done the King, the honor of the Queen – but what are airy words that might suffice to heal such grievous harm?"

"Just, say you're sorry," says Jo, and a wave of the mask in her hand. "No need to make a big deal out of it." The mane of it, lazily a-sway. "Tell me, we're done, I'm gone, it's all good."

"Is it? Really? All of it?" He leans back, against the desk. "But what of it if I don't?" His smile fades. "For there's the rub of the green, you see: I won't."

"Apologize," says Jo. "Say you're wrong, Chazz. Because you're wrong."

Looking down, his pink hands clasped before him, "Mine office," he says, "was restored to me, when off the yoke was struck from about this very neck – by none but our very King." Looking up, to her. "We would do well, Huntsman, to address each other thus, and what we'd be about."

"Well," says Jo. "Okay. Devil. But I'm not going to kill you."

"A truth, in point of fact. You must destroy me, rather. I've been dead; death didn't still my tongue."

She lifts her hand, the mask in it, fingertips glimpsed through the eye-holes, thumb curled between two crudely chiseled teeth. Then tosses it aside, the mane of it trailing a dark comet falling to hit the floor, an echoing clack, a puff of dust. "I'm not," she says, "that's, not gonna happen."

Blinking, he looks up from the crumple of mane to her hand that threw it. She's turned away, to flip idly through the folders and photos in an opened drawer. "Perhaps," says the Devil, "his majesty was, unclear, in his remit?" And then, "This matter must be settled!" he cries. "Without my contrition, only my silence will suffice!"

"Or mine," says Jo. She's tugged a photo free, sepia-tinted, creased, a group of men in sweaters and padded breeches posed about the landing of some great staircase, mustaches and center-parts, a bowler hat, and the one in the center holds a football, white letters painted over its seams, PFCC. "It is supposed to be a duel, right? Trial by combat?" Peeling translucent tissue from another photo, yellowed, two women in aproned dresses on a sidewalk before a storefront, the hand-painted sign above the door that says Eat. "Not an execution. So I might lose."

Hoarsely, hushed, the Devil says, "Unthinkable."

"What," says Jo, "that you might be right?" Tucking the photos back in their folders. "What are you trying to do, here," she says, turning about. The circle of filing cabinets about them. "What the hell is all this?"

"Huntsman," he says, "forgive me," his voice returning, "I've not followed your career with the avidity that it perhaps deserves, but: I can't possibly be your first?"

"You aren't," says Jo, flatly.

"Then you must know, the quarry is most dangerous when cornered in its den. Yet," he's headed back behind the desk, stiff black wingtips placed among the scattered photos with exaggerated care, "in you walk, daisy-fresh, cucumber-cool, you spurn my last request, demand of me my reasons, why – my garters, stars, and coronets!" He stops there, the desk between them again. "I almost begin to think you hope, against all hope, to talk me out of that which I needs must, now I've taken the wheel."

"If I haven't got a hope," says Jo, "you might as well humor me. I mean, we can spare a few minutes?"

A single bark of a laugh from the Devil, and he turns to open a drawer in one of the cabinets behind him. "If the minutes be but few," he says, flipping through the folders within, "I'd better show, not tell. I am often accused of verbal imprudence," and he tugs a folder free, "of slathering a dozen over what's best said with one," laying it open on the desk, "but I ask you: what use parsimony, when something so simple as this is worth a thousand of them, or more?"

She reaches over to take the photo he holds out to her. Three women, all in black, walk down a meander of paving stones set in a scrap of yard, the first the youngest, black dress shortly tight, eyes hidden behind black sunglasses, long dark hair beneath a broad flat hat, the next in a black suit, flared trousers and a smartly tailored jacket, a bit of veil about the brim of her black slouch, and finally the eldest, white hair done up under a trim black pillbox, and a nondescriptly sensible black dress. Jo turns it over. On the back a worn black-letter stamp says Oregonian, and under that in red ink a date, 4/6/73. A strip of typescript peeling loose from ancient blotches of paste, a caption: L to R Duenna Perry, d. – Mrs. Richard Perry (Arabelle) – Isobella Perry / Richard Perry funeral (departing). She looks up to see him, smiling, arms folded, pink hands tucked away. "What is this," says Jo.

"This," says the Devil, a gesture about, "is aptly enough termed a morgue, though the singular designation is, perhaps, misleading: these were painstakingly secured from the archives of two dozen newspapers, or more – "

"Why this one." She holds it up. "Is it that she's, I mean, it's a recurring thing?" She drops it to the desk between them, the folder laid open on the desk, the other photos within, three women in rich pastels about a banquette table, three women in sepia'd, antique blacks, three women, three women. "I kinda got that already."

"One of our great mysteries," says the Devil, "and already you kind of get it."

"What does it have to do with you stepping to the King," says Jo.

"The King?" says the Devil. "Huntsman – have you spoken with the Queen?"

"What," she says, "today?"

"Since morning broke."

"I haven't had the, I had to go and, and, I don't, have to," she says. "You're wrong. Flat-out."

"You've spoken with the Gammer, though."

"She, they, told me where to find you."

"Of course. But tell me: have you spoken with the Bride?"

Jo's scowling, now. "I think I've maybe said two words to her, since she got here – "

"I do not mean the charming lepidopterist from Detroit," says the Devil. "I mean, and here I speak quite plainly: the Bride." And then, as she looks away from him, down to the photos on the desk, he says, "Are you starting, now, to rather kind of get it?"

"Well," says Jo, "that's, that," and a rip of velcro, one hand worrying at the cycling glove about the other, "that's not, what you said this morning, which, that she wants to stop the King. She doesn't. That's what you've got to walk back."

"Then *prove* it!" He pounds the desk. "With your blade! Upon this body! Let there be no doubt!"

"Not gonna happen," says Jo.

"Hunts end in death, Huntsman! Or do you think to set aside your duties as lightly as you do your badge?"

"Apologize," says Jo.

"*No!*" roars the Devil.

A deep breath, and she shakes her head. "Okay," says Jo, "all right, then I guess we're at an impasse," and the Devil leaps.

He leaps, pushing up over the desk in a tidy tumble, hanging there an instant impossibly arms spread wide and legs drawn up, and then his shoulder dips a dancer's roll to sweep a shining black shoe round and out a kick that doesn't landing crouched hands slap the floor for balance head a-tilt, ducked aside, drawn back from the tip of the blade she's pointing at his throat.

"There it is," he says. And then, a careful swallow, "Such clarity, pressed into the moment by the enormity of what's to come."

She lifts her sword away, long, straight, harsh light chasing down the edges of it, swirling the basket that guards her fingers lightly gripped about the wire-wrapped hilt. "You startled me," she says. "That's all."

"That's all?" he says, drawing back as he stands. "That's all? You pulled steel from the very air. What might you produce if you were, let's say, alarmed?"

Jo closes her eyes, her sword leaned up and back against a shoulder. "All right," she says, and opens them. "Thank you," she says, "Devil, for your apology. The King will be pleased." And with a shrug she turns and walks away, out between a couple of cabinets. The Devil stands quite still a moment, then, with a shiver, starts forward, "Huntsman!" he cries, heading after.

She's marching away across the enormous, empty, bright-lit room. "Huntsman!" he cries again. "You cannot do this!"

"Watch me!" she calls back.

"It is a *lie!*"

"So?" She stops, turns back, "Whatever it is you're trying to prove, Chazz, nobody gives a damn!" Dropping her arms, her sword held loosely at her side. "Everybody's, embarrassed – they're gonna jump all over the slightest chance to get back to business as usual. And one way, or another, I'm gonna give 'em one." Jabbing a finger at him, across the emptiness. *"That* is my fucking duty," she says.

He rushes at her, but stops as she steps back, free hand held up. "I will call you out," he snarls. "Before court and Queen I will name you a liar. As you love her – as you *love* her, Huntsman! Think! How it will *crush* her, to see you as you are!"

And she tips back her head, a shudder of laughter boiling up to a whoop. "You!" she cries. "You don't know a goddamn *thing!* About me, about her, about *any* of this! Not a goddamn thing!" Walking away, turning about again, pointing her sword back at him, "Just say you're fucking sorry. We're done."

"As you love her," he says, and his brow knits, his eyes blaze, *"half* so much as I do, *strike*. Me. *Down!"*

"No!" she bellows back. Lowering her sword. "You apologize," she says, "or I go out there," sword swung back, pointing to those bright front doors, "and tell them all you did. There's two ways this goes down – that's it."

"Put that away" – a Scream – unfinished Business

"Put that away," says the xo.

"She has a name, you know," says Moody, elbows on the table, delicately fingering the pommel of the poignard balanced on its blade-tip before him, turning it slowly about, the long and tapered edge of it gleaming, and the wire wrapped about its handle.

"You named your knife," says the xo. He's in the doorway there, looking out from the dim little cabin onto a porched bit of yellowing deck, the placid river just beyond, greyly green. His anorak dappled in chocolate-chip camouflage, the furred hood of it laid back, a ruff about his shoulders.

"Boat has a name," says Moody.

"It's a boat," says the xo. "They're coming. Put it away."

"Lucinda," says Moody, twirling the knife about again. "Why are we on a boat, anyway." His black T-shirt plain, his worn jacket of army-surplus green.

"I'm not gonna ask you again, dammit," says the xo.

"A few manners go a long way," says Moody, tilting the knife back and forth, the tip of it dimpling the table's dark veneer. Footfalls clomp the dock without. The xo says, "Moody, please. Put Lucinda or whatever the hell away. There's that old saying, about knives, and gunfights?" A tinny electric bell ding-dongs, and "Come on in," the xo calls out, without taking his eyes off Moody. Moody slips the blade back in its sheath. The xo nods, turning away to greet the first man stepping onto the deck, tall and broad, straining the shoulders of a shiny blue suit. Long mustaches droop about his mouth, the tips of them weighted with a couple of heavy grey beads. He nods once, stepping aside as the second man enters, shorter and more slender, Agravante in his blue and white striped suit. "You must be the Executive Officer," he says, with a quick squeeze for the xo's proffered hand.

"Yessir," says the xo. "Chad."

"And I am the Viscount Pinabel. This, the Anvil;" a nod to Pyrocles beside him, "you will take instruction from him, when I've instructions to give," and Pyrocles' mouth tightens at that, a pinch of a frown.

"I," says Moody, "am the Dread Paladin."

They turn to look at him, sitting there, at the table. The xo clears his throat. "One of our jefes, sir," he says.

"Ah," says Agravante. "Well. The Anvil, here. Rest assured: when he speaks, it is with my voice."

"All due respect, sir," says the xo, "but it's your money we'd be listening to, mostly." He gestures toward the table, and his tight white scar lopsides his welcoming smile. "Something to drink?"

"We're familiar with the broad outlines of your arrangement with the Duke," says Agravante, who doesn't move to take a seat. "We see no need to alter the particulars."

"Well, see," says the xo, "that arrangement with the Duke, we hadn't altered in quite some time. Being an established relationship." He folds his arms, leans back, half-sitting on the table, and

Moody behind him. "Market being what it is, we'd want to talk about upping the retainer."

"And we'd propose something of a trial run, as it were, before commitment," says Agravante.

"Well, without a retainer, prices *do* go up a bit."

"As you require," says Agravante, a dismissive wave of his hand, but Moody's leaning forward, "Hang on," he says. "Viscount, that's like a Vice President, right? And used to be we worked for a Duke?" Looking up to the xo. "What are we, getting demoted?"

White-gold dreads brushing his shoulders, blue eyes weirdly pale in the dimness, "It really is quite simple, Paladin," says Agravante. "The Duke's now gone, and the Duchess too wrapped up in court intrigues to find your services to be of any use."

"I dunno," says Moody, as the xo mutters something tersely pungent. "A Duchess," says Moody. "Sounds like more fun."

"Jo Gallowglas is many things," says Agravante, "but I'd hardly call her fun," as he turns back to the xo, but there's a pop of a laugh from Moody. "Danny," says the xo, a warning in his tone, but "Jo?" says Moody. "That's the Duchess? Jo?" And then, when no one answers, "A girl named Jo. Isn't that funny?"

"Maybe now's not the time," says the xo.

"I used to once know a girl named Jo," says Moody. "Jo Maguire." Looking past Agravante to Pyrocles, whose mouth's set between those drooping mustaches. "Wouldn't *that* be funny," says Moody.

"I believe," says Agravante, "that is the name inscribed on the cards she carries in her purse," and Moody laughs again, leans back, looks up to the xo. "I get it, now, why your old man wanted me along."

"You mean to tell us that you know the Duchess of Southeast?" says Agravante.

"Oh," says Moody, grinning, "me and Jo, we go *way* back."

"Hold still," says someone, the clatter of dropped blades, rising smoke, a scream, get her down, she's on her knees, her belly, cheek pressed to polished concrete streaked white with dust, mud, the door flare brightly shadow bulked is walking across the ceiling toward her, where she's lying, on the falling massive bell-shaped lamp up from the floor behind him crashing fountain sparks that drift quite lazily back up and up she makes me dizzy turn about, flip over, this is she's the one the gunshot, yes, does she could she I don't know, black shoes trousers squatting, blue and white and yellow flowers, idiot, reaching for her sword-hilt, get herself killed, hold her, roll her on her back and black smoke whirls before her eyes, about her wrists and arm, her shins and shifting lifts her yanking over and she kicks, she can hear us, black smoke whips about her ankle, hear us she can see us, as he's leaning over, black smoke trails and tatters of it swirl about the crimpled eaves of hair untouched left still and calm in the ruffling fluttering shut up hold her is it yes it's open up, make sure, make sure, those thick-fingered hands push her chin to one side grip the placket of her red red shirt and once more there's a scream, she's screaming, and as he yanks a button popping free he says, Mr. Keightlinger, his mouth full of black smoke, "Hold still."

Dull whump, and he shivers, but when dirty smoke billows from the front doors, the roof, he steps out of the grass, into the empty lot, his eyes on the heavy gold watch about his wrist. Every hand on the face of it pointing quivering at that big box of a store.

"Shit," says David Kerr.

Breaking into a jog, a lope, a flat-out run for those doors hung slackly open in that great oblong thrust above the high flat roof, and behind it, the towering pillar of smoke. Wading over the threshold through that smoke, slapping at tatters of yellow-white flame that lick at his sleeve and trouser-leg, toss his unruly hair, he yelps, ducking, stumbling out into the enormous open empty room, sparks everywhere and the sizzle and popping bangs of dying lamps. A scrap of paper flies past, another, more, he grabs one out of the air, a photograph stiffly glossy, two men in a canoe before a grand stone arch. More photographs, and more, tumbling, skirling, scraping the floor, here and there burning, flaring, wild shadowy flocks of them lofted, sculpting the gusts and blasts of a raging windstorm and there, in the eye of it, over toppled cabinets and the fallen bell of a lamp, hangs a man all in black his feet churning the air, reaching, grasping, wailing, yanking himself about with the effort of clutching the photos that whirl just out of reach.

"Hold still," says someone loud enough to carry over the wind. A zipping rip of cloth. A big man kneeling darkly crouched over something, red shoes kicked out a-sprawl to one side of him, the gleam of a blade. "Well, do something," that loud voice again, and Kerr, reaching for the bezel of his watch, finds his feet no longer on the floor, turned about his hands whipped back a grunt and slap, photos against his chest, photos clinging to his arms, the side of his face, a yelp from the Devil over across that room. More photos flutter snap to press against him trembling, he's lurching himself around in the howling wind. Mr. Keightlinger below spreads that undone red shirt, that ripped black T-shirt, Jo's eyes wide mouth working a word unheard, and those spatulate fingers press and twist her skin. Kerr hung above a lapped and bristling mass of photographs plastered to his torso, more photos slithering his arms one bending lifted close a hand to grab to peel to rip away the photos crumpling themselves into his mouth, a desperate gulp of air, a single shout, "Lu!" or maybe liu, or leu, it echoes, a distorted clang, and Mr. Keightlinger looks up, startled, as the wind

Kerr's feet hit the floor, he stumbles to his knees, an elbow, clang and crash the Devil falling from the air, the rustle flutter patterfall of hundreds, of thousands of glossy photographs dropped all at once. Scrape and squeak of shoe on concrete Mr. Keightlinger standing, looking about that enormous, empty, silent room. "Where!" he cries, a forlorn yelp, and then, *"Come back!"* a ragged shout. Kerr pushes himself to his hands and knees and *"You!"* roars Mr. Keightlinger, rounding on him a kick to his belly over and tumble, grunt. Hauling him up, handfuls of beige fleece, "I'll," says Kerr, but an arm swings back for a punch to his gut, "What did you," Mr. Keightlinger's howling.

Kerr says, "I'll speak another," and then the next punch lands. Kerr grunts, coughs. "You couldn't," Mr. Keightlinger's saying, arm cocked.

"Sure I would," says Kerr, grin crooked.

"Hey. Fucko," says Jo Maguire.

Mr. Keightlinger drops Kerr, backs away. Jo's marching toward them, rent shirts hung open, sword in hand. "Come back," says Mr. Keightlinger once more, to none of them in particular. *"Please."*

"What the hell," says Jo. Over behind her a scrape of metal pop and clatter, the Devil, rolling over.

"You have it," says Mr. Keightlinger. "You're the one that has it."

"That's not all I have," says Jo, lifting up her free hand.

Something rustles in the drifts of photographs, and Kerr looks back and forth, from her to him, to her again, but there, by the toppled cabinets, the skull mask lifts itself, the mane of it drawing itself together as it leaps across all that empty room, a thunderbolt to her hand.

"My morgue!" the Devil's roaring, kicking over a tumult of wrenched and broken cabinets.

"You," says Mr. Keightlinger, to Jo as she fits the mask over her head, as the mane climbs up and up, a great black banner flying. "Stay alive," says Mr. Keightlinger, backing away. "And you," he points to Kerr, who lifts a useless hand. "I won't forget," says Mr. Keightlinger, turning, loping away, off toward the broken doors.

"Your heart!" cries the Devil, staggering, slipping on photographs, stooping to snatch up his cutlass, "in my hand!" as he levels the blade at Mr. Keightlinger's retreating back. *"Now!"* And slashing the air with it leaps over the photos after him at a run.

And Kerr, Kerr's fallen, scrambling back, Kerr's staring jaw dropped at Jo Maguire, Jo Gallowglas, Jo the Huntsman of the Court of Roses, under that swelling thunderhead that roils the bells of the remaining lamps, swallowing the light, lifting, pointing her flashing blade, "Devil," she says, and the word booms. And as the Devil stops, looks back, eyes widening, she says, "We ain't done."

And he smiles. "Of course," he says. "The knave will keep." A jaunty salute of his cutlass, and he sets off, charging back across the room toward her.

That mane hangs in the air above them, lazily coiling about as she ducks, sidesteps his first wild chop, his second, clang and scrape she catches the third, steel screeching as she pushes, he shoves, she stumbles blade whipped wide as both hands gripped his next cut slashes her shoulder to hip she's falling, heavily, a gasp, and all that mass of mane drops from the air. The Devil steps back, panting, blinking. Swallowing as he takes in the basket of wiry strands a-bob in the air before him, at the end of the blade jammed through his chest. It sinks with him as he falls to his knees, reaching. The blade wobbles, shifts, drops suddenly in a spatter of something wet and black to the floor, by an angled jawbone bristling with golden teeth. The mask falls from Jo's face with a horrid echoing clack.

Blood wells from the long clean slash across her breast and belly, dark slicks of it already swamping the photographs crumpled beneath her. Kerr kneels over her, looking about, hands hovering uncertainly over throat and wrist, she jerks, a bubbling splat of a cough, and he yelps. Wisping up from her chest the barest tendril, too faint to have any color at all. "Oh, shit," says David Kerr. "*That's* it. That's what he meant."

Jo drags up her sodden hand, presses the heel of it a squelch to her breast, tamping it back down.

"I can't," says Kerr, "I'm sorry, there's no way I can call an ambulance. They're not equipped. *I* should be running for the fucking hills," but her head's rolling back and forth, no, no, as her other hand wrestles something up, her phone, lighting up under a film of red. Holding it up to him. "Luys," she just manages to say. "The Mason. Call," her voice catches, "Luys."

And now the blue is almost gone from the sky, a lemony pale above that shades down through lime and lavender to oranges, to wild magentas that cling to the bottoms of a shadowed flotilla of clouds, down and down to the molten gold still burgeoning over beyond the roofs and towers, the far-off hills, and off behind it pinkly greens through purples unearthly, stately, down into a rumor of the darkness that's to come. He slips around the corner of the low white warehouse as across the way a streetlight flickers to life. The empty street, the bare sidewalk, the warehouse wall painted over the length of it with a sprawling mural, figures and scenes that lap one over into another, masks and blocks, flames, a gnarled and squamous root-shape crowned with a forest, all the rich colors of it leached away in the deepening dim. Another wall over across the street, grey and blank but for a simple sign, Multnomah County Department of Community Corrections, it says, Probate and Parole. He hunches under the hood of his grimy sweatshirt, hands wrapped around whatever it is he's carrying, and heads quickly down the open stretch of sidewalk, toward the row houses at the end, the cluster of recycling bins, but even before he's halfway along there's an engine-chug, a pickup truck turning the corner ahead, and he stops in the glare of its round headlights. It's an old truck, an aqua blue weirdly luminous in the gloom, fenders scabbed with rust. "Hey," says somebody, the driver, through the window rolling down, "hey," as the truck stops there beside him. "Christian? The hell you doing over here? You know my word only goes so far."

"You hold my money," says Christian, tipping back his head, looking out from under his hood. "Not my feet."

"I hold your money," says the xo, companionably enough, "and you know if you need anything, all you have to do is ask. Just like I know if *I* ask *you* for something, you'll bring what you got to the table." There's a shadow just past him, someone else in the cab. "Now get over here," he says. "We been looking for you all afternoon."

"Who's we," says Christian. "Who you got in there with you."

A chuckle from whoever it is, the shadow in the passenger seat. "Oh," it says, "oh that's Shizzt, all right," and Christian closes his eyes with a shiver. The passenger door opens with a scrape. Christian hurriedly takes the shoe he's holding, wrapped in his hands, the oxblood black in the darkness and the buckle of it gleaming, and stuffs it into the pocket in the front of his sweatshirt, and his hands in after. Moody steps around the front of the truck, lit up suddenly by the headlights, "Shizzt the Drow," he says, his hands spread wide, welcoming. "How the hell are you."

"We ain't got nothing to say to each other," says Christian, looking down, hunching over the bulge of the shoe in the pocket of his shirt.

"Now don't be like that, man," says Moody. "You *know* I didn't do half a what they said I did. That's why I'm out so early. Good behavior, and all kind and manner of false pretenses and shit." A step closer, and Christian lifts his head up, glaring out from under his hood. "Now you," says Moody, a hand up against the light, "you ain't changed a bit. But Bambi Jo?" And there's that chuckle again. "You seen her, lately? God damn." Another step closer, and there he is, right there by Christian, one foot up on the curb. "Tell me," says Moody. "How the hell you think she's doing, these days?"

THE SILHOUETTE IN THE DOORWAY — ECHOES

Ysabel, a silhouette in the doorway, and behind her the hall, stellated by those strands of little yellow lights. "Jo?" she says. "Are you awake?"

From the mounded white comforter, blued in the darkness, a sigh resolves itself into a word: "Yes."

"I wish you had come," says Ysabel, stepping down as she kicks off her shoes, clump-thump. "The piano, in this one song," and she twirls about, white coat slipping from her shoulders, flump to the floor. Careless drips of golden glitter spangle her bared arms, her thigh, down about her knees. "It was magnificent," she says, sitting at the foot of the futon.

"There's the, Samani? In the morning? Knighting of knights? Luys is gonna be here in, stupid early," grabbing her phone from the clutter on the table by the futon, ghostly flash of her face in the light of the screen. "Three hours," she says, putting it back.

"You might've brought him with you. Made a night of it."

"Some of us need our sleep, your majesty?"

"Sleep, your grace, is highly overrated." Ysabel undoes a knot at the back of her neck, and peels the lacey overlay of her brief dress from the glossy chemise beneath. "As well you know," she says, dropping the overlay to the floor. "Do you still mean to propose your friend for office?"

"Ah, he said no, and took off, but," and Jo rolls over, under the comforter. "I got Sweetloaf out looking for him, just in case."

"Sweetloaf?"

Darkness shifts as Jo sits up a little, "Yes," she says, "Sweetloaf," and then, falling back, a shadow on the pillows, "the hell do you care, you're not even going."

"I *do* care," says Ysabel, leaning back against the wall, closing her eyes.

After a minute or two, another sigh from under that comforter, "Christ, if you're staying, get under the damn covers. Make me nervous, just sitting there like, what are you, Ysabel?" Jo sits up again, switches on the anglepoise lamp on the table by the futon. There at the foot of it Ysabel's squirming out of her chemise. "I'm not sleeping in this," she says, dropping it on the comforter. "Besides," a brow cocked at Jo's bare shoulder, her breast, "when in Rome."

"And of course, you went commando," says Jo, as Ysabel crawls up the futon. "And you reek, of cigarettes, of booze, of, of pussy – "

"Jo!"

"You do!"

Ysabel leans close, to nuzzle Jo's cheek, "Intoxicating, isn't it," she murmurs. Stroking that red hair spread out in the lamplight. "Don't," says Jo, gone suddenly still.

Ysabel lets go, sits up, "Jo," she says, "I would never," and "I know," says Jo. "I know." Looking up to Ysabel, those short black curls touched here and there with white. "What," says Jo. "Ysabel. What is it."

"I," says Ysabel, looking away.

"Is it Chrissie? Did you leave her in your room again, or – "

"I sent her home," says Ysabel, "but, I, I," the dim glow of the hallway out there, past the half-closed door. "Does it hurt?" she says, turning back to Jo.

"Does, what – hurt?"

"Your," and Ysabel waves a hand, vaguely, over Jo, "condition. Does it hurt?"

Jo says, *"That's* what this is about?"

"Well, I, I worry, I do." Her hand laid gently over Jo's heart. "I do care."

"So you can't bear to let me sleep."

"You *owe* us, Southeast." Stern words belied by a gentle smile. "You told your Mason, before you told your Queen."

"Well, I, yeah," says Jo, "he is my, ah, my, my – "

"Your lover."

" – I was gonna, more like say, lieutenant?" The sour twist of her mouth. "What's that Mafia word. Consigglesomething. Consorleoni?"

Ysabel, pressing softly with her hand, says again, "Does it hurt?"

"Sometimes?" says Jo, looking down at Ysabel's fingers. "Mostly, it's just, like, a chill. But I can forget it's even ow, okay, yes, you do *that,"* laugh and tussle, rustle of bedclothes, a shimmer of falling gold knocked loose from Ysabel's skin, "that's not *it,* you can *stop!* Now!" the last words spiking, slap and shove and tumble, and Ysabel gasps, "What," says Jo, hands lifting away as Ysabel sits back, "I saw it," she says, "I think."

"Yeah?"

"A glimmer."

"Like soap."

"A rainbow."

"But you look at it."

"There's nothing."

"Sometimes," says Jo, reaching out, "it's easier to see," switching off the lamp, "in the dark."

"I don't," says Ysabel, black hair lost in the shadows, her hand a shadow on the pale, blue-tinged ground of Jo's chest. "It's gone," she says.

"Quicksmoke," says Jo, her hand covering Ysabel's.

"The whirlwind, in a bottle."

"Christ," says Jo. "Don't remind me."

"The fire enfolded, from before the world was the world."

"Echoes," says Jo. "Your father called them – "

"I have no father."

"Okay, uh, John, John said – "

"The King Before."

"The King," says Jo, "Before. Yes. Called them echoes." Her hand, clasping Ysabel's. Fingers twining. "I am," she says, "so fucking sorry."

"What on earth for," says Ysabel, with wonderment.

"That he went after you," says Jo. "The magician. I – you, you shouldn't've had to – if I'd told you, but," as Ysabel stretching out lays herself down, her head on Jo's shoulder, "I should've told you. I should've. Before he – but I didn't – "

"Jo."

" – I had no idea he was even still here – "

"Jo, it's only logic, that he'd come to look for it first in me," and "I know," says Jo, "but if I'd, I," her arm coming up about Ysabel, "I'm so sorry," and Ysabel's saying, "he hurt no one, he barely even spoke: mostly bluster. It's all right. It's all right. I was more concerned," a little laugh, "with what my mothers meant to do." Her hand, squeezing Jo's. "I am all right," she says. "But you should know. He'll come for you, next."

"Yeah," says Jo, looking away. The shadowed walls, the windows streaked with streetlight.

"All this time," says Ysabel, "you've carried it," her thumb, lightly stroking, there between Jo's breasts. "Why didn't you tell me?"

And Jo says, "I was scared."

"Oh," says Ysabel, pushing up, "oh, Gallowglas," leaning over, a hand to that red hair, black in the blackness. "How could you ever be frightened of me."

"Not of," says Jo. Looking up, past Ysabel's shadow. "For." The dim ceiling above. "You were," she says, "gone."

"I fell," says Ysabel.

"It, this, stuff. This smoke. It eats things, out of the world. People."

"I fell, into myself."

"You were gone."

"I fell, but you came for me."

"Before that," says Jo. "Before that. Before your, the King, before he found me, you were – nobody, they all, didn't know you. Luys. Marfisa. The, Mooncalfe, and, and Leo, nobody – "

"Jo."

"Sweetloaf! Nobody, no one," pulling her hand free, sitting up, away from Ysabel, "you were *gone.*"

"Jo," says Ysabel.

"This, stuff," says Jo, and her wavering hand closes in a fist, presses knuckles sharply to her sternum. "Lenses, he said. And mirrors. Breath. That's what holds it, he said. But it also," that fist, twisting, and she winces, "makes a shell, for itself? From what it takes. It makes a shell, and *plants* itself," her eyes, her face crumpling, shoulders hunching, knuckles digging and she groans, "it's *sleeping, here,* in my *heart,* and I don't know what will happen when it wakes," shuddering, *"up,"* and a hiss of breath, but Ysabel's grabbed her arm, pulled that fist away, pulled Jo close her arms about her, "But I'm here," she's saying, "I'm here, Jo, I'm here," kissing her, her forehead, a hiccuped sob. "I'm here," she whispers. "Jo. Know this." One hand slipped between them, laid against Jo's breast. "I am," says Ysabel, *"so much bigger than that."*

Jo pulls her close, arms tight about her, crushing Ysabel's hand between them, "It's just," she says, eyes squeezed shut, "I, I love you," a breath, in Ysabel's ear.

And Ysabel's arms about Jo, and her mouth turns to find Jo's mouth, and a kiss, and another kiss, another, and just the barest motion of her lips against Jo's lips: "Thank you."

And you wonder
Will I leave her—
But how?
I cross over borders
But I'm still there now.

—the Russian

NO. 27

" – tends to crumble – "

THE ROOM IS BLUE, and dark, and very quiet. At the foot of the pallet mounded with white pillows under the angled ceilings he's sitting, and dark hair eaves his shoulders, a great beard brushes his chest, his back and upper arms are hatched with more hair curling with the curves of sagging muscle, down to his thick round waist. His legs are folded tailor-fashion, bare feet tucked under bare thighs, hands held loosely open on his knees, his cock a-jut, tip of it darkly swollen, glistening, there before his thick-furred paunch. Mustache wide in a simple smile beneath eyes simply, gently closed, there between his beard, his hair, serenely still, so very quiet.

Explosions rip the television screen, chatter of gunfire, Angels comin thick an fast Sarge, and the guy on the beanbag leans back and forth, thumbs and fingers frantically working the controller in his lap. The view on the screen wheels, jerks, dials and meters in the corners whirling, flashing, galloping along in a tight-packed herd of wildly colored centaurs, garish pastel zebra stripes, neon leopard spots, Appaloosa rainbows, all wrapped in khaki saddlebags, human torsos draped in bandoliers, big guns in their outsized hands, Get to cover! Under the cable! Your six, your six! and another explosion. "Shit!" he yelps, tap-tapping, laughing, "Shit!" Over across the room a woman's headed toward a grand dark staircase, and the other man in the room looks away from the screen, starts after her, "Ellen," he says, dodging around a dark wood column, "hey, Ellen, wait up." She stops, a couple steps up, looks down at him. "How long, exactly," he says, "is he gonna be staying here," and he points, up the stairs, past her. She shrugs. More explosions, more gunfire, the guy on the beanbag whoops. "Long as he needs," she says. Her black hair spiky short, the inky lace of tattoos edging the collar of her running shirt.

"It's just," he says, at the foot of the stairs, tall and heavyset, cardigan blue. "The occasional overnight guest is one thing, but – "

"My room, my friend, my business," she says. "You won't even know he's there, Dan, unless you go out of your way." The loudest explosion yet, and "Shit!" yells the guy on the beanbag. The television's gone red. She's turning to climb the stairs. "Ellen!" says the man in the blue cardigan, starting up, "Ellen, he was, what the hell was he doing, wearing my shirt?"

She looks down at him again, and maybe shrugs. "Looks better on him," she says, and up she goes, up another flight, up under the very peak of the house. At the end of a cramped hall a door, cut at an angle the top to fit the slope of the roof.

The door to that blue room opens, and she steps in, a shadow dressed in black, flashes of silver piping, "Phil?" she says. "You're, ah, oh." Stretching out a foot to prod the black huddle of a discarded suit, there on the floor by the door. Splash of yellow within, and blue and white, a rumpled aloha shirt. "Hungry?" she says. "I was gonna go for phở." Still in the doorway, hand on the jamb. "Did you want some?" Creak of a floorboard as she steps back, out into the hall. "I'll bring some back," she says. "You're welcome to half the bed, if you need it." The door swings shut. The latch clicks, quietly.

Rattle of glass, yellow bin in his hands, blue letters along the side say Portland Recycles! Clang and clink he sets it down, chock full of bottles, brown glass and green, clear, four or five of them wine bottles long and slender, the rest soda bottles, beer. Squatting he pulls out a wide-mouthed jar, the label mostly torn away, and holds it up in the light. "Fuck," he says, setting it down. Smacks it, topples it, sends it rolling a hollow rumble away down the linoleum clunk against the wall. "Fuck," he says, again, rattle and clink, and "shit," and then "damn."

Over by the floor-length curtains a brown and green sleeping bag, someone in it, rolling over, a voice, sleep-muzzled, "What."

"Bits," he says, "of *pickle,*" waving a hand, and dark hair swings about the shoulders of his warm-up jacket, blue and grey.

"So rinse it?" The sleeping bag hunches and flops open, whoever's in it sitting up, a woman, wrapped in a puffy pink and orange parka. "Why should *I,*" he's saying, "why couldn't *they,*" and he shoves the bin, a chiming crash. "We'll just have to get some. Bread-and-butter pickles. Trader Joe's."

"You want to," she says, and she's pinching the bridge of her nose, "you want to buy a new jar of pickles, and, what, eat them all, or throw them out, and the rinse the jar, because you don't want to rinse the jar?"

"The label on that one," he says, and then "dammit! It's the perfect size." Stomping the length of the room to snatch up the jar, and then through the door. Clomp and clatter, a squawking wrench, the rush of water.

She sighs, crawls out of the sleeping bag, long yellow hair a-dangle from the parka's fur-lined hood. She slips on a couple of red canvas shoes and heads off carefully through the garbage strewn across the floor, more bottles, empty, all sizes and colors, glass and plastic, quart-sized cartons and half-gallon cartons and little pints and half-pints, cereal boxes and pasta boxes stacked and wrapped together with blue masking tape and black friction tape, towering masts of emptied rolls of plastic wrap and toilet paper, paper towels, plastic tubs tall and squatly broad, whole ranks of them that say Nancy's in letters of various hues, all laid out in a relatively tidy grid, narrow paths between and through them all where she places her feet, aglets of her undone laces clacking against the floor, until she reaches a wide cleared curl of an aisle of sorts, edges marked with long strips of more blue tape.

He's at the sink, fiercely scrubbing the jar, "Basic civic *duty,*" he's saying, *"think* of other people, come *on.*" Slamming the jar on the counter by a dozen or more empty jars and bottles, scrubbed clean, gleaming. Yanking the faucet to shut off the water. "Luke," she's saying, "Luke," and he looks up to see her there, hands stuffed in the pockets of her parka. "The hell you wearing that for," he says, scooping wet shreds of label from the sink.

"It's freezing," she says.

"You know why it's cold," he says, dropping the mess plop in a swollen garbage bag that yawns there on the floor.

"So I'm wearing this."

"You look ridiculous." He shakes the slop off his hand.

"There's still a smell," she says. He's headed past her, out of the kitchen. "Luke," she says, following, "Luke. We're gonna need – "

"Don't," he says, kneeling by an untidy patch of garbage.

"We're gonna need money," she says. "Rent. The fifth. It's next week."

"We're always," says Luke, "gonna need," plucking up a cereal box, "so get a job," he says, grabbing another, a clownishly colored bird on the front of it.

"I *had* a job," she says.

"Jessie," he says, "don't, just," and he looks up, a shrug. "Your sister's gonna be here soon. Right? So maybe she'll have something for you. For us."

"My," says Jessie, frowning. "Luke, now is not the – "

"Don't," he says, leaning over to place one of the boxes right next to a yellow plastic jug.

"The first order of Business" – at This table antique Punk bullshit – the Basics of Security

"The first order of business," says the man at the head of the table, "in any face time we take with potential occupancy partners, we need to assess how the anticipated anchor's gonna impact their appraisal and availability approach." It's a long table, a slab of wood the color of pale flesh, polished to a striking gleam that's broken here and there by a phone or a computer tablet laid before this person or that, until down at the very other end of it, a couple of comb-bound reports bristling with post-it flags, a spill of colorful diagrams, a worn redweld holding a couple of file folders upright, a small black notebook splayed open, the wispy scratch of a fountain pen, APPRAISAL written in ruddy black ink, AVAILABILITY, then three sharp underscores. "It's not," the man at the head of the table is saying, "that we anticipate an antagonism toward the anchor, on the part of any potential part-ners?" His flat grey suit's a touch too big, the collar of his soft blue shirt's undone, his sparse beard neatly trimmed. "But by anticipating," he says, "their respective stances vis-à-vis their individualized brand engagement profiles which, let me assure you, we will be reviewing in a thorough manner before we, we take up any," he's trailing off, "tête-à-têtes," blinking quizzically. The room about them's walled in cool sheets of green-tinged glass on all four sides and more beyond refracting, reflecting, shimmer-ing desk lamps and fluorescents, computer screens, heads popping up over cubicle walls, turning, following the figure swimming up through them, one glass door after another opening before her, "I," says the man at the head of the table, "excuse me," as the final glass door swings open, she's sweeping into the room, Ysabel in her long white coat. "I tried to tell her," someone's saying, a receptionist maybe, bobbing in her wake, and "Do you mind," says an older man, halfway down the table, a hand on his phone on the wood, but she's glaring at the very other end of the table. "How *dare* you," she says.

"Sorry, folks," says Lymond, screwing the cap onto his fountain pen. "Think we might have the room a minute?"

"I, um," says the man at the head of the table, "we just got started?"

"And we'll get right back into it," says Lymond. "I'm really looking forward to hearing more about this brand engagement. Now," pushing back his chair, "if you don't mind," but already they're filing out, shirts and blouses of dull green, milky blue, an intrepid puce, awkwardly around past Ysabel all in white. "Um," says the man who'd been at the head of the table, in his flat grey suit.

"Thanks," says Lymond, cheerfully. The green glass door swings shut. "How dare I?" he says, to Ysabel. "I'm the King. A certain latitude's expected."

"You could've gotten her *killed,*" says Ysabel.

"They're watching, you know," he says, tucking a report into the redweld. "Go on. Lean over the table. Slap me. That should be enough to undo all his sacrifice secured."

She blinks at that, draws back. "Sacrifice," she says.

"He thought of it as such," says Lymond, stacking up those diagrams, tapping their edges against the wood. "Now. Slap me, or turn about, and go home."

"Not until you explain yourself, brother."

"Oh, Ys," he says. "If you would play at this table," he's tucking the diagrams into a file folder, "you must pay attention." A wince, as he sets the folder aside. "We find ourselves upon a crux: the duel between the Devil and the Huntsman redounded to our favor, yet the wound's but freshly healed. Any sudden shift might tear it right back open." His hands, folded together before him, a thumb pressed tight against a knuckle. "Is that what you would have?"

"I've seen the wound," she says. "He nearly cut her through. The owr does what it can," and she looks up from the tabletop to meet his eyes, one brown, one blue, both cold. "She sleeps. She's been asleep since the Mason brought her home." Leaning down now, both hands planted on the glossy wood. "I'm doing you a courtesy, by answering a question I assume you would eventually have asked?"

A bitter something of a smile. "How is Jo," he says, "how Jo is, I know how is our Gallowglas: loyal, and effective. I trusted her to do what needed doing, and she went and got it done. Now," over her sharp intake of breath, "I ask, once more. You know what is at stake. Do you mean to stand against any particular point of our plan?" Leaning in close. "Slap me," he says. "Or go home."

She steps back, she turns away. Before she can open the green glass door he says, "Take care, sister, where and when you might vent any further displeasures?" Looking down, at his folded hands. "Our tantrums are expensive."

"You've no idea," she says, "what could've spilled from her heart, had his stroke been a whit more true."

She opens the door. He shifts his thumb. The thin line of a neat straight cut along the edge of his forefinger, sewn with tiny beads of dark red blood. He lifts it to his lips. "Um," says someone, the man in the flat grey suit a touch too big, peering into the room. "Everything good?"

"Paper cut," says Lymond, waving him in. "C'mon, let's go. Take it from the top."

Well and I don't know, dim voices floating up through floorboards loosely laid across the joists, *not* what we discussed, poets and junkies, epic, like some, there's a mirror, there's no one in the mirror, there's a crack in the glass of it jagged, chased and dappled, splotched with gold, a spangled haze, such a history, working together, that didn't work, a drip-drip trickle from the faucet, puddles on gold-streaked marble about the sink, but there, it's gonna be epic, dust gone dark to grey, to black, a lump of it mucked up under the mirror, with the shreds of a burst plastic baggie, this, or this, or this. There's music, too, loud but languid, strummed guitars, a melodeon, but she's sitting up in the dark, her head in her hands, and there is no mirror, no light, no sinks or water, no marble countertop, but there is the dust, spangled, glimmering in the milky cloud of her hair, and still the music.

"Well if we have to have a name," says Gloria Monday.

"It's something to put on a poster," says the woman sitting on the nubbled pea-green couch, one hand braced on the curled handle of an orthopædic cane, a big brown scaley purse in her lap.

"Well if that's all we want," says Gloria, wrestling to one side a great stretched canvas, a twirling figure calligraphed in slashes of black, to reveal another propped behind it, the next wild scribble of dance. She steps back, behind a tiny silver camera atop a stolid tripod, stoops to peer through it. "We could call it the Lawn," she says, snapping a picture. Straightening, she looks back and forth, from the painting, to the image of it, now on the enormous white-framed monitor behind her there on the worktable.

"As in get off the?" says the woman standing off to one side, her long black coat done up with brightly silver buttons, and a little grey snap-brim hat on her head.

"That's not what we discussed," says Anna in her houndstooth trousers, narrow black-rimmed glasses glaring in the light.

"The *house,*" says Gloria, taking hold of the canvas. "Run-down and falling apart and poets and junkies and twenty bedrooms to one bathroom and full of," lifting, "epic," hoisting it aside, "legend, and, and art," to reveal the next. "The Lawn," says Gloria Monday. Her feet are bare, laddered tights printed with overlapping gears, her vast white T-shirt says Robot Fightin' Boots.

"I liked Weatherall's," says Anna. "If we're going to change it."

"Yeah, well," says Gloria, stooping behind the camera again.

"Sounds like some Harry Potter shit," says the woman in the long black coat.

"*Jilting* of," says Gloria, snapping another picture. "*Granny* Weatherall? Been a while, since you been in high school?" The woman on the couch snorts up a laugh, sits up, hefting her cane. "How about," she says, pointing the wide rubber foot of it out, toward the cavernous space beyond, "this building," the boxes, equipment, the bulks of whatever it is under tarps shoved off to either side, stacked in the stalls that one by one march down the long high walls, "the history," soaked in soft grey light depending from up under the rafters, the windows there scrubbed clean of filth, scraped clear of paint, "a name should honor that."

"It was a warehouse for vegetables," says Gloria.

"A farmers' market," says the woman on the couch, "built by Italian immigrants, working together. Cooperatively."

"Snot Market," says Gloria, "Grime Market, *that* didn't work," grabbing the next canvas, "Pus Market has a certain punch," hauling it aside, "but *Anna* didn't like any of those, and anyway it's antique punk bullshit. Effluvial Plane I kinda liked, but that's too, *much,* y'know?"

"How *old* are you?" says the woman all in black.

"*Fuck* you," says Gloria. "*That's* how old I am."

"Gloria," says Anna.

"No, *fuck* this," snarls Gloria. "We got the space. We're doing the thing. It's gonna be epic. And you can either get on board, get your, people, involved," the woman on the couch, clutching her purse, "you can write about it like you know what's gonna happen," the woman all in black, hands in her pockets, smirking, "or you can scramble to catch up after, like everyone else."

"Ms. Thorpe, we must apologize," says Anna, after a moment, but "No, no," says the woman all in black, "tempers run hot and you let them out and that's fine, and then you stop and you take a deep breath and you *think*. Maybe you do this, or maybe tomorrow you're kicked out for squatting. You don't – "

"Hey, Anna!" says Gloria. "What's the owner got to say, about us being here?"

"There are no objections," says Anna, but Thorpe looks away, rolling her eyes. "I did my homework," she says, lifting her little grey hat, "or I wouldn't be here at all," scratching her head, her dark hair short, swept back. "You're Suzette Wilson, you're Tom Wilson's daughter, and I'm sorry for your loss, but the title to this pile is hardly as clear-cut as," but Gloria's saying, "This, this is *my* place," as Thorpe says "that's before we even get into the questions of insurance, and zoning, and inspections," but Gloria's shouting "S1! Last Thursday! The Teahouse! You think *they* waited around for fucking *paperwork?*"

Anna and the woman on the couch, watching them both, Gloria seething, Thorpe settling her hat on her head, "Well," she's saying, tucking her hands in the pockets of her coat, "S1 is street-legal now, yeah, and the Teahouse? That was in Sellwood? Long gone. And you have any idea how much the merchants on Alberta pay the city for extra cops?" A shrug, and that smirk warms to something more sympathetic. "You want to beg forgiveness instead of ask permission and I can respect that, but there's this delicate balance. You gotta be big enough to get noticed, but you can't be so big you get noticed, you know?" Looking out, over the cavernous space below. "And all this you want to do in a week." Turning back, hands spread in a hapless shrug, a burble of sound, "I like you," she says, "I do, I like the idea," looking up. It sounds like someone's singing up there.

Up there, up at the edge of the planks laid across the joists, up by the brief ladder bolted to the wall a couple of long bare legs kicked over and orange underpants, ee, ee-oh nor, the keening voice a grunt, doo da-da dee, doo da-da dee, down the ladder to the walkway up there, a wild mad cloud of white-gold hair, "and quickly was received, enthusiastically," and Thorpe looks down, over at the paintings leaned, at the image on the enormous monitor. "Some say that it had more to do with her," the singer's making her way, hand on the railing, "improper sense of dress, than her talent, or her diligence," opening a door up there, painted with letters that possibly once said Ranchers, or Gardeners, and closing it muffles her song. "I'm sorry," says Anna, drawing back their attention. "It seems Marfisa forgot we were meeting this morning."

"I've seen," says Thorpe, "I've heard her, before."

"Salt and Straw," says the woman on the couch, but then, lifting a finger, "no, that's the ice cream."

"She kinda came with the place," says Gloria. Up there a crash of water, flushing, that door opens, Marfisa's stepping out, "Cartier Bresson!" she shouts. "Max Ernst, Paul Eluard, George Bataille," as she's making her way back along the wall above them. "Their misogyny really irritated her, but she wasn't, she," stopping, standing there, wavering a little, looking down at them. Absently scratching just beneath a breast, and sunlight flashing from the gold dust spangling her skin.

"I heard you play once," says Thorpe, abruptly.

Her wide smile spreading, Marfisa tips back her white-gold head, "Lee, ee-oh nor!" she sings, reaching for the ladder. "Lee, ee-oh nor!" Climbing back up toward the makeshift floor above.

"Stone and Salt!" says the woman on the couch. *That* was it."

Ding the microwave, she opens the door of it, reaches in with a hot pad for a steaming pink mug that says Sophia & Dorothy &

Blanche & Rose. In she dunks a purple octopus infuser, dandling its delicate chain a moment. Color blooms.

Out of the kitchen, across the living room, dark wood paneling, grey-green shag, shuff and snap of her slippers into a nook of a hall, too brightly lit. She nudges open a door left ajar, into a small dark room lit only by sunlight staining the edges of heavy curtains drawn, and almost entirely filled by a great wide bed. "I've brought tea," she says, setting the mug on the nightstand in the corner. "Hey." Sitting on the edge of the bed. "I called Reg," she says, reaching along the margin of the thick dark comforter, and a gentle stroke for the blond head there, turned away. "Told him we'd need another week. He wasn't happy, but hey. Fuck him." Tucking a lock of her own hair, as blond, as straight, behind her ear. "Chrissie," she says. "Chér."

"I don't want any tea."

"Yeah, well," says Ettie, and she gets to her feet with a sigh. "This would be why I stick with men. They can't break your heart."

The door swings open, for a moment all's revealed, scarred floor and drifts of grit against the bar, peeling dimpled paint along the front of it and its cracked vinyl bumper, dust furring the bottles along the top shelf, the washed-out flyspecked neon lights, the bartender, spiky hair flared palely to a golden brown, hand up against the raw daylight, skinny arm festooned with shadowy tattoos, "Jacks?" says Jessie, blinking, but the light's swallowed away as the door swings shut, and dimness closes about the warm neon, the sparkle of glass, the rattle of drums and a couple of jangled chords, bubbling bass, "Jackie?" says the bartender, his hair gone black. "Ah, naw. She ain't here."

"Oh," says Jessie, in her puffy pink parka. "Sorry. I thought," and she shakes her head, Americans were thus denied, someone's singing, with the guitar and the drums, all right to travel to the other side. "She usually works mornings," says Jessie. "Any idea when she's in next?"

"No, see," says the bartender, "I mean, she's not here? Anymore?" Folding those skinny arms, leaning his elbows on the bar. "And we can't be giving out people's schedules, come on. Basic security."

"I'm a friend," says Jessie, and then, "I used to dance here? About a year, year and a half ago. Went by Rain?"

"If you're a friend," says the bartender, "I mean, she left, what, right after the holidays? Two, three months ago? So, I mean," and he spreads his hands. "Want something to drink?"

"Where'd she go?" says Jessie.

"I don't know, Eugene or something? But even if I did I couldn't tell you, because, security, you know. Coffee? Anything?"

Betcha my life, there'd be no violence there, and she opens her mouth to speak but everything lights up again, washed out, as the door swings open, two women, raincoat, trench coat, gym bag and backpack, nodding to the bartender who waves hello as they head through empty tables past the empty little stage, toward the nondescript door back there. "How about Chilli," says Jessie. "He back there?"

"He, naw, Chilli, we're," the bartender jumps as she walks away, "we're under new management," he calls after her, "so," but there's confusion by that nondescript door as it opens, those women stepping through around and past a man who's stepping out, brown leather vest and rich red hair flopping from a widow's peak, "I need you to," the bartender's saying. Jessie waves him off. "It's Gaveston," she says. "I know Gav."

But Gaveston's holding the door for someone else, a tall woman in a white track suit, short hair greenly yellow, and Jessie stops short, in the midst of the empty tables. "Chariot?" she says. The tall woman's saying something to Gaveston, as she heads off past the little stage. "Iona?" says Jessie, and the tall woman looks over to see her there in pink. "Oh," she says, stopped short. "Rain."

"Is she here?" says Jessie. "The," a cough, "the Princess? Uh, Queen? Ysabel?"

Iona's shaking her head, "I'm merely here on her behalf," she says, stepping away, but "Iona," says Jessie, "Chariot, tell her, please," and Iona stops, looks back. "Yes?" she says.

Jessie looks away. "Nothing," she says. "Don't tell her any-thing. Not even, that you saw me."

"As you wish," says Iona. Jessie's still looking away, there among the empty tables. I'd want the giddy-up, the guitar jangles, I'd want to live it up, I'd want the pick-me-up, and the nondescript door back there's now shut. The bartender isn't behind the bar that flares, scoured once more by daylight as Iona opens the door outside. She steps through, the door swings shut, the darkness returns.

Nox Sea Raid say the letters punched in light across the screen. Choose Your Squad swooshes in below. A husky contralto says Set em up Sarge over the speakers, and the guy on the beanbag thumbs and clicks the controller in his lap, wheeling the view on the screen about a motley crew of centaurs, each stepping up to present arms as the focus settles fleetingly on them, uttering a catch-phrase, Rock an roll, rack em and pack em, they will fear my song, buzzbombs why's it have to be buzzbombs, reportin for beauty! rock an rack em rock an pack em why's it have to fear my rock an roll an reportin! "This is gonna suck," says the guy on the beanbag, "I need more'n one tank for this." Wrinkles about his eyes and gin-gery stubble along his jaw. "Whaddaya think," he says, looking away from the screen, "would a Mixolydian," but there's nobody beside him, there's a man headed away, over toward the grand dark staircase, dodging around a dark wood column, his sweater bulky, red, he's looking up to the woman stopped there on the stairs, black trousers, a bowtie unclipped about her winged collar. "Long as he needs," she's saying, and "Oh," says the guy on the beanbag, turning back to the screen, "Ellen's home." Clicking through the figures on the screen, rock an roll, reportin for beauty, they will fear, "The hell was he doing, wearing my shirt?" and the guy on the beanbag looks up again at that, the man in the red sweater a step or two up the stairs, and Ellen above him, maybe a shrug, "It looks better on him," she's saying, turning away. Why's it have to be, says the centaur on the screen. Rack em!

"Quite distressing," says the older man, there in the wingback chair. "Though one does not wish to play the churl. A certain degree of disarray must certainly be allowed, given the shocks – the challenge, the duel – "

"Allowed?" says Agravante, there by the yellow stone fireplace, an elbow up on the mantel, and the older man takes a sip of milky tea from a thin bone china cup. "How is the King's champion, by the way?" he says.

"Death's door," says Agravante. There on the mantel by his elbow a fiendish little basket-box, carved from a chunk of dark red wood. "Shame," says the older man, shaking his head, stiff grey curls swept back, and the collar of his shirt undone, a blue scarf knotted tidily about his throat. "Though it is distasteful, how they might linger, on that threshold? Neither here, nor there," and another sip of tea.

"What is it that distresses you, Medardus," says Agravante. White-gold locks tied neatly black, his grey suit shot with blue.

"It's a delicate question I'd have answered, Pinabel," says the older man, setting the cup in the saucer on his lap, clink. "Does the King yet mean to pursue his bold vision?"

Agravante's brow pinches. "Of course," he says. "Insofar as I know."

Medardus smiles. "Delicately put," he says. "It's been two days."

"These things take time."

"Two days," says Medardus, "since he took from me mine offer," knobbled fingers closing in a fist, drawn up by his yet-mild smile. "And not a word said since."

"There's much to be considered," says Agravante. "Four of you do vie for her hand."

"Please, Pinabel," says Medardus, dropping his hand, and a clatter of cup and saucer. "It's an indulgence to pretend the choice isn't manifestly clear – that mine is not the best offering."

"The best, perhaps," says Agravante. "But sufficient?" A slatey shoulder shrugs.

"The King would demand more?"

"How can I answer that," says Agravante, "when I know nothing of what you've promised, or he might require."

"Nothing," says Medardus, still smiling. "Such a delicate word." Setting cup and saucer on the low table between them. "I would hope," he says, "it could always be said that the Hound has done well by Medardus," and he knots those knobby fingers in his lap. "Much as it can be said, to a surety, that Medardus has done well by the Hound."

Rather carefully, Agravante does not smile at that, or nod, his shoulders do not move, nor does his arm, there by the basket-box. "Of course," he says.

"But it's also said," says Medardus, "that a fear grips your court: that the line is not unbroken. That the Queen, despite her, prodigious recovery, has no Bride of her own. That your King's hand, howsomever reluctantly, is forced. That he means," and here Medardus leans forward, elbows on knees, "to take the Princess for himself, and that is why our offers go unanswered." Sitting back, a dismissive fillip of his fingers. "Or so it's said."

"By some," says Agravante.

"Indeed," says Medardus.

"But not to me," says Agravante.

"Ah." Medardus pushes himself to his feet. "Tell me," he says, as Agravante leads him out of the little drawing room, "how fares the Count?"

"Grandfather?" says Agravante, pushing open the sliding wood-paneled door. "He sleeps." Beyond, a narrow hall, in the shadow of a long straight staircase.

"Oh," he says. "It's you." A glass of wine in his hand, something dark. "She isn't here."

"She will be, soon enough," says Marfisa, muddy boot up on the side porch step. "Jason, can I just, wait inside?" The collar of her sheepskin coat turned up, loose white hair stirred by a gust. He steps back, the door held open, his lips a sour purse between his mustache and his dull red beard.

Up the steps into a mud room, painted blue, forgotten coats and a tangle of umbrellas, a scooter, a chalkboard palimpsested with to-dos and shopping lists, "Ah ah," he's saying, pointing, thick-lensed glasses blanked out by the ceiling light, and she scrubs her boots against a mat before stepping up into a kitchen to the left there, ruddy stove and a steaming pot of something, stainless steel refrigerator hung about with coupons and note cards, a calendar, a math test festooned with red checks and gold stars, past a breakfast bar sloppily piled with newspapers and a box of soda cans, into a narrow sitting room, a low brown couch, a girl tucked at one end of it, under a red and yellow blanket, and pink headphones startling against her dark hair, watching something on the tablet on her lap. "Grace," says Jason, still in the kitchen, but she's already snatching off the headphones, a burst of chirpy music, as Marfisa steps about the low coffee table. "Hey, Mar," says the girl on the couch, and "Grace," says Jason again, "upstairs," as Marfisa sits herself at the other end. Something bulky's tucked in her coat, she leans over the table, pulling it out, a flat paper sack that spills out a sheaf of handbills, goldenrod pages splashed with black lines, a dancer rendered in calligraphy, and each marked by the green dot of an eye. "Oh, hey," says the girl, springing from under the blanket, all elbows and knees and clattering headphones, "is that," says Jason says "Grace!" again, but she's already scooped up a handbill, turning it over and back again, nothing else to it but little pull-tabs at the bottom, each printed with an elaborately arabesqued question mark. *"You're* putting these up?"

Marfisa shrugs. "You've seen them?"

"Yesterday, at Mississippi Pizza?" says Grace. "Did you hang 'em there?" Marfisa shrugs again. "The Mercury just had a thing about these things, like how nobody knows what they are, or who's, it's, it's you! You're doing it! Is it like, are you putting the band back together?"

"Grace," says Jason.

"What," snaps Grace, rolling her eyes away.

"Upstairs," he says, "now. Flashcards till dinner."

"Jason," she says, but she's kicking off the couch, scooping up the tablet, stomping around the table when back that way there's a clatter and a squeak of hinges from that side porch, "I'm home!" cries someone, and "Carol!" cries Grace, turning on a dime, scampering off past Jason, through the kitchen, "Guess who's here!"

Marfisa leans forward, slipping the handbills back in the sack, not looking up at Jason looking down at her.

And there's Carol, by the breakfast bar, setting a brown leather book bag on the carpet. Draped in a brown and yellow striped serape, her dark hair neatly short. "Mar," she says. "How are you."

"Well as I might," says Marfisa, looking up, pushing back a wave of white-gold hair. "What would you say to a chance to sing again, together?"

A hallway narrow, dim, dark doors to either side, silvery numerals set in the walls by each, slender 1s, a wiry 7, great round-bellied 6es, an 8, a 9. Iona in her yellow track suit leads the way around a corner, stops before the door at the end of the hall. 620, the numerals beside it. She plucks a white card from a pocket, holds it up before slipping it into the slot above the knob. "I miss keys," she says, as the lock chunks, a green light flicking on. "These may be better, but not in any way that matters." She opens the door. "Go on," she says.

Within brown walls and gold, bathed in daylight hazed by yellow curtains drawn over corner windows. A comfortable yellow chair, a reading table and a lamp, unlit. A wide bed draped in blue and brown and at the foot of it, sat tailor-fashion, Ysabel, in a white chemise, and soft white leg-warmers thickly rumpled. "Starling," she says, with a smile.

"My Queen," says the Starling, a shadow there by yellow Iona, black jeans, black sweatshirt, the hood of it up. "This is not our usual Thursday," she says, in not much more than a whisper.

"This isn't a Thursday," says Ysabel, nodding to Iona, who steps out, closing the door behind her. "This is a whole week-end, if you'd like."

"But I must dance, ma'am," says the Starling. "Today and tonight, at the club, and Saturday – "

"It has been cleared, with your, manager," says Ysabel. "You're free, till Monday."

"Free to be here, with you," says the Starling. And then, "If it's just to be the two of us?" Her words worn thin.

"If you'd like," says Ysabel. "Or, step back through that door. The Chariot will happily take you anywhere in the city you may wish to go."

The Starling reaches for the strap of the black gym bag slung from her shoulder. "I don't mind," she says, "being with you. I'll just go change," but "No," says Ysabel, quickly, "Starling, no. Put that down. Sit with me."

"My Queen," says the Starling. "I am not who I am, when I'm with you."

"Please," says Ysabel. "Sit."

The gym bag slumps to the speckled brown carpet. Stepping over, the Starling stands a moment before the foot of that bed, and Ysabel sat there, smiling up, but then she turns, the Starling, and finds the yellow chair behind her, and sits, a darkness in that weak light.

"I'm glad you came," says Ysabel.

"My Queen desired it," says the Starling.

"I thought," says Ysabel, looking away. "I'd thought today that I might dance for you. I have danced, you know. At a party. She said I was quite good."

"Of course," says the Starling.

"I settled on an outfit," says Ysabel, looking down at herself, "nothing too elaborate," and "Good," says the Starling, "but," says Ysabel, "I've been flummoxed by my lips. What should the color be?" A hand, lifted to her mouth, her hair, "White?" she says. "To go with the ensemble? Or would that be too much? Would a simple red be enough?"

"No one pays attention to the lipstick," says the Starling.

"You do," says Ysabel, quickly, even sharply, and then, "You take such care, with yours."

That hood shifts, down, to one side, dim light passing over her chin, the tip of her nose. "White's better for the stage," she says. "Too bold for such close quarters."

"A simple red it is."

"Your majesty is sad," says the Starling, then. "Why should that be?"

"I," says Ysabel, shoulders lifting, and her chin, a retort swelling but then suddenly pricked, deflating, and she looks away. "Affairs of the city," she says.

"Not the heart, then?" says the Starling. "Nor the hips?"

Ysabel untucks herself, a bare foot lowered to the carpet, and her hands on the edge of the bed. "Tell me," she says. "Do you know the smell, of blood?"

That shadow sits up. "I do, ma'am," says the Starling.

"She sleeps," Ysabel's saying. "Peacefully. Her wound is poulticed with a fief's portion. The bleeding's long since stopped, but," and she takes in a deep breath, shivering at the top of it, a sigh, "wherever I go in those rooms I still can *smell* it, that – *tang*, like an armor hot from the sun, and I," but the Starling's standing, stepping over, she kneels at the foot of the bed, reaches for a hand that Ysabel lifts away, "here I am," she says, "holed up in a hotel across town."

The Starling sits back on her heels. "Would you rather go to her?" but Ysabel's shaking her head, "The Mason," she says, "watches over her. She wants for nothing. I am," but then she stops, and the Starling catches her hand, draws it down, covers it with her own. Ysabel says, "My brother once told me," but then she stops again, blinking rapidly, looking down at the Starling looking up from under her black hood. "He was once a little boy," says Ysabel. "Did you know that?"

"The King," says the Starling, "yes, ma'am, of course. I remember those days."

"Not even a Prince, just an infant, he came to me, in the little garden, and took my hand, and asked me, sister, why are you crying?" Turning her hand in the Starling's hand, taking hold of it, squeezing. "And I said, because I do not wish to wed. But I am the Bride, I said, and one day a King will come, and I must take his hand. Whether I will or no, I must, but he," looking away, "he swore to me, then and there, most earnestly, that *he* would one day be the King, that I might never need take anyone's hand."

The Starling says, "And he did just that."

"My brother," says Ysabel, "the King, this," and her eyes close, the lashes of them shining, "city," she says, and her mouth closes about another, unsaid word, she swallows, and a lick at her lips. "Jo," she says.

"My Queen," says the Starling. "I will go, and change, and dance for you, to take your mind," but "No," says Ysabel, leaning forward, her hands on the Starling's shoulders, "do not change, do not dress, do not perform," lifting a hand, right to the very hem of that hood, but then pulled back, withdrawn. "I would see you just as you are," she says, her hands once more in her lap.

"But, my lady," says the Starling, and she reaches up to draw back that hood. "I am always as I am." Black hair uncurled, slicked back, clipped down to stubble along her temples, about those ears. Her cheeks, the line of that jaw. The nose. Those eyes, only a hazeled hint of green. Thin lips unpainted, up-turned, parting as Ysabel leans close to say, "And you are with me," and then a feathery kiss, tugging at the Starling's hands, lifting, the Starling who stands up before her, and her hands fall to the Starling's hips, rough black denim, the belt loops, her thumb, the wide leather belt, looking up, those green eyes. She yanks at the bulky black sweatshirt, "Get this off," she says, and the Starling lifts it up and off and tosses it aside. Bare now from the waist up, and the torso of her lean and long, and her long arms sinewy lowering, curling, Ysabel's darkly hands caught up against the smooth pale chest of her by those wide white hands, and the backs of them snarled with thick blue veins.

"Now would you have me go and change?" murmurs the Starling.

"But you are beautiful," says Ysabel, slipping her hands free, reaching for the tongue of the belt. The buckle jangles. "Majesty," says the Starling, "I am many things, but," and a gasp, at the kiss pressed there below her shadowed navel, as those black jeans loosen, lop, as Ysabel's fingers dip within to uncurl a palely slender cock, and a stroke for the lengthening lift of it, "oh," says the Starling, "my Queen, you needn't," as her hand cups Ysabel's face.

"But do you want me to," says Ysabel, and the Starling, shivering, nods. "The principles, I should think," says Ysabel, "are essentially the same?" And a lick of a kiss for the tip of it, there on her palm.

Pinned to the pole a mulching bark of posters, flyers, handbills, postcards, lapped and shingled one over another, rain-dimpled, sun-faded, twisted, torn, defaced, Thrash or Die, April Showers Burlesque, Snap! at the Holocene, Anodyne Presents, Missing Dog, Laughing Horse, Drum Circle Saturday Rain or Shine, Cinco de Mayo on the Waterfront, big black letters on an enormous sheet, Grupo Samurjay, Grupo Maravilla, Los Supremos de Los Hermanos Flores, Woodburn Rocks. As the bus pulls away she's pushing back her black hair looking up toward the top of that slithery bristling treeline, there where handfuls of old notices have been ripped away leaving crowded dozens of denuded staples, glinting, by a metal sign that says No Parking This Block, a relatively fresh sheet of goldenrod paper, mad black scribbles limning a dancer, a single eye of bright green ink. She reaches up, to the pull-tabs fluttering the bottom of it, each printed with only an elaborately arabesqued question mark. Her other hand holds fast a black leather knapsack slung from the shoulder of her slick black jacket. Her glasses with thick black frames. With a sudden yank she rips the handbill down.

A broad porch with four front doors set one right next to another, and she unlocks, slips through the third of them, and up an immediate steep staircase, narrow between dark walls, unlit, that yellow page bright in her hand. Around the wall at the top of the stairs through an open room a couch the floor before it piled with cardboard boxes into a long hall once painted white, some time ago, lit by daylight seeping in from somewhere else.

At the end of it a dark room, curtains drawn, and she closes the door behind her, a shadow in the shadows. Flump of the knapsack, dropped to the floor, creaking footstep, the thick click of a switch. Light blares from naked bulbs in the fixture in the middle of the ceiling, pink springs from the walls all whorled curlicues and faded bouquets, the bed there, skewed bedclothes striped dull brown and beige, and on the floor at the foot of it a great conical pile knee-high or more of gleaming golden dust.

She steps around it, jacket half-unzipped. A ridge of the pile has settled, slumped, dust trailed over the floor away from it, and the goldenrod poster drops, crumpled, from the hand she's lifting to her throat, to the bit of black lace tied there. Steps back, around the bed. She grabs a little hand broom from the nightstand. Kneels down by the pile. Begins to sweep up the goldstuff, careful with each thread and grain.

Eyelids a-twitch, lips parting just to say not even a whisper, maybe a number, counting, nine or ten, eleven, those lids blink open over mud-colored eyes that swivel, narrow, try to focus, a gleaming edge there, mirror-bright, shifting as she blinks the length of it flat and smooth and slender, somehow deep within it coiling whorls of light and dark chased up and down a shallow groove that cleanly stretches up and up to a glittering net there on the pillow, wiry strands that knot a cage about a simple hilt she jerks away, kicks back sitting up, "Shit," she says, as the sword's tangled in the sheets, teetering at the edge of the futon. She's bent over, thin white T-shirt, wine-red hair, rubbing her shin, a thin dark line of blood beading down by her ankle, "Shit," she says, again. Snatching the hilt she whips the blade free from the sheets, "this fucking," but it turns in her hand, a wrench and away it flies across the room to crack and a wibble it's stabbed the white wall there by the plain black scabbard, hung from a nail, and the painted skull-mask also, the mane of it stirred by that thrust. Jo blinks. "Okay," she says, to herself.

Without, the hallway's dark, the little lights strung along the ceiling unlit. The kitchen beyond is empty, only glancing daylight and shadows. Jo leans over to knock at the door across the hall, "Ysabel?" she says, turning the knob. The room within all yellow and white, gauzy curtains, big bed neatly made, the armoire shut, and nothing draped over the dressing screen in the corner. "Ysabel?" says Jo again, but something, she looks down. Something lightly, barely there, faintly wisps, like down, like ash, falling from, brushing her foot, past her knee, caught there in the hem of her T-shirt, falling from, she lifts it, peering down at her belly beneath, and the line that climbs it packed with an ashen crust and a last few spangles of gold and, she touches it crumbling, flaking away, the pink skin taut beneath.

Back against the jamb. Dropping the hem of the shirt her hand to her breast, and quick wincing shallow breaths. Lurching up across and over to the dresser, a bouquet of heavy-headed peonies pink and yellow, she grabs a small brass box and pries it open, frees a cigarette, and a ragged book of matches.

The hall, the back room, dark, the back door and out, outside, out in the grass, under the sky, sunlight and blue sky, and glowering clouds behind, white and blue and grey and blue and greenly black, swollen with the coming rain. Fitting the cigarette to her lips but even as she opens the matchbook she's falling to her knees in the lushly green, soft grass out to the parapets to either side, and she coughs up a sob, another, doubled over on her shaking shuddering self, her hand a fist to her chest.

The cigarette falls white to the grass before her. Feathers of grey-white ash caught about it, and sparks of gold.

A call behind her, muffled by walls and doors. Sitting up she catches, holds her breath. Swallows. A slam back there, distant, bump of a footfall, she wipes her eyes with the back of her hand and leans forward getting her feet under herself but the back door bangs open boot-thump someone shouting and she springs up turns her arm flung out the sword

The sword in her hand –

Her hand, her arm extended shoulder dropped her torso sidelong and her front foot planted, off leg leaned back straight and true, off hand slung back to balance the thrust that's ended sword-tip snagged in a corner of his unzipped shortwaisted jacket yanked up one side he's twisted, turned away from it, both arms flung up and alarm gently folding his face.

"Oh God," says Jo, dropping the blade, the ring of it soft on the grass.

"You're awake," says Luys, lowering his arms. Brushing the front of his soft brown jacket, his finger finding the hole punched there. "Your coat," says Jo, "I'm so, sorry," but "No sin espinas," he's saying, almost to himself, holding out a hand, "You are awake," he says, but she rushes past that hand to crash into him tumbling her arms about him there on the rooftop under the clouds, she's kissing his throat and then as he lowers his head she looks up to kiss his mouth, his mouth.

EYELIDS A-TWITCH – PLAYED AGAIN
HOW SHE MIGHT HEAR – "THE HELL WITH THE MILK"

EYELIDS TWITCHING over mud-colored eyes that widen, startled, but then she smiles, stretching under the comforter, lifting her bare arms up and out and sighing deeply, turning on her side. There's Ysabel sitting on the floor by the futon, chin on her folded hands. "You're awake," she whispers.

"Yup," says Jo, reaching out to stroke her cheek, leaning in for a kiss.

"He isn't," mutters Ysabel, against her lips.

Jo rolls back. There on the other pillow a cap of black hair turned away, a broad brown back, hillocks and bunches of muscle soft and still. "Poor tuckered boy," she says.

"This must be the first he's slept since you were struck."

"He stepped out, just for a minute, and that's when I woke up. He was, so apologetic," her hand laid gently on that great shoulder.

"Come," says Ysabel, getting to her feet, and Jo rolls back, looks up to her standing over the futon, a bulky fisherman's sweater over a loose white gown, a hand held out. "I'm," says Jo, the comforter clutched to her chest, "I need to," and Ysabel steps back, "If you must," she says, headed for the door. "But come."

Jo sits up. Drops the comforter. Luys doesn't stir. She's looking down, at the clean pink line drawn down her skin, and her fist pressed over her heart.

Up the thin white T-shirt from the floor and over her head she's standing, the light about uncertain, shrouded in the doubting rain outside. On the wall there by the door the painted skull-mask and its mane hung motionless, and slung from its leather strap the plain black scabbard, and snug within, her sword.

"Ysabel?" she says, hand on the knob of the door across the hall, under the little yellow lights, but a wrenching screech from the bathroom, the crash of water, the light bright within. Jo lets go of the knob.

Ysabel's already doffed her sweater. "Go on," she says, over the rushing water, wrestling with the gown she's tugging up over her head, letting it drop, and only a bit of mushroom-colored silk and ivory lace about her hips. "You," says Jo. "You want to. Turn, some owr." Sitting with some care on the edge of the tub, her hand, hovering uncertainly before her breast. "Look, if this is about replacing what you had to, I mean, for me, there's still, the surplus? From a couple weeks ago?" Ysabel's stepped away, toward the sink, the jagged oblong of mirror set in the wall above it. "Unless – Christ, Ysabel, how much did it take to sew me up?"

Ysabel's picked something up, a small blue balloon tied off at one end, swollen with liquid weight. She slops it into Jo's hand, and "This," says Jo, poking it with a finger, "this is a condom."

"I've been," says Ysabel, "with the Starling."

"Oh," says Jo.

"We must do right by her."

"Okay," says Jo, the condom in her hand. "But – "

"With all that we've been able to do, with the turning, with surpassing our mother and restoring the, the city," and she sighs. "We," she says, quietly, under the churn of falling water, "I, wronged Chrissie. I would not do that, to the Starling."

"Okay," says Jo.

"I would give this back to her as gold, and set her free."

"But," says Jo, "I mean, right now. You want to do this."

"Are you up for it?" says Ysabel. "Are you still in pain?"

Jo leans back, over the steaming tub, twisting the faucets squeak and groan. "Eh," she says, as the flow of water gurgles to a stop. "Mostly tired. Shaky, weak-as-a-kitten tired. Which, I mean, I just woke up, you know?" One last twist of the faucet.

"You were strong enough to bear the Mason's weight," says Ysabel, in the silence.

Jo sits up. "The fuck is that supposed to mean," she says.

"Show me," says Ysabel. "Your wound." Stepping close, taking Jo's hands in her own, and that small blue egg clutched between them. "Show me how it healed."

Jo steps back, lifts up the hem of her T-shirt, and Ysabel kneels then on the white tile before her, and strokes that faintly puckered seam, stitched up from crease of thigh and up across the belly. "Your skin," she says. "It remembers."

"This time," says Jo, letting the shirt fall, but Ysabel catches it, lifts it up again, "don't," says Jo, but "Show me," says Ysabel, and "I *did*," says Jo, stepping back, away, but Ysabel stands, tugs, "the rest of it," she's saying, "what did it do," and Jo catches Ysabel's hand, "hey" and "stop" and "don't" as she yanks and twists, "I must see it!" cries Ysabel, "What is over your heart!" and that little blue balloon squirts free to arc to fall to burst there on the floor.

"Shit," says Jo.

The deflated condom, darker now, the knot skewed by a rent, the milkily viscous splotch frothed desultorily with bubbles popping as it spills lazily into the grout between tiny hexagonal tiles.

"Shit," says Jo, again. "I'm, I'm sorry." Stepping back. "Can you, I mean, but you can just, get more. Right?" One small step, a shift of weight, back in. "Right?"

"Gallowglas," says Ysabel, quietly, still looking down at the mess. "Leave us."

"Gah," she says, shutting the big front door on a dripping susurrus, shaking herself from her sodden coat. "Wasn't it, like, seventy-five yesterday, or something?" Unwinding a gauzy stretch of scarf. There in the open collar of her white shirt a thicket of black ink, leaves and branches, a songbird's beak.

"Hey," says the big man coming up to her, there by the grand dark staircase, "we need to talk." An explosion rattles the windows, and "Aw, crap," she says, "is he playing that *again?*" Leaning past him, "Hey!" she yells, at the guy on the beanbag before the garish television screen. "Turn that down!"

"Ellen," says the big man before her, shawl-collared sweater over a T-shirt that says Dave's Dog Dave. "It's about," and he points up, at the ceiling, "him."

"Yeah?" The receding rat-a-tat of gunfire.

"How long, exactly, will he be staying?"

She shrugs. "Long as he needs, Dan."

"I don't mean to tell you your business – "

"So don't," she says, stepping up onto the stairs, but he moves in close, "None of the rest of us *know* him," he says. Another dulled whump of explosion. "My friend," says Ellen, "my room, my," she frowns, looks away, "business," she says, taking another step up.

"Ellen!" says Dan, starting up behind her. "Ellen, what the hell was he doing, wearing my shirt?"

She's still frowning, looking down, at her feet on the stairs, at him below. "You know what he was doing, Dan," she says, and up she goes.

A single glass vase, a singular stalk of artificial pussy willow, and bolted to the wall above a wooden sign, scrolled edges and gilt letters that say Rooms 201 – 209, Rooms 221 – 232, and frilly arrows pointing left and right. She scoops her phone out of her pink and orange parka, flips it open, thumbs to a text message that says only 213. Snaps it shut, heads off to the left, pink and orange and white yoga pants, red canvas Keds, her yellow hair loose about her shoulders.

Cream doors to either side down dull beige walls. She stops by the one that gilded says 213. Tips her head back and forth, shakes out her hands. Unzips her parka, and underneath a white sports bra, her midriff bare. She knocks.

The man who opens the door's a tangle of blond hair and a big blond beard, and his white blouse half undone. *"Not* here," he says, and then, relaxing, "Oh?" he says.

"Harper," says Jessie, her smile tight, her lips shellacked a glossy pink, her eyeshadow pink and a glittery silver frost.

"Rain," says the Harper. "Been a while."

"I went, last week, down to the club," she says, and "New management," he says, with a weary shake of his head. "I know!" says Jessie. "The Stirrup. Can you believe it?"

He steps back, opening the door. "Wouldn't give you a slot, would he."

"He told me where to find you," says Jessie, stepping in.

"You smell like a lollipop," says the Harper.

"Like it?" Past a bathroom and a closet the room opens up under bright ceiling lights, a low dresser, an exorbitant television set, a couple of queen-sized beds, one mounded with stacks of white boxes, and on each of them a photo of what's presumably inside, keyboards, music players, remotes, phones, and the other bed a rumpled mess of blankets and pillows piled, a plate of crumbs, an empty soda bottle clinked beside. The Harper in that white blouse and his bright green boxer briefs, his bare legs blondly furred. "Did I wake you?" says Jessie.

"You, who worked your way up under a Duke, a Queen," he says. "Must you now go trawling for humble knights?"

"Chilli," she says, "can we just do this?"

"Do what, my – ah, forgive me." He combs his fingers through his beard. "Away from court as I am, I've no idea of the current fashion in addressing former concubines."

"Rain," sighs Jessie, "is fine." Her hands in the pockets of her parka.

"Then, my rainy Rain," says the Harper, "a hundred other clubs await, and none of 'em run by me; go! Dance!" and a magnanimous sweep of his hand toward the door. "You have my blessing."

"But I need the money, now, is the thing."

"Now?" A scuff of laughter. "I'm not a bank."

"Why not?" A deep breath, pink-shaded eyes a-squint, "You forget, Chilli. I've seen the dukedom's books. I know what you bring in, running girls."

He folds his arms. "You want me taking care of you."

"I want you to give me two thousand dollars," says Jessie, and he guffaws. "Tonight," she says. "And then, this weekend, I work for you. Whatever I make, it's yours. Send someone with me," she says, as he rolls his eyes, "if the word of the Hawk's widow isn't enough. Come on, Chilli. If you have half an idea what you're doing, it's," and her pocketed hands open up the parka, "a sure thing," in a shrug of a display. "What do you think?"

He steps over to that enormous television, and the dresser beneath. Kneeling, his hands on the knobs of the bottommost drawer, "I think I got it covered," he says, and with a grunt he pulls it out.

Within a cloud of taffeta fluffed about a length of smoothly gleam like polished wood, and when it rustling moves Jessie gasps, there's an ankle, a foot, a thigh and hip, a figure jackknifed forehead to knee lifting up and up a leg unfolding elbow wrist a hand stretched up and out and Jessie's stepping back, a groan, a pop of wood, silver glitters, pushing rolling turning standing up, a woman in a cocktail dress of mirrored sequins, smiling woozily, blond hair in squiggled curls. "It's time?" she says, a breathy squeak.

"A couple hours yet, sweetling," says the Harper, still sat on the floor, holding up a pair of silver slingbacks. "I thought you might like a walk about the lobby, or the lot?" She's leaning back, lifting a foot, slipping on a shoe. "See what you turn up on your own." He holds up a white keycard. "Use the room next door."

"Nifty!" she says, turning to go, a couple inches taller now, and a strut in her step. "Hel*lo,*" she says, smiling brilliantly at Jessie.

"No more than an hour," calls the Harper after her. And then, "So," he says, still sitting on the floor, to Jessie, still staring. "Two thousand dollars, or," a nod at the door, swinging shut, "just the wear and tear. Which do you think?" The drawer, still open beside him, fluffs of taffeta drifting about the depression left crushed in that nest. The drawer above it, closed, the same width, the same height. "Well," she says. "You could," and she shudders, looking about, the bed mounded with boxes, the other bed messily rumpled, the Harper on the carpet in his bright green briefs. "Leo," she says, and a scowl creeps over his face, "Leo," she says again, "tolerated your pimping, but this – "

"The Duke is gone," snaps the Harper, "and desperate times call for measures desperate. If they will not let me fight for my honor," and a hand on the carpet now, and he's leaning on that hand, "I'll buy it back, instead."

"Buy it?" she says. "Even Bruno would, would balk at this. What were you *thinking,* what, that *Jo,* would have anything to do with this? With you, after she heard about this?"

He lifts that hand from the carpet, a fist now about the stubby golden hilt of the sword he swings around and up as he pulls himself to his feet. "And how would her grace come to hear about it?"

"What," she says, "what're you," as he steps close, as she steps back, brought up thump against the door, "kill me?"

"A step, a shift of weight," he says, the scalloped tip of his sword slipped between the pink and orange placket of her parka, there to crease the gore of her bra. "I won't just," she says, looking right into his pale blue eyes looking right back at her. "There'll be blood," she says.

He rocks back, sword-tip slipping free. "A tragedy's been writ, and played out many times, that ends with a woman's body in a dumpster. And here's you, dressed for the part! The police might not even bother to file a report."

"Oh, Chilli," she says. "Chilli, you damned fool. It's not the police." Shaking her head as he pulls back another step, and his sword with him. "It's Ysabel," she says. "The Queen. Falling on you, to avenge, her love." But her voice quavers as she says it, and the corners of her eyes do shine.

The demure brown of the door melts into the brickwork about it as he closes it, and locks it with a key on a lanyard about his neck. Works his head back and forth, shakes out his arms, couple-few jogging steps in place there on the sidewalk. Turning about to set off he yelps, leaps back, "Excuse me," says Marfisa, stood not an arm's length away, hands in the pockets of her sheepskin coat.

"You always," he says, hand to his chest, deep breaths, "sneak up, like that?" Taller than he seems at first, his dwindling hair clipped close.

"I wanted to let you know," she says. "Tomorrow night, we're hosting a," and then she stops, frowning, as away off a block or so a clattering crash, "a, ah," she says, "a sort of, gallery opening," and he shakes his head at that. "You make any noise," he says, "we call the cops." There's another rumble and crash. "The hell?" he says, looking away toward the corner.

"There'll be," she says, looking off away too, at the echoes, "live music," but he's waving a hand, "If there's *any* kind of a disturbance," he says, "I don't care if you own the block, we're calling the cops. Okay? Thanks for the warning and all, but – "

"This isn't," she says, sharply, and then a shake of her white-gold head. "I'm here to invite you," she says.

"Invite?"

"Both," she's saying, but a rapid thumping's started up, around that corner. "Excuse me," says Marfisa, turning, striding away, and "Both?" he says, frowning, but she leaps at a yelp from faintly off that way, around the corner, down the slope along the looming blue-grey bulk of the warehouse, that thumping getting louder, a roll of cyclone fencing leaned up against the wall there, and an old worn sign tipped on its side that says Wilson Properties, and someone's screaming. Marfisa kicks off the bundle of uprooted fenceposts ringing under her bootheel up to crouch on a shallow threshold jutted beneath the door cut into the wall there, three or four feet up, and her fist a clang of a knock, and still the banging, the screams, the roaring rush, like wings. Gripping either jamb, leaning back knee cocked and up the sole of her boot, boom, another, pop the door. She shoulders her way in.

Dust and litter and pieces of paper, a tarpaulin skirling, madly rips of wind through all that cavernous space, she throws up a hand, "Hey!" she hollers, "Anna?" and over by the green couch another shriek. She bulls her way through the flapping hurricane, "Gloria!" An answering "Mar!" from there in the corner.

"What happened!" she cries, stooping beside them, huddled under a stretched canvas borne up on Gloria's broad back.

"She didn't get the milk!" wails Anna, head on the floor, hands over her head.

"The fuck with the milk!" roars Gloria, and they're pelted with handfuls of nuts and bolts. Marfisa ducks as her bright white hair flies up, a turbulent cloud that skeins itself into knotted hanks and *"Damn* you!" she bellows, "You *dare!"* At that the litter all about them drops, and a thunderous silence. Marfisa stands there, panting, as Gloria heaves the canvas up and over, helps Anna to her feet. "Hempen!" cries a voice out there, and "Hampen!" another, over that way, and "Hempen! Hampen!" again, and again, Gloria peering wildly about, that first voice crying "Neither!" over the boxes tumbled, tarps askew, "Neither no more!" and "No more tread!" and "No more stampen!" echoing about, and "What the hell?" says Gloria.

"Shut up," says Marfisa.

"Hempen!" this voice, and "Neither no more!" that, and "No more tread nor stampen!"

"Where did they," says Gloria, and "Shut *up,"* says Marfisa, and "Hempen!" cry the voices now in unison. "Hampen! Neither no more tread nor stampen!"

"Shut up!" roars Marfisa. *"Now!"* Grabbing the handrail of the skeletal staircase, those voices a cacophony again, "Outlaw!" and "Bandit!" and "Exile!" echoing as she climbs, steps clanging, "Enough!" she hollers, up there on the walkway, a hand on a rung of the brief ladder bolted to the wall. "I will show you the law!" she calls down. "I will show you who's without it!" She starts climbing, up toward the makeshift floor of planks above.

"We are so fucked," Gloria's muttering, "we are so fucked, we are so fucked," and "Would you please *stop,"* snaps Anna.

"Hilda's here in an hour, in an *hour* to load in," says Gloria, kicking at the trash. "How the *fuck* are we gonna, how the fuck, how – "

"Perhaps," says Anna, still looking up, "next time, you will remember the milk."

"The *hell* with the *milk,*" says Gloria, and the light changes.

The light changes, softly golden falling now to warm away the shadows, gloss Gloria's black hair, to ruddy Anna's mousey brown and glint her glasses. Down there, out in that cavernous space, things move and shift as people stand, three four five of them stepping out, looking up, lit by a seeping summer twilight. Up on the walkway there's Marfisa, holding up a shallow wooden box, and the lid of it open, and the low bright sun within. *"Here!"* Her free hand scoops up sunlight, flings it out, clouds of buttery sparks that arc, that fall, an afternoon in fireworks. "Take it up!" The box snaps shut, light shifting as the brightness starts to melting settle. "Clean up your mess with it," she says, setting the box at her feet, "tread it, and stamp it," as she stands back up, a wooden bat now in her hand, "and what is left, is yours!" Clang the bat against the railing, as toppled boxes rustle upright, as tarpaulins loft into place, as those scraps of paper and canvas sullenly sweep themselves away, as Gloria's turning about, eyes wide, as Anna turns away, her hand to her mouth. Light congeals to wisps of glistening fog, streaming, swirling, and one more clang of the bat against the railing. "There is more," cries Marfisa, "where that came from!"

THE QUESTION MARK – LA DIFFÉRANCE
LAISSEZ-MAJESTÉ – WHAT SHE MIGHT ASK

THE QUESTION MARK's elaborately arabesqued, a boteh of curli-cued ink on the goldenrod tab he holds up, fingers glittering with silver rings, an ankh, a skull, and the nails of them a deep chipped purple. "But where's the question," he says, turning it over. Setting it down on the bedspread by the handbill, a slashed sketch of a dancer, and one green dotted eye. "The answer's pretty clear, tomorrow night, Southeast, Italian Public Market, Gardeners' and Ranchers', what does that even, you're, you're rubbing off, you rubbed off on me. Ranchers." He sighs. "Ranchers' what.

No. The question." He hasn't looked up yet, his long black hair hung about like curtains. "Where is it, when is it, no. Am I, no, no, not that, not am I going, if it was then the answer." His black T-shirt says Good-bye Robot Dinosaurs in round white letters. "The answer would be," he says, looking up. Past the handbill, spread out one atop another a pair of neon green tights, some stockings lacy black but also bright pink fishnets, a tumble of skirts, blue denim and calico patchwork, emerald crinolines, and propped in the corner where the bed's been jammed a fluffy orange sweater, a yellow slicker, an unlaced corset printed with faux-embroidered flowers. Set atop it all a pink meshback cap, the front and bill of it a hash of pink-and-black camouflage. "You could go," he says. "You should go. Go on," he says. "Go. Go."

Rustle and scrape of cardboard against the floor, stiff paper crinkling, he lays his head back down, dark hair lankly coiling among the cartons, the boxes, the denuded tubes of plastic wrap and tinfoil, jugs and tubs and bottles stood up about him. "Ten years," he says, "it wasn't ten. It was three." Holding up a hand above his face, turning it over, indistinct in the darkness. "The chair," he says. "The chair. Only fourteen, ever," lowering his hand, wiping his lips. "Made," he says. "Was it even three?" A key rattles in a lock, a knob turns, a latch disengaged, his hand slips to his throat where a shadow's suddenly slashed, dark enough in this light to be red. He sits up, hacking, gagging, "Luke," Jessie's saying, she's there, all white and pink and orange, "Luke, are you okay?" Leaning over him, there in the wide clean curl of aisle through all that sorted trash.

"Yeah?" he says, both hands tentatively pressed to his unblemished throat.

"What were you," she says, her hand on his shoulder, but then, leaning close, "you found it?"

"Maybe," he says. "It might be."

"It's so close, to the river," she says. "You said it was Eastside, but this, this is right here, so, close," looking out over the wide grid of garbage, stretched out to the floor-length curtains there along the wall, and her lips purse, quivering.

"I don't know for sure," he says, but her quiver's become a giggle she's trying to stuff back in with her hand to her mouth, "What," he says, "what's so funny?" and then, "Why are you dressed like that?" Her parka's fallen open about her white bra, her bared belly. "What have you gone and done," he says.

"What'd I do?" She pulls a manila-wrapped brick from her parka and tosses it into his lap. He starts back, hands up, "What," he says, and "Rent," she says, "a couple weeks' groceries, at least. That's what I did."

The crackle of the glossy clear tape wrapped about it. "Oh," he says.

"Pretty sure it's a one-time deal, though." Her smile's faded away. "So there's still work to be done."

"Well," he says, "it's like I told you," but then he stops. "It wasn't you, was it."

"What?"

"It was her. I told *her*, that maybe, when *you* got here, you'd have something for us."

"Her," says Jessie, flatly, frowning.

"You look so much alike," he says. "The makeup – you look, older." He sets the paper-wrapped brick aside. "Just about her age," he says. "Just *like* her. I should've known. You would try to pull something like this."

"Luke," she says, but he lurches forward, hand up, a finger before her lips, "No," he says. "Call me Lake."

"Lake," she says, still so flat, so seamless and so smooth.

"So I know it's you," he says.

"It's," she says, "me," and then, a hitch in her voice, "Lake," she says, "Luke, Lake," and a flutter of that laugh returning, uncertainly settling in a mouth that curls in a slowly sidelong smile. "Hi," she says. "Should've known I couldn't fool you," and a shake of her head, her yellow hair pale, the flash of glitter about her eyes. "How's," she says, and a deep breath, "my sister. How's," blink, "Jessie."

"Your sister," he says, and his smile's a gentle, softening thing. "She," he says, "came along, at just the moment I needed her, and she gives me," his hand, on her knee, "she gives me just what I need."

"So that's the difference," she says. "I don't, I don't give. I take."

"Take what," he says, but she pounces tackling toppling him, crumple of cardboard squeak and crackle of plastic crunch she's kissing him, he tears his mouth away, "The city – "

"Fuck it," she snarls, hand tangled in his hair, yanking his head back to bite at his neck, he yelps, he sighs, he whoops as she kisses him, his bearded chin, his mouth, his hands at her shoulders to haul at that parka, she sits up, shrugs it off, tosses it away, crash a taped-together tower of towel rolls and egg cartons, "Luke," she says, then "Lake, Lake" as he grunts *Lake,* " and "no," she says, "get out of there," slapping the fingers he's slipping into her pants.

"I should maybe give," he says, "if you're gonna take," and she laughs. Pushes herself up out of his grasp to loom over him, slinking her hips side to side, thumbs in the waistband of her pants tugging swaying curving over and down, and down, stooping to free this foot, that, in her flat red shoes. "Careful," he says, but standing athwart his hips she winds up and whips her pants away, and crash an enfilade of plastic bottles, "Shit," he says, sitting up, looking over, but she grabs the back of his head, fingers twining in his slickly heavy hair, wrenching him around, "Fuck it," she says, dragging his face to her belly, "go on," and she closes her eyes as he opens his mouth, as his hands grip her buttocks, sprawl over the glistering rays of red and yellow bursting from the burning heart on the small of her back. Shivering she rocks her hips, shaking out her yellow hair, but he twists his head free, she slaps at him, lets out a seething groan as he pulls away, looks up, his beard askew. "Hey," he says, and "Dammit!" she snaps, and "She never told me, what do I call you? What's your name?"

And panting through a churlish snarl, her pink and silvered eyes unsqueezing, opening, she unbites a glossy lip that gathers itself for a disappointed moue, or maybe a smile, she looks away, opens her mouth to say a word she doesn't speak, shakes it away with a cough of a laugh, "Lake," she says.

"Tell me," he says.

"Okay," she says. Looks back down to him, and all trace of anything gone from her expression. "How about," she says. "Call me Jezebel."

That skinny, tattooed arm doesn't move from across the nondescript door, "Not backstage," he's saying, "no, you're not."

"I have something to give her," says Ysabel. Up on the little stage behind her a woman in a silvery bikini's hanging upside-down from the pole, spinning up and up and a bellowing chorus huffs over skittering handclaps, let them all talk and discuss what they want, until she hikes up her carouselling legs to plant her lucite soles on the ceiling, I'm gonna do what I like, 'cause I'm free! The audience is roaring, stomping, cheering. "Do you know who I am?" says Ysabel, leaning in, looking up.

"Not a dancer," he says, applauding with everyone else, letting out a piercing whistle. Ysabel in her long white cardigan watches him a moment, looks to the door, then reaches out, opens it, steps through.

A narrow hall, quite dark, the crowd's roar and the music thumping, dulled, "Hey!" the guy with the skinny, tattooed arms, crashing in after her, grabbing at her, "You can't come *back* here!"

She says, "Let. Go."

A moment there, the two of them, Ysabel's white-draped arm in his fist dark with ink that sweeps and curls around the wrist, the forearm, twining waves like teeth, like dark flames, like the shadows of the bones beneath. "You can't come back here!" he says, again, finally. Still holding her arm. "We can't have any disruptions!" From off down the end of the hall behind her a derisive snort, there's women in the doorway there, lace and plaid and spangled sequins. "Let go," says Ysabel, again. The light about them shifts, the door behind him's opening, "Look, lady," he's saying, "I gotta," but "What is this," says someone else, gruffly, behind him.

"Sorry, boss," says the guy with the tattooed arms, shifting his grip on Ysabel's arm, reaching back for the knob to the nondescript door. "I'll have her out in a – "

"Your people need educating, Stirrup," says Ysabel.

That man back there steps out, not especially tall, his face fleshy, his red hair dark in the shadows flopping from a widow's peak. "Majesty," he says, and the tattooed guy whips his head around at that, "Oh you have got to be," he says, but the man with the widow's peak doesn't blink, or shrug, "Jeffers," he says, "collect your things. Get on home."

"Aw, boss," says the tattooed guy, "you can't fire me. Not over – "

"Fire you?" says the Stirrup. "Heavens forfend. We'll call, as soon as the schedule opens up again."

Jeffers flings Ysabel's arm away, and a stomp, *"Bitch,"* he snarls.

"Jeffers," says the Stirrup.

"Fuck," says Jeffers, and then the nondescript door swings open on the applause of the crowd, the thumping banging music, the dancer in her silvery bikini, mopping her forehead, and a wad of money in her hand, "Gina!" she yells, bumping into Jeffers, "You're up!" Turning about, looking about at them all crowded together in the dark and narrow hall, "Shto zhe?" she says, as a woman in a short kilt and a tight white blouse squeezes past Ysabel, the sweaty dancer, glares pointedly at Jeffers in the doorway, and the faltering applause behind him.

"Jeffers," says the Stirrup again. "If you're not working, you shouldn't be backstage. Go on, Gina. The rest of you, get out there, work the room. You too, Rocky."

"Dammit, Gav," says the silvery, sweaty dancer, as the woman in the kilt heads out into the club. "I just got done!"

"So I'm sure half the room wants to buy you a drink. Go on."

A bustle of confusion, then, as they all make way around each other in the narrow hall, heading out one by one past Jeffers watching each of them pass by, into the press of the crowd, the whoops, the sneering jangle of guitars, with their government grants, someone's crooning, and my IQ, they brought me down to size, academia blues, the door swings shut, thump and dull, and only the two of them left, Ysabel all in white, and the Stirrup in his leather vest, his red tie half undone.

"I'll only be a moment," she says.

He says, "As your majesty requires."

The dressing room is small, the walls of it black, and lamps ablaze about a row of mirrors. At the end there against the far wall, sitting on a short red velvet chaise, the Starling, her black hair short, swept up in front, a tidy stack of curls, and her eyes a startling green. She's smiling, lips painted lushly gold to match the gold streaked up her arms and daubed about her nipples, and a thick stripe of it down her belly, gleaming against her darkly olived skin.

"I see you're dressed," says Ysabel.

"I'm never not, my Queen."

"The," says Ysabel, her hand comes up, a cup in the air, "breasts, are maybe a little small?"

"Better for dancing," says the Starling.

"Is *that* my problem."

"I'm certain it's but mine." The Starling turns back to her reflection, framed in a clutter of stickers and notes. "I hadn't thought to see you again so soon."

"Is it only of a Thursday I'm to see you?"

"Your majesty may see me as you wish," says the Starling, tilting her chin, lifting a tiny brush to her brow. "I quite enjoyed our weekend."

"I've something for you," says Ysabel. In her hand a plastic baggie, stuffed with golden dust.

"But," says the Starling. "I've already, I received – I already have, so much."

"This," says Ysabel, "is, yours," setting the baggie on the counter beneath the mirror. "None other's. No liege to portion it out, no knight to cede it to you. Yours alone."

"You," says the Starling. Setting down the brush. Reaching out to stroke the plastic with a gold-nailed finger. "You took. This." Looking up to Ysabel. "All this came from what you took?"

"It happens, at times," says Ysabel, looking away. "Such an abundance, at the first few turnings." Her smile is tight. "This is your banner, Starling. Freedom. Beholden no more, not to anyone."

"But when it's gone?"

"Why, then," says Ysabel, "I'll, turn you more. Whatever you need. Whenever it's needed. Think of it, Starling," she says, stepping close. "You wouldn't have to dance."

"I like to dance," says the Starling, reaching down to her gym bag.

"But you wouldn't *need* to," says Ysabel. "Dance whenever you want, wherever you like."

"I like it here," says the Starling, pulling handfuls of darkly filmy stuff from the bag, winding it about. "I like an audience."

"Then stay, if you like. But because you like, and not because you must."

She's draping the smokey stuff about her arms, arranging the fall of it over her lap, "I have never known of a gift so rich," she says, looking up, and those green, green eyes. "I can't possibly accept."

"Of course you can. How could you not?"

She lifts the stuff up along her shoulders, lays it over her breast. "Time passes, my Queen," she says. "Time was, my liege was the Dagger, when he was Sidney, and he came to me often, in this very room. But time passed, and my allegiance was passed to the Harper, and a better knight, by far, than the Dagger: he came to me only the once." Her gold-streaked fingers find ties there by her collarbone, and begin neatly to knot them. "And now, but these last two weeks, I am the Stirrup's," she says. "And he is as much better a liege than the Harper, as the Harper was the Dagger." She stands then, the Starling, and the shadowy stuff drapes about her, a gown that falls from her shoulders to brush her feet. "Or as your Duchess, my Queen, is, than the Duke was, before her." The gold paint beneath it glimmers as she takes a step toward Ysabel, limning curls of breast and belly, shining brightly where the gown parts there about the pout between her thighs. "Time passes," she says, "and with it, fancies pass. What would become of me, my

Queen, if I took up this banner," a touch, for that golden baggie, "only to find when it had gone that yours had, too?"

"I would, never," says Ysabel, and then, "as I told you. Whatever you need, whenever – "

"My lady, I," says the Starling, loudly, "would always," more quietly, and a deep breath, "kiss your mouth, when it is turned to me, and pillow your head on my lap, but can you as you stand there answer true, that you do love me?"

"That," says Ysabel, so quietly, so carefully, "is not a question for you to ask."

"And this," says the Starling, pushing the baggie away along the countertop, "is not a gift for me to take."

She slips past Ysabel then, her loose gown trailing, a wake of smoke, settling a-float about her as she stops in the doorway, looking back to Ysabel unmoved, a hand on the counter by the baggie. "I'm on after Gina," says the Starling.

Ysabel nods. "Of course." Taped there to one side of the mirror, larger than the notes about it, a sheet of goldenrod, a handbill, printed with a single scribble of a dancer, and one green-inked dot of an eye. "Your hair," says Ysabel.

"Ma'am?" says the Starling.

Ysabel turns away from the mirror, all in white, her long white cardigan, her blouse of lawn, and her white jeans. "It should be long," says Ysabel. "I'd see myself as once I was, and will be again."

That gown shifting, flowing as she lifts her hands to her hair, those black curls pushed back and back, and down, and down, pushed back and out and up, and tugged, and let to fall then, an artful tangle of curls about her shoulders. "As your majesty wishes," says the Starling.

The explosion rattles the speakers, and the sound of the door opening's lost in the din, but he sees her there, turns his head to look, then the rest of him in that bulky grey hoodie that says RCTID. He heads off across the low room columned and beamed in dark wood to where she's mounting the steps of a grand dark staircase, "Hey," he says, rat-a-tat of gunfire behind him, "hey, Ellen. Ellen!" and she stops up there, a hand on the railing, looking back, tattoos like a lace of ink about the collar of her sweater. "What the hell was he doing, wearing my shirt?"

"What?" says Ellen, after a moment.

"When he showed up pounding on the door last," and he stops suddenly, blinking, "last," he says, again. Another explosion from the television set, and the guy on the beanbag yelps. "Last week?"

"What are you, what are you saying, Dan," she says. "What the hell."

"I almost got it" yells the guy on the beanbag, "God damn, man, God damn!"

"Why is he, why was he wearing my shirt, Ellen?" says Dan, but he's looking away, off at the television screen.

"You want your shirt?" says Ellen. "I'll go get your fucking shirt." And up she goes, and up another flight, down a narrow hall beside the stairwell, fingers rap-tapping impatiently on the banister, at the end of the hall a dark doorway, and the next flight up, she steps in, steps up, stops, "Wait," she says, "who – how?"

A shadow's sitting on the steps there, swathed in pearly grey, a woman looking up, her dark hair all in tiny screws swept back, pinned up, her big eyes sleepy. Reaching up for the railing bolted to the wall, pulling herself to her feet with a grimace of effort, waiting a moment, pointedly, for Ellen to step back, to clear the doorway.

"Who are you," says Ellen.

The woman in pearly grey looks back, clutching a bundle of black cloth. "You're welcome," she says, her voice at once both rich and hoarse.

"What?" says Ellen, but that woman's walking away down the hall, along the stairwell, her heavy gait listing to one side. Ellen looks away, up the next staircase, heads up them quickly, up under the very peak of the house. At the end of a cramped hall a door, cut at an angle to fit the slope of the roof, that she opens on a blue room brightly lit, and the only shadows on the clean and gleaming depthless cloudless color of it from the pallet out in the middle, pillowed in white, and the big man stood up naked before it, brown hair in eaves about his head, and the great ruddy beard brushing his brown-furred chest. "Phil," says Ellen. "Phil, what the fuck. Phil."

"Ellen," he says. "I needed time. I am so sorry, but I needed time, and it is so quiet here."

"Who was that," she's saying, stepping into the room, past the aloha shirt left by itself on the floor, "the woman, what's, what the hell," and "It's all right," he says, "It's all right. I did it. I did it."

"Did what?" says Ellen.

"I quit," says Philip Keightlinger.

BOOM & BANG & RATTLE & CRASH

BOOMING BANGING RATTLING CRASH she yanks down the overhead door to close with a clang, driving home the bolt with a shove, snapping shut a conspicuously shiny padlock. Up out of the dying echoes a slender guitar-line picks its way to a shambling arpeggio, out in the cavernous space all around the low walls of the narrow stall about her, lined with framed, postcard-sized drawings of street corners, storefronts, houses hatched in ink with fiendish care. She stumps her way through confetti and bobbing drifting balloons, blue and white and silvery mylar, skirts of her high-waisted gown bobbing and belling, her long black hair threaded with silvery ribbons and gathered in two great hanks.

Next stall over, the door's already closed, an enormous photo hung over it, all silvery black bared legs and buttocks bunched and ropey with muscle in a plié, filmy skirt lifted high by a rusted hook at the end of a heavy chain. A woman stands before it, black jeans, a slick black jacket, turning at the rustle of skirts, "Oh," she says, "are you closing? Is it time to go?"

"We'll probably shut the lights off, in a bit?" says Gloria Monday, and off behind her that guitar's settled into a swaying round of strums and plucks, climbing and falling and back again. "But we're not yet kicking anybody out."

"Okay," says the woman all in black, and then, "but, do you need any help? Sweeping up, or anything?"

"What, this?" says Gloria, kicking a blue balloon away. "Nah, we got this, thanks." She bustles out into the open cavernous warehouse, her skirts dragging glitter across the concrete floor, shining in pools of harsh light from the fluorescent bars racked here and there, the ceiling far above, lost in shadow. The raised stage at the end of the space ablaze in spotlights shining on the canvases displayed there, leaned up against the worktable, a couple of stools, the nubbled green couch, each other, the splashing dancing figure leaping twirling spinning from one to the next. "Actually," the woman all in black is saying, hurrying after, "I was, curious? Some of the galleries, are, ah, empty," she looks back, at the stalls that brightly lit march one by one down the long high walls, "I was wondering, who do I talk to? About, about maybe showing something? Sometime?"

"What?" says Gloria, and then, "Oh! Oh, yeah, no, that would be me. Any of us, really." There's a kid sitting on the edge of the stage, curled about a big-bellied acoustic guitar, and Marfisa sits beside him in her sheepskin coat, swaying back and forth, a hand up to hold onto Carol's hand, Carol stood behind them in a gown of greens and purpled blues, her eyes closed as she harmonizes with Marfisa, no woman, no cry; no woman no cry. "What do you do?" says Gloria. "What is it you want to show?"

"Photography," says the woman all in black. "Stuff I shoot, that I see, when I'm walking around the city. I'm trying to play with color?" She holds out her hand. "Petra," she says.

"Well hello, Petra," says Gloria, taking it. "Gloria Monday. Bring 'em by sometime, there's pretty much always somebody here. Because that's what this is all about, you know? Working for each other? Those of us who know?"

As Petra heads off to climb up on the stage, gazing up at all those canvases, Thorpe saunters up, that trim grey snap-brim hat on her head, and silver buttons winking down the front of her long black coat. "Was that an actual sale?" she says.

"Somebody else to show," says Gloria.

"You had, what, a dozen people here tonight? And how many of them want to hang here, too?"

"It was damn well more than a dozen," says Gloria. "You better not put that crap in your column."

"I'll write whatever I damn well please," says Thorpe, with a smirk. Pointing. "But hey, looks like Hilda's maybe chatting up another new exhibitor for you."

Over by the big main overhead door, half-raised, an older woman's sitting in a wheelchair, a big brown scaley purse in her lap, speaking with a wave of her hand and a shake of her head to a tall woman in a pale blue ski jacket, her blond hair chin-length, severely straight. A spotlight shining on the wall behind them lights up a giant curl of a question mark, painted with elaborate fronds and spots over a much older sign, faded, worn, that once said Eastside Italian Market & Grocery. "Hello," says Gloria, heading over, "Ms. Donovan, hey."

"Gloria," says the woman in the wheelchair.

"Are *you* in charge here?" says the woman in the ski jacket.

"Sure," says Gloria. "Why not. Gloria Monday."

"Stephanie," says the woman in the ski jacket. "Stef, Stef's fine. So, so this. This is all about her, right?" She holds up a crumpled goldenrod handbill. "You're doing, something? About her?"

Gloria nods. "She asked you? So you know?"

"Know?" says Stef, says Ettie. "Know what? It's my sister. She has my sister, and I don't, I don't know. What to do. At all."

Suppose we have a mold that produces faulty bricks, and the flaw in single bricks can be modeled with the words *tends to crumble on the left;* if we then build a wall with these flawed bricks, that wall may or may not be flawed; also, the flaw may or may not be modelable with the words *tends to crumble on the left;* but even if it is, it is still not the *same* flaw as the flaw in any given brick; or the flaw in the mold. Keeping all these states clear and unentailed, despite the accidental redundancies of the language we can use to talk about them with, is the way out of most antinomies.

—Ashima Slade

NO. 28

" – Hands of an Angry – "

THOSE WICKED TALONS – AN AVERAGE FOOT – HARSH LIGHT ON STEEL
IT SHOULD BE LOOKED AT – PERQUISITES – "JUST HOPE IT'S ENOUGH"
WHAT ONE DOES – SIX OF THEM – MILO, DUB, JONESY & GOOSE
A CAPITAL SUGGESTION – NO SHOUT, NO CRY, NOT A WORD
WHO HE IS – 20 OR 30 FLOORS BELOW – "IS THAT A GOOD THING?"
SOMETHING NICE – DUST & DARKNESS – AT THIS HOUR
A HANDFUL OF CITY – 20 FUCKING MINUTES
THE JINGLE OF THE BELL

THOSE WICKED TALONS blackly shining relax their hold, lift, stretch, and he leans back, hands up in abeyance, as they re-settle about the wooden dowel, rasp and clack, two curled about the front of it, and two behind. The insistent buzz of the electric lantern by his knee. He leans in close again. Wrapped about the knobbled yellow-grey leg above those talons a bit of olive canvas, and with great care he pinches it, the gleam of a brass snap wink-ing in the shadow of his thumb. His other hand up to gently steady the feathered bulk looming above. Somewhere up there a shining eye, blinking, unconcerned, and the black curl of a wicked beak.

Setting the buzzing lantern on a rickety table of old grey boards, a crumpled leather notebook there beside it. That olive strap in his rough-edged palm, and pinned to it a dented metal capsule of that same olive color, absurdly small against his finger-tips. Head tipped back and a breath sucked through his teeth, he sets to carefully unscrewing the wee top of it.

A bit of yellow ribbon just a couple inches long, unrolled, weighted down at either end with pennies, and tiny symbols scratched in brown ink down the length of it. He's squinting at them, writing pairs of characters on a leaf of the notebook, IS, LK, CI, GF, FO. Off in the shadows back behind him cages creak, a rattle of chains, claw-clacks and the fluffs of settling wings. He's circling letters, sketching arrows and lines from this one to that, then lifts the pen, looks up, peers down at the floor there by his booted foot. He's returning to the page when it happens again, the faint knock somewhere below, but then there's the crash of breaking glass.

"Come on, Moody," says the man in the chocolate-chip camouflage anorak. "You honestly telling me you can't pick that rinky-dink thing?"

"I can open any damn lock made by man," says the man in his worn surplus jacket, kneeling there in the doorway, and "Shyeah," snorts the old man wrapped in a filthy thermal blanket, leaning back against the storefront's unlit window. Moody spares him a glance from under the brim of his black leather hat, and then looking up, over his shoulder, to the man in the anorak, "So maybe this one wasn't made by man," he says.

A scuff as the man in the anorak steps in, swings a hand, knocking that black hat off Moody's head. Moody surges to his feet, but then the fourth of them, the kid leaned up against the fender of the old pickup truck, says "Maybe there's a doorbell," a bit loud, and then, when they're all looking at him, "since we're being so polite."

"Kid's got a point," says Moody, with a chuckle. "Told you he was sharp." He scoops up his hat from the sidewalk. "Jasper, if you would?" to the old man, who pulls a crowbar out from under his blanket and slaps it in Moody's hand, and then quickly steps away from the window.

"Oh *hell* no," says the man in the anorak, and Moody favors him with a sharp smile, "No?" he says, an elaborate shrug, crowbar a-dangle. "You *are* the Executive Officer."

"Just get us inside," mutters the man in the anorak.

That first shivering crack hits under the arcing painted letters that say George's, just above where it says Shoes Repaired. Crouching Moody slings the crowbar back for another blow, crash right through a broken ringing jagged guillotine blades of it dropping smash, whooping, "Hah!" belts Moody, jabbing with the crowbar to knock out this dangling shard or that.

"Let's go, let's go," says the xo, waving them on.

The dark front room within, glass crunching underfoot, Jasper's blanket snagging on the window frame, "Shit," he's saying, yanking, more glass crashing. Moody's stepped right up to the counter, dropping the crowbar, clang, he's hauling himself up and over. The xo, over by the front door, squinting at the lock, and the fourth of them, the kid in his grimy sweatshirt, hood of it up about his head, he's just standing there, in the middle of it all. "The fuck," says Moody, picking something up, dropping it in the shadows. "Shoes."

"It's a shoe shop," says the xo, his hand held over the knob of that door.

Jasper's picked up the crowbar, he's leaning over the counter, trying to jam an end of it into the drawer of the cash register, blanket slipping from a shoulder. "And none of 'em pairs," Moody's saying, "buncha goddamn orphan garbage shoes," hurling off another, and another, shoving a pile of them all at thunderous once. "Hey," says Jasper, looking up, "there's maybe five bucks in here."

"So *take* it!" snaps the xo. "Nobody ever said he was any *good* at this shit. Fuck it up! Break shit! Come on!"

The kid's squatting over a battered, lop-tongued work boot, that's landed on the broken glass before him. The toe of it scuffed and sharply creased, drily flakes of pale brown leather, emptied eyelets, the heel of it almost pulled away entirely, there, where brightly worn nail-tips glint in the streetlight. It jumps as the cash register topples to the floor, a ringing, jangling crump, and the kid tugs the hood of his grimy sweatshirt down about and over his face. One dark hand comes down, reaching out, has almost taken hold of the boot, when the lights come on.

"Shit!" yelps the xo. Jasper's already legging it, crunch of glass and his blanket lofting as he leaps out the broken window. At the back of the store a dark hand flat against the wall by the light switch, a beaded curtain parting about the bulk of him in a T-shirt yellowed with old sweat, bare head darkly bald above a circle of crisp white curls, and a dark electric lantern in his other hand, and he's glaring, ferociously, at the kid, who's jerked to his feet, whose hood's fallen away, who's staring, wide-eyed, back.

"Moody, dammit!" the xo's yelling.

Moody kicking shoes away's swooped right up next to the bald man and a gleaming silver length of knife held right up under the bald man's chin. "Moody," the xo's saying, "come on, man, this is outside the scope," but Moody's shaking his head, "No," he's saying, "no, he knows just what the hell this is, and what happens if I," and then a lurch, as the bald man steps close, as Moody jerks back, that knife-tip pressed again against the loose skin of his throat. The beaded curtain clattering to a close. "I wonder," says Moody, low and quick, "do you know, already, which bone it'd be? Something from the foot, I bet. All those metatarsals and cuneiformes, seven thousand fucking bones in the average foot, and does it ever bother you? Walking around on a goddamn shattered Ming vase, sewn up in a leather sack?" But the bald man steps up again, and stepping back Moody stumbles over the tumbled shoes and falls back thump to his butt on the floor. Shaking out his arm the bald man lets something drop through his fingers, a flare of light a rod of metal whump the head of it hitting the floor, a crown of flanges nicked and gleaming hefted looping tightly swung about and up to catch Moody right in the grunting belly doubled bang back against the counter and down, coughing, groaning, the knife still in his useless hand.

"Oh, hell," says the xo.

"Get," says the bald man, lifting his mace, *"out,"* pointing it at them all, "of my. *House!"*

HARSH LIGHT ON STEEL – IT SHOULD BE LOOKED AT PERQUISITES – "JUST HOPE IT'S ENOUGH" – WHAT ONE DOES

HARSH LIGHT ON STEEL, his blade the length of it broadening from pointed tip to palm-width ricasso, there about the flatly cruciform hilt held lightly in both his gauntleted hands, hers a shorter, slender thing, needle-whip and wick about in her one hand netted by the glittering silver guard of wiry strands, thrust and thrust and slipping slice, and each assault brushed off by the merest twitch of his long impassive blade, that here and there tips forward, a simple riposte, wildly batted back, and every steely strike another clang wrung from some antique carillon.

She steps back, away, around, feet bare on polished concrete. Restlessly jagged slashes at the air. Her free hand in a fingerless cycling glove held up against her chest, her plain black T-shirt, her black tights, her wine-red hair. His bootheels click a stately tempo toward her, his blade held up and straight ahead, the flat of it parallel to the floor, tip of it squarely toward her eyes, one of his elbows crooked up at an angle, tight white tank and brown jeans and his cap of black hair shining. Jo springs right, jogs left her shoulder dipping, swing and up a thrust he bats aside with a slight twist, his sword still high, still flat, still stepping toward her, click and click as she scrambles back. "You let me control the field," says Luys.

Another long step back and right again a straight hard thrust scraped off the tip of his blade turned to parry, to slice past, to poke at her. A leap back, her back toward the big white suv parked near the wall, her blade up at an angle, guarded, "Like a goddamn tank," she says.

"At least make me work for it," he says, "my lady," click and click, blade up, elbow cocked.

She bounces up on her toes arm high a cut over the top at his head and he yanks his grip up to catch with the forte of his blade but she pivots her cut licking under, a thrust that shoulders dropped he dodges just head back arm snapped straight, a riposte, and "Shit!" yelps Jo skidding a stumble-step back her shaking sword swept around and up, and trembling up between them. His blade still high and flat, his elbow cocked, eyes dark over his impassive mouth.

"Does it hurt?" he says.

"Yes!" she snaps, blade dipping, jerked back up again.

He nods. He claps his hands together, stepping close, tugging one of his big cuffed gauntlets free to slap to the floor. He reaches out to take her arm as her blade-tip dips, drops, and his bare hand peels back the sleeve of her T-shirt, careful of the darkly trickling blood. She hisses. "It doesn't look so bad," he says. "Come, let's sit you down." Leading her back toward the suv, and the low-slung car beside it, reddish-brown, with a black stripe along the side. She lays her sword on the roof of the car, and he helps her up to sit on the hood. He's let the other gauntlet fall, and in his hand a plastic baggie, an eggshell's worth of golden dust. "You'll need to take that off, my lady," he says. "Your shirt."

"Just," she's saying, fingers curled to tug finickily at the sodden sleeve, hissing, "work this up," and "It's too high, on your shoulder," he says. "Take it off. I can help," and "No," she says, "no," a hand up, "give me a sec," sitting forward, wriggling the T-shirt up and over, "shit," she says, T-shirt clutched to her chest, blood seeping darkly down her arm. "Go on," she says.

He leans close, a scoop of shining dust in his fingers that he presses to the hole in her shoulder. She sighs, a long and settling breath that leaves her slumped on the hood of the car. He lifts his hand, gently brushing a wisp of something from the smooth unblemished skin. The blood already drying.

"My lady," says Luys. "Let me see it."

She lifts her head, and something of a glare.

"My lady, please."

"You stuck me, just so you'd have an excuse – "

"No," he says, quickly. And then, "Please," but she's already dropping the shirt to the floor as she sits up straight, and running up her belly from the waistband of her tights a faintly puckered seam, pinkly pale and up, up to where, canted in the middle of her breast, an ovoid pucker maybe about the size of a thumb, sheened with a faintly rainbowed slick against the rippled skin about it. "Well?" she says. "What do you think? Any bigger? Smaller? Well?"

He straightens, steps back. "You should have that looked at," he says.

"Yeah?" says Jo. "You got somebody in mind? A quicksmoke specialist? Good with parasitic shit from before the dawn of time? Give me their number, I'm all ears."

"You must take care," he says, turning away.

"We were just banging around with live steel!" she says. "You stuck me," her hand on the tacky blood on her arm, "less than a foot away from that thing? That's taking care?"

He looks back with a small, tight smile. "My blade goes where I will it, lady. We were in no danger."

She grabs his hand, yanks at him, "So you *did* stick me on purpose!" she says.

He takes her hand. "An opponent," he says, "will make a cut like that to weaken you, and distract you with the pain of it."

"I've been cut before," she says, wryly sour. "Once or twice. I know what it feels like."

"But this time," he says, her shoulders in his big hands, "you raised your blade up after, ready for what I'd do next."

"Yeah, I did, didn't I," slipping from wry to sly. "And that over-under feint!" His elbow, in her gloved palm. "I *finally* got you with that."

"I could not parry it, but I did dodge it," he says, as she tugs him closer.

"You had to stick me to get me to back off," she says, her hand on his hip.

"That you did, my lady," he says, just before she kisses him.

"Your grace should not be skulking in a basement," he says, stooping to reach for his jeans.

"Well I wouldn't call this *skulking,*" she says, sprawled naked on the hood of the car.

"You should have a hall," he says, stepping in one foot, the other, "for sparring, for revels, and for holding court," tugging them up about his hips.

"I don't know," she says. Tearing open the velcro on one of her gloves, "It's actually," she says, resettling it, closing it up again, "I like it down here. It's, oddly, it's private. In kind of its own way. We can do the Apportionment stuff down here. And Bruno doesn't mind me using his office, when I need it. And we can, spar here, whenever," sitting up with a stretch and a flash of that pearly scar, and a very contented grin. He's tucking in his white tank top. "Any other revels, I mean, really, that's more Ysabel's department?"

"You've revels of your own to keep," he says, buttoning up his fly. "With your men."

"I wish," she says, sitting up abruptly, scowling, "you wouldn't," feet on the bumper, and then the polished concrete, "you know," she says, grabbing her T-shirt from the floor, "they aren't *mine,* Leo's the one who – "

"You are the Hawk, now," says Luys. "You're the Huntsman. You are Southeast, lady, and her men are yours."

She closes her eyes at that, she opens her mouth. She bites her bottom lip, and a deep breath in, "I," she says, "am starving." Picking up her tights. "What about some breakfast. Jam, up the street." Stepping into her underwear, pulling them up. "Waffles," she says. "I'm buying."

Stepping out of the shower stall, drying his armpits, crotch and thighs, his buttocks and the small of his back, up to ruffle what's left of his hair, and then wrapping and tucking the white towel about his hips. Opening the medicine cabinet, reaching past a blue plastic pillbox for the shaving bowl, the safety razor in its plastic case, when he stops. Closes the cabinet up again. Eyes his reflection, fingertips rasping the stubble that darkens his cheeks.

He slips through the white curtain drawn about the toilet, the sink, the glass-walled shower, out into the white-painted loft, and the clerestory high above, shining down the length of it. At the far end by the bed in all that light there's Pyrocles, pulling on a blue shimmer of jacket over his dazzling white shirt, "Oh," says Becker, resettling the towel about himself, tucked below his bit of belly sucked in, "you're not working the garage today?"

"Unrest, between North, and Northeast;" says Pyrocles, as Becker pads toward him through all that falling light, "my lord has called for his gentlemen."

"Unrest?"

"Bluster only, and again, but we are to meet on it, nonetheless." Pyrocles smiles, and those pewter weights at the ends of his mustaches sway as he shakes his head. "I'm only in danger of boredom."

"You can't, you can't wear that suit," says Becker, frowning. "I had it out, I was gonna make a run to the dry cleaner's on my way," but Pyrocles holds up a hand, "It's all right," he says. "It's all taken care of."

"Huh," says Becker, stopped there at the foot of the bed.

"Yours, too." Pyrocles smooths lapels, checks his cuffs.

"My clothes?"

"All taken care of," says Pyrocles. "Something of a perquisite." Stepping close, a hand to Becker's shoulder. "And there's breakfast on the counter, if you'd like," and he leans close for a kiss that Becker distractedly returns. And then he's off, pale shoes clacking, past the kitchen nook, the white curtain about the bathroom, to the loft's door, that mighty thing of beams and planks.

"Breakfast?" says Becker, frowning, to himself.

A thready stream of smoke pulled up and up till there, up there, just out of reach, a sudden curl, a spill of it seeped in a light-struck haze that can't relieve the gloom. "Why come to me?" says the man leaned back against the desk, his vest and trousers of an understated plaid.

"Well," says Jo, laid out across the sofa, pillow under her head against the slatted wooden arm, "I figure, if he's got a phone, you've got the number." Lowering the cigarette to her lips for a long slow crackling drag.

"Your grace," and he takes in a hiss of a breath, weighing words. "It's not so simple." On the desk by his hand a tumbler of ice and brown liquor. "To go to such trouble yourself, in such a matter? It would seem," and he picks up the glass. "Unseemly," he says, and sips.

"A phone call," says Jo. "So, what. I should have Luys do it?"

"Much the same? He does speak with your voice."

"Neat trick, that," mutters Jo. And then, hiking up to look over the arm of the couch at him, "Are you seriously telling me, Bruno, that one of the, ah, my guys, my knights, I can't just, call him? On the phone? When I need to tear him a new one?"

"There are protocols, ma'am," he says, with a shrug. "People will talk."

"I *want* people to talk about this."

"You want them to tell the right story," says Bruno, and another sip. "If there were a function, you were both to attend? So that the arrangement of the meeting doesn't overshadow the reason for it." Setting the glass back down. "The Samani would've been ideal."

"Yeah, or, I could go down to the Devil's Corner, maybe buy a drink, bump into him coming out of his office except, wait a minute," she sits up, "oh, yeah – we fired his sorry ass."

"We had our reasons," he says, brushing down the front of his vest. "Perhaps," looking away, "if your grace were to unfold a few more particulars?"

Jo stubs out the cigarette on a flower-rimmed saucer scarred with old burns. "I need to find out exactly what he got up to, with the dancers, while he was running the club."

Ice clinks as he lifts the glass again. "The usual, I suppose." And then, as she looks at him, "Your grace is hardly naïve."

"I'm not a chump, either."

"Of course not."

"The Starling," says Jo, still giving him that look, and his glass halfway to his lips, "told the Queen," and that glass droops, "that the Harper came to her, once."

"Came to her?" Up the glass again, and this time he drains it. "What does that mean?"

"That's what I'm gonna ask him." Standing abruptly, "Tell you what," she says, checking the time on the screen of her phone, tucking it away in the pocket of her jacket. "Her majesty dropped this in my lap, so I'm gonna drop it in yours." Heading past him, toward the door there, lit with a stippled pane of glass that says, reversed, Bruno's. "Tell him whatever you want, he's won the fucking lottery, I don't care, just get the Harper in a room with me by, let's say, tomorrow night?" She opens the door. "Call me when you've got something."

He's looking down, hands on the edge of his desk, and a judicious nod. "Of course, your grace."

On the screen a photo, Jo and Ysabel, cheek to cheek, black curls trapped lopping over the upturned collar of Ysabel's white coat, and she's almost smiling sidelong at Jo, her short hair brown and tufted up every which way, her eyes crinkled, smiling wide, directly into the camera, out of the phone she's holding in her hand. The clock over their heads says 15:48. Tuesday, April 10. She thumbs it, and the screen goes black, and she tucks the phone away again in the pocket of her butter-colored jacket. An elbow on the standing table that runs the length of the sunstruck store window, and a big red cup of cappuccino, the leafily patterned foam of it already disturbed. "Hey," says somebody behind her, but gently. "How're you doing."

He's tall, the man behind her, not looking at her but back, over his shoulder, at the rest of the sparsely dim coffee shop, the long wood tables, the quietly hulking coffee roaster in the corner there, and sacks of beans about it. He wears a beige fleece pullover, the half-zip open over a blue-striped shirt, and his dark hair's slicked back, and he looks down at the heavy gold watch about his wrist before offering up a wryly tossed-off smile.

"David Kerr," says Jo. "Boy Wizard. How's it hanging."

"I really," he says, stepping close, "really," elbows on the table, "don't like that word. Wizard. Makes it all sound like some kind of roleplaying game which, I assure you, it is not."

"So what would you," says Jo, "I mean, what even is it that you do?"

"What the hell does anybody do? I try to stay comfortable. But you," he sucks his teeth, "you make me uncomfortable."

"It's a gift," says Jo, lifting her cup. "But now I'm wondering why you came over to say hi." A sip, that he watches intently, following the cup back down to the tabletop. "How is it," he says.

"The cut?" she says. "It's healing. It's healed, pretty much. The quicksmoke?" and Kerr looks up, sharply, at that, looks about, over his shoulder, "It's, fine, it's, you know," she says, "it's not leaking, or whatever. Nothing's, gone, nobody's gone."

"Due respect, Duchess," says Kerr, "but you'd never know. Whatever this shit touches, it's not just gone. It's like it never was. You could've walked into that warehouse with a whole crew backing you up and if they caught even the slightest wisp of that stuff," he looks down at his watch, and up again at her, "it never happened like that. They're gone, they never were, and you always went in there alone, and nobody'd ever be able to tell the difference because they. Never. Existed," his knuckles knocking the table lightly with each word, "and no one could ever know otherwise."

"Except me," says Jo.

"Well," says Kerr, after a blink or two. "You're the shell. It's not gonna eat you until it's done, and ready to – "

"No," says Jo. "I mean," and she lifts a hand, wrapped about in a fingerless glove, reaching for something, a moment, "when," she says, "he dumped the stuff, the wizard, on the bridge – "

"Leir," says Kerr.

"Leir," says Jo. "It took him. And Ysabel. Before it," her gloved hand, closing in a fist, "got stuck, in me," that fist, over her heart, "and for a while, it was like that, like she'd never been. Nobody knew. Except me." He's looking her in the eye now, and he's frowning. "But she went somewhere," says Jo. "They both did. A place, and, I, went there. And we came back. And everything went back to how it'd been."

"So that's why you're so complacent?" says Kerr.

"I'm scared out of my fucking mind," says Jo.

"Okay," says Kerr. "Okay." Leaning down, shoulders hunched. "Have you seen Keightlinger, since then?"

"Who, the one with the beard?" Kerr nods, and Jo shakes her head, "No," she says, "no, thank God. What the hell did you do to him?"

"Something stupid," says Kerr. "Just hope it's enough." Straightening, stepping back from the table, from her, "Look, here, let me," he says, "in the, ah, just in case. If you, find you need help. Just, say my name. I'll, I'll be there."

He's turning to leave, but "David," says Jo, and he looks back, "Well," he's saying, "actually," but "Thank you," says Jo. "For shutting him down, but also. For being there. To call Luys. Because I, I never think, about backup."

"Yeah," says Kerr, stepping away. "Well."

Grunt and grunt and a guttural *"shit"* and a bubbling squeak of a giggle. Reflections flicker in the glassy dead expanse of a television screen in time with the shrilling jounce of bedsprings. There's two in the room, queen-sized, heads against the wall there, and the one over closest to the window with its curtains drawn has piled atop it boxes small and glossy black, printed with swirls of stylized smoke in different neon inks, chartreuse and orange, leafy green, magenta, teal, and scattered among them plastic clamshells that seal up ranks of little amber vials, Red Tobacco, say the haphazardly pasted labels, Matcha Menthol, Grand Reserve Gold, Seabreeze Mojito. The grunting's a groan now, low, drawn-out, the giggling a squealing breathless round of "Yes!" and "Yes!" and "Yes!" Chilli's flat on his back on the other bed, eyes grimaced shut and blond hair dank with sweat, one hand knotted in the sheets and one hand up, holding tight the arm of the woman astride his hips, her blond hair bouncing in squiggled curls, a babydoll nightie slipping from her shoulders, "Shit," he's saying, "shit," and "Oh, yes!" she cries, wide-eyed, but she stops with a jerk looking over her shoulder half-turning hunched up on a knee, "Hel*lo,*" she says, smiling brilliantly. "Shit!" roars Chilli, kicking scrambling back up the head of the bed, the weight of her gone, she's gone, "Shit!" he's yelling, swiping at the air, at the filmy stocking drifting in languid folds to his lap, the glossy page torn from some magazine he bats way, "shit," he's saying, "shit," sitting up, bent over, panting.

"Harper," says the man at the foot of the bed, a sword in his hand.

And screeching something incoherent Chilli naked uncoils to his feet the room lit up in a burst his hands above his head bring down the heavy blade of his short sword with a "hup" from the man who ducks to one side, his own blade coming up from under, piercing Chilli's chest. He lets go, steps aside as Chilli blunders past to crash into the dresser, and the enormous television wobbles. He turns about, that blade stuck clean through, the elegantly simple hilt of it maybe a half a foot out from a wetly yellow wound, and rising and falling with his ragged breath. "Disarmed yourself," he spits, but that man's pulling a handkerchief from a pocket of his understated plaid vest, and as he steps close Chilli drops his sword from fumbling hands, reaches for that shuddering hilt, but that man's pressed a hand to Chilli's chest, the handkerchief wrapped about the base of the blade, and Chilli's hands slackly fall as shove and a grating scrape the blade's yanked free. Chilli slumps back against the dresser, and the television wobbles again. "You're pathetic," says the man, wiping his hands on the handkerchief.

"Bruno, come on," says Chilli, panting. A hand up to that wound. "You didn't have to do her like that."

"You didn't have to do it at all."

"What am I supposed to do?" Chilli pushes past him into the space between the beds, falling to his knees. "Ever since that *bitch* – "

"*Harper,*" says Bruno, quiet and cold. "Every time you've been given some responsibility, an opportunity, you've pissed it away. Come to find out today that the Duchess was right to demand your ouster from the club;" and, as Chilli looks back with a jerk of his head, cheeks angrily mottled over his yellow beard, "you only went and diddled the Starling," says Bruno.

"That's," sputters Chilli, turning about on his knees, "that's what you do!" The wound oozing stuff like honey, spun the color of milk, unheeded down his ribs to plop on his bare thigh. "It comes with the office!" In his hand that torn page, crumpled, thin and glossy.

"Not the Queen's favorite, you blasted fool," says Bruno. "Now. Here is what you will do." His narrow shoes step close. "The Duchess has taken to sparring in the mornings, with the Mason. At the residence. You will go there, tomorrow, around ten of the clock. You will throw yourself at her feet, and you will take what you have coming." Those shoes step back, away, leaving behind a faint imprint in the ecru carpet. A door opens, closes. Chilli's spreading flat that page, smoothing the crinkles, a sumptuous boudoir, a woman, knee up on an overstuffed footstool, a brief nightgown, squiggles of blond hair, the words about her, lace-up corset-style, daring, dramatic, adjustable straps, matching panty, imported nylon.

SIX OF THEM – MILO, DUB, JONESY *&* GOOSE
A CAPITAL SUGGESTION – NO SHOUT, NO CRY, NOT A WORD
WHO HE IS

SIX OF THEM in the room, and him, slouched in the doorway, hands tucked in the pockets of his grimy sweatshirt. "That you spend time," the withered old man is saying. "And I pay money, for that time." A low, incantatory growl, a bellows-rasp of breath between each phrase. "That I buy, your time. How. How can I, buy time." Sunlight glowers behind heavy ruddy drapes drawn over a picture window. "Hand me some time. Put, in my hands, an hour of your day." He's sitting in the big brown leather recliner, leaning forward, soft shoulders warmly wrapped in an old quilt. "See what good," he says, and under the quilt a hand jolts, and another wheeze of breath, "it does. Either of us. Some of you." One of those eyes squinted shut by a snarl of wrinkles, radiating from that sunken nose. "Think it's your effort. Not time, but labor. Work. That if you try. That if you strive. That's what I want. That's what I pay for. But I don't. *Pay* you. What I want. What I want."

The xo's there, across the room, frowning around the stiffness of his scar, and three men on the couch, the two of them at either end upright, elbows on knees, the one in a soft plaid workshirt, a steaming cup in his hand, the other in a brown and blue down vest, empty hands scraped rawly red about the knuckles, and between the two of them Jasper, leaning forward, elbows on his knees, grizzled head in his hands. "We, built," the co's saying, from his recliner, "the finest country, the shining city, our green Jerusalem. We did that." One hand springs from the quilt, clawed in a fist. *"No* one paid us. No one. Paid. Us." There in the corner, Moody sips his coffee, watching the xo, who's watching the co. "We built it. It was ours. Until the others came, and *took* it."

At that, he pulls his hood up, ducks back around the doorway, away down the unlit hall. Back in the sunlight, Moody smiles over his cup. "Even so," the co's saying, that hand of his drooping, "even so. With every advantage, in their grasp. The, laws. The rules. Politicians. Media. The, the," and he pulls that hand of his back under the quilt. "The rules," he says. "The rules."

"The banks, Dad," says the xo.

"The banks!" spits the co, trembling, coughing. "The banks," he says, again. "Even with, all this. Even with *every* advantage. Our country, in their hands. Smirking. *Laughing,* at *us*. Even with all that, it's, still, there. We can." That hand, working its way free of the quilt again. "Pay you?" he snarls. "Your time? Your labor? You take it, you take it and you go out, and you *take* it! You build it up again! *Rip City!*" That hand of his, upthrust, a fist, and after a moment over on the couch a raw-knuckled fist is lifted, and the hand that isn't holding a cup is wadded, help up, and a nudge for Jasper between them, who shakes his grizzled head. "Go and *get it!*"

A general exodus from the couch, bump and stumble and one or the other of them helping Jasper to his feet, the xo waving them over, rubbing his chin. Moody's looking across the room to that unlit hall beyond, but the co's reaching up out of the quilt about him, grabbing at Moody's sleeve, "Where is everyone?" he says, his voice gone querulously thin. "What happened?"

"It was a fine speech," says Moody, plucking at that hand. "Very inspirational." The xo's jabbing a finger, making a point, looking from the one man to the other, as Jasper opens the front door, a blare of daylight. "Where is everyone?" the co says, again. "The jefes? Where is everybody?"

"They're here," says the xo.

"Where was Milo?" says the co. "Where was Double-Dee?"

"Dub was, Dub was here, Dad," says the xo, kneeling by the recliner. "Dub just left," but the co's saying, "Where's Jonesy? Where's," and "Jones," says the xo, taking his hand, "Dad, who are you," as the co says, "where's the Goose?"

"Dad," says the xo. "Goose died, like, two years ago. Two and a half years ago."

Down the unlit hallway, out onto an awkward corner landing, Moody cup in hand is careful of the plywood ramp laid over the steps down into the kitchen. Through that, down another short flight, a door at the end half-open, and sunlight falling from a small window set high in the wall. "Hey. Shizzt," says Moody, setting his nearly empty cup down by a limp black duffel. "Hey," he says again, nudging open a louvered door, a small closet, and there's Christian in his grimy sweatshirt, sitting on the floor of it, beneath a mirror pasted over with stickers. "Weren't thinking of sneaking out, were you?" says Moody, and Christian hunches further under his hood. "You always was smart," says Moody, hunkering down in the doorway. "You know this is your best play, you know this is where it's going, and we all know you're gonna help us get there. So I know you know better than to go walking out in the middle of a sermon, yeah?" His thin lips curl companionably as he tries to peer under the margins of that hood. "He ain't talking about you. You get that, right? You get he's talking about the Russians and the Vietnamese, he's talking about the fucking Mexicans, for Christ's sake, he ain't talking about you. You're smart. You're good – "

Christian's hand catches Moody's, that was reaching for that hood, "The fuck you know," he growls.

Moody yanks his hand free, standing, stepping back, and his reflection in the mirror lapped by the peeling stickers on the glass, black and grey and here and there some red, and the letters on them white and silver and black, shaped like blades, like bolts of lightning, like letters from old Bibles, the Boreads, they say, and Sheriff Pain, Article xviii, Hróðvitnir. "I know you're pathetic," he says. "You're weak. You never had the guts to go join a gang of your own. Your mother never had to get around to kicking you out of the house. This is all you got now, and I'm the only one here who's got your back. So. Get up off that skinny black butt and get upstairs and make yourself useful, that's what I know."

He opens the glass door off the sidewalk, steps inside, a wall of mailboxes, six of them, dully stainless steel and sharp corners and scuffed plastic over handwritten box numbers, and around the corner a short flight of steps up to a landing at the base of a steep staircase, and Jo, sat there, her sword in its scabbard across her lap. "My lady," says Luys, all in browns. "I had not meant to make you wait."

"No," says Jo, "no, you're fine," and sighing, looks up the switchback stairs. "Chrissie's here."

"What, again?" says Luys.

"Still," says Jo, getting to her feet, her red Chuck Taylors, her baggy black jeans, her tight black T-shirt. "Let's get to it." Swinging her sheathed sword up to rest on her shoulder. "Unless you'd rather skip straight to waffles?"

"As my lady wishes," says Luys.

"One of these days," says Jo, headed for the door, "I'm gonna get you to admit you want something I don't wish."

Outside, and the wall of the building rising white and green beside them, and across the street the dark empty windows stretching up, plastered with signs, Now Leasing, The 20 on Hawthorne, Units Available. Jo up under the latticed fire escape is saying "So how do you know?" Looking back over her shoulder. "What gives it away? Nine times out of ten I can't get you to bite on a feint. What's my, whaddaya call it. Tell."

"I couldn't say," says Luys, with a bit of a smile.

"You couldn't, you couldn't say. That's some good teaching, there."

A shrug of those broad shoulders. "I merely know, my lady, when you mean to strike, and when you do not."

"Okay, so, wait, so yesterday," says Jo, planting herself, reaching out to stop him, "did I really get you with the over-under? Or did you just not take the block so you could set up the cut?"

"My lady," says Luys, nodding at something past her, behind her. Jo turns. Down at the corner there's a garage door, set at an angle, a couple of recycling bins blue and olive in a slice of shade. Beside them a boy's leaned back against the wall, brown bomber jacket and his brown hair in a wilting pompadour, an arm crooked over the hand-truck there beside him, loaded with a large plastic tub, a couple of pink boxes, a pallet of water bottles and atop it all a tray of paper cups of coffee. "The hell?" says Jo. "Sweetloaf? What is all this?"

"Hey, boss," says the boy, pushing off the wall, "sorry, yeah, I don't have a fucking key for the big door, and I didn't want to try to wrestle this fucking thing through that fucking little door there, and," but Jo's talking over him, "No," she's saying, "no, Sweetloaf," and then, to Luys, as he stoops to unlock the garage door, "Is this your idea?"

"It's none of mine," says Luys, hauling up the door.

"So there's towels," Sweetloaf's saying, with a kick for the plastic tub at the bottom of the stack, "for sweat, I guess, or if you spill any fucking water," a slap for the plastic-wrapped pallet of plastic bottles, "lots of water, and hey, Mason, I know you like those fucking Staccato donuts, but my connect's with Voodoo, and these are fucking good, fucking primo," and Jo says, "Hey, Sweetloaf," but he's saying, "and of course coffee, can't fucking go without coffee," and "Sweetloaf!" says Jo. "Why. Did you bring. All of this. Here?"

"Shrieve said to," says Sweetloaf.

"But there's just the two of us," says Luys, frowning, as Jo says, "Bruno," and then "shit," and then she's headed off under the door, down the ramp within, "My lady?" says Luys, and "There fucking better be more than just the two of you," mutters Sweetloaf, but there's a clangor echoing down there, steel on steel, and Luys starts running after Jo, "Gallowglas!" he's yelling, "Gallowglas approaches!"

"Can I," says Sweetloaf, "a little fucking help, here? Hello?" Lifting the tray of coffee cups with one hand, grunting as with the other he leans the handtruck back and wrestles it around, trundling toward the ramp, "No, seriously," he's muttering, "fucking thanks."

Around and down the precipitous curl of the ramp the garage opens and stretches out under the length of the building above, fluorescent lights, polished concrete, the suv and that low-slung, muscular sedan. Milling about there, half of a dozen turning, lifting fists and weapons in salute, a burble of "Your grace" and "Duchess" and "My lady!" as Jo stalks toward them, "Okay, so, ah," she's saying, stepping into the midst of them all, "gentlemen, ah, folks," a blink, "I'm guessing the Shrieve told you guys to show up?"

"And a capital suggestion!" cries a man in a blue-and-white striped sailor's vest, whipping his rapier back and forth, and "A dash of finality to spice our play," says a shirtless man, the sleeves of his orange coveralls tied about his waist, and a short wide-bladed sword tipped to his forehead.

"Yeah," says Jo, still looking about.

"Is there some concern, Duchess?" says the burly woman looming over them all, her long hair dyed a watery green, and a barbed harpoon leaned up against her shoulder.

"What?" says Jo. "No, Peg, no, we're all," and then, raising her voice, "there's refreshments, everybody, avail yourselves, and I guess there's towels? I dunno. Sweetloaf!" Beckoning him over, and he sets down the coffees as the knights, murmuring, laughing, approach, and hustles through them, followed closely by Luys. "Get upstairs," she says, quick and low in his ear, "and make certain Iona is with the Queen."

"What?" he says, too loud, alarmed. "Boss, why?"

"Just do it."

"What is it, lady?" says Luys, as low and close, as Sweetloaf hustles off.

"Chilli isn't here," she says. "But he will be. I need to know who in this room is with him."

"He's much on the outs, since the robbery," says Luys. "The Cater and his cronies," he's nodding at the man in the sailor's vest, raising a paper cup of coffee to them, "have made their disdain clear."

"Well somebody's up to something," says Jo. "Watch my back."

"My lady," says Luys, with a disarming chuckle, "no one would dare."

"Hey, Astolfo!" Jo's calling, and she lifts her sheathed sword from her shoulder. "You want to show me how those shield-thingies work?"

"Is her grace quite certain she doesn't mean Medoro?" says the man in grey sweats, sipping carefully from the cup in his buck-lered fist, and "No," says Jo, "my grace does not, Medoro's the Axle," and the man in the grimy T-shirt lifts an exaggerated hand to his breast, "and you're a fucker, fucking with me. C'mon, let's go!" One hand on the hilt of her sword, the other about the beaten metal throat of the scabbard of it, as amidst laughter and claps and backslaps he steps out into the open space, tightening the straps on his bucklers, the one on his left hand edged with a sharp polished rim, the one on his right bossed with spikes. "But wait," says Jo, and he stops. "You got the ante?"

"Ante, ma'am?" he says.

"A pinch of owr," says Jo, "or thereabouts, in case you poke me. Can't have a Duke bleeding all over the floor now, can we?"

"But, your grace, that's hardly fair," says the Cater, stepping up with a broad smile to temper his stern judgment. "We pay to cut you, but if we are cut instead – we're done for!"

"Don't think of it like that, Connie," says Jo, turning to him. "Think, instead, that I will lose a knight – which will hurt me quite a lot, seeing as how I'm so fond of all of you." Luys stifles a chuckle at that, as the rest of them turn from one to another, uncertain, hesitant. "So, what, too spicy, folks?" says Jo, drawing her sword. "Come on! Try to get as close as you can without touching – anybody trust their skills enough to play?"

Luys says, "Perhaps, my lady," but the Cater laughs, a sharply cornered bark, "Mason!" he cries. "You've had her every morning of the week! Let the rest of us have our," but he stops, brought up short by the tip of Jo's sword, lifted in a sweeping arc to wind up there, an inch perhaps from the end of his nose. The chuckles of the knights behind him turn to whistles, cheers, a booming "Ha!" from Peg. His smile widens, his eyes flash, his rapier whips up whick-whack knocking her blade aside and a hasty riposte that sends her leaping back. She stoops to lay her scabbard on the floor, then steps back again, to the side, leading them both out into the open space. "So tell me," she says, "Connie, how long you been fencing?"

"Why," he says, twisting to follow her prowling steps to one side, then the other, "I cannot remember a day I've not held this hilt in my hand."

"Well I've only been at it about, six months," but already Jo's lunging, high over his blade twitched around and under as he lifts to parry the feint and whooping he skips back, slashing the air with his rapier. "So go easy on me," she says, settling into en garde with a grin.

"Of course, your grace," says the Cater.

Whick and snick thin scrapes and snap his needled blade against her slender steel, the wisht of his rope-soled espadrilles on polished concrete, the squeak of her red Chucks. He's pressing her, quick thrusts that lick at her quartered parries, rapid enough she doesn't have time to riposte, retort, reply, a constant clash till back she steps and back again and he doesn't take what she cedes. He lowers his blade, guardedly, and a quirk of a smile. "Six months?" he says.

She shrugs.

"Who's next, then," says Luys, "to try her grace's hand," but even so the Cater's blade-tip loops high and then a lazy fillip about Jo's frantic parry to hitch back under and plunge home, canted at an oddly hilt-high angle, and gasps about as breaths are caught. Jo looks down the length of his steel to that needlepoint plucking a belt loop of her jeans.

"The distracted hunter," says the Cater, stepping back, "might be caught in her own snares," and lifts his rapier in a salute.

Jo coughs up a wry chuckle, "Okay," she says, "okay," whipping her sword back, shaking out her wrist, "point taken." And the eruption of laughter at that, which she joins, after a moment. "So who is next?" she yells out over the ruckus, "who's gonna give me another pointer?" But even as she bites her lip looking off away at that with a wince they're all turning about, squeak and rustle in the fallen hush, and the clink and faintly chime of weapons gripped more tightly, swung about and hefted, at the ready. No shout, no cry, not a word is spoken, but there he is on the rise of the ramp where it swings out of the garage, one foot forward, lower than the other, and his hip slung back, his empty hands at his sides, his white blouse open at the throat, laces loose a-dangle below his big blond beard, his matted tangle of blond hair, Chillicoathe, the Harper.

"Shit," says Jo, under her breath.

"Hey," says Chilli.

That growl's coming from the throat of green-haired Peg. "You," snarls the Cater, there behind Jo.

"Me!" cries Chilli. "Am I not a knight yet in this company, and as game to play as any of you?" and his empty hands spread wide.

"Oh, it's not play we'd be about," says the Cater, and he points his rapier past Jo, up at the Harper, and Jo's looking from the Cater, to the Harper, to Luys. "Who would you have as your second?" the Cater's saying. "Oh, but who here would stand as second for the likes of you?"

"My *second?*" cries Chilli, with an overabundance of alarm, as the Cater steps past Jo, his sword still up and out, "You've disgraced this company," he's saying, "your weakness, your cowardice insulted our Duke, our Queen, and I would see it proved upon your body," and a slash, at the air, and another, "as I should've done, weeks ago!"

"Well if that's the matter," says Chilli, looking about at the rest of them, "what say you, friends? Anyone willing to help the Cater out? To step up, and stand as my second? Gerlin? Medoro? Peg Greentooth? Anyone?"

The man in the orange coveralls steps out of the little crowd of them, his short wide sword held low, and a nod as he heads past the Cater to the Harper's side, "Pwyll!" says someone, Astolfo with his bucklers, but the man in the coveralls holds up his free hand, "I do this office," he says, "that we might see this done," and Chilli welcomes him with a sweep of his arm, "You're welcome none-theless," he says, still smiling. "Hold up," says Jo.

"Who then will stand for me?" cries the Cater with a show-man's flourish, and even as Astolfo, and Medoro, as Gerlin and Peg lift up their hands and weapons, "Hold it," says Jo, louder, "that's enough, you guys, okay," stepping out between the two of them, "enough!" Standing before the Cater now, her free hand out toward Chilli. "We are *not* having a fucking rumble today, is that clear?"

"Your grace," says the Cater, "I must insist," but "My lady," says Chilli, "his insult will not be borne," and "it is an affront to" and "demand satisfaction" and "stood there like" and "blade and body" and "sneering clown" and "here and now" and "Enough!" bellows Luys, off to the side of all of them. "Gentlemen. The Duchess has spoken."

"Your grace will not deny me satisfaction, surely," says Chilli, waving him off.

"You and me, in a minute, Harper, we're gonna have words. Until then, shut the fuck up."

"My lady is yet young," the Cater says, "and as new to the reins as the hilt. Let me shoulder this odious chore – I'll cut him down, to the size he would affect!" But even as he's lifting his rapier again, Jo's glaring at him over the shoulder of her sword-arm, "I hunt for the King," she says. "Don't you ever even *think* you can tell me what I have or haven't done," and he's blinking, his face goes blank, "Ma'am," he says, "I would never," but his sword's still pointed past her, at Chilli, who lifts his hands and claps them together in a flash of light, to draw out between them his short and heavy sword, one hand now wrapped about the golden-pommeled hilt, the other stroking the flat of the blade of it down to its tip and off. "My lady, please," he says, and his shaggy yellow head is slowly shook. He looks up to her. "Do not ask me to set this aside."

"I ain't asking, I'm telling," says Jo. "Christ, Chilli, this is one hell of a long way to go to get out of talking to me. Put it away. Put them all away!" Swinging about to encompass the lot of them, that glowering arc arrayed behind the Cater, swords and bucklers and steel rod and harpoon a-bristle. "Lower your goddamn weapons! This is *not* how we are doing things today!" And her own sword droops. "I *swear!*"

"Please, my lady," says Chilli then, behind her now, quite calm, his sword held high. "Let me show you who I am."

Jo looks from the Cater to Chilli, then, and "Not like this," she says, but *"Villain!"* cries the Cater. "Reprobate! Cack-handed milk-sodden fustilarian!" And Chilli, swelling up with a great breath, lets it out all at once, *"I want my coat!"* he roars, and leaps in swinging.

20 OR 30 FLOORS BELOW – "IS THAT A GOOD THING?"
SOMETHING NICE

TWENTY OR THIRTY FLOORS BELOW the river a sheet of noontide gleaming, bridges marching out into the brightness till, far-off, the great arch of the northern freeway, laden with crawling traffic, and off to the left a cluster of towers, stepped red brick, high and white with darkly narrowed windows, glassy and green-clad, topped by a slanted deck of solar panels, and away beyond them all one lone tower of coppery pink glass framed with pinkly amber stone, stood up tall against the green hills beyond. "It is a matter of some delicacy," says Agravante, somewhere back behind him. "Hence, the apartment."

"My lord?" Pyrocles turns away from that wall of glass, the city below, his brow quizzical. "There is some issue with the construction?"

"No, no," says the Viscount, shaking his head, white locks brushing the shoulders of his slate-grey suit, "all is well here, finally. No; our matter is for elsewhere, and tonight – but its delicacy dictates that our meeting not be marked."

Pyrocles in his pale blue blazer looks about the empty room, the sweep of glass, the stretch of glossy dark wood floor to the clean bare kitchen island there, between him and Agravante. "How would it be that meeting m'lord in his new tower might go unmarked?"

A nod from Agravante then, and something of a smile. "It's always been a source of some small consternation, that you are sworn to Southwest, yet live three blocks north of Burnside."

"An accident of geography, m'lord," says Pyrocles, "the garage, is – "

"Of course, your garage," Agravante holds up a hand, "I do not mean for you to lose your garage. But you are one of my, grandfather's, finest and most true of knights. You deserve an address within the demesne," and that upraised hand swings wide, encompassing the space about them both.

"You would have us move, here," says Pyrocles, still frowning.

"If you like," says Agravante. "Keep the loft as a pied-à-terre," he says, setting a ring with a single key on the island, clink. "Or stay there; use this for entertaining. The occasional night away from your boy. I'd have it known: the care I take, of those who serve the Hound. The Sapper's just across the hall," he says, "and the Trident a few floors down. The Serpent, too."

"He's not a boy, m'lord," says Pyrocles, stepping toward the island.

"Not a boy?"

"Becker," says Pyrocles. "Is not a boy."

"Of course," says Agravante. "Your very own Gallowglas. Well!" Pushing the key across the island toward Pyrocles' hand. "Now that our reasons for meeting are established. I've work for our low friends, and arrangements for you to make."

"But delicately," says Pyrocles, without reaching for the key.

"Anvil," says Agravante. "Pyrocles. I know you've no taste for skulduggery. I assure you, were there any other way," and he elaborately sighs. "The insult to the King, the Queen, but most of all our new Princess, Annisa – and in my own house! My very sitting room! But made by one without the niceties of our court – "

"Who," says Pyrocles, taking up the key.

"Medardus, the Lake Baron," says Agravante. "I will tell you what must be done."

"You should come away upstairs," he says, the scabbard in his hand. He leans close, and after a moment sitting there on the polished concrete she looks up. "Yeah," she says. "Okay."

"Leave it," he says, but she shakes him off and picks up the slender glittering curl of bone, a rib, tarred along the edge there with something thickly black. Looking about as she gets to her feet, turning away from the hand he offers once more. The garage about them empty, otherwise.

Down there in the open room, Iona all in yellow, and Chrissie a shimmer of white there beside her, and also Ysabel, looking up as they step through the door, "Jo!" she cries, but Luys's arm's about her shoulders, he's steering her through the kitchen, into the short dim hall, pushing open the door to her room, and the daylight cooled by white curtains. She wavers in the doorway, his arm still about her. Before them the sword, sunk half the length of its whorled steel blade in the wall, and the gleaming hilt of it even now seems to thrum. On the floor below it the painted skull-mask, tipped over on the black coils of its mane, grinning up at them with those crudely chiseled teeth.

"Does this," says Jo, "I don't get it. Does this mean. Did I, is that, is that a good thing? Did I break it? Is it done for? Is it gone?"

Luys kneels there to pick it up. "It merely fell, from the wall," he says.

"So I just, it," says Jo.

"You hurled your sword away with such force," says Luys. He holds up the mask to her hand that reflexively takes it, and as she looks down to see what she's holding, he stands, he seizes the hilt of her sword there, "If you don't mind, ma'am," he says, bracing his other hand holding the scabbard against the wall, and pulls it free with a clatter of bits of sheetrock.

"Don't," says Jo. The mask falls to the floor with a soft clack. "Don't call me ma'am," she says, turning away, the futon there, sinks to her knees on it. The bone she's still holding, glittering, stained.

"As my lady wishes," says Luys. He holds up the sword, angled to peer down the flat of the blade in the light, turning it over. "Don't," she says, "call me," as he's wiping the length of it clean on the sleeve of his T-shirt. "Just," she says, but there's Ysabel bursting into the room, stooping by the futon, reaching for Jo's hand, "What happened!" she cries. "What's wrong, Jo, talk to me, are you hurt," and Jo says, simply, "I killed somebody." Luys slips the sword into its scabbard, and leans it there against the wall.

"The Harper?" says Ysabel, a hand on Jo's shoulder.

"Connie," says Jo.

"Conary, the Cater," says Luys.

Ysabel looks from the one to the other, and neither of them looking back at her. "What did he do?"

"Nothing!" says Jo. "Not a goddamn," as Luys is saying, "He stood against your grace with steel in his fist, and did not put up when told."

"He shouldn't've," says Jo, leaning forward, away from Ysabel, "I didn't have to," as she sets the rib-bone down on the night-stand, clack. "I know," she says, "we're not, gonna call the cops, for this sort of, but, so, I mean, your brother?" Looking back, over her shoulder, at Ysabel in gauzy white, a gown loosely draped about her white satin shift. "Only I'm the one *he* calls, when he needs to, when somebody, and I have to, but I can't, so, I mean, who do we call?"

"Jo," says Ysabel, gently, "I don't understand what you – "

"I *murdered* him," says Jo.

"Forgive me," says Luys, "but your grace did no such thing."

"There wasn't," Jo's saying, "I didn't," lifting her hands to her face, "they were just, fighting each other, I told them to stop but they were striking at each other, around me, and I, I just," her hands pushing up and back, through her wine-red hair, "and they all just stood, there, all of them, staring," and "I'm sure it was an accident," says Ysabel, stroking Jo's cheek, but Jo starts back from the touch.

"Your grace is Gallowglas," says Luys then, "the Huntsman of the Court, the Hawk's Widow, and the Queen's Champion. You are the Duchess, ma'am. You are Southeast. Sunward of the river, below Burnside Street, your word is law. Your sword is law. What you do, is law."

Jo blinks. "I can't, just," she says, as he steps away from the wall, toward her, kneels beside her. "Yet you have, my lady," he says, taking her hand.

"Christ," she snaps, jerking away from him, "can't you just, *listen,* for once," pushing up to stumble off the futon, away from both of them, "and *talk* to me, like a goddamn, normal," looking wildly about, heading abruptly for the door, the hall, Luys lurching to his feet but stopped, suddenly, by Ysabel's hand laid softly on his arm. He looks down at her, those green eyes, those lips flatly determined, and then he looks away, he steps away, but doesn't follow after. Out there, a door slams.

A pale hand waved before his face, and nicked about the knuckles with old cuts, a dozen or more, red and dead-skin white and tiny and precise, and something older, darker, a burn healed long ago, perhaps, down by the wrist, close to the face of a heavy gold watch. So Becker sighing sits up, leaning with the motion of the bus, thumbs something on his phone, plucks the buds from his ears as Kerr swings into the seat next to him. "So how's Intro to Early Education and Family Studies going, huh? Did you get Washington, or Lopez? Because I hear Lopez can be a *real* hardass."

"I hadn't said your name," says Becker. "Not once. So whatever you think is going on – "

"Can't I see an old friend who happens to be on the same bus and just come over and say hi?" Kerr's grin is sharp, his eyes bright, his curls coming unsprung in his slicked-back hair. "Geeze," he says, loosening the knot in his bright green tie. "So paranoid."

"I don't know what you think you, you're getting, out of this stalker bonhomie, but trust me," says Becker, "it's counter-productive."

"I told you," says Kerr, and that grin softens, slips. "I need you for something. It's a good place to be – my heart has only your best interests in mind." His grin's become a smile now, for Becker, Becker by the window in his soft plaid overshirt, his rusty red T-shirt. "And you, chasing yours – I gotta admit, I was wrong. It's been good for you." And then what's left of Becker's hair stirs as Kerr hauls himself to his feet, steps aside in the aisle, "Your stop's coming up," he says.

"Shit," says Becker, grabbing a blue knapsack, climbing out of the seat. Kerr grabs his arm as the bus snorts itself to a stop. "Go ahead and grow the beard out," he says. "It'll look good." Letting go. Becker backs away a couple of steps toward the door as others are getting up, shifting about them. "And treat yourself!" Kerr calls after him. "Something stupidly nice, okay?" The doors open, front and back. "Do that," says Kerr.

"Well it's a question of goddamn logistics," says the XO, throwing his hands in the air. "This has to be done tonight?" And Pyrocles nods, there in his pale blue blazer, hands clasped behind his back. The XO leans forward, elbows on the table, his sleeveless workshirt, his red cap that says Game Redneckognize Game over the bill. "Why," he says.

"The Viscount wishes it," says Pyrocles. "Do you mean, then, to say you cannot do it? Or you will not?"

"Can't, won't, shit," says the xo. "I got a street address. I ain't never been there, I don't know the ins and outs, I don't even know what the guy looks like, I mean – "

"You will know him, I am certain," says Pyrocles.

"You know," says Moody, over there, other side of the table, "a lot of people call this the Stars and Bars? But they're wrong." His back to them, he's looking at that great flag pinned to the back wall of the cabin, a red that's bright even in the shadows, criss-crossed with star-spangled bars of blue. "*That* was a flag looked so much like the ol' Stars and Stripes they ended up shooting themselves, both sides, Second Battle of Manassas, you can look it up. So Stonewall Jackson goes and asks his right-hand man, one G. Gordon Georges, what's the way to prevent such an unfortunate occurrence from ever occurring again, and Georges, see, he used to be second in command on the Monitor – "

"You got a point, Danny?" says the xo, and a peevish look over his shoulder.

"He doesn't like this," says Moody, still looking up at the flag. "He doesn't approve." Turning then, and looking straight at Pyrocles, and he isn't smiling at all, under the sharp beak of his nose. "He doesn't want it done, at all."

"What I wish is immaterial," says Pyrocles.

"And this was a naval flag," says Moody, a thumb over his shoulder at the flag now behind him. "Which, I mean, we're on a boat. The house, at this address. Got a front door?"

"It does," says Pyrocles.

"And is it right up on the street," says Moody, "or set back, or," and Pyrocles says, "Off to the side. There are trees."

"Well there we go," says Moody. "Easy-peasy!"

"That's getting in," says the xo. "How the hell we getting out?"

"It's Lake fucking Oswego," says Moody. "They won't be looking for white boys pulling a home invasion. They'll be looking for African-American thugs," and he archly turns the phrase. "Hell, we got the truck – they'll be looking for feral Mexican gardeners! We've got this," he says, to Pyrocles.

"Whoa, hold up," says the xo, leaning back from the table. "We ain't got nothing, not a damn thing, not until we talk specifications, and payment. This shit is well outside the scope."

Pyrocles loosens one hand from behind his back to set in the middle of the table a thick roll of bills wrapped about with a rubber band, and the xo eyes it, but doesn't reach for it. "Same as with the shoe guy?" he says. "Smash shit up, take whatever's valuable?"

"The house is to be burnt to the ground," says Pyrocles, "and everything in it. No one is to be, killed. The man is to be beaten, but you are not to cut him, and do not strike him about the head." He delicately tips the roll of bills over, toward the xo. "Another will be brought to you," he says, "when it is done."

"Well, shit," says Moody. "Guess we're gonna need some, whaddayacall it. Accelerant."

Dᴜsᴛ *&* Dᴀʀᴋɴᴇss – ᴀᴛ Tʜɪs ʜᴏᴜʀ
ᴀ Hᴀɴᴅꜰᴜʟ ᴏꜰ Cɪᴛʏ – 20 Fᴜᴄᴋɪɴɢ ᴍɪɴᴜᴛᴇs

Dᴜsᴛ ᴡɪᴛʜɪɴ, ᴀɴᴅ ᴅᴀʀᴋɴᴇss, the lights from the parking lot outside barely reaching the stack of drywall, the buckets, the mound of garbage there beyond, gutted boxes, shucked plastic clamshells, shriveled and crumpled plastic and paper wraps. They look about as they file in, one by one, Pwyll in his long embroidered coat, and Medoro in his work jacket, Astolfo in his sweats, Gerlin with a stained apron about his belly, Peg Greentooth, her hair gone black in the shadows, and bringing up the rear in his short brown jacket Luys, who closes the scuffed glass doors.

Out across the darkness of that great empty space a single light, a desk lamp back there, perched atop a lone, mostly intact filing cabinet, dimly illuminating a twisted tangle of torn metal and some great fallen bell, and Jo, in her black T-shirt, her black jeans, sitting on an upended drawer, smoke curling from the cigarette in her hand. "Come on," she says, leaning down to stub it out, then flicking the dead butt away as she stands. "Over here. Careful of the pictures."

Scattered over the filthy concrete, the edges and the corners of them caught in the weak light, a thousand photographs, and another thousand, and more, and they pick their way across the room from one clear spot to the next. "You're gonna step on some," says Jo. "Can't be helped. It's okay. Just, be careful. Okay," she says. "Okay. I ain't Leo," and she's looking about them as they look from one to another, "I think we're all pretty clear on that," and it's nothing like laughter, or even smiles, but still the rustling, the relaxing, the settling that spreads among them, and "I don't know you," she says. "I didn't come up with you. We never hung out together. I never did what you do, and you don't do what I've done. I don't know you, and that's," she's looking away, aside, "I'm not your Duke," she says. "I'm the Duchess. I stand with the Queen. I hunt for the court." Her hands, wrapped in fingerless cycling gloves. "A couple weeks ago," she says. "Here." She looks up, at them all. "I was about, the King's, business. And I thought I had it under control, but. Things got out of hand. I cut the Devil down. And then, this morning."

"My lady," says one of them, Peg, but no more.

"This morning," says Jo. "I thought I had the situation under control. It got out of hand. And now the Cater's gone. What I brought you here to say," and then she shakes her head, "what I mean to say, to you, is it won't happen again. You, have, my word."

And Luys says, after a moment, "Of course, my lady," and the rest of them, following after, my lady, your grace, yes, yes, my lady, of course.

"Now, the pictures," she says, and they step back, look down, rustle and crumple. "Something the Devil was working on. And I don't know, maybe whoever it is who owns this place, maybe they're still trying to figure out what happened here, maybe they don't give a shit, maybe they haven't even noticed, I don't know. But we can't just leave 'em here."

"Ma'am?" says Pwyll, the Cinquedea.

"So I'm gonna ask the Mason to get these all together and hauled away back to the, ah, residence," says Jo. "Don't, worry about keeping 'em in any kind of order, we just want to get it all out of here, but, I mean, if they're too, burned, or something, just, just leave 'em, we're not trying to wipe out any trace," she's looking past them now, "just, get as many as we can," a wave out over them all, those scattered, fallen photos, and then she starts off, walking away.

"Does your grace mean," calls Medoro, the Axle, after her, "for us to pick these all up?"

"That's kinda the idea, yeah," says Jo, looking back a moment. "Might want to see about getting some light, first? And some boxes?"

Luys says, "All right, of course, I'll have Sweetloaf round up some otherwise idle hands. Spread out, to size up the scope of this task, and then Spadone, you'll negotiate a crew with the Soames."

"Shouldn't we ought to run this through Bruno?" says Gerlin, in his stained apron.

"The Duchess didn't ask the Shrieve to meet us here tonight," says Luys. "We'll handle it ourselves."

Jo's lighting a cigarette, off toward the doors there. She looks up as Luys comes close, photos crackling under his feet. "It's not what you had in mind, I know," she says, softly, snapping off her lighter.

"There are people, for this sort of work," he says, quietly. "If you'd let me know." And then, "What can you possibly mean to do with all of this?"

She sucks the coal of her cigarette to life for a moment. Blows out a cloud of smoke.

"Are you well, my lady?" he asks, and then, quickly, as she looks away, "I only ask because you left in such a temper, this afternoon." And then, his hand laid gently on her arm, "I worry about you, Jo."

She looks at him then, in the darkness. "Don't," she says. Stepping away, from his hand, from him, from the rest of them muttering back there in the shadows, away off toward the doors.

"A cool head," he says, and then from his knobbled fingers that tiny scarlet figure trembling drops, straight to the tiny frozen waves of the sea below, clack and tumble. "Though a steady hand," he says, "is also of some use," and he reaches down to pluck it up again. Frowning over the board spread out upon the low table, the ocean before him, the mountains rising a rumple of snowy grey on the other side, the forest, the desert, the river between, and all stitched together by a dusty road. "Clothilde," he says. Two cities, each made up of cunningly joined hexagonal tiles of tiny palaces, temples, arcades, favelas, the one there scarlet, where the river flows down from the mountains, the other a soapy viridian, spread along the margins of the bay. "Read me again, his last move?"

"The Poet, Grandfather," says the woman curled in the brown leather armchair opposite, peering at the sheet of onionskin in her hand, "to one eight nine point nine, thirty-seven aught, north by east." Her feet tucked under her thighs, and a lacey shawl about her shoulders.

"Blasted Rufer notation," he says, reaching along the thick wooden frame of the board, carved with obscure characters, a sentence, or an equation, twining through a repeated pattern of egg-and-dart. He flips a switch with a hefty thunk, and tiny white lights blink on, a grid spread across the board, shining in the blue, the yellow, the green, the grey and the brown, though here and there a point is dimly amber or entirely dark, and one of them there by the red city's winking, on and off. "Umf," he says, his hand, that little scarlet figure, hovering over a yellowing ridge, dithering between two pinpricks of light, "there," he says, setting it down amid other figures red and green and Ah, me, sighs a scratchy voice from the speakers set in the board's frame, the only Emperor doesn't glitter. "What were his rolls, again?" Wrapped about in a dark blue dressing gown, and his curls are stiffly grey, swept back from his forehead. Five dice are laid on the table by the board, three of them glossily black with white pips, one glassily clear, the pips but chiseled notches, and the last is larger, an angular icosahedron, bright red, its triangular faces printed with astrological symbols.

"Three, one, four, a six, and Ninurta," she says, reading from the onionskin.

"Then I do have it right," he says, looking them over. "Now: we must formulate our response. And I must admit, the temptation to reply in kind to such a cheeky provocation," his hand trembling over that grouping of red figures, a Tinker-Prince, a Hedgewych, a couple of Jugglers and leading them all the red Poet, there on the slope of the ridge held by a lone green Beast, "is overwhelming, but one must be wary of the pitfalls of intemperate overreaction. Thus, the cool head," but off back that way somewhere a simple descending chime rings out, and he frowns. "I wonder who that could be," he says, as Clothilde gets up out of her chair, "at this hour?"

"Good lord," says Becker in that brightly empty room, his reflections turning with him, a confusion of light in the sweeping wall of night-struck glass.

"Yes," says Pyrocles, there by the clean bare kitchen island.

"I mean God damn," says Becker. "And back there?" Pointing to the darkened hallway on the other side of the island.

"Two bedrooms," says Pyrocles, "one with a view," and Becker's already dashing off that way, and Pyrocles with a sigh and a small wry smile heads after him.

Through that doorway a narrow hall jogs back, past a couple closed doors to open on another big and empty room, unlit, and the sweeping wall of glass looks out on the lights of the city beyond, the ruddy shine of a main thoroughfare, paralleling the dark river below, and the lines of lights of streets stretched out beyond, and here and there the bright white shine of this intersection, or that, and off to the left there the winking lights of construction cranes, and the bridges streaming red and white, and the blazing towers of downtown.

"Oh," says Becker. "Wow."

"Do you like it?" Pyrocles, his footsteps cushioned by thick white shag, his arms coming about Becker's waist.

"We'd have to never turn the lights on," says Becker, his face in the shadows brushed with amber and with gold and blue, and his eyes. "So we could always see this." And then, "Oh, but I *like* the loft."

Pyrocles, his chin on Becker's shoulder, murmurs, "Did you see the bathroom?" and Becker, turning to look at him, says, "No damn curtain?" and Pyrocles smiles. "A proper door," he says, "and a full-length tub, and a gym, a pool, the rooftop garden," the weights on his mustaches gleaming.

"And this is closer to Sylvania," says Becker, "just a bus ride down," and then he laughs. "No," he says, "it's just, I saw David again today, David Kerr. On the bus," and as Pyrocles stiffens behind him, "oh, but it wasn't, he was an ass, yeah, but it was like he was apologizing? Or conceding something, I don't know. But he said, he told me to treat myself." Settling back again against Pyrocles. "So. What do you think." Looking up, and back. "Should I grow a beard?"

"You would look," says Pyrocles, smiling again, "in your plaid, like a lumberjack."

"The lumberjack, and the knight," says Becker. "In our metropolitan penthouse."

"We should go," says Pyrocles, after a moment.

"No," says Becker, "no," looking back for a kiss from Pyrocles. "We could see just how soft this carpet is," and another kiss, and Pyrocles loosens his grip about Becker's waist. "You always get so sleepy, after," he says.

Becker turns to face him, to hold him in turn, "You worry so much, about me," he says. "I can worry, too. I've got a pill with me. In my bag."

Pyrocles says, "You do."

"Always," says Becker, and a kiss. "You never know," he says, and another.

"Shizzt!" the bellow, from deeper in the house, "My drow!" and "Yeah, yeah," mutters Christian in his grimy sweatshirt, the hood of it up, and his hands stuffed in the pockets. "You got this?"

Halfway up the spiraling cantilevered stairs, all hand-painted tile and wrought iron, Jasper wrapped in his filthy blanket nods, a revolver loosely in his hand. Sitting at the foot of those steps the old man in his dark blue dressing gown, the tall woman shivering in her lacey wrap, and their hands bound up in clumsy mitts of clingfilm. Another bellow, "Shizzt!" from off that way, and Christian heads back through a kitchen white and terra cotta tile and a smashed bottle of something pink and sticky puddled on the floor, down a few steps, past a pool table, into a cozy library, intricate rugs and orderly volumes lining built-in shelves and a rich brown leather sofa and Moody, standing over a low table. "This asshole," he says. "Look at this. This asshole plays D&D. Really fucking fancy asshole D and goddamn D."

The board laid out on that table, thick frame carved with its egg-and-dart, the bas-relief land within, mountains and ocean, forest and desert, cities and river, red and green.

"Moody, man, we gotta finish up," says Christian.

"I read about this," says Moody. "Only fifty of 'em ever made." He grabs a figure from the board, a green Beast, and the speakers set in the frame let out a scratchy roar. Moody jumps, startled. "Based on drawings from the Book of Voynich," he says, and whips the little figure away.

"Please don't," says old Medardus, in the doorway behind them.

"Shit," says Christian, "fucking Jasper," but "Don't what?" snaps Moody, and leaning down he snatches up a handful of figures, and the board lets out a muddled yowl. Medardus starts away from Christian, "Please!" he cries. "I have been playing that game for seven years now," wincing as a little red figure bounces off his shoulder, "with the King of Fountains," and another figure, green, plaps his chest there, bared by the loosening collar of his gown. "Please," he says, lifting his plastic-swaddled hands.

Snarling Moody turns and slams a hand onto the board, grinding crunch of porcelain snap of wood and splintering plastic hauling up the tiles of that green city, and a piece of water with them, turning to hurl them but "No!" wails Medardus, jerking forward, fumbling over the back of the sofa feet kicked up and groaning rolling over. Moody laughing steps aside, leans over to rain bazaars and fortalices down from his fist until a lurching thrash knocks him back unsteady bang against the table pieces clattering away. He sits abruptly, and smashes the board with a dying squawk from those speakers.

"Shit," says Moody, and then another laugh, "you stupid son of a bitch," he says to Christian, still stood there, hands in his pockets, "you're about as useless," and then Medardus howling flips up Moody's legs with his swaddled hands, sends Moody over and whooping off the table, crash, Medardus up on his knees now face a rictus breath a keening rasp, those bound hands rising and falling like a club, "Whoa, hey, whoa," Christian hopping over the back of the sofa, squeak of leather, Medardus falling as Moody growling pushes up and a steely flash, mirror-bright, but then out that way somewhere shouting and a sudden loud bang. They all stop. Medardus his legs held by Christian rolls heavily off Moody, flat on his back and panting, and letting go the handle of the knife that pins the dark blue gown to his breast.

Staring at the hilt of it wrapped about in glittering silver wire Medardus, his eyes wide, whispers, "You are not mortal."

"I *know* what I am," grunts Moody, "and I know what *you* are," then looking up, over his shoulder, at Christian on his feet and backing away. "But what the hell are you?"

"I'm just, me, man," mutters Christian. "I'm just me." Raising his voice, eyes wild, "You wanted me in all this! You did!"

"The hell you got in your pocket, boy," says Moody, but before Christian can do more than stuff his hands back in them there's the xo in the doorway, gas can in his hand, "Let's go!" he's yelling, "It's lit!" But his face falls as he looks over the sofa sprawled there Medardus and Moody, the knife, and as he steps into the room, "The hell," he says, it's then that Medardus coughs, a thick wet gag of a sound, and Moody scrambles back, and the knife drops to stand an instant on its tip before slowly leaning turning falling softly clink to the rug by a glittering bit of bone, and it's then that Christian springs away, past the xo, running, out into the thickening smoke, away.

"It smells of cooking meat," says the man at the head of the booth, his suit a windowpane check in grey, his ivory vest striped with blue, his face hidden in the shadows from the lamp hung low over the table, the low dark room behind him, amberly dim and almost empty, a lone couple dancing too slowly there to a languid calypso beat, the crooning fragrance on the wind, could be as exquisite as this. "Sit, if you're gonna sit," says Chilli, his arms folded, and a not-quite empty glass before him.

The man in the suit swings himself into the booth, sits himself down, leans forward into the low light, Bruno, an elbow on the table and his thumb to his teeth. "We could've met at my offices. There's a couch. It's perfectly safe; she doesn't have anyone watching it."

"It's not her I'm worried about."

"Don't hint," says Bruno, sharply. "I can't abide hints. Say what you mean, or let go."

Chilli leans close, light swooping over his yellow beard. "You sent me in there to get got. Only a miracle of incompetence that I'm still here to lift a pint."

"Here," says Bruno. "Not out by the airport, sweeping rubble." But before Chilli's frown can find a question, another arm slips into the light, burly, tattooed, the hand of it setting a fresh glass on the table filled with thin cool gold, and Chilli lifts the almost empty, drinking off what's left. "You want anything?" he says, setting the glass down with a thump. "I'm buying."

"I'm not thirsty," says Bruno. And then, as the empty glass is whisked away, he says, "One of the differences between us, Harper, is I make a point of knowing when I'm not invited, and to what." Looking off out the window there, the parking lot beyond, lit up a garish red by some enormous neon sign. "I'm a businessman. Nothing more. I sent you there because it was asked of me. But because I am a businessman, when something happens, I look for the best angle to play. And because I am a very good businessman, I have the resources to play any angle very well indeed."

Chilli takes a thoughtful sip. "So if it'd been me, instead of the Cater, you'd be having this conversation with him."

"It would've been more brief," says Bruno. "He already worked for me."

Another pull from his glass. "Yesterday, you told me every time I got something, I fucked it up."

"Well," says Bruno. "Now there's two of us, hoping I was wrong."

The showerfall cuts off, and he whoops, a sound much too loud for the space. The slender door pops open, pebbled glass of it wobbling in the frame, "Fuckin' A, man," Sweetloaf, leaning out of the shower stall, groping for the white towel neatly folded on the little countertop right there. "Just, pouring hot water over your fucking head? For, like, twenty fucking minutes?" Patting down his narrow chest, vigorously rubbing his thick wet hair. "Fucking vacation, man." Holding the towel up before him, looking about the cramped trailer, curtains drawn and only two lamps lit, up there in the little dining booth in the nose of it, and back behind, over the low bed in its alcove, and Luys laid out on his side, atop the umber comforter.

"Ah, fuck," says Sweetloaf. "Not again."

Luys propped up on an elbow shrugs his meaty shoulder, his grin rather pleased with itself, and his cock a startlement of brown against the black curls there, the tip of it discreetly peeped from out its cuff of foreskin.

"I know," says Sweetloaf, "you and Mom are having some issues, but – "

"You oughtn't to call her that," says Luys, and his smile sours.

"And you ought to tell me where my fucking pants went. Sir."

"Your pants," says Luys, sitting up, "were filthy, and your shirt was filthy, your jacket was filthy, and your shoes," and another shrug. "They will be clean in the morning. You might as well relax."

"Relax," says Sweetloaf. "Yeah. Right." Letting the towel drop, and his own cock already stirring. "Not that I'm saying no, mind. But I just had a fucking shower. You're gonna get *me* all filthy, and sweaty, and sticky," and "You should feel free to take another shower, when we're done," says Luys.

"I don't know, sir," says Sweetloaf, a knee up on the bed. "I don't fucking know. *Two* fucking vacations in one night," as Luys pulls him down.

Bare knees on the unfinished floor, "ticket," he's muttering, "placket," arms spread wide, head tipped back, dark hair unruly with curls, "racket, rickets, rickety tacky, pocketa ping, pocketa pocketa queep!" and hung in the air before him a heavy golden watch, shining in the cold light somewhere off behind him, a piercing silver shine that strikes bright gleams from the blankly empty windows lining the far-off walls, "Tin," he says, "Rin Tin, Tintin," and his sweat-sheened chest jerks hauling him up, "Tiki Tiki!" he cries, "Tiki Room!" and then sitting back on his heels again, slumping again, "a lady's hat," he says, "slack, slacker slake slacking, no slacking, slack," and again he jerks upright, up on his knees and shouting at the ceiling, "Please! No slacking, please!" falling back down, and his arms drooping, and his fingers brushing the ash-dusted floor, and all this time his eyes are closed, and all this time the watch hangs steady before him, fixed, unmoving, gleaming in the bright white light, "United," he says, "ain't really," and then, muttered quick, "Rikki-Tikki-Tavi, don't lose that number, Rikki-Tikki-Tavi, you're so fine, Rikki-Tikki-Tavi, mongoose is gone, won't be coming 'round, and the organization," he opens his eyes, "ain't really organized," and one hand whip-quick leaps to catch the watch as it drops.

The room is dark.

"Shit," says David Kerr. "Okay." Breathing heavily. Leaning over to crush a burning ember with his fist. "Okay," he says, again, and he fits the watch about his wrist. The hands of every dial on its face point down, at six, at six, at six. "I guess we're doing this," he says.

THE JINGLE OF THE BELL over the door, and the whole crowd filling that front room turns, green work shirts and blue, brown coveralls, uniforms in black and taupe and white, breast-pocket insignia and badges and nameplates, here and there a plain white T-shirt, or dark blue, and styrofoam cups in every hand, and they're staring at him in his grimy sweatshirt, the hood of it up, his hands in the pockets of it, the door propped open against his shoulder, and the street behind him filling with morning light.

"Come in if you're coming," says Gordon, stood behind the counter laden with almost-empty donut boxes and a couple of platters and a box of coffee. Christian steps inside, the door closing behind him, and shakes off his hood. "You already got the window fixed," he says.

"You here to kick another hole in it?" And then, "Hold up, hold up," as a muttering murmuring unrest sweeps through them, "let him be, let him be."

Christian looks warily about them all, shifting and looking away from him, a sip here, a cough there, and then a woman in blue coveralls, her hair under a kerchief, lays a hand on the arm of the man beside her and steps back, gently urging him back with her, and across from her a burly little man in a boilersuit steps back, and yanks the elbow of the much taller man beside him, until an aisle is cleared through that small front room, and chest swelling with one great breath and both hands still in his pockets Christian steps along it up to the counter, and then with some effort tugs from the pockets a shoe that he sets down by a platter still holding a handful of pinwheel sandwiches. It's a simple, well-made shoe, of shining oxblood leather, closed with a single monk strap.

"What's that," says Gordon.

"I figure," says Christian, "you got a shoe shop."

"Where'd you get it," says Gordon.

"On the MAX. It was just, right there, on the seat. And I knew it, I figured, I better pick it up and, keep it."

"Train," says someone behind him, and "A road," says someone else, and "What time was it?" and "Train *station*," says somebody, "more like a *crossroads*," and "What time of day?" says the tall man, again, looming over Christian's shoulder.

"Dawn," says Christian. "First train of the day. Well? This mean anything?" And then, looking about, "I got bad people coming after me. You know what I mean. So what does this do? What does it get?"

Gordon steps heavily back around the worktable mounded with shoes, back toward the beaded curtain there, and the wall lined with shelves, partitioned into cubbies, stuffed here and there with mismatched pairs of shoes. Runs his hand down a column, works a pair free, comes stumping back up to the counter. Sets them down: a wedge-heeled leather pump the color of a decent-enough cognac, and a shining oxblood monk-strap.

"That's it?" says Christian, as Gordon lifts the pump away, tosses it to the pile behind him. "The other shoe? Man, they don't even fit!"

"Welcome to Portland," says Gordon, gruffly, and Christian starts back, *"Fuck* you," he snarls, and then leaning in again, a fist on the counter, "welcome to Portland, I been living here most of my damn life!"

A snort then, behind him, a chuckle, a titter, a chortling guffaw, an outright hoot, all of them now, shaking heads, a stomp of a foot, slap at a knee, laughing, laughing at him.

Arsenal Against All Odds (3.44)

Three Four Fire (3.45)
1. Strapping Mines on Babies
2. Stepping on Bugs
3. Stifling All Forms of Ambient Life

Fast Car in the Hands of an Angry
Pessimist (4.22)

Five Hundred Rounds of Howitzer Ammo
on the Vatican Alone… (2.59)

A Weekend Spent Smuggling Bad
Musicians into Great Britain to
Undermine the Economy (5.31)

Suicide Option (2.09)

—the Bulldaggers

Killing Everything in Sight
(side two)

NO. 29

" – shiver & headache – "

PHOTOGRAPHS SCATTERED OVER THE FOLDING TABLE, silvery black, ivory, muddy sepia, that one there tinted almost red, creases burring the corners and a long fold right through the middle of a group of men, their shapeless suits a black gone rusty brown. A stolid doorway behind them, columns rising up past a lintel carved with simple Gothic letters, Scottish Rite of Freemasonry. One of the men is tall and broad, his hatless hair bright white, and the younger, slighter man beside him laughs under the brim of a neat derby hat. The third of them's quite somber in a simple jacket buttoned up to his throat, and something in his hands, but there the photograph's been scratched, the ruddy tones of it scraped away.

Out under fluorescent lights, Ysabel approaches, wrapped in a filmy gown, feet bare on polished concrete. In one hand a glass half full of milk. "Jo?" she calls. "Jo?" Laying a hand on the high-backed black desk chair pulled up to that folding table, starting back at a bubbling grunt of a snore. Jo's slumped over the photos, one folded arm a pillow, and a bottle there beside her, almost empty. Ysabel picks it up, brow quirking at the stylized yellow bee on the glass of it, the label that says Evan Williams Honey Reserve.

She sets the milk where it had been, and strokes Jo's wine-red hair. Presses a kiss to her cheek. Straightening, she looks over the boxes stacked up against the back wall, regular banker's boxes white and brown in mostly regular columns, four or five high, and some on the floor before them, and by the table, lids loose or propped open, and within them, so many more photographs.

As she leaves, she tosses the bottle into a blue recycling bin with some force, and a crash of glass.

WHITE LINES GLEAMING, burnished by candlelight, angles that frame her belly, her breasts, her throat and face, her eyes closed below severely straight bangs, long yellow hair gathered by wide white ribbons in hanks over either shoulder. She's laid back, settled against curves of golden brown, shadowed leg along the pale length of her atop the pillowy comforter, hip and belly, shoulder, dark arm curled about her, laid over that white paint, a brown hand tucked there, just between her thighs. She sighs, tilts up her head. "She'll come around," she says.

"Your sister?" says Ysabel, above, behind her. "She seemed fairly adamant."

"You didn't even ask the question."

"It," says Ysabel, "it isn't that important, really."

"How can you say that?" Twisting, squirming about, "No, I meant," says Ysabel, and then, "careful, you'll smear," but "All our life," she's saying, "all our life!"

"And yet."

"No!" Chrissie's sitting up on an elbow, glaring down at her. "No! Even," she says, "when we used to," but she blinks, "swim," she says. "When I." She looks away. "When she."

"Used to swim," says Ysabel. A smudge of white paint there on her breast, and flecked with gold. "But you don't, anymore? Did you forget?"

"Racing," says Chrissie, still looking away. "Competitively. We did, we used to, we were, a scholarship. Couldn't afford college, otherwise."

After a moment, Ysabel says, "What happened, when you used to swim?"

"Have you, do you swim? Laps, I mean, not a lot of people race."

"I can," says Ysabel.

"It's just, how easy it is, when, there's, there's other people, they're all around, there's even cheering, sometimes. Announcements, over the," waving a hand, "PA. But you can shut it all out. It all, goes away. It's just, you, and the water. For the sprints even, but especially the distance races, and you're all on your own, cut off, it's, easy to get, lost," and a sputter of laughter, at Ysabel's smile, "I mean, in a pool, but, all those laps? Up to sixty, in a twenty-five meter pool?" Looking away again. "So there's signs."

"Signs," says Ysabel.

"Like a small whiteboard, or these plastic numbers you can swap out, or leaves, you can flop over, to change the number? And you stick it in the water, so you can see, as you're coming in to the wall, what lap you're on. So you don't get lost." Grinning at herself, but biting her lip. "But. Every race, see? She never missed one. Every time I swam a distance event, an eight hundred, a fifteen, when they let me, no matter what she had to do, she was there. Holding the sign. Keeping track."

"She didn't swim?" says Ysabel. "I thought you both swam."

"It wasn't fair," says Chrissie. "It completely wasn't fair." Looking down, idly stroking the blurred white paint that slants up past her sternum. "It wasn't even her pot, it was Jeff's, but – zero tolerance, you know? She lost the scholarship. She had to drop out."

"But you stayed."

"I stayed. Another, I – three semesters. We weren't going back."

"But, you did drop out? You stopped swimming."

A sigh. A kiss. "It bulks up your shoulders, distance swimming. If you don't keep it up, you lose that. And anyway," another kiss, "she was, we could, we were making better, well. More, money. Dancing. So."

"So."

"So she'll come through," says Chrissie, and lays her head on Ysabel's breast.

Some time later, she sits up, alone in the wide white bed. Ysabel, in candlelight, wraps herself in a filmy gown, "I didn't hear Jo come up," she says.

"What?" says Chrissie.

"I'm going to check on her."

"Oh." Chrissie flops back down on the pillows, rolling over. "Jo." Those white lines carefully skirt an exaggerated lip-print drawn in red ink there, just below her breast. "Don't worry about the bedclothes," says Ysabel, "though you could get cleaned up, if you wished?" And she opens the door and steps out, into the hall.

Head back hunching grunt and tendons stark he's squatted bare feet flat on the carpet jerking buttocks hands on hips she's curled beneath him turned about her weight on her shoulders head a-cant and fingers at her red-painted lips legs loosely flopping cooing breathless slapping squeaking pop and slap that freezes suddenly silent, pop-eyed rictus skewed up in a corner of the screen, fishnet foot kicked up, fingers clenched and gripping dimpled flesh of thigh her eyes round in surprise beneath blue-painted lids. "It's machismo, it what it is," says the man on the big dark bed. "We're not *supposed* to show you this, so we're gonna *prove* we're showing it to you. So throw out any artistry, anything that might come off like a trick, even a simple edit and you'll go aha, you cut there, you're hiding something, I got you. Spell's broken." His voice pitched to carry across that dim room lit mostly by the skin on the screen. "Nothing's staged, there's no attempt to move you, evoke anything, carry you anywhere, because every effort's bent on making sure *you* see that *these* people were moved, went there, beyond any shadow of a doubt. So chuck 'em in a room, shoot whatever happens, there it is," he lifts a tiny silver remote, "under the lights." Those bodies lurch into motion, squeal and slap and grunt and smack as the view wheels, freezes again, blur of thigh, rimpled glisten of condom, arc of belly. "I mean, budget, sure. Budget's a factor. But beyond a certain point," folding his hands up, behind his head, "budget's a fucking excuse. If you've got something to say, you say it, you work past that, you find a way." The hair on his head too slickly black, his chest too wispily grey, his belly slack and his lolling cock, his limply legs, his angled feet. "It's not without its charms," he says. "But it's crap. It's all crap."

"Even the tasteful, feminist stuff, Reg?" says someone on the other side of the half-open door there, light blazing on white tiles within.

"Crap!" he says, sitting up, tossing the remote clink to the bedside table. "This is, this ought to be," he's getting up, he's crossing the room to that enormously lurid television, "the art of utopia," he says, and he clicks it off, plunging the room into shadow. A slap of a laugh from behind that half-open door. "No, think about it," he says, heading toward the bright slice of light on the carpet. "Utopia: you've settled your basic physical needs, safety and security all sewn up, you've clawed your way to the top of Maslow's hierarchy." The tile white under his feet, smokey grey up the walls, pebbled amber glass of a shower stall. She's there before the sink, black towel about her hips, and her belly, her breasts, her throat and her face painted with angled swaths of black, sheenly smeared with handfuls of greasy white cream, long yellow hair tied back with a wide black ribbon. "Huh," he says. "Those really aren't extensions."

"Tricks of the trade," says Ettie, rubbing cream onto her cheek.

"I like it long," he says. "Where was I. Needs, right, so! You've actualized yourself. Transcended yourself. It's all good! There's no loss to mourn, no lack to salve – what *art* do you make, then?"

"Pin-ups and money shots?" she says, daubing her face clean with a grubby white towel. "You're talking about pornography, Reg. Come on."

"Haven't you ever," he says, "described a dessert, as pornographic?" Stepping close. "Sensual. Pleasures. Evocations of, of those pleasures," his hands uncertain, "of desire, of fulfillment," one setting on that hip-slung towel, "do you realize, the pornography we see? Every day?" He leans close. "Menus," he murmurs. *"Catalogs."*

"You're insane," she says, rubbing at a stubborn blotch under her ear.

"It's *obscene,*" he says, looking down, there, on her side, just below her breast, an exaggerated lip-print, cartooned in red, unsmeared with cream or paint. "You missed a spot," he says, fingertips brushing the kiss but "Don't!" she jerks about, slapping his hand away. "Sorry," she says, as he steps back. "I'm sorry, I – "

"Look," he says, quite curt, his eyes gone stern. "Whatever it is, between the two of you? Fix it. Because, let's face it. On your own?" Looking her up and down, her one hand clutching the towel. "You're talented, sure, you're good. Very good. But your tits are too small, your legs are too long, you've got that nose, and the overall," waving a hand, "resting bitch gestalt. But together?" Spreading his hands, a shrug. "Together, you're spectacular." Stepping back, toward the doorway. "I'm paying for both of you. I'm going to get my money's worth."

He steps out, and shuts the door, gently.

Leaned against the fender of a sleek sedan, he's not too tall, somewhat stout, arms folded in a sleek grey suit, grey shirt, grey tie. Watching a white suv rumble down the narrow, buckled street under the lights fixed to the deck of the bridge above. It wheels into the space beside him, next to one of the slender, sharp-edged concrete piers. The rear door pops open as the engine cuts off, a high white boot slips out, and a bared pale thigh, brief white shorts and thin gold chains a–dangle, white halter deeply scooped and draped in a loose hood up about the black lines painted framing breasts and throat and cheeks, and straight yellow hair caught up in hanks by wide white ribbons. Coming around the back of the suv, as tall, as slim, as severe, but dressed instead in black, black boots and shorts, black hood, angled white paint, and something of a smile about her lips.

"What do you think?" says Ysabel, still in the back seat of the suv.

The man in the grey suit snorts. "Mama Rave and the Ravettes," he says.

"Darling Mr. Davies," says Ysabel, climbing down out of the suv. "It *is* the Montage." Ivory trousers bell about her ankles, and a long sleeveless tapestry coat, unicorn and maiden in a garden, picked out in colored thread on an ivory field. "Nice shoes," she says, and he turns a foot, displaying his black and white spectators. "I doubt anyone will notice," he says. "They'll all be staring at you."

"Why else go out, if not to be seen?" says Ysabel, but he's offering his arm to the woman in white, "Shall we, Ettie?"

"Oh, he's gotten better at this," she says, taking his arm.

"He's paid attention," says Ysabel.

"You were both trying too hard, in the other direction," he says, as Chrissie all in black takes his other arm. "Occupational hazard," she says.

"It's nice to see you both together again," he says, as they set out, under the bridge, and then, a moment later, a bit too loud, "I don't see any deathless paintings down here, at least?"

Ysabel brushes her fingers against the pier they're passing, sprayed with a tangle of initials in bright orange, and a glyph in red, two dotted eyes cradled in a wide simple smile, and then she steps out into the street, "Look at them!" she cries. Throwing a bare arm up, a sweep of her hand, the slender piers rising abruptly to massive concrete caps that brace the girders of the bridge, thrumming with traffic, far too much weight to be borne up by such stalks. "Would you adorn this, with art? So graceless, so out of proportion – pieces, from a kit, slapped together and on to the next, like any other dreary overpass. Only a generation after the Lovejoy Ramp," and as she's speaking, Reg has freed his arms from Ettie and from Chrissie, leaving them on the sidewalk to step out into the street beside her, "and already they've forgotten how to listen. As if they know more about the building of bridges than the bridges ever could themselves. And yet," she says, "even in such a benighted space," her gesture now toward the corner there, three storeys of red brick building, upper windows dark, but down here in the shadows lamplight warmly shines over benches and small potted plants, muffled music, the laughter of someone stepping out of the door set in the corner of it, under signs that say Montage. "Commerce thrives," says Ysabel.

"It's one restaurant," he says. "The building's in dire need of restoration. Otherwise?" Looking about. "You-store-it warehouses, wholesale office junk, a parking lot – is that one of yours?"

"An art studio," says Ysabel, pointing up the street to a low green building behind them, "the wonders that might spring, from soil such as this."

"Yeah," says Reg, looking past, across the boulevard beyond, to a pocket of grass, the crook of an onramp, a low tree harshly topped with green by streetlight, deeply shadowed beneath, where a cluster of makeshift tents has been staked and tied together, yellow tarps and blue tarps and plastic sheeting lit up within by flashlights and by camp lanterns, and shadows moving about. "I wonder. Let's get ourselves inside."

Heads turn as they make their way through the ochre dining room, chairs scrape here and there, pushed back for better views from long tables laid with white cloths and sparkling glassware, Chrissie and then Ysabel, Ettie, finally Reg, as orders shouted in the open kitchen, scrape and chop, a rush of flame, music loud and someone's singing ai mambo, mambo Italiano! They're led to a long table against the far wall, beneath a monochromatic cartoon of the Last Supper. Ettie and Chrissie slip around the end to lay hands on the chairs there, standing, being seen, as Ysabel and Reg sit down across from them, and then they sit themselves, shoulder to shoulder, a regiment of emptied wine bottles lining the shelf above their hoods, the black one, and the white. "Flatiron steak," says Reg, waving away the menus their server's trying to hand out, "rare as it's legal, and a Ross Island iced tea. Girls?"

"Soup, or salad, sir?"

"Skip it," says Reg, a bit terse. "Girls, what will you have?"

"Hoppin' John salad," says Ettie, and "Two forks," says Chrissie.

"Something to drink?"

Chrissie opens her mouth to say something, but looks to Ettie first. "Water," says Ettie, and Chrissie, shrugging, nods.

"Pesto mac," says Ysabel, handing her menu back up, "and surprise me with something that has your vanilla vodka."

"Splitting a salad?" says Reg, as their server heads off, and "We aren't hungry," says Chrissie, and "We're just here to look pretty," says Ettie. "Go on, do your business."

"But you are our business," says Ysabel.

"Yeah?" says Ettie, but "Look," says Reg, "I know you're ducking my calls. You think I'm angry. There's been skipped appointments, lost opportunities, but remember: I work in a creative industry, too. I understand the process. Sometimes, it takes time. I respect that."

Ettie says, "You're about to drop a but, aren't you," the both of them looking at him.

"But," he says, a bit theatrically, as glasses of water are set down, "there's money at stake, and money to be made. For all of us. That needs to be respected, too."

"I have, perhaps," says Ysabel, "been guilty of monopolizing your attentions." And then, to Reg, "Christienne has been most helpful in getting my foundation off the ground."

He looks at her, blinks, "Your," he says, *"foundation,"* and then he rocks back in his chair with a rumbling wheeze of a laugh, "you are a piece of work, you know that?" he says. "Why the hell can't you go to your brother and tell him you don't want the damn thing demolished? He can just, shut it all down! Problem solved. Art saved."

Smiling just, she says, "But there's money at stake, Mr. Davies. That must be respected. If I go to him as a sister – now that mother has retired, that would be all that I am. But if a foundation comes to him," and her drink is set before her, tall, pale yellow, clinking with ice and a bright pink straw, "backed by concerned citizens, members of the arts community, sympathetic stories in the press, some of his own investors," and she leans forward, for a sip.

"Some of?"

"You can't think you're the only one I'm meeting with."

"I do, actually. I do." Shaking his head, stirring his own drink tall and amber with a purple straw. "Cards on the table," he says, lifting his glass for a gulp. "I donate some money to your effort to save the Lovejoy Ramp, lend you my name, say something nice in public, and you get out of our way," he's looking across to Ettie now, "let us get back to doing what we'd already agreed to do," and to Chrissie, in her black hood, her white paint, sat across from Ysabel beside him, who lays her hand on his a moment, "The one," she says, "has nothing to do with the other," and as he's turning, frowning, "What?" he's saying, Chrissie leans forward, blurts out, "We don't want to do it anymore. The photos, the movies," but Ettie's saying, "We didn't say that," and "we want to do *our* show," says Chrissie. "*Our* way. We can do that, now."

"Whoa," says Reg. "Okay?" Spreading his hands, smoothing the waters between them all. "There's still some misconceptions. This is all, photos, whatever, you're in charge. If you'd come to one of the meetings I'm setting up for you? The one, Tuesday, came down from Seattle, total punk-hippie chick, Femmerotic, her thing's called. Totally tasteful. Completely feminist. Nothing you wouldn't be comfortable with, okay?"

"Comfortable," says Chrissie, sitting back.

"Nothing's comfortable, under the lights," says Ettie, looking to Chrissie beside her, leaning closer, shoulder to shoulder. "You look so pretty when you smile," she says, and they're both smiling suddenly, great wide sparkling grins. "Why don't you put an arm around her," says Chrissie, and she does. "Oh, that's great."

"Put your hand in her lap," says Ettie, and she does. "Go on, a little higher."

"You don't really *have* to," says Chrissie, tipping her head back, hood falling, baring her throat, "but it has to *look* like," and "Give 'em what they want," growls Ettie, as Chrissie curls her lips, an exaggerated moue, "Oh!" she says then, sitting up, leaning close. "I know we said you wouldn't."

"We'd never ask you to cross a line," says Ettie, black paint brushing white.

"But if you'd just," says Chrissie, the tip of her nose just by Ettie's. "Like you were about to."

"As if you just did."

"Just to see."

"We wouldn't use it."

"We wouldn't *have* to use it."

"Just once," says Ettie, but then Chrissie turns aside, "So long as you're comfortable," she says, as Ettie sits back. Chrissie lifts her hood up into place, smoothing the hanks of her yellow hair, and those smiles are gone, and their blue eyes flatly cold. "It doesn't matter what we say when we shake hands."

"The photos are all that ever gets seen," says Ettie.

"If we aren't the ones calling the shots," says Chrissie.

"What's shot is what gets called," says Ettie. "This isn't our first rodeo."

"But that's what I'm talking about!" Reg leans close, both hands on the table. "Did you hear? How quiet it just got, when you were," and his fist thumps once, a chime of glassware. "Attention was paid! And that kind of, charisma," he looks back, over his shoulder, and then to them again, "that magnetism, that can be monetized. Hell, it could be weaponized!"

"It will end up pointed," Chrissie's saying, but "That's it, isn't it," says Ettie, and "at us," says Chrissie, looking to her with a questioning frown, but Ettie's looking at Ysabel. Glaring, even. "That's the question, isn't it," she says, as Ysabel unperturbed looks right back. "That everyone wants to talk about," says Ettie, "but nobody wants to actually, like, talk about."

"Everybody?" says Ysabel.

"Do you want to *see* me," says Ettie. "Do you want to see *more* of me. Do you, do you *want,*" but Ysabel's shaking her head, waving a hand, "It's not enough," she says, "to ask the question. One must attend the answer."

"Yeah?" says Ettie, shrugging off the hand Chrissie's laid on her arm. "Well, attend this: no. No, I don't. You absolutely terrify me."

Chrissie's staring, aghast. "Wait," says Reg, "what?" Ysabel's lifting her half-drunk glass. "What we call beautiful, we do quiver before it," she says, and sips.

"Yeah, well, sometimes we quiver because it's fucking *wrong,*" says Ettie.

"Would somebody please tell me," says Reg, but there's his steak, sizzling, swooped in, set thump before him.

A portrait propped on the mantel there, white beagle spotted black and tan, stood proudly in a field, trees low in the distance and a sky full of brushstroked clouds. The hearth beneath of yellow brick, fire chuckling on the grate, two wingback chairs pulled close before it, upholstered in pale pink with white roses. To one side a fussy credenza topped with cut glass decanters, to the other a low shelf, a single line of books, all of a height, and bound in the same blue leather. He runs a hand along the back of one of the chairs, looks about the room again. The fire shifts, settles, sparks pattering up the flue. His great beard is the color of mahogany, and his little round sunglasses in this uncertain light might well be green or purple.

The door rasps open, there's the Viscount Agravante, white dreadlocks touched with gold tied back, a salmon dress shirt open at his throat. "Mr. Keightlinger!" he cries. "Of course I remember you. Forgive the delay; I was upstairs, attending to Grandfather."

"How is he?" says Phil, says Mr. Keightlinger.

"He sleeps," says Agravante. "Something to drink?"

"No," says Mr. Keightlinger, after a moment. Agravante's pouring something clear into a glass. "Sit," he says. "So." Corking the decanter. "How is Charles."

"Charles? Was," says Mr. Keightlinger, "not Leir." His hand still on the back of the chair. "Leir was a wig."

"You don't say," says Agravante, plucking an ice cube from a bucket. "A wig?"

"Do you have the boon?"

"You haven't taken your seat," says Agravante, coming around the other chair. "Are you certain I can't offer you anything?" He sits. "Tell me, Mr. Keightlinger. Do you have any family?"

"The boon, sir, that was given to you last year. Do you still have it?"

Agravante sips his drink. "I know you are not a rude man. I cannot abide the ill-mannered." A gesture, toward the other chair.

"In my work," says Mr. Keightlinger, as he sits, "I have been many different people. Some had family. I couldn't say which were real."

Agravante lifts his glass, a salute. "You're a magician, aren't you. Magicians rarely have family, in my experience. You'd rather wield blessings and curses, than homilize about them."

"As you say, sir."

"As I say." He chuckles, and leans forward to set his glass on the low table between them. "They know you, family, better by far than anyone else, but that knowledge fixes you, holds you fast. It squeezes. And yet," sitting back in his chair, "when allegiances follow fortune, and philosophies change with the cut of one's suit, still: one's family is always one's family. There's a comfort to be taken, in that."

"I wouldn't know, sir."

"Of course. Of course." The crackle of the fire. His elbows on the arms of the chair, his fingers steepled. "I was to hold the boon, and keep it safe, and undisturbed, until he asked for it again. You," those fingers tip, point, "are not he."

"As I said, sir, Leir was, a mask, an illusion – "

"A wig, yes. Am I not bound by the word I've given a wig?" A shrug of those hands. "Perhaps your companion from that evening could resolve this dilemma."

A rustle of that beard, as his sunglasses turn from the fire to Agravante, the lenses settling, for the moment, on green. "You know where he is."

"Do I." He picks up his glass. "As to what was given me, it's on the mantel," and there, set before the portrait of the hound, a fiendish little basket-box, "safe," says Agravante, as Mr. Keightlinger leaps to his feet, "and undisturbed."

Mr. Keightlinger turns it over in his hands, the dark red wood of it seamless, corners knurled, faces carved with simple, stylized shapes, a mountaintop, a raindrop, a sunburst, a quartered circle. And then he lifts it up and brings it down, crack against the mantel, and up again and down, a splintering crunch. He swallows it up in both his hands, prying with thick fingertips, a grunt, arms trembling, a sudden twist and a snap like a branch, breaking. One of those hands lifts away from the other and in the palm of each a jagged half of basket-box, edges red, the hollowed wood within a smoothly yellow.

"Where is he," says Mr. Keightlinger.

"Who," says Agravante, serenely getting to his feet.

"Where!" Thrusting one empty half of the box at him.

"The box was kept safe, and undisturbed," says Agravante. "As to what was held within," and a shrug, stepping back as Mr. Keightlinger hurls that half into the fire. "If he does not like what I have done, why, surely he'll return? To let me know?" The sliding door rasps open. Mr. Keightlinger's leaned against the mantel, the other half still in his hand. "Do be so good as to show yourself out," says Agravante.

HAND IN HAND – TWO STOREYS, OR THREE
HOW IT WORKS – COMMITMENT – THE WHAT OF THE BANDIT

HAND IN HAND from glaring sunlight wisp of bare feet thump of shoes, a sudden swell of darkness as the door swings shut behind them, shadows to foil yellow hair and gleaming shoulders, arms limned with the last of that thin-stretched light. "Wait," says Ettie, pulling Chrissie back to her, pulled close, and arms folding about and cheek by cheek, an embrace there before a washer and a dryer, hidden away under a drape of patterned cloth. And then, "How could you," she says, stepping back.

"She asked."

"It's been two weeks."

"I know."

"How could you *possibly.*"

"It's been two weeks."

"God," says Ettie. "You smell like a piña colada."

"We burn so easily."

"You'll spoil the look."

"It's, like, SPF 150 or something." And then, "You could lay out, too – "

"As *if,*" says Ettie. "You left!"

"She asked."

"She's asked a lot of people!" cries Ettie. "Whatever it is. I've met some of them. They all," and then, throwing up her hands, "dammit, she broke your heart!"

"But my heart isn't broken," says Chrissie. On her side, there just below her breast, an exaggerated lip-print drawn in a red gone black in the shadows. Ettie shakes her head. "You're, you're under a," she says, "it's like, she casts a – "

"Magic?" says Chrissie, catching her hand. "C'mon," she says. "I'll show you some magic."

Hand in hand out into a hallway under strings of little yellow lights, a confusion of doors, Chrissie's hand on the knob of the one to the left when one of the ones to the right pops open on white tile and Jo, blinking, all in black but her red Chuck Taylors, her wine-red hair, frowning as she takes in the two of them, severe yellow hair and blue eyes startled, Ettie in a black tank top and yellow tights, and the pale bare length of Chrissie, opening the door. "Oh," says Jo, "um, hi," but Chrissie's pulling Ettie in after her, "so you're, ah," Jo's saying, but Chrissie slams the door, leans back against it.

"Who was that?" says Ettie.

"That was Jo," says Chrissie. "You know Jo."

"Right." Looking about, the white walls, the high wide bed piled with white pillows, long white curtains drawn over the windows. "The surly housemate." Ettie parts them just enough to look out, down, the cars parked along either side of the tree-lined street below. "So this is where the magic happens," she says, letting the curtain fall from her hand, turning back to Chrissie, leaned against the foot of the bed. "Where's your things? Your clothes? Your underwear, dumped all over the floor? The lavender oil, the wobenzyme, you left all your supplements, I don't even want to *think* what you're doing to our hair," but Chrissie's saying, softly, "I have a shelf in the medicine cabinet, a drawer in the dresser, and I have," standing, stepping across the white rug, *"we* have," she says, laying her hand atop the dressing screen there in the corner, a simple frame of white-washed wood, and panels of plain linen. "This," says Chrissie.

"I don't," says Ettie.

"Watch," says Chrissie, slipping behind it, ducking behind it, a rustle, a thump, and then from the other side of it slips a shining black boot, planting its outrageously thick sole, wobbling a moment shift to find a balance bared knee thigh up the hip a black skirt shinely vinyl clinging corset-tight about her breast and up a hood to swallow head a blank glass diver's mask that's sweeping, back and forth, arms held out in tight black sleeves stretched down and down, past hands and down to join an empty swaying loop swung back and whirling forth and up, a tottering wide-hipped step, that cyclopean eye tilting, tipping, looming close. Ettie takes hold of the mask with both hands, tugs it awkwardly up, there's Chrissie, blinking, holding still as Ettie peels the bottom of the hood down past her chin, freeing a delighted smile, "See?" says Chrissie. "See? Baba Yaga!"

"La cabane sur des pattes de poule," murmurs Ettie.

"Allegro con brio!" cries Chrissie, lurching back, those thick soles clomping in time. "We can even," swinging the loop of her arm again, "have the sleeves linked, like a chain. The twisting and binding dance? All seamless! They won't rip! And the quick-change, at the end?" Quick mincing steps close to Ettie. "Think of something. Anything." A hunch of a shoulder, offering the loop of her arms for Ettie to take. "Don't tell me. Just, keep it in mind, and come on. Step back with me."

Ettie lays a hand on the slick black sleeve.

Together to the screen, then, and Ettie leads the way, backing behind it, "There," says Chrissie, sidling sidelong in those boots, stooping, and a rustle. The curtain stirs before the window, the merest shift of air in that white room, and the afternoon light.

First one, then the other, out from behind that screen, their yellow hair quite long now, past their chins, brushing bare shoulders and down, each in the same brief chemise, bluely translucent, skirling about their hips, their buttocks bare, and their long bare legs, their bare feet soundless on that rug, their faces hidden by black domino masks, eyes covered over by wide white lenses, wickedly surprised, laughing, and a fluttering rush of words between them, "comic strip" and "yes, indeed" and "exhibition!" and "inappropriate for dinner" and "but a dance?"

Shuffle-step, twirl, hands catch hands to pull close, each archly looking away, a push apart to spin about, but there, oh there, under an upraised arm, she stops, a sudden hitch in the works. Seize and yank to crash together arms about pressed tightly, masks clacking nose to nose, their lips a fierce quick kiss.

Then Ettie shoves away, turns away, steps away, toward the window.

Chrissie peels the domino from her face. "We can *do* it," she's saying, "we can do it *all.*" Tossing the mask to the bed. "Maybe she can't give us nearly as much money, but think of what we won't have to spend!" Holding out her hand, but Ettie's white-eyed mask turns back to her, that blank gaze a bit downcast, and Chrissie follows it back along her outstretched arm to her side, the lip-print there, just visible through the gauzy chemise. "Oh," she says, "oh, that isn't, we were just, it was a game, this morning, she drew it there, with a marker, it'll wash off," and then, "I can fix it." Looking about. "I can fix it." Over to the dresser, lifting aside papers, a glossy contact sheet, thumbnails of bridge-columns circled in red, "Aha," she says, and holds up a fat red marker. "Go on," she says, to those empty eyes. "Take it off."

Ettie crosses her hands, tugs the chemise up and off, drops it to the rug. That mask still fixed in place. Holds her arm up and out of the way as kneeling Chrissie leans close, a hand on her belly, marker hovering, "Here we go," she says, and sketches quick a curve of lip. "Just the same," she murmurs, and another stroke of the marker. "Just the same."

"Huh," says the woman in the long, silver-buttoned black coat, stopped on the landing, a hand on the railing of the next flight up. "I would've sworn, in court, this building? When we were outside, it only had two storeys."

"Three one two," says Ettie below her. "Third floor."

That next flight ends in a narrow landing, just large enough for the both of them to stand before a plain brown door. Black numerals, 312, hung above a peephole, the rim of it pitted with rust. The woman in the long black coat lifts a hand to knock, but reaches instead for the little grey hat on her head, resettling it, dimpling the pinch in the crown. "Ready?" she says to Ettie behind her, in a pale blue ski jacket, yellow tights. Ettie just reaches past to rap smartly on the door.

It's opened by Iona, tall and broad, her close-cropped hair a virulent chartreuse, a white bolero jacket over a white and gold maillot, and golden basketball shoes on her feet. "Goodness," says the woman in the long black coat, and then, "hi. Anne Thorpe, to see Ysabel Perry."

"Her majesty's expecting you," says Iona.

"Majesty," says Thorpe, with a hint of a smirk. And then, "This is my assistant," with a gesture back to Ettie, "Stephanie, ah, Stephanie – "

"Halliwell," says Ettie. "Stephanie Halliwell."

"They're in the garden," says Iona, stepping back to let them in.

"Garden?" says Thorpe.

Down a hallway under strings of yellow lights, opening the last of the doors at the end there, and through a narrow dark room, bulky machines stacked up under patterned cloth, and opening a door at the other end on a blare of light that washes over as they come out on a little wooden porch, a single step down to lush grass spread out to low parapets, here and there islands of the building's infrastructure, a ventilator hood, chimney pots, the bulky box of a fan. Wooden tubs hold small trees brightly green, and a raised bed there bubbles over with flowers, pale daffodils and tulips red and violet, a froth of pansies orange, yellow, pink and white and just past that two Adirondack chairs, unpainted, draped with thick white towels. On the one laid out on her back is Chrissie, eyes closed, shining slickly pale, the other Ysabel, a gleaming golden brown. "Oh, hello," she says, sitting up on her elbows. "I wasn't expecting you so soon." The both of them quite nude.

Thorpe struggles with her smirk. "We can, wait inside," she says, "or come back later," but "No," says Ysabel, "no," reaching for a pair of smokey aviator sunglasses. "Unless this makes you uncomfortable?"

"Just trying to figure out if this is more Helmut Newton, or LaChapelle," says Thorpe, watching as Iona drags over a couple of floppy white hassocks. "Oh," says Ysabel, "you know these first really sunny days. The temptation's always to overdo it." Thorpe drops heavily into one of the hassocks as Iona adjusts the fit of her bolero. "Something to drink?" Ysabel's saying.

"Shall we take your coats?" Thorpe shakes her head. "How about you, Ettie?"

Chrissie opens her eyes. The shadow looming, blue ski jacket, Ettie fiercely haloed, and whatever her expression might be lost in all that glare.

"It is good to see you again, Ettie," says Ysabel.

"Her assistant," says Ettie, abruptly, stepping out of the light. "I'm her assistant."

"Of course," says Ysabel.

Chrissie sits up, an arm folded under her breasts, hand pressed to her side, as Ettie lets her blue jacket drop to the grass. "I'll have one of those," she says.

On the table between the Adirondack chairs a couple of cocktail glasses, something palely green in each, though much less in the glass on Ysabel's side. "Gin and absinthe, darling – a Dortmunder, isn't it?"

"Dorflinger," says Iona, stooping to pick up the jacket.

"Do make another," says Ysabel, "for everyone," but Thorpe's shaking her head again, "Just water, for me," she says, and "Of course," says Ysabel, "certainly, but make her one anyway, in case she changes her mind."

"I never drink when I'm working," says Thorpe. Her smirk has curdled.

"Is that what we're doing?" says Ysabel.

"In theory."

"How *does* this work, then." Ysabel lies back in her chair, reaching over to lift the lid of a small brass box, there by her glass, fingering out a cigarette, a ragged matchbook, and "Well," says Thorpe. "I ask you a series of pointedly leading questions, which you just as pointedly ignore in favor of your own narrative, and whether that's a meandering stream of consciousness, or a smoothly machined message that will not be derailed, I guess we'll find out soon enough. Then, because this is entirely on spec, a couple weeks, a couple months, whenever I manage to place it, I'll write something that paraphrastically bears little to no resemblance to whatever notes I bother to take today, which matters less than you might think, because whichever editor will massage the piece beyond all recognition to fit whatever they had in mind when they bought it. Now. If you're lucky, they'll spring for a round of fact-checking, but don't let it fool you: what seems perfectly, straightforwardly correct by itself in a question comes out utterly, improperly off in an expository paragraph, and you'll demand a correction, which maybe they'll print, but who gives a shit, since nobody who reads the original piece will ever notice it, and anyway all anyone ever remembers is the headline spat out at the last minute by an intern who only ever skims the first couple of paragraphs of whatever the hell this will end up being. So." She smiles, she shrugs. "Shall we get started?"

Ysabel tilts her head, blows out a stream of smoke. "What about pictures?"

"Pictures," says Thorpe. "Is that why you went to all this," a hand, waved about, a chuckle, "that, all that comes much later in the process. If at all. And the art director will set that up. If they even have one. Nothing to do with me; I'm just the writer."

Laid back in her chair behind those amber glasses Ysabel lifts her cigarette for another drag, and the crackle of the coal at the end of it. "I meant," she says, "pictures of the Ramp. The columns beneath it. The artwork, that I want to talk about. That we want to save. Even if you have no say over artwork, perhaps looking them over might help you focus your, what's the word, pitch?" Another drag. "Is that the word?" And then, "I can go put on a wrap, if you'd rather."

"No," says Thorpe, and "no," and then, "all right," leaning forward on the hassock, "sure. Let's see 'em, if you got 'em."

"Chrissie?" says Ysabel, those amber glasses still fixed on Thorpe. "Could you hand them to me, please?"

Chrissie, still sitting up, still folded about herself, leans over, lifts her glass from from a crisp new manila folder on the table, the sheen of it blemished by a single drop of something, liquor, sweat, oil. Ysabel takes the folder from her and opens it in her lap, and within are five or six black-and-white photographs, pillars shadowed by the deck of a bridge overhead, set in cracked pavement, and murals on each of them, a scribbled bird perched on a bulbous nose grown from a scraggled sketch of a tree, a faded hint of a swan above a sheet of simple music, a monstrous owl of ribboned feathers, clutching a pen, above a scroll marked with words, till he dead. She hands one to Thorpe: a chalk-robed hermit pushing against the very edge of his column with a staff, a lantern held up by his shortened arm. "Huh," says Thorpe.

"These are just a few," says Ysabel. "I had them blown up, as examples." Iona's stepping off the porch, a tray in her hands laden with fresh cocktails. "There are seventeen distinct pieces, on a dozen columns, painted, or drawn, I suppose, some three generations ago – "

"By Athanasios Stefopoulos," says Thorpe, "who worked as a night watchman for the railroad, back in the day. Just passing time between trains." A hand up, waving away the tray Iona proffers. "I've been known to do the occasional lick of homework."

"We called him Tom," says Ysabel.

"Did we," says Thorpe, as Chrissie suddenly swallows what's left in her glass, then lifts Ysabel's away, clearing room as Iona sets down one by one filled glasses, astringently green in the sunlight.

"Back in the day," says Ysabel, as Ettie snaps out a hand to Chrissie, "Come on," she says. "The columns are well-known," Ysabel's saying, "an unofficial landmark of the city, appearing in a number of films, some quite famous," but "Come *on*," says Ettie, her hand still outstretched. Chrissie's turned away, she's handing the empty glasses up to Iona. "Let's go," says Ettie.

"I'm enjoying myself," says Chrissie, laying back on her towel. "The Ramp," says Ysabel, "well, the Viaduct, I suppose, to be pedantic," but Ettie seizes one of the full glasses from the table and drinks it off at once. "There," she says, daubing her lips with her wrist. "We're even." Her other hand still held out.

"The Ramp," says Ysabel, "is due to be demolished in July."

"By your brother," says Thorpe.

Ysabel inclines her head, a point of order, "The Department of Transportation has the keeping of the Ramp," she says, "as they maintain the, infrastructure," savoring the word, "of all the bridges that the city owns."

"It's gonna be knocked down by a contractor working for the River District development consortium," says Thorpe, "if we're gonna be pedantic."

Ettie hurls her glass to the grass, "We're *going home,*" she says, snatching at Chrissie's hand, but "Don't be ridiculous," says Chrissie, slapping her hand away, and *"Girls,"* says Ysabel, then.

"*Fuck* you," snarls Ettie.

Those amber glasses turn, look up to her, the smile serene beneath them. "Tell me, Ettie. Have you checked your messages?" Thorpe's looking down, at the little grey hat in her hands. "What?" says Ettie, after a moment.

"Have you checked your messages?" A fleeting lick of her lips. "I believe Mr. Davies has been trying to reach you."

"Ah, he's texting, emailing, he's pissed because we're totally blowing him off," that last, forcefully, to Chrissie. "All these meetings he wants to set up, with photographers?"

"Actually," says Ysabel, "today, I think you'll find he wants to know if you are free for dinner." Thorpe turns away, looks over her shoulder at Iona, waiting patiently by the porch. "Dinner," says Ettie.

"We're meeting tonight, the two of us, you see, and thought it might be swell to have the two of you along. It's in a restaurant," a mocking lilt to that smile now, "in public. Chrissie? Why don't you take your sister inside, to find something nice for you both to wear tonight. Leave me and Ms. Thorpe to finish our discussion without distractions." Chrissie's already getting to her feet, and "Um," says Ettie, taking the hand Chrissie holds out to her, "wait," stumbling as she sets off after Chrissie across the grass.

"I prefer Miss Thorpe," says Thorpe, then.

"Miss?" says Ysabel. "How charmingly old fashioned."

"Nah, it's just – when I commit to a bit? I *commit,*" says Thorpe. "Now. This Mr. Davies? Is that Reginald Davies? High-end niche marketing guru, budding property developer?"

"You *have* done your homework," says Ysabel.

Here there are languid golden blossoms stuffed with soft cheese, and shards of pastry topped by baked apples and onions, misshapen little waffle-lumps under clouds of cream and fresh berries, piles of nuts that shine stickily, dustily dulled with spices, palm-sized tarts filled with savory custards of yellow and pale green and pink, toast soldiers smeared with smashed green peas and twists of mozzarella, yellow leaves of endive cupped like boats, freighted with glistening cabbage and broccoli slaw and shreds of pickled carrot, but it's a tight-wound knot of crispy noodles, stickily clung with finely chopped herbs, that she plucks up, turns over, "These look good," she says, popping it in her mouth.

"It all looks good," says Luys, hands in the pockets of his brown jeans.

"I don't see the Duchess," she says, chewing. Her hair strung with beads, bare chest darkly freckled.

"You're Zeina, the new Mooncalfe?" he says, and she nods. "Perhaps it's best she's indisposed." He steps back from that laden table, all in brown, deep brown blazer, shirt striped brown and cream, into the crowd that mutters about the high wide room, a great wall of glass curving above them, dark trees beyond, and away past a glimpse of city the lone tooth of a snow-capped mountain. A brief nod as he approaches the only chair in the room for the Marquess, stood there in a slim grey dress, her only jewelry the vambrace strapped to her forearm, and the Soames in a green plaid suit, a meshback cap on his head, Trucks That Mean Business, it says, over the bill. "Mason!" he cries. "Has the Duchess arrived?"

"She is indisposed, my, ah, Excellency. I'm to convey her apologies."

"Shame," says the Soames. A burst of laughter from the Viscount yonder, throwing back his white-locked head, clapping the shoulder of the short wide knight beside him. Still chuckling, he approaches the chair in his blue suit, a colorless drink in his hand, to stand there by the Marquess, "Mason," he says, "good of you to fill in," and "She is indisposed," says Luys, but catching himself, a tight nod, "of course, m'lord. I will do what is asked of me."

"You'll do fine," says the Viscount, as the crowd all about shifts, turns, falls still. The King's stepping out of the hall there, into the high wide room, his white dress shirt, his black trousers, his coat of shimmering gold and black, his shock of orange hair bobbing with greetings, handshakes, a wave for someone across the press of them all. A woman in a purple gown, black scarf wrapped about her hair, leans close as he thanks an older man in a bucket hat, to whisper something in his ear. The King straightens, she daubs something white from the corner of his jaw, he grins, and a flash of something sheepish. And then more nods, more hellos, more shakes of hands until "Okay!" he says, and a single sharp clap. "Let's get this audience started," and flipping up the tails of his coat, sits him down. "We have a letter," pulling a folded sheet from a pocket, "well, an email, from our cousins Sigrid and Clothilde, offering gratitude for the condolences we have expressed, at their tragic loss."

"Would we had more to offer than condolence," says the Marquess.

"The police have had had no luck?" says the Viscount, silkily.

"This is no matter for police," says the Marquess, sharply.

"No?" says the King. "The assailants were mortals."

"Hounds, majesty," says the Marquess.

"She means a bunch of bums and beggars, sir," says the Soames then, "will do for cash, when owr's short for my boys."

"Southeast has been known to make use of them," says the Viscount, and Luys speaks up, then, "I assure you, sire, all, the Duchess has not – "

"Hold a moment, Mason," says the King; "these waters are more deep than they first seem. You know these hounds, Soames? They have a kennel?"

"A house in St. Johns, sire," says the Soames, "on Leonard Street," but the Marquess says, "It's not the kennel we should seek, majesty, but the leash, and the hand that loosed it."

"We know enough of husbandry to follow a simile," says the King, sitting back, tucking the paper away. "Which of them do we think, then? Alaric? Alphons? Euric?"

"Perhaps, sire," says the Viscount, "we should think beyond the Barons?"

The room about's gone breathlessly still. Luys opens his mouth, but closes it at a look from the King, who says, "You'd have us look to someone in the room?"

"Of *course* not," says the Viscount, a hand to his breast. "The Baron Medardus was poised," and his look slips from the King to the woman stood behind the chair, in her headscarf and her purple gown gone redly iridescent, "to make a great leap up. Any of the great and growing number of players ranged about our city might've feared such a shift in our balance."

"Are we grown so precarious?" says the King. "Very well. Soames: beard these hounds in their kennel, find this leash, follow it back to the hand. We would have news for our cousins when next we speak. You'd make an amendment, Linesse?"

The Marquess, swallowing something, shakes her head quickly.

"In the which case!" says the King, and a clap. "What new business for the court?"

The stirring of the crowd then, looking about to see who might be next to speak. The Viscount with a winsome shrug says, "Perhaps it's best if Southeast were to address us?"

"Mason?" says the King, but Luys shakes his head, "My lords and ladies, sire, her grace has nothing to impart."

"But good sir knight," says the Soames, "what of the bandit?"

The gasps, the looks, the murmured asides. "It *is* all that anyone might speak of," says the Viscount. "Why, but moments ago – Gwenders! Gwenders, come away from those hors d'œuvres a moment, come here," and the shuffling, the chuckling at that, the steps and turns about, there's an older man in a bucket hat, windbreaker and cargo shorts, brown socks and shower slippers, "Excellency," he says, studiously avoiding Luys's dumbstruck glare.

"You were just telling us," says the Viscount, "you were robbed this very morning, weren't you."

"Late last night, as might be counted. In through the back gate, off the alley, and out laid my boys with that bat o' hern. Great flopping head of a horse. Threatened the glassware, and mine own noggin, did I not bring direct the Addition's portion, or that as left on't."

"We hope your lads are recovering," says the King, and Gwenders nods, "Gracious to've asked, sire," but the King's continuing, "Ladd's Addition, though, correct? In Southeast?"

That's when Gwenders looks to Luys. "Aye, majesty," he says, "but it's Hob's own, getting word to her grace these days."

"Gwenders felt he might do well to bring the matter before the court," says the Viscount, "and I couldn't but agree."

"Majesty," says Luys, but the Soames is speaking over him, "Masked bandits, muggings and assaults, home invasions, murther – "

"Tom Thomas, please!" cries the King. "You'll frighten the horses. Now, Mason: you wished to make an answer, for Southeast?"

"Only to assure the court," says Luys, "we are determined to find, and to stop, this bandit," but there's a "Ha!" from someone, the Mooncalfe, prowling there behind the Marquess. "Of course, of course," the Viscount's saying, the drink in his hand a banner he's lifting, "but you must admit, for a month or more," lowering the glass to point to Luys, "this horse-headed brigand's eluded your every determination."

"But we know the outlaw's name," says Luys.

The Viscount blinks. "You do," he says.

"Marfisa, sir. Your sister. That once was Axe, to your Handle."

The glass droops, forgotten. "You are mistaken, sir," says the Viscount, his voice gone hoarse. "I have no sister." A deep breath, gathering himself. "A woman did fill that office once, it's true, but she turned her back on us all. I gave her the cash myself to board a bus, to anywhere. Points east." A smile, for the crowd. "She always wished to see the Apple Courts."

"I have fought her before, Excellency," says Luys. "Blade or bat, I know her arm."

"You are mistaken!" roars the Viscount, and there in his free hand the flash of a long-bladed dagger, but a bellow from the King, "Enough!" on his feet now. "Put up, Agravante!"

The crowd drawn back from them both, the Viscount, blade in one hand, his drink the other, Luys, half-crouched, his both hands up and empty.

"We are the Court of Roses," says the King, his blue eye and his brown both coldly furious. "We speak with one voice. We act toward one purpose! We lift this city up, and with it, all of us!" One hand sweeping up to point, "Mason!" he booms. "You will convey our displeasure to the Duchess. Axehandle!" Swept back, the Viscount agog, *"You* will speak with your sister."

"Majesty," says the Viscount, "if you mean this bandit, who only preys across the river, in Southeast – "

"You will speak, to your sister," says the King. "Are we understood?"

"Majesty," says the Viscount, with a nod. The King pushes past, out into the crowd that parts before him, and the woman in the purple gown follows him out of the high wide room, into the hall beyond. The Marquess all in grey nods curtly at something said by the Mooncalfe at her side, the Soames leans over, arm about the shoulders of the short wide knight, his bald head ruddy. The Viscount turns to Luys, smiling now, though his face is pale. "Did I not tell you?" he says. "You did do fine." Hoisting his glass to drain it off with a clink. "But one word of advice," he says, leaning close. "Learn to read the room. An invaluable skill, if one is to continue playing at this level." And off he goes with a lurch, through the dispersing crowd.

"Take care" – the Safety of the Space
this is Their plan

"Take care," says the woman in the mirror, and he lifts the razor from his lathered cheek. "I realize," he says, "you people get a lot of mileage out of pretending you never have time for the niceties?" Dipping the razor in foam-swirled water. "Whatever you're up to being too important. But, I mean, really – a closed bathroom door. Is nothing sacred?"

A shrug of her pearly shoulders. "Your majesty is alone, here." Her voice rich, her lips painted brown, her large eyes smiling. "Well," says Lymond, tilting his chin, "I'm headed down to a crowded audience in a minute. Make it quick."

"This briefing is a courtesy," she says, hands clasped behind her back. "You are advised of an operation currently under-way in your city, to secure an item of paramount importance to global security; you're assured that every effort will be made to secure said item with the minimum necessary dis-ruption."

Lymond takes up a towel to blot scraps of lather from his face. "If minimum disruption's risen to the level of informing the mark, I'd guess a couple strands of haywire've already popped loose." Leaning back against the sink, folding his arms, his dressing gown printed with antique travel postcards.

"Our agent in the field abruptly resigned. We've had to adjust our approach."

"And, presto: you've got a false flag, to drape over any further cock-ups. Neat." Clapping his hands, a hollow pop in these close quarters. "Tell me, which corner of the alphabet soup are you? FBI, CIA? DEA? FDA?" Her eyes still smile, her hands still clasped behind her back. "Okay," he says. "All right. I at least get to know what the item is. Courtesy surely extends so far?"

"A verse," she says. "Of Antethesis."

He looks off to one side, sucks his teeth, "That," he says, "explains a thing or two. Calls another couple into question, but there you go. Who has it."

Those smiling eyes, those clasped hands.

"Who's got the verse," says Lymond. And then, "Is it Jo?" She looks down. "Jo Gallowglas?" Looks up, all trace of her smile gone. "Not too hard to guess," he says. "That disruption damn well better be minimal, Agent Whoever-you-are – "

"How do they not smell it on you?" she asks, and he draws back at that, blinking his one eye blue, his one eye brown. "The rust," she says.

"Living, here, as we do," he says, "we're all brushed by mortal-ity. It lingers, in the nose."

"Some more than others, perhaps," she says.

"I think you think you're threatening me."

"Call as many of them to you as you might," and she sighs, "open the door as you will. Send them off to wherever you must. You know as well as we do that all you are depends on us. That if we were no more, you would never have been." Another shrug of those padded shoulders. "We will employ whatever means are necessary to secure the item," and she turns to open the door.

"Secure," he says, and she stops, her hand on the knob. "It's an interesting choice of words – neutralize, eliminate, remove, destroy, though destroy's hardly euphemistic enough, contain, I suppose, would've worked, or sequester, but you went with secure. Interesting." She isn't looking back at him there by the sink, but she hasn't turned the doorknob, either. "You don't want to get rid of it. You want to use it. You might be worried about it, but it's not the existential threat you just so thuddingly alluded to. Is it."

"Tell me, King of Roses." She turns to him, the door unopened. "Have you ever been to Mars?"

He leans back at that. "No," he says, "no, can't say I have."

"There is a glacier, in the shadows of the Micoud Crater," and her eyes are smiling again, "far to the north, where summer dawns last forever. The air is terribly thin, but as it warms to the rising sun it stirs, and the dust that covers the ice," but she stops, she looks away. "Keening isn't the right word. So thin, so faint, so hard to hear, but sharp enough to cut glass, and a moan so low you feel it in your boots. The songs are never the same, but they are gorgeous, unearthly, unspeakably haunted." She reaches for the knob again. "The Micoud Crater's still a very quiet place, you see. Utterly empty. So rest assured, majesty: we have our eye on the long game, we take great care, and we will not be caught off guard."

"That's," says Lymond, "all right, well. I guess I've been briefed. Will you," but she's opened the door, she's stepping out, "be joining us," he says following her into an empty hall, and no one to either side. She's gone. "Guess not," he says.

"A cup of coffee. A venti vanilla latte, to be precise." She looks down through her black-rimmed glasses at her hands, folded one over another in her black-jeaned lap. "I guess," she says, "she didn't want to pay. She just didn't want to, so, for a, a five-dollar cup of coffee, she asked me, she, asked me." Looking up at the rest of them now. "And she kissed me. And ever since," she swallows, "I, I saw her, once more, after that. We, um. She was." Looking down again, forelocks of her black hair tucked behind an ear, a bit of black lace about her throat. "I don't think I'm ready to talk about that, yet."

"That's fine, Petra," says Anna, but "You *saw* her again?" says Gloria, perched above them all, on the edge of the stage. "Because I mean I ran into her a couple of times after, but I never – "

"Yes, *thank* you, Petra," says the older woman by Anna, her hand on Anna's knee. "We certainly mustn't push anyone, beyond what they're comfortable with." Her unkempt hair a grey-dusted red, her bulky overshirt spangled with flowers like old wallpaper. "This must be a safe space for sharing the experiences we've had with what we all share."

"Not *all* of us," says Gloria, kicking her bare feet against the brick. Under a cavernous black hoodie her white T-shirt says Kitten Parkour, and in the darkness behind her, the canvases leaned up against one another, and each splashed with a figure leaping twirling spinning from one to the next. "If it's not safe *for* all," the woman by Anna is saying, "it's not safe *at* all."

"She means me," says Ettie.

Across that circle of a dozen or so sat on folded chairs she's slouched in hers, long legs stretched out in yellow tights and thick grey leg warmers, a pale blue ski jacket slung behind her. "She never asked me for a thing."

"So why are you here?" says a woman off to the left, shredded jeans and long dark hair, and Ettie says, "You know, that's a really good question," as the woman by Anna leans forward to say, "Why not start with your name."

"I was here just last," says Ettie, "week," a hand to her forehead, sighing, sitting up. "Stephanie Halliwell," she says. "My sister, Christine, she's the one who, who should be here."

Off to the right, a woman in a denim dress says, "You're strippers, right?"

"Burlesque artists," says Ettie. "Featured performers. Choreographers and curators, musicians, entrepreneuses. Movie stars. Just saying stripper, chère? Leaves out a bit."

"But you take off your clothes, for money?" says the woman in the shredded jeans.

"We're very good at it," says Ettie.

"How did your sister come to meet her?" says a woman whose hair is strung with dirty rainbow threads.

"We're putting together a show?" says Ettie. "She's one of the sponsors. Maybe. They started seeing each other, which isn't necessarily smart, but it happens, and as long you remember the ultimate point," she spreads her hands, looking about the circle of them all. "But one night, one morning, really, Chrissie comes home, despondent, and I, I guess that's when she got asked, or whatever?" They're all sitting up at that, sitting back, looking away, a nod, a sigh here, a flicker of a smile there, all of them but the one woman, her chair pulled back almost out of the circle, wrapped in a long black coat, and a little grey hat on her head. "Chrissie literally stayed in bed for, like, a week after that. And I figured, I don't know. It's a bad breakup. This has happened before. But. But this," her shoulders rise, a deep breath in and out. "It was like, and I swear, this is what happened: I felt a chill, all over my body, the hair stood up, on the back of my neck," her hand reaching up, falling away, "and then, and then there was a knock. At our door. And nobody knocks at our door, unless it's pizza." Smiles and shrugs and nods, a half-voiced laugh, rippling among them all. "Nobody knows where we live, it's one of the rules, it's sacrosanct. But still. Somebody is. And what do you do, when there's a knock?" Looking about. "You answer it. And, I mean, I knew, who it was. The chill, the shiver, I knew. Even though I knew it was weird to know. And it was like, I thought, maybe, it would be okay, she, she couldn't come in. If she wasn't invited. Like a vampire. Like she was a vampire. I could talk to her. I could turn her away, it wouldn't do any harm, just to open to door. So I did." Another rise and fall of her shoulders. "And she walked right past me. I didn't say a word, she just," and Ettie swallows. "And not, five minutes later. My sister. My twin – since we were born? We have spent every day of our lives together. Twenty-four seven, we, we live together, we work together, add it up, I think, all told, there's maybe six weeks? Seven? When we weren't in shouting distance of each other." Head lowered, eyes closed. "Not even five minutes after I opened the door, they walked out. And I haven't spoken to my sister in thirteen days."

"She's with her," says Petra, all in black.

"She gets to be with her," says the woman in the denim dress.

"I want her back," says Ettie, looking up to Gloria. "You said you'd help me get her back."

"We'll talk about that in a minute," says Gloria. "Anybody else? Want to share?"

They're milling about the one end of that cavernous space, still close by the ring of chairs, the sunlight falling diffidently from up under the rafters. Ettie stands one hand on the back of her chair looking off toward the stage, where Gloria's hopped down, she's talking to the woman in the long black coat, and there's Marfisa beside them now, in a bulky blue sweatshirt. "I didn't mean anything, by that," says someone, and Ettie shakes her head, looks away, the woman stood beside her, in the denim dress. "I've seen you dance – that bit you did, with the Batwoman, and the Joker?"

"Alice," says Ettie. "Batwoman and Alice. And Prince. Yeah, that got us a C and D, but the C and D got us a post on Boing Boing? So it worked out okay."

"Cool," says the woman in the denim dress, her thick dark hair cut short. "Bobbi," she says, and a sideways shrug.

"Enchanté," says Ettie, and then, "How did you get into all this?" Over there, silver buttons flash as the woman in the long black coat turns, scoffing at something Gloria's said. "I used to work at Mary's," says Bobbi.

"Oh," says Ettie, but then her attention snaps back, "oh," she says.

"Yeah," says Bobbi. "Anyway, she was there, the night of the fire."

"I," says Ettie. "Wow. And she, and you," but Gloria's calling, "Ettie, hey," waving her over, and "I should, ah," says Ettie, and Bobbi nods. Shrugs. "Next time," she says.

"Do you know Anne? Anne Thorpe?" Gloria says, as Ettie approaches. The woman in the long black coat holds out a hand and Ettie clasps it, after a moment. "Should I?" she says.

"I don't really need to be known," says Thorpe, with a single firm pump of her hand. "Only read. You're Étienne Limoges? One half of the scandalous Sœurs Limoges?"

"Oh!" says Ettie, brightening. "You write about music, you're a music critic! For Anodyne!"

"For anyone who'll pay," says Thorpe.

"Anne," says Gloria, grinning broadly, "is writing a story about her."

"I'm looking into it," says Thorpe, as "Story?" says Ettie, looking from Thorpe to Gloria, to Marfisa behind them, leaned back against the stage, and a nod of that white-haired head for Ettie.

"Ms. Ysabel Perry, scion of the Acme Parking fortune," says Thorpe, "has announced an initiative to stop, or at least delay, the destruction of the Lovejay Ramp, which they're doing for the whole Old Town rejuvenation, the Brewery Blocks, the Pearl District, all that. Save the Lovejoy, or something. She could use a little pizzazz in her PR."

A brittle look crosses Ettie's face, that does not smash into a scowl or a snarl as she turns to Gloria. "This is it?" she says. "This is your plan?" To Marfisa. "To help each other? To be useful?" To Thorpe. "You're gonna write a goddamn puff piece?"

"Hear her out," Gloria's saying, but Thorpe says, *"She* might want a story about her conservation efforts. I'm after the story about," and a tossed-off wave of her hand, "this."

"This," says Ettie, "what this, what are you – "

"All of this!" says Thorpe, a bit too loud. "This whole, *all* of you. There's a story here. I want it." Resettling the little grey hat on her head. "I don't have the faintest idea yet what I'm going to *do* with it, mind. But I'm going to meet her this afternoon, at her apartment. I understand your sister's staying there?" And then, as Ettie's looking from her to Gloria, to Marfisa, and back, "I thought you might like to tag along, as my assistant. Which, you won't have to do any assisting. Strictly an unpaid

internship." Thorpe chuckles. "A tissue-thin ruse, to get you in the door. See what happens."

Ettie blinks. Marfisa's smiling. "See?" Gloria's saying. "Told you we'd cook something up."

"Okay," says Ettie, to Thorpe, "but aren't you scared? That she'll ask her magic question, or whatever?"

"Maybe," says Thorpe. "Are you?"

"It's been a while," he says, leaned back against the white-tiled wall.

"It's only been a couple of weeks, Phil," she says, sat back against a thick wooden leg of the enormous butcher's block. "Actually, I think it's been two weeks exactly."

"No, I mean," he says. "Since we did that." His great beard brushing his chest, his bare shoulders hatched with curls of dark hair. "It doesn't have to be a thing."

She sighs, heavily, "Of *course* it's a thing." Her shoulders, her upper arms, her back and her breasts thicketed with tattoos, calligraphic vines and branches, leaves and flowers, and creeping crawling peering within so many animals and little birds. "You think you can just, wait, figure out how *I* feel about it, so you can maybe ease it into some equilibrium that slopes whichever way *you* feel about it." She leans over, reaching for a discarded thermal shirt, her undone jeans slopping about her hips. "Saying it's not a thing is about the most useless thing you could say."

"I don't know," he says. Closing his eyes. "How I feel."

"I thought," she says, wrestling her way into the shirt, "you were ready to talk."

He's pulled something from a pocket of the dark grey windbreaker sprawled on the floor beside him, a pair of sunglasses, the lenses small and round and purple. "I am talking," he says, as he unfolds them.

"And I thought you quit," she says, getting to her feet.

"I did," he says, looking up at her buttoning her jeans, fastening her belt. "I can't do what I did. I can't hear myself think, anymore," and then he looks down, and lifts the sunglasses to hook the spindly arms about his ears. "It's quiet, but it's so *quiet,*" he says, leaning forward, elbows on his upraised knees. "I'm useless, to them." She's leaned back against the butcher's block, arms folded. "So I quit," he says, looking up, the glass green over his eyes. "But they think he's dead and gone. My friend, who it turned out wasn't my friend. The one I left on the bridge. But he isn't gone. If he were gone, I wouldn't know his name."

"Charley," she says. "Charlock."

"So they're wrong," he says. "He isn't gone. So," and he sighs. "So. I don't know if that," a wave of his hand, "was something we should've, I should've, you need the, *I* need to, leave you the space, you need, to, to," but "Phil," she's saying, "Phil. Phil. If I need space, trust me. I'll take it." Turning about, her back to him, a scrape as she takes up something from the butcher's block. "So you're gonna go, is that it? Look for this guy, that isn't dead? See you when I see you?" It's a broad-bladed cleaver she's picked up, handle braced against her palm.

Mr. Keightlinger's frowning. "No," he says, "no," as he drags a black T-shirt to him across the floor, "I know where he is," he says. "I've always known where he is."

Gloved in pinkened Mail – a Kept eye – Asymmetry

Gloved in pinkened mail the metal slipping scrape against porcelain smear of a stain she shifts she grabs the pipe there bracing grunt and push back slap and groan his hands her hips her jeans about her knees his knees her belt a-flopping jangle keys or change in a pocket ringing snort and slap and slap again and "shit" she says and "there – like that – you" head hung low her hair quite short and spiky black the apron slung about her neck hung loose the ties undone her arms are folding pushing back against the bulk of him plowing groaning "skotosch" he says, or something like it, "hwikaz, witting" tossing his head that beard of his jutting "sulnthaz!" he roars, "Suntchazi!" jerking hammering clenching squeezing shaking her head she's "no" she's "not" she's "dammit, dammit" as she slaps the slaps the white-tiled blood-smeared wall she's hunching back against he shakes his shaggy head his brown hair whipping free of his loosening ponytail stuttering working a stilling slap and hitch and "don't" she blurts as he's leaning back his undone head eyes closed his mouth a-gawp his body rocking with the force of her shoves back again and again and her bare hand slapping "shibal" she spits and "shibal!" and he opens his eyes, seize and slam and meaty slap she coughs or sobs a grunt her breath a hiccup caught a tremor shivering shake her knees her hips her mail-gloved hand about the pipe and her pealing cry.

Across the stretch of concrete gleaming under fluorescent lights those boxes against the far wall, regular banker's boxes white and brown stacked four and five high in mostly regular columns, and set up before them a folding table and a high-backed black desk chair. Jo's tugging, pulling one of the boxes from the top of a stack, tipping it forward and down, up on her toes to get her fingers in the handles on either side before pulling it free, the weight of it a sudden swoop that swings her about with a grunt, heaving it up to brace against her belly as she hauls it to the table. Her oversized sweatshirt blue, and it says Brigadoon! across the front of it, and off that way the click and tap of footsteps breaking into a rush, "My lady!" cries Luys, hastening down the length of the garage, but she's already dropped the box by the table, she's dropping herself in the chair with a squeak and a sigh from the vinyl cushion. "There are those," says Luys, slowing, "who should help you with, those," even as she's throwing back the lid of the box.

"You look nice," she says, lifting a handful of photos to her lap.

"The audience, at noon today," he says, smoothing the front of his deep brown blazer, his shirt striped brown and cream.

"Yeah," she says, flipping one by one through the photos, plucking one from the handful, tossing it to the table, a silvery image of two women holding a large umbrella up over their heads and a third, all in black, to one side. "You got it covered, right?"

"I wish you would reconsider, my lady."

"I told you," she says, "if you're gonna, I mean, my liege. It's a less, confusing, way to, I mean, I looked it up."

"My liege," says Luys. "It would be best for all if you were to attend."

"Mason," she says. "You'll do fine. You're my lieutenant, you speak for me. Everybody says so." Flipping another photo over, and another. "The Vice Duke," she says, "Duke of Vice." And then, her grin folding itself away, "That didn't, that, came out wrong."

"There will be questions."

"So answer 'em. If you can. If you can't," and she shrugs.

"There will be decisions, to be made."

"So *make* them! God *damn,* Luys," she slaps the photos down on the table, "you *know* this shit. Better than I do. If you can't make the call," and she throws up her hands. "I am good for one thing, in all this. One. With the mask, and the sword. He needs me for that, well, he knows where to find me."

He looks down. She starts rifling through the photos, spreading them over the top of the table. After a moment, he says, "As my liege wishes."

"Damn straight," says Jo.

White apron streaked with red, the clean long slender knife in one hand, the other in a bulky mail glove, links of it pinkly slicked. She wrestles the leg about, skin of it yellow, mottled with brown bruises, deftly slices the flesh, then flops the bulk of it over, continuing that slice around above the trotter. Sets the knife aside to take up a small bone saw, which she fits in the cut, and begins to hack through the bone with quick squeaking strokes. Her black hair spiky short, and frilled about the collar of her white thermal shirt a thicket of black ink, leaves and branches, the beak of a bird. The bone cracks apart, and she tugs the trotter loose, sets it aside, looks up to see him there across the butcher's block, plain black T-shirt, dark grey warm-up jacket, his bushy beard the color of rich mahogany, his hair tied back in a club of a ponytail, a pair of small round sunglasses perched on his nose, the lenses greenly purple.

"Phil," says Ellen. And then, "You shouldn't be here."

"Story of us," he says. "For what it's worth, I'm ready."

She sets the bone saw aside, clink.

"You said, come back. When I'm ready," he says. "To talk."

"Let me finish this," she says, picking up the knife.

She's leaned half the front seat back, not quite supine, she's laid back wrapped in a pale blue ski jacket, white blanket over her lap. The rearview mirror's skewed to look back and up at a long low building painted white and widely trimmed in green, and all the windows dark in the low morning light but the top storey, the third storey, where yellow lamps shine behind white curtains, and the rooftop garden beside it strung with little lights ablaze, and a woman standing there, her black hair short, wrapped in a filmy white gown, smoking a cigarette. Someone's tapping on the passenger window.

She sits up, then reaches over to wind the window down an inch or two, peers up through the gap at the woman leaning down out there, sheepskin coat, palely blued cloud of hair. "Hey," says Marfisa. "Stef. May we speak?"

She pops the lock, and Marfisa pulls the door open, her hair lighting up golden white as she climbs in, choking up on a baseball bat to pull it in beside her as she settles on the passenger side of the seat. Something flops in her lap, a rubbery empty horse's head, the bulging dark eyes, the limp snout. "Keeping an eye on them?" she says, stooping to look back and up through the driver's side window, the long low building across the street, white and trimmed in green, and all the windows lining the two storeys dark. "Not much going on."

Ettie leans back, out of the way, "Look," she says, pointing, "up there, look," and Marfisa leans further, over her, awkwardly twisting to look up and out through the skewed rearview mirror. There's the building, long and low, and there's the third storey, lit up against the deepening dawn, and two figures in the garden now, another woman, yellow hair severely straight, an embrace, a kiss.

"Well," says Marfisa, sitting back on her side of the car. "That is a clever trick."

"*I* didn't," says Ettie, "it's just, the mirror. Could be any mirror, for all I know."

"Or only the mirrors of old automobiles, perhaps," says Marfisa, stroking the white leatherette of the dash. "This is a formidable machine."

"Got us to North Dakota and back. Twice," says Ettie. "But you didn't drop in to compliment our car."

"I was visiting, with friends," says Marfisa, "and happened by – but I do want to speak with you, about the gallery. They'd – we'd – like it, if you were to come back."

Ettie looks away, up into the mirror, "It's like I told Gloria," she says. "You talk too much. You meet, and you talk about your feelings, and you argue and you yell and then you have a meeting about the yelling, and I just, I don't have the," she closes her eyes. "Patience," she says.

"You'd rather watch?" says Marfisa, and Ettie opens her eyes, glaring up at her. Marfisa smiles, but it's wistful, too weak to reach her eyes. "Do you know who she is, that you are watching? That woman, with your sister?" Leaning over again, looking up into the mirror. "She is her one true love. The queen, of her world." Sitting up, leaning back. Ettie looking down, away. "Just as she is of Gloria's," says Marfisa. "And Anna's. And of mine, as well." She opens the passenger door abruptly, shifts the bat, propped out against the sidewalk, but stops, sitting there, and both feet still in the car. "We can all help each other," she says. "Help her."

Ettie's eyes have closed, again. "By talking some more, I bet."

"There might even be some yelling," says Marifisa. "But come, this morning. For tea, or coffee, if nothing else. But what we have to talk about, today, I think we will all find – useful."

She climbs out, steps away, off up the street. Ettie shakes her head. After a moment, she leans way over, reaches out, manages to snag the door. Pulls it shut.

Snip snip, the wee silver scissors in her hand, snip, and bit by bit short black curls tremble and fall. Snip. She pinches a wayward sprig, twists them together between thumb and forefinger, tugging aside, scissor-blades brought close to goosefleshed skin, snip. Holding the tuft up before her lips, she puffs, they fly away, she leans in close to blow again, clearing the strays, and that brown belly shivers, and those thighs, "That tickles," says Ysabel, annoyed.

Chrissie blows once more, a giggled flutter, "But I've got your attention."

Ysabel looks away from the contact sheet she's holding, glossy in the harshly immediate light of the bedside lamp. "What are you doing down there? You'd better be keeping it even."

"I wouldn't dream of messing up perfection," says Chrissie. Naked, and curled on her side, her knees up on the pillows. "But I could," combing the trim little thatch with her finger-tips, "denude you, if you'd like?"

"Is that what you'd like?" says Ysabel, circling with a fat red marker one of the images on the sheet, a column shadowed under a bridge. "Perfection, that you wouldn't mar, but you'd raze to the ground. As it were."

"Only if you want." Chrissie pillows her cheek on Ysabel's thigh, and just the lightest of touches for the furl of lip below that thatch, and Ysabel shivers again, but shifts, her foot, her knee, her legs apart. Her filmy gown undone, splayed open, and her breasts and belly bare. "The fashion," she says, "is to go without a frame, is that it? These days?"

"For us," says Chrissie, fingers lazily circling, "it's more of a uniform? No shirt, no pubes, no service," and she snorts up an awkward giggle.

"You aren't the funny one," says Ysabel. A squeak of the marker circling another image, a scribbled bird. "Remember that."

"I know," says Chrissie, and a sigh. "I know."

"You've no tattoos," says Ysabel. "Or piercings. Aren't those part of the uniform, as such?"

"Our ears are pierced," says Chrissie. "But we did that when we were twelve. That's part of our thing, though. It's in the name? Sœuers Limoges. Flawless," her fingers, pale, "porcelain," stroking the olived shadows about the navel before her, "skin."

"But what if you wanted a tattoo," says Ysabel, setting the contact sheet aside, capping the marker.

"I don't."

"But if you did."

"It would be," says Chrissie, and then another sigh. "The mistake too many people make," she says. "It shouldn't be, just a mark here, a mark there, whatever. Willy-nilly. They need to be, the body, the whole, the whole effect, needs to be considered. And we would," she says, "it's just, simpler? Not to." Her hand on Ysabel's hip, now. "On you, I mean," she says. "Something bold, but a single color, a pattern, all the way around," a gesture, a circle, "geometric, but asymmetrical." Looking back up the warmly lamplit length of her, that hand settling once more by those short black curls. "Definitely, for you, asymmetry."

"But I don't want a tattoo," says Ysabel. Sitting up on her elbows, shrugging her gown back up on her shoulders, "Hold still," she says, and "What are you," says Chrissie, as Ysabel pops the cap off the fat red marker. "Hold still," she says again, leaning over.

"Ysabel," says Chrissie, "what are you drawing?"

"If you struggle, or laugh," says Ysabel, but then she jerks up, holding the marker away, "if you do *that* again," she says, "I'll *definitely* mess it up," and Chrissie quivering with stifled giggles lifts her hand away, stretching away along Ysabel's out-stretched leg, a stilling sigh, but then as Ysabel's leaning down again a fresh shudder, a laugh blown out through her nose, her firmly smiling lips, her eyes clamped shut, "Are you quite through?" says Ysabel, marker still held high, and Chrissie nods quick and tight. "A deep breath in," says Ysabel, "let it out, and hold *still.*" She leans over, and sets to with the marker.

"I'm so," says Chrissie, "happy, that you asked me. To come back."

"Are you."

"And if you, asked her. I'm sure. She'd say yes."

Ysabel looks up at that, at Chrissie's yellow hair, her eyelids shut, still bluely shadowed, her dreaming smile. "Is *that* what this is about," she says, and leans down again, to draw a careful curve.

"What," says Chrissie, still smiling.

"You've shared men with her," and a stroke of the marker, and another, "but she's never shared a woman, with you."

"That, that's not, no," she says, and Ysabel lifts the marker away again, "not at all," says Chrissie, her arm about Ysabel's leg.

"But it is true," says Ysabel, leaning down again with the marker.

"It's, the," Chrissie says, "the nature of the, industry, the uniform," and she laughs again, briefly, "Hold still," says Ysabel, "we're both," says Chrissie, "comfortable with," and she sighs, opens her eyes. The marker's paused again. "There's never been a woman before."

"I find that hard to believe," says Ysabel, stroking, daubing.

"If you asked her," says Chrissie, "I know. She'd say yes," and a squeeze, a kiss pressed to Ysabel's knee. "Because you are."

"But why should I," says Ysabel, lifting the marker away. "I have you." Lying back. "There," she says. "Willy-nil, and un-considered, but rather a bit symmetrical? If I do say so myself."

Sketched in red on Chrissie's flank, just below her breast, an exaggerated lip-print, a pout of a kiss. "I see," says Chrissie, and a long and languid stretch. "So now you're marked," says Ysabel. "You're mine." She sets the marker aside and lifts a leg up and over Chrissie's yellow head, shifting her hips as Chrissie reaches around, "Like *that*," says Chrissie, and a long, slow lick, "was ever in doubt," and Ysabel shivers.

Some time later, Chrissie says, faintly, but quite distinct, "What time is it?" Alone in that wide white bed. The lamp snuffed now, and the room gone dark. Ysabel lets the curtain fall from her hand, steps back from the window. "It's tomorrow," she says.

Chrissie sits up on her elbows, opening her eyes quite wide, a quick shake of her head as if dashing something off. "How long have I been *awake?*" she says.

"Come," says Ysabel, taking up her gown from the foot of the bed. "Let's go watch the sunrise. It's going to be a beautiful day."

THE HAT IN HIS HAND

THE HAT, THE HAT HE TAKES IN HIS HAND, stretches it out and turns it over, and then hiked up on his toes leaned up against the woven metal cheek he perches as high as he can that hat atop the giant face. It's a pink meshback cap, the hat, and the front and bill of it hashed with pink-and-black camouflage, and when he lets go it slides down the massive brow and tumbles from the bulbous metal nose to his feet. "Fine," he says, and scuffs a kick at it, "fine!" Staggering back from that giant, empty-eyed face. Stadium gates loom behind it, a great sign atop them that says Jeld-Wen Field, and the marquee beneath it, Portland Timbers vs. LA Galaxy, Saturday April 21, 7:30 kickoff, and then a dim round clockface pinked by streetlight, hands pointed at a quarter of three, or thereabouts. The starless sky above a black gone vaguely brown by those lights of the city still shining.

He snatches up a swollen garbage bag bouncing off his stumbled steps away across the plaza, swinging out as he turns to look back across the street, the great white wall of the building there rounding the corner as if it's turning its back, dotted with small anonymous windows, some here and there plugged with the boxy grilles of air conditioners, but most of them empty, even the glass gone, and all of them dark, unlit. An orange trash slide depending from a second-storey window, feeding into a hulking brown dumpster, ReBuilding Center, says the sign hung from it, DeConstruction Services. He throws up his hand, middle finger raised and waved at that wall, those windows, that dumpster, "Fuck you!" he roars. "Theodofucker!" The faint buzz of streetlights, a fan running somewhere, or maybe the wash of traffic, blocks away.

Lurching across the intersection, the one street curling away from the stadium, the arc of rails set in the pavement, he trips over the curb into a train stop, and shoves his hand in the garbage bag as it twists about, untwists itself, pulling out a handful of clothing that he lets drop, one by one, a pair of tights, one long sock, a T-shirt, a corduroy skirt. Draping a beige bra over a green junction box. His fingers glitter with silver rings, a snake's head, an ankh, an eagle in flight, his black jeans ripped at the knees, his black T-shirt that says Decisive Action by Western States, his dark hair dangled from his head hung low. He drops more clothing in his wake to the sidewalk, the rails, the pavement, more socks, more T-shirts, a loose-knit shrug, some complex contraption of ribbons and hooks and panels of satin and lace. Between him and the empty street now an aisle of young trees freshly planted, newly leafed, and he hangs more clothing from branches as he goes, a pink fishnet stocking, a pair of boxers printed with cavorting cats, a crumpled crinoline skirt, a gauzy blouse, until he sticks his hand in the garbage bag and rummages around and comes up with nothing, nothing left at all.

He leaves the empty bag at the corner.

A couple of low steps. Leaning way over bracing a hand he sits him down, wincing. Two stolid wooden doors behind him, signs hung there, No Smoking, No Vaping, No Solicitation. He shivers, folds his arms about himself. Leans against the base of the column there, to one side of the steps. Closes his eyes. The column, slender, rising up and up past a grimy, shadowed lintel to a curled Ionic capital. There are letters carved in the lintel, over the doorway there, but whatever they might say can't be made out in the darkness.

English, which can express the thoughts of
Hamlet and the tragedy of Lear, has no words
for the shiver and the headache. It has all grown
one way.

—*Virginia Woolf*

NO. 30

" – on pretending that – "

THE LOCOMOTIVE stubby, boxy, there between brick-walled warehouses, an idling rumble so large and full they step around, move through it, a dozen or so in coveralls, toward the lone boxcar coupled to the end. A couple clamber up on the walkway running back up the side of the locomotive to knock the panels of it, peer in the vents, wreathed in the streetlight tangled on steaming exhaust. The rest cluster about a sliding door in the side of the boxcar, splashed with graffiti. A lever's thrown, latches undone with booms that echo under the rumble, that door slides open even as an overhead door grates up on the warehouse there, snort a forklift pulling out onto the loading dock, and shouts, arms waving, someone in coveralls leaping up on the dock to confer heatedly with a man in shirtsleeves. The woman behind the wheel of the forklift holds up a clipboard. The rest of them all in coveralls form up a line across the street, from boxcar to loading dock, hup! a shout as swung from the boxcar comes an enormous burlap sack, hup! as it's caught and passed to the next, and the next, even as a second swings out, a third, as the first's heaved up on the dock, neatly dropped on the forklift's waiting pallet, and the next, with grunts and whups of bags passed hand to hand down the line. I'm the man, someone chants, the publican man, and others join in, that waters the workers' beer! Yes I'm the man, the middlin' man, that waters the workers' beer! What do I care if it makes them ill, or it makes them terrible queer, I've a car and a yacht and an æroplane, and I waters the workers' beer!

Past the warehouse, deep shadows of an overpass, a cast-iron streetlight stands sentinel on high. Two men beside the balustrade up there, couple-three yards above the snoring locomotive, watching them unload the boxcar, another hup! and a hitch in the line, someone slaps the fender of the forklift, the load lurches, lifts, the motor whines as it backs away. From the boxcar tumbles a fresh pallet, grey scraps of lumber nailed ruthlessly square, falling edge-on into the waiting hands of the line to be caught and awkwardly rolled like a cornered wheel up to the loading dock tipped, falling, bang! into place. In its wake the heavy sacks resume their swinging, tossing progress, I reaches my hand for the water-tap, and I waters the workers' beer!

"Boys wanted to put on a show," says one of the men up there. "Send it off in style." His suit a greyly green, his black meshback cap that says FTZ-45 over the bill. "Last delivery by rail to a factory in the Triangle. End of an era."

"Triangle?" says the other man, sweater the color of oats, shock of hair gone dull in the streetlight.

"The Northwest Industrial Triangle, sire? This vitiated district of your demesne, that we have faithfully served so many years?"

"It's called the Pearl District, Tommy Tom," says the King. "Has been since Nu Shooz had a hit."

"Pearls," says the Soames, looking out over the warehouse rooftops. He lifts a hand, a benediction, "Well, they'll grow in peace. These crusty oysters won't anymore be troubled by the clamor of honest work."

"You wax elegiac," says the King. "When this ramp comes down?" A gesture for the viaduct stretched out toward the river, the bridge, the unlit hulks of warehouses below. "When the condos finally go up, all at once? These old oysters will need gutting, renovating, replacing. Construction's honest work." A sidelong smile. "And as clamorous."

"Construction ebbs and flows, majesty. And when it's done, it's done."

"When it's done, Tommy, there'll be a brewpub. Fifteen hundred barrels a year." Pointing to the bustle below. "A grocery store," waved at an empty warehouse, "a twenty-storey tower," up along the viaduct, "anchored by the first brick-and-mortar of a major online retailer. And running down Lovejoy, right under our feet? The first new streetcar line in any city since the war! Art galleries, design studios, turnkey manufactories, software ateliers, fulfillment conciergeries, small presses for video, paper, internet, small-batch distilleries, pickleries, roasteries, perfumeries," leaning out over the stone balustrade, reaching for what's to come, "creative engineers and fashion directors, indigenous restauranteurs and industrial docents, network cartographers, data sculptors, experiential curators, ten *thousand* people, right here, and all they might ever need or want but a block or two away."

"Stevedores," says the Soames. "Wharfies. Dockers. Teamsters and bullockers, outfitters. Firers. Conductors and yardmasters, longshoremen, switchmen, brakemen and signalers, porters, bulls," as below, the forklift's hauling another load away, into the warehouse, and another empty pallet's tumbling down the line of laborers, I puts in strychnine, they're chanting, some methylated spirits and a drop of paraffin!

"Tell me, Tommy," says the King. "Did you ever meet Pearl?"

"Pearl, sire?" says the Soames. "Can't say I have."

"You seem quite close to the Viscount, these days; I wondered how far back that might've been the case." And then, still lightly, smiling, "Do you really believe the Duchess set the hounds on Medardus?" That smile slips away. "Or, to be more precise: did either of you believe, that I'd believe."

The Soames says, "She did spend time with a number of the hounds, my lord. In her days on the street, before she caught your sister's favor." Still looking down at the laboring line. "Perhaps they did not do so at her direction, but still, I think, we'll find: with her license."

"License?" says the King. "I'd no idea she'd annexed Lake Oswego. I can figure the Viscount's play in this, Tommy, but you? You surprise us. You'd throw away your sterling word for a bit of backup in your beef with the Marquess."

"The Duchess, sire," says the Soames, "we all see how your sister does dote on her. And she did love the Duke, and he loved her, but – she is a Gallowglas, for all that. Who knows what mortal fears might drive her, and to what?"

The King turns about, his back to the stone. "Four terminals," he says. "Rail yards in Brooklyn and Northwest. The airport, Swan Island, up to your eyeballs in the ten-year and twenty-year development plans, a place at court, and a full share of the Apportionment. No other Soames has risen so high, Twice Thomas, nor done so much for his people."

"It is as nothing without your majesty's generosity," says the Soames.

"Yeah," says the King. Pushing off the railing then, headed away, hands in pockets, down the ramp, the shadowed street below. The Soames folds his arms. The sacks keep piling up, huff and grunt and slap, there isn't the profit there used to be, in watering workers' beer!

She sits up abruptly, at the table neatly stacked with photographs, siennas, rusts, dull greys, a fumble of her fingers, peeling away the one stuck to her cheek, an image of men in old dark suits on steps before a stolid door, and part of it scratched or scraped away. Blinking thickly at an empty drinking glass, a ring of milk left at the bottom. Turning with a jerk at the footfalls that ring across polished concrete, a man in brown shorts and a brown work shirt, clipboard in his hand, "Your grace?" he calls, down the length of the garage. "Jo Gallowglas?"

"What?" snaps Jo, standing up from the high-backed black desk chair.

"Apologies, ma'am," he says. "There was no one to sign for this," and "What?" Jo's saying, as he holds up a white envelope, "message, ma'am."

"Who from," she says.

"Ah," looking down at his clipboard, "Beaumont," he says. "Christian Beaumont."

Becker's eyes are closed, but his brows lift in surprise or delight perhaps, at something in a dream, a deep breath in through his nose and out through lips hatched about with stubble, pressed together to shape a word he doesn't speak. The shuff of bed-clothes, crisp linens striped with indigo. His eyes blink brownly open as his face arranges a consternated scowl, a grimace as he lifts his head, a wince as he props up on an elbow, looks down the length of himself softly pale in the buttery daylight, boxer briefs pink and black in the clutch of those widely grey-furred fingers crumpling, tugging, grizzled scalp a-bob, blue eyes lifted up to meet his, as from between those lips slips out his cock, stiff enough now to sway over swell of belly, and long grey mustaches trailing, weighted to either side with pewter beads that drag up his skin as Pyrocles smiles and says, "Good morning, beloved."

"Oh," says Becker, falling back to the pillows, but then, when Pyrocles takes him in his mouth again, "no, wait," lifting a weak hand, thumb to a cheek, to the corner of lips that swerve to kiss, "not yet," says Becker. Rolling away, reaching over, as Pyrocles lays him out to one side on those blue-striped sheets, the leanly naked length of him a-gleam in the suffusing light. Past him a sweeping wall of glass, and out across the river the city edged and cornered shadows hazed by steaming cloud, shreds and lines and clots of trees gone grey and yellow and blue in all the pale and chilly morning light stretched parlous thin through all that air from the one sharp far-off mountain. Becker pokes to life a glassy black phone upright in a charging stand, a snapshot appears of the two of them side by side in a red leather booth, 07:07, say the numerals over the photograph, and Fri, April 20. Sets it back by the books stacked there, the titles along the spines that say Fifty Early Childhood Strategies for Working and Communicating with Diverse Families and

Parents to Partners: Building a Family-Centered Early Childhood Program and Remote-Controlled Childhood? Combating the Hazards of Media Culture. "We've got time," says Becker, plucking up a purple squirt bottle from beside the phone. "Plenty and to spare. Tell me something."

"You'd have me speak?" says Pyrocles, taking the bottle Becker hands him.

"Tell me something," says Becker, "about, about Vergina."

"Where the Argead rule," says Pyrocles, beaming.

Steaming mug of coffee set before him on the counter, there by the white-framed platter of his phone. He pushes back his stark white cuff to check his watch, and the hands of every dial on the face of it tremble, twitch, spin wildly about. He lifts and levels his wrist above the counter and two dials, three, snap to a stop, hands pointed away across the U-shaped counter, past the griddle there in the midst of it, the man in a grubby white shirt and the ring and scrape of his spatulas, past the woman in a fuzzled blue cardigan, "Denver omelet," she says, setting a plate before the man there on the other side of the counter, taking up his fork, past all that to the door swinging open in its dull red frame, the jingle of the bell, the big man stepping through, dark grey warm-up jacket over a plain black T-shirt, bush of a beard the color of mahogany, sunglasses small and round and purpled green.

Kerr lowers his wrist as Mr. Keightlinger heads down the counter, past empty stools, the windows bright with neon signs against the morning, Open, they say, Fuller's Coffee Shop, "Sit anywhere you like," calls the woman in the blue cardigan. Kerr tucks his phone away in the pocket of his light fleece jacket as Mr. Keightlinger rounds the corner toward him, stops at the stool beside him, one big hand leaned against the counter, and Kerr looking up opens his mouth, "Get you anything?" says the woman in the blue cardigan, bustling over.

Those green sunglasses turn away from him to her. "Ice water," says Mr. Keightlinger, and sits himself on the stool.

"You're late," says Kerr. "You look like hell."

"I failed," says Mr. Keightlinger.

"You, what, you couldn't get it? Or does he not have it, any-more."

"He still has the boon," says Mr. Keightlinger. "The boon is empty."

"He, it, so. Oh." Kerr lifts his mug. "He's out. Oh that is infin-itely worse."

"He's still somewhere in that house. We would know otherwise."

"So he's, he's trapped?" says Kerr. "He's still contained? Okay," and he downs a slug of coffee, leans forward, both elbows on the counter, "okay. The math hasn't changed, then. He's still out of play."

"I'm going back tonight."

"What? No, no, tonight, tonight is the night. That trigger has been pulled." Kerr leans back as the woman in the blue cardigan sets a glass of water before Mr. Keightlinger. "It's like I said from the jump," says Kerr, quiet and close. "We take this, this *thing* out, first, nobody has it to play with. Not your friend, not your former employers, nobody fæside, not us, but, I mean, *I* didn't have any plans for it. You know? So we take it out, tonight, and *tomorrow* we go to that house, we find your friend, we take care of him then. Or maybe the day after. Take some time off, in between. Maybe a nap?"

"What if your plan doesn't work," says Mr. Keightlinger.

"Work?" Kerr snorts. "Tell me, you know anything about nuclear bombs?" A muffled buzz from from his jacket pocket, and he pulls out his phone, "Mechanically speaking, they're terribly simple." Glancing at the screen. "Not a lot of moving parts to not work." Slipping the phone away again. "You just, you take your two pieces of uranium or beryllium or whatever, and you just," pressing his hands together, a slow clap, or a prayer, "get out of the way. Let it happen. Boom."

Those purple lenses shift their gaze from the counter to the glass of ice and water. "We must be certain," says Mr. Keightlinger. "If it can't be tonight, it will have to be this morning. Right now." Greening as they turn to look at Kerr. "You owe me."

"I owe you *squat,*" says Kerr. "Look, I'm sorry, I said I was sorry, but you were trying to kill me. I think my response was entirely proportionate."

"You wouldn't have died."

"Yeah, well," Kerr gets up off his stool, "maybe next time your whatever-the-fucks start stuffing photos down somebody's throat, you take a moment to make sure everyone's clear it's all less-than-lethal." Pausing there, by Mr. Keightlinger's hunched bulk. "I'm sorry," says Kerr, again. "Look. I got shit to do, you got shit to do, this, this was an idea, but it's not gonna," hands cycling uselessly, spreading in a shrug. His phone's buzzing again, but he's pulling out his wallet, laying a couple of bills on the counter by Mr. Keightlinger's elbow. "Buy yourself some breakfast," he says. "If you come to your senses, you know how to find me."

The woman in the blue cardigan steps over as Kerr yanks open the red-framed door. "Something to eat?" she says, over the jingle of the bell.

Mr. Keightlinger looks from the bills on the counter up to her, the light sliding over those sunglasses. "Bacon," he says.

"Desks, chairs," the voice comes from just outside the door there, "credenzas, shelves, barrister bookcases," just visible over all the tarp-mounded, tightly packed shapes of various heights, mostly tall, at least an arm-span in length, but only a foot or two wide at most. "Filing cabinets. A flat file, there, is a monstrous inconvenience, a useless block of wood to be removed before you renovate, repurpose, demolish," the rasp of a key in a lock, "but a month or two on a ship to here, some spit and polish," sharp squeak of a knob, scrape of the door, "that block of wood is just the thing an architect's wanted for the front room of their live-slash-workspace townhouse." The shorter man in the doorway there tucks a key away in the pocket of his marbled silk vest.

"Flat files?" says the taller man, yellow beard pale in the shadows, yellow hair tied in a knot.

"These aren't flat files." Bruno, the Shrieve, squeezes his way into a narrow aisle between tarps, careful of his vest. "I don't get it," says the Harper, Chillicoathe, turned sideways to press in after. "You clean 'em up, but you can't possibly be making enough to cover the cost of getting 'em here. Unless there's a lot of really stupid architects? I mean," as Bruno looks back, "here or there, a thing's worth what it's worth. Right?"

"Spoken as a brigand, not a businessman." Bruno lays a hand up on a tarp-draped corner. "The worth of a thing's not fixed within, to be measured with scales and calipers. It's found in relationships, between those that have the thing, and those that want it. Granted," leaning close as his voice takes a conspiratorial turn, "there are such things that by their nature implacably alter the tenor of those relationships – think, perhaps, of a traitor: how much he's worth to his liege, and how much to his master. Help me with this." He's seized the tarp, and Chilli, frowning, reaches up for the other side. Together they haul it heavy down to the floor in a whirl of dust.

The wooden cabinet shining still, panels along the front of it white enamel, filigreed with intricate wooden lacework, and a pitted brass socket there by Chilli's shoulder, bare threads where a fitting's been stripped away, its match by Bruno, still with a brass-shaded lamp that might've cast light on the long and gleaming lid that Chilli, with a look to Bruno, reverently lifts. The keys beneath, eighty-eight of them, yellowed ivory, and dull black. "Pianos," says Chilli, looking up, at the oblongs crowding the room. "They're all pianos."

"Uprights, spinnets, pianos droits;" says Bruno, "I began by buying up office furniture, but in every city and many of the sizable towns, rows of old terrace houses were being demolished to make way for modern council estates. And in the front parlors of these terrace houses, gathering dust since the days before television, before the wireless, before electricity," he reaches across the front of the piano, sliding the central panel to one side. The man within snorts himself startled awake, white-haired head laid back against the rows of hammers poised against tautly angled strings. "Spruce!" he blurts, and coughs, patting the pockets of his crisp white shirt, arms tucked close within the cabinet's confines. "Spruce," he says again, "from the forests about Old Tjikko, long may he reign," and fits a monocle to his eye, "chilled in the hold of an old steamer down through the Baltic and the cold North Sea. Mahogany from Brazil, that baked in breathless heat across the Atlantic, between the Pillars of Hercules and up the Balearic to Marseille. Iron," his smile is beatific, "scraped from Erzberg's slopes, spun to wire in Vienna and brought by rail across Venetia and Sardinia. Sugar pine from the very wilds of Northwest America about us now," reaching out of the cabinet to gently stroke the keys below, "stacked for a harrowing, storm-wracked voyage all the way around the Horn, only to end up a century later right back where it began. The ebony veneer from too many different pieces of wood, some of them once keys from other instruments, but not an ounce of ivory to be found: the natural keys are topped with porcelain, which has left them with the occasional chip and crack, though not a piece is missing."

Chilli's stepped back, pressed against the draped piano behind him. Bruno's tugging something from another pocket of his vest, a tiny glassine envelope. "I've kept in tune as best I can," says the man within the piano, with a gesture to the strings arrayed behind him. "Shall I play you something? In a rag-time, perhaps?" Bruno steps close, holds up a fingertip glimmering gold, which the man in the piano seizes and brings it to his lips for a kiss, and a slow and savoring lick. "They don't need much," says Bruno, as he plucks that monocle from limpening fingers, slips it back into a pocket of the man's white shirt. "Mostly, now, they sleep." He gently slides the panel shut, as the man within lies back against felted hammers. "So tell me, Harper: how much would you say I paid for one of these, when I first began to bring them over?"

"I don't," says Chilli, looking at that panel, looking about, all the other pianos crowding them. The tarp, on the floor. "All that work?" he says. "Two hundred, three hundred dollars. Three hundred."

Bruno shakes his head. "You haven't listened," he says. "A house, a hundred houses, to be torn down? Dozens of blocks of wood to be removed? Ten pounds, *they* paid to *me*. To haul them each away. Thirty dollars, at the time." Kneeling then, he takes up the tarp in his hands. "I've since sold a number of them," he says, "for a great deal more than that. If you would?" Chilli stoops, takes up the other end of the tarp. "But now it's all plastic and computer chips," says Bruno, as they lift the tarp up and over, settle it, smoothing, patting it down. "Pianos genoux," he says, with one last tug.

On the table between them a thick roll of bills stood upright, a truncated gnomon. "Go on," says the man sat beneath the flag pinned to the back wall, "take it," but the silhouette in the doorway shakes a head, once, and doesn't unfold his arms. "You were told," he says, voice full of gravel. "No one was to be cut. No one was to be destroyed." Sunlight leaks through the door behind to strike gleams from the beads at the ends of his mustaches. "What you did was, unacceptable."

"Well we ain't accepting it!" The man at the table slaps it once, there by the roll of bills. "Go on, take it back. It's all there."

"The cash is not at issue."

"The cash is a pledge. We take this very seriously. The guy responsible? Moody?" Sitting back, lifting his hands, "We cut him loose." Those hands settling back on the dark veneer of the table, to either side of the bills. "What he did, he did in the heat of the moment, but that's no excuse. Something goes that wrong, we do whatever it takes to make it right." Sliding the bills away across the table. "That's what you can expect from this relationship."

"That relationship no longer obtains." The silhouette turns for the door but the man at the table springs up, reaching out, "Wait!" he cries, "wait," hand stopped short of the shoulder of that shadowy blue suit coat. "It's a," he says, drawing back, "to speak frankly, it's a cash flow issue. The retainer, we, we need the retainer. For the next few months, to, it's, it's a," looking down at that roll of bills, "cash flow," he says.

"Which has no bearing on his excellency's decision." Pyrocles opens the door, and steps out onto a porched bit of yellowing deck, then across a gangplank onto the grey boards of the wharf, and the forest of bare masts all about.

"Felt good, didn't it?" says the man falling into step behind him, light fleece jacket over a gold striped shirt, blue tie loose about his stark white collar. "Telling him off like that."

Pyrocles looks back over his shoulder, leaps away, turning in a crouch, "Melanchlœnidon!" he roars, wheeling a greatsword around and down as Kerr with a yelp skips back, "Whoa! Whoa!" Peering out from behind his leather satchel held between himself and the tip of that long blade held before his eyes. "I ain't nobody, man," and he gingerly pushes the blade aside with the edge of a hand. "Nobody at all. And ain't nobody gonna tell nobody nothing, okay? You don't have to worry about nobody one bit," and Pyrocles straightens, lowers his arms, "I mean," says Kerr, "it was always you, y'know? Never a contest." He's looking from the glare in Pyrocles' eye to his empty hands to his feet and back again. "I wasn't into him, not like that, not for that." A scrap of laughter. "You're the one to make him happy, and that's," looking away, back toward the houseboat, a shake of his head, "I know what you've had to do, to make him so? Make sure he takes his medicine, every night? So it has to feel good. Shutting them down like that." Pyrocles' grimace is softening, under those mustaches. "So now you don't have to *tell* him about it all. And I *know* you were fretting over *that.*" Kerr steps close, and a hand on the shoulder straining that blue coat. "You should treat yourselves. Take him out tonight. Remind him why you're doing all this. Take him back, to where it all began."

"The rabbits' church?" says Pyrocles then, with a frown.

"No," says Kerr, "no, that was the meet-cute. I'm talking first date. I'm talking Goodfellow's. Take him to Goodfellow's," and Kerr steps back, "I mean, nobody tells you what to do. Am I right?"

Pyrocles nods, slowly.

Couple of chiming steelpans and a rubbery bumble of bass, a saxophone lilting from the clock radio on the counter, he's looking from the shoe in his left hand, a lop-tongued work boot, toe of it scuffed and sharply creased, to the one in his right, a grubby sneaker, laces striped with old black stains from the eye-lets, canvas frayed away from cracks in the rubber sole. A deep breath, and he sets them both on the counter, looks up to the old man stood across from it, who shakes his bare head darkly bald above a circle of crisp white curls. "Nope," he says.

"Man, what the," says Christian, slumping, a sigh, he folds his arms, draped in a bulky green pullover two sizes two large. "I don't get it."

"You will," says Gordon, picking up the boot, chucking it over the counter to thump to the mound of shoes on the worktable back there. "Don't force it. Take a minute. Look at the tenny," and rolling his eyes, shaking his head, Christian glares at the shoe left on the counter. "Close your eyes," says Gordon. "When I say boo, reach back, let your hand grab the first shoe it wants. Close 'em boy. Go on," but Christian swells up at that, "God*dam*mit," he snarls, "stop *calling* me that!"

"And I told you," says Gordon, "take those words out your mouth. They aren't for the likes of us."

"I ain't no damn *boy*," says Christian, drawn back. "Sure as shit ain't yours."

"Who else gonna take you in hand? Show you what's what?" Bam, the heel of his hand on the counter, the sneaker jumps, "Go on, get up, walk out of here. Get yourself to your mother's house, wherever that is. Catch a bus to St. Johns or Gresham, go on. Walk up to her door. Ring the bell. She won't know you from Adam, you hear me? Her boy, her boy's in the ground, or worse, and you? You some punk, hustling loose change, sell her some cigarettes, maybe some magazine subscriptions, cut her grass, she got any. You fell out of the world, boy. You ain't going back. So instead of bulling your way through like you know what's what, maybe sit down, shut up, listen when you're told. Now." Gordon steps back, folds his arms. Nods at the sneaker. "Match that shoe."

Christian drags a breath in through his nose, then turns abruptly, grabs something from the pile back there, spins back to slap it down by the sneaker, a garish running shoe, stripes and cheetah spots in yellow and vermillion. He eyes them both before lifting his hand away, shaking his head, "Shit," he says.

"Now, wouldn't be too bad," says Gordon, "if they wasn't both for the right foot." Picks up the grubby sneaker, heads around the counter, drops it on that pile. "It's not there's only the one shoe in the world that does the trick. It's like people that way. Most any one of 'em can make do with just about any other, with a little effort, a little," trailing off, he looks away, looks up. "Forget that. Nothing like people at all." Back around the counter, that old work boot in his hand. "Still. Some pairs definitely won't never work, but some," setting the boot down on the counter, by the running shoe, "most definitely do."

Christian says, "I don't get it."

"You will," says Gordon, sweeping the pair of them off the counter, heading back toward the shelves partitioned into cubbies, many already filled with similarly mismatched pairs. "No, I mean," Christian's saying, "why do you even bother? I mean, they come in, they have a shoe. You find the other shoe, now they have both. So why even bother with, that, with the matching?"

"Sometimes," says Gordon, and a grunt as he squats to reach a slot close to the floor, "it's as important, what's left behind," tucking the pair away, "as what goes on ahead."

The music's changed, thump of drums, hesitantly simple piano. "So that high-heeled thing," Christian says, "with the other sandal, that's on me, too? Something I left behind?" A shrug from Gordon, still on his knees. "You tossed it back!" says Christian, looking back at that enormous pile. "I gotta go find it again?"

"Went out the door already," says Gordon. "Couple-few days back. Older white woman, nice coat. Left that tatty old golf shoe, which ain't never walking out of here."

"So I'm supposed to go find her?" says Christian, throwing up his hands. "How does this work? What the hell am I supposed to do?"

"I told you," says Gordon, still on his knees. "Don't talk like that."

"Don't swear? Or what? My tongue turns to stone? My hair catches fire?"

"Cuss all you want, boy, but hell? Damnation? Salvation? That don't concern the likes of us. So put any notion of supposed out of your head, except how you're supposed to learn to match up shoes. Now go on, pick another one, let's see," but a bell out there jingles, Christian's looking away, toward the door at the front of the shop. "All right," says Gordon, bracing a hand to push himself up, "see to whoever that is," catching the work-table with his other hand, shifting his balance, but Christian's shaking his head, and Gordon lifts himself to see Jo there, in her leather coat the color of butter.

"I don't think she brought a shoe," says Christian.

"Gordon," says Jo.

"Grace," he says. Turning toward the beaded curtain back there, "I'll go put a kettle on," but "Actually," says Christian, "we could just, go out back," and then, to Jo, "You got any smokes on you?"

Gordon folds his arms, frowning. Jo's looking away with a sigh.

"OH" – HOW DOES SHE EVER
BLOOD & WATER, LILIES, GLASS – THE POINT OF DREAMS

"OH," says Jo, and then, "that can't be right."

"Holed up in St. Johns, with Chad and his dad. I was up there a couple weeks, sleeping in the damn, the dang basement." Christian takes a drag from the cigarette and holds it out to her. "I'm supposed to be quitting," she says as she takes it. "He got ten years. No way he's out so soon."

"Good behavior," says Christian, and Jo snorts smoke. "Danny fucking Moody?"

Christian takes the cigarette back. "Maybe he broke out. Maybe five-oh's closing in. Hard target search!" Another drag. He offers it to her, but she shakes her head, "It would've been in the news," she says.

He lets the butt drop, grinds it into the mud. "Film at eleven."

"The hell you were doing up there, anyway," says Jo. Looking away down the unpaved alley, crowded by garage doors, high back fences, drifts of green grass up to the knee. "Two fucking *weeks?* The hell, Christian? You walk away from me, you walk away from everything I was gonna do for you, you walk away and you fucking go to the goddamn Dread fucking Paladin?"

Christian turns away. The gate behind them, leaning drunkenly from a single hinge. "Say what you like, the xo still runs the gutters. And for a racist motherfucker, he never stiffs me on what I bank with him?" Tucking his hands up under his bulky pullover, winding and unwinding. "I was gonna sleep up under the Marquam, but then he went and told me Moody's back," his elbows pulled in tight, "so I went elsewhere. Out to Avi's, for a couple days?" and Jo laughs then, "Jesus," she says, "he's still," and "Yeah," says Christian, "only, Roadhouse? It's streaming on-line now or some shit. No way you wear that tape out. So after a couple of days I head back into town, and that's, that's when," a deep breath, "I went to St. Francis, to get some food. No jefes, right? But there's the xo, tooling by in his truck, and Moody's with him, and Moody," Christian shrugs. "Wants me."

"The hell for?" says Jo.

"Help him get you," says Christian.

"I," says Jo, "me," and her eyes go wide, she steps back, hands up out of her pockets, but Christian's turning aside, laughter blooming in his throat, and he tips back his head to let it out. "You actually *thought,*" leaning over, a shove at her shoulder, and *"Fuck* you," says Jo, shaking him off.

"He *is* after you," says Christian. "Has a *serious* mad-on for you, but he ain't doing shit about it. Two weeks we sat in that fucking basement, the co wheeling around upstairs. Every now and then we'd step out. Do a mischief." Looking up, through that gate. "Smashed Gordon's window, one night." And then, with a tilt of his head, "Hey," he says. "What kind of shoe did you have?"

"What?"

"When you first got in all this, Duchess. What was the shoe you had? And the match, that didn't match. What did he have?"

"I didn't," says Jo, "I, I have no idea what's up with that."

"Then, how the, how'd you, get into this?"

"How do I ever get into any goddamn trouble." She pushes the gate open. "I picked a fight with a psychopath. Come on," and she steps through.

"Come on?" says Christian, scrambling after. "Where?"

"Back to Plan A," Jo says, heading up the length of the lot tuffeted with soggy grass, up toward the old unpainted brick building, the flight of stairs bolted to the back of it. "You come stay with us, at least until we figure out if he's gonna pull anything," and "Jo," says Christian, but "if there's any danger," she's saying, and he grabs her arm. "Jo!" he says. "I'm fine. Here. It's good."

"You have no idea," she says, and she opens the door.

"I can take care of myself!" But she's stepping inside. "Dammit! Jo!"

Within, a kitchen, cramped, scuffed linoleum, dark cabinets, Gordon in his blue shirt there by the stove. "Grace," he says. A kettle's hissing to itself on a reddening eye.

"Gordon," she says. "I, ah, we appreciate, what you've been able to do, but Christian, he's gonna come back with me, now."

"That so," says Gordon to Christian, who's looking away, the beaded curtain off down the hall there.

"You don't need any more trouble," says Jo. "This is on me. Goes way back, before either of us had anything to do with any of you. It's on me, so I'm taking care of it. I've got you," she says, to Christian.

"Come here, boy," says Gordon. In one hand a little paring knife.

"I can, go watch the front," says Christian, and a step toward the curtain.

"Mr. Beaumont," says Gordon, beckoning. "Something the both of you need to see."

"Gordon," says Jo, but "Porter," he says, "we're gonna be formal and all. Mine is an open house, your grace. All are welcome, no one is turned away, and nobody leaves without they say so. We clear? Now give me your hand, boy."

"Why," says Jo.

"Gonna show you a thing, like I said." Gordon takes Christian's hand in his, and lifts that knife. "Then you make your call. Go, or stay."

"The hell, Gordon," says Jo, but Christian sucks in a breath. Gordon sets the knife aside. There's a trickle from the nick in Christian's thumb, a milky bead that rolls down to dangle, swelling, touched with gold, from the edge of the heel of his hand.

"This goes back, too," says Gordon. "Way back. And it's nothing to do with your troubles. Now go on home, Gallowglas. Back to your unwed Queen. Leave us to get along as we will. Your friend," and he holds out a clean white rag, "will look to himself."

After a moment, Christian takes the rag.

Leaning back in the swivel chair, stockinged feet crossed up on the desk, not a smile so much as an air of being on the verge about her mouth and eyes. "David," she says.

Kerr lets the leather satchel slip from his shoulder. "Don't like the view from your office?" A glance at his watch. Twenty of eleven, though a couple of smaller dials spin loosely about.

"You aren't returning my calls." Her hair's cut short, in curly spikes the bright red of her lips. "You really should return my calls."

"What is this, Avery," says Kerr.

"There's expectations, of every contractor. It's why we have contracts. Each obligation set down in black and white so all parties can agree, what must be done, and how, by when and whom," a rolling gesture to emphasize each point, and now she lowers her feet, sits up, "what happens when it doesn't. You don't report. You don't check in. You blow off staff meetings, you – "

"There's nothing to report!" says Kerr. "Avery. I, lay the groundwork. So you can knock it out of the park. Any campaign – "

"I know what you do, David."

"*Any* campaign that needs me to scramble three weeks out is in serious trouble. You're not in serious trouble. He could totally blow the debate, he'll still clear fifty-two, fifty-one percent. So no run-off, in November. So you don't need me coming in Wednesdays and Fridays to say what I said six months ago, last year, it's all done! You listened, you mostly did what I said, yay team! It's a waste of everyone's time."

"Then we're left with a – "

"Who is this for?" says Kerr. "These ambush theatrics. It's just the two of us in here, and you've got to be smart enough to know this does nothing for me. Are you bucking yourself up with this little show? Because, I gotta tell you, that really – "

"We're left with a question, David," says Avery firmly. Her mouth and eyes are nowhere near a smile, now. "If you *are* done, why should we keep you around?"

"Well," says Kerr, "that contract also specifies payments, bonuses – "

"And you've established you're in breach."

Kerr closes his eyes. "You have got to be fucking kidding me. The debate – "

"But I thought he couldn't lose, even if he blew it. Thanks to your hard work." She leans down, working a foot into the straps of a spindly black heel. "It's nothing personal, David." Leaning over to the other side, her other shoe. "I'm sure we'll work together again. Soon." Standing, she hands him a blank white envelope. "You're very good at what you do." And out she goes.

"Well, shit," says David Kerr.

A smash of glass out there, a splatter, a shriek, the comforter tumbled tossed up Ysabel springing the length of her arm out snatching a wrap of white lace striding quickly out the door as Chrissie sits up yellow hair askew about her squinted face, "Ysabel?" she says, softly muzzy. Someone's wailing out there, and wracking, yelping sobs. Chrissie kicks herself free of the bedclothes, crouches naked by the wide white bed, rummaging through scraps of discarded black clothing, "Dammit," she's draping an awkward halter about her neck when the cries out there redouble, words can be made out, such a fucking *God*

damn, she scrambles to her feet, cords of the halter dangling loose by the exaggerated lip-print cartooned in red on her flank. "Ysabel?" she calls, out the door, down the hall, into the kitchen, slick of water, shards of glass, the broken stems of a dozen lilies, waxen white-gold petals splayed and crushed. Jo sits on the floor in her coat the color of butter, her back to the breakfast bar, hands held one clutched up in the other and blood, red blood runneling, splotching her coat, her face screwed tight with pain. Ysabel wrapped in white lace kneels on the low steps beside her, murmuring something, and "Oh," says Chrissie, "oh, that looks," gingerly stepping about the smashed vase to grab a dish towel from the handle of the fridge, "*Stupid fucking what* did I," Jo's choked growl, and Chrissie kneels at her other side heedless of the water, the flowers, the glass, "let's get some pressure," she says, but "Jesus Christ!" spits Jo, jerking away.

"I'm sure," says Chrissie, "if we could just – "

"You want to pretend to help?" snarls Jo. "Put on some goddamn pants."

"I," says Chrissie, "I just," but Ysabel takes the towel from her slackening hands. "Go," she says, her eyes on Jo.

"I could," says Chrissie, "sweep this up for you, at least let me – "

"Go," says Ysabel. "Away. *Now.*"

Chrissie, slowly, climbs to her feet. A long step over the worst of the glass, then – quietly – out of the kitchen.

"Well," says Ysabel. Blotting the worst from the gash across Jo's palm, but fresh blood wells up there between thumb and forefinger. Jo takes a ragged breath, "I've ruined your lace, what is that," she says. "A peignoir? I don't know all the," wincing as Ysabel winds the towel about her hand, "It's a wrap," she says, "and at the moment, the least of my concerns. Hold that. I'll fetch some owr. You'll be fine." But she doesn't get to her feet, and Jo opens her eyes. "What the fuck are we doing, Ysabel?"

"Pitching a tantrum, it seems." Ysabel looks over the spill of water and lilies. "A shame. Today's bouquet was lovely, I thought."

"I punched him in the nose, is the thing," says Jo. "I mean, otherwise? I'd tell you, sure, maybe I saw him get cut or something, scrape a knee, but I wouldn't be sure. Maybe I was just making up what I wanted to remember. But. First time we met? We just met, and he cracks some stupid, bullshit joke, and I punched him, and what squirted out," she holds up that reddening, tight-wound towel. "So. Today?" she says, closing her eyes. "When he?" Lowering her hand. Ysabel catches it, lifts it gently back upright, "Hold that above your heart," she says.

"What do you know about hearts," says Jo.

Ysabel lets go of her hand.

"He's gone, isn't he," says Jo. "Christian." That hand up by her shoulder. "I mean, whoever that is, it looks like him, it talks like him, knows what he'd know but it isn't, it's, one of you, dressed up, like, and – "

"Jo," says Ysabel.

" – he's dead, he's dead, I knew it, I knew he was dead, last year, that *stupid fucking hunt,* I never," looking away. "I *never* should've said yes."

Quietly, Ysabel says, "Do you mean that," but Jo's catching her hiccuping breath, "Or is it," she says, "is *that* it, that when you die, if you die and you're lucky you come back, as one of you," but Ysabel starts forward, seizes Jo's unwrapped hand in hers, leans close, a kiss for her forehead, "Feel," she says, "the warmth of me, my flesh, my breath – you know I am no ghost," and Jo, blinking her wet eyes, "My God," she says, "do you love me."

"Of course," says Ysabel, cradling Jo, "there can be no question," but Jo twists away, "I," she says, and "you, why, why," says Jo, "did you pick him," pulling back, "not me?" Her head against the bar now. Ysabel setting back on those low steps. "Christian fucking Beaumont. He gets in, he gets to go on, with his shoes and whatever and I'm stuck, here, with, with this?" Holding up the blood-soaked towel wrapped tight about her fist. "And Frankie?" she says, and her eyes close up about tears. "And Danny goddamn Moody," she says, and a tremendous sob. "Jo," says Ysabel, leaning close, but that fist, that fist, Jo opens her eyes, "Because you *need* this, don't you. To answer every insult. To *be* the *law.* While you – "

"Jo," says Ysabel.

"While *you* lie about, pretending to be queen."

Ysabel looks down, away, to one side. Puts a hand on the floor, the water there. "I will," she says, lifting her hand, planting it again, "I will fetch the owr," she says, pushing herself to her feet. "To stop the bleeding."

"I'm not the only one," says Jo, gathering herself. Ysabel holds out a hand, "What do you mean?" she says, but Jo holds her one hand in the other, twists away from Ysabel's help as she stands, "Ask your brother," she says, pushing past Ysabel, out of the kitchen, into the hall, through the door to her room.

"My brother," says Ysabel. "Jo?" And then, "Jo, who is Danny Moody?" And a mutter, to herself, "You're not making sense." And then, plaintive, faltering, "Gallowglas?"

That door bangs open. Jo in her blood-splattered coat steps out of the shadows, and in her bloodied, towel-wrapped hand the skull-mask, crude teeth thickly lined with black ink, long black mane dragging the floor, the water, the flowers, the clink of glass.

"Where are you going," says Ysabel.

Jo hoists that mask. "See about getting rid of this," she says. Her hand on the knob of the door to the apartment. "I'm," she says, looking down. "I, tell, Chrissie. I'm sorry, I was, she was just," but then she opens the door. Looks back over her shoulder. "Let her go home, Ysabel," she says.

"Wait," says Ysabel, *"please. Stop,"* but Jo steps out, she's gone.

"Few things," she says, "make any sort of sense now," as she pokes the glowing embers on the grate, stirring sparks. "Then, I might take up my bright sword, my sturdy burgonet, draw on my gloves and take down my whip from over the door," a scrape of metal as she sits back. Her left arm sleeved in gleaming plate, cop and pauldron, vambraces and cowter. "My mare without, eager for the narrow road, and the morning at our backs." Her hair a close-shorn cap, warmly grey in the firelight. "The very bushes would lie flat for us, the streams shrink for us, and men and women bow as we passed. They knew their manners then, and what was proper to a knight. But now that I've a banner of my own? The crowd about me, mewling their every need to me, as if I were the source and sovereign remedy, and I must," closing up her gauntlet in a fist upon her knee, *"listen,"* she says, with a soured look.

"The irony's not lost upon us," says one of the women on the sofa behind her, and her long white hair's unbound, left loose to float in wisps about her head and shoulders. "The crown of even a Marquess has some heft," says the other, white hair tightly bound in ruthless braids.

"I sleep now," says the Marquess. "Since I came back to life, I sleep most every night, and I have dreams." She hangs the poker from its hook there by the fire. "Or rather – I know that I *have* dreamed. I wake up, I come back to myself, deviled by these scraps of, not even memories: colors, mostly. A sense of motion." Clank and squeak she lifts and opens her fist, as if tossing something into the air. "I don't see the point of them."

"And yet," says one of the women. "But," the other. They sit with their backs against the arms of that sofa, brownish pink, their legs curled up together under a knitted afghan, a god's eye, neon-bright.

"Last night," says the Marquess, "and the night before, the same still moment surfaced from all that huggermugger. I stood, or seemed to stand, on the parapet of a tower, high above the city, but no such tower exists. The sun shone, but through a haze, not fog, or clouds, but smoke, as if siege-towers burned at our gates, and the light was at once too bright and dim. But I could see the river, the waters of it risen to swallow bridges, to fill streets and lap at windowpanes, and the flood was dark and red in that awful light, like rust."

"Blood, I think you'll find."

"Rust's why blood is red."

"But fire's what makes rust."

"Oh, now *that's* a reach."

"What does it mean?" says the Marquess, turned about on the hearth now to face them both, the one of them carefully shaping a nail with an emery board, the other peeling a green apple with a little silver knife.

"Nothing."

"Everything."

"We'll know soon enough."

"Unless we don't, of course."

"True, true."

That armored hand closes up again in a fist.

She's pulled on black jeans, and a loose white cardigan over the halter, but her feet are bare on the lush grass. She's looking down at them, at the grass, and her yellow hair has fallen before her face like a still straight curtain. The sky above a cloudless blue impassively clear, the flowers that fill the raised bed richly white and pink, bright orange, yellow. A latch clacks, hinges squeak, she lifts her head hair swinging, the door there's opening under the awning of the little wooden porch, and Ysabel black hair streaked with silver in the shadows, lace wrap splashed with something, blood. "Oh, God," says Chrissie, "is she, are *you* okay?" but Ysabel's lifting a hand heavy with light, gold streaks and clumps of shining dust, "Come," she says.

A lurching step across the grass. "Ysabel?"

"Do you love me."

"Of course," says Chrissie, another step, another. "Yes, Ysabel, I – "

"Do you want me."

"I, but, what," says Chrissie, as Ysabel seizes Chrissie by a belt loop with that gold-clotted hand and stops her sputtering with a kiss. "Do you *want* me," says Ysabel, dragging her hand up between them, smearing Chrissie's belly with light, her chest and throat now shining, golden, her eyes closing, lips parting, a breath, but the word, trembling, will not come, she nods instead, quickly, frantically: yes.

THE GARBAGE BAG'S almost empty, but it sways heavily as she shifts it over by the others, stuffed full but much lighter, there by a half-dozen cardboard boxes. Straightening, hand on her hip, baggy black T-shirt, bit of black lace tied about her throat. The windowless room close about her, lit only by the lamp on the floor. Wild shadows loom up the dusty walls. She kneels by that limply weighted bag, unwinds and spreads it open, and the light that dapples up a spill of softly golden morning reflected off calm water, and her eyes drift shut, her shoulders settle, a deep breath in. Footsteps crackle outside. She twists the plastic shut, a sloppy knot to swallow the light, and shoves it under the other bags.

"Hey, Petra," says Gloria, there in the doorway, tie-dyed coveralls, the top of them unzipped over a T-shirt that says Skunkguckin in hand-scrawled letters. "Wanted to see how you were settling in. You've got power up here, good – are you sure you want this room? We've got plenty with windows, you know. If they're painted over, we can get 'em cleaned. All kinds of stuff we can do."

The woman all in black straightening, stretching, "I want," she says, "to hang pictures? My shots, so it's all, the city. Inside? Sort of?" Folding her arms about herself.

"Do you need blankets?" says Gloria. "It's still a bit chilly at night – we've got a bunch of space heaters. Did Anna tell you about the flatpacks?" and then, as Petra frowns, "Come on, I'll show you," beckoning, out into the hall, "a desk or two, couple dressers, some shelves, leftovers from our last IKEA run," sunlight shining from the grimed-over window down at the end, "though we won't even have to go out there once we get the broadband and the wifi sorted," ducking a sheet of the dull beige paint that's peeling in desiccated swathes from the walls and ceiling. "Them and Amazon? We can get whatever we need, delivered right here. Which is good, since we don't have a truck," turning ahead, around a corner, Petra, jogging after, "Gloria!" she calls out, footfalls crackling on fallen paint.

Around the corner, a couple of steps down a short flight, Gloria's looking up at her, expectantly, and Petra folds her arms about herself again, "I don't," she says, "I can't really, the room is a godsend, a lifesaver, literally, I can't, I, thank you. I just," as Gloria turning takes a step up toward her, "I really can't, afford? To do anything like that now. I mean, I'd be out on the street, if you hadn't," but up another step, Gloria's saying, "No, no, you don't understand: it's covered. It's all covered."

"Covered," says Petra.

"Anything you need. New camera? Film? If you shoot that? A laptop, maybe. Whatever. Let me know." Leaning close. "We will make it happen."

"Covered," says Petra, again, unfolding an arm.

Down the steps into a foyer floored with tiny yellowing tiles, "That's the whole point," Gloria's saying, "what we're trying to do here," back past the staircase under a low long arch, "take what happened, what's been done to us," out into the cavernous warehouse, shadowy stalls marching up the length of those high walls, "and make," she says, a hand up, her pace faltering, "something," looking up toward the raised stage at the end of the space, the man there, his back to them, stood before canvases leaned one against another, the painted figure dancing from one to the next. "Can I help you?" calls out Gloria.

He turns about, grey jacket, bush of a beard, small dark sunglasses. "You were with the Mooncalfe," he says.

"Can I help you," says Gloria, sharply.

He nods, he sighs. "Marfisa," he says. "The Axe. Sister of the Hound. It is of paramount importance to the universe entire that I speak with her." And then, "Marfisa?" he says. "She is quite tall, her hair, white – I'm told she lives here, with you?"

"There," says Gloria, looking up, to the rafters, the shadows.

Mr. Keightlinger plants his hands and hops himself lightly onto the stage, up past the canvases to the skeletal staircase against the wall. "Gloria," says Petra. "Are you sure?"

"Not now," says Gloria, watching him climb to the walkway. "The ladder," she calls out. He puts a hand on a rung, looks up. Starts to climb.

It's dark, up under the rafters. The makeshift floor of planks smothered under intricately patterned rugs laid one atop another, and a futon on the rugs, and Marfisa, white-gold hair ablaze in the light from the lamp up on a corner of a low shelf crammed with books. She sets aside a paperback curled and worn, Abby Tinker, say the once-gilt letters on the cover, Cynara's World, and watches as Mr. Keightlinger climbs up onto the rugs, unfolds himself, shoulders hunched, head ducked, but looking up at the ceiling, just above them, full of stars.

The ceiling's filled with stars: thousands of them burning, coolly, red and orange, green, blue, white, but mostly gold, spangled in whorling drifts and shoals, great wind-licked curls, so many and so bright, and yet so faint their light can barely reach his shadowed face.

"You used to work with the magician," says Marfisa.

"I," says Mr. Keightlinger, lowering his sunglasses, turning away from that ceiling so close, so far away. "Need your help. Your brother – "

"I have no brother."

"The Handle," he says. "The Hound."

"I've left all that behind."

"He has," says Mr. Keightlinger, "meddled with something terribly dangerous."

"There's nothing I might do to help with him." Marfisa takes up her book.

"You can open the door to the house for me."

A moment, then, before Marfisa looks up, with a shake of her head.

"Tell me," says Mr. Keightlinger. "Who else is in that house, besides your brother?"

"He's not," says Marfisa, but then, a hitch of her breath, "Grandfather," she says.

The sun so bright, so high above, so thin but piercing through the cleanly blue to strike staggering gleams from towers crisp against green-draped hills. The spatters on her butter-colored coat have paled to a shade of mud, the dishtowel dark about one hand, her head down stalking her way across the great wide bridge past idling cars and trucks, stalled by some snarl in the traffic ahead. The mane of the mask in her other hand drags the sidewalk in her wake.

The wisp and scratch of the mane, and the scuff and slap of her shoes.

Stopping she looks up, shading her eyes with her towel-wrapped hand. The susurrous breeze can't manage to stir her hair. The unruffled river below too bright to look at directly. She steps from the sidewalk to the concrete deck, peers through a sunstruck windshield at the seats empty within. Heads from the stilled sedan to grasp the bed of the high-wheeled pickup next in line. No one's up behind the tinted glass of the rear window of its cab. Past a low-slung empty roadster, the bus there one lane over, Don't Let LOL Become DOA, the seats through the windows above the ad all empty, and no one at the wheel. Up on the bumper of a town car, onto the trunk of it grunt of shocks as she leaps onto the roof, a crumpling pop as it settles under her weight. Two lanes stretch bumper-to-bumper down the length of the bridge, but silent, empty, still. The towers ahead, and the hills, the sun, the swoop and wheel of freeway ramps behind, the bridges to either side, and only the bright river lapping below.

She lifts that mask up high. The mane skirls, more from the motion of her arm than any breath of air. She holds it high, and then she pulls it down with both hands, and fits it over her head.

The black mane lofts up huge and high, spreading, growing, a sail, a wall, the shadow of it a darkness eclipsing bridge and river, thunderhead uncoiling far above as out she throws her arms, jaw dropped beneath the teeth of that mask, she's howling and the sudden blare of horns, rumble and snarl of engines, someone's yelling down below, laughing she's catching the mask as it tumbles from her face, leaping a bounce from hood to sidewalk and running, running as the rain comes crashing down.

"Holy shit," and the peals of steel guitar squeezed through a tinny speaker dissolve in a squawk of static. Scrabble of plastic and cardboard someone clambers out of a lean-to strapped to the high wire fence along a sidewalk, filthy jeans and a jacket of army-surplus green, big black hat, he comes up by the woman there in a purple rain shell and sagging khaki shorts, she's pointing, but she doesn't have to, boiling up over the trees, out over the river, the bridges, a wild black cloud that climbs to swallow the sky as a great wind rises whipping their clothes the tarps behind them even the gravel scuttling flap and crash a sheet of cardboard bellies up from the ground, clings to the fence, "Wow," says the woman, the word lost in that buffeting roar and he falls to his knees, cheeks shining wet, throat jumping, "Moody," she says, loudly, "Moody!" over his hoarsely yawp, grabbing his shoulder as the first fat drops begin to fall, but he swings a shove of a punch at her, she skips back, "Fuck you," she screams as he tips over flop to the mud-dening dirt, she's stooped over crawling under the tarp, *"Fuck you!"* as he hauls himself up on all fours, retching, green jacket plastered with flower petals wetly pink and white, and more falling flying wheeling through the rain.

Floor-length curtains drawn along the wall, faint light seeping from some device away off in the kitchen, garbage in heaps and mounds all over the floor, she drops the yellow plastic recycling bin with a clinking crash. Red Keds unlaced, legs streaked with mud or something, pink and orange parka shining slickly, dotted with wet flower petals. She kicks that bin over by a bare foot jutted from under a tumble of trash, tin cans and plastic bottles stripped of wrappers, cardboard cartons, plastic tubs, eggshells and screwed-up twists of plastic wrap, paper, balled-up foil, splat of vegetable peels and coffee grounds pattering as he lifts his head, long brown hair damply lank, "What," he says, blinking, "Jes? That you?" But she's headed off toward the kitchen.

When she returns, she's lost the parka, she's swigging from a green glass bottle, he's picking over the garbage in the bin, "This it?" he says. "It's crap." The clatter growing louder without. "Is it raining?" he says, peering at her wet hair, and the petals caught in the strands. She empties the bottle, whips it away to crash among all that garbage, "Crap?" she says. "You want some beer?" Planting a Ked on his bare chest, pushing him back, down, to squat over him in the darkness. Rucking up the hem of her dingy tank top over her hips. "You miserable, filthy shit," she says, and a spurt, then a jet of piss splashes his matted beard, and he opens his mouth to gulp it down as rain pelts the glass without.

White apron streaked with red, slender knife in one hand, she steps from the white-walled back room gleaming into the dimmer, wood-trimmed storefront, past a young man in a white shirt, sleeves rolled above his elbows, down the length of the chilled display cases filled with slabs and cuts of meat, thick steaks wetly red, and piles of sausages, a tray of dark-jeweled livers, kebabs bright with cut peppers and onions and mushrooms and spangled with green herbs, richly hued prosciuttos and jamones, out onto the floor past a customer or two toward the windows, streaked with rain and petals, the crashing bouncing clatter of rain on the sidewalk and street out there already faltering, the light already shifting, the late sun struggling out from under those lifting, parting clouds. "Wow, that was, intense," says a customer behind her as the last flowers drop from the dying wind. "Oh, Phil," she breathes, a whisper to herself, "this better not be you."

Rainwater puddles the floor, soaking the xes of blue masking tape laid here and there, and sodden petals pink and white, the occasional dark red, trail from the double doors to where she's sprawled, her back against the mirrored wall, pale splattered coat splayed open, and her crudely bandaged hand in her lap. The mask on the floor there beside her, stiff black mane spangled with water, and petals in its strands. She looks up as a man steps into the wide room, close-cropped balding hair and a salt-and-pepper Van Dyke that frames a soured mouth, a paper cup in his hand, and another clamped in the hook he holds out to her. "What's the other guy look like," he says, as she takes it.

"No, it wasn't," she says, sniffing, sipping, wincing, "it was, a, a vase." Another sip, eyes widening, a stiff swallow. "I broke a vase."

"Still. Better get it looked at," he says, but she laughs, "This?" Lifting her clumsy mitt of browned towel. "I just need to shove it in a bucket of glitter. I'll be fine."

"I'd say don't be stupid," and he crumples his emptied cup, lets it drop. "But that train's left the station. What did I tell you? First thing!" Turning away, he aims a kick at a soggy clump of flowers. "Do *not* get mixed up in this shit!"

"Oh, Jesus fucking Christ, Vincent, I am sorry." Jo pushes herself to her feet. "Where's the fucking broom."

"Don't you," spinning about, "laugh this off," stepping close, she lurches away to bump herself back-to-back in the mirror, "don't you *dare,*" he's saying, "dragging that goddamn thing back in here," his hook pointing at the mask there on the floor, "you *stupid,* thoughtless girl, you don't have the *sense* God gave a pea," but "You told me," she's saying, "you told me they'd take one look at me, one look and they'd cut me open and steal my lunch money."

"Yeah, well," a deep breath, "they still got time."

"Eleven," she says, flatly, starkly. He draws back, frowning, "Eleven?" he says, and a glance at the mask. "Eleven," he says. "The hell are you – are you, you want to compare *body counts?* Girl, I have," but her face screws up and a single tremendous sob shakes her shoulders jumps her throat her head knocked back against the glass a retching cough her hand up curling down about herself a snort of breath she shivers with the effort to hold, to press, to clamp. "Eleven," she says, letting go. Lifting her head. "Directly, with the sword, or, because, I did, something stupid? Or I was scared. Angry. Stupid. But also, because I was," a shuddering breath, "told to. The Devil. I can't, I can't keep doing this."

"But you're in it," says Vincent, voice gentled to a rasp.

"I want out," she says. "I want to quit."

"You can't."

"You did."

He steps back, looks down, the puddled floor, the strips of tape, the petals. "What I did," he says, "that's easy. Just, walk away. Drop everything. Take off. Leave 'em in the lurch, alone, let him fall, don't look back. Try not to look back. If you do," a deep breath, "I wouldn't call what I did quitting, exactly." Turning back to her. "You tell yourself you're ready, you know what it means. That you'll never see her again. But you aren't. You never will be. It will never, let up, the shock of realizing over and over you will never. See her. Again. So," he says, blinking rapidly. "There's that." The doors behind them rattling, someone's trying the knobs. Someone's knocking. Jo steps away from the mirrored wall as Vincent turns away, heads for the doors, "Hang on!" he calls as the knocking becomes a pounding, booming. Jo stoops there by the mask. The mane of it stirring as she picks it up and turns it over in her hands. "I wasn't kidding, about the broom," she says. "I'll clean this up."

"You're gonna need a mop," says Vincent, undoing the lock, opening the door. "And careful with the tape. I am not about to reblock Titus."

Jo looks up, blankly, at the man stood there, grey jeans and a soft yellow shirt, his hair a shock of pinkish orange, "Hey, Dad," he's saying, "is she," and then, as she's getting to her feet, the mask in her bandaged hand, "Huntsman!" he calls. "Are you well?"

That black mane sways as she takes a halting step toward them both. Shakes out her free hand, lifts it, and light flares in that wide room.

HER SWORD – THE RICHES OF THE CITY
PEABO'S LEAF SPRING – "IT'S ALL GOOD"

HER SWORD the blade of it harshly bright from clean straight quillions set above the glittering wiry net of the guard about her pronated hand up and out to the tip of it quivering just a foot or so from his throat, his chin lifted up and back, his eyes, one blue, one brown, unblinking, fixed on hers. "Gallowglas," he says, and just the touch of a question to his tone.

"Jesus, girl, put that away!" Vincent, eyes wide, beside them.

"You lied to me," she says, to Lymond, to the King.

"I assure you, we have not."

Her other hand still wrapped in that bloodstained towel held low, fingers and thumb clamped tightly about the chiseled teeth of that skull mask, the mane of it dangled just above the puddled floor. "You kept things from me," she says.

"We have been as clear and open in our dealings as any ruler might," he says, but she's lurched forward and a whick of her wrist that shivers the sword to whip the tip of it snag and slice, he jerks back hand up across to clutch his shoulder sleeve there torn, and a yelp from Vincent. Jo lowers her hilt, draws back her blade, the tip of it dulled by a smear of red.

"But I showed you that the day you took your charge from me," says Lymond.

"What the hell," says Vincent, off to the side, as "You didn't *tell* me," says Jo. "You didn't tell me what it means. That you could *take* this from me!" Hoisting the mask, the mane of it limply swaying. "That all this time you could've done this shit your*self!*"

"Huntsman," he says, "your grace," lifting his hand from his shoulder to hold it slickly red between them, there by the mask, "even if this meant what you think," wincing as he grips his wound once more, "I could not hold your office. A king might no more be gallowglas, than a gallowglas a king."

Vincent, stepping close, says, "Let me take a look at that," but Lymond turns his shoulder away, "Dad, please," he says, and then, "Jo. You took this office from my mother's hand. You sought the mask yourself, and you've done well by it, and yet – if I could take it from you?" She's lowering her blade as he steps toward her, and reaches out his free hand to grasp hers wrapped in the bloodstained towel, and the mask a-sway between them. "But I can't," he says. "You are the Huntsman. The hunt is yours." Removing his bloodied hand once more from his shoulder, folding it with his other about her makeshift bandage. "But," and he takes in a deep breath. "It's your other office that concerns us, now. You were missed at court, yesterday."

"Luys," she says, a croak of a word.

"The Mason was game, but we needed Southeast," he says. She looks away, steps back, tugging free her hand, her sword and the mask held low as she's shaking her head, "Jo Gallowglas," says Lymond, "there is a threat, to your quarter, and our Queen. We understand you wish to set aside your duties; we sought you out today to ask you to come back with us, to," he blinks, a hint of a frown, "where it all began," he says, "to, to Goodfellow's house. We would go to Goodfellow's house. To show you something there, of duty, and our need. Shall we dress our wounds, and go?"

Her back to them both she lifts up her bandaged hand and holds the mask there a moment, then lets it drop, clack, to the floor, that mane slumping in a tangle. "How'd you know you'd find me here?"

"Christ," growls Vincent, "you have any idea the ruckus you made with that thing? All anybody'd have to do is follow the damn rain."

"Yeah?" says Jo, looking back, over her shoulder.

"He called me," says Lymond. Jo nods at that. "While he was getting the bourbon," she says. "I didn't know you guys were speaking to each other." Vincent, glowering, shakes his head, "You scared the living *hell* out of me, girl," he says. "Coming in like that."

"I'm sorry," says Jo, looking down. "I'll go with you, majesty, but first," lifting her red-shoed foot.

She lifts her foot, she brings it down, a stomp of a step on the mask, crack. It breaks, snap a jagged feathery line of torn papier-mâché from jutting tooth a-curl through cheekline up to wrench an empty eye-hole apart, that last clinging twist of forehead parting as she kicks the pieces away, dead black hair whirling petals skidding through rainwater clink against the mirrored wall.

"I won't kill anyone else," says Jo. "Not for you, not for anybody. Not ever again." Looking up to the King. "We still good?"

He lifts his head, a slow nod, "The hunt is yours, as you see fit, Huntsman," he says.

"Yeah, well," she says, and a restless slash of her sword before she heads, abruptly, out through the doors, into the hall.

"I'll send someone round to clean this up," says Lymond, after a moment. "It'll be like it never happened." And then, "Dad?" But Vincent doesn't turn to him, or nod or shake his head. He's still staring at the pieces of that mask.

"Thank you, Mayor Beagle," says the man at the one end of the stage, as the woman, by far the slightest figure up there, settles back on her stool, her suit a royal purple, a weighty pearl necklace draping her black turtleneck. Sipping some water as the applause smatters away. "Mr. Killian," says the man at the end of the stage, looking down the line of them. "Your response?"

One of the men stands up from his stool, quite tall, his suit more grey than navy, features sharp, "Thank you," he says. His narrow black-rimmed glasses like a squint. "And I'd like to thank the Mayor, of course, for such a sterling example of the consistency, of leadership, she provides. And for all the differences we each may have with her," a sweep of his arm for the rest of them on their stools lining the stage, the high white columns behind, "we must admire that consistency. You can almost set your watch by the moment when, in a soaring bit of oratory, she will reach into her pocket, as she just did, and pull out those stirring words attributed to Charles Erskine Scott Wood," he spares a smile for her behind him, "Good citizens are the riches of a city. It's a fine line; a noble sentiment – so much so it's inscribed on the base of Skidmore Fountain, just a few blocks away." Looking out over the audience, past the bright lights. "Certainly, we've a great many riches piled up in here tonight." A chuckle stumbles through the crowd, trips over itself, falls away. The man in a neatly pressed plaid shirt on the stool by the Mayor scribbles a quick note to himself. "But my response? Well, your honor, fellow candidates, City Club," spreading his hands, taking them all in, "so what." Letting his hands fall. "So what," he says, again, into the dead silence of the hall. "Four thousand people out there in this rich city, tonight, will sleep without a bed of their own. Less than two thousand will have a bed at all, in one of our overburdened shelters. Seven hundred families, with children, out there, tonight, without a home. Tomorrow, seventy thousand people will wake up in this city to go out and try to find a job, any job, and another hundred and forty thousand will go to work in jobs far beneath their abilities, for much less than they're worth. And thirty thousand people out there, thirty thousand good citizens, have given up looking for work at all. Is this," looking about the dark hall, "how we spend," stepping up, toward the edge of the stage, away from the other candidates, "our riches?" He lifts his hands, presenting his point: "We can't keep on like this," he says, a clipped statement of fact, the edges of his words a bit dulled by amplification. "Good citizens are the riches of a city, it's true," he says, "but it's not enough to pile them up and dust off our hands and say, we're done. Riches – *wealth* – must be invested. Put to work. To make this city bigger, better, richer than before. Good citizens of Portland!" And he lifts his voice, and his hands. "Let's put ourselves to work!"

It's a moment before the applause begins, and swells.

"No, no," says Lymond, "this way," and Jo turns from the porch to follow him down a walkway along the front of the big white ramshackle house, perched high above the corner, the sidewalk, the cars parked below. Tiny colored lights string bannisters and window frames, and candles burn on sills, but no movement's glimpsed behind gauzy curtains, no shadows on drawn blinds. Lymond turns into a darkly narrow alley between houses, lined with rolling garbage cans of green and blue, a neat rank of yellow recycling bins half-filled with empty bottles. "Anybody home?" says Jo. Instead of her bloodstained coat she wears an oversized hoodie, hands stuffed deep in the pockets. Lymond's already around behind the house. No walkway here, just a sketch of a path leading steeply down, between concrete foundation and ivy-laddered fence. "This way," he calls, already down where the path peters out on the sidewalk. He's swapped his torn yellow shirt for a hoodie of his own, pulled up over his shock of hair, a darkly anonymous silhouette. Dirt scrabbles as she hurries after almost to slam into him, stood waiting, hand on the knob of a red-painted door. She looks out at the parked cars, the empty intersection, the old green house cater-cornered across, first storey thicketed with scaffolding. "Could've just walked down the sidewalk," she says.

"Then this might not've been here," says Lymond, opening the door.

Down a couple of steps into a basement apartment and a crowd about, chatting quietly, couches and sofas, small tables with flickering candles, "On water lying strong ships," someone's saying, quite loudly, a guy lit up in the corner, "and men in weakness skilled reach elsewhere: no prouder places from home in bed the mightiest sleeper can know," he's reading, from a slender book held theatrically. "This simple joy," murmurs Lymond, leaning close. "To walk into a room, and not be known. To not be, for a moment, King. Or Duchess." Straightening as that guy in the corner belts out, "but a fountain without source, legend of mist and lost patience," and somebody's making his way toward them, a small man all in black, spreading welcoming hands. "Never lasts, of course," says Lymond.

"You majesty," says the man all in black, "your grace," quietly, unobtrusively. "What a surprise."

"Pleasant, I hope," says Lymond.

"My house would brook no other kind. Food? Drink? A bit of poetry?" That guy in the corner's emphatically declaiming, "And the dusty eye whose accuracies turn watery in the mind," as Lymond shakes his head, "Just a bit of business upstairs, if we might. Perhaps after?"

"Ah, if after's but perhaps, might I bend your ear before?"

Lymond looks to Jo, who shrugs. That guy in the corner holds up his book, "Like an island with no water round in water where no land is!" The applause is sparse. More people are looking to them by the door, as Lymond and Robin Goodfellow head off to one side, someone's waving, getting up from a couch, it's Becker, beaming, and Pyrocles in his blue suit getting to his feet, ducking his head in a bow as Jo holds out her hand for a shake, "Your grace," he murmurs, and then Becker's wrapped his arms about her in a sudden clap of a hug, "Damn, it's good to see you!"

"You look, you look good," she says, "is that a beard?" What's left of his hair's slicked back, and his loose shirt's of a berry-colored plaid, "Life as a duchess must treat you right," he's saying.

"It's," says Jo, looking away a moment, the guy over there's saying, "a custard made from the pink powder bought at the store," and she takes a deep breath, "it's a challenge," she says, a half-hearted gesture, a deprecated smile.

"How does Peabo's leaf spring by you, lady?" says Pyrocles.

"The what now?" says Becker, looking to him. "You're fixing her car?" Back to Jo. "You have a car?"

"He means my sword," says Jo. "It," she looks down a moment. "It's done everything I've asked. You're, ah, your hammer's true, Anvil."

He smiles. "Your grace is kind."

Over there, Lymond's shaking Robin's hand, "I think that's my cue," says Jo, stepping back. "Business upstairs."

"Well," says Becker, "come back down when you're done!"

"We've been told there'll be dancing," says Pyrocles.

"If we don't have to take off," says Jo, "I'll come back down, sorry," she nearly bumps into, steps around a stolid woman swathed in pearly grey, her dark hair tiny screws, "but this custard is too fine!" cries that guy in the corner. "Sorry," says Jo, past a dark man draped in a long white shawl, a shirtless woman, arms bound in pink fishnet, a man in beige fleece checking his watch by a man trussed in slashed denim and electrical tape. There's Lymond, holding out a hand. "Shall we?" he says.

Up a tightly switchbacked flight of stairs, walled in framed illustrations of moths as if specimens pinned to the paper, colors of earth and stone and bark and dying leaves, there's silver though, and neon spots of pink and yellow, and now white gold and tiger-stripes, butterflies in a sunburst of orange that cools through ruby and amethyst to emerald, sapphire, onyx, and at the very top a cloud of opals about a door that opens on a toothpaste-colored kitchen, brightly empty. "Beer?" says Lymond, opening the fridge.

"If you think it'll help."

"Can't hurt," he says, handing her a bottle. "Through here," and a gesture with his.

The wide room beyond, windows lit with candles and strings of light, the hearth at one end cold, swept clean, and nothing else but the upright sword out in the middle of the floor, a neat ring of charcoal burnt about it, the blade of it straight, the hilt wrapped in white leather yellowed with hard use. "Marfisa's sword," says Lymond.

"I figured it had something to do with this."

"You've seen it before, I know."

"I was here when it happened." She swigs from her bottle. "Well. Not in the *room.*"

"Six months, it's stood there, and no one will go near it. Rather crimps Goodfellow's style." He hunkers down, there by the blade, careful of the char. "She could put out her hand whenever she wished, and draw it forth," a gesture with his bottle, "but instead, she's made do all this time with a bat, and a mask."

"She's pretty damn good with the bat."

"She's an outlaw, and she steals from you."

"Oh, Jesus, it's a," waving her bottle, "grief she's got, with one of the guys. Chilli. The Harper. Kind of an asshole. She's trying to make him look bad – whatever she takes, we've covered."

"Have you spoken yet, with Gwenders?" he says, and as her frown turns quizzical, he shakes his head. "You should've been at court, yesterday." Rocking back to sit upon the floor. "You might replace the owr, but not morale, or respect. You must put a stop to this."

"And I told you," says Jo, looking away, out a window. "No more assignments. No little chats. I'm done."

"I don't mean a hunt, Jo. Or a duel. Even with the mask, you'd be hard-pressed to take her. No," setting his bottle down, pushing up on a knee, "I'd have you bring her back. Go and speak with her. Tell her: put out your hand. Take up this sword. Be our Axe, once more."

"And that's it," says Jo. Still looking out the window. "Just like that, she's back in it."

"She exiled herself," says Lymond, getting to his feet. "She's the one to undo it."

Jo throws back the last of her beer, turns away from the window, her face in shadow, "Why do you do this?" she says, and a wave of the empty bottle. "You're not one of them!"

And Lymond laughs, a sudden gut-busting eruption that knocks back his head, rocks him back a step, "Jo," he says, catching his breath. "I'm the King!" That sword, shining behind him. "And kings are among the loneliest people in this world." Stepping close, a hand to her shoulder, "It's perhaps why we so treasure our friends. Take your time; think on this charge. Go home to sleep on it, if you would. Come find me when you've made your call." Lifting his half-full bottle, waiting, until she desultorily clinks hers against it, and then, with a nod, he turns to go.

She watches him walk away, loosely waving her empty bottle about, until he's stepped through the doorway to the kitchen, and then, a swing of her arm, "You son of a," but she doesn't let go, doesn't throw, turns about. Crouches, leans forward on her knees, close by the sword. The steel of it sleek, whitely silver in the lights, but brightness snags in sparks from dings and nicks in the edges, and scoring the face. "Somebody's been busy," she says, reaching out a hand, settling, with a ripple of her fingers, about the yellowed hilt. Squeezing, bracing herself, but she doesn't pull, doesn't shift it, doesn't move it at all. Lets go. "Shit," she says, pushing up on her feet, stalking back to the window. Heel of her hand against the frame. Forehead against the back of her hand.

"Hey."

She pulls back, blinking. A golden watch, waggled right by her face. "Let's go," and the watch drops away, "Wait," she says, "wait – what time is it?"

"Come on." He's in the shadows at the foot of the stairs.

"Come on where," she says, heading over, heading up after him. "What the fuck is going on?"

"It's Becker. We've only got a few minutes."

"What, what about Becker? Hey!" The syllable flatly loud as she springs after him, grabs a wrist. "The hell *time* is it?"

Jerking his hand free, "It's not that kind of watch," he says. Tugging a white cuff over the face of it. "Listen," he says, coming down a step closer to her. "I can talk just about anybody into almost anything, you give me room enough to work. But what I *can't* do," taking her hand in his, "what I can't do is actually talk somebody into *actually* falling asleep. Just not boring enough, I guess. So I slipped him a mickey. He's hitting stage three any minute now, and you need to be as close as possible when that happens. Okay?"

She nods, slowly, in the dim hallway. Looks back, the light coming up from the stairwell there, and shadows all about from fleshy lobes and fronds, and curling stalks that grow in ghostly patches up and down the wall. Someone yells below, a floor or more below, and a crash. "I think the Anvil might maybe've figured out Becker isn't coming back with that martini, so we've got time pressure from a couple of vectors, can we," she nearly trips over a ruck in the rug as he tugs her in his wake, "I think it's," stopping by a doorway clustered about with mushroom caps brown and black and grey, trembling, a scramble up the wall, fishscale gleam and a flicker of too many legs. "Yeah," he says, turning the knob, but "David," says Jo, "wait. Something's – off."

"*Listen,*" says Kerr, a flash of anger, suddenly smothered. "What he's got? What he has, it can't *stand* what isn't right. What doesn't belong. And what's in *you,*" he taps her, once, on the chest, she winces, "*that* doesn't belong *any*where. Ever. At all. So." He opens the door.

Shelves lined with the thin spines of vinyl records, and a low-slung hifi cabinet, and Becker sprawled on the carpet before it, headphones on his berry-plaid chest, the coils of its cord, mouth open, eyes closed, an etched glass goblet overturned by nerveless fingers.

"He's okay," says Kerr, reaching back for her, but "whoa," he says, "whoa!" drawn back, she's wavering in the doorway, head drifting back and blinking forth, in her hand the hilt of her sword, and the blade of it scribing drunken loops and curls. "Jesus!" says Kerr. A slam somewhere below, another shout. "Put that away," he says, reaching carefully this time to pull her inside, closing the door quickly, quietly, click. "You don't need it," he says. "It's all good."

"I can't," says Jo, planting after a moment the swordpoint in the carpet by Becker's foot. "I can pull it out, but I still can't," legs folding, a slow-motion crash to her knees, "put it back, it goes wild, I might," a deeply shuddering sob, "I might *hurt,* somebody," leaning her weight on the sword like a staff, coughing up a laugh.

"It's okay," says Kerr, "it's all right, it's all good," helping her to lie down by Becker, chiming clank as her sword falls to the carpet, he doesn't fight her as she grabs for the hilt of it, drawing it close, he's gently shifting Becker to lay his head atop Jo's chest, Becker stirring, mumbling, homina frazz, "There," says Kerr, soothingly stroking Becker's cheek with the back of his hand. "There. It's all good." Another door slams, out in the hall now. "Becker!" the roar, and a murmur too low to make out much more than reassurance. Jo closes her eyes. "Here we go," says Kerr, softly, kneeling over them both, hands held out above them, just in case, footsteps without and the doorknob rattles, someone's pounding, "mongoose is go," says Kerr, eyes widening, fingers trembling, "oh," as thunder bursts, and Avery stops, a hand on the passenger door, as Killian in his grey suit ignores the thunder, smiling for the three or four photographers on the sidewalk, and Vincent pauses, bottle in one hand, cork in the other, then pours more whiskey into his mug as thunder shakes the futon frame to scrape the blue wood floor in that high blue room, Ellen a shadow on those sheets white in the streetlight, thunder troubles the garbage piled about Lake crouching lank-haired, naked, over Jessie sprawled in sleep, and Moody wakes with a start under blue plastic, balling his fists over his ears as the thunder swells, and Petra B looks away from her phone in that windowless room, to one of the garbage bags piled with the others, and gold-crusted fingers digging, working, snarling against the throat she's kissing Chrissie grunts and clenches, straining with the thunder to let out a settling breath, and wheels squeak as the CO shifts in his chair, looking up and around with a worried scowl as thunder shakes the kitchen window, and the jangle of chains, explosive fluttering, keening screams as Gordon walks the line of cages, soothing, shushing under the thunder the pianos draped in darkness unmoving but the strings shiver within, a polyphonic chorus to haunt the room, as the doorknob crunches, and Lymond throws open the door, and the thunder claps and rumbling dies away.

"Beloved!" cries Pyrocles, filling the doorway behind him. "Majesty, is he," but Lymond's sagging, slumping, collapsing to the carpet there by Becker, and the headphones, and the goblet, and Pyrocles falls back. "No," he's saying, out in the hall, "oh, my Becker, oh no, my King," his back against the wall, papered with intricate art nouveau browns and beiges, greens in abstractly fungal patterns, shot through with silver threads.

THE ALARM CLOCK

THE ALARM CLOCK blinking 12:00, 12:00, the blue glass reading lamp unlit. The paperback book, flocked with mold, the cover of it faded, Chanur's Legacy, it says, just legible. She tosses it to the wrought-iron bed, kicks her way through the clothing strewn about the bare wood floor toward the only flat wall in that round room, the plain wood door and not one of the half-open casement windows, the quiet night without.

Down tightly winding spiral stairs, hair a white-gold cloud in the shadows, her grey overshirt, black boots quiet on the hallway rugs. One hand idly brushes the wall below a line of portraits in darkly ornate frames, a portly white-haired man in an antique suit, sat before a pigeonholed desk, holding up a feathered pen, a gaunt man in a flour-dusted apron looking away from tins and pans and spatulas on the board below his outspread gnarl-knuckled hands, a stoutly white-haired woman in a brassy cuirass and a polished morion, gauntleted hand holding an outsized compass above a calligraphed parchment map, a fat man crowned with tangled white hair, swaddled in blue robes, his ring-bedecked hands clamped tight about the leashes of the wolfhounds at his feet. Down the long straight staircase to the front door, set with an arc of frosted, leaded glass, that she opens quietly just enough to see him there on the front porch, waiting, grey jacket, bush of a beard, small round sunglasses. "Upstairs," she murmurs, stepping back to let him in. "To the right, the second hall," but they're both brought up short. There in the shadows by the staircase, white locks unbound, his belted robe pale blue, Agravante holds a cut glass tumbler in his hand. "Sister?" he says, roughly. "Magician? What is the meaning of this?"

"Go," says Marfisa, stepping up to block her brother, letting the bat drop into her hand, choking up on it as Mr. Keightlinger hurries up the stairs, "Wait!" cries Agravante, but Marfisa knocks him back with a short sharp jab at his chest, and the clink of the ice in his glass. "You *swore,*" she says, and another jab, "that boon had naught to do with us!" He wards off another blow with his forearm, she shifts her grip and knocks the glass from his hand, smash against the wall. *"What have you done to Grandfather?"* she roars. He ducks under another swing, comes up with a long-bladed dagger in his hand, swipe and thrust, and she leaps back. "Awake!" he cries, swinging, thrusting. "Fear! Fire! Foes! Awake, to me!" She parries a blow with her bat, whock, and another, but then they both freeze, as thunder washes through the house, rattling windows, creaking the frame of it, knocking something to the floor in another room.

"Earthquake?" says Agravante, when the echoes have died.

Marfisa shakes her head. "Thunder," she says.

"It never thunders here, like that," he says, and someone screams upstairs.

Up the stairs leaping two and three at a time the bat in her hand he's racing after, robes a-flutter, as folk uncertainly gather in the hall below, two women in periwinkle dresses, a man in blue scrubs and a tall white toque, another man, his blue vest open, tie undone.

Down unlit halls, round corners, footfalls muffled on long pale rugs, "Grandfather!" cries Marfisa, but "Wait!" cries Agravante. "Stop!" She flings herself shoulder-first at the door at the end of the hall to pop it open shivering splintering frame, "Don't!" cries Agravante, too late, stumbling into her, catching hold of her arm where she stands stock-still in the doorway.

Curtains drawn in the room beyond, and no lights lit, a bed surmounted by a tumbled mass of blankets kicked aside, pillows knocked to the floor by the body sprawled there, splayed legs trembling, foot a-twitch with one last kick. Grey jacket soaked in something, blood, black as that T-shirt. A snorting, huffing hock and swallow, something's crouched over the body, over the head of it, shadowy, huge, "Grandfather?" says Marfisa, her voice quite small.

Something looks up, with a shrug to wipe a sheen from what might be a mouth. A growl, almost a word, "Child," and then, "children," shadows shifting as something rears up, wavering, "forgive me." The head of the body below twisted aside, throat and chest torn open, that bush of a beard soaked in blood. "He was, a friend? Of mine, but," the wavering trembles, collapsing over the body, and a snuffling, coughing gulp. "I just *woke up,*" the growl gurgling, rising, climbing into a wail, "and I am *so hungry!*"

When the baby is born there is no place to put it:
it is born, it will in time die, therefore there is no
sense in enlarging the world by so many miles and
minutes for its accommodation. A temporary
scaffolding is set up for it, an altar to ephemerality—
a permanent altar to ephemerality. This altar is
the Myth. The object of the Myth is to give
happiness: to help the baby pretend that what is
ephemeral is permanent. It does not matter if in
the course of time he discovers that all is ephemeral:
so long as he can go on pretending that it is
permanent he is happy.

—Laura Riding

NO. 31

" – marble sends regards – "

The body
  The water
    The sun

        The air
          Those teeth
           The light

the body on the blue tarp, draped in filthy fleece, bone-bleached chinos, the one foot laced in a torn leather shoe, the other gone, that trouser leg knotted off just below the knee. Glint of gold about a wrist, a watch. The only sound a lazy lap of water somewhere below.

"You can't," he says, "think of it like that. The past is *not* another country. You can't *go* to the future. They're *directions*. Not places."

She steps off the little wooden porch, sinks to her knees with a crackle of dead dry grass before a broken wooden tub. Ragged red Chuck Taylors, black boxer briefs, broad straw hat. A single sob heaves up shoulders burnt a ruddy brown, her back, her legs. Running from the waistband of her briefs a pale seam pinkly white against her sunbrowned belly shining up and up to the thick green stub of a stem, freshly broken, rooted in a gnurl of flesh on her breast.

"David?" she says. He's slumped in the high-backed black desk chair, photographs spread over his lap, under his unmoving hands. Hazed by light from windowed walls that narrow to a windowed point in that open room. "David," she says again, there in the kitchen, black shorts, red shoes, the broad straw hat, and something else, a flower a-bob there by her chin, bloomed delicately pink from a long green stem coiled once about her shoulders, and rooted in her breast. A scuff of something underfoot as she heads down from the kitchen, blue glitter brightly scattered on the steps.

Rustle she pulls the folded tarp from a narrow closet crunch as something heedless falls in its wake. Sunlight blares through windows all about, and drifting scrims of dust. Bundling the awkward tarp under one arm she brushes the flower irritatedly from her face and heads out past a tipped-over bucket, a rack hung with yellow track suits, white piping shrouded in dust, past drywall patched with curdled plaster, out onto the landing, and staircases up and down, and the chuckle and slap of water somewhere below.

Paddling her canoe through sunstruck wavelets up to the point of the corner of the building that rises up white and green, she slews about with the rough-hewn paddle to slow a rush of water sloshed before half-open doors of mud-flecked glass. Stashing the paddle in the bottom of the boat she reaches up and back for the frame and muscles bunching in sunburned arms leans, levers, wriggles the slender canoe around to pull herself backwards through the doors. Click-clack, a sign hung to one side, Sorry We're Closed, it says.

Gliding back past mannequins knee-deep in scummed-over water, polyester finery gone dank, racks and shelves of clothing mud-soaked, rotting, clouded glass case filled with spills of beads, sunglasses tumbled in amber and tortoiseshell, clouds of chiffon scarves, sparkling bangles and baubles, the occasional fallal, geegaws, trinkets, slow currents roiling in her wake. Lifting off her hat she leans away from the flower by her chin, looks ahead over her shoulder to eye her stately progress through another doorway, into a trash-choked hall, until the stern clacks gently against a submerged crate. Clambering adroitly hat in hand from canoe up over stepping to the ottoman beyond a squelching leap the landing there, slimed with mud, stairs rising steeply, high and dry, to a second floor, and a third.

"Jesus," she says, and "fucking" and "oh shit, you fucker, *move.*" With a skronking wrench the outer glass door shivers in against the weight of water shoved and sloshing falling through she's spitting getting her splashing feet under herself dark hoodie soaked, black jeans sodden, fighting her way to the landing high and dry enough, "shit," she says, but "Wait!" he's pushed in after, churning up muck-slicked waves, falling to cling to a crate there by the wall of mailboxes, "Jo!" he yells, but she's scrabbling up the stairs to the second floor. He splashes after white shirt translucent beige fleece slopped over his shoulders up the dripping steps, "Jo!" Lunging to clutch an ankle tripping her bang to her elbows, *"Think,"* he's saying, as "Dammit!" she kicks herself free, "there's *no one here!"* he cries, but she's up on her feet, "Ysabel!" she bellows, from the next landing up. "Iona!"

"Shit," he says, tugging back a waterlogged cuff to check the golden watch about his wrist, and every hand of each of its dials hung slackly loose. "Shit."

Through the dead grass past a rust-mottled air vent toward the body on the tarp there by the parapet, she kneels to stroke the sunken cheek, "You stupid," she murmurs, "stupid," as she takes up a wrist, brushing back what remains of a fleecey sleeve to reveal that watch. Supinates the wrist to pick at the latch until it springs open, loosening the golden band, and the watch slips off to drop into her palm. She peers at the face of it in the shade of her hat, four or five dials each hashed with tiny numerals, signs and sigils, and all the hands pointed up and up, to twelve, to twenty-seven, to the tops of their dials, even the single ornate sweep hand above them all. "Stupid," she says, again. "Never should've," but the rest is blown away by a sigh. Lifting the edge of the blue tarp crinkling over the body, reaching to grab the other side. The watch chimes then, softly.

She freezes, bent over the body. Looks down without moving her head to the watch, tilted just to see the sweep hand swinging down to point toward something behind her, off to the left. The quiet lap of water far below's disturbed by the faintest flickering hum. Slowly, so slowly she turns enough to look back over her left shoulder, where it hangs a few feet back, a central mass maybe as big as the palm of a hand, glossily carapaced, and waspish bodies, four of them, depended from the quarters of it, each twitching a-shiver with flickering wings, lacily rainbowed, too many too fast to count. She tenses as it swoops just a few inches away, spun about to bring one of those bodies to bear. She leans back her head, tipping the brim of her hat out of its way. Closes her eyes as it settles on her shoulder, a great four-taloned claw clamped about her upper arm, her back, her chest, the buzzing stilled, those wings now visible, four sets of four each, veinily transparent. The clicking as tiny legs dimple her skin. It noses closer to the broken stem rooted in her breast, and she sucks a sudden breath when black eyes open as that snout rears up, legs cycling before they seize her ragged stump, and squeeze it, drops of sap flicked up to what might be a mouth.

"Oh," she says, "oh – "

It kicks off in a blur of whirring wings, wheeling about to zip up and back, slip to one side, nose toward what's laid out before her, but quickly now she settles the tarp to drape the body completely, and it turns away, spins about lifting, and she sits back on her heels to watch it accelerate away. Snaps the latch of the watchband closed about her fingers. The hands of it all swing slackly loose but the one, that sweep hand, still steadily pointed back behind her, off to the left. She looks back again. Nothing now but the little wooden porch in the awning's shade, the closed door, the building beyond.

With a grunt she heaves the bundled body up onto the parapet, swings it out, away, lets go. After a moment from down below a splash. She's already sat herself on the parapet, hat in one hand, watch about the other. She turns herself about, elbows braced, legs a-dangle kicking once, pushing herself away to let herself drop and then, a pause, the splash.

"Orthogonal," he says. "Hyperbolic orthogonal, rather." His voice unmuffled by that tarp. "Since we're abstracting a pseudo-Riemannian manifold down to a, a pseudoholomorphically symplectic curve, and I've always liked that about math? If anything threatens the elegance of your equation, you can just," he smiles, or seems to, "forget about it." Laid out in the bottom of the canoe. She's perched in the stern, braced against the gunwale to cant the boat to one side, driving it sluggishly forward with awkward curling strokes of the paddle. "So throw out the space-like dimensions, height, breadth, width: fuck 'em. Focus on the timelike: now," and he leans forward in the big black high-backed chair, fingers pinching a point before his eyes, "before," a wave off to his left, "and after," a gesture right.

"What have you done," she says, lifting the lid of one of those boxes stacked about. Blue glitter slithers to the floor. He slaps it shut, knocking the lid from her hands. "You might as well ask who drowned the world," he says, leaned heavily on his makeshift crutch.

"Future days," she mutters. The bow of the canoe now pointed past those spiky hillocks ahead, leafless crowns of submerged trees. She rests the dripping paddle on the gunwales.

"They're gone!" he roars, pounding up the stairs after her, grabbing her arm. She shoves, slap of wet clothing, "whatever's up there," his gritted teeth, "fuck you," she snarls, shoves him against the wall, "it *isn't them,*" he says, catching her hand. She yanks back, drops to sit on the steps, "think," he says, sitting back in that chair, "of time as a line. We'll keep it simple. Time is a line, and now?" His hands suggest a line in the air, string a point on it, shrug. "Thing about now is, now doesn't move. It can't. It's *now*. It's the *line* that moves," sweep of a hand from right to left, "bringing what's to come, letting go of what has been. What do you think," lurching away from the box with a hop-skip, crutch and foot, over toward the windows, "about a hundred feet? How many icebergs even *is* that?"

"All of them," she mutters, digging in with the paddle again, past the cool shadow of an apartment block, out over unruffled water like milky mud stretched vastly out before her. Far-off, ahead, towers rise grey-glassed and white, and further off, to the right, the towering arc of a bridge still high and dry above the water, past green-glassed towers and girdered infrastructure sunk deep, overwhelmed. To her left, another bridge risen up from the middle of the swollen river to almost reach the steep far bank. She savages the water with the paddle, swinging her freighted bow toward it, toward another set of girdered towers, angled stubs that jut from the water there and there before the empty freeway bridge. "All of them," she says, but he shakes his head under the tarp, "Precisely," he says. "The thing about now is, we experience the moment, the instant, the point, but it's really a plane. To keep it simple. I mean, where the line of time passes through it?" Poking the palm of his hand. "A point, sure. But looping out from that," his poking finger lifted in a swoop, "perpendicular to, *orthogonal* to that line, etched across the plane of now: what might've been. What maybe could. Every moment," he says, sitting back in the chair, "carries with it everything that led up to it, and anything that might come of it." Leaning on his crutch there by the windows, sunlight dappling his face.

"What the *fuck* is this," she growls when he opens the door.

"Good to see you, too," he says, slumping with studied insouciance.

"The *fuck,* David!" Thumping the door with a fist, rattling the numbers nailed to it. She reaches into her unzipped hoodie to yank down the collar of her white T-shirt. He frowns, peering at the blemish on her breast, the puckered skin, the greenly yellow leaf uncurling from it. "Well, damn," he says. "I guess we know now we're not inside of *that.*"

"You're so full of shit," she says, unzipping her sodden hoodie. "You fucked with this," click-clack she taps the hard little lump on her breast, under her wet white T-shirt, "and it did what it does, which is contain the fuckery." He lets out a single flat laugh, turning away from the windows on his crutch, "If that's taken us inside of it," he says, and a nod for the flower grown up straight and tall beside her chin, "then how is it in here, with us?"

The canoe's slipped into still water, in the lee of one of those girdered towers, a breakwater of junk, branches and broken timbers and picked-over flotsam. Caged in the girders high above a great counterweight, storeys of concrete once painted red, now covered over with crawling black shapes blurred by buzzing wings. "Well," he says. "We're fucked then, aren't we."

"Should've gotten some dry clothes."

"I wouldn't go back there, if I were you," he says, and she stops, dripping, there in the kitchen. "That's," she says, looking into the open, sunlit room beyond, "those," as he pushes past, down the three low steps, among the regular banker's boxes white and brown stacked about, on the floor, on the sofa, "the photos," she says. "The Devil's morgue. Someone must've brought it all up, before the flood."

"You haven't heard a goddamn thing I've said." He sits back in the chair. Lifts the lid of a box, water puddling at his feet. "There *is* no back. We can't *go* anywhere. All we've got is now." Leaned on that crutch. "It's just, a different now. But the problem is, whatever it is that *makes* it different?"

"What have you done," she says, red shoes spangled with blue glitter, that flower pink grown up out of her half-zipped hoodie.

"The math. Can't. Tell," he says, knocking the lid of the box by his knee for emphasis. "Whatever we use to try to grab hold of it, points, vectors, planes or manifolds, pseudoholomorphic curves, whichever way we run the equations, forwards, backwards, now or later, *doesn't matter*. You can't tell. The math," a lop-sided shrug, "forgets."

A hawk screams somewhere, and those black shapes leap from the tower to a sudden thunderhead, a bombilation rising in volume, falling in pitch as they swoop overhead, dip toward the canoe, the tarp-wrapped body within. She lifts her paddle, holds it warily, as she glides closer to the tower, "Hrif!" someone cries, a figure up there, hanging off a ladder, glint of sunlight on goggles. "Hrif!" Someone else, scrambling toward her over the junkpile.

"What did you do," she whispers under her broad straw hat, the stem of that flower grown long enough now to loop, once, about her shoulders.

They've wrapped the body with bungee cords about the tarp, the one of them goggles pushed up, a couple faded T-shirts one over another and arms wound about with strips of filthy cloth, the other in dusty black rubber waders, dark shoulders shining, floppy grey bucket hat. She's perched above them, leaned back against a girder, red shoes braced on an angled beam, "I did what I had to!" he shouts, through the tarp. "I figured it out! How to make it *matter!*"

"Gheupo we!" The body jerks, bungee cords lashed to a cable yanked taut, gears creaking. It begins to spin, slowly, as it's lifted.

"I know how this ends, David," she says, as he lurches toward the chair, as he sits back in the chair, as he spins that high-backed chair about, idly, with one wet hand. "You're gonna die here," she says. "Right there."

"But I figured out how to make it *back,*" he says.

She shrugs.

"Topat wel," says the one, pushing back the bucket hat. The other's halfway up the tower, guiding the body past the enormous counterweight, and the buzzing crowd eddies about, skirling, whirling up to settle in crawling clusters at the top of that tower, waiting. "Dal, dam timon, the time, 's good. Hungruz, kenk, kenkru? Grows," he says. "Topat wel. Gedhlei. Good."

"Yeah," she says, hopping off the beam, crash and crunch through the junk.

"You'll be back," he says, leaned on his crutch, sat in that chair, dripping among all those boxes.

"Yeah," she says. The towers of downtown so close across the water, brick and crowned by a ziggurat, high and white with darkly narrow windows, grey and topped by the tilted black wing of a great solar panel, and pale smoke drifting from beneath it into a white sky filled with droning black shapes swelling the flocks that circle above, but ahead, behind all that, rising into the haze from the flood, a lone tower of ruddy amber glass framed by dull pink stone all flatly sunstruck bright, and tethered far above a garden, a sudden burst of color against the sky, circling a castle of yellow stone, all on the back of a shining silver zeppelin.

From behind her, the call, "Medheigh!" She waves without looking back. Plants a foot in the canoe scraping against drift-wood, balancing a moment. Red shoes, black shorts, the broad straw hat. Stump of a stem at her breast, gold watch flashing about her fingers as she reaches for the paddle. Leaning into a kick of a shove, pushing out over

the water brown and oily sunlight-frothed, sluiced into the bucket by a current slow and strong. Twang of the rope as she pulls it hand over hand up through the pulley, wobbling, sloshing, white plastic striated with hard use. Wrapping the rope about one hand, letting go with the other, leaning out over the drop to grasp the bucket's handle, balancing rope, pulley, bucket, herself, she shifts, hauls, releases a screech of the pulley the bucket slopping in through the window.

Leaned against the weight of it she makes her way past a wall of silent grandfather clocks out into a broad dim showroom broken up in niches and nooks by arrangements of furniture, settees and love seats, end tables, coffee tables, rugs laid showily atop the dull grey carpet, a phalanx of loungers, a couple chaises longues. Her red shoes, black jeans, dark hoodie. A row of free-standing fireplaces, red brick and white and yellow and grey stone, white tile, smoked glass, gleaming chrome, but every hearth is cold. At the end a wide white plaster mantel, elaborately molded, and four or five mounds of blankets and pillows laid out before it.

Long windows at the front of the showroom glazed with sunlight, and another line of fireplaces there, faced out toward the empty street. She sets the bucket down before a pot-bellied stove at the end, with a ramshackle sheet-metal chimney run up and back to a hole punched in the wall. Dry wood stacked beside it, split and neatly trimmed. Protecting her hand with the cuff of her hoodie she levers the door open, eyes the glowing embers, stuffs in a log, and another.

The water in the bucket brown, but slicked with hints of rainbow.

On the mantel off to one side a tall stainless steel pot, a couple of skillets, a plate of something, draped in crinkled plastic wrap, a misshapen loaf of stuff the color of old ice that quivers as she digs her fingers into it, scooping off a goodly corner, rolling it into a fatty ball with her fingertips. Holds it over the bucket, lets it drop. It floats a moment before with a sizzling plop it sinks, scarring the muddy water with white bubbles. She leans back against the mantel, stretches out her arms, grimacing, shaking out her hands. The bucket gurgles, spits up more bubbles that pop with a smokey haze. The stove sighs, the chimney tocks, once. An ethereally slender man shuffles up, quilt about his narrow shoulders, blinking behind thick spectacles. "Bout done?" he says, looking over the bucket.

"Give it a minute," she says.

A girl approaches, long dark hair and a cropped white tank, "Where's the coffee?" she moans.

"In the jar," she says, snagging a tin cup from among the pots and pans.

"You ain't even made it yet?" says the girl, rolling her eyes. "Water's not done," says the slender man. The girl stalks off. She scoops a cupful up from the bucket, sips, then gulps it down, clear water trickling from the corner of her mouth. "It's done," she says, dropping the cup.

"You want some coffee?" he says, as she steps away.

"Can't stand instant," she says.

"But it's all that's left," he says, gaze mournfully rounded by those spectacles.

Brown water sucks at the pole as he shoves the raft along. Greenery draping the banks of the gulch to either side, buildings stood up beyond, the blankly grey warehouse looming behind them, red letters unlit say Gordon's Fireplace Shop. His loose white shirt, his cargo shorts, his spectacles blanked in the light. She's up toward the front, dark hoodie, black jeans, by someone bundled in blankets, stringy iron-colored hair spread thinly from the scalp, and a bald man, brown-shouldered, pin-striped vest and trousers. The girl laid on her belly on a towel in the middle of the raft, and rainbow-colored ponies cavort across her underwear. She's writing something in a fat little journal with a silver pen.

The water broadens as the gulch bends to the right, and an onramp lifts ponderously from the middle of it, pavement cracked and yellow grass sprung up. He pushes along from bent to bent until the ramp is high enough to slip beneath, out of the sun, and as the shadow falls the girl on the towel rolls over, looks back to him and his pole with a glare that unfolds in a wide-eyed smiling gasp. "Fairies!" she cries, pointing.

A dozen maybe, clustered about each other against the underside of the ramp, black bodies formless, clickery scratch of claws, humming of unseen wings as one and then another drops, snaps to, zigs and zags. He plants the pole, dragging the raft to a sloshing slowing stop, and the man in the vest gets to his feet, and she does, too, the both of them eyeing the buzzing, whirring mass. Something's glistening in the middle of them all, a grey wet shimmer, "Think it's a big one," says the man in the vest. The girl laughs. "Look!" she cries. "Look!"

One of them hovers before her, bobbing as one of its waspish bodies curls under itself, jerking as wings strain to take up the slack, the one body grasping toward its opposite, legs extending up and down to meet with knitting clicks. "Oh, look," says the girl. Something growing glistens there, too grey to shine in sunlight bounced off smooth brown water. The stuff's flicked up to hang a moment as it unfolds itself, wheeling away as that ball drops neatly to her upheld hands, a greasy plop that quivers as she clutches it carefully to herself. "Wow," she says.

The chainsaw rattle, the two-stroke growl, the rest of them kick off the underside flipping and falling in swarming whirling streams out into the sunlight up and gone. The stuff they've left behind distends, an egg, a teardrop stretching threads of itself still clinging to concrete, "Watch it" and "Don't bump" and "Whoop!" as it drops thump to the middle of the raft, "Whoa" and "Got it!" and "Wait a minute, wait" as wavelets disturb the brown placidity about them, slopping over the boards of the raft to soak their feet, the blankets, the towel, "My journal!" cries to girl, but she holds it out to her, and the pen, rescued from the water. The girl beams, clutching them to her chest with her sloppy handful of stuff.

"This is plenty," says the man in the vest, hunkered over the splattered bolus.

"So let's go back," says the girl, pressing her handful into it, arms streaked luminous grey.

"It's too much," says the hatless bundle hunched at the front of the raft.

"We said we'd all go," says the man with the spectacles.

She says, "I want some damn strawberries."

"And fish," says the hatless bundled. "But it must be kept safe."

"From what?" says the man in the vest with a snort, and "We can just cover it with the towel," says the man with the spectacles.

"They'll *know*. They'll all know."

She says, "So somebody takes it. We'll just find more."

"This is enough for *days!*" cries the girl. "We can just, go back, fuck off, who cares? Strawberries." Stepping to the edge of the raft. "I mean," she says, "I could fucking *swim* back – "

"Lauren," booms the hatless bundle. "You are not to dip one *toe* in that foul brew."

"Yessul," mutters the girl, skipping down the line of grandfather clocks, bare feet silent on the carpet, "check it from the inside," she sings to herself, past the nooks and niches, "step up to play," past the fireplaces dark and cold, "come on strong, hold on tight," up to the front of the showroom where someone sits before those sunfilled windows, dark hoodie, black jeans, she patters up all in a rush, "that boy's gonna make you scream tonight! Hey," she hunkers in her cartooned underwear, "something I wanted to ask you." Reaching for that hoodie. "What do you have on your – "

"Don't," she says, knocking the hand aside.

"Okay," says the girl, sitting back. Swinging her skinny legs around, wriggling bare feet filthy, catching them in her hands as she leans forward, "I used to have a pair of red shoes."

"Did you," she says, gripping the rough-hewn paddle, ragged red Chucks braced against the gunwales. Her broad straw hat, the broken stem jutting from her breast. Watchband gleaming about her fingers. To her left the dull pink tower rising, and the tether climbing higher, but to her right the river opens, stretched off in a side-channel, a steeply green-walled gulch, gated by a tangle of freeway overpasses and bridges risen and fallen from the dull brown endless water. They drift into her

wake as she paddles past, even as that tower seems to stay fixed,
turning only slightly, to follow her.

Twist the berry thumb and forefinger pinch the stem, pluck, a
tiny thing in her palm, bright red peppered with black, a fade of
pinkish green about the cap of it, but she's swung her hand over
the plastic bucket by her knee, maybe a third full already, she's let
it drop, her other hand already reaching for the next berry, the
next plant. Lined across a gentle slope long low-mounded rows of
low and dusty plants, and narrow dusty paths between each row,
and just ahead a knee-high concrete wall. As she plucks the last
berry from the last plant before it she hoists the bucket up to balance
on its crumbling top, then sits herself beside it, swings her red-
shoed feet over. The dusty ground beyond's a foot or two lower,
but lined with more rows of dusty red-dotted plants. In the
shadows to the right there, neat piles of old brick, an even stack of
whitely desiccated lumber, ruthless coils of wire, what's left of
the house the wall once supported. A couple people ahead,
crouching, kneeling, making their way along their rows, reaching, plucking, filling buckets and boxes, a half dozen more, seven,
eight, to either side of this foundation, through a similar space
beside it where another house had been, now filled with strawberries. These fields bordered above and below by the broken
pavements of empty streets yellowed with dust and old mud.
Another block below of houses razed and dry soil tilled and
low plants mounded in long interrupted rows, and yellow
grass beyond, and then trees black and green below, falling away
to the valley floor, houses down there and buildings, and brown
water pooled in dendritic fronds along low streets. Far off away
on the horizon an abruptly upthrust tooth of treeless grey-brown
stone, a single mountain, utterly bereft of snow. She heads on
down her row through the former crawlspace, turning leaves
with care, plucking berries darkly red, leaving behind the pale
ones white and greenly pink. Those ahead already climbing up
and over the foundation wall, leaving her behind.

The man in the pin-striped vest steps heavily down the slope, one arm up to steady the laden flats balanced on his shoulder, his other slung low by the weight of a full bucket, a red bandana tied about his bald head. "Fujiwara-nota!" he calls, to the small crowd gathered by the rickety wagon at the bottom of the field, couple-three women in print dresses, a blouse, some broad-brimmed bonnets, the slender man in his cargo shorts and his loose white shirt, the girl's there, too, sat tailor-fashion by the bundle of blankets, writing in her journal. The older guy who turned at the cry peers up, skin crinkled about his eyes. His brown jeans shiny with old grime, a yellow kerchief about his neck, black fedora tipped back on his head. "Arrie gato, gozeye mas!" calls the man in the vest, "Fujiwara-nota!" and the older guy rocks back with laughter. "Not bad!" he booms. "You'll soon sound like a Yonsei!"

The man in the vest sets his bucket down by others clustered there, and then the flats he's carried. She's coming down after him, buckets heavy in either hand. "Want us to go back out?" he says, straightening, thumbing a trickle of sweat from his brow, but "Nah, no," the older guy's saying, "we already got more than we could ever eat. Somebody's got to learn to make strawberry wine, eh, Baba?" The woman in the blouse waves a dismissive hand. "Brandy even," says the older guy, taking one of the buckets from her hands. "That'll use some up. Come on, Jonny Pulliam's gonna be here by nightfall, and a metric butt-load of seriously fat fish. Let's get these berries loaded, run 'em down to the compound, and then do nothing at all except maybe keep an eye on the grill till he shows."

She stumps over to sprawl on the curb by the girl and the bundle of blankets as they start heaving up buckets and flats onto the wagon. "Hey," she says, pulling a wadded handkerchief from her hoodie. "Lauren." The girl ends a sentence with a flourish and looks up, scowling, capping her pen. She's unwrapped the handkerchief to reveal a half-dozen little berries, perfectly red, and the girl squeeps and grabs them up, pops one in her mouth, "Oh," she says, rolling her eyes, *"so* good," chewing, swallowing with a humming moan, "Pru," she says, "Pru, they are *so good,"* holding one out to the bundle, the

stringy-haired scalp tipping to free a spindle nose from a blan-
ket-fold, chapped lips parting about sharp yellow teeth that
take a berry, gingerly, from the girl's hand. The wagon's creaking, getting under way, the older guy and the man in the vest at
the beam at the end of the tongue of it, bracing themselves as
the slender man and the woman in the blouse push. The girl
flings her arms about her, "You are the *best!*" and "Lauren,"
she says, "hey, Lauren," as the girl sits back, peering, pointing,
"What's *that,*" she says, curious, not at all unfriendly.

She looks down at her T-shirt under the unzipped hoodie, at
the spot brightly there, the point of light that doesn't shift or fall
away as she turns about, that's shining out from within her shirt.

"Jo?" says the girl, but she's scrambled to her feet, stepped
away, she's yanking at the collar of her

A crack in the thumb-sized rainbowed slick that's otherwise
smooth against her skin and shining out from it a spark of
golden yellow light and uncurling up from within a tender
greenly yellow leaf, another

"Jo!" cries the girl as she falls to her knees, her hands and
knees heaving once a hacking spitting cough of something
slimily yellow, and a deep breath scrapes the back of her throat.
"Are you," footsteps behind her, rustle of clothing, blankets,
"Oh" and "Is she" but she pushes herself to her stumbling feet,
"Wait! Jo!" but she waves them away, heads off away, up the
dusty street, faster and faster toward the dark trees and the sky
so white above and the flaring brilliance of

THE SUN

the sun shining down through concrete pillars that support a
tangle of onramps and offramps knitted against the white sky
above scoring the brownly dappled water with shadowed maps.
Quick chopping strokes of the rough-hewn paddle scoot the stern
of the canoe about a curl of a turn to the right under a low bridge,

skidding through shadow and back out into dazzling bright. She keeps her head down, shaded by the brim of her broad straw hat. Another bridge ahead, even lower, anchored to a grassy ridge just breaking the water's surface, and she ducks forward as the canoe slips under and past with the last of its momentum.

A lapped lagoon beyond, pavement rising up from under her to crest that grassy yellow slope, a sudden shore crowned by dark trees, and splashing and peals of laughter echoing. She swings the paddle out and around, suddenly wary. Past a skeletal stand of drowned trees, the rusted tops of a couple of sunken fence poles, there's a fold in the shoreline, a shallow pool snug against the sudden loft of the ridge, and a half-dozen kids splashing and laughing, dark against the bright water, the yellow grass. Falling silent as her canoe drifts up crunching snagged to a stop on the shore. Red shoes splashing she drags the canoe higher onto the grass, drops the paddle clattering into the belly of it. "Need to keep your ears open," she calls down to them. "Eyes peeled. Moody'll come down and get you."

They laugh, all of them, the boys with black hair closely clipped, the girl with her curls tied up in beaded twists, even the toddler, clapping pudgy hands and kicking up water, "He ain't come down in years," says one of the boys, shading his eyes to peer up at her, and "Everybody knows that," says another.

She looks down at the watch about her fingers, then up, to the bridge above, winding together with all the others to flow toward the swooping arch of the freeway gathering itself to leap across the water. "Years," she says.

"Reverend Turner keeps the calendar," says the woman leading them down the dim hall, "oh, my, yes. Fifty years since the flood, and almost fifty years again, it will be soon," her head wrapped about in brightly colored scarves, and more bright cloth swathing her shoulders, drapes of shimmering yellow, orange, red, "when the waters recede, and Vanport stands once more." Doors open on spacious rooms, unlit to the left, but those to the right have windows, filmy curtains, sunlight, beds neatly made with white sheets and brown blankets and about each bed more curtains that might be drawn, or left pulled back, and this room has five or six cardboard boxes filled with books, and the next a small table overwhelmed with framed photographs, the next's awash in plastic and wooden toys in strong primary colors, and conversations still as they approach, and folks look out at them as they pass, his footsteps loudly clattering, those stovepipes clamped about his shins. "We'll know for certain when we see it all come back, of course, but by then it'll be too late. A time, and the times, and the dividing of time." The hall opens out in a sharp corner, turning, sunlit rooms continuing around to the right, walls falling away to the left, a counter instead, a chrome rack hung with soft suits in singly rich colors, magenta, pale green, luminous blue, a man sat in a desk chair, another man in a faded blue smock stood beside him, scissors in one hand, a comb the other, a third man looking over the intricate game of solitaire laid out on the counter before him, behind jars and vials and little pots of powders, salves, creams and oils, and a small sign propped by a dead computer monitor: Lew's Man Shop, say white plastic letters neatly pinned to black felt. "He's usually here in the afternoons," she says.

"Brady?" says the barber. "He's off in the courtyard, seeing to Ike and that rabbit of his."

"Thought he was up with George and Howard today," says the man in the chair.

"Ain't no rabbit," says the man laying a card down with a snap. He frowns almost immediately.

"A busy man, our reverend," says the woman in headscarves, turning back to the two of them, waving them on, him skinny, dark hair tucked under the colander on his head, the plastic bin in his hockey-gloved hands cloudily greasily filled with something heavy, the color of old ice, much like the bin in her bare hands, her dark hoodie half unzipped to leave room for the flower grown there, delicately pink, at the end of a stubby green stem poked up from the ripped collar of her T-shirt. "But, oh, yes, my dear," the woman in headscarves is saying, "decades since He moored His castle in the skies above, and sent His cherubs to us with their manna, but only months remain until Vanport returns, and He steps down to begin His glorious reign."

"Decades," she says, mostly to herself. Down the next hall, the sunlight less direct here, cooler, but still the stilling conversations, the wary, watchful eyes, not glaring, not quite staring, the women in a circle with a quilt upon their laps, the man poised on a credenza with a hammer and his lips about a couple tiny silver nails, the old woman peering out from behind the plastic curtain drawn about her bed, sparsely curls rinsed blue, the toddler goggling as they clanking pass. The hall opens out in a wide foyer, walled and doored with smokey glass, and slow dust a-drift through lowly desultory light. A quiet bank of elevators there, and a long rack that holds perhaps a half-dozen bicycles before a row of dark and empty vending machines, and a small sign of black felt on a stand at one end, Thos. Shine Parlor & Bicycle Shop, say neatly pinned letters of white plastic. "Through here," the woman's saying, "through here," scarves and wraps still bright in the dimly amber, but there's a squeak and a patter of running feet, "Randy!" someone's calling, "Randy!" and there's the toddler running out into the foyer, a man hustling behind, "Sir Bob!" cries the toddler, arms out wide to crash into a hug about the skinny guy's pipe-clamped leg.

"Hey, little mister," says the skinny guy with a smile, looking down past his heavy bin. She sets her own bin on the floor, then takes his, and stiffly he drops to one clanking knee, clink of the glass bottles in his canvas rucksack. She's set his bin on hers, straightens, leaning annoyed away from the flower that brushes her chin. "Sorry," the man's saying back there, "sorry, Randy, you come on back now," but from off that way here comes striding a short man regal in pastoral lavender, a couple three people behind him, "Pearlie Mae!" his voice large and rich, his thick spectacles gleaming. "Is everything all right?"

"Of course," says the woman in headscarves, "it's all fine, Bob's just brought us more," but those spectacles've turned to her, they're all looking at her now, sunbleached, sweatlogged, the only spot of color about her that pale pink flower, the bright green stem.

Clank and scrape the skinny guy pushes himself to his feet beside her. "Since when is your name Bob," she says, quietly sidelong, and "Later," he says, with a warning lilt. "Who's your friend then, Bob?" says the man in the lavender suit, that rich voice filling the foyer without being raised. The skinny guy turns to her, but it's then the toddler lifts a hand and says, much too loudly, "She has a flower!"

Hand over her heart, clenching the flaps of the half-zipped hoodie, pushing the flower back, away, stepping back from the hockey-gloved hand held out to her, but the woman in head-scarves kneels, an arm about the toddler, "Isn't it a wonder?" she says, smiling.

Clattering spokes, whizz of chains, bicycles soar up the empty street, houses to either side giving way to low buildings, a yellow warehouse with a sign that might once have said Rebuilding Center, a giant guitar hung in the window of a pale blue building says Black Book Guitars, the windows of the next shop walled up with books, Reading Frenzy, says the sign over the door. Unlit neon in a dark window once spelled out Bridge City Comics, faded signs say The Meadow and Mississippi Chiropractic and Laughing Planet. A chittering flock of songbirds erupts as they wheel past a line of trees before a looming block of apartments, a tipped-over sandwich sign on the sidewalk, an arrow pointed uselessly off toward a Rental Office. A blackly four-lobed shape floats up against the white sky laboring under the sheen of its wings as those songbirds settle, chirruping, in their wake. He's pumping, pushing heavily, the clank of the stovepipes clamped about his shins, the enormous pot lid strapped to his chest, the rattle of empty bins and clink of glass in the panniers behind him. She drives ahead, coasts behind, churns her pedals to catch up once more, the flower laid back against a shoulder, fluttering with speed. A lone car slumped in the next intersection, a van that says We Deliver For You by an abstract eagle-shape in blue on its side. She slows as he grinds on, she circles the van in a swoop of a turn, stood up on her pedals, looking it over. The tires long since gone, and the glass of its windows, the front of it crumpled, scorched. "Hey!" she calls, flatly loud, pumping her pedals, flower bobbing as she pulls away. "Hey!" Catching up halfway along the next block, more low buildings, a storefront painted bright sky blue, dotted with cartoon clouds. "Why were they calling you Bob?"

"Well," he says, opening the door, and the jingle of a bell, "I used to work with Gordon. So."

The floor's covered with mismatched shoes set left by right, brogue by sneaker, clog by chukka, cracked and grimy boat shoe by gleaming patent mule, creamy slipper by ankle-strapped stiletto, weather-beaten boot next to a peep-toed alligator wedge. He hops clang and crash from this gap to that cleared spot, toward the counter, she takes long, teeteringly awkward steps after, empty bins in her hands. "He's not here now, is he?"

"No," he says, shaking off a hockey glove. "Everybody was gone when I, uh," he pulls a crumpled running shoe from his rucksack, "the boxes, they don't show up anymore, either," tosses it to the mound of undifferentiated footwear on the worktable behind him. "I still see a shoe here and there out there, though, just, sitting on the sidewalk, or whatever? So. Figure I'll keep my hand in," but there, on the green-cushioned pew, an older woman sits, hunched in a puffy winter coat, her hair the color of iron, cut short.

"But you're out here by yourself," she says. A half-empty glass on the teal formica before her, a hand up by her shoulder, the flower safe behind it.

"So, what," he says, "I should, move in with them, at Emanuel?" In his hand a glass half-full of something thinly pink. "I don't know. I mean, we help each other out, sure, but. Different worlds, you know?"

She shrugs. "There's other folks out there."

"Yeah? Anybody bother you, when you were up on Tabor?" he says. "Down the Gulch?" She shrugs again. "Because," he says, "you know, it's really pretty quiet," setting his glass on the table by the open bottle, the small plate piled with wobbling grey. "Moody aside."

"That's a pretty big aside," she says.

"Yeah, but, even he's calmed down? These days. And besides," sitting heavily on the edge of the bed, all that makeshift armor scrape and squeak, "it's not like I'm by myself, now. Right?"

In her torn T-shirt she sits up on her knees behind him, peeling away at the grubby tape that straps a pot lid to his shoulder. "Been a while since you've had this off, huh."

"Sorry," he says, looking down, "for, uh, the reek?"

"I don't know," she says. "Sweat, hot metal, plastic – better than rancid river mud."

"Yeah?" Looking over his shoulder. "Well, you've got that flower, making everything smell sweet," turning creak and clunk, "Frankie, wait," she says, but "Jo," he says, his bare hand gently on hers, and smiling just enough to bring out a dimple, there and there.

"Months, decades," she says, lying back on rumpled blankets, "whatever," T-shirt gone now, too, black jeans on the floor there, bare feet grimy, grime and old dirt streaking the skin of her, shins and thighs, limning creases, her knees and hips, elbows paler than forearms, shoulders, throat and face burnt ruddy, sunbleached hair sweat-salted spread over pillows as she turns on her side to face him, "I'd still kill for a cigarette."

"Not what I thought you were gonna say," arms up folded beneath his head, still mostly strapped and crimped in his suit of junk. "Know what I miss the most about it?"

"Frankie," she says, with a warning edge.

"When you're waiting for it to kick in," he says, "when it's too late not to do it, and just any minute now it's gonna come on like a movie, you know? All smooth and cool and every move you make, just like you meant it, and everything in the world's gonna do just what it's supposed to, the way it's supposed to, and even if you fuck it up it's clear you did that for the kick, you know? It's," she's pushed up on an elbow, leans over flower pulsing, "it's all *lubricated,*" he says, and she kisses his mouth. "That's what I miss," he murmurs.

She kisses him again. "Does it still hurt?" Her hand on the pot lid strapped to his chest, but the woman on the green-cushioned pew lifts her head, "He didn't have to end up like this!" she croaks. "It was you. It was all your fault!"

Cages hang from chains bolted to the beams above, nine of them in rows of three set close together across the width of the

382

sleeping porch, bottoms about at shoulder-height. She crouches to pass beneath them, careful with her flower, red shoes scuffing scattered dried seeds, tiny packets of needled bones and matted rotten fur twisted in weird sigils. She's pulled on her underwear, her dark hoodie. Low table at the end of the porch, sleeping bag neatly rolled, she bumps a cage as she stands upright, clank and groan of chain set slowly a-sway. Something within the cage, a crumpled sack once perhaps as long as her arm propped up by twig-like bones, shriveled talons whitely grey at one end, and feathers broken and fallen away from it, and only the beak still cruel and sharp.

"I couldn't, I didn't know," he says, at the other end of the porch. "There's no doors, on the cages, see?" Pot lids gone from his chest, his shoulders, shirt unbuttoned, ducting still crimped about his forearms, legs clanking as he steps close to the cages between them. "I tried, I did. I, I made sure there was water, and I, when I could, I brought him mice? And a dead bird, like, a robin or something? And I talked to him, I did, but I don't, I don't know why he stayed. I don't know why Gordon left him behind. I don't," he's in shadow, indirect sunlight behind him hazed by floating dust, but still a glint on his bare chest, darkly wet, a line, she blurts out, "You slept up here," and a glance for the sleeping bag at her feet. "Didn't you." Looking back through the cages to him.

"Yeah," with a rising lilt, not quite a question.

"That was his room," she says. "That was his bed, where we."

"Jo," he says, "I don't," she's pushing between the cages groan and popping clang, they crash together behind her, she shoves through the next row, scattering seed and straw, "Shit!" he yells, those massive cages striking dully sour peals that far too huge and squeal of links and straining beams she's through, he reaches after her, she's out the door. "This isn't yours!" she yells, over the clamor, "None of this!" too quickly almost falling down the steeply switchbacked stairs, bouncing out splash through the beaded curtain into the front room, and silence. He turns about, there in the middle of those neatly lined shoes, chinos faded, fleece of his beige pullover worn thin about the elbows, frayed along his

upturned collar. "That got loud," he says. She stands there, blinking, pink flower brushing her chin. He checks his watch.

"How long," she says.

"Since the last time you took off?" he says. "Couple of days."

"Months."

"Whichever. Listen – "

"You're dead."

His brow cocks at that. "No," he says, "I'm just not there.
Here. Listen – "

"I wrapped you in a tarp! I took you to – I'm going to – it's,
I don't," she says.

"You're seeing what you see," he says. "You haven't even
asked about my foot."

"It happens sometime after *this* damn thing is gone," she says,
a hand lifted to cup that flower. He claps his hands soundlessly,
once, "Jo!" he says, sharply. "I'm about to lose the connection.
Pay *attention.*" His shoes aren't there, among those other shoes.
His chinos are fading away. "Come back," he says, faintly.
"Come back as soon as you can." The sunlight shining through
him now, "I figured out how to," and then there's nothing left
of him but the glint of his watch, left hanging in

the air, a towering arc to leap the wide river below, and at the very
top two flags still limply fly. She stands in the shadow of a slender
overpass, ragged red shoes, black briefs, the broad straw hat in one
hand, the gold watch wrapped about the other. Pavement
stretches cracked and crumbling before her, yellow lines and
white baked almost away, just ahead a single skid mark, each
nubbin and crease printed clearly on the concrete, a swerve to the
left that ends at the guardrail. To the right, another lane rises at a
slightly steeper angle, climbing to cross over hers up ahead, just
before that towering arc, one deck of that great bridge stacked

atop the other, and the next cool patch of shadow. A deep breath, and she drops to one knee, bending her head. A hand lifted to cover the broken stem on her breast.

"The hell is that?" he says, looking up as they come out from under the trees. She swings back, lurching toward him, dark hoodie, black jeans, fists balled, "You *don't,*" she snarls, "you don't *talk* to me, you don't *follow* me," he's smiling, "Jo," he says, "you keep the *fuck* away from me," she says, "I *ever* find out how you did, *what* you did," and "Jo," he isn't looking at her, "you," she says, "I am gonna fucking *kill* you, you goddamn – "

"Jo!"

"What did you do to them!"

"*Who!*" he bellows, she throws up her hands, spins away, turns back, leaning in, "Becker!" she yells. "Lymond! *Everyone!*" Echoing up and down the empty street. *"Where did they go!"*

He bursts into laughter, doubles over, hooting, hacking, gasping for breath, "Me?" he manages to say. "What did *I* do? Jo. *Look.*" Waving an arm for emphasis. "They didn't go anywhere."

The street drops away from them down a slope between two- and three-storey buildings and stands of trees to a calm flat plane of water swallowing doorsills and then windowsills, and then the islands and reefs of upper storeys, roofs, treetops out to that tower risen from the water, ruddy amber glass framed by dull pink sunstruck stone, and far off past it the arc of a great bridge gathering itself to leap the flood.

"We did," he says, the laughter still in his voice. *"We did."*

Tethered high above that tower a glorious tumbled garden of flowers floating, a castle of yellow stone gleaming against the white sky, a shining silver zeppelin undergirding the greensward.

On her knee on the crumbled pavement head bowed her lips move, whispering, and as she lifts her hand from her breast the last word can just be made out, please, as that hand closes in a fist and muscles straining, jaw set, she pulls down nothing from the air, not even a flash of light. She doesn't look up when she opens her eyes. She looks at the face of the watch in her palm, the hands of it slackly swinging. "Well," she says, as she gets to her feet, "back to plan A."

"Big One?" he says, looking around. "But there'd be more damage. Buildings, roads – same if Yellowstone blew, plus," looking up, squinting at the glare, "we wouldn't have such a pristine sky. Nah, my money's on a catastrophic melt. Methane outgassing from the Siberian tundra, ocean acidification run amok, hockey stick becomes a space elevator straight to hell, and are you *listening* to a goddamn *word* I'm saying?" She's stepped away, her back to him, looking at something in her hand. "You got a signal on that thing?" he says.

She shakes her head, tucks it away, a slim black phone. Steps out into the middle of the tangled intersection, right up to the verge of that opaque brown water. "I can wade maybe a few more blocks," she says. A tall sign that says 2 BIG MAC FOR $5 planted right where a drive-through lane rises from the flood, circling round the back of a dark and drily empty fast-food restaurant. "Gonna have to swim to make it to the 405. At least, I guess, we know *some* time passed?"

"Since when?" he says.

"Since," she says, "before, this." A wave at the water. "Happened." Her gesture ends up pointing up, but she's turning, looking away, looking back, off to the right, across that intersection, past a triangular slice of park. "That wasn't here when we left."

He peers up at it, a dozen storeys or more of blue-grey glass stacked on the corner, grimly similar storefronts lining the sidewalk, unobtrusive signs tucked here and there, cracked plastic letters that say Boise Fry Company, Tropical Smoothies, Parking, Hot Lips Pizza over an exaggerated cartoon lip-print leached of color. "Huh," he says.

"I know somebody who lives there," she says. "What used to be there. What's supposed to be there." Her ragged red shoes slowly, deliberately make their way along the long unwavering ramp held out over the water toward that great bridge, but hitch once, faltering, a step that doesn't swing forward, that pauses, that returns to the crumbled pavement. Sweeping off her broad straw hat, tipping back her head, eyes closed, under the white sky. Sweatlogged hair crumpled on her shoulders, the green stump on her breast now edged with brittle brown. The shadowed mouth much closer up ahead. Plastic sheeting's been hung across the roadway, and down the sides of it, tenting the lower deck.

"Moody!" she calls.

There's no response.

They lie on dusty pavement wet beneath them, water seeping from their clothing down the slope to where it dips below the muddy flood. He sits up, white shirt clinging translucent, scoops up a sodden wad of beige fleece, futilely sets to wringing out what he can. "That," he says, a grimace of effort, "was foul." Spitting. He shakes out the pullover, drops it plop to the pavement. "Look, if you're expecting a text from somebody, I've got bad news."

Laid back, she's holding up her phone, still dry. On the screen of it a photo, her brown hair short and tufted, cheek to cheek with Ysabel in her white coat, long black curls, sidelong, knowing smile. 35:B, say the slender floating numerals of the clock above their heads. Baldr's Day, Eighth of Ever. 87%, say tiny numerals by a battery-shaped icon. She thumbs it off. He checks the golden watch about his wrist. "So what's the plan, mastermind?"

"Plan?" she says. She's closed her eyes. "The plan is, I go across the bridge to high ground, head south, figure out how to get over I-84, maybe the bridge at 12th is high enough? But I can swim that easy, if I have to. Keep going down, till I get to the apartment. Get inside. Get upstairs. If she's here," opening her eyes, getting to her feet, "she's there."

Still sitting he shifts, turns to follow her as she walks away. "Not sure I agree with you a hundred percent on your theology there, Jo," he says.

"I could give two shits," she says, striding on.

"Hey. Hey! We came here together!" as he stands, "Wherever we go? It's together!" as he snatches up his pullover. "You're dead," she mutters to herself, but "Mastermind!" he yells. "You happen to notice what's up ahead?"

The ramp they're on climbs higher out of the water, and to the left another climbing higher till it crosses over, there, one deck above the other where the bridge takes a sharp turn to the right and the towering arc of it leaps over deeper water, falling short of that far side, where ramps unwind themselves, reach out straight and true for the greenery edging those ridges, but the bridge, the bridge: white plastic sheeting hangs from the upper deck, the limply cloudy length of it tenting the lower.

"Somebody's up there!" he cries.

"Yeah?" she says, without looking back. "Maybe they got something to eat."

The tapered poignard mirror-bright beneath her chin, "Hot damn. At last. At long God *fucking* damn last, *hot* damn." He tips back his black leather hat. "As I live and breathe, Bambi. How the hell are you."

"Moody," she says. His smile flicks away. "You know the law!" he snaps, pressing close. Wrapped in a jacket of army-surplus green. "No! Real! Names!" She leans back from the knife, but her blinking eyes are fixed on his, not the blade. "You," he snarls, "you will *give* me my *due,* bitch."

"Dread Paladin," she says, and "Damn *straight,*" he says. The man beside her with the damp beige pullover coughs up a laugh, "I'm sorry," he says, and they both look at him, "but that? Is the stupidest fucking, and today, has been a *wealth* of stupid, fucking, I mean," as the blade-tip turns to him. "Dread?"

"The hell are you?" says the man with the knife, and she says, "The Wizard," and "Jesus fucking *Christ,*" says the man with the pullover, "how many times I have to *tell* you," but the little guy beside him in a tight T-shirt yanks his arm, and "Shut *up!*" says the man with the knife. "You know who she is?"

"Of course," he says, twisting his arm free, rubbing his wrist. "She's, uh," looking her over in her dark hoodie, hunched, arms folded, drawn away from the figures behind her, the one with the thick chain hanked about a fist, padlock clipped to one dangled end, the other leaned on a scuffed length of plastic pipe.

"Well?" says the man with the knife.

"Bambi," he says, "right, she's Bambi, call me the Wizard, sure."

"You *can* learn. Good. Because there's rules, out here. Tell him the rules, Bambi."

"No snitching," she mutters, still looking down. "Never talk to a cop. Respect the lifers. No real names, never talk about where anybody sleeps. No flirting, with your brother's girl, your sister's boy. Never steal from" but he joins in, shrieking over her, *"Never* steal from *family!"* Jabbing the knife at her. "She ran away from home, she came here, and we gave her a *new* one! *I* gave her a *family!"* The others of them all stood or sat in a ragged circle among the supermarket tents, the shopping carts lashed together, draped with sunfaded blue tarps, a little town sheltered by great cloudy curtains of plastic hung from the deck above. "But she had to go and run away again. Took a government handout for a room in a box. You went and got yourself a *job.*"

"How long'd you end up doing down in Salem, Moody," she says.

"I ought to beat you down by the tracks *myself,*" he snarls, lurching close, "let those goddamn buzzards pick your bones. I ought to," drawing back, "but, shit. World's ending. We can afford to be magnanimous, *right?*" Spreading his arms to the listless slithering flap of plastic curtains. "So!" Stepping close to the man with the pullover. "We'll just tax your sorry ass. Let's have that fancy watch."

"What?" he says, still holding his wrist. "No, that's," looking over to her, "not gonna happen."

"Oh you do *not* want to say no. Tell him, Bambi."

"I can't give you the watch," he says. "Ask for something else. Anything," and he hold his hands very still as that knife reaches toward him, a swallow as tink the tip of it touches the glass of the dial, "Jo?" he says. "Hate to ask, but any time, you know?"

"I can't," she says, her arms still folded, and "Can't, wait, what?" says the man with the knife, as she says, "don't you think I already tried?" Hood falling back, blinking quickly, mouth set tight. "I can't *reach* it. I can't find it, it's not there, I don't, I don't know," and the man with the knife is smiling again. "So!" he says. "Give me the watch."

"Well, first, it's not a hey!" as the guy in the tight T-shirt grabs his elbow, "It's not mine to give!"

"It's mine to take," says the man with the knife. "Hand it over. Maybe we'll let you go on over the bridge."

"Paladin," she says.

Rustles and steps a clink of chain that plastic pipe lifted as she pulls something glassily black from the pocket of her hoodie, "Hold up," says the man with the knife, "hold up," and then, "a phone?" he says. "The fuck am I supposed to do with that?"

She thumbs it to life.

"Oh, Bambi," says the man with the knife, leaning close. "Oh, that is adorable. You got yourself a girlfriend."

"She's," she says, but then she pushes the phone at him. "Tax me. Let us go. You'll never see me again."

"Oh, but I will," he says, his hand on hers. "Any time I want. Long as the battery holds."

"Moody," she says, again, lifting a hand watch wrapped about her fingers to part the heavily translucent curtains that hang across the road. No one stands guard on the other side. No one moves among the litter of tents beyond, no one's peering out from behind a flap. A shopping cart's been knocked over. Splintered wood pallets, broken glass. One of those tents still lashed to its frame, but upside-down, stubbed pegs stuck useless in the air. A boot tipped over, filthy green jeans, a khaki coat in a rusty splotch of brown. Those curtains with a shuffle fall shut behind her, hung breathlessly still down either side of the bridge deck. Another body crouched, one running shoe still on, another puddle of blood. Two more wrapped about each other under a sticky, bunched-up blanket, another just beyond, head at an impossibly wet angle, thick chain flung off just out of reach, almost beneath the turning, twisting, she shakes her head, she looks away. "Oh, Moody," she says.

His black leather hat's fallen to the pavement, there by the knee of the man sat tailor-fashion, silver stripes of his green track suit dull in the dim, head bowed, a pair of blue and white headphones over his ears. She kneels before him, trying to meet his eyes behind his sunglasses, careful of the sword laid on his knees, the long blade of it and the golden pommel both stained darkly red. She starts back when he lifts a hand, wrapped in a fingerless cycling glove, but he's reaching for those headphones, burst of noise as he lifts them away, "Forgive me," he says, "but fighting," his words wheeze, "your folk is such. Butcher's work."

"I don't," she says. "Do I know you?"

"Huntsman," he says, gazing up at her through jagged lenses tinted green, like pieces of broken bottle. Beneath her straw hat her haggard face. The broken stem lodged in her breast. "You've," he says, "changed, but," fighting for breath, "hurry. We haven't." And then, "You must."

"Hurry," she says, standing. The watch about her fingers.

Twisting, turning, the body wrapped in a jacket of blood-soaked army-surplus green hangs leaned forward from a dull green-grayish cord that's wound about the chest, up under dangled arms, stretched taut to the pale green girder above. The head flopped forward. Her free hand, shaking, catches one of those dangled hands, lifts it limp, her other hand fingers stretching the golden band of the watch enough to slip it over those fingers, past the knuckles, scraping back the drying blood. Snapping the latch shut, the body swaying, bumbled against her with the effort, "God!" she spits, steadying the weight, patting at the pockets of that jacket. Up close the dull green cord's quite iridescent, browns and purples, reds, oranges chase each other up and down the glistening length to where it's swallowed by the bloody jacket, the once-white shirt beneath. She tugs something, a stiff weight from a bloodlogged pocket, lets it fall a brightly clang to the pavement, long, tapered, the silver handle wrapped in wire.

"You'll need a blade," he says.

"I don't want," she says, stepping back. "I know Lucinda. I remember, but I don't," she frowns. The sword on his lap, his hands in those fingerless gloves, grey and black. "I used to," she says. "I had a pair of gloves."

"You will need gloves," he says, and coughs.

But she peels the jacket open, reaches for the pockets within, this side, that. Steps back. The body left to sway a ponderous pendulum from that taut-stretched cord. The phone in her hand, one corner of the glass of it webbed with cracks, a crooked line jagged up to the top. She closes her eyes, opens them, thumbs the button at the bottom of the phone. Nothing happens.

She falls to her knees.

Some time later she takes a deep shuddering breath. "There's no flies," she says, to herself. "Where are the flies." Sitting up. Rip of velcro as she tightens the closures on her fingerless cycling gloves, black and grey. Scrape of steel she takes up the bloodied silver poignard. Knife in one hand, phone in the other, she heads over to the edge of the deck, to the cloudy plastic aglow with sunlight whitely without. Tucks the phone away in the waistband of her briefs. Turns the blade and lifts it a swinging punch, rip, she snatches the tear to pull, yanking with rustles sharp like clattering falling sheeting popping loose to slump, a clamorous collapse, crumpled to the guardrail, leaning slowly weight of it pulling over and down to the water below, "Come on!" she screams. "Come on!" The light pouring in, the towers of downtown rising from the flood. The body behind her turning slows abruptly, an arm slipped free of the twisting cord that tips the weight of it sideways legs a-dangle lift, and the hair flops back from the ruin of that face, but still within all the blood the lips are parted in a smile about

THOSE TEETH

those teeth that gleam in sunlight hazed through windowed walls that narrow to a windowed point. "You're not," she says, coming down the low steps into the open room, hat in hand. "I was here," she says. "I've already been here."

"You came back," he says, the words slipped carefully through such long teeth. "Remember?"

"I wrapped his body," she says. "I went to get the tarp, I brought it here so I could drag him down the," looking back, over her shoulder, "hall, why did I come back?" Brushing her cheek a flower, delicately pink there at the end of a green stem sparsely leafed, long enough to coil once about her shoulders, rooted in a pucker on the slope of her breast. "Who knows?" he says, climbing down off the high-backed black office chair. "One last look about the place. You're going back!" He sets the wide-bladed cleaver down on the box before him, by a small glittering bit of bone. "We're going back," he says, pushing back his tattered cuff to check his watch. "That's what matters."

"You're dead," she says.

"You keep saying that," he says. "What I have to keep asking myself is how I can hear you, if it's true." His beige pullover rent to shreds, he's leaning on a makeshift crutch.

"Whatever it is you do, it doesn't," she says, "it's not, gonna work, and I come back here, why do I keep coming back?" Looking about the sunlit room, the boxes stacked about. "The last time, the last time I come back here, you're in my chair," she points, "and I wrap you in this plastic tarp from downstairs, and, but then, I *came back in here,* and there was, there's gonna be, this tiny guy in my, chair," and as she falters, he smiles, much too widely about those teeth. "Don't," she says. "Stop doing that." And then, "I know you," she says.

"Eleleu, ie," he says, quietly. "Jo. *Jo.*" Snapping his fingers. "Of course you do. Don't get lost now."

"Shut up, David," she says. "I'm talking about him. You're both here. Sort of. You will be."

"But I'm dead," he says. "And you haven't even asked about my foot."

"What is this," she says. "Why am I here. What did you," she's stepping in among the boxes, and he hops back a step. "Figure out," she says, looking down at the lid of the box between them, the cleaver on it, and the bit of bone, all spangled with blue glitter. "Is it the photos? Is it, that's, why would somebody go to all the trouble. Pictures, of Portland, how we, know it, remember it, so that, what, makes a difference. Right?"

"You haven't heard a goddamn thing I've said." Thump of his cane, hop-step toward the windows, "Every moment already holds within it whatever might've come before. All of this," leaning lurch as he waves that crutch spinning about to thump catch himself, "already here," he says, "there's no difference." Thump, hop. "But you're close."

"What have you done," she says, lifting the lid of that box with a slither of blue glitter, tink of bone against blade, he slaps it shut, knocking the lid from her hands. "It's not the photos," he says. "It's the box. *Think!*" Waving his free hand gleam of the gold watch over those boxes. "*Who* went to all this trouble? *Who* brought them all upstairs, and saved them from the flood? Who cleaned them and sorted and filed them away?" He's standing on the sofa behind him, among the boxes there, an elaborate shrug of don't ask me, his smile somehow hapless despite his teeth. "Who stayed behind to do all that?"

"What did you do," she says, red shoes spangled with blue, that flower pink beside her chin.

"What I had to," he says, resting his free hand on the lid of that box, his weight on his hand. "Took *forever*. I had to be so, inhumanly patient. But I did it." Looking up, lifting that knobbled knurl of bone, spangled with silver, dusting his fingertips with glittering flakes of blue. "I caught him. And he told me where he slept."

"Slept," she says, flatly.

"Don't you get it? They never slept, before they came here. Now, some of them, all they *do* is sleep. And they have to sleep *somewhere*. Boxes!" Setting the bone back down. "Cabinets. Cupboards, drawers. Footlockers," looking about, "closets, hell, there are *so many* of them. And they all need someplace to call their own, where they can go, to dream – don't you *get* it? It's too *small!*" Thumping the lid of the box for emphasis, the shreds of what's left of his pullover a-flap with the force of it. "He couldn't *possibly* fit in this. But he *did*. It's a bubble, of somewhere else – of space! Not time, not time at all. And if we can get in *there?*" He's peering out from behind him, crouched on the arm of the sofa now, twirling a finger by his temple. "We can go anywhere. Jo. Anywhere. We can go *back*."

"What was his name," she says.

"All we have to do," he says, but "*His name,*" she growls, and "I," he says, looking down at the bone, the cleaver, the box. "I don't see what," and then, his shoulders slumping, "Inchwick," he says, looking up, but she's closed her eyes. "David," she says. "I'm not going back." A deep breath, and she opens them. He's slumped in the high-backed black desk chair, lost in the sunlight hazed through windowed walls, hands not quite folded together atop the photos spread over his lap. "David?" she says, sweeping off her hat, and he takes it from her and lays it on the sofa, then takes her hand in his, much smaller, and roughly red about the knuckles. "Then what happened," he says, carefully, through those teeth.

"I'm gonna go to the top of Big Pink," she says, still looking at the body in the chair. The flower's as high as her eye, and the stem of it long enough to drape, once, about her shoulders. "She's up there, I know she's up there. Should've known that as soon as I saw it."

"So you've spoken with the King."

"I, guess? That would make sense, but – no, wait. He's not, up there? With her?"

"There are rules."

"Yeah," she says. "Right. Rules. So he's the one who tells, who. Will have told me. What to do."

"You'll come back."

"I came back."

"Here you are."

"Yeah," she says. "I was gonna, I'm, I need," she swallows, looks down at him. "The watch," she says.

"By all means, take the watch."

"I should," she says, looking up, "do something for him," but she falters, blinking. The chair is empty.

"You wrapped him in the tarp already," he says. "That you went downstairs to get?" She's shaking her head, but he's rattling on, "You've already hauled him away outside, you're almost good to go, the only way out is up and we're all onboard with that, but you came back in here for one last thing."

She says, "What."

"Lean down, if you would?" he says. "I can't quite reach," and when she does so, hesitantly, bent forward at the waist, he gently takes the stem of that flower between thumb and forefinger. "Actually," she says, "that's," but as she tries to straighten he tightens his grip, hand a fist about the stem now, "Hey!" she slaps his shoulder, pushes him away, but he's opening his mouth.

Lobed petals delicately pink unfurl in curling layers from a tight-packed central bud within to open and open up and out until the outermost ring's laid almost flat atop five green long-pointed septal leaves, and she spreads her fingers to push it, gently, away, out of her face, "I'm sorry?" she says, looking up, then shaking her head, irritated. The flower's bobbing back against her cheek.

"Proof of residence," says the woman, peering down from up behind the podium, a slab of pink-tinged granite trimmed with greening copper.

"I haven't," she says, looking down at herself, that sparsely leafed stem awkwardly swallowed by her half-zipped hoodie, stiff with dried mud, her bare mud-spattered legs, her ragged red shoes. "It's been a while since I got a gas bill," she says, "and unless you've got a working DMV somewhere up in here?"

"Your claim to passage," the woman up behind the podium with a white-gloved hand lifts a piece of paper to read from it, "is that you are within her heart." Lays it aside. "You must provide proof of residence to redeem your claim."

"I, did I," frowning, a shake of her head, "did I say that? That doesn't, I don't – "

"You would establish another claim to passage?" She sits up, leaning over the edge of the podium, her jacket a silvery pink, trimmed and epauleted with white cord, the breast of it festooned with ribbons and medallions, and the orange beret pinned at a distracting angle to her whitely silver hair.

"I don't," she says, looking past the podium to the dark hall beyond, the bank of elevators. "Is she, can you at least tell me if she's even up there? Can I get a, message to her? Or something?"

"To whom," says the woman, still leaning over the edge of the podium.

"Ysabel. Perry. Ysabel Perry. Is she – "

"Queen of All? Mountain-shod, Sun-clad, the Star-crowned Lady, who is never but Maid and Mother and Loathly Crone? The Acme, the Zenith, the One True Only and Ever for Always?"

"I," she says, "well, I was the Gallowglas? I hunted for the King. I was the," pushing that flower away again, "I was the Duchess of Southeast. The, the Widow, of the Hawk."

"None of which," says the woman, sitting back, "is sufficient to redeem your claim to passage."

She turns away abruptly, flower swaying. The light about is thin, shining up from water unseen below to slip uncertain through walls of coppery glass. "If I could just," she says. One whole pane there's been knocked out, a makeshift balcony of planks and bungee cord lashed to the frame. "I haven't seen her in," she says, "ah, shit," and breaks into a run thump of her shoes on filthy carpet driving around and past that podium toward the elevators head down grunt arms flung up stumbling headlong sprawling falling to tumble roll fetch up against the wall as the woman drops down from behind the podium, bustling quickly over crook of the cane in her white-gloved hand shoving her sitting up back and down against the carpet, holding her there, "You may. Not. Pass!" she cries, but there's a sharp "Hey!" from someone else, and she lifts the cane, straightening, reaching up to make sure of her orange beret. "Majesty," she says.

He's not too terribly tall, draped in a kaftan of leafy greens shot through with golden thread, and his hair's a mop of artful tangles blackly drooped about his shoulders. "Just, show her the phone," he says, not unkindly. "The lock screen? That photo of you and Ys, that's enough, that's all she, Jo?" Her head back against the wall eyes closed she draws a breath that shakes with the sob that screws up her face, that coughs out of her, that leaves her gasping. "Oh, Jo," he says, kneeling before her, and then, "Leave us," he says, and there's steel in his voice.

"Majesty, I could not possibly – "

"Take a fucking break, Mousely. They're not exactly beating down our doors anymore. Go for a swim or something." Half-turning, to face her. "Give us the room."

"Majesty," she says, and a curt little nod.

"Jo," he says, taking her hand in both of his. "There are rules. Rules not even a king might break." He smiles, but it does little to light his face. "The flower's spectacular. You certainly took your sweet time getting here."

"I didn't," she says. "I didn't know. It, it didn't, I," but "It's all right," he's saying, squeezing her hand. "It's all right. Is it lost? Gone for good? Can you get it back?"

"You're not," she says, then, and then, "you, you're Lymond. You're Lymond."

"Well," he says. "When I'm at home." That smile again. One of his eyes might be blue, and the other more a brown, but it's hard to say, given the uncertainty of

THE LIGHT

the light, bounced from water to glass, reflected, refracted, tinted and coppery softened, dimmed, steeping the shadows about them both. "Five hundred years?" he says, sat on the carpet, back to the wall beside her. "Fifty." A sigh. "*I* don't know."

She says, "Is she up there? Is that where she went?"

"I was so angry at them both," he says. "Vincent, for just, quitting, walking away from a fight, but John for forcing the fight in the first place. I wasn't on his side, or his side, I was – I wanted to go back, to before there were any sides at all."

"I even," she says, "made it over to our old place, our first place, in the Kafoury building? Just in case, I mean, maybe, but it, there was nobody there. And I tried to find the vc. Back where it all began, right?" Leaning away from the flower, shoulder brushing his. "It's gone. Somebody put up a fucking skyscraper."

"I wish you'd seen it," he says, her hand in his. "When it all finally came together? It was, it was glorious. It worked. It worked!" A giddy little laugh. "So many of them came, from all over the world," looking up, "and there were rooms enough for them all."

She says, "This time, this is the time he's gonna be dead. I don't," a deep breath. "I don't wanna go back." Closing her eyes. "But I have to go back to get the watch so I can get the phone so I can get past whatshername." Looking slyly over at him. "Are you sure you couldn't just, let me slip past? Right now?"

"Well, I put on the mask," he says. "I figured, I don't know," and a sigh. "I'd sweep it off, at just the right moment. Shame my father for not being there. Stop the King in his tracks." He closes his eyes. "But it all happened so fast." Looking down at his hands, folded together in his lap. "I think he knew it was me, in the end. I think, he *let* me win. And so," lifting his hands, ta-da, "here I am."

"It feels like I've been here so long," she says. "This sun."

"She's waiting for you. I can tell you that. But there are rules."

"I don't like his smile."

"I called them here," he says, sitting up. "I opened the door. I saved them all, every last one. *Fuck* Mars!"

"Lymond?" she says. "What's going on?"

"Oh, probably a couple more days. It's nice, isn't it?" Looking down, at her flower. "Getting a glimpse of what's to come."

"Not all of them," she says.

"What I can do," and he gets to his feet then, "is hook you up with a canoe. That should let you get around a little faster, anyway."

"Not every last one," and she takes his hand, and lets him pull her up.

"You do know where it is."

"Why did he do it?"

"That I might be King," he says, leading her toward the empty pane, the makeshift balcony. "Wait a minute," she's saying, as they step outside. "Didn't I come here in a canoe?"

Stowing the rough-hewn paddle she pauses halfway up the rickety ladder, leaning over the gunwale to look down the two or three storeys she's climbed above the dripping guide-rope lifted off the water's surface as she strokes and kicks through pale brown water, flower floating in her wake, the slowing canoe bumps a couple of kayaks thump and wobble, a neatly knocked-together raft among those empty little boats that choke the water about the mud-scummed base of the towering wall of pink-bronze glass, mossily tarnished where wavelets lap, the boats knock hollowly. A bloodstained poignard in her teeth she reaches for the makeshift balcony lashed above her head, she hauls on the guide-rope, she takes long careful dripping steps from gunwale to bobbing deck, scrambling up from the rope ladder onto that narrow balcony lashed to the broken window, pulling herself from the milky muddy water kick and splash, leaping the final step to the floating dock butted up against the glass that anchors the guide-ropes stretched out to styrofoam buoys, the focus of that abandoned flotilla. Her dripping jeans, her bare legs dry, the black glass phone tucked in the waistband of her briefs, her wet hair darkly shining under the high white sky, the broad-brimmed hat that shadows her face and shoulders, the stump of the stem rooted in her breast, the flower gleaming with water droplets almost white in the brightness. Red shoes squelch as she heads across the dock, drily quiet across the balcony, squeak and clack as she starts up the ladder, clink of glass as she steps through the missing pane, "Hello?" she says.

"Lymond?" she says.

As and as she walks heads across the filth across the grimy carpet, "I. I was the. Gallowglas," she says, she says, "the Huntsman. I am here. The Duchess of Southeast! The Hawk's Widow! Her Champion! *I am here!*"

There is no response.

"Shit," she says, she says, "ah, shit," she says, and. Heading around and past the toward the podium past to the elevators grunt she stumbles sprawling headlong hands and knees the knife skitters bounce and tumble to fetch up against the wall. Black phone held tight. Deep breath sighing, she rolls over and rolling over sits up, lifts her hand sitting up, her hand coming up to push away a flower, there is no flower.

"Ysabel?" she says, getting to her feet. Getting to her feet.

The stairwell's dark. Water drips echoing somewhere far below, and the shuff of her footsteps, climbing, until somewhere up there she stops, and sits herself on the steps. She takes off her straw hat, blots her forehead with a gloved palm, leans back, looking up at the flights above still left to climb. What little light seeps through doors propped open here and there up the height of it all makes it all that much harder to see. She lofts that hat out into the stairwell, whirling up in the weak light to wobble slip and fall away quickly lost and gone.

The stairs end under a low ceiling, a nondescript door held open by a folding chair. Beyond a catwalk over dormant gears, slack dusty cables, quiet engines half-seen in the pooled brightness at the end, where one more flight of stairs climbs into dazzling sky. She pauses at the foot of them, in the last angled fall of shadow, the colorless light beyond, above, and the climbing curve of thick-twined rope that thins into a thread, lost to sight long before it reaches the silver belly hoving into view, the underside of that far-off castle, fringed by the greenery of its gardens. Up the steps, up and out onto the roof of that tower a dizzying height above the water caramel yellow under the blank haze, cradled by the rumpled folds of hills, their trees long since scorched brown, interrupted by pockets of empty houses, shelves of condo-miniums broken along this ridge or that, the great leaping arc of the freeway bridge, plastic sheeting ripped and dangled from the deck of it, and clouded crawling with swirls of black specks, and then lines and blocks of rooftops flat and peaked, and upper storeys, and the round tops of a row of grain silos, irrupting the endless stretch of smooth calm water. Turning about, the towers of downtown enormous gnomons against the haze, the curve of that other freeway bridge, and the girdered spires sunk before it, clouded about by smudged arabesques of more specks and sparks, and far off out there past the water a sharp mountain at the edge of the world, harsh grey without a hint of snow. She comes out onto the roof, away from the steps, the rope descending from straight above to end in a mighty anchor bolted to the buckled, rumpled concrete there by the antenna knocked askew, topped by a dead warning light, and the white rock shaped there, a bird, much too large to be a bird, smooth rounded shoulders with not a suggestion of feathers but angled chevrons carved in the broad stained breast. The little man kneeling before those cyclopean talons looks back at her over his shoulder. A great flower's laid on the cracked concrete, a handspan or more across, delicately pink, the long stem of it thickly limp, sparsely leafed, browning at the broken end of it.

"Eleleu," he says, through all those teeth.

The head of that eagle turns, a grate of stone on stone, stark beak, blank eyes aimed square at her.

Head low feet pound she comes for him. He ducks under the lifting groaning grinding wing spread up and out to halt she ducks around and under there he's stepped up on the anchor seized the rope in both his hands she's running as he opens wide his mouth and

the sound

bites, head whipped to one side spun away as the freed rope drags a yard or two along the roof, sliding away toward the edge, "No!" she cries, slither and slip of the rope off the edge of the roof away and gone she's running, running leap onto the parapet and kicking launched out into the air the water far below she's falling hands she's reaching grasping seizing hands the frayed end of the rope she's holding, holding, swinging, swaying, kicking out over the city drowned below, arms straight up over her head the pink-bronzed tower so far too far away, below, her eyes squeezed streaming shut her muscles bunching arms and shoulders pulling, pulling, holding, folding as she hauls herself up her face now at the level of her hands at the end of that rough rope, and then, swung and swayed and twisted about she lets one gloved hand, flung up clutch to grab to higher hold, a gasp, her other hand up after seizing holding fast. Inch by inch, hand over hand, up the rope a vast pendulum swung from the castle drifting far above until, until the soft-fuzzed end of it thumps against her foot, her kicking red shoe wound about, her both feet now, clutched together, and the rope between them, clinging glove and forearm elbow thigh and knee and shoe.

The towers and the brown hills falling away, the water passing beneath and now that higher ground, houses and empty streets, trees still dark with leaves, the mountain twisting about, absurdly sharp, too close to be so far away, and then the city again, behind. She lifts her feet, knees bent a kneel to draw them up, clamped higher about the rope, standing herself then, up higher, lifting her hands one the other to clutch up higher up the rope. And again. And again, feet and knees, hands, muscles bunching, shifting, jaw set, knife jammed through the waistband of her briefs, by the black phone snug against the small of her back, and the frayed end of the rope left twitching and jumping in her wake.

The light's changing as the castle drifts on, dimming, coalescing above the hills behind the dwindling city in a point too bright for the yellowed sky. Something flickers in those shadows, billowing slow coils that churn, dissolving into whirls of specks that surging flurry closer, closer, she closes her eyes as by the dozens, the thousands they swarm, black-lobed bodies spinning glossily beneath the threnodic roar of those shivering wings, a terrible soaring storm of them mounting the length of the rope, rushing away up toward the castle. An eddy peels away, gusting back down to the weight of her dangled to gyre about, fetch up in jerking halts, hovering, dropping and jagging close, startling away. One struggles insistently to hold itself before her face until she opens her blinking eyes again to see it wings too fast to be but rainbowed blurs, light glinting off the cockpit surmounting the central mass of it, obscuring the helmeted figure within, the flash of the silver needle it raises, sat astride the high-backed saddle strapped between those glossy wasp-bodied lobes. That lance tips over, pointing down, the buzzing rising as it heels over, tinny knock of a fist against the cockpit glass, pointing down, pale underside of its wide-brimmed hat lit up in carnival colors by instruments within. Below, past her feet, far past the tufted end of the rope, far below the streets have unwound themselves from a close-packed grid to sparse threads laid through dry fields, dark lines and clumps of trees and only now and then a house, a barn. The flash of that tiny lance again, pointing once more down, and then the figure leans back in the saddle, sawing the reins, flicking an array of switches, rolling, pitching, yawing away, each of them spinning, lifting in fits and starts, scraps of ash climbing an updraft, leaving only the creak of the rope, but something's changed, something's changing, the sound of it, the tension, the air about her, looking up, the castle shining closer now, and growing closer, larger, too quickly, she clings to the rope watching helplessly as it swells, the flowers of its gardens, the golden towers above, pennants snapping in the wind, all occluded by the shining belly of it, white stone, polished steel, woven aluminum, titanium ribs, the whole of it slowly starting to spin as she's twisting, twirling with the growing speed of the rope drawn up into the zeppelin's hull through a hawsehole tiny in that vast expanse, but there's something, she blinks, cheek pressed to the shivering peering up the taut length to that small whiteness against the silver, a circle, a disk, an inverted cone cuffing the rope that thrums with the speed of its passage through a far too narrow notch in its center.

"Oh," she says, or "oh, God," or maybe, "no."

Leaning back from the rope but there's nothing, nothing but the spinning ocean of light and shining silver, cloud and stone and the white guard at the center of it all hurtling toward her. Trembling leaning further back "oh, shit" her hands slip once a jerk feet cycling trying to turn herself about feet-first but it's all so fast, too sudden, smack and bellow slam into wrenched about shoes against booming skin of it skidding the notch at the top the groaning rope arms braced and screaming jerking rope slips once through her gloved hands buckling knees and rip and slam against the clean white guard the rope wrenched out of her hands and slipping sliding falling out over all that

One last frantic kick that knocks her out and up enough just enough her flailing slap and grab the edge swung out a grunt heeled up but one hand slipping she's slipping she lets go the one hand reaching for the knife in her waistband windmilling arm up driving it point home into the crump of plastisteel steamed papyrus the mithriluminum punctured yes but holding, holding, hand on the hilt, the rest of her dangled over nothing at all.

The last of the rope slips bumping frayed end up through the guard and whips away, gone.

The flat wide cone of that guard's hung at an angle on a slender pylon jutting from the silver stone foundation wall, ten feet below that hawsehole. Ragged holes punched along the surface of it, four or five in an irregular line, the last of them still plugged with the wire-wrapped handle of that knife. She's laid on her side on the pylon, holding tight to a cross-bar, one leg bent, a foot hooked through the notch in the top of the guard. The haze has faded, light sharpened, crisp blues and greys now etch the slopes of clouds. Here and there among them float other yellow castles, and the bright flowers of their gardens, and brave pennants. It's breathlessly quiet, but for the chatter of her teeth, and her hair is stiff with ice. In the hand close by her face she holds the glassy black phone.

A face appears at the hawsehole, peering down the ten feet to that pylon, the damaged guard, "Aiw!" jerking back thump of a helmet against the hole's rim. Some heated discussion ensues. Her teeth have stilled.

Scuffle and thump, feet emerge from the hawsehole, pale bare strapped in leathern sandals orange coveralls a shining foil pressure suit, dangled there a moment thick bit of rope, knotted every foot or so, a coil of air line red woven aluminastic, "Yjb elayna," and a burst of static, "razgonyat!" Climbing floating leaping lithely down to land step grab the pylon. "Dap. Dedap!" Kneeling folding hands together lifting a finger to an ear, hidden behind a light-glared faceplate, "Penquepel," the voice, rotely bored, devoutly murmured low and close, "sothe for to seyne, muy dolzhniy. Plaiqwel?" Standing then, adjusting the fit of the breechclout, tool belt, paying out the air line, holding tight that simple rope ladder, floating stepping over her to the top of the guard. Wrenching the knife free with a shocking sound, whipping it away, blood-browned wire-wrapped shining tumbling flying falling kneeling to reach up, take hold of a sun-ruddied arm clamped tight about the brace, gently work it loose. Looking up, lifting a hand to the ear again, bowing the head, a kiss for a wrist, shadow nodding behind light-struck glass, "Five by five, Medheigh."

Straightening bracing wrapping a loop of rope about an elbow to plant a boot a sandal a callus-horned foot and lean into a shoving kick that sends

They'll name a city after us
And later, say it's all our fault.
Then they'll give us a talking-to
Yes, they'll give us a talking-to
'Cause they've got years of experience.

—*Regina Spektor*

NO. 32
" – only to sit – "

Crash the glass and splintering wood she's through and falling, swaddled in curtains ringing ripped and twisting snap through cracking branches thump and rolling down the slope below, Marfisa finds her feet bat in hand and white hair ghostly in the darkness, leaping down the hillside away from the back of the house to the shadows under the trees, curtains left sprawled on the grass, and from the broken window high above a howl of anguish, of terrible, heart-cracking rage, and

Herwydh, arranging flowers, blinks in wonder at her hands, pale among the blossoms on the counter, then looks up to see Powys at the sink in a blue-shadowed apron, paused in the act of wiping out a pan, "Something's happened," he says, and slap and rustle from the hallway strung with yellow lights come running Costurere and Aigulha, aprons and mob caps, tape measure fluttering about Costurere's neck, "We fell out!" she cries, and "What's happened," says Aigulha, glumly, as

a dozen pianos play at once, astringent ringing, sludgy rumbles, skittering trills and scales and maybe even chopsticks in there, hearts and souls, and Bruno, the Hawk's Shrieve, stood in the midst of all those tarp-draped cabinets that shake, rattle, jerk with the force of the sounds pounded out of them, eyes squeezed shut, hands to his ears, mouth gaped in a bellow drowned by that ruckus, and he pulls from a vest pocket a tiny glassine envelope and tips it over his palm, but what drifts out's not glittering gold but feathery ashen grey, falling so lightly, without the weight to settle on his skin, and

Lewis David Coffey, long since retired, stumps across the unlit parlor, lifting an arm to lay clink against the glass of the picture window not a hand but a hand-shape, cast in bronze and beaten with whorls of puckered dots, and outside only a slightly inclined street steeped in darkness, a couple of houses across set close, clapboard and shutters and a dark tumble of hydrangeas, and wails and moans are sobbing through the wall, Meganissi! comes the voice of old Cass nan Sinann from the next apartment over, Fonissa! Artemita! Hush! as

embers crackle, dying on the grate, but the Marquess Linesse, Helm of the Court, has set the poker aside, on her knees she turns from the hearth, "Hello?" she says, and what little light's left gleams the points and edging of the plate that sleeves her arm, "Who's there?" she says, when the sofa to one side creaks, a shadow sits abruptly up at the one end, and another at the other, and they both of them begin to scream, and

Mrs. Upchurch, Frances Upchurch, though that is not her name, regards the intricate graph on the screen of the laptop before her, red points and crosses and green lines rising and falling in sinuous curves that climb from left to right until almost at the edge a frantic leaping abfusion of data that collapses into a single flat red line, shaking her head, those tiny corkscrew curls all brown and gold a-swing, ignoring the phone that's buzzing on the table before her, as

the terrible rage of that anguished howl echoes away in the hall and a shadow, hugely uncertain, turns from the jagged glass, that's a foot that plants itself on the long pale rug, a hand that braces some unspeakable weight against the wall, those are eyes that blinking take in what they can, squinting at the sight of the broken door askew in its frame at the far end of the hall, and beside it in his blue robe, a dagger in his hand, the Viscount Agravante, Handle of the Axe, agog at what's forming in the darkness before the broken window, and that's a throat that rumbles, coughs, spits from what's becoming lips that sneering roll about a syllable: *"You."*

"He's awake" – Breakfast – 3 Questions

"He's awake."

Pewter beads at the ends of his mustaches clacking thump against his shoulder as Pyrocles turns, blue suit shining, away from the sword thrust upright in the middle of the room, floor charred in a circle neatly all about, toward Robin Goodfellow all in black in the archway under the stairs, and brusquely past him into a dark hall papered with overlapped labels from wine bottles, beer bottles, bottles of bitters and liqueurs, past the white door hung with a sign that says Employees Must Wash Hands, past three men sat upon the floor, heads drooped, lolled back, hands in laps or laid on the knees of ragged trousers streaked with drying paste, over and between their outstretched legs to where a puddle of light's seeped past the jamb of a second door, pushing it open, stepping into a small room lined with books, and more books stacked on a couple of wing chairs, and the narrow tables to either side, "Becker?" says Pyrocles. "Are you within?"

Becker's head appears above the high back of an oxblood leather sofa, what's left of his hair slicked back, cheeks hatched with stubble. "I just," he says, "I'm sorry. Woke up." His shirt of berry-colored plaid unbuttoned, dark hair sparse about his clavicle. He pulls it closed, looks down, about, "I can't find my phone."

Pyrocles steps close, holding something out, "I kept it safe for you," he says.

"Safe," says Becker, sharply, taking the phone. "And you are?" But then he looks away from Pyrocles' pale eyes, "I'm sorry," he says. "I'm a little, disoriented. I'm not – sure? Where I, am, or how I got. Here."

"You've forgotten," says Pyrocles.

"I must've had something fierce to drink last night," says Becker, swiping at his phone. Frowning. "Is this some kind of joke?" he says, looking up. "How the hell is it already April?"

Tripping he staggers naked back through the garbage crumple of slithering pop of plastic crunch and she pushes herself upright, untwisting her dingy tank top, "What the *fuck*, Luke."

"*Lake!*" he snarls, crouched there, dark beard lankly wet. "It should have been simple," he mutters. "What have you done."

"Me?" Jessie kicks garbage away, red Ked flopping unlaced on her foot. *"Me?"* Another kick topples boxes, scatters cans across what's left of the gridded stacks, the ragged lines of garbage that stretch across to where he squats in a shallow crater of trash. "You got the name wrong," he says. "Isadora. Lucette. Lizzie, Annabelle, *Jezebel.*" A sneer hunches his mustache. His hand shifts from knee to lap. "You never took this seriously."

"My *name,*" she says, "is Jessica Vitaly." Looking away, the floor-length curtains behind her. "I have a, *father,* and a mother, a stepmother, and a mother I haven't seen in twenty years, I have two little brothers, but I do not have, I *never* had, a *sister.*"

"If you weren't going to play, you shouldn't've played. Who taught you," raising his voice to cut her off, "who *taught* you, to drink? To smoke?" Getting to his feet. "Who showed you how to walk in heels, to shimmy those hips? Who first put on your lipstick?" Wide step over a berm of garbage, softening cock a-wobble. "Who taught you to yearn, to crave? Who else could've been the first you ever wanted, and wanted to be?"

"You're not," she says, her anger taken aback to bewilderment, "I don't – "

"You never answered the question," he says. "And now the spell is broken. You could have been with me, up above the river, under the earth, where it's three but not ten, and only ever," she coughs, he blinks, "fourteen," but she's quivering giggles bubbling up abruptly hiccuping, a whoop leaping out of her, swallowing guffaws enough to say, "Shut *up*. Shut the fuck up, Luke." Kicks back through the garbage toward the drapes, the sleeping bag spread open and the parka puffy pink and orange that she seizes, shoves her arms into the sleeves, laughter fled she's trembling waving an arm about loose cuff flapping wet with something, *"Shit!"* Stoops to scoop up wads of trash, food wrappers and newspaper, plastic bottles whip and clanging cans flung at him, "God!" she shouts, and "You!" and "Fuck!" bouncing off his arm his hip he ducks a cereal box blue tape flapping smash of a glass jar, she's screaming, hands on her knees now, twist of cellophane ghosting about her, still a thumping, rapid banging, someone's pounding on the other side of a wall.

"Shit," she says, when the pounding stops. Snatches up a crumpled sheet of paper, goldenrod stained dark at a corner, most of the pull-tabs at the bottom torn and gone, and the figure splashed across it in black ink. "You," she says, she starts to say, but then she stuffs it in her pocket and sets off, too quickly, heedless of the garbage slipping underfoot. "What was that," he says, lurching after, "where are you," seizing her hand, "Jez!" yank and twirling stumble by the door, "Fuck you," she snarls, grunts, hauls him into a levee of flattened cardboard crash, and the pounding starts again. He sits up, knocking coffee grounds from his beard. "Jessie," he says. "I don't want to hurt you."

She gets back on her feet. "That's what you all say." She opens the door. "Every single motherfucking last one of you."

Leaned on push brooms, a mop propped in a bucket, tool belts about hips or shoulders, wiping a plaster-smeared trowel, hefting a spool of glossy blue cable or a dripping plunger, all of them looking to the raised stage at the end of the cavernous warehouse, the canvases displayed there, the dancing figure ink-splashed on each, and before them Gloria Monday, long black hair shining under racked fluorescent lights. "Is it the milk?" she says, too quietly, and then, a bit louder, "We've been leaving out the milk."

A man steps up, bouquet of wire-caged lightbulbs clutched under one arm, his other hand held out, a little plastic baggie, a nod, go on, take it. Gloria holds it up in the light, peering at the ashy dust within. "I don't get it," she says.

He turns away, bulbs chiming, they're all turning away, someone's ducking under the half-raised overhead door there, Marfisa, sheepskin collar upturned, white hair twig-matted, freighted with rain. They press close, tool-clank and step-scuff, and the flutter and crinkle of baggies, of glassine envelopes in hands outstretched, and all the dust within unsparked grey ash. She pushes through as they hurry hustle step back out of her way, past Gloria turning "Mar?" to the skeletal staircase foot-steps clanging up to the walkway, where Anne Thorpe in her long black coat peers blearily at two men in smocks by a door freshly painted, purple and green, and baggies in their hands with wet brushes, past and up the ladder bolted to the wall, up and up to the planks laid over joists a ceiling up and over.

"Okay," says Gloria, "it's all right," calling out, "she's here, everybody! Marfisa's here. She's gonna," and there's Anna, in a checkered nightshirt, Petra B in a wine-colored robe, slipping into the crowd. "She'll sort this out," says Gloria, and then an anguished cry rings out from above.

The stillness that follows a breath stretched much too far until in a rush it's all let out, a keening howl, and a shape's whipped over them all from the shadows of that attic, shallow flat and tumbling a box, and the scramble as they hasten from where it will fall, push and scuffle catching help each other back and away from the splintering crack and cloud of what it held, of dust, softly falling through harsh light, shadowy flakes of dull sparkless ash that settle on the concrete, and still that horrid ululation.

"Oh, no," says Anna, staring at the broken box.

A wincing grunt, he reaches for his lap, the head there tousled dirty-gold hair bobbing as his hips jerk on the d un-colored chaise. A yellow tie draped over his shoulders, collar open, cheeks grizzled with stubble brownly shadowed in the low light of the dressing room, "Brother!" he calls, hips lifting, a spasmed grimace. "In here! Not a drop," to the woman sat up between his knees, back of her hand pressed to her lips.

"You've seen it," says the man stepping in, "have you? Haven't you?" Blue dress shirt, salmon tie neatly knotted. "You spoke to Harfang. Dandyclaw? Dandyclaw saw what, yes," holding a small but ornate brass headset to one ear, he's nearly shouting into it, "*All* of it? You're certain?" and, with a nod, he taps it, and looks down to the man on the chaise. "Mousely says the Champoeg vault's still whole and hale, but everything else…"

The woman in her gauzy caftan gets to her feet, hand still over her mouth. "Break your fast, Rhythidd," says the man on the chaise, buttoning up his trousers.

She plucks the headset from Rhythidd's ear and pulls his mouth to hers, and with a lick he takes her kiss, leans into it, shovels his tongue in her mouth to slurp and swallow, and lets go. "Autophagy's at best a short-term solution, Welund," he says, and licks his lips.

"Any solution's short-term, in the long run. Now let Wilolly be about her business, and you about yours, that we all might get on with our days."

"M'lord," she says, and reaches for Rhythidd's hand, but he lifts it away, to the knot of his tie, "What news of the King, brother?" he says.

"He passed the night at Goodfellow's," says Welund, with a shrug.

"And her majesty?"

"Only that she has met the King, and they are to go to the house in King's Heights," says Welund, buttoning up his shirt, "to which, as soon as I've restored myself, I shall repair, and you to the Hound in Goose Hollow, and then, dear brother, why, *then* we shall know the news."

"But what of her amanuensis," says Rhythidd, as Wilolly looks over her nails.

"If you mean the Gallowglas," says Welund, adjusting the drape of his tie, "she is as yet unfound; if you mean some other, why, we should know, soon enough, if you would not mind," and he holds out a hand, an importunement, and after a moment Rhythidd nods. Wilolly sinks to her knees, and then the jingle of a buckle, undone.

Leaf-bladed shears part to bite the belt about those hips, saw through it, chew on down the seat of those grey trousers winey brown with blood. Peeling up she lifts out sopping the tail of a black T-shirt, gathered with the warm-up jacket in her blue-gloved hand, and slits her way up the broad back, more blood oozing from jammy clots with every cut. Gingerly through the collars of jacket and shirt, shying from the matted hair still tied in a stunted club of a ponytail, but despite her care the head does wobble on what's left of the throat. "We're going to have to strip the carpet out," says the woman behind her, hugging a bolt of white lawn to her breast, "we'll never get it cleaned," stepping back, "not with-out," but a crunch underfoot, she looks down, swinging the bolt of fabric out of the way, to see a pair of sunglasses dappled with blood, one purple lens intact, the other greenly shattered. "Oh," she says, as the woman with the shears yanks cloth away from back and buttocks bared a mottled expanse of bruise, "oh, *why* are you still *here!*" and squats beside the body to unroll the snowy lawn.

Downstairs, Agravante still in his pale robe looks from the ceiling back down to the thin glass tube in his hand, capped with cork, sealed with dark blue wax. Holds it up in the sunrise streaming through the windows there, but the thread of dust within's still coldly grey. A guffaw rumbles from the shadows well out of morning's reach: "You'd weave another circle round me?" A bone clatters the length of the dining table between them, chunk of vertebra spangled dully silver, rolling a die to wobbled stop by the flared end of an ulna flaking green. "Better make it fast, this time."

"You've had enough?" says Agravante.

"Enough?" growls the other. "What does that even mean, enough." A lick of shadow, a hand perhaps, pressed to the table.

"If I said no, would you offer me another? How many do you think I could eat, before they broke, took off, left you flat? Not nearly as many as it would take to finally get you on your feet yelling stop, you monster, *enough.*" Leaning close, to the very edge of the morning light, "You God damned idiot. The hell were you *thinking,* cuckooing me out of my egg like that?"

"Certain," says Agravante, "oracular powers, are said to accrue to one such as yourself." His gaze blank, his face slack, all framed by matted white hair. "Properly tended."

"Properly?" That grinding laugh again. "Well *some*body sure as shit kicked your plan in the toilet. And you, you were gonna dip your thumb in the cauldron – you went and put your foot in it!" Something in those shadows starts to swirl. "Well. Tell you what I'm gonna do: I'll tell your future, here, now, for free. In a minute, after you've answered three questions, you and me, we're gonna get up and go for a ride. How's that for an oracle?"

Agravante says, "You'll frighten the horses."

"Ha! Okay. First: is there still a Court, and a Queen?"

"Insofar as I know," says Agravante.

"Such a bravely ironical tone!" Whatever it is lurches, rears up to crumble in the shadows, but the voice without a trace of effort continues, "And would that be Queen Arabella? Queen Duenna? Or Queen Ysabel?"

"Ysabel," says Agravante, leaning forward, squinting against the light, but he jerks back when the shadows fall over a chair, lean on it, splinter it to kindling. "Who's the King?" that voice, quite cheerful as the whorling twisting suddenly stops. A floorboard creaks with a shift of weight. "Well?"

"Her brother," says Agravante. "Lymond." And then, with wonder in the word, "Grandfather?"

"Hardly," scoffs the other, stepping into the light, shooting the cuffs of a crisp white shirt from the sleeves of a navy suit, the tie black, the belly round, the head pinkly bald, but for an ivory crown of hair. "Though I see how you could get confused. Now!" A sharp clap. "Get dressed. We're off to see the neighbors."

1510, says the scrap of paper in her hand, and 201. Across the street a small sign elegantly plain over demure glass doors says 1510 – the Hawthorne. "Huh," says Ettie, in her black shorts, her cropped blue sweater.

The doors are locked. A small black speaker on the wall beside them, and a keypad, she presses 2, then 0, then 1. The pound key, after a moment. A click, and the timbre of the stillness shifts, opens with a faint hiss. The loud burr of something ringing, then another click. That hiss still tugs the air. "Hello?" she says. "Starling? It's, ah, Stephanie. Étienne Limoges?" A truck sighs down the side street, chasing its morning shadow. "Hello?" she says.

A beep, and the latch of the glass doors disengages with a thunk.

Up a switchbacked flight of stairs to a courtyard mezzanine, and more doors of demurely clouded glass, a bicycle hung upright, a rainbowed parasol furled against an unlit grill. The door at the end, opening slowly as she approaches, has the numerals 201 set in the brick beside it. The woman stood there wears a blackly simple maillot, trimmed in lurid pink, her dark hair pixie-cut. "Starling?" says Ettie. "I would've called," but the woman's turning away. "Can I come in?"

Past an unused coat closet an emptily spotless kitchen, bamboo and stainless steel. A sturdy pole's been bolted floor to the low ceiling's edge. Ettie steps around it into an open space that leaps two storeys up or more, the front wall unbroken glass that looks out over the street below. In the sunlight a couple of sleekly angular chairs, and sat to the left a thick-set woman in a white lab coat, black leather satchel on the floor by her sensible shoes, and to the right a young man, shirtsleeves gartered, scissors and threadhanks and papers of pins tucked in the bib of his leather apron. A beat thumps quietly somewhere, and an airy drone of pipes, a crooning monotone, these are your broken arms, all a the legs a Irish kings, these three sad things. "Starling?" says Ettie.

Smack and squeak of skin on steel the woman in the maillot's grabbed the pole and leaning away spins about it, follow me now, this is me and the dead boy talking, twisting and dip and smile, this is me when I'm ten. When she comes back around her hair is blond and severely straight, this is me lying in bed when I'm old, mountainous veins in my hands, bracing she hoists herself upside-down to clamp her thighs about the pole, give me an inch and I'll go for your throat, Ettie's looking from pole to chairs and back again, "Hello? Starling?" Up the wall to the left a minimalist flight of steps, concrete planks bannistered by slender cable, leads back up to a bedroom lofted over the kitchen. "Hello?"

The woman in the lab coat turns over an empty hand. The front of the young man's apron's dusted with powdery ash, a torn plastic baggie crumpled on his knee. The woman in the maillot's upright again, curling an arm, legs more tightly gripping the pole, leaning back and back, free arm swooped offhandedly to slow her spin, lowering the yellow flag of her hair to the floor. "I need to speak with you," says Ettie, looking up, pitching her voice up and out. "It's about my sister." The music's come to an end. "I know," says Ettie, "you've seen her, with Ysabel. I know you can get to Ysabel." The woman in the maillot's pulled herself back upright and in, spinning faster now and faster, scraping thump the trembling pole. The man in the apron leans forward in his chair. The woman in the lab coat's looking out the window. Faster, as Ettie takes a step away from the stairs, toward the pole, faster clang and squeak a clap of closing air the woman's gone, pole still thrumming in her wake. Something clack a bounce across the kitchen floor, a bit of bone, and Ettie shrieks. The man and the woman still in their chairs, and her eyes are closed, his cheeks wet.

"Oh my God!" cries Ettie, climbing the steps too quickly, stopping halfway up, "my God, if you just, if that," starting up again, toward the bedroom loft, "Starling? Starling!"

Sitting up amidst a bewildering tangle of color and pattern the Starling lifts a corner of satiny pink to her shoulder, across her breast. "Leave," she says.

"Oh," says Ettie, a hand, both hands to her mouth. "Oh, what has she done to you."

"Done?" the Starling growls. "What has she *done?* Withdrawn her favor. *From us all.*" Leaning forward on the bed, "You would *go* to her? Foolish mortal. Your sister," reaching down to snatch up a blue-black garment, a bulky hoodie, "has been let go, as have we all. She is free, or lost, and gone," pulling it over herself, settling the hood over short black silver-shot hair, "so go. Leave me to myself."

"No," says Ettie, stood there, unmoved. "No." Lifting a hand, an offer, a welcome, a request. "There's, some people you should maybe talk to," she says, quietly, but firm. "Come on. I can take you to them."

Stumbling over meandering stones, "Hey!" he's frogmarched across a scrap of yard, "Not so rough!" up to a yellow door, of a house much like the others on this side of the street. The Chariot Iona, hands on his shoulder, his belt, hauls him up onto the threshold, his dark hood falling back from an up-thrust shock dyed orange-pink. Shuff of slipper, click of heel they follow, Ysabel a briefly loose chemise of white, laced and hemmed with pale gold ribbons, and Chrissie all in black for dancing, reaching to catch a hand, tug Ysabel to a stop, there before the house. "What are we doing here?" she murmurs. "What's going on?"

Ysabel smiles as if to reassure, steps close, a hand to Chrissie's chin. "When I find out," she says, "I'll put a stop to it." Chrissie looks away. Ysabel presses her kiss to a cheek. Parked along the curb across the narrow street a couple of suvs in black and stern brick red, a silvery grey roadster, a blocky hybrid blue and white, and the high stone wall rising, and tangled thickets and trees, half-glimpsed gardens that climb the slope above.

"Ma'am," says Iona, a meaningful hitch her her hands occupied by his shoulder and hip, and a pointed glance at the door. "Of course," says Ysabel, stepping onto the threshold, but before she can reach for the knob it's swung open, "Majesties!" cries the woman stepping out, into morning light that sets off in the purple of her gown a seemly riot of yellows, greens, reds and sheening blue, dazzles the silver thread picked through the black scarf binding her hair. "You've come with the sun, to resolve a most uncertain night."

"Yeah," says the man in the hoodie. "About that." Wincing as Iona shakes him, once. "Highness," says Ysabel, and a gesture within, "if we might?"

The woman all in purple steps back, door held open, but her smile has faltered to a frown. "Ma'am?" she says. "My lord? Lymond? Is something here amiss?"

"My, sister," says the man, "is," with a jerk to free himself from Iona's clutch, "understandably!" brushing, resettling his hoodie, "overreacting, perhaps, a tad, to the, *uncertain,* uh, nature, of what's, occurred," trailing off as the woman in purple with a rustling drag steps close, looks up, into his blue, blue eyes. "My lord," she says. "What is it you call me?"

"I, what?" He blinks. "Call you?"

"When we speak together, lord. After court, or over breakfast."

"We, ah," another blink, and again. "You, and I."

"You did send for me, sir, from the Court of Engines, did you not? Surely you have not forgot my name."

He looks away, and something comes over his face, those eyes, his mouth cast slyly wry.

"Âna Annisa hight," she says, and offers him her hand, "Ray," he says, and takes it with a shrug.

"A pleasure to meet you, sir. What has become of your brother?" she says, to Ysabel, who looks down, to Chrissie's hand in hers. "We do not know," she says. Looking up. "We begin to think he doesn't, either."

"Actually," he says, but she's kept on, "His majesty left to meet our Gallowglas last night, who was, distraught." Letting go of Chrissie's hand. "Now she is gone, and he is gone, and this," a sidelong look, "is all that's left. We mean to bring him within, and examine him closely, to learn what we might before this news might spread."

"Ah, lady," says Annisa, suddenly grave. "If such was your design, I fear you've come too late."

Past her, down the hall its gleaming floor opening out into the wide room under the great curving wall of glass, the hush

of conversations held in abeyance, and the Gladius, the Byrne
and the Oubliette, the Sovnya, chin tucked behind a shining silver
bevor, the Fauchard, the Pilot, all craning to peer back up the
hall, and the Gaffer in his pea coat, clay jug in his hands, the
Mooncalfe barefoot, holding a green plastic bottle, and the Mason
all in brown, and a simple silver thermos, and taking one hesitant step into the hall, the Guisarme Welund in his linen suit,
his yellow tie.

"They've come in fits and starts throughout the night," says
Annisa, "since that uncanny thunderclap."

"If so," says Ysabel, "so be it," and she strides toward them all.
"We've enough for a quorum. Come! Bring him, before my
council!"

"It's," he says, waving his hands up above that shock of orange
hair, "it's, it's either day or, or it's night, or," dark hood lowered, a cowl about his shoulders, "and when it's night? There's
snow, feet of snow, snow like maybe back in Paul Bunyan's day
or something, I don't know, but, when the sun comes up? It all,
it melts. And there's, the water, then, it's like, a hundred feet
deep? I don't know. Five, six storeys downtown, whatever that
is. And the days, the days last for, like, weeks, months, I don't
know. Not like I have a watch," pushing back a cuff to show his
naked wrist. "Not like it would do any good. And there isn't a
cloud in the sky, but until the sun finally, finally starts going
down, and then it gets cold. Fast. Everything freezes. And it
starts to snow." Sitting back in his chair at the head of the table.
Behind him, past the credenza laden with cold silver chafing
dishes, the vertiginous drop, the dark trees, the rooftops gauzed
in mists steamed away by the rising sun. "Anyway. That's
where I was, when I was him. So I figure, now I'm me again?
He must be there."

"And, forgive me: you are?" says Welund, sat to his right.

"Ray," says Ysabel, stood to his left, leaned against the back
of a chair.

"Yeah," he says, leaned forward, and the heels of his hands against his eyes. Pushing back his shock of hair, "I'm on the ragged edge, here. Can I get something to drink? Some juice? Water?"

"How do we get there?" says the Gaffer, hunched over in his burly pea coat, "Or, I suppose, how does he come back?" and the Mooncalfe snorts. "You think he means to come back," she says, beads clacking as she sagely shakes her head.

"Tell us," says Ysabel, leaned over her chair-back, "who else was in the room, when you became you again."

"I," says Ray, and a sigh. "Like I told you," he says. "The big guy, the one with the mustache. Whatsisname, was at the church that time."

"The Anvil Pyrocles," says the Mason, halfway down the table to the right.

"The Anvil. And that other guy, who was also at the church, laid out asleep on the floor. And, and it was, like, the saddest, the most terrible thing in the world, that he was," a shrug, "asleep," he says, looking up to Ysabel. "She wasn't there," he says. She looks way, to the Mason, who's looking at the thermos set before him. "I haven't seen her," a breath, sucked in, "since the last time I was me."

"My lady, we've gotten all we might, I fear," says Welund, spreading his hands, "for now; for now, my lady, we must discuss what we'll do next."

"Time enough, yet, for that," she says.

"Lady," says Welund, gently. "Every ounce and drop of due respect, and more besides, but: your people need you, now."

"Is that so," she says. The table quiet a moment, the air quite breathless. Morning rises through the trees below. "Seriously," says Ray, "a glass of water," but Welund says, "My lady, you must know it is."

"What my people need, Glaive Welund," and she reaches for the jug there by the Gaffer's elbow, and reflexively he lifts a hand, then draws back, sits back, chagrined, "is the owr," she says, "that I provide." Lifting the jug. "We may speak freely, here." Setting it down, in the middle of the table, before them all.

"If you were to turn even a thimbleful, ma'am," says Welund, the timbre of his words dropped, clipped, "it would tell us much, of what we face."

"It would tell you whether I might yet make more," she says. "We've not forgotten how my, how our mother was treated." He pushes back his chair at that, gets half up out of it, "My lady!" caught in that moment, not sitting, not standing, a hand on the arm of his chair. "No one doubts your fecundity," he says, pushing himself upright.

"She does," says the Mooncalfe. Between her hands a squat plastic bottle, the label of it peeled away in strips that litter the table before her. "It's why she's so keen on her Gallowglas." Looking up, to meet Ysabel's green gaze. "You need your crutch," she says.

"I need," says Ysabel, cold and terrible, but then she closes her eyes, swallows, with a small tight smile. "We understand your office must be filled," she says, to the Mooncalfe, "but must you fill it with such zeal?"

"If it's amanuensis you require," says Welund, "what on earth's the matter with the blonde, upstairs?" Sitting him back down. "Why else bring her?"

"Accept, Glaive Welund, that there is much about which you know little enough, and that about which you know nothing at all." Pulling out her chair, she sits, and winds up a trailing ribbon in her lap. "Today," she says, looking up, "you find yourselves without a King, and a Huntsman. I have lost a brother, and my most beloved friend."

The Gaffer leans close. "We do have you, ma'am," he says.

"So, are we," says Ray, "are we done?"

"No," says Ysabel. "You saw something. You heard something. You *know* something, whether you know it or not. *Some*thing that might help. When you, when you became yourself again, and opened your eyes," she shakes her head. "Before that. The moment *before* you came back. What's the last thing you remember? I must know!" she cries. "If they've gone there, I must know. Was it hot? When you left? Cold? Day? Or night?"

"It, it doesn't work like that," he says, "and anyway," he points down the table, finger crooked up, "I think she's trying to get your attention?"

At the back end of the porch Iona's stooped, halfway down the stairs, beckoning awkwardly, "Ma'am?" coming down a few steps more, straightening as she does. "Your pardon, ladies, lords: the Pinabel has come."

"Southwest, at last," says Welund. "Tell us, Chariot: has the Viscount come himself, or is it but another ambassadour with a bucket?" The Mooncalfe rolls her ostentatious eyes at that, and the Mason shakes his head.

"Neither, sir," she says. "It is my lord the Count."

"Oh," says Welund, after a moment.

Up the stairs, out into the wide room under the great wall of glass, the Glaive, the Gaffer, the Mason, the Mooncalfe, and Ysabel behind them, paused on the top step as a voice floats to the top of the murmurous clamor, "poached in virgin olive oil, and grits simmered in cream." She closes her eyes. "A salsa verde, perhaps," that voice continues, "chopped herbs, and just enough oil to loosen them." She sets off toward the armchair there, the little table by it, and Chrissie sat back against the arm of it, ankles crossed, phone in her hand. "Peppers and garlic, a bit of sugar, added to fermented fish sauce," and Ysabel leans close to her, "You mustn't sit on the throne," she says, quietly, a hand on Chrissie's elbow.

"How long's this gonna take?" says Chrissie, getting to her feet. "He's making me hungry."

"Take yourself downstairs, to the porch," says Ysabel, as quietly as before. "Go, now. Iona is below, you'll be quite safe. Don't worry," and her fingers to her chin, but Chrissie steps back, "I wasn't," she says, "but I am, now."

"It will all be over soon enough. And then you'll eat." A gentle push, to send her along, and Ysabel watches as Chrissie, halt-ingly, crosses the room between and among them chuckling and murmuring to stand a moment silhouetted by the climbing sun at the top of the stairs, and only when she starts down does Ysabel look to Agravante, suited in pale blue, and the other beside him, in navy. "Majesty," that voice, "forgive us," that pink-cheeked smile, that wild crown of ivory hair. "I was regaling the court with a hypothetical breakfast," those round pink hands are neatly folded before that firm round belly. "To, maybe, restore us all, so we can work out what's been done, and what we have to do."

"We offer our condolences," says Ysabel, to Agravante, "on the loss of your grandfather."

"Loss?" says Agravante, and a cough, a swallow, "majesty, what, what an odd thing to say, when he stands awake before you, for the first time in months."

"Does he?" She steps close, a hand up, against the light. "The face," she says, "the face works. The hair is quite good. But the voice?" She shakes her head. "You'd have a sauce of *fish*, at our table?"

"Fish?" says the other, and then, "oh, the sauce: fish blood's hardly *blood*, girl. It's garos. Kê-chiap." A sweep of one of those hands. "A palate expands, with age. What else is it for?"

"Do you hear?" she says, to Agravante. "It's off. All," stepping back, "just a bit, off," and then, "some of you! Attend: we'd have this juggler removed." Looking to them all, arrayed about that wide room, stiffly still, and silent. "He thinks he's being wicked, but he's actually quite dull. And small."

"I know not what you mean," says Agravante, and "We mean for him to go," she says. "*You* might stay, if you wished."

"It's sadly clear," says the other. "Her majesty's been rattled by the ruptures of the day. The failure of the, the owr, the loss of the King – tremendous blows. Take a moment, child, and come back to yourself. Look at me." Those pink hands pressed to a white-clothed breast. "You know me. You know who I am."

"A princess," she says, "might familiarly be a child, but a queen? A queen is never familiar. He knew that." Stepping close again. "Of *course* I know you. I couldn't say your name – I might've head it once, in passing, perhaps? I never bothered to learn it." Close enough to loom, stooping, hands on her knees, and his pink cheeks splotched with red as he looks up to meet her cold green eyes. "But had you truly thought," she says, "I could ever forget your stench?"

A roar swells up that's swallowed, with a grunt. For an instant shadows seem to shiver from that squat form, lightless motes that leap and spin and dissipate, a glowering haze that's gone even as it appears. "Lady!" cries Welund somewhere off behind her, but the other's speaking words that grate as they're pushed between those lips, "You will *not* speak to *me* in such a fashion," but a crack of laughter, there's the Mooncalfe dancing up, blade in either hand, tip of one of them chivvying, urging Agravante back, "how *dare* you," and her second blade swung up to cross the both of them now a scissors parted for the other's throat. "There's no gallowglas about," she says, "but I'm willing to work around that."

"Fauchard!" cries Ysabel. "Gladius! Byrne! Shall Northeast's ambassadour seize all the glory?"

Thump of boot, chime of mail, they step up, and sunlight brazing blade-edge and spear-tip.

"Sheep!" bellows the other, hastened back up the hall with Agravante, and Ysabel striding in their wake, the Mason racing ahead to the door, and the rest of them clank and rattle a thicket of pole-arm and spear-haft behind her. "Sheep, the lot of you! You don't have the stones to leap after a new shepherd!" Shadows spill over the other's face, his white shirt as the Mason opens the door, and sunlight sluices down the hall. "I look forward to the day you come to rue this moment, O Queen! *Pray* you do not fail your flock. Pray you do not falter any single step!"

"You have a choice," she says, to Agravante. "You may stay, or you may go."

"Lady," he says, blinking in the sunlight, "please. Let us work together, to," but she nods, and the Mason shuts the door between them.

"Good lord" – the Water's depth – the Offer on the table
to Have or to Eat – "Everyone is welcome!"

"Good lord," says Arnold Becker in that brightly empty room, and only a white leather couch on the white shag, before a sweep of window.

"Yes," says the Anvil Pyrocles, there by the bare kitchen island.

"You, I, I mean, we?" says Becker, "Live? Here?" Pointing, to the unlit hallway on the other side of the island. "There's more?"

"Two bedrooms," says Pyrocles, and then, "I might move my things to the other, if that would," but Becker's already heading off, past the island, and Pyrocles follows with a sigh. The cabinet under the sink stands open, and nothing within but a spray-bottle of some cleaning solution.

The narrow hall jogs back past a couple of closed doors to open on another room filled with morning light, a round bed strictly made, crisp linens striped with indigo, and three men, one of them in a simple black suit, and a slender, older man in a chef's coat, and the third of them seated on the foot of the bed, clean workboots and yellow coveralls unzipped, empty sleeves wound about his waist, head hung low, his shoulders broad, sunbrowned. "Oh," says Becker, in his berry-colored plaid.

"This is the room we share," says Pyrocles. Slipping off his blue suit coat he holds it out, to the man in black. "Though I'd happily sleep in the other, love, if you would be more comfortable."

Becker says, "But," in a far-away voice, "this isn't my room," and then, louder and more close, "my *place* – " He starts off around the bed. The man at the foot of it looks imploringly up to Pyrocles. Somewhere out in the main room a harsh buzz. "How did you know?" says Becker.

"Know what, my love?"

"*How* did you *know?*" Becker turns, holding up a book, Parents to Partners, says the cover, in brightly colored letters. Building a Family-Centered Early Childhood Program. "That this, that, if I ever quit my crummy-ass job, that maybe I could," lowering the book. Setting it back on the nightstand with the others.

"It makes you happy," says Pyrocles. "And you are so very good with the children." Something out there buzzes again. The man in the chef's coat shakes his head, folds his arms. Becker's pulled a phone from his pocket and hesitantly, tentatively sets it on the charging stand by the books. Starting when it snaps perfectly into place. The screen flashes to life, a snapshot of Becker and Pyrocles side by side in a red leather booth, 09:13, the floating numerals, Sat, April 21.

"Five months," says Becker, dulled.

"Anvil!" a bellow from the other room. "Present yourself!"

Out in the kitchen Agravante's by the island, ring of keys in one hand, and his countenance is stern, but Pyrocles looks past him to the two men on the white carpet, the Serpent slender in a suit of blue-black denim, the other in navy, a hand on the Serpent's hip, and sunlight in the crown of ivory hair. "Your grace," says Pyrocles with quiet wonder. "I had not looked to see you up and about."

"It was just a nap," says the other, with an indulgent smile. "You all make out like I'm back from the dead."

"You are such a welcome sight, lord," says Pyrocles. "It almost undoes the misery of the morning. Excellency," he turns to Agravante, "of course I stand ready, for whatever is required. I ask only that I might – "

"Ask?" snaps Agravante. "What would you ask, when your King's gone missing, your Queen's gone mad, the very spark of us wasted away to ash and you, sir knight, would ask – what? What is it you ask?"

Pyrocles somberly expressionless, the shirt of him strained by the breadth of his shoulders, his strong neck. Silvery close-shorn stubble, his long grey mustaches, and those pewter beads can't quite catch the light in this dim kitchen. "Her majesty, my lord?" he says.

"Mad as a goddamn hatter," says the other. "High on her own supply, spouting the most fantastically paranoid bullshit – she had the gall to throw the two of *us* out on our ears!" The Serpent shakes his head, appalled. "And the court! Indulging her delusions, *encouraging* them, toward some," letting go the Serpent's hip, those pink hands reaching, "ill-gotten gain, in uncertain times. We must save her from herself, *and* them. We need men, and quickly."

"Even with our full thirteen, it's us against a city," says Agravante. "I mislike the odds."

"Not the *entire* city," scoffs the other. "We don't need an army. Just enough to handle a handful. More than us two, any-way, and these fine two – you got anyone else stashed away in this tower?"

"What of the Lake Barons?" says the Serpent, a squeak in his voice.

"No," says Agravante, flatly, but "What about them?" says the other. "Go on."

"Forgive me, excellency, your grace," says the Serpent. "But they're much vexed, over the murther of Medardus, at the hands of Southeast's hounds. We might, help each other? Press us each our suits?"

"My lord," says Pyrocles to Agravante, but the other slaps the island countertop, "Ha! I love it! Roll up with the suburbs behind us, go in hard and fast before they know what's hit 'em, and we *take* her!"

"My lord!" says Pyrocles, and the other's antic grin unspreads, tempers itself, "All right, fine, we *secure* her *person,* let's say. How's that?" Clapping Pyrocles' shoulder. "Man up, sir knight. There's work to be done!"

"Pyrocles?" A small voice, off to one side, the dim hallway, Becker, and Pyrocles' blue suit coat in his hands. "Are you going somewhere?"

"Shortly," says Agravante, gruffly solicitous, "and not for long. Serpent," he says, heading toward Becker, "take his grace down to the car. We'll follow after," reaching out to take the coat from Becker, "I wish to help the Anvil see that his companion's cared for."

"Don't dawdle," says the other.

"My lord," says Pyrocles, when the door has closed. "If any one of them were to discover – "

"How, discover?" says Agravante. "Discover what?" Turning from Becker, holding the coat out to Pyrocles. "There's nothing to discover. But still: I think you begin to see how deep the water is, in which we swim."

Tension holds it, gravid, vaguely sinking, a slick-sealed bolus whitely gold that slowly rolling stretches from curl of dimple down and down, this cyclopean teardrop hung a-float between

folded knees, threads caught in languid ripples, swirls unskeining tugging spinning till with a soundless gasp it implodes,
swell of it drifting from itself, a creamy cloud thinning to milk
in dissipating swirls, a haze that licking gilds her thigh, her
belly where the bathwater laps, her elbow and her shin.

"That it?" says Chrissie, crouched on the bathmat by the tub,
holding out over the water a plastic bottle empty but for one
last clinging drop. Ysabel's fingers stir the lazily vanished
opalescence. "I mean," says Chrissie, "do I wait? Should I pour
some more?" By her feet a thermos, a small clay jug, a pyrex
bowl, the bottom of it coated with a viscous milky film, just
touched with gold. "I, I don't know." Setting the bottle down
on the mat. "What I'm doing, here. Ysabel?"

"It will not turn," murmurs Ysabel.

Up she pushes, water a-slosh, and out she dripping climbs,
heedless of Chrissie fallen back on her hands. Across to a counter,
the mirror above it, swiping aside her reflection to paw at the
medicine cabinet clatter and crash, combs falling, a shaving
brush tumbling into the sink, a jar of something purple smashing
to the floor. "Ysabel?" says Chrissie, shivering, looking to the
scatter of black clothing by the toilet, the white chemise draped
over the seat of it. "Can we, can I go?" Ysabel's found a safety
razor. Chrissie snags with a toe a bit of black lace, drags it across
the floor, slips it on to pull it up, standing to "Jesus Christ!" see
Ysabel slash her palm with the loosened blade and watch, impassively, as the wicked yellow-edged cut oozes not-quite gold.

"I almost thought I'd see red blood," she says.

Chrissie steps back, knocking the pyrex bowl aside with a ringing slop, "What," she bumps into the towel rack, "what *is* that?"

"Chrissie, Christienne, O Sœur Limoges," stepping close,
"you know what I am. You know *who* I am," that hand held up
between them, and Chrissie shrinking away, "I am the Queen
of Heaven, the tear the Sun let fall, and I put the Moon to
shame. I am the lure from paradise. I am a wonder, among
flowers," the litany a murmur, and Chrissie squeezes shut her
eyes. "I have been in the Llyn, and in Cær Vivien, I have
mounted the bridge over the Somme, and lain where warriors

fell," and Chrissie violently starts as that hand's laid sticky against her cheek, and the milky runnel drips to her breast, her belly. "Roses grow where I set my feet, and a diadem of unworked gold is fitted to my brow, and in my merest spittle," pressed close, nose by nose, lip to lip, "have you tasted cloud-spun honey," and a kiss, and Chrissie groans. "Tell me, then," says Ysabel, a whisper, "sweet mortal, oh my pretty dancing girl," another long abandoned kiss, broken when Chrissie twists her mouth away to lick at, slurp that wrist, the palm, "tell me," says Ysabel wincing, "while I yet have this mean power left to me, answer me this: do you, Christina Halliwell, do you," and again a kiss, "love," and a kiss, but then a hitch in her breath. Ysabel opens her eyes. Pulls back just enough to see Chrissie against the papered wall, wrists pinned up above her head, eyes closed, lips parted, searching, glisteningly smeared.

Ysabel lets go, steps back. Chrissie lowers her hands. Wipes her mouth. "What just – "

"Go," says Ysabel.

"But you're hurt." She tries to clasp that shining hand, but Ysabel twists away, *"Go,"* she says. Chrissie reaches after, catches her wrist, "You need help," and the sharp pop of a slap, her head rocked. "From *you?*" says Ysabel, free hand held up, ready. "You tried. You failed. Now go."

Chrissie blinking rapidly looks down, then kneels, to begin to gather the rest of her clothing.

By the door she stops, looks back, black halter about her neck, tights over an arm, shoes in her hand, and her phone. "So, I mean, uh," she says. "What do I tell them? I mean, they're gonna want to know what, what happened?"

The one hand cradled in the other Ysabel takes a deep breath, wavering with the effort of it. "Whatever you like," she says.

"*Quite* mad," says the other, leaned back before the crowded table that nearly fills this cramped room, and shelves to one side stacked with industrial-sized cans of food, Mutti Polpa, say the brightly colored labels, Jay Brand Sliced in Syrup, Swati Green Chili, Freshly Canned. A huddle of yellowed aprons hung in the corner there. "She insists I am not myself, which is absurd: who else could I be?" A downward twist of those lips, an upward eye-rounding cast of brow, a shoulder lifted, a shrug for them all, Agravante and Pyrocles, Serpent and Glaive, Coltello, the Baron Alphons red-faced, black band about one sleeve, and the Earl Alans his eyes alight, reaching for a basket of naan, stone-faced Baron Euric in a vest of green and yellow fleece, and at either corner of the head of the table, short Sigrid in a tight black dress, and the Baroness Clothilde, tall, her leather jacket black. The other leans forward, jostling a dish of rich red chutney, "I don't mean to make light of this state of affairs. It *is* distressing. But it could be managed – if it wasn't for certain opportunistic parties."

"Rabbits," says Euric, gruffly, and "The Marquess Helm," says Alphons. "That Gallowglas," says Sigrid, arms folded, and Clothilde's hand upon her elbow. "What?" says Alans, chewing.

Pyrocles says, "My ladies, we do not know of Southeast's involvement."

"Nonetheless," says Agravante, "is she with us, here?" Ignoring Pyrocles' sudden look.

"If she were," says Clothilde, "we'd have words." Sigrid nods. Alphons shakes his head. "I gotta say," he says, "I don't see the part we play in this mishegoss. She's not our Queen."

"She is, she was, she will be again," growls the other, waving a hand, but looks are exchanged. "You mean to reopen discussions of Apportionment?" says Sigrid. Alans, reaching for the chutney, says "Oh, not *that.*"

"Your grace," says the Glaive, his tin plate empty, but the other swivels about, "Crisis?" glaring at each in turn, "Opportunity. Opportunity? Advancement." Sitting back. The wall behind covered with posters of richly colored doe-eyed figures drawing swords, bows, holding court, smiling beatifically beneath prismatic sprays. "Do I have to spell it out for you."

"Wouldn't hurt," says Alphons. "If the basic terms haven't changed, then I think," looking about, "I can speak for us all when I say: neither has our answer."

"The rent," says Euric. "Too damn high," and Alans says, "We *settled* this."

"My lord," says the Glaive, "if we might focus," but Sigrid at the head of the table says, "Actually, there is something – "

"Enough," snarls the other, and then, in the silence that follows, "Help us; get thanked. *That's* the offer on the table. Take it or leave it but do it *now,* for God's sake."

"My lord," says Pyrocles, quietly, and with some concern.

"Thanked," says Alans, with elaborate distaste. "How, exactly?" says Alphons.

"In a manner commensurate with your efforts," says the other, but Euric's shaking his head, "Terms," he says. "Conditions. Details," and "I don't even unbutton my cuffs without a pre-nup," says Alphons. "Pay as we go," says Alans, reaching for the curry. "It works. It's been working. Why talk about anything else?"

"As my cousin was about to say," says Clothilde, but plates and glassware ring as the other slams a hand on the table, "This is so *desperately simple,* people!"

"Perhaps, your grace," says the Glaive, "if we were to hear them out? Just for the moment? It might possibly speed things along," and the other waves a dismissive hand, all right.

"Your grace is too kind," says Clothilde.

"Before we take up new terms," says Sigrid, "we ought confirm arrangements already made," but Alphons shakes his head, and Euric grunts, and Alans groans, "Why? We're good!"

"That arrangement was never arranged," says Aphons.

"Our offer was accepted," says Sigrid.

"Unlike yours," says Clothilde, to Alphons, "or yours," to Alans, "and yours," to Euric, "was burnt to ash and ground underfoot."

"Your Grandfather Baron's offer," says Euric, as Agravante's fist clenches by his plate, "but he's no longer here. Nor the King, apparently."

"Yet here we sit," says Sigrid, "idly to determine the fate of one Queen, and one court. Why not another?"

"Oh!" cries Alans. "Oh, I get it!" but then his look of triumph crumbles. "Wait, you can't do that. Who'd take her hand?

You?" to Clothilde. "It isn't fair." Folding his arms. "We have to start over."

"Much as it pains me to admit," says the other, "I've got no idea what we're talking about. Another Queen?"

It's the Glaive who leans forward, looking up the crowded table to him. "Annisa, my lord. Late of the Court of Engines."

"We met her this morning, at court," says Agravante.

"I've been asleep half the year," growls the other. "I didn't know half the people in that damn house."

"She was sent for, and paid for, at your suggestion, Grandfather," says Agravante.

"A possible new Bride, my lord," says the Glaive. "Should the Perry line have proved played out."

"But it didn't," says the other, scowling thoughtfully. "Maybe. So. You might maybe have a spare?" Pyrocles closes his eyes at that. Euric blinks, once. Sigrid shivers and the other looks up and around at them all. "Her brother meant to set himself up as High King, didn't he," and then, "my memory is addled," he growls. "Not my wits."

"He meant, good sir," says Alphons, "to endow a second court, here over the hills."

"A grateful court," says the other, and Euric snorts.

"Why should we not have a High King?" says Sigrid. "Or Queen," says Clothilde. "Roses are as worthy as Apples," says Alans, "or as the Wind, or Gold, Angels – "

"One thing at a time," says the other, loudly, standing with the scrape of a chair. "First, we secure the Queen, *and* this new Bride. Then maybe we see what it takes to restore the," a wave of one pink hand, "stuff, and when we know what it is that we've got, *then* we sort out who gets which part," squeezing between chairs and wall toward the door, "but. Make no mistake, gentlemen, ladies," looking about at them all, "whoever's in the room when we do that? Is who has a say in how we divide and decide. So talk it out," rounding the corner, there at the head of the table, "come to whatever arrangements," a hand on the back of Clothilde's chair, "we roll in an hour. High noon. I'm just gonna get me some air."

Out in a narrow hall, door closing click behind, to the left a sparsely peopled dining room, front windows brimming with golden light that gleams the table-tops. To the right an abrupt little kitchen, three men in stained white aprons busy at a stove there, ladling green curry into a dish, scooping spices orange and clayey yellow into dented bowls. The other steps close to the stove, sniffing what simmers in a tall pot, "Hey!" yells the man with the ladle, "vamos! Sal de," faltering as the other reaches into the pot, wincelessly stirring the thickly orange sauce with pink fingers, dredging up a morsel of something, chicken, popped between pink lips. "Pretty good," chewing, swallowing, then, with a groan, "I swear to God, if I have to choke down another fucking lump of tofu," and a shake of that white-crowned head. "Habla Inglés? Anybody?" Licking those fingers clean, and the three of them speechlessly staring. "Enough to get by?" And then, leaning conspiratorially in, "I want to *rip their fucking throats out.*" Nods, straightens, adjusting the knot of that narrow black tie. "I mean, it'd be like candy floss compared to the real thing, but they will *not* stop talking, you know? But," folding those hands before a wolfish grin, "patience has its rewards. I have been turning it over in my head since I woke up, spinning it around: should I have my cake? Or should I eat it?" Those folded hands tip to one side, then the other, "have it, eat it, have it, eat it, what do they go and do?" The hands spread, the grin opens in delight, "Here, Mr. Leir, we'll give you *two* pieces of cake!" and a giggle, "Two!" They look to each other. The curry bubbles. The other reaches in for another piece of chicken. "This, this is good. Burn sneaks up on you. God *damn,* I needed this. So thank you. Thanks."

"Madre de dios," says the one of them by the little bowls of spices, when the other's left. "Qué gilipollas."

A half-dozen long flat cardboard boxes stacked on the floor, and they stand about, a half-dozen or so, coveralls and tool belts, dungarees, workshirts buttoned to the throat, and Gloria Monday in her laddered tights, squatted by the boxes, slitting packing tape with a butter knife. SVÄRTA, say the simple blocky letters printed at one end. "You don't need all that," she's saying, wrenching the lid of the box up, slicing a last lingering strip of tape, "it's all, it's ready to go, you just," chiming clunk and a rip, she's prying open a smaller cardboard box tucked within, "put it together, there's instructions, and all you need is," holding up a little plastic baggie, and inside bolts and nuts and a couple of Allen wrenches. "And maybe a screwdriver? Phillips head, I think," getting to her feet. Knuckle of Tit says the handwritten scrawl on her oversized T-shirt. "Okay? So we're staging the mattresses downstairs when they get here, and the bedding, so, get the frames assembled, and, we'll start to put it all together!" She tosses the baggie to the woman across from her, who startled catches it, safety glasses pushed up atop her curled black hair. "Maybe, scrape the paint off the windows, too?" says Gloria, headed for the door there, the hall without. "Let a little light in? Get it all, get it looking nice?"

"I hope you know this is a waste of time and money," says Anna low and close as they head down the hall, her shoes sensible, her skirt windowpane, a yellow scarf about her throat, but "I don't wanna hear it," says Gloria, headed past the freshly painted wall a zig-zag of rainbowed angles down a short flight of steps.

"They can *sleep*," says Anna, hushed but forcefully, *"anywhere,"* leaned out over the balustrade.

"That so," says Gloria Monday, on the landing below.

"A cabinet, a drawer," Anna coming down the steps toward her, "a box or a crate, any little corner."

"You have a bed."

Anna stops so suddenly she almost stumbles, clutching the bannister, "I," she says, primly regaining her composure, "am not a domestic. Gloria," her steps stately down to the landing, "I know you think you're doing them a favor, but honestly. They won't know what to make of it. It's just not what they're used to – a corner, tucked away, out of sight, as they should – "

"Yeah?" says Gloria Monday, sharply. "And how's that gonna work if all your magic's gone?"

She heads down into a foyer crowded with people hauling limply heavy bundles, plastic-wrapped mattresses they stack below the stairs, "They're early!" says Gloria. "That's great, yeah, right there," and then, calling back to Anna, trailing after, "thank God at least the bank still works?" as they pass under a long low arch, "And the internet, and trucks," out into the cavernous warehouse brightly lit by racks of fluorescent bars, and sunlight streamed through windows high above, the stalls that march up the length of it, hung about with photographs and cartoon-bright paintings, folks in coveralls stood about a sculpture like a varicolored pile of pillows, and more, so many more milling among the long tables set up out on the open floor, laden with jugs of water, urns of coffee and hot water, plastic cups, torn-open boxes that spill forth packets of nuts and chips, raisins, popcorn, protein bars, and also platters of sandwiches, and mounds of paper napkins. "My God," says Gloria Monday, half to herself, "they just keep coming, where are they coming from?" and Anna looks up and away with a sigh. Gloria in her T-shirt and tights steps into the thick of it, black locks shining loose, her short-trimmed bone-bleached bangs, waving on, urging on, calling out "yes" and "that's it" and "go on, there's plenty, and milk, too," point-ing out coolers on the floor there, small red-and-white cartons tucked in shoals of ice, "take what you want, that's it, yes, go on! We're *working* on it," she says, to the older man wet-eyed beseeching, holding an empty plastic baggie out to her. "Honest," she says. "Until we do, please. Feel free. You're welcome, here."

"Of course, ma'am," he says, and a brief small smile to answer her wide bright grin, "You're welcome," she says, she cries out, "You're all welcome! Everyone," she says, turning about, moving on, "is welcome! You're new."

The woman before her, red Keds lolling unlaced about her feet, bare legs streaked with filth, yellow hair in tangles lank about her shoulders, pulls from a pocket of her pink and orange parka a crumped sheet of paper, goldenrod, something grimy's stained a corner, and half the pull-tabs feathering the bottom torn and gone, but splashed across it black ink dancing calli-graphic, a figure marked with one green dot of an eye. "Actually," says Jessie Vitaly, "I think I'm late?" Looking away, over the heads of the crowd, to the stage at the other end of the warehouse, and the canvases displayed there. Over by the big overhead door half uplifted, Ettie holds a hand up against the sun's glare, "Oh, who is that," she says, peering across the crowd at the woman in the parka there by Gloria Monday.

"When we danced at Devil's Point, her name was Rain," says the Starling close behind her, hood up over her hair.

"Right!" says Ettie. "She left to work for Leo. Okay."

"*You* danced at Devil's Point?" says Anne Thorpe in her long black coat, a box-cutter in one hand, and a half-dozen undone plastic packing straps a-twitch in the other. "Wonders never cease."

"*She* does know our lady," says the Starling, and a nod at Jessie across the room, "but as for the rest, these urisks, clods and hobs?"

"Yeah, this is, this is new," says Ettie, and then, with a side-long look, "almost like something's happened, yeah? Hang on," turning away, digging a phone out of her back pocket, "oh my God," she says, "oh my God," swiping, whipping it up to her ear, "Chrissie? Chrissie, is that you?"

Petra B slips through the crowd, past Anna, past the overloaded tables, and Gloria Monday taking Jessie's hands, the last of the stalls there, hung with oblong abstracts steeped in rainy colors. Her T-shirt's baggy, black, a bit of black lace tied about her throat, and a garbage bag, almost empty but heavily, tightly swaying, the excess plastic of it wound up in a sloppy knot clutched close as she heads from the tables toward the overhead door, the Starling pushing back her hood, looking down as Ettie steps away, "no, don't go home," she's saying into her phone, "call an Uber, I'll tell you where, are you ready?" and Thorpe, waggling her handful of straps, wait, trying to take it all in, "Petra," she calls, "hey, Petra," but past them all to the skeletal staircase footsteps clanging up to the walkway, past the painted door to the ladder bolted to the wall feet and one hand leaping, catching, the other careful with that garbage bag, up and struggling up to the planks laid over joists a ceiling rough above her clung there, swaying the weighty bag back and forth to reach it up and over past the ceiling now a floor.

It's dark, up under the rafters. Petra B crawls onto the planks, gets crouching to her feet, stooped under a dark and starless ceiling. Steps onto the rugs laid before the futon there, against the far wall by a low shelf crammed with books. Sets the garbage bag down. "Marfisa?" she says.

The hunched and mounded quilt on the futon doesn't stir.

"Marfisa," says Petra, "I think, there's something you should see." Dragging the slithering weight of the bag closer over the rugs. "The first time? The first time, she gave me a kiss for a cup of coffee. I've told that story before. But the second time?" Sits tailor-fashion, on the rugs there by the bag. "She was lost, frightened, alone, she needed somewhere to go – "

"She has never been alone," the voice a grief-roughed growl.

Petra's hands settle in the darkness on that garbage bag. "She needed somewhere she could go, so I took her back to my, well, the room I was renting, and we, I mean, I guess we, you know – "

"You spread yourself beneath her devastating kiss, and licked in turn the dew from her thighs, and cooed and sighed together in exquisite agony," Marfisa rolls over, sits up in the darkness. "You *fucked,* coffee-girl."

"We made love," says Petra B.

"You're hardly unique among us in that regard."

"Yeah, but, this?" undoing the knot in the neck of the bag. "This is what I wanted to show you. This is what happened." Unwinding the plastic, spreading it open. "It's still happening," she says.

Light dapples up, a spill of softly golden morning reflected off calm water, and there's Marfisa, white hair a cloud about her slackening face. Answering the dawn a pinprick of light struck from the ceiling, and another, cool dim stars of blue, and white, a dozen more, and more, and "Oh," says Petra B as red and orange and green now glimmer to life, and gold, so many gold, hundreds that suddenly wink out, snuffed by a crumple of plastic in Marfisa's hand.

"This," she says, in the darkness, "is from that night?"

"Yes," says Petra B.

"And you've kept it, all this time? You brought it here?"

"What does it mean?" says Petra B.

"That there's yet hope," says Marfisa, quiet, calm, and sure. "Here," she says, and hands the wadded neck of the bag back to

Petra. "You kept the secret this long. Keep it an hour more, or two. I will return, or you will know for certain all is lost."

In one swift motion she slips away, over the edge of the floor and down.

A Knock – happening at Once

A knock. "Majesty?" pitched to carry through the door. "I mean to come within." Ysabel, sat naked on the closed lid of the toilet, looks up as the door opens, "You would dare," she says, "come gowned and trammeled to my presence, here?"

"Your pardon, lady," and a rush of taffeta underskirts as Annisa kneels on the bathmat, bowing her black-scarfed head. "Needs must. You're required below."

"Required," says Ysabel.

Butterflies of silver thread sparkle through that scarf as Annisa looks up. "Requested," she says. "I'd help my lady dress, if such were to be your wish."

"And are you now my mistress of the robes, or of the stool?" says Ysabel, as Annisa plucks up a scrap of lace and satin. "I am my lady's servant in all things," she says, brushing one bare foot, and when Ysabel deigns to lift it, slipping the underwear on and up, hands brownly warm against cool olive shins. "Your point is made," says Ysabel, getting to her feet, pulling the underwear up about her hips. "It's him, isn't it," she says. "He's come back."

"Yes, ma'am," says Annisa, fetching the chemise, trailing pale gold ribbons. "He waits without, in his car."

"Persistent," says Ysabel, pulling the chemise over her head. "And is he really not the Pinabel?"

"He really isn't," says Ysabel, tugging and settling.

"And the King is not the King." Annisa gets to her feet.

"And the medhu will not turn," says Ysabel, "and the Court still has no Bride." Looking to Annisa then, all in purple and black under the yellow light. "Yet you're still here. Is that not strange?"

Annisa blinks slowly, once. "Do you mean to say that we are rivals, now?"

Ysabel laughs.

Downstairs a crowd fills the long hall, Sovnya and Fouchard, Chariot and Pilot, Gladius, Byrne, Oubliette, hands filled with pole arms and with swords. "My lady!" they cry, as Ysabel appears, her briefly loose chemise trailing undone ribbons, "Majesty!" they cry, and "Hail! Hail, the Rose!" She lifts a hand. They fall silent. Annisa, rustling down the stairs behind her. "How many has he brought with him?" she says. A moment passes before the Chariot speaks up: "Three cars' worth, ma'am. More than a dozen."

"And what has become of our Mason?" she says, looking about. There's the Gaffer, the pole in his hands topped by a heavy brass hook. "Left, ma'am," says the Fauchard, her pike leaned against the padded shoulder of her maroon jacket. "To resume his search for the Gallowglas," says the Guisarme, in his linen suit.

"And the Mooncalfe?"

"Gone, to bring word to the Helm, my lady," says the Chariot.

"No one thought to lend her a phone?"

"My lady," says the Guisarme, soothingly, stepping close, "it's only a few Houndsmen, and some from the Lake, or over the hills. My brother Rhythidd is among them — let me go to him, and with him to the Count. I might yet speak a word in his ear, to cool the heads of those without, that — "

"There's to be no congress with the thing that calls itself our cousin," she says, and he nods quickly, stepping back. "It is not the Hound Pinabel, restored to health; the Count is gone, eaten up by that — thing." Shivering she folds her arms about herself. "It bedeviled us last year. Our sudden loss of, power, this morning, is, doubtless, due to its return. It means to extinguish us. Iona," and the Chariot nods, "put out the call to our knights not here, the Patch, Escuchon, the Sequin and Seax, and have them come presently. Welund," and the Guisarme looks up, "speak your word in the ears of the Helm and the Mason: have them come, in strength, as soon as they might. Gaffer Boggs," and the Gaffer blinks, surprised, "if any others from the North might come, let it be now. Some of you, go: rouse the domestics, and set them at the windows, to keep watch – incredible as it may seem, our neighbors have been bewitched. Soon enough, that thing will goad them into striking this house, or it will strike, itself. So." Looking up to meet the eyes of him, then her, "Hold," now him, and him, "this," she says, and looks back, over her shoulder, "door." Turning to Annisa, holding out a hand, "Princess," she says.

"But my lady," says Annisa. "You are hurt."

She's looking, they're all looking, at the glistening cut across Ysabel's palm, edges of it puckered, scabbed with white.

"But a scratch," says Ysabel, turning to offer her other hand. "Come."

Out into that wide, now empty room, the two of them under the great glass wall, Ysabel staring up into the cloudless sky, and Annisa trailing after. "I reached out, I squashed it, with these fingers," mutters Ysabel, curling shut her white-crusted hand. "Why did it not stay dead?"

A squeak, a shift, a shock of pink-orange, peering around the back of the armchair. "Just, ah, letting you know, you're not alone in here."

"Get," snaps Ysabel, *"up,"* starting across the room. He shrinks back in the chair, hands up, "whoa, whoa," says Ray, "hey, it's the only place to sit!"

"It is the *throne,*" she snarls.

"Oh," he says, sitting up. "Oh." Getting to his feet. "Sorry."

"Did you leave Chrissie alone down there?" says Ysabel, heading past Annisa toward the glass balustrade about the stairwell to the porch.

"What? No!" throwing up his hands. "She left *hours* ago."

"She – did," says Ysabel, turning back. "Why are you still here."

"Why?" says Ray. "Your brother's had my carcass up here the past however the hell long, and I doubt he was paying my rent. I got nowhere to go, nothing in my pockets, and no idea where my next meal's coming from. Why not stay?"

"You should've left," says Ysabel. "It's too late, now. It's here."

"What?" he says. "What's here?"

"Majesty!" cries Annisa.

Up from the porch below Agravante white locks swept back rushing past the balustrade, "Lady," he says, quickly across the room, "do not cry out," seizing Annisa's wrist, pulling her rustle-stumble to him with a shriek she swallows as he brandishes a dagger. "Do not cry out," he says, again. "Whoa, shit," says Ray. The Serpent's slipped up after Agravante, and with footfalls that shake the glass the Guerdon, silver-headed hammer in his hands. "We would not harm you," says the Viscount, to the Queen.

"Then put up your weapons, my Handle," she says, heading toward them both, pale ribbons trailing. "I see it in your eyes," she says. "You know that's not your Grandfather, but you don't know what it is. You don't know what it means to do."

"My lady, what I know," he says, holding Annisa close. "I know today things are not as they were the day before. I know our power is lost. And I know we will do whatever we must to keep you safe. Both of you," looking to Annisa beside him. "Come with us, I beg your majesty. Fighting will only peck the world to pieces."

Ysabel steps back, takes in a breath, "My knights!" she cries. "To me!"

Several things happen at once. The Serpent leaps from behind Agravante slender sword up and back, bellowing Chariot and Gladius pound into the room, whip and clang of steel, Agravante's withdrawn, Annisa with him, the Pilot, the Byrne, the Oubliette pole arms rattle and clank, the Guerdon's hammer brightly high. More knights spill into the hall, Sovnya and Guisarme, but looking back, her sword swept back, his hands up ducking as men in blue suits scramble after, Sapper and Coltello, Trident and Arbalest, Basilard, Anvil, Euric and Alphons, Clothilde, the Gaffer stumbled among them all, and *"Okay!"* a roar, the other pushing through the fray. *"Enough!* That's *it!"*

Blades stilled, some lowered, some warily held. The Pilot sits heavily, gripping the ricasso of the blade stuck through his belly. The Serpent a hand to his throat, wet stain spreading down his denim jacket. Agravante still tightly holds Annisa, glaring at the spears that bar his way. Ray's crouched by the armchair, hands up, looking about in terror. The Coltello and the the Chariot sink in each other's arms, rapier through a shoulder, knife sunk to the hilt in a thigh. Ysabel untouched stands in the midst of it all, glaring at the other, who stoops over a groaning Gaffer and says, not unkindly, "You did fine. You did what was asked of you." Clapping the Gaffer's shoulder, "It wasn't enough, but that's not your fault." Straightening, looking up just as the baseball bat takes the Guerdon in the back of the head.

He topples not even a hand flung out to catch himself. Marfisa in her sheepskin coat springs over him catching his silver hammer as it clangs to the floor, bat in her other hand swung to catch the knees of Sapper and Arbalest, doubled back to thrust the butt of it into the Trident's groin. She darts through the gap their falling makes, skidding on one knee beneath phalanxed pole arms across the polished floor to spin up on both feet hammer out and bat, fetched up before Agravante, Annisa shoved behind him, his dagger held high.

"Boo," says Marfisa.

"Outlaw," snarls Agravante.

"My lady!" cries Marfisa, turning away from him, hammer and bat at the ready against all those weapons lifting, turning, pointing toward her, a ragged arc about her, before her, between her and the long hall dimly yawning, between her and the stairwell yonder. "Somebody *get* her!" the other hectoring sing-songs.

"My queen," says Marfisa, with a smile for Ysabel, her arms about herself, and stricken with a most wondrous look. "All is not lost," says Marfisa.

"Anybody?" says the other.

Marfisa hurls the hammer gleaming at them stumbling back in disarray, tosses the bat to Ysabel, then flings herself shoulder against the armchair, shoving, groaning, scraping, pushing as Ray scampers away she's picking up speed almost at a run one final desperate step that slams the chair into the great glass wall that rings and shivers a gong but does not break.

"Get her!" the other screams.

Ysabel swings the bat wildly at Agravante neatly sidestepping, Ray crouches ducking his pink-shocked head, the knights set to, too close together to hack and swing lurching forward, yanked back, tripping over each other. Marfisa grunting plants her feet, seizes the chair by its overstuffed arms, hauls it up, leaned way back against the weight of it tottering forward slam the base of it stubby legs crack against the glass and one long uncertain step back she plunges forward again to crash the chair against the great sweeping window that

bursts –

Shards of glass pelt the trees below the floor Marfisa lets the weight of the tumble dropping chair away and gone she wobbles staggers back from the bouncing clattering smashing edge, turns, glass glittering on her sheepskin coat, shining in the white cloud of her hair, and in the middle of all that holds out her hand.

Scuff of slipper clatter of bat to the floor Ysabel kicks off across the room. Agravante white locks flying lets go of Annisa, lunges after, comes up short, and the seething surging knights, the other stood among them, that slumped white crown of hair, the rage and the dismay struck through those black eyes watching her hurtle herself into Marfisa's arms, Marfisa already leaning back, over and out the topple and down, clutching Ysabel close, coat wrapped about her as twisting turning they fall through snap and cracking branches to the glass-littered slope below.

Sʜᴇ sɪᴛs – ᴡʜᴀᴛ ʜᴀs Bᴇᴇɴ Lᴏsᴛ – Aʟʟ ɪs Wᴇʟʟ

Sʜᴇ sɪᴛs leaned back in a nubbled green armchair, Marfisa's sheepskin coat about her shoulders, bare knees scuffed, gleaming under the too-bright fluorescent light, hands restless in her lap. "It's all right," murmurs Marfisa, knelt before her on the grimy carpet. "Petra's coming. She'll be here in a minute. You'll see."

"It hurts," says Ysabel, her voice quite small.

"I know, lady." Stroking once those short black curls, and here and there a sprig of silver. "But you're safe. Everything's going to be fine." Pressing a folded towel to Ysabel's throat, her cheek.

"Everything *hurts*," says Ysabel, green eyes blinking, dull.

"I know, my lady."

The freshly painted green and purple door flies open, Gloria bursting into the little windowless room, "What the fuck," she's saying, "what the absolute fuck, you brought her *here?*"

"Not so loud," says Marfisa.

"*Fuck* loud," growls Gloria, "*fuck* you, fuck *this,* this, this *this* is why we, this is the whole *reason, this* is," but Marfisa's lifting one of Ysabel's hands to the towel, pressing it close, to hold it, getting to her feet, "she's, *she* is why," Gloria turns to follow her, "we're here, in the first place," as Marfisa gently shuts the door. "If you keep on like that," she says, hand still on the knob, "everyone will hear."

"*Fuck* everyone," snarls Gloria. "What were you *thinking.*"

"You died," says Ysabel, letting the towel fall wetly heavy to her lap.

"What?" says Gloria, after a moment. Staring. "Jesus Christ," she says. "That's fucked up."

"Yes," says Ysabel.

"It's fine," says Marfisa, kneeling, taking up the towel. "Nothing's wrong." Pressing it back to the seeping white-lipped gash. "It's going to be fine." The door she closed cracks open. Anna slips within, closing it behind her. "My lady," she says, ducking her head. "You're hurt."

"We jumped out a window," says Ysabel, but "Stop *doing* that!" snaps Gloria, rounding on Anna. "That deferential *bull-*shit. You're gonna undo *everything* we've worked for, here."

"There's no need to be so strict," says Anna, adjusting her glasses. "Yes, there is," snaps Gloria.

"She has nowhere else to go," says Marfisa. "That's not our problem," snaps Gloria. Anna's hand leaps to her mouth. "Do you love me, Gloria?" says Ysabel.

"No!" snaps Gloria. "What the hell kind of," and then, "question," she says, and stops. "Oh," says Gloria Monday.

"So," says Ysabel. "There it is. That's it." Holding the towel to her throat. Smiling nonetheless.

"The hell it is," says Gloria. "You don't get to wave away everything you did to us like that, you have to," but *"Stop!"* cries Marfisa, still kneeling before the nubbled green chair.

"Ladies," says Anna, "you mustn't," but Gloria, looming over Marfisa, "The fuck do you know?" she says. "You never took the work seriously. Always sneering, at the art, you roll your eyes every time Addison leads a session, you don't give a *shit* about what we're trying to do here – "

"I'm not here for the work," says Marfisa, quietly. Looking up. "You brought that. When you came. I was here already."

"This is *my building,*" says Gloria Monday.

"Ladies!" cries Anna.

"Jessie," says Ysabel, looking past them all. "Hello."

"Hey," says Jessie Vitaly in her pink and orange parka, her back to the door she's just swung shut. "Good to see you." She's looking down, at the carpet.

"And I am happy to see you," says Ysabel. "I'd thought you'd left."

"Where would I go," says Jessie. Looking up then, to Gloria, to Marfisa. "The crowd, out there. I think they maybe know you're here?" A glance at Ysabel, then back to Gloria. "Thought maybe somebody should let you know."

"Like she gives a shit," mutters Gloria. Marfisa surges to her feet, "Take that tone once more, child," she growls, but "My ladies, do not do this," says Ysabel, and Marfisa stops.

"Our world ended today," says Ysabel, wanly pale in that green chair, sodden towel pressed to her throat, the flank of her chemise translucently stained, still smiling. "Let's not fight," she says.

Click of the latch, and Jessie steps away from the door swinging open again. Petra B steps inside, the almost empty garbage bag in her hand. "My lady," says Marfisa, and sits on the arm of the chair, "my queen, it's as I said." Petra kneels before them unselfconsciously, unwinding the throat of the bag. "All is not lost," says Marfisa. The too-bright light in that cramped room takes on a faintly golden tinge. Anna gasps. "Holy shit," says Gloria.

Ysabel bends down, dropping the towel to the carpet. Reaches into the bag to lift out a shining pinch that she presses to her cheek, her throat, draws her smearing fingertips down, erasing the gash, eating up the sticky sheen with crawling sparks. Spreads what's left across the palm of her other hand,

and the dry white-crusted scab flares up a sunly bright that leaves them blinking. Stretches, tips her head this way, that. "Well," she says, sitting back.

"It's from that night," says Petra B.

"Your first gleaning," says Marfisa. "Almost a full portion, as strong and bright as when it first was turned," but Ysabel's shaking her head, with a sigh, "And there will be no more," she says.

"You can't know that," says Anna. "Not for certain."

"Of course I can."

"So now you're *completely* useless," says Gloria, and Marfisa braces herself to get to her feet, but Ysabel lays a hand on her knee. "The paintings," she says, "on the stage, below. Those are yours?"

"Yeah," says Gloria, after a moment.

"You have a good line," says Ysabel, sitting up. "You should find a new subject. There is a crowd below?" she says, to Jessie, who shrugs. Ysabel gathers up the garbage bag, "May I?" she says, to Petra, who nods, sitting back on her heels. "My lady," says Anna, "I did for your mother, I'll do for you," as Ysabel gets to her feet, *"any* of us might stand amanuensis for you, ma'am, we can," reaching for her, "ration out what's left, a pinch at a time, and try again, until we get it right – my lady!" as Ysabel opens the door. "Please!" At that, Marfisa closes her eyes.

"There will be no rationing," says Ysabel, looking back to them all from the doorway. "No husbandry. This," hefting the almost empty bag, the weight of it swinging about, "this is extravagant," she says. "Or it is nothing."

Out onto the walkway, above that cavernous warehouse, the dozens of them below all turning to look up at the ring of her footfall in the sudden, echoing silence. "My people," she says, too quietly, and a crack in her voice, she takes a breath, "My people! All of you. All of you who, who could. Be here. My, people." Looking down. The heavy bag still turning slowly in her hands. "Today," she says, "has been a terrible day. We have lost our King, my brother. We have lost a peer, our Hound the Count Pinabel, two," she says. "Two peers. We've lost our Huntsman. The Duchess, of Southeast. And we've lost," closing her eyes, "ourselves, the part of us that makes this, this world," looking up, "this unbearable world," out over them all, "worth the bearing." The thick-necked man in grey coveralls, Brether Ned, the woman by the tables, Meg Mullach, paused in the act of adjusting her wide red suspenders, Thorpe in her long black coat, her little grey hat, and Cherrycoke beside her, tool belt slung from a shoulder, and sharp-chinned Jenny Rye.

"I have failed you," says Ysabel, the Queen.

From the room behind her Marfisa steps out onto the walkway, and Petra B. "I have, done things," says Ysabel. Gloria pushes past Anna, stood there in the doorway. "Terrible things," says Ysabel, "unforgivable, things." Jessie, arms folded, head bowed, behind Anna. "But my one regret," looking to them beside her, behind her, "is what I could not do." A briefly bitter smile. "I failed you. And tomorrow, you will go," Cragflower in his red apron, blinking quickly, "you will find another queen," Offa beside him, taking his hand, sky-blue polo and chinos, "another court," Lustucru in a grease-stained T-shirt, Trucos and Getulos in their paint-smeared smocks, "another city, a finer one, than this," they're all looking down, shaking their heads, "No," says Templemass, and "No!" cries Big Jim Turk, "My lady! No!" She grips the rail before her with her free hand, "I am *sorry,*" she says, not loudly, but the cavernous room falls silent. "I am sorry," she says, again. "But that is what may come. But what may come will come tomorrow, and tomorrow," her smile is bright now, "tomorrow is not tonight!" She lifts a handful of light from the garbage bag. "Tonight!" she cries, and the whole room takes a breath. "Tonight, we once more say what's never once been said. Tonight we shine a light that never once was seen. Tonight!" Her hand too brightly full a sun above her head. "Tonight, we tell them," a deep breath, "we tell them *all,*" she says, terrible and stern, "we are. Still. *Here!*"

Hurling the light, reaching for another handful, hurling that, again, soundless sunbursts into countless wheeling sparks that, burning, fall, that falling slow, that float, cinders of light, billows of brilliant golden smoke, arcing comet trails of morning light that softly overwhelm the harsh white buzz of the fluorescents, that seep into upturned faces, reaching hands, that dazzle eyes, and then the shouts, the laughter, the scraps of song, whoops that break out as she hurls another handful, and redouble as she hoists a bare leg over to perch half-sat upon the rail she clutches with her light-soaked hand. Marfisa starts toward her, but the sound that's rising from them all, louder and more loud, a nameless shapeless vowel lifted to meet those drifting settling stars, then slipped into a dizzying ululation that rings up and up to meet her as she steps out into the air, onto those skerries of light.

Laughing, singing with them as they take up another swooping pass of that simple phrase, throwing back her head as it climbs to its keening peak, throwing back herself as it croons away again, pillowed in all that glorious light, and the ribbons of her ruined chemise twine loosely languidly weightless, the garbage bag in her lap spilling light. She wrestles it open, and a galaxy's unleashed, a milky gold too bright to look on swirling all about her in curling threaded arms that drooping sag even as those hands, those faces, those mouths below begin to rise, and every color tumbling from the stalls so richly weighted full to overflowing glimpsed through all the light. Marfisa reaches after her, Jessie ducks her head, Anna beside her an arm about her, and Gloria halfway down the stairs, agog at her canvases on the stage, and Petra B's already lost in the crowd, the crowd, Luchryman and Umlauf, the Buggane, Charlichhold, Iemanya, Gordon there by Hilda in her chair, still dubious, even now, and Manypeny, Sweetloaf's got an arm around the Blue Streak's shoulders, both of them lustily singing along, and Carol with them trying to keep up, and little Sproat twirling with Addison, Herwydh with blossoms in her hair, and Bobbi just looking, looking about, hands folded over her heart, hands, so many hands, that pluck stars from the air, that swing plastic baggies like nets through roiled and coiling light, hands that brush those floating ribbons, let them trail through fingers, a slipper caught as it falls, hands that yearning touch her, ankle, elbow, knee, her hip, her shin, her shoulder, hands that take her settling weight, that ease her down, hands she kisses each in turn, hands full of light. Another round of that simple phrase vaults up, and Ettie looks up after it, and Chrissie still in black, leaned back in her arms, smiling small and somber, reaching out to Ysabel among them, Ysabel her chemise undone, limbs splashed with light, Ysabel her green eyes shining, Ysabel her kiss, and Ettie's laugh of delighted shock muffled by another, the three of them pressed together among them all, four, the Starling not so tall, hood pushed back by shining hands, her short hair silver-shot, her green eyes shining and her wet cheeks in the light about them all that swells so bright, that chorus soaring up and out, away over the streets, across the river, up even into the hills the faintest echo of it, and kneeling the other looks up at the sound of it, from the remains of the throne broken on the grass so far below, just in time to see a bloom of golden light smudging the night so far away, above the streetlights and shadowed trees. Standing, stepping back from the precipice edged with broken glass, a gust of wind tousling that crown of ivory hair. Scowling at them all arrayed there, knights in blue suits and fleece vests, weapons put away, some stood waiting, some sat upon the polished floor, some on their knees. "I thought you said it was all gone," growls the other.

"It was," says Rhythidd, in his blue shirtsleeves. "It is," says the Gaffer, knelt in his dark pea coat. "Turned to ash in our hands," says Agravante, and Pyrocles beside him.

"Well, she got more," says the other, stumping back toward them, crack and pop of glass underfoot. "We're gonna have to do something about that."

"But my lord," says the Serpent, his denim stained. "If her power is restored, then all is well!"

"Restored?" snarls the other. *"Restored?* You think, after what's happened, after we did what we've done, we can just, what, kumbaya ourselves back to, back to," one pink hand waving about, *"normal? After this?"* That pink hand slung back, at the empty wall, the shattered, glass, the missing throne. "'Cause let me tell you, boys and girls, normal ain't coming back. Normal's toast. Welcome to the brave new world." That hand swung back around, those fingers crooked, "C'mere," to Ray, there at the one end of the crowd. "C'mon, come here. I ain't gonna hurt you."

Ray lets go of Annisa's hand and sets off, hesitantly, across the room. As he nears the other he lifts up his dark hood over his bright hair, but then almost immediately lowers it again. "I, um," he says, but, "It's all right," says the other, that pink hand lifted, turned to clap Ray on the shoulder. "Go on. Tell them. *Tell* them."

"My lord!" cries Iona, on her knees before Agravante. "Your grace," someone else, Euric.

"Tell them who you are," says the other, not unkindly.

"Ray, Ray Miller," he says, and a quick look back at them all. "Look, I just, want to go. Okay? I'm done, I'm done with all this, I can just, walk away. Okay?"

"Okay? Okay?" says the other, pitched mockingly high, and then, "You're done. Done with what?" A shake of his shoulder, gasps and murmurs from the knights and peers, *"Tell them,"* snarls the other.

"I, um," says Ray, but Welund steps from his brother's side, "My lord," he says, "enough. Whatever has happened, whatever has been done, this," reaching out to them both, imploringly, "was your King. *Is,* our King. We must respect that."

"Yeah?" says the other, lifting that other hand, the one not clamped about Ray's shoulder, whipping it suddenly across the margin between them, but not a sound of a slap. Instead, as the other holds that other hand high, Ray takes a gurgling retching breath, a bubbling cough, and a look of such disappointed shock as he tries to catch the blood that falls from the line across his throat. The other lets go his shoulder and Ray sags, legs folding, torso toppling, head hitting the polished floor with a thunk, a splatter.

"Do kings do that?" says the other, turning away from them all, lifting that hand to lick, quickly, the blood from the wicked shard of glass pinched between thumb and fingers. A shudder of delight. Deftly tucking the glass in the breast pocket of the navy suit coat, adjusting the knot of the narrow black tie, turning back to them all, the body between them, crumpled, still, but for the flickering darkness of spreading blood. "Somebody," says the other, "clean that up."

But suppose there are Red and Green and Yellow,
that you feel them.
Then suppose you had a lamp
bigger than you to lean against,
a dark maroon red carpet to sit on
and a blue teacup large as your chest.
Then imagine, like me,
you were made of gold,
that you were willing to be idle
and were the one to come after Man.

—Dennis McBride

" *– carnival was ringing –* "

"On a scale of one to ten" – entirely too Sweet
a Jagged crack – the Man in the Chair – as she Passes
a Rasher of Bacon – Rip City! – Eatum-Rite & the Duckwall Bros.
the Color it was – Stockings, red and black
cooling Their heels – a timorous Glaive – the Question
the Color it is – Pounding, pounding – non sum qualis eram
thrice Setebos – the Gold, the Gold
"Come and get it"

"ON A SCALE OF ONE TO TEN," says Becker.

"Yeah?"

"On a scale of one to ten," says Becker, "where one is very dissatisfied, and ten, ah, is very, very satisfied," leaning close to the monitor that fills his narrow carrel, "how," he says, "would you rate your satisfaction with, with your, ah, the welcome, you received, from the reception team?"

"Reception team. What's that."

"Ah, that's what it says, sir."

"Yeah, but, what *is* it? Is it like when a company decides they won't call their employees *employees,* so, they're like, associates, or cast members, or compadres, or whatever? I mean, reception team. The heck is that? The receptionist? Whoever it was gave me the new patient questionnaire?"

"It's," says Becker, "whatever it means to you, sir."

"Well, that's stupid."

"Sir," Becker adjusts the microphone of his headset. "Your experience with Pet Depot was, was yours, it was singular, unique – "

"Really?"

" – but if we take enough of those experiences – "

"I would've said it was pretty friggin' generic. Pardon the French."

"If we rate enough of those experiences, sir, measure them, consistently, systematically, we help Pet Depot better determine, ah, where they're doing well, and where they need to improve, in providing service to, ah, pets, and their people."

"Pets and their people." A snort. "That yours? Or is that just what it says?"

Becker drops the headset on the keyboard, frees a wrist from the tangled cord with a jerk. Twiddles his mouse, clicking, closing windows one two three on the monitor. All about people are pushing back chairs, getting to their feet, slipping into rain-shells and light jackets, zipping up hoodies, backpacks, each before their own kelly green carrel, just barely wide enough for a monitor, a keyboard, a phone. "Good job," says the kid who steps out from behind the one desk in that narrow office, making his way upstream as they file past toward the door, "not bad," he says, "nice numbers tonight, good job, Crecy." His discretely checked shirt of blue and green at odds with the silver dots on his tie. "Hey," he says, crouching by Becker's chair, and Becker still sat in it. "Yeah, I know," says Becker, reaching for his messenger bag.

"No, you did okay, just," says the kid, a hand on the back of Becker's chair, "don't try so hard."

"Don't try so hard," says Becker.

"Yeah," says the kid. "With everybody, it's like, you have to do whatever you can to make them understand. Why we're doing this. Don't, you know. Try so hard. Just ask the questions, take down the answers, move on to the next." Lifting his hand away when Becker pushes back his chair, gets to his feet, looking down at the kid. The knot of that tie's too wide for that skinny neck. "Tell me," says Becker. "How long have you been managing this shop?"

"The phone room?" Pushing upright, a shrug. "Couple months."

The dining room is very bright and loud with laughter, folks sat and stood about a long table piled with books, a slither of unopened mail, half-empty glasses and half-laden plates, clink and clack of plastic and stainless steel, "Not till the third episode," and "Only if you don't touch!" and "They're painting it *beige!*" and "Who had the mushroom bacon?" Becker's in the unlit parlor, there by a couple of bicycles, a sandwich board that says Piano Lessons, Weekday Appointments, a low couch piled with coats. Arms folded, he watches a minute, maybe two, before somebody looking away from a joke catches sight of him, "Becker!" she says through her chuckles, and more of them, "Becker!" and "Hey, Becker!" and then, all at ragged once, "Happy Birthday!"

"It's not my birthday," he says, tugged into the light, the crowd. "It's not *any*body's birthday," says someone, and, "Well, not anybody *here,*" says someone else.

"I was merely reflecting, on Slack," says a woman from across them all, in the archway that leads to a kitchen, "that I didn't get to do much of anything for my last birthday, and Erick agreed, and Amy chimed in – "

"I *never* chime."

" – and anyway, it snowballed."

"Didn't you get the email?"

"I've been at work," says Becker.

"So *anyway,*" says the woman in the kitchen, waving a spatula, "pannenkœken! Savory, or sweet?"

"What?" says Becker.

"Pfannkuchen sind Liebe!"

"Pancakes for everyone!" says the woman with the spatula. "Do you want 'em savory? Or sweet?"

"I want," says Becker, stepping back into the unlit parlor, "maybe, I'll just, head upstairs. Keep it, uh, *try* to keep it, down?"

The futon's shoved against one wall of that little room, curled along one edge to make room for a cinderblock shelf just long enough for a dozen or so albums, a handful of books, a sleekly slender turntable, a reading lamp, the only light. Something's softly playing, a smoothly tempered jazzy line, past Hebrew kings and furry things to the birth of humankind. A thickset man in a long grey cardigan steps on the futon, over the messenger bag there by the pillows, gingerly making his way with a green glass bottle over the blanketed stretch to the window there, wide open.

Out on the tarpaper roof Becker's laid flat on a rumpled quilt. The thickset man steps through the window with exaggerated care. "Arnie," he says, sitting heavily, ostentatiously offering the bottle, "and if you're gonna call me Jimmy, I can call you Arnie."

"I didn't call you Jimmy," says Becker.

"I rest my case. Here," waving the bottle, "cidre doux. Which, apparently, means entirely too sweet. But a nice fizz." Becker takes the bottle, but sets it off to the side. "Well," says Jimmy. "You're a real stick-in-the-mud tonight." Tenting the skirts of his cardigan over his knees. "You're going to have to talk about it, sooner or later." And then, when Becker doesn't, "You dropped off the planet, Arnie. Quit your job. Got a new phone and didn't tell anybody which, believe me, I understand the impulse. But the only reason nobody thought you were dead was Elspeth happened to see you out on the town with a particularly fine specimen of silverback sugardaddy and, forgive me, Arnie, but I honestly didn't think you had it in you." Tipping a fond look at Becker, who's looking away, out over a dark backyard that glimmers with light and laughter from the party below. "And just as suddenly," says Jimmy, "just as *abruptly,* here you are. Back – back! – back in the low-rent groove!" he croons. Trees and houses silhouetted by streetlights that smolder too brightly for the stars above, so faint, so few. "What happened?" says Jimmy.

Becker sits up, legs folded tailor-fashion, elbows on knees, fingers against clean-shaven cheeks. "I don't know. I just," a deep breath taken in, a plosive sigh. Those fingers sweep up through what's left of his hair. "The last time I saw him, the look on his face," he shakes his head. "Whatever it was," says Becker, "it was, unforgivable."

Jimmy leans close. "You, Becker, did something unforgivable," he says. "Details, darling. Details make the story."

"Details," says Becker. "There's a lot I just, I," arms folded, still looking out into the darkness. "I don't remember."

"Drugs?" says Jimmy, with delicately skeptical excitement. Becker picks up the bottle of cider. "Yeah," he says, handing it back unopened. "Sure. Drugs."

"Well," says Jimmy, sitting back on his elbows, "as I said. Mysterious depths, Arnie. I never would've guessed," settling himself on his back, squirming his shoulders to smooth out the quilt, cupping his hands to pillow his head, "ah," but then the one hand leaps to point, "look!" and Becker follows it just as the shooting flash fades away, a thin faint line of light drawn down the sky, low over the trees.

"How about that," says Jimmy, lowering his hand. "And I'll even let you have the wish, generous soul that I am."

Flare from the tip of the tapering blade to the hilt of it wheeling falling fast, light stretched a line drawn down the sky to stop with a sudden crumpled pop, that building there, an angled bulk two storeys tall, or three, wedged into an awkward intersection, a little garden tucked on the roof of it. The poignard's plunged upright in unkempt grass, and what can be seen of the blade is mottled with dark blood. The wire that wraps the hilt glintingly underlit by the streetlights below. A susurral thrum of traffic, engine-rumble, tire-whir, the sound of music somewhere, a beat too far away to resolve, the sudden rising rush of air through leaves, a disorganized stumbling thump and fall, a low, bewildered groan. Rustle of grass bent, shoved aside, she pushes up on hands and knees, rolls heavily over to sit, that knife stuck there between her shredded soles of red canvas and cracked rubber. Leaning forward, shirtless back ruddy even in this dim light, she lays a hand wrapped in a fingerless glove on the hilt, firmly still against the swaying grass. Cranes back her head, looks up, the starless night sky rusted with city light above.

"Shit," says Jo Maguire.

A Jagged crack – the Man in the Chair
as she Passes

A JAGGED CRACK across the black glass face of it, and she takes
great care, laying it on the pillow, inserting the power cord. Knelt
there, wavering, exhaustion perhaps, sagging with sudden relief
when the screen of it flickers to life, a black bitten apple on a white
field. A photo appears, herself, brown hair short and tufted, cheek
to cheek with Ysabel, long black curls, knowing smile. 12:19, say
slender floating numerals above. Friday, May 4.

Steam billows from the shower, but she's by the sink, long robe
of buffalo plaid tied off about her waist, empty sleeves a-dangle.
She's smearing creme over her sunblasted shoulders, wincingly
persisting till she catches sight of herself in the artfully oblong
mirror, ragged hair, that nose, her thin-lipped grimace. From the
rumple of robe about her hips a faintly puckered seam runs pinkly
up and pale to an ovoid dimple the size of a thumbprint, sheened
with a vague iridescence, canted in the middle of her breast.

Wrapped in that robe, squatting in the doorway, she works a
plug in a socket. Strings of little yellow lights flick on. Up then,
across the kitchen, past a dead bouquet, the counter littered with
desiccated petals, brown–pink, black–purple. Down the three low
steps into the open room beyond, windows left and right in walls
that narrow to a point, and at the top of the room a great dark
chair. Knee on the cushions, leaned close to the window, she looks
down. A car preternaturally silent passes through the intersection.
The marquee of the theater across the way is dark, but the letters
can still be made out, Reds 600, Cinco de Mayo la Batalla, 930.

A pot left on an unlit burner, and something dried within rattles
loose when she picks it up, sets it frowning in the sink. Shakes out
a wadded dishtowel, folds it, leaves it a neat little square on the
counter. Opens the fridge on a shrunken lemon half, a couple of
wilted scallions, some cans of diet cola and a cardboard takeout
box. A slender carton of milk, red and white, Alpenrose, it says.
She pulls it out, pinches it open, tips it over a blue-lipped glass, but
what pours out is thickly lumpy slopping, fouled, she hurls the
carton splattering away to drop a-splot in the sink.

The high wide bed is neatly made, white comforter draping the foot of it, white pillows piled at the head, but the dressing screen's knocked over, linen panels awkwardly folded over themselves, whitewashed frame askew. White trousers crumpled and a coil of measuring tape, tumbled lace and satin. She's there in the doorway, by the dresser, another dead bouquet atop it, and a small brass box. Six or seven cigarettes within she stirs about, plucks one, and a ragged book of matches.

Into the room across the hall, around the futon, cracked phone still charging on the pillow. She wrestles open the window at the end there, rattle and grind of the sash. Sits herself on the sill. In her fingers the soft spark of a cigarette she doesn't lift, or look at, she doesn't look out, across the darkly empty street, one lone window lit in the apartments opposite, the banner hung that says, Now Leasing. She isn't looking at the stark white wall of her room, or the plain black scabbard hung there, empty, from a single nail.

She stubs out the cigarette. Drops it out the window to the sidewalk below. Parts her robe just enough to thumb the enameled nodule there against her breast. A wince, a shudder, she closes up the robe, and then her eyes.

Starts awake, sunlight blazing the lozenge, a riot of birdsong. Closes up her robe. "Shit," she says. Leans over the futon, thumbing the phone to life. 06:31, say the numerals on the screen. Saturday, May 5.

"Shit," she says.

Dressed now, black jeans, black T-shirt, stood in the sunlit kitchen. Blue-lipped glass still there on the counter, carton still in the sink, the glaze of drying milk. A look back down the hall, lit by those little yellow lights, half-closed doors at the end of it. She lifts her right hand, turns it over and back again, pronated, supinated, fingers wriggled, curled in a loose grip. For a moment she holds herself quite still, feet planted, eyes closed. Reaching for something, arm quivering with the effort of it, until her hand squeezes in a fist, her arm drops. She sighs.

Crashing out the back door, off the little wooden porch, across the potted lawn, past the patterned bronze chiminea, cold and dark. Crouching there, between a couple of raised beds, elbows on her knees. Takes hold of the wire-wrapped hilt of the poignard, thrust upright in the unkempt grass. Yanks it free.

Back inside, down the hall, into the kitchen, past the counter and the bouquet, past the steps, she yanks open and out the door to the apartment. Down the steps to the landing below, two plain brown doors, she knocks at one of them, gently, "Iona?" she calls, tucking the blade in the back of her jeans. "Chariot?" Trying the knob, jerking her hand back when it turns and the door cracks open. Within unpainted walls patched and seamed with unsmoothed plaster, a freestanding rack hung with tracksuits, three or four, yellow and white. "Iona?" she says, again. And then, more quietly, "Ysabel?"

Down the last steep flight, into the lobby, the hall behind her, boxes stacked along one wall, a wooden crate, an ottoman abandoned with a broken leg. She leans on the crash bar of the door outside and steps into the sunlight, the wall of the building rising brown and darker brown behind her, and signs filling the storefront windows across the street, Opening Soon, the letters tastefully slender, Boxer Sushi. She closes her eyes and slowly opens up her arms, a diffident breeze stirring her sunbleached hair.

Heading toward the garage, one arm outstretched, fingers trailing along the brown, brown wall, tap, tappity-tap, tap. Down the drive, around and down the precipitous curl of the ramp, the basement opening out under the length of the building above, polished concrete shining under fluorescent lights, a ruddy, lowslung sedan there, parked at an angle across a couple of spaces. Beyond, stacked against the back wall, banker's boxes white and brown in mostly regular columns, four or five high, a couple left on the floor by a simple folding table, a high-backed black office chair turned away, and someone sitting in it.

"David?" she says, pitched to carry, blinking at the echo. And then, much more quietly, "Luys?"

He's asleep, the man in the chair, and short enough his feet in once-elegant brogues are left to dangle, but the fingers of his hands so long and slender, laid over the photographs on his lap, black and white, sepia, dull silver.

"Inchwick," says Jo.

He jerks awake, wiping his mouth with the back of one of those hands, blinking. Catching sight of her he flings himself from the chair rolling back, photos scattering flutter to his knees with a grunt, pressing his forehead to the floor as she skips back, "Hey," she says, "hey," the chair fetching up against the boxes. She squats before him, "Don't," she says, "you don't have to," reaching toward him, drawing back, "come on," she says. "You're Inchwick, right? Get up."

"As your grace would have it," he says, pushing himself upright, "though that the mouth of one such as herself should come to be troubled by the shape of the name of one such as this," and he shakes his head hung low, "what, oh what has come of this vale of tears."

"That's," says Jo, "kinda what I was," leaning forward, trying to catch his eye, giving up, sitting back. Tugging, smoothing her black T-shirt back into place. Leered across the front of it the face of a red devil, marred by silkscreen craquelure, and her hand stops, splayed across it. She looks away. "Where is everybody?"

"Your grace," he says, eyes still downcast, "but everybody's such an amorphous and an expansive assembly, difficult to pin down –"

"*Everybody,*" she snaps. "The Queen. The Chariot. The, who-ever, washes the dishes, does the, the, the apartment's *aban-doned,* Inchwick. Please. They're all gone. Everybody's *gone.* Except, except you." Leaning forward. "You're here," she says. "You stayed."

"Of course," says Inchwick, head a-bob. "Of course. This one could do no less, your grace."

"Don't," says Jo, "don't say that."

"But, your grace," he says, and "I'm *not,*" she snaps, hands up for emphasis, and he looks up enough to see her shirt. "I'm not the Duke!" she cries, as he knocks his forehead back to the floor. "I'm not, it's all," the heel of her hand to her breast then, and a wince.

"But," he says, his voice quite muffled, till he lifts his face, "your grace did save the morgue."

She opens up her eyes. He's turned half around, looking back to those boxes stacked along the wall. "For that alone," he says, "this one should serve my lady till the end of all our days."

"I didn't," she says, half-says, and then, a deep breath, "Inchwick," she says, with terrible patience. "What happened to the Queen."

"The day your grace disappeared, my lady, if such a one as this might be forgiven for saying so," he turns back, head ducked once more, "the King passed, too, and every grain of owr in the city was turned to dust with the grief of it. The Queen in her majesty did with an insuperable effort bring forth one last wonder, and did portion it out, in a warehouse toward the river, but," he's lifted one of those hands to his mouth. "It was not enough," he says, breath catching on the word. "Not nearly enough." A sniff. He blots his cheek. "Her majesty keeps something of a court there, now. The old Eyetalian grocers', on Taylor."

She gets to her feet with a squeak of her shoe. He pushes himself up as she steps away, "Your grace!" She stops, looks back, "what is to be done," he says, "with your grace's morgue?"

"It's not," she says, shaking her head, a sigh. "Keep it safe," she says. "If it, ah, starts to rain? Like, a lot?" She shrugs. "Get it upstairs."

"As my lady would have it," he says, and bows to her as she leaves.

Blocky columns swell in the gloom to groin a lowering roof, and nestled among them an archipelago of candles, guttering wicks in limpid pools, reefed and shoaled about by congealing wax. That lambent glow sheens silks smooth-woven, roughly raw, in purples, magentas, gold, cushions heaped and bolsters, wraps spread, draped, tumbled over thick-piled Turkey rugs the patterns of them breathing in the play of light, light that lends a warmth to olive skin, and pale, that snags black curls artfully tangled, shot here and there with sprigs of silver, that serely slicks severely yellow hair, that swallows, recedes, laps shadows pooled about soft curving plains, abruptly muscled ridges, escarpments of elbow, shin, chin. Ysabel asleep in the midst of them all, her pillow the Starling's belly, the Starling her arms flung wide, face tipped up, eyes closed, and such a smile of contentment there, glazed with drying white, a frost clung to the stubble that roughens her cheek. Étienne between the Starling's canted knees, one pale sugar-crusted hand reached over Ysabel's waist to hold her sister's hand, Christienne in Ysabel's arms, her sleeping yellow head against Ysabel's brown breast, her spume-caked thigh nocked between Ysabel's thighs, and there a confusion of milk-dusted feet.

A hand on one of those columns, barely touched by that flickering light, Marfisa turns away from them, slipping ghostly into the shadows. Back through the columns toward a thinly seep of daylight limning the nosings of steps that climb into a somewhat brighter light, falling from the foyer above. She stops a moment, hand against the wall, feet on different steps, sleek running shoes, black tights, grey tank, her wild white hair hung low.

Into the foyer, brightly blue graffitied with primary colors, lines and shapes, corpulent miens of exaggerated joy, surprise, exasperation, a tree that scales one wall, leaves and fruit of it trowels and rakes, shears, empty gloves, hoes, hammers, and up the other wall a ziggurat of rough red bricks that somehow become the lines and knots of a net flung high above the stairs and filled with fish, with stars, bones, coins, and painted over the ceiling far above the keel and churning wake of a ship. She crosses yellowing tiles, past the stairs, under a long low arch lit by glowing tubes along the floor, and out into the cavernous warehouse, brightly sunlit. Most of the stalls that march the length of it have been opened to the outside, and clusters of people are sat or stood together among the art, speaking softly, laughing quietly, sipping coffee from paper cups, or tea, dozing in the sun, bent over tools laid out on folded towels, screwdrivers and crescent wrenches, awls and chisels, clamps, taking up each in turn to be checked, adjusted, polished, snapped home in a toolbox or a belt, cleaning brushes in a bowl of cloudy spirits, sluicing paint from roller sponges, mixing color in a pot, dollop of umber in the carnadine, genially disputing a paint-spattered sketch, but conversations falter as she passes, laughter trails away, focus shifts, returns, drops to the task at hand, the cup laid by. No one looks to her, but all watch as she makes her way, footfalls quiet in those shoes, out into the open area before the raised stage, past that main overhead door rolled all the way up to the skeletal staircase there, under the faded painted letters that once said Eastside Italian Market & Grocery, onto the walkway, up to the door there, freshly painted purple and green. She takes hold of the knob, and opens it.

"No, no," Gloria Monday's saying, leaned against an escritoire, "where are we gonna *put* 'em. It's not like we have a conference room," and Anna Nirdlinger, sat on the nubbled green arm-chair, holds up a placating hand, "It'll be fine," she says, and adjusts her narrow glasses. "Perhaps the upper gallery."

"Put whom?" says Marfisa.

"Still smells like God knows what," says Gloria to Anna, and then, "Where's her majesty?"

"She yet sleeps," says Marfisa, and Gloria snorts. Her oversized T-shirt in a pulpy font says Dick Storm in South America. "Put whom," says Marfisa again, more sharply.

"Her lawyers," says Anna.

"Your liege?" says Marfisa.

"Our *bank,*" says Gloria. "They'll be here after lunch."

"Why," says Marfisa, frowning. "Why would they be coming?"

"*That,*" says Gloria, pushing away from the escritoire with a creak, "is the ten thousand dollar question. *That* is maybe some-thing her ostensible majesty could weigh in on. Share her *thoughts.* Maybe give us some insight as to what's maybe in play, here?" Stepping closer to Marfisa. "So maybe you might could go *back* downstairs, and *this* time you could ask her, politely, please press *pause* on the orgy, just for a minute, so she could," and her head whips back with the crack of a slap, "the *fuck?*" she snarls.

"You would do well," says Marfisa, lowering her hand, "to ameliorate your tone."

"You don't *touch* me," spits Gloria. "Not *ever,*" and *"Ladies,"* says Anna, hands on her knees as if about to stand.

"I swear to God," says Gloria, rubbing her cheek, "I am *never* gonna understand," braced against the escritoire, "what it is you see in that colossally. Useless. *Bitch.*"

Anna leaps up, stepping between them, "She is," she says, turning to Gloria, "our Queen."

"Yeah?" says Gloria. "What has she done for you lately? I'm *serious!*" leaning to follow Marfisa, who's turned away. "*She* isn't up here, taking people in. *She* isn't holding this place together with her bare hands and takeout," as Marfisa yanks open the door, "it isn't *her* name on the goddamn credit card!"

The door slams shut hard enough to bounce open again. Marfisa's footsteps ringing on the walkway, rattling down the stairs. Gloria stands in the doorway a moment, looking out over them all below. "I wish," says Anna, behind her, and then Gloria slams the door shut again.

"You wouldn't," says Anna.

A RASHER OF BACON – RIP CITY!
EATUM-RITE *&* THE DUCKWALL BROS. – THE COLOR IT WAS

THE RASHER OF BACON limply sheens those fingers greasy with scorched fat, those lips already parting for another bite, "You sure?" A gesture toward the platter heaped with bacon before them all. "Cooked to perfection. Gotta admit," polishing it off, "you people set your minds to something, you do it right. No matter what." The platter's the only food on the long table, the plates before the rest of them all empty, cups and glasses sparklingly clean, napkins neatly folded, cutlery untouched. "Anybody?" A look for each of them in turn, the Glaive to the left, striped sleeves pink and white, the Guisarme in linen to the right, and beside him Mousely in a pink suit, clutching a sleek aluminum briefcase on her lap. Beside her the Chariot Iona, uncomfortably buttoned into a yellow blouse, and then Luys, the Mason, in a brown chamois shirt, and across from her the Gaffer Boggs, black turtlenecked, and the Soames himself, Twice Thomas in green tweed. "Going begging," says the other, white shirt blazing in the sunlight. Stood behind each of them, at the edges of the shadowed porch, men in blue suits, hands behind their backs, Guerdon and Net, Trident and Serpent, Alphons, Anvil, Alans and Shield.

"My lord," says the Axehandle Agravante, sat at the foot of the table, his suit perhaps of the darkest blue. "If we might dispense with the matter at hand?"

"What I don't understand," says the other, reaching for another piece, "is how any of this does any of us any good." Munching thoughtfully. "Girl already owns the whole damn building."

The Guisarme snorts. "Tom Wilson," says the Glaive, "the girl's father, held controlling interest in a group invested in developing the property; actual questions of ownership, of the land, of the structures, and so forth, and so on, are, shall we say: murky."

"The north end of the block," says the Guisarme, "the restaurant, the abandoned bar, the apartments above, all held by Southeast. Her father's grandiose plans for the parcel had long been thwarted by the Duke's refusal to part with them, at any price."

"That's not gonna be a problem anymore though, is it," says the other, and Luys leans forward, "If it means," he says, "an end, to the Queen's mad dalliance, and brings her home, to us," sitting back, with a sigh, "then you shall have it."

"So we got us a plan," says the other. "Rickety, but actionable. When do we kick off?"

"My lord," says the Axehandle, but "This very afternoon," the Guisarme's saying. "We've already arranged a rendezvous," says the Glaive.

The other laughs, a bark that crumbles into chuckles, climbing again in spiraling giggles. The Gaffer, starting, looks up to meet the Chariot's blank gaze. The Mason's hands to either side of his plate, a bit of leather tied about one wrist. The Soames looks up over his shoulder to the Anvil behind him, the Anvil looking down at his black, black shoes. "All *right,*" says the other, pushing back from the table, "let's get 'er done."

"My lord," says the Axehandle again, as they're getting to their feet, "if I might?" A nod for the shining case that Mousely clutches close. "Do we think that wise?"

The other scowls. "We think it's necessary."

"It's the last of our stores, my lord," says the Axehandle. The Gaffer looks with alarm to the Soames, who looks sharply at the Mason, who glares at the Guisarme, who lays a hand on Mousely's shoulder. "If something were to happen to it," says the Axehandle.

"Nothing will," says the other, with a smile for the Glaive, and the Guisarme. "Y'all won't let it." And then, a hand slammed to the table, "Gentlemen! The point is not to make this girl's day with a shiny new fortune. The point is to isolate your Queen, disband her cavalcade, and bring her home. And if this rickety-ass Plan A don't work," a pink hand lifted, a gesture, for that briefcase. "Best have a Plan B riding on your hip. Trust me, folks," that gesture withdrawn, "ain't nobody gonna like Plan C."

"We'll have your assurance, sir," says the Mason, voice gruffly raised. "No harm will befall her majesty."

They all look then, Soames and Chariot, Gaffer and Mousely, Glaive and Guisarme, from the shadows at the foot of the stairs to the other in the sun.

"Well, shit." The other reaches for more bacon. "Pretty much up to her, now. Isn't it."

Up the stairs then, and out into the wide room, and what had once been a great curving wall of a window shattered, as open to the air now as the porch below. A breeze luffs the Serpent's hair as he takes up a position at the edge of it, where the floor's still mottled by old rain, as more men in blue suits accompany the rest of them down the front hall. Agravante stops there, in the middle of the empty room, looking down. Another stain blots the floor there, darkly ruddy, dulled by hapless scrubbing.

Out of the wide room, down the hall, past the front door where stone-faced Euric's standing watch, but turning from him and up the enclosing spiraling staircase, steps quick, down another hall, dimly lit, and photographs hung to either side, a weed-choked vacant lot, a white house stark against an oncoming storm. At the end of it the Laguiole stands by a closed door, and as Agravante approaches, she slips a key from a pocket of her wide-shouldered pink coat to undo the padlock bolted to the door. He passes through, into a room almost entirely walled behind a canopy of white netting. A lamp shines within, and fluttering shadows lop before him, butterflies, their brilliant colors banked by gauze, impressions only left of black and red, of black and yellow, of orange and gold. "Highness," he says, as the door's closed behind him, and the sound of the padlock fitted to its hasp. The lamp-light's occluded by a shadow standing, approaching the netted canopy. "Excellency," she says.

"I trust you slept well?"

"One needn't trust," says Annisa, hoarsely. "I do not sleep." The papery sound of butterfly wings, their whispery alightings.

"The Laguiole," he says, "the Ronca: they see to your needs?"

"Whichever of them currently looks to the bathroom could stand a lesson or two in mopping," she says.

"This privation will soon be over."

"What need of soon? Unlock the door. It might be over now."

"Highness, the lock's for your protection. Surely you must see that."

"What I see," she says, and the shadow of her shifting, and a sigh. "It's not my person you'd secure, but my promise. Until the Queen's returned, you clutch me close not for my safety, but your own." Her shadow blurring as she steps back. "I am your just-in-case."

He folds his arms, and if he'd been about to smile before, there's no trace of it now about his lips. "Whichever case might come to pass, highness, you're almost certain to end up with a crown – hers, perhaps; or a new one, of a new court, of your very own."

He knocks once at the door, and a key-click, a hasp-rattle. "Do you know, Viscount," she says, "Grandson of the Hound – I almost believe that you believe such a simple lock would stop him."

He looks back as the door is opened. "You mustn't worry yourself, highness. On this, you have my word – you've nothing to fear."

"Tell me, excellency," she says, as he steps through the door. "In all your experience with queens, have you ever known a one to see the folly of her ways?"

"*Rip City!*" he roars, and wipes spittle from his chin. "Rip City!" sitting up in that big brown recliner, shoulders swimming in a grey-beige sport coat. "Nineteen seventy-seven," he says, "we had, we had *giants,* in those days." Legs lost in the quilt across his lap. Jasper's by himself on the couch, wrapped in a filthy blanket. "Men who played the game. They played hard, but. They *played* the *game.*" Wrinkles sour about the CO's sunken nose. "Didn't give a *good* God *damn* about the money, or the drugs, or, or. Or." Jasper's grizzled head nods along, his half-full mug of coffee half-forgotten. "Bill Walton! Dave Twardzik!" That soured face turns up. "Walton! *Hurling* a rock from the other side of the court to make the damn shot. Rip City!"

"Dad," says the XO, over across the room. "That was Jimmy Barnett, Dad."

"Bill!" The CO's eyes bulge as he sucks in air enough to finish the name. "Walton!" Sport coat shoulders lurch, lapels swell with another labored breath. "Hit the bucket at the buzzer! Won the damn game! Won the championship, first time in the show!" Jasper sits back, sips coffee, looks from the CO to the XO, whose fingers are at his temple, pressing an ache, "Walton was on the championship team, yeah, Dad," he says, "but it was Barnett hit the long shot that started Rip City."

"Barnett! Barnett, you ignorant – Barnett was traded after one season! Nineteen goddamn seventy! To the Warriors!"

"And that's when Rip City happened, Dad," says the XO, pushing off the wall, heading through the sunlight slicing the ruddy drapes. "Against the Lakers. And we lost." Squatting before the recliner. "And Bill Walton was a fucking draft-dodging hippie. Come on, let's get you back to – "

"I ain't done yet!"

"Dad, come on." Dropping the quilts to the floor. "Nobody's here. No sense – "

"Whose fault is that! Nobody's here. Why do you think that is? There were *men,* in those days!"

"*Dammit,* Dad! Let me just," and a ringing clunk, "ow!" Coffee slops the quilts. The XO lifts a hand to his head looking up, "Jesus!" to see Jasper behind him, staring at the unbroken mug in his hand, mumbling something, "wanteda hear a rest of it," maybe.

"Give me that!" snaps the xo, reaching for the mug, grabbing Jasper's wrist, "the hell are you trying to," reaching across to seize the mug itself with his other hand, "you're as bad as him, I swear – "

"Chad," says the co.

Letting go of the mug, the xo looks down.

"Chad," says the co again.

The xo lets go of Jasper's wrist. "Dad," he says, "Dad, I'm sorry, but – "

"Whose fault is it?" The co's voice is quiet now, and almost gentle, as he sits up to look down at the xo. "That nobody is here. Why is that, exactly?"

"I told you, Dad. I told you Moody was a bad idea. I told you not to bring him in on this." The xo lifts up his head, but the co's raised his voice again, "Bad idea!" he cries. "Bad idea! Who the hell else had any good ideas around here, huh? Who hooked us up with them new boys, after Duke kicked it? Who set us up with that sweet deal? Who took a beating for us when he went inside? The Dread goddamn Paladin, that's who! There were *men! Giants!*"

"He *lied,* Dad," says the xo. "He's a liar." But he doesn't look up, to meet the co's glare. "He's the one fucked the deal up for us. He fucked *everything* up with them that's in it." The co looks to Jasper, nodding, once. "He's the reason," says the xo, "Dad, he is," and then with a sideways sweep of the mug Jasper clonks the xo's head again, knocking him to his hands and knees.

"So?" The co bends over the edge of the recliner, wheezing. "*So?* If that's what's going on, why the hell are you just sitting there, whining? If that's the way it is, boy, what the hell you gonna do about it?"

Somewhere above a ragged chorus of pianos honky-tonks its way through chords too jangly to be sombre, too stately to sprite, chasing each other up and down the scales. "Hello?" calls Jo over the clamor, sunlit street too bright behind her, but the devil on her

T-shirt clear enough in the shadowy vestibule. "Luys?" To one side rows of Mason jars filled with keys, sorted by size, price tags about the necks of them, quarter each, seventy-five cents, a dollar. To the other a file of unhung doors canted one against another along the wall. Sunlight desultorily browses past bins of door-knobs and drawer-pulls, glass and crystal glinting, polished brass and dented, plain turned wood, smooth porcelain, some painted with leaves, or hearts, or brush-stroke flowers. "Bruno?" says Jo. Above cabinets crammed with tiny drawers of screws and nails and nuts and bolts and hooks hang pressed-tin signs, Hood River Pears, they say, and Gosling Northwest Apples, Eatum-Rite and Blue Goose, Duckwall Bros., Kiyokawa Family Orchards. "Anybody?" In one of the angled doorways leading further in there's a boy in a brown bomber jacket, aghast. "Sweetloaf!" she cries, but he darts away, "Wait!" She sets off through that doorway into a room thronged with bone-dry toilets, sinks on teetering pedestals, white enameled tubs lined regally behind them. Sweetloaf's ducked through the next door into a crooked hall, couple of steps round a corner the one way, a dead end the other, two doors, the signs above them pictures of a screwdriver and a wrench. Jo looks back and forth, pianos clanging somewhere up away, but then the cry "She's back!" rings out from around that corner.

Around the corner, into a trapezoidal room, the ceiling lost in shadows, a thicket of broken furniture climbing one wall. A long oval table, topped with glass, littered with paper plates, napkins, empty soda cans, a couple pizza boxes, and pushing back their chairs, getting to their feet, the Cinqudea in his orange coveralls, the Spadone his apron dingy with old grease, an older man swiping the bucket hat from his head, the Harper there, his yellow beard, Sweetloaf turning at the foot of it to look back to her, eyes wide. At the head of it Bruno, the Shrieve, in his moleskin vest, "My liege," he says, quite grave, and bows his head, and they all bow their heads.

"Jesus," says Jo, "you don't, come on guys. Guys," as your graces and my ladies mutter from them all. Sweetloaf blurts, "Your hair's fucking different!"

"Yeah, well," says Jo. "Stuff happened."

"Your grace need not explain," says Bruno.

"Actually," says Jo, "the last thing I had to eat? Handful of strawberries. I couldn't even begin to tell you when that was." She nods at the pizza boxes. "Any of that left?"

"Strawberries," says Bruno, "yet tartly pale, and ramps, the first raisins soaked in last year's vinegar," he opens one of the boxes, "new cheeses wrapped in lemon leaves, and flatbread charred in cinders: an excellent breakfast, for a day on the road." He shoves it down the table toward her. "All we might offer your grace is last night's pizza. Sweetloaf, fetch something to drink."

Jo snags one of the remaining slices as Sweetloaf with a bob of his matted pompadour bustles away. "So," she says, chewing, swallowing, "what's with the concert?" pointing to the distantly crashing pianos above.

A dismissive shake of Bruno's head, "Merely a household dispute."

"Yeah?" Another bite. "Nobody's doing the dishes anymore, are they."

A look, from the Spadone to the Cinquedea. The Harper snorts. "There are those that are restive," says Bruno, looking up, "and more," a shrug, "who've left their station."

"But not you boys," says Jo, looking to the older man, the bucket hat back on his head. "You're not one of the boys."

"Gwenders, ma'arm," he says, with a nod.

"Right," she says. One last bite. "The Ladd's householder." Dropping the pizza rind to the box. "I was supposed to come talk to you."

"I'ud nar dream t'impose, ma'arm," her says, but she holds up a hand, "I said I would. I didn't. I'm sorry. But it's been a little," and she sighs. Looks to Bruno. "Luys didn't leave," she says.

"He's at council this morning, your grace."

"Without the King?"

"It's Pinabel leads the council, for now," says the Harper.

"Agravante," says Jo, skeptically flat. "On the throne."

Bruno shakes his head. "The Count, my liege, is awake."

"The throne's broken," says the Harper.

"Oh," says Jo. Sitting abruptly. Sweetloaf sets a glass before her, sparkling water, choked with ice. "But the Queen," she says. "Is safe."

Bruno opens his mouth to answer, but "Seized," says the Harper. "By the bandit. Just after you left." He takes his seat, and after a moment so do the Cinquedea, and the Spadone. "Bandit," says Jo. "You mean Marfisa."

"Ma'arm," says Gwenders, taking his seat with a nod.

"But it's okay!" cries Sweetloaf. "You're back! You're fucking *back!*" Slapping a hand on the table, and Jo starts. "So it's *all* gonna fucking be okay! Just, we can just, go and fucking *get* her," blinking, "her, her majesty, and, and everything can just," brushing back his pompadour, "go, go, back, to how it fucking," sigh, *"used* to be."

"There is no more used to be," says Bruno, still on his feet.

"The owr," says Jo, and they look one to another, stirring in their seats. "Except," she says, leaning forward, an elbow on the table, "there was more, wasn't there? After it all went poof?"

Again, the looks passed back and forth, and the Harper sits up, opening his mouth, but "Not even a firkin, your grace," says Bruno. "Left whole by some mystery, burnt away in a night. We have heard her majesty's tried to turn more, and failed."

"Okay," says Jo. "Okay." She drinks down half the glass of water, ice clinking, wipes her mouth with her wrist. "I need somebody to find me David Kerr. A, uh, a magician, worked for the mayor, or a guy running for mayor. He," hand to her breast, heel of it pressing there, above the devil's leer. "He made whatever happened, happen. Also," her hand laid back on the table, "you need to find Arnold Becker. Lives with that big knight, from Southwest. Pyrocles. Used to work with me at, actually, you should also look for Guthrie? Ah, Bill, Bill Guthrie. Is anybody taking this down?"

"Becker was found at Goodfellow's, that night," says Bruno, and sits him down. "The good Sir Anvil took him home."

"So that's a start," says Jo. "He was there, with me, and David, when it happened. David," she sits up. "He might not've made it back. I don't know. We need to know."

"Back," says the Harper. "From where."

"When," says Jo, standing. "Bruno, tell me. When did you paint the building?"

He frowns. "Ma'am?"

"The apartment building. When did it get to be so fucking brown."

"I, I would have to make enquiries, your grace. It's been so since we bought it."

"Huh," says Jo. "Okay." Lifting the back of her T-shirt. "One more thing. Find me a sheath for that," and she sets the poignard clink upon the table, blade of it streaked and darkly blotched, spotted with orange here and there. "I don't want to cut myself."

"My liege," says Bruno, a hint of a question.

"Where's your fucking sword?" says Sweetloaf.

"If I need that," says Jo, "we really *are* screwed."

STOCKINGS, RED AND BLACK – COOLING THEIR HEELS
A TIMOROUS GLAIVE – THE QUESTION – THE COLOR IT IS

STOCKINGS, THEIR RED AND BLACK stripes tugged out of true by someone else's fingers that close suspender straps, smooth the blackly satin garter belt, tug the red coatee into place. She lifts her arms as they do up golden buttons, heavy like the gold braid burdening her cuffs, spattering the glossy bill of her red cap, set at a jaunty angle. Those fingers settle the golden hawks pinned to either point of the coatee's collar, straighten with a tsk her cap. She laughs, lips expertly red. Her sister sat beside her, lining her lips in a blazing mirror with a burgundy stick, her legs stockinged and gartered with polished boots laced up her shins, her coatee slung on the back of her chair, her cap on the counter before her. "Smile!" says Chrissie.

"No," says Ettie, capping the stick with a disdainful moue.

"Go on," says Chrissie, and Ettie does, a sudden, glorious grin, ostentatiously effortful, blatantly cruel, washing away to strand her stony affect. Costurere with a last pat for Chrissie's

474

coatee leans between them, rustle of white, bloomers and camisole, mob cap on her mousey hair. She takes up a little pot and a tiny brush, kneeling there by Ettie, who holds her half-done lips quite still as brilliant red's applied. "It was easier, when we had the screen," says Chrissie.

"It was easier with the owr, miss," says Costurere, with a last deft twist to shape the Cupid's bow. "If I'd be permitted to say so." Standing, she reaches for the coatee, but Ettie pushes her chair back, "Go on," she snaps, "I can put on my own damn jacket. Go help her," an irritated gesture flung away to the Starling there among the candles, laid out on rugs and pillows and clouds of gauzy black tulle, Aigulha knelt beside her, sheer white shift and a mob cap of her own, painting a bare brown thigh with lines of icy silver. Ettie's working an arm into a sleeve of her coatee, turning about, wrestling with the other until Chrissie shifts the shoulder of it just, lifts it into place, steps close enough to begin to button it up. Ettie submits with a grimace.

Light approaches, away across the basement, a fluorescent lantern swaying in the hand of Big Jim Turk, and the silent lightning of Petra B's camera, capturing in stutter flashes white robe loosely belted, silver shot through short black hair, Ysabel against the darkness, colors about her warming, softening as she steps into the nimbus of those blazing lights. "Ladies," she says. "They're here. Five minutes." Aigulha steps up to unbelt the robe and draw it from Ysabel's shoulders. Costurere gathers a handful of underwear, a fold of something demurely striped. The Starling gets to her feet, working her head from side to side, shaking out her flashing arms and legs. Big Jim holds his lantern high, a pair of mallets in his other hand, his kilt of khaki corduroy. Chrissie does up the last button. Ettie rolls her eyes away, "The hell is she getting us into."

"It'll be fun," says Chrissie, pressing close, bills of their caps clicking, tipping, lips brushing carefully painted lips. "Spectacle."

"Under the goddamn lights," mutters Ettie, and then, as Chrissie steps away, "and we aren't getting *paid!*"

"Let me guess," says Anne Thorpe slyly, and across the stage Anna shudders. "You." Pointing to Welund, sat at the one end of the nubbled green couch, linen discreetly rumpled. "You're a lawyer. But you?" Craning over, looking past to Rhythidd at the other end, resplendent in a lustrous blue coat over pink and white stripes, a slender silver watch about one wrist. "I mean," sparing a glance for the Serpent and the Shield, watchfully still behind them, "y'all're easy. You're muscle." Mousely in pink, sat on the couch between the brothers, silver briefcase in her lap, pillbox hat on her head. "And you're the help. But you?" Rhythidd favors her with a sidelong look. "You're the money," says Thorpe, "but not, like, middleman money. You *are* the money. I can smell it from here. Which rather demands we ask the question," pressing her hands together, "why are *you*," pointedly ignoring Anna's bespectacled glare, "cooling your heels for the likes of *her?*"

"A fair point," says Welund, with an indulgent smile. Rhythidd looks away with the slightest roll of his eyes. "I'm certain her majesty will only be a moment longer," says Anna, smoothing her houndstooth skirt.

"Don't let's forget Miss Wilson," says Thorpe with a smirk.

"Of course," says Welund. Rhythidd looks at his watch. Mousely jumps, startled, the Serpent stiffens, the Shield shakes out a hand, as from somewhere above an unearthly alto note is lifted, held out over the empty warehouse, a note that fluting modulates, becomes a word, a phrase, "A thogha na mban," and Rhythidd tips back his head, "ná tuig-si féin," Welund leaping to his feet, "do shlad go n-déanfainn air æn t-slíghe," stepping out to the very edge of the stage, peering up. On the walkway above, in a gown of greens and purpled blues, Carol strains to shape those words, "le cam, le cleas, ná beartaibh claona," eyes shut tight, and stood beside her in a baggy grey suit coat Marfisa, white hair undone, a set of pipes under an arm and Carol's hand in hers, fingers intertwined. As the song rings out, from all those stalls below step hobs and clods, domestics, in boilersuits and yoga pants, denim jackets and work shirts, blouses and paint-drabbled coveralls, "tu-sa agus me-si bheith," and Marfisa lets go her hand, hikes the sack of the pipes up under her armpit, the drone back over her shoulder, "a mhaighdion mhaordha," the mouthpiece to her lips and the chanter in her hands, "air feadh ar saoíghil," and she begins to play.

The arch at the other end of the warehouse flares and pulses now with licks of light, with the rising pop and thump of drums, the whip and lash of Christienne and Étienne in coatees and caps high-kicking, flames streaming from the torches they thrust and withdraw, thrust and withdraw to the cracking rhythm of the Bullbeggar's bodhrán, the sonorous thump of Big Jim's big bass drum. Following after a tall figure wrapped in a black hoodie, skirted in black tulle, marching with stiff precision as Petra B darts about, camera snapping away. Pipes and drums climb to a summit that collapses, beats redoubling, notes tumbling, somewhere a tinwhistle joining the fray, and the hoodie's whipped away, black gauze a cloud unspooling, the Starling leaping, twirling, black hair twisted in a bun, silvered limbs flashing in the sunlight and the fluorescent light, battling swords a-clash, bright spears leaping to a shout, moonlit hind brought shining down in a clearing as the song of them falls to a halt with her, and only the drone of the pipes, the tinwhistle's eerie echo, mallets and tipper held high, those torches, all of them motionless but for their labored breath, the glisten of sweat, those candescent flames.

Ysabel steps from the neon-brushed shadows of that arch.

Short black hair brushed back, her coat dress of sombre chalkstripe, black Chuck Taylors laced upon her feet. A smiling benison to either side as she makes her way up the aisle, and to either side then heads begin to bow, Sprocket and Manypeny, Bellman, Lustucru, Teacup Tall and Templemass, knees are taken, Fell Swinton, lucent Himmelbirb, trembling Charlichhold, Getulous and Trucos and looming Meg Greentooth, and on the stage Rhythidd, the Glaive, stands up from the couch, "Majesty," he says, so loud in that rustling silence. Taking a knee by the Guisarme Welund, already kneeling, and the Serpent and the Shield bow their heads as Mousely scrambles to bow without getting up or letting go the case. Anna ducks her head. Thorpe smiles behind her hand.

"Welcome!" cries Ysabel, as they all about her stand back up again. "Welcome, to our guests," lifting a hand, "and to our host!"

Up on the walkway the painted door swings open and out she steps, Gloria Monday, stately, plumped in a black high-waisted gown, jet-black hair threaded with white ribbons and gathered in two great hanks, short bangs freshly pinked, arms socked in black and white stripes one gripping the railing, the other hitching her skirts so she might make her way down the skeletal stairs.

"Miss Wilson!" cries Rhythidd, as loudly as before. Gloria stops, halfway down, scowling. "We would not trouble you," he says. "We'd happily meet with you upstairs, within."

"You wished an audience, gentlemen," says Ysabel. "You shall have it, before our court. Press your suit."

Glaive Rhythidd takes a breath, almost a shrug, very well, and steps back to sit on the nubbled couch where the Guisarme's already sat, Mousely all elbows and knees between them. "We have broken with the Mason, ma'am. He's agreed Southeast shall release the properties at the top of the block to us, that we might work with you, Miss Wilson," looking over and up, "to help you make your father's dream come true."

A look comes across Gloria's face at that, and she begins to laugh, a soundless rippling quiver that hitches her shoulders, tips back her head, erupts in a glittering spray, whooping as she lurches, slapping the railing, "My *God,*" she says, and the light catches the letters embroidered in silver thread over her bosom, OKBUMR. "My father's *dream,*" and she waves a hand over them all, "was to flatten the whole damn block, pour a big flat concrete pad, float a couple-four storeys of cheap-ass shitty balloon-frame condos, with cheap-ass shitty vinyl siding, and those cheap-ass fucking windows, and, and, my father's *dream,*" she sneers, "was *bullshit.*"

A stillness seizes the cavernous room, as a smile quirks the corner of Ysabel's lips.

"Child," says the Guisarme, "do not be so quick, to spit on opportunity. The monies to come from realizing even one such dream are enough to leave one in comfort the rest of one's natural days," but Gloria's shaking her head, "I'm *already* rich," she says. "Asshole."

"You are to be commended, gentlemen," says Ysabel. "Placing these buildings in Gloria's hands will go a long way toward securing what's been built here. A truly generous gesture."

"Ma'am," says the Guisarme, "it's not that we," faltering, looking to the Glaive, who smoothly takes up the thread, "I am afraid, majesty, it's not so simple as that. We cannot freely make a gift of these properties to the girl – there are obligations to fulfill, investors that must be satisfied – "

"Twice now," says Ysabel, "Glaive Rhythidd, in this audience, have you said you are afraid." Stepping closer to the stage. "We might begin to doubt your courage, were we not confronted by this insinuation, that you might not do as we have said you would." Her smile is guileless, open. "If such is so," she says, "you would be right, to be afraid."

"We *may* not, ma'am," says the Glaive in his blue coat. "Not might. *Can*not. There are laws, that must be followed."

"Bonds of mortal toradh, ma'am," says the Guisarme, "if you will."

"You are also," she says, that smile quite gone, "to cease any efforts to demolish, dismantle, or destroy the Lovejoy Ramp."

The Guisarme moves to respond, but shuts up his mouth at the Glaive's slightest gesture. "Of course, ma'am," he says, they both say, and bow their balding heads.

"What I will, is done," says Ysabel. "Now go, and be about the doing of it."

An ugly snort from above. "Fucking yahoos," says Gloria, and then, as that entire room looks up to her on the stairs, "what, did I say the quiet part out loud?" Flinging a gesture over the stage below. "*Look* at them! Second they get out the door, they're gonna figure out a way to fuck us."

"There, actually," says the Guisarme in his linen suit, "there is," getting up from the couch, kneeling before Mousely, sat stock still. "There's but one matter more, ma'am," he says, resolve a-firming as his patter smooths. "We'd prove detestable ambassadours, to leave without leaving a gift." Squatting, tugging the silvery case from Mousely's rigid grip.

"Brother," says Rhythidd, so quietly.

"It's all right," murmurs Welund, laying the case flat on Mousely's knees, undoing the latches, click and clack. The sighs that thrill that cavernous space as he lifts the lid, spilling golden light.

"We know," says Welund, turning, standing holding aloft a couple of plastic bags, brightly full. "We know what it means, to see golden promise turn to ashes in our hands. When first the Apportionment thinned, and threatened to wither altogether, we devised a plan, my brother and I: a storehouse, without the city, where we might set some of our portions aside against another such day," and he thrusts up his laden hand. "It survived!" Swaying those bags from side to side, a beacon bright enough to warm those upturned faces, the hands that lift, that reach. "Enough to support the court," he says. "Enough to return you all, and keep you, as you ought be kept, enough to – "

"Enough?" cries Ysabel, and the swoop of the room's attention, down from his hand to her before them all, pressed close to the stage. "For how long?" says Ysabel, and some of those raised hands falter, drop, even as the Guisarme lowers his bags. "As you portion it out to peers, week after week, and they to their stewards, seneschals, and knights," turning to look to the crowd of them thronged about, "and they to their henchmen, housekeepers, cooks and valets," catching the eye of one, then another, Iemanya and Bluelock, Glenn, the Dinny-Mara, Little Conway Coolidge, "to janitors and chambermaids, plumbers and electrickers, gaffers, tapers, bootblacks and chimblesweeps, scullery boys," smiling when someone cries "Yeah!" and another, "Oh, yes!" and "A portion! Give us a portion!"

"How long!" she says again, and then, cutting through the rising clamor, *"How many times?"* Speaking to them all from her little space before the stage. "Even at just a mean pinch for each, a crumb at a time, how often could it all be handed round until you're left to sweep that one last golden speck from the corner of a cold and empty vault?"

"No!" cries someone, and someone else moans. "A Queen might come," says the Glaive, patting Mousely's knee. "Whenever she wished," standing, "to plenish our stores again." Stepping up, beside the Guisarme, who lifts the bags again, to cries of "Yes!" and

"Now!" and "Oh, yes!" Chrissie's jostled as the Primo Rivas shoves past reaching for that light, Herwydh there, catching her balance in Umlauf's wake, and Lupe Lupita, the tears in Christian's eyes, Gordon's scowl, Biscuit clapping his big hands together, the pop of them loudly, slowing, stopping when no one else joins in.

"She might," says Ysabel, and there are whoops, "but when she does, *if she does,*" and at that a stillness raggedly settles over them all. "If we did," she says. "Those who serve our enemy? Would find themselves without."

"My lady," says the Guisarme, tenderly. "There is no enemy."

Ysabel steps into the crowd that makes way before her. "What if she doesn't, though," she says, and though her voice has quieted, her words still carry. "What if we, what if, what if *I,* cannot." Turning back to them on the stage, and Gloria on the stairs, Marfisa and Carol high above. "That's the question, isn't it. Why you cling to the skirts of that monster, and pack up those last few dimming scraps in a stiff steel case. What if this," looking now about her, "is it?" Bwbach and Cherrycoke, Offa and Ssidi Kur and stoop-shouldered Quilibet. "Our reign's been brief," she says, "not six full moons, and yet," closing her eyes with a shiver as a hand takes one of hers, Chrissie slipped through them all behind her, "I've already lost my King, my Huntsman," opening quickblink eyes, "the throne itself," squeezing Chrissie's hand as more of them press close, Alanbam, Meguis, Botté and Jeaneatte with her wildered eyes, Guytrash and thick-necked Brether Ned, Petra B her camera forgotten against her hip, little Sproat and Schuka reaching for her hands, her fingers, her shoulders, the sleeves of her coat dress. "We have no Bride at our left hand," she says, "but two bent Crones do shadow our right," gazing up at them, Welund agog, Rhythidd looking away. She takes a step back toward the stage, and all those reaching hands fall away. "If the very wellspring of our toradh has run dry," she says, "if the bond is truly broken – are we yet a court?" Folding her arms about herself. "Are we not a Queen?"

A moment, and another. Rhythidd coughs. "My lady," he says, "you – "

"Pack up your dross and go," she says.

The vehemence, then from the crowd, she flinches, "No!" and "Oh, no!" and "Stop, my lady! Wait!" the surge of them desperate pressing her stumble-step close, hands braced on the edge of the stage, "Or, or stay!" she shouts. "Stay! Stay! Stay here," she says, to Welund, to Rhythidd there above her, as the shouts and calls falter away. "With us. Make do, with us. See what comes next."

"Majesty," says the Glaive, but he's looking out, over, past the crowd in motion behind her. She turns, Ysabel turns, but they've already stepped aside, stepped back, cleared a path. Stood in the slice of sunlight under the big main overhead door, all in black, hands in her pockets, "Uh," she says, "hey," says Jo, Jo Maguire, Jo Gallowglas, Widow of the Hawk, the Queen's favorite.

Slap and squeak of footfalls pelting Ysabel flings herself past all of them, and Jo steps up to meet her, colliding, twirling, stumbling, leaning, laughing, together.

Leaned against the column a dozen canvases or more, almost as tall as she is, awkwardly wide. The painting on the first one's stark enough to make out in the darkness, slathered black and red on white the suggestion of an arm, sleek lines there a throat, a chin, a head tipped back, pillowed in madly scribbled hair, and gazing out the lone green dot of an eye. She tips it forward enough to see the next one, similar, a leaping gesture, an imperturbable green dot, the next, a twirl, the next, clack of the wooden stretchers loud in the shadows.

"Huh," says Jo Maguire.

The shadows wheel and sway as cold light blooms behind her, and she lets the canvases drop back to the column, turning away. Out past the blazing mirror of the dressing table someone in coveralls hoists a trouble light on a tripod, over the dying candles, and two more, three approach through the copse of columns, hauling in long flat cardboard boxes that they set down by the rugs and pillows with weighty thumps. Someone kneels, unfolding a clever little knife, and sets to slitting the boxes open. BRIMNES, says one of the flaps, in simple blocky letters. The others pull out long dark planks and set them precisely on the floor in a choreography of lift and step and swing and duck. "Uh," says Jo, taking a step closer, "I don't, ah, Ysabel, I mean, her majesty," as they set to work about those planks, inserting dowels, turning cams, fitting them together as a broad shallow box, "she was supposed to – "

"Excellent," says Ysabel approaching, her brief coat dress, those flat-soled shoes, "though the headboard should point north." One of them licks a thumb, holds it up, then points, nodding, and they all stoop and lift and turn the frame a few degrees, hup! Two more approach with a mattress wrapped in plastic, "Oh," says Ysabel, "it's not quite ready, set it there," gesturing, and more of them now with plastic-wrapped stacks of bedding, great soft unslipped pillows, an enormous white duvet, "careful," she says, "the floor's not perfectly clean. I told them to get white," she says, "it seemed easiest," turning with a smile toward Jo, "but we can always change it later," her smile, furling, "if we," falling away, as she takes in the look on Jo's face.

"Leave us," says Ysabel, the Queen.

And chime of tool and scuff of boot, clack and thunk of plank, they do.

"Oh," says Ysabel, when they are alone. "My beautiful Huntsman."

Jo looks down. "I broke the mask," she says. "I lost the sword." Stood there shadowed before the blazing lights about the mirror. "But you're still here."

"Of course," says Ysabel. Stood there by the tripod, and every line and stitch of her chilly pricked by its argentine light. "Where else would I be?"

"Up?" says Jo. "Away?"

Ysabel steps toward her, and holds out a hand. Jo steps up to take it.

"Day?" says Ysabel. "Or was it night?" And then, "You look like you got some sun."

"He's back, isn't he," says Jo.

"You saw it?" Ysabel's other hand grips Jo's shoulder. "It didn't harm you, did it?" Jo with a wince shakes her head, her other hand coming up between them, pressing a moment to her breast, there, just about the devil's brow. "It's *terrible,*" Ysabel says. "Everyone insists it's just the Count. No one will believe me when I tell them. They put me off. They *indulge* me. But," tipping back enough to look her in the eye, "you're back," hand lifting from Jo's shoulder to her cheek, "you're here, now," hitching up to press a kiss to Jo's forehead, tilting, tipping down, but Jo turns her mouth aside. "I can't stay," she says.

"Of course you can," says Ysabel. "Don't be foolish. There's no one to take care of the apartment. Your things can be brought over as soon as there's a place to put them. It needn't be down here – there are so many rooms! Jo. Jo, you must."

"I must," says Jo, pointedly flat. Letting go. Stepping back. Her hands crumpled in her black T-shirt, twisting the devil's leer. Yanking it up, higher, enough to show the nodule over her heart, the color a dulled mirror in this light, and Ysabel's hand to her mouth, blinking quickly. "I can't," says Jo, and lets the hem of her shirt drop.

"Nothing will happen," says Ysabel.

"It already has!" cries Jo. A sob hunches her shoulders, she wraps her arms about herself, squeezing as she dips her head, hauls in a breath, "two weeks," she says, and another breath, easier, more of a sigh. Straightening as Ysabel steps close. Takes her hand. Jo's looking past her, over her shoulder, the cold light, the half-built bed, "You were gone," she says, the words small in her mouth. "You left." Ysabel's arms about her waist. "I chased you," says Jo, "but you," closing her eyes as closer still, cheeks brushing, lips, "took off," says Jo, and a kiss.

"Then that is how I know," says Ysabel, "it was but a bad dream."

"I don't know how I got back."

"You woke up!" Ysabel wipes her cheek with the back of her hand, then Jo's, brushing away a tear. Jo shakes her head away, "The magic's *gone,*" she snaps, and Ysabel laughs, a giddy bark of surprise, delight. "Why then, your grace," she says, and lays a hand on Jo's breast, "we've nothing to fear." Jo looks away, but doesn't let go. "Ysabel," she says. "Ysabel, the apartment. What, what color was it? The building?"

"The color?" Ysabel frowns. She's looking at her hand, laid flat on that black T-shirt. The back of a finger a-glimmer, a golden spark caught in the fine hairs below a knuckle.

"Ysabel?" says Jo.

"It's white," says Ysabel. She sluices the corner of her eye with her little finger. "With green trim." A cloudy droplet clings to the tip of it, and she reaches it to Jo's cheek, dredging up the runnel of a tear-track there.

"What," says Jo.

Ysabel shivers. Holds her hand between them, fingers curled but the smallest, and trembling there at the top of it a scatter of tiny, shining kernels of gold.

"Oh," says Ysabel. "Oh, my."

POUNDING, POUNDING – NON SUM QUALIS ERAM
THRICE SETEBOS

POUNDING POUNDING, hurling herself against the demure brown door, "You *must!*" she cries. Adjusting her baggy grey coat she rattles the knob that will not turn. *"Open!"* she roars, kicks, hurls herself again. It shivers inward, tripping her staggering into a stairwell with a spray of splinters, "Hello?" she calls, pushing back her cloud of white-gold hair. Something saggy flops in her other hand.

Up the stairs then, pounding, back along a balustraded hall past the first door, ajar, to the second. She smacks it with the heel of her hand. "Open!" she calls. "I must speak with you!" Pounding. "Hello!" A deep breath. "I know you are within," she says, more quietly. "It is of vital importance that I speak with you."

Clack and scrape, the rattle of a bolt. The door opens enough to show a man peering over a taut-stretched security chain. "You shouldn't be here," he says, low and close.

"But I am. I bear news of utmost importance."

"I don't give a shit if it's life or death," he hisses, "if you wake her, I'm gonna," but then he catches himself, deflating.

"It concerns the roof over her head," says Marfisa, "the floor, beneath her feet."

He leans close to the gap, scowling. "How did you," he says. "Who *are* you."

"Eddie?" a querulous voice from somewhere behind him. He sags even more, shaking his head, dwindling hair of it clipped close. "Nothing, ma'am," he says. "Solicitor. Go on, now. You need your rest."

"Nothing, *hell,*" that voice. "Go on. Let 'em in."

She lifts a hand, the one with its floppy bundle, as he gently closes the door, but the chain scrapes loose, the door opens again, wide now, he's stepping back out of the way, careful of the shelves, and all the books.

The walls of the room are lined with shelves dark and pale, unpainted, brightly varnished, a stretch of metal shelving painted industrial mint, all filled stuffed crammed with books, with hardbacks wrapped in tattered jackets, glossy library plastic, pebbly leather, with paperbacks stacked and piled, spines curled and cracked and scored into illegibility, page-edges rumpled, foxed, rigidly cut, greying with old ink, covers creased and flaking, torn, stained, faded, dulled, worn away, but the names, still, the names, Pauline Elizabeth Hopkins and Charlotte Perkins Gilman, Andrea Hairston and Begum Rokheya Sakhawa Hossain, declaimed in block capitals, Mrs. H.A. Dugdale, Suzette Haden Elgin, Balaraba Ramat Yakubu, curling in fanciful scripts, Mariame Kaba, Xiaolu Guo and Nalo Hopkinson, Mikki Kendall, Vandana Singh and Nnedi Okorafor, worked into elaborate designs, painted into the illustrations, Tanith Lee and N.K. Jemisin, Benjanun Sriduangkæw, P.C. Hodgell, shaped with tiles or threads or circuitry, Tananarive Due and C.L. Moore, Octavia Butler, Shalija Patel, some of them written in the same peevishly careful hand on spines repaired with duct tape, friction tape, masking tape. Out in the middle of it all a grandly overstuffed love seat piled with pillows and boxes and stacks and pads of paper and primly sat at one end of it a tiny woman bundled in a pale blue quilted housecoat, a pad of yellow foolscap on her lap, her bare brown feet tucked into a shallow tub, the water in it bubbling about them.

"Ma'am," says Marfisa, stock still before her.

"What is so all-fired important," that voice now loudly creaky, those eyes peering up through Coke-bottle lenses, "has you banging down my door like this?"

"My lady," says Marfisa, "Abby Tinker," sinking to one knee there on the cluttered carpet. "I love your stories," she says, an elbow on her knee.

"Yeah, okay," says Eddie by the door, starting toward Marfisa, "let's go," laying a hand on her shoulder. She stiffens. "Next time, write a letter," he says. Abby Tinker on the loveseat shakes her head, and he lifts his hand away. "You had something to tell me about my apartment," she says, leaning forward. The thrum and chuckle of the water in her bath.

"This building," says Marfisa. "The men, who hold it. Have the keeping of it. They will come to you, and say to you, that you must leave. What I would tell you," she looks down a moment, takes in a breath. "What I am here to tell you, my lady Tinker, and also you, Edward – this building," she says, "now belongs to *us*. And these rooms, your rooms, we'd give to you, that you might freely stay, so long as you would wish. No matter what those men might tell you."

Abby Tinker takes up the pad from her lap and sets it to one side, screws the cap back on her pen, "Now," she says. "Setting aside for a moment the question of whether you *can* do such a thing." Leaning forward, closer than before. "Tell me why you would," she says.

"I heard you read once." Marfisa unfolds her floppy bundle there on the carpet. "The Whorlagig Road. Planet Chooseday, Klaatu Gawd. The Excellent Canopy. Cynara – the Herd!" Smoothing it flat, her rubbery horse-head mask, the limp snout of it, those bulging eyes. "Your stories are my favorites," she says.

"You heard me read?" says Abby Tinker, those glasses turning up to look to Eddie. "You must have been a bitty little thing."

"When I learned that you lived here," says Marfisa. "You're why I stayed. You're why I'm here." Her hand on the mask. "You're why I wear this."

Abby Tinker lifts a bare foot dripping from the tub, plants it on the carpet, bracing herself to lean down from her perch to take up the mask in a leathery hand. "I am not as I was," she says, half to herself, "in the reign of good Sinara. Would you look at this, Eddie?" Holding up the mask. "She wants to be a Horse."

"Fuck you, you're not here, fuck you, you're not here, you're not here. *Fuck* you," wetly shredding the fricative, *"fuck* you, you're not here, you're *not fucking here!"* Wiping his wrist across his mouth, dragging in a hissing breath, shoving away the hand she lays on his shoulder. She sits back on squalid cardboard, wrapped in a purple rain shell, grey-callused feet pinched by lime green flip-flops, flat little bottle clutched to her chest. Pit River Vodka, says the label. Blue plastic tarp snaps and rattles overhead. She takes a swig. "Moody, baby," she says, "you got to stop this. It ain't good for you." Another. "Tell me," she says, "where'd you go. Where you been the last couple weeks."

He wheels, eyes wide, mouth snarled. "Where's Lucinda?"

"What?"

"Lu! Cin! Da!" Shoves her toppled rolling through the blue tarp with a grunt. She stiffly gets to her feet, bottle still in one hand, pebbles and wet grass clung to a knee. The blue tarps slung from a slender tree to the pole of a No Parking sign, a makeshift tent between street and sidewalk. She lifts a flap to see him frantic, rummaging through a bucket, dumping filthy clothing from a garbage bag. "Moody," she says, all her wheedle gone to steel. "Stop."

"The Sikes-Fairbourne!" he says, breathless. "About yay long," holding up his hands, a span between them. "Only fourteen of them, Ada? Ada!" Snapping his fingers under her nose. "The hell you staring at?"

"That's a nice watch," she says.

Loosely golden, heavy about his wrist, he shoves back the cuff of his army-surplus jacket to gawp at it, the wide flat face, three small dials set within the largest, each of them hashed with tiny numerals, letters, other inscrutable symbols, the slenderly fili-greed hands of them held quivering still, pointed this way, that, but for the single majestic sweep turning slowly above them under the crystal of it. He gingerly settles his thumb and middle finger on the golden bezel of it, forefinger stroking the face, and it chimes, softly. His fingers leap away. The hands of it swing wildly about but for the sweep, which has stopped, pointed right at him.

He looks up at her.

Gasping she drops the curtain, blotting out the sunlight, leaving only the bedside lamp in that dim room, all beige carpet and vaguely striped wallpaper. Blots her forehead with the back of her hand. Tucks a sprig of corkscrew curls behind an ear. She steps to the foot of a queen-sized bed draped with blankets a touch more brown than the carpet and opens a glossy laptop, looming over the light of its screen. Types a brief command. A graph appears, a flat red line crossing from left to right with a hiccup there, a scurry of green and red and orange unknotting, retwining, wobbling wind-ing tipping until at the right edge it explodes, a luridly unskeining rainbow leaping and diving for asymptotes. She touches the screen and the lines dissolve to clouds of points, diamonds, crosses, exes, lurching to the left as the graph updates, and again, as numerals appear in and about the thronging constellation. She picks up a phone from the bedside table, dials a number, then an-other. "Setebos," she says, and then, "Setebos, and Setebos." Waits a moment. "It's back," she says, and terminates the call.

In the shadows below a splintered wrack, torn upholstery, draggled filthy stuffing, yellowed spears of grass grown up and through it, and all the shards of glass. He's stood in his dark blue suit at the edge above it, among juts and angles of more broken glass. She crosses the empty floor toward him, squeak of her golden basketball shoes, yellow blouse uncomfortably buttoned, but stops her long white skirt a-slosh at the sound of voices raised below, one fucking job, give a shit, growling up from the stairwell to a you! before muttering back to indistinguishable menace. She starts across the room again, more slowly, less certain, stopping suddenly when he looks back, a wry smile under his mustaches. "Chariot," he says.

"Sir Anvil," says Iona. Stepping up beside him, at the edge. "You overlook our wreck," she says. "Someone should have cleared that days ago."

"No," he says, lifting his chin to point out over the light-struck trees, the city beyond, smoldering in sunset. "I look to him."

"Him, good sir?" Her chartreuse hair gone weirdly pale in the uncertain light.

"My lord," says Pyrocles. "My love. He has forgotten me," a shrug, "he's forgotten us all. But when the Queen's brought back — when the owr's returned," he says, and again a growl from below, a shout, a screeching howl cut suddenly short. Iona steps back from the edge, looks up, away. Pyrocles, blinking rapidly, ducks his head, brushing his mustaches with a knuckle. "I will see in his eye once more that he knows me," he says, as footfalls climb the steps from the porch below. There's Welund in his linen suit, and Rhythidd frantically impatient up behind him, stumbling heedless past him, staring at what's clutched in both his hands, a curve of bone, a rib, glittered with pink. "Go on," snarls the other, coming up after them, sleek aluminum briefcase carelessly depended from one hand, "slink on out of here!" And then there's Agravante, bringing slowly up the rear. "Next time," the other's saying, "next time you fuck up like this. Next time you *lose* your fucking *nerve. Next time it's gonna be one of you.*"

"My lord," says Welund, there in the doorway to the hall, and Rhythidd gone on ahead.

"Oh, don't worry," says the other, handing the briefcase off to Agravante. "It's perfectly safe. Now *go,*" and that one word a thunderclap in this wide room, and for an instant sparks flare about that squat round body, crawl through the crown of ivory hair. And then the other's smiling, "All right!" and pink hands clap. "What's next?"

Iona looks to Pyrocles, who doesn't look up. "Next, my lord?" says Agravante, briefcase cradled in his arms. That smile upends, a frustrated scowl. "Plan," says the other, "C," each syllable deliberate, a stone in a well. "What are we *doing*. To make it *happen.*"

"We, ah," says Agravante, "must," a breath, "reach out, to the peers, assemble vehicles, matériel – "

"Then *do* it!" snaps the other. "Reach out! Assemble! Is that fucking thing *leaking?*"

The shine of the briefcase shifting, has shifted from colorless silver to buttery gold against the pink fingers reached out to touch it, snapped back when the light flares not from the case but the air about it, and "My lords," says Iona then, hoarse with wonder.

Out there, past her, past Pyrocles and the broken wall of glass, past the silhouetted trees dissolving in the softly rising dazzle, the ruddy light of sunset swallowed by a light more brilliant and more gold, a gentle summer sunburst just across the river, fading even as it warms their faces, dimming, gone.

"Majesty," says Pyrocles, the word a merest breath.

"Not again," says the other, and then, an avalanche crash to fill the words, *"not again!"* Quasars scratch the air and shadows scribble, the hair unraveling, those pink hands loosed, that shirt too loud, *"How!"* The ringing echo of the cry and all that energy a breath sucked in, light and shadow collapsing to a hard round belly, white shirt a bit too bright, bald head flushed pink in an ivory crown. "Go and get her," says the other, a simple exhortation. "Bring her to me. Now."

THE GOLD, THE GOLD – "COME AND GET IT"

The gold, the gold that spills from her hand a glittering trickle to the brilliance mounded in that wooden tub, "After all that."

"Yes," says Ysabel, laid back among the rugs and pillows, wrapped in a white robe.

"You said it was broken," says Gloria Monday, empty hand on the edge of the tub. "Done." Still in that black gown, and still with ribbons in her hair.

"I said *if*," says Ysabel. "*If* it were broken. *If* it were done. Would you stay. And the answer was yes. Even so. But now," her black hair shining, wet, her hands, her throat, her bare shin streaked and gleaming gold, "the toradh is restored."

"We must've been reading different rooms," says Gloria, stepping away from the tub, past Anna there in her houndstooth, her narrow glasses. Jo in the shadows, buttoning up her jeans, braces herself. "This," says Gloria, "is fucking unbelievable. This cannot fucking be believed." Anna lifts a cautioning hand, "Gloria," she says.

"You know what's up there?" says Gloria. "You know how all this started? Why?" A step toward languid Ysabel. "It was all the people, all the *women*," says Gloria, "you fucked over, with your fucking goddamn question. Me," she says. "Marfisa. Bobbi, and Anna," Anna looks away, hand to her brow. "Julia? Tully? Petra, and Miriam, and every, everybody else who's up there, now," as Ysabel sits up then, looking to her with those green, green eyes, "who washed your dishes, or, or cooked you something, folded your fucking underwear, *slept*," turning to Anna, "in a goddamn *shoe*box, and *you*," whirling back to loom over Ysabel, "said it was all *done!*" Jo gets to her feet. Gloria straightens, steps back. "I guess that was bullshit."

"They have all," says Anna, adjusting her glasses, "*we*," she says, "have given freely, of, ourselves." Nodding, to the tub full of gold. "That gift will be honored."

Gloria snorts. "You nearly had a fucking *riot* before. The hell you think is gonna happen when you just, walk that shit upstairs? You have to stop. You have to *think* about what – "

"Tell us, child, what we must do," says Ysabel, and the flames of the candles about her gutter, and tremble back to light.

"Oh, *fuck* you," says Gloria, and Ysabel surges to her feet, "There is *nothing* we must do!" she bellows, a step toward Gloria falling back before the advance. "We," cries Ysabel, "are Queen!"

"You and what army," mutters Gloria, but Ysabel's turned away. "Send for my dressers," she says, "and once I am dressed, send for those enough to carry this portion up to the main hall. The white suit, I should think, if we have it; something white, and gold."

Anna, nodding, says, "Miss Monday's not without a point, ma'am." Gloria glares. "There are," and Anna takes a breath, "but few enough," she says, "peers within, to steward an Apportionment."

"The Bulbeggar, the Mooncalfe," says Ysabel with a shrug, "the Dagger – and, of course, Marfisa, will make for more than enough. Oh, but send for the Starling, first: I'd see her restored to herself before the portion's handed round."

"Ma'am," says Anna.

"And of course, if there's the slightest breath of trouble," Ysabel turns away from them, "we've also our Huntsman – "

Gloria looks up. Anna takes a step.

"Jo?" says Ysabel, to the empty shadows. "Jo?"

A crumpled cigarette smolders in fingers spangled gold, the hand there on her knee, black jeans brightly dusted. Sat on the low stoop, soles on the sidewalk, music dimly thumping somewhere up behind her, keyboards trilling, lyrics loudly whispered over cries and cheers through the ash and acid rain, I don't care if the germs eat our books and our brains, all I want is to echoing back through the blue-lit foyer, the climbing murals of tree and ziggurat, the silhouette in the open doorway, "You ever gonna get around to smoking that?"

Jo looks back, sighs, offers up the cigarette. Slip and shuff of bare feet, slickery rustle of leather pants, a brown hand plucks it away. Beads in black hair clack as a drag's taken in, that shadowed head tipped back to loose a long, soft cloud. "I have nothing against you," says Zeina, the Mooncalfe.

"I know," says Jo.

"But," says Zeina, another drag, "I can't help feeling," another cloud, "it's maybe the other way round?"

"Nothing personal," says Jo. "It's just, your predecessor," wave of her hand, looking for the next word.

"Is deceased," says Zeina, offering the cigarette. Jo shakes her head, but takes it, "I want to quit," she says, "but if I do?" Hand drifting back to her knee. Rising thread of smoke from the coal. "Damned if I know what I'd take up next," she says. Lifting it to her lips, a slow, considered gesture. A drag. The beat still thumps behind them, a different piano over gyring strings and a piercing falsetto never let you go, tomorrow's party will never end and the whoops and shouts. "Well," says Zeina. She's looking at the gold that clings to Jo's hands, her knees, that's caught in her sunbleached hair. "You did it."

Jo nods. "Get yours?"

Zeina shrugs. "There's time enough," she says, "and plenty."

One last drag, and Jo drops what's left to the sidewalk. A white SUV with discreet gold trim pulls up to the curb. Jo gets to her feet. "Iona?" she says. The passenger door opens.

"Luys," she says.

"My lady," says the Mason, stepping from the truck, hand on the door of it to brace him in his wonder. "I'd been told you had come back, but still – I hardly dared to hope."

"Told," she says, as the other doors open, and men in blue suits pile out. "Duchess!" cries the Chariot, chartreuse head popping up from the driver's side. "Welcome home!" In among the blue suits there's the Stirrup in his brick red vest, and the Axle's helping Sweetloaf climb out the back. "What is happening," says Jo. "Luys. What's going on."

"Good Sir Mason," says the Shield in his blue suit, a phone held away from his ear. "The Viscount asks, are we in position."

"A moment," says Luys, stepping close to Jo. A hand to her shoulder, "Soon enough," he says, "all will be well."

"No it won't," she says, ducking out from under.

"Sir Mason," says the Shield again, and "A moment, sir!" snaps Luys, stepping after Jo, but that's when Zeina shouts, "Gentlemen!" Up on her feet in the doorway now, and everyone stops. She lifts her left arm, pointing the rapier in her hand. "Everybody here for your portion, line up in an orderly file to the north, one! By! One! Anybody here for anything *else?*" Shaking out her right hand, she grips and twists a second rapier from the air. "Come and get it," she says, settling into her stance.

"No!" cries Jo, a hand at the small of her back.

Flash of slender steel those two blades whick and whack as Zeina Mooncalfe catches the Trident's short sword knocked aside she lurches rapiers whirling over around as she arches back under the Serpent's cut with a twist of her hips a leap to plant herself riposte

"I said no!" Jo bellows.

into and through the Serpent's breast. Gurgling his blade drops a-clang to the sidewalk his knees, grasping for the needle-whip even as it slips away. A "La!" from the Mooncalfe as a bit of glimmering bone bounces to the stoop at her feet.

"Enough," says Jo, quietly, but the word still cuts through the grunts and shouts, and the thunderous crashes and sharp clangs within. They all eye not her but the sword in her hand, the steel of it whorled with dark waves and light, the hilt she grips so simple, so straight, guarded about by a net of wiry strands that glitters even in this darkness. The Mooncalfe settles in a wary crouch, one rapier low before her, "Well," she says, the other up and back, "want to dance, Gallowglas?"

Jo steps back, and again, bump her back to the side of the suv. Slowly, slowly she sinks, drawing the sword back to herself until her knee brushes the sidewalk. The Mooncalfe quivering scowling shifting her grips on her hilts, and the jagged little carpal bone spangled with blue by one bare foot. Someone shouts within, behind her, and a crowd roars. Jo lays the sword on the concrete before her, the faintest clink of steel. Lets go. Gets to her feet, looking about, Iona to the left of her, Luys to the right, and all those knights in blue suits. Sets off with a lurching clockwork step, pushing between Alans and the Guerdon, away out into the empty street. "Gallowglas!" cries Zeina behind her. *"Huntsman!"* But someone shouts, and the light changes behind her, warming, growing, and before her all the suddenly awestruck knights begin to bow their heads, and slowly take their knees.

Walking away from the warehouse lit up against the night behind her, stepping into the shadow of the warehouse across the street, silent, still, unlit. Creative Woodworking NW, says the round wooden sign on the small wooden door of it, brightening in the brightening light. She doesn't look back, her step doesn't falter, her arms come up to wrap about herself, her head lowers, she puts one foot in front of the other until

"Jo," the voice behind her, and she stops.

"Jo," says Ysabel again, and she turns.

Stood there in the air behind her, loose white trousers, billowing blouse, her hands apaumy and her dangling bare feet slathered with dripping with gold, and shining, shining, stepping down to the pavement, just, and it's lit up like a summer's day. Jo closes her eyes. "Please," is all she says, but

"Don't you love me?" says Ysabel.

And I am nothing of a builder,
But here I dreamt I was an architect,
And I built this balustrade
To keep you home, to keep you safe
From the outside world.

—*Colin Meloy*

The text has been set in Tribute, a typeface designed by Frank Heine from types cut in the 16th century by Françoise Guyot; specifically, a specimen printed around 1565 in the Netherlands.

Kɪᴘ Mᴀɴʟᴇʏ lives in Portland, Oregon, with a cartoonist, an aspiring large and exotic animal veterinarian who loves animals, and (at last count) two cats and one hamster.

He may be contacted via email at kipmanley@yahoo.com. His general-interest website is available for viewing at www.longstoryshortpier.com.

CITY *of* ROSES

Season Two: SPRING; SUMMER

VOL. 3

IN THE REIGN
of GOOD QUEEN DICK

THE THIN ICE — VILISSIMA *&* INFIMA — TWO SWEETEST PASSIONS
ONLY BORDERS LIE — TENDS TO CRUMBLE — HANDS OF AN ANGRY
SHIVER & HEADACHE — ON PRETENDING THAT
MARBLE SENDS REGARDS — ONLY TO SIT
CARNIVAL WAS RINGING

COMING SOON

VOL. 4

-or BETTY MARTIN

UP AND STAND. — MANY CHRISTIAN EYES — SO POWERFULLY STRONG
AND 'THIRSTY WILDS' — EKUMEN AIN'T EVERYTHING
BEAUTIFUL, WE ARE — DIRTY WHITE NOISE — ARMS—LEGS—HEAVEN
SUN, DUST, SHADOW — THE FIVE POINTS
THAT WAS THE RIVER

9 781734 945232